BRIDGES THAT STAND

BRIDGES THAT STAND

▼

James D. Folger

Writer's Showcase
San Jose New York Lincoln Shanghai

Bridges That Stand

Writer's Showcase
an imprint of iUniverse.com, Inc.

For information address:
iUniverse.com, Inc.
5220 S 16th, Ste. 200
Lincoln, NE 68512
www.iuniverse.com

ISBN: 0-595-18917-2

Printed in the United States of America

DEDICATION

▼

To all fliers, and the ground crew personnel, and the Operations personnel who served with B-26 Bombardment Groups in the Ninth Air Corps in the European Theatre of Operations, and to the B-26 crew with whom I served: Eugene Miller, Frank Kepner, Maynard "Red" Graham, Eldon McGoey, and Francis Schmuck.

EPIGRAPH

---▼---

"The beginnings and endings of all human undertakings are untidy, the building of a house, the writing of a novel, the demolition of a bridge, and eminently, the finish of a voyage

John Galsworthy, Over the River.

FOREWORD

———————▼———————

Below are the remarks of Professor George Logan Price* Creative Writing department, San Francisco State University, regarding my short story, *Venison*.

"Shades of Walter Clark. This could be a great entrance to a story. *You can* write. You have the firm foundation on which to build precariously."

Professor Price was the winner of the James D. Phelan Awards in Literature for the short stories:
*The Hunters
*Fat Tuesday
*Nical and the Dolphins

From a six page handwritten letter from Professor Walter Van Tilburg Clark* discussing a story submitted to him while taking Directed Writing for Individual Students.

121 Hawthorne Ave.
Larkspur, California

Dear Jim Folger,

"...Like everything else of yours I've read, including earlier drafts of this story, the writing is clear and well paced and the sensory rendering is excellent. That's proof enough to my mind, that your work can have a future. You have beyond question, the power of observation, the feeling, the kind of memory which more and more seems to me the natural attributes without which even the most earnest labor can't get far..."

Sincerely yours,
Walter Clark

The Ox Bow Incident
The City of Trembling Leaves
The Watchful Gods and Other Stories
The Track of the Cat

ACKNOWLEDGEMENTS

▼

My special thanks to Kathleen Bettis, MLS, Boise, Idaho, who edited, and offered valuable criticism.

For his unflagging patience, humor, and encouragement to stick with this project, I thank my friend and neighbor Doc Takeda, a member of the famed WWII 442nd Regimental Combat Team. He was wounded while participating in the rescue of the lost 36th Infantry Division in France, earning the Purple Heart, and he was awarded the Bronze Star.

Newton Gann: for technical advice. He flew combat missions with the 9th Air Corps, served in the Army of Occupation, retired as a Air Force Major, earned The Air Medal with clusters He retired as an Engineer from The Boeing Aircraft Co.

Ernest A. Lindner: a B-26 Bombardier—Navigator in the ETO, and an Observation Group Leader during the Korean Peace Action. Awarded the Air Medal with clusters, the DFC, and the Purple Heart, Ernie is a retired Air Force Captain, and a retired businessman living in Glendale, California.

Mr. Hank Burrows, WWII historian, qualified critic and friend, and a decorated member of the 517th Regimental Combat Team offered many insights regarding combat stress and its affect upon young civilian-soldiers.

B-26 pilot, retired Lieutenant Colonel Joe Dressel, was the winner of the Air Medal with clusters during WW II combat, and gave advice on the technical aspects of flying the Marauder, as did the late Mr. Jack Cayot, a B-26 pilot, who was shot down in Italy, and spent eighteen months as a prisoner of war.

D-Day P-38 pilot Bob Clark flew 200 combat hours both from England and France, and was awarded the DFC, the Silver Star, and the Air Medal with clusters.

R. Owen Barnes, M.D, provided medical advice. Crystal Goss, rendered the translations.

Special thanks to Marjorie Ann Folger, my spouse of over five decades, and the loving mother of our four daughters, who as a homemaker supported my business career and tirelessly edited and re-typed dozens of manuscripts for outdoor magazines and newspapers, back before computers and word processors.

Bridges That Stand
Introduction

▼

This is a story about the youthful crew of a WW II medium bomber, a B-26, named DIANA, and it is about the girls they love. Trained to skillfully cope with the challenges of aerial combat over the skies of Nazi Germany, they discover they are ill prepared to assume the role of conquerors. Because these fliers have not accumulated enough "points", they cannot go home. They become a part of the Army of Occupation.

Marshall Sunder is the Bombardier-Navigator of the crew. His hunting experience with his father and uncle prepared him for the stress of combat. His vulnerability as a young man is revealed when he falls in love with a German girl, Kristine, forbidden by the "No Fraternization" regulations. Tragedy transpires: Death, revenge, hate, cruelty, invades his life. He tries to cope with condemnation. He seeks forgiveness. He experiences infatuation and lust, as well as respect for several women, as Kristine, Lorelei, Nausicaa, Eileen, Paula, Carla, Martha and Jeanette each impact his life.

The nicknames of the B-26, Martin Marauder, a medium bomber, were derisive, humorous, and most often painfully accurate. Manufactured in the Martin plant in Baltimore, Maryland, it was early on called The Baltimore Whore because it had "no visible means of support." With its short wing span it was the fastest landing and fastest sinking airplane designed in WWII. If reference was made to The Flying Prostitute, to the B dash crash, to The Widow Maker or to the Flying Coffin, it was commonly understood that the airplane was the Martin Marauder.

The sleek design of the airplane was esthetically pleasing: the rudder, the vertical stabilizer, was tall, aggressive, appearing to lean into a combat readiness. The fuselage was cigar shaped with cone shaped ends, supported by relatively short wings which in turn supported 2800 horse power twin Pratt and Whitney engines, each the equivalent of a locomotive engine, which spun thirteen foot six inch propellors. It rode on a tricycle landing gear, and was flown by two pilots. The other crewmembers were the bombardier-navigator, the flight engineer, the radioman, and the tail gunner.

It took exceptional ability and coordination plus courage to pilot the sixteen tons of metal, rubber and fabric worth almost a quarter of a million of dollars. The pilots knew that they had to be master of their ship or it would master them, with tragic results.

"One a day in Tampa Bay," was a grim quotation uttered by other pilots and fliers upon learning that another flier was a crew member of the Marauders being flown from McDill Field, Florida. Much of the selection of crews and their training as a team began at Lake Charles, Louisiana, where the direction of the runways from which the new pilots took off, crossed Lake Calcasieu in the direction of the Gulf of Mexico. The loss, the failure of one engine, on take-off often resulted in a fatal crash in the lake or the gulf.

As demanding, thus dangerous, as the airplane was, the fliers respected it, and became defensive when its characteristics were criticized by "outsiders." The fliers and the ground crews were proud to be Marauder Men. Other fliers were astonished to learn how "hot" it landed, flaring out at a 130 plus miles per hour just before touching down.

The B-26 medium bomber crew is stationed at an air base in Denain, France, north of Paris near the Belgian border. DIANA is painted on the fuselage beneath the first pilot's window on the port side of the airplane. It is crewed by the first pilot, 2nd Frank Mueller, the second pilot 2nd Lt.

Gary McAdam, Bombardier-Navigator, 2nd Lt. Marshall Sunder, Engineer, First Sgt. "Pop" Skidmore, Radioman, Sgt. Jim Frantz, and tail gunner, Sgt. John Dublin. Their average age is twenty-one. John, the tail gunner is seventeen, and "Pop" the engineer is twenty-seven, thus his nickname.

Unlike some branches of the military, fliers do not always heed the protocol of rank, and they often arrive at their own comfortable manner of addressing one another, especially within the confines of their battle - home, the bomber.

Lt. Frank Mueller is from Topeka, Kansas. His parents are wheat farmers. Married just before going overseas, Frank's wife is Diana. It is the prerogative of the first pilot, the pilot occupying the port-side seat, the captain of the ship, to name the bomber.

Lt. Gary McAdam is from Chicago, Illinois. He has a twin brother, Sean, in the Navy, and a sister Debbie. His father is in the construction business. The identical twins were influenced by their parents to go into different branches of the service.

Lt. Marshall Sunder, is the only child of merchants located in Chico, a small town in he upper Sacramento valley of Northern California. Basically, a hardware and farm supply store, the business is known as Sierra Mercantile.

First Sgt. Ed "Pop" Skidmore is married. He and Paula are the parents of two year old son, Tim. Their home is in Los Angeles, California. When drafted, he was employed as a salesman for The Rainbow Paint Co., making sales promotion calls on contractors and retail stores.

Sgt. Jim Frantz is from Rochester, Minnesota. His father is a pharmacist and owns a small drug store. His mother occasionally helps in the store but is a homemaker, and cares for a younger sister, Heidi.

Sgt. John Dublin is from Alva, Oklahoma. His father is an English professor at Oklahoma State Teachers College. His mother tutors English and math at their home. His older brother, Jeff, is in the navy.

World War II in Europe is in its final stages.

Contents

▼

CHAPTER 1

▼

REVEILLE

Three loud knocks by a heavy fist preceded the opening of the thick barracks door. Chilly, sharp air, carrying with it the odor of high-octane gasoline, sliced past the Duty Sergeant, filled the room and gripped the ears and faces of the sleeping fliers.

The roaring of the huge Pratt and Whitney engines reached from the flight line to the barracks. Barely awake, the fliers listened, waiting for the cough, the sputter of a faulty engine: engine failure that could mean death. The Duty Sergeant removed one glove and located the light switch, flipped it and shouted, "Okay, warriors, drop your cocks and grabs your socks! Breakfast in thirty minutes, preflight in one hour and Axis Sally will tell you where you're going."

"Go away, Attila!" Gary McAdam shouted. "Turn off that damn light."

"Yes sir!" the sergeant shouted. "OKAY, Let's hear three more voices!"

"Okay, yes, okay!" the voices of Marshall Sunder, Frank Mueller, and Wally Sullivan finally responded before the sergeant was satisfied he'd done his duty.

Marshall Sunder remembered the knocks on the door of the bunkhouse in Oregon. *It's dad and Uncle Bruce and it is time to have breakfast, gather up our rifles and ammo and our saddlebags. Out in the corral we'll saddle our horses, steam rising from their warm bodies as they munch grain. We'll load our saddlebags with a rain-slicker, a lunch and a jug of water and a towel to clean blood off our hands if we shoot a buck. Each horse has a name. Dad will ride Ace and Emil will probably select Neptune for me.*

Marshall threw back the blankets and looked around the room. Frank was the pilot of their B-26 bomber and as with the horses, the airplane had a name; theirs named after Frank's wife, Diana. Instead of saddles, the bombers had seats, and instead of saddlebags, a bomb bay in which were placed eight five-hundred-pound bombs. Instead of grain, the huge engines were fed one-hundred octane gasoline.

"Damn, I wish we were going deer hunting. This blowing stuff up is getting old," Marshall said.

"We're halfway home. Number twenty-five today," Frank said, then yawned and stretched. The fliers began to sit up and move out of their beds. Four officers occupied the combination bedroom and living room, furnished only with a large table and five chairs, a bathroom with one sink, and a shower. Two officers shared ample space within the two large side by side closets.

"See if you can get Sally, " Marshall said.

Frank Mueller turned on the radio. It squealed, squawked, hummed, buzzed, and finally the syrupy, sweet, feminine voice of Axis Sally gave the weather report, and said, "Okay yanks; following these announcements, I'll play, as requested, Glenn Miller's Sunrise Serenade, and while you are listening, remember, back home, your wives and sweethearts are keeping the Four—F guys happy in your beds." She laughed and then said, "Seriously, I suggest that all members of the 493rd Bomb Group just roll over and go back to sleep. Our aces and 88's await anyone foolish enough to try to reach Ulm. And think about this, fly today and there'll be no

Moonlight Serenade for many of you! So, close your eyes! Sweet dreams, and now here's Glenn!"

"Turn her off," Marshall grumbled.

"No!" Wally said, "I love that Sunrise Serenade."

"I'd like to lay that Nazi whore!" Gary said, then laughed.

"Who wouldn't you like to lay?" Wally asked. Wally was the copilot of another crew, but the room accommodated four, so most crews were split up. Wally was compatible with Frank's copilot, Gary, and Marshall, the bombardier-navigator.

After D-Day, they'd moved from England to a new base a hundred miles from Paris, near the Belgian border. Having lived together for several months, at the new base, their routine for use of the facilities had fallen into a pattern, uncomplicated and convenient, reflecting the tempo of their personalities. Just as airplanes traveled in a traffic pattern, so did they. There were no conflicts as they took turns using the toilet and wash basin.

"Look at old Wally," Gary said, "combing his hair with that wash cloth."

"Dumb shits like you caused me to lose my hair," Wally retorted.

Gary laughed, lathered his cheeks and square jaw with soap, then placed the brush back in the mug, and began to shave. "Aren't you about ready to finish your tour, give us a buzz job and head home, Wally?"

"It's number forty-eight today. Yep! Two more! Then I'll be back home thinking of you, Gary, all clean shaven, your hair parted, flexing those big biceps, while you're sitting in some Stalag, eating saw dust!"

Frank and Marshall overheard the exchange and smiled.

"Poor Wally, he'll be home and the war will end and we'll be stuck here, having all the fun, looting, raping, stealing paintings and drinking schnapps," Frank said.

"You don't really think they'd keep us here after the shooting stops, do you Frank?" Marshall asked.

Frank smiled and shook his head. "No, Marsh. The ground pounders will get that duty. We're fliers, not policemen."

Marshall looked into Frank's steady gray eyes and felt he must know that for a fact.

"This is an air medal mission coming up. Who wants to join me in Li`ege?" Gary said. "I got transportation all lined up."

"I told the Spike I'd show him around," Marshall said. "It'll be his fifth."

"Hey, Marsh," Wally said, "I understand they're putting Spike and a Norden in my ship today. Think your protégé is ready?

"Certainly! Spike had a Circular Error of under a hundred feet back at Childress. What happened to your guy?"

"Poor Moose. Ruptured an ear drum," Wally said. "Grounded for awhile."

Frank tucked in his shirt, hooked his belt tightly around his thirty-two inch waist and said, "Well, let's hope Spike won't have to use that Norden today. Rumor has it that we are flying lead for our flight."

"You're right, and me and Duffey will be in the slot, nice and tight."

Gary rinsed off his razor, replaced the mug, combed his hair and said, "Come on you guys, back to the serious stuff. Anybody want to join me? The Mademoiselles await!"

"Sure. Spike and I'll join you. Got anything lined up?" Marshall said.

"You betcha! My girlfriend Ginger has a sister, damn near as pretty as she is, and I told you about her mother, Marsh. Let me introduce Spike to them! Man, he'll die and go to heaven!" He puckered his lips and whistled. "God, what a body. She has to be in her mid-thirties. I'll take the mother any day and you guys can fight over the sisters!"

"Christ, Gary, isn't there anything on your mind except sex?" Frank said.

"Sure. Breakfast and getting back alive from Ulm," Gary said, then laughed loudly.

"Damn, it is cold!" Wally said. He lit a cigarette.

"Wally, did I tell you about my last visit to Li`ege?" Gary said.

"Yeah, but tell me again. I want to see how you change your wild tale. Your fantasies are what keep me going!"

"Ha!" Gary exclaimed, as he pulled on his shirt, "That's funny. It was 'wild tail' all right." Spelling out 'tail', he laughed loudly. "Honest to God, with Ginger it was just one long, never ending orgasm. They just ran together. Finally I conked out and next thing it was morning and here we are in this nice big bed, a huge down comforter floating over us, both naked as jay birds, and there's a knock on the door and Ginger says 'come in', in French of course." Gary paused as he buttoned his shirt and tucked it into his trousers. "It was her mom with three cups of coffee on this tray, and she smiles at me and sets the tray down and Ginger introduces us. Geez, I'm wondering what kind of a mess I've gotten myself into this time. God, I hope I'm not getting trapped into marriage."

"Hurry up," Wally said. "You're getting me all excited. That truck will be here in a minute."

"Well, we sip the coffee and Ginger and her mom are whispering and giggling and all of a sudden Ginger reaches over and throws the sheet and comforter back and I'm rigid as a broomstick and try to cover up, and they both laugh," Gary laughed. "Wally I couldn't make up something like this! I don't know what they said but her mother drops her bathrobe and she's a duplicate of Ginger. Incredible figure, AND," Gary raised his voice, "she climbs into the bed on the other side and I'm suddenly engulfed between these two luscious, voluptuous, soft, warm, sweet smelling beauties. It was real, Wally!" Gary exclaimed.

"Gary," Wally said, laughing loudly, "I know you are full of shit but I love to hear you tell about your imagined love life."

Marshall brushed his closely—cut, brown hair, shaved and checked the hair above his upper lip. Still coming in blonde. He'd grown a mustache, and although his hair on his chest was dark and curly, the hair above his lip was not visible. He'd used a soft lead pencil trying to darken it, but embarrassed by Gary's teasing, shaved it off.

Frank, lean and the tallest of his crew, slouched slightly. It was the bold Gary that said, "Hey skipper, stand up straight. Are we too heavy for you?"

"Too many years following a damn plow behind a stubborn mule, Gary."

"Look at this Mauldin cartoon, fellas," Wally said, holding up a copy of *The Stars and Stripes,* "those poor ground pounder's are covered with mud from head to foot, unshaven, eating K rations, and you guys look like you're going to the prom!"

"Wally, after this mission, I'm going to go into Paris and take one of those sight seeing tours. Want to join me?" Frank said.

Wally hesitated, lowered his head, "Sounds great, sure, providing I can get a pass," Wally said, then very quietly added, "You know Frank, This damn war's about over. Christ! I'd hate to be the last guy killed on the last fucking day of this thing!"

"Come on, buddy, you're too damn ornery to get it! Hell, you'll be out of here in a couple of weeks, if not sooner."

Unaware of the conversation, the others left the room. "Marsh," Gary said, "I bet Frank and Wally buy some French postcards!" He laughed loudly.

In the darkness outside the barracks door, a six by six truck awaited, its engine idling. As fliers were dressed and ready, they climbed into the truck, sat shivering for the short ride to the mess hall. There they disembarked. Following their steamy exhalations, and rubbing their hands together to warm them, they entered the mess hall.

Inside, the fragrance always seemed the same; always the odor of fried bacon, and there were the trays of scrambled powdered eggs suspended over the hot water basins, and pitchers of orange juice and tomato juice. Apples and oranges were in pyramid stacks and many of the fliers would take a couple each and stow them in their pockets. Stamped-out, stainless steel trays were stacked and the fliers fell into a line, took a tray, a knife and fork and pushed their trays along the track, advising the servers how much or little they desired of the eggs and fried potatoes and bacon and toast.

White porcelain coffee mugs and clear water glasses were on the tables, with the pitchers of water and of hot, steaming coffee. Many of the fliers sat and stared at their coffee mugs, avoiding thoughts of the imminent danger. They lit cigarettes, a few smoked cigars, but there weren't many pipe smokers. Some visited with other fliers at the table. Most were quiet, and Gary delighted in revealing his love life to anyone who would listen.

Gradually they departed for the briefing, and at the exit, each flier was handed two candy bars. Energy food, they were told.

CHAPTER 2

▼

THE BRIEFING

There was no great rush to move from the mess hall to the auditorium—type building where they would be briefed for the day's bombing mission. In the chill of early morning darkness, they strolled, ambled; now in groups of three, walking rather stiffly, Marshall observed, recalling his dad's pace when they walked to the Baptist church. Some held their lit cigarettes, not puffing at them, and there was a perceptible lowering of their voices, of the timbre, as they indulged in small talk, but prepared themselves mentally for the serious business ahead. It was common knowledge: some would not return.

Marshall, Frank and Gary selected a position midway in the line of rows of wooden benches and sat together as a crew-threesome, as did most of the other officers. The fliers scanned the room and when they made eye contact with a friend, they'd raise a thumb, or form the V sign with their fingers, smile and look back towards the blank emptiness of the concealed map. In a nearby building the enlisted men were similarly being briefed on the day's mission.

At one end of the prefab building there was an elevated platform, a stage, and behind it on the wall was the large map of Germany, now concealed by a plywood structure, a covering, supported at the top by spring loaded hinges.

"They ought to install some fans to blow this damn smoke out of here," Marshall said, coughing.

"Nervous in the service time," Gary said, then chuckled, "Got to do something to get your mind off it."

"Cigarettes are too good for bartering for me to smoke them," Marshall said.

"We've been lucky," Frank said, "But Lady Luck is impatient with carelessness. Let's pay attention."

"Roger," Gary said. Marshall was always amazed by Gary's personality change. One hour ago all he did was gab and joke about his love life. But once inside the briefing room his demeanor changed. If Frank was wounded, it would be up to Gary to fly *DIANA* back to friendly territory, and to land her unassisted.

The Operations Officer, Major White, appeared suddenly and without hesitation hopped up the few steps to the platform and then strode to the edge of the covered map. He held a pointer in one hand, looked out at the audience of fliers. He smiled and said, "Good morning gentlemen. This won't be a milk run, but we don't think you'll encounter a single fighter out there."

With fifty-five missions behind him, he would still occasionally go on a mission as an observer, not in one of the pilots' seats. He said he felt it was his duty to know what was going on, out in that other world. Major White unhooked the covering and swung it upward so that it revealed the map, covered with a plastic overlay.

From the group of fliers a few moans emanated, and someone said, "Flak Alley again," but silence prevailed, broken only by a cough, or the sound of a pencil being tapped against a clipboard.

A wide, black-grease-pencil mark led from their base near the small village of Denain, in France, north of Paris, near the Belgian border, across the edge of Belgium, then zigzagged around known heavy flak areas, finally to Ulm, where the target would be the marshaling yards, the roundhouse in particular.

"The positions of their eighty-eight's are based on yesterday's Intelligence. As you well know, they're still capable of moving those installations overnight."

"Meteorology tells us you've a C.A.V.U. day with a fifteen-knot wind out of the north, which won't help the bomb run time, but that may change as you get near the target. The Ordnance guys are now loading eight, five-hundred-pounders. You're scheduled to drop from thirteen thousand, five hundred feet. I'd suggest a drift reading about five minutes before the I.P."

"Any questions, so far?" Major White asked and looked into the young faces of the pilots and bombardier navigators. He studied their faces, *Christ; some of those guys still don't have enough of a beard to shave.*

"Hey, Major White, sir. I've got two questions?"

"Okay, shoot."

"Why the hell did we hear about Ulm from Sally? And why is the flak getting thicker if they're whipped?"

"I'm your operations officer, not Intelligence, and I'm as pissed off as all of you guys. Honestly, I think Ulm was a lucky guess. The heavies went in there yesterday and did a lot of overall damage. We've got to do the real precision work today. As mentioned earlier, the heavies reported no fighters. As for the flak, the Germans seem to be trying to save what's left of the fatherland. Finally it's their land they are fighting for and unfortunately, they still have plenty of ammo for the 88's."

"Any more questions?" He looked around the room.

"If your craft is damaged, head for France, not Switzerland. We can find you in France. Getting you home from the Swiss gets complicated. Neutral, as you all know."

Major White then read from a clipboard the names of the pilots that would lead the various flights. Four B-26's were in a flight, and Marshall was pleased that it was reaffirmed that Frank Mueller had been chosen. All bombardier-navigators were qualified to do their job with the Norden bombsight, but often the bombardier-navigator who was not in a lead ship did not have a bombsight and, using a toggle switch, manually released his bombs when the lead plane's first bomb appeared as it fell from the bomb bay. The experienced commanders knew that this procedure resulted in the tightest possible pattern of bombs. Of the six aircraft, two were equipped with Norden bombsights. In the event the lead plane was damaged, the crew with the other Norden was prepared to move into the lead slot. The crew of Duffey, Wally and The Spike were assigned that responsibility. Ample navigation responsibilities occupied the bombardier-navigators without bombsights.

"Okay fellas," Major White said, "I expect to see all of you back here this afternoon, and just for you, we've a group of Parisian dancing girls, a magician, and a fine, real swinging, big band waiting for you!" He smiled at his audience. *Each of them thinks the other guy will get it, not him*, then he saluted, turned and left the platform.

There was a scattering of applause, a few laughs, and one flier was heard to say, "Some incentive plan!"

As they began to file out of the room a corporal stood by the exit holding a large box of candy bars. "In case you didn't pick up any after breakfast," he repeated as the groups moved passed him. If a flier took a candy bar, the corporal would say, "Good luck, sir."

Before returning to their barracks to put on the warm, heavy flight gear, most of the fliers stopped at a tent. Often it would be occupied by a Roman Catholic Priest, a Rabbi, and a Protestant minister. Each Chaplain stood behind, or near their respective altars, and would say a short prayer with a flier. Sometimes the meditation and prayer duties would be handled by just one chaplain. Marshall, Frank, and Gary always approached the Protestant Chaplain and listened with bowed heads as he read from the New Testament.

The three moved on, allowing other fliers in line behind them time to visit their chaplains. A tall stocky flier exited the tent about the same time and suddenly bolted around the corner of the briefing building. He quickly reappeared, and moved a few steps out ahead of the threesome, walking alone.

"What the hell was that all about," Frank said.

"Don't you know Greg Cook? He was a star fullback at U.S.C." Gary said. "I saw him do that one other time and I was alone. He walked up beside me and said. 'This is just like waiting to run through the tunnel out onto the field when we played Notre Dame, actually any team we played. I always, I mean ALWAYS had to throw up. Then everything was fine. It's damn sure embarrassing.'"

"All I could say was, 'oh.' I didn't think he wanted me to say 'sorry,' or anything like that. I hear he's a hellova good pilot."

"Never got sick, but my hands still get kind of cold," Marshall volunteered, "For me it's a hunting trip. My dad and Uncle Bruce trained me to hunt."

"I've got one goal. Get *DIANA* and you guys back safely so I can be with my other Diana. Otherwise it's just a high risk job," Frank said.

Gary spoke. "For me, it's one mission at a time. Today we bomb Ulm. Then it's Lie`ge and then it's Ginger."

"Catch up with you later, guys. I've got to get my maps, and the calculations for my computers entered," Marshall said.

"See you back at the barracks," Frank said.

The bombardier-navigators all went to a large, separate room where they spread out their maps, on tables and some on the floor and plotted their courses to the target. Every few inches Marshall entered the reciprocal headings so that he could give a heading to Frank or Gary anywhere along the designated flight plan, in the event they were hit and damaged and had to try to return to the base.

Marshall studied every inch of the course they would travel and circled small bridges over rivers and streams, which had continuing roads. He selected three targets-of-opportunity, in case he could not drop his bombs on the primary target. Marshall spotted The Spike on the other side of the room and when he turned he saw Marshall. They smiled and exchanged V-signs formed by their fingers atop raised arms. Marshall closed his brief case and departed.

Frank and Gary were almost dressed for the mission when Marshall arrived back at their room. When they were all ready they joined other fliers outside the barracks where a six by six truck was parked, its engine idling. In the east, the sky was pink, and the stars faded. Nine officers each studied the sky, then climbed into the back of the truck, lifting their legs with the heavy flight boots, helping each other get settled, all wearing heavy flight clothing, tight-fitting leather hats with sewn-in ear phones. Each wore a chest holster holding their .45 Colt. It was a short drive to the flight line.

"Well, *DIANA* awaits," Frank said, "Let's hop a jeep and see how our guys are doing."

Frank and Gary rode to within a few yards of their B-26, *DIANA*.

"There's Pop supervising those ordnance guys," Frank said.

"How do things look, Pop?" Frank asked.

"She's about loaded up and I checked out the engines awhile ago. I gave them the acid test. Smooth as Gilbey's gin. Good flight-crew. And I filled those thermos jugs with hot coffee for you."

"Let's check out the shackles," Marshall said, "And you've got your emergency screwdriver someplace?"

"Roger, and with a tight fit."

Both walked to the front of the B-26, touched the nose wheel then hoisted themselves up into the pilot's compartment. Marshall tossed his parachute chest-pack onto the seat of his chair in the navigation department. In the bomb bay, Pop and Marshall began to check the shackles holding the bombs, making certain the wires were attached that would be responsible for activating the little propellers which in turn would arm the bombs.

"Fifty-caliber ammo all hooked up properly?" Marshall asked.

"Roger," Pop said. "Jim and John have checked their machine guns. Everything checks out okay."

"Marsh?" Pop asked, "Is this going to be a tough one?"

"Don't think you'll even have to touch those fifty-calibers, Pop, however you be sure to wear that flak suit. I think we can fly around most of it, but it could be rough at the target. You got your rabbit's foot?"

"Never without it," Pop said, laughing.

"Would you mind emphasizing to Jim and John to wear those flak suits. The other day I overheard a gunner say he wasn't afraid of flak." Marshall paused and looked into the questioning eyes of Pop. "Nope, wasn't Jim or John. Just a reminder."

"Roger. Hell, Marsh, I'll ORDER them!" Pop said and laughed. "Anyone not afraid of flak is stupid!"

Marshall laughed too, and thought, God, I'd love to have a set of those big white teeth. Pop opens his mouth, his blue eyes twinkle, and everyone wants to laugh with him.

Both Frank and Gary checked and double-checked every nut and bolt of the landing gear, and they checked every moving part of the nose wheel mechanism. They checked for fine hairline cracks, and for oil or grease that shouldn't appear, and they checked the tires and walked around the aircraft peering up at the bottoms of the wings. Flight crews had already done this, but Frank was the final authority about whether *DIANA* would fly.

Finally they were all aboard and seated and they listened to the roar of the huge engines, and at last they were taxiing to the take-off position. They hoped for some head wind. They all remembered too vividly the B-26 that had an engine fail just as it had become airborne with its landing gear raised. The bombs didn't explode, but the gasoline ignited and did explode when the plane crashed, and then *DIANA* lifted off a few seconds later, flying through the black smoke.

During take off Marshall sat in the navigation department in a high-backed steel chair. He looked towards the tail and across from him sat Jim Frantz, the radioman, his chair also positioned to protect their backs if they crashed and survived. Pop was strapped into his seat behind the copilot, and John was in the stinger, looking past his twin fifties at the B-26's following *DIANA*.

Occasionally, Marshall mused about the various degrees of danger associated with the B-26. When they arrived at Shreveport, Louisiana, where the crews were assembled and they had their first tour of the B-26, it hadn't occurred to him that there would not be an escape hatch in the nose. He knew there was one in the B-25, and the B-17, and the B-24. But there was nothing he could do about it, except pray that he'd never have to try to climb up out of the nose if the plane was diving. If McAdam was helpless, Marshall was trapped. Unassisted, he wouldn't even be able to push back the foot pedals, much less slide McAdam's chair.

At least they had installed that nice door of plate steel, half-inch -thick that he could swing closed when he was in the nose. Good protection for Gary's precious groin! And there was nothing he could do about the danger in taking off and landing. Up to Frank and Gary. And there was nothing he could do about the engines. He understood car engines. Loved the purr of his Model A, and if there was so much as a strange cough from one of the Pratt and Whitney's, well, they all jumped. Pop was a stickler. He worked with the flight crews. He understood the magnetos and the pressure gauges. Marshall had never taken the time to become an expert with the engines. His own responsibilities were enough of a concern. Why worry about things you have no control over, he concluded.

Finally they were airborne. Hell, that's half of the danger behind us already. Now if those pilots are as good as Frank, they can cuddle up nice and close, overlap the wing tips a bit, but I hope the bastards don't plow right on through us. It happens. Marshall recalled the day that Frank came in a little too hot and Marshall thought they'd be grinding metal of another B-26 with their thirteen foot, six inch propellers, but Frank cut power and they fell several hundred feet, and then finally rejoined the flight and got into position.

It wasn't until they got home safely that Frank said, "Christ, that was too close for comfort this morning."

There wasn't anything to add. Pop, Gary, and Marshall all nodded, but said nothing.

Shortly after takeoff Marshall moved from the navigation department to a kneeling position behind the pilots, shoulder to shoulder with Pop. Both Marshall and Pop liked that position where they too, could watch the horizon and see the individual flights of the B-26's of other squadrons, all members of the 493rd Bomb Group. Finally a box composed of the squadrons moved towards the target.

It was time for Marshall to enter the nose and he asked Gary to slide back his seat. Marshall pushed the foot pedals aside, squirmed, twisted his shoulders sideways, and half dragged his hips and legs behind him, his big insulated boots finally disappearing from Gary's view. In the nose, Marshall felt comfortable, with an unobstructed view of space, from horizon to horizon, now eight thousand feet above Belgium. Soon they'd be over Nazi Germany.

CHAPTER 3

▼

A TARGET OF OPPORTUNITY

Thick amber smoke, not unlike that rising from the burning rice fields fired after the fall harvest on the flatlands west of Chico, darkened the morning horizon over Bavaria. Distant black spots, unattached, at eye level, grew larger, then dissipated and became a part of the dirty smoke already saturating the air. It was the Germans' flak.

The spots always reminded Marshall Sunder of the fly specks on the window of the pool hall next to his dad's mercantile store and of the days he stood and stared up at the great rack atop the head of the mule deer mounted high on the wall, hoping now to get back alive, and again hunt big mulies with his dad and Uncle Bruce.

Above the level of the smoke the sky was clear and blue. The meteorology guys were right. With one hand Marshall shaded his eyes from the white sun. He scanned the one hundred and eighty degrees of horizon available to the scope of his vision, partially limited by the aluminum wall beside him and the cable-lined bulkhead behind him.

Then he looked at the map he held in his hands and at the zigzag lines drawn across it, put his finger on a spot, looked out ahead and downward at the neat, symmetrical patterns of the forests, the brown fields, the plowed black lands and at the white, divided-lane autobahn curving, turning, following the gentle contours of the earth west of the Rhine, guiding them now as a navigational aid accurately towards their target.

Leaning forward slowly, balancing his torso, burdened with a heavy flak-suit, Marshall looked downward and off to his right. A few yards behind him in the plastic nose of another B-26 he saw a hand moving back and forth slowly. Marshall acknowledged by waving back.

Behind them the B-26 flown by Duffey and Sullivan with Spike, was below and behind them in the number four, or the slot position, as it was known. Spike will be okay, Marshall thought. He'd checked him out carefully. Spike: what a hellova nickname. He wished that he'd never mentioned it. It had just slipped out—the reference he'd made about the cattle rancher's back home calling a virgin buck a spike. Marshall had been allowed to join his dad on the hunting trips to Oregon and had a couple of four pointers to his credit. None of the hunters would shoot a spike, or a doe. Hell, every buck deserved a chance to propagate itself. If a forked-horn hadn't gotten any, that was his own fault. But you had to give a spike a fair chance. Well, after Spike's Air Medal mission, his fifth mission, Marshall had promised to check him out in Lie`ge. He'd introduce him to some pretty Mademoiselles. It'd be up to him. But they'd probably call him Buck after a weekend leave. Marshall chuckled.

Marshall Sunder looked back at the horizon. The spots were still there, larger now, and the bank of smoke was closer. Beside him the pointed white hand on the black face of the altimeter had stopped revolving and hovered at fifteen thousand feet.

Marshall laid down the map and put his cold hands beneath his armpits to warm them. He wanted to blow on them but couldn't. A gray-rubber oxygen mask was strapped to his face. He felt as though his entire body was bound together so it wouldn't burst and fly apart. His feet were buckled inside of heavy, fur-lined flying boots resembling the weighted shoes of a deep-sea diver. He kneeled and rested his buttocks against the stout shoes. His back was bowed from the weight of the downward pull of the steel flak suit that hung from his shoulders.

Beneath the flak suit was a tight harness with rings to hold his chest pack, and beneath the harness was a shoulder holster carrying his loaded .45. In a pocket of his green woolen shirt he carried the small book, a condensed New Testament, that had been given to him by his mother and she had marked the place he was supposed to regularly read. Its cover was a dark camouflage green, tight fabric, with a small gold cross on the cover. He always took it on a mission. He'd promised he would.

Atop a leather helmet that was buckled beneath his chin and which encased tiny speakers was strapped a steel helmet. Around his throat an inch-wide, gray elastic band was stretched, pulled tight and hooked, holding pressed against each side of his Adam's apple, two nickel -sized sensitive discs; his throat microphone. A hand switch was at his side.

Across the top of the black, crackle-tone finish of his Norden bombsight, out beyond the cigar shaped Plexiglas nose of the B-26, Marshall could see the high rudders and the wings of the bombers of his own squadron and those of other squadrons now surrounded by the black spots, all in flights of six, at different altitudes, moving in tight formation, their wings almost overlapping, changing their course and altitude constantly, steadily boring through the air with the same precision displayed by the high-kicking Rockettes that Marshall and Frank and McAdam had seen in New York City before shipping out.

Within the sun-brightened nose it became suddenly darker and Marshall's mind again lied to him as it had done on twenty-four previous missions.

"Don't you get panicky when they're shooting at you?" Spike had asked him when he joined the squadron and Marshall became his mentor.

"Sure. My brain seems to need a flak suit of its own sometimes," he said. "I just imagine I'm on a hunting trip. It's kind of like having my own personal camouflage."

Turbulence of the explosions shook the airplane and black smoke parted, dissipated, as the Plexiglas nose bore through it. *It is the shadow of a great Canada honker that has flown close to the car. Geese, thousands of them, are slapping their wings against the waters of Tule Lake. They are moving forward, rising, crying out their plaintive honking call, blackening the sky, circling now, seeking their leaders, forming premature V's, waiting for the cold air from Canada to send them farther south. Dad is driving slowly so that we can see them and hear them. Late tonight we will turn off of 139 onto a dirt road and drive to Izee. Emil will be waiting at the ranch.*

Shadows from their great wings darkened the sky. Deep shade momentarily filled the nose of the bomber. Don't kid yourself, he thought. The goddamn krauts are tracking your flight now, have found your altitude and figured your course and the 88's are bursting closer.

In the space between the gray rubber oxygen mask and the rim of the leather helmet perspiration began to form into small beads that trickled down inside his mask. It cooled him, then chilled him. Removing a glove, he wiped away the wet stuff, rubbed his hand on the woolen flight suit, looked at his palm and it seemed too white. He replaced the glove. His eyes darted sidewards at the oxygen valve and he saw the pulsating indicator. He was breathing. The instruments told him everything.

Beside him the tools of his trade were stacked. The C-1 and the C-2 computers and the E-6B. There were notebooks with white print on black pages giving data for all of the bombs. There was a navigation log and sharpened pencils and shiny chrome-plated divider, a compass and rule and multicolored linen-backed maps.

There was a notebook full of photos of the target area, taken from all angles. Everything was set. All of the information garnered from his charts and computers had been entered into the secret guts of the Norden, the disc speed, the drift, figured and preset, the trail-arm adjusted and the motor had been turned on to keep the instrument warm.

Only the bombsight and the two great engines driving the propellers were allowed the luxury of warmth. When the airplane had pierced the invisible, vertical wall, dividing friend from foe, and crossed the bomb line to enter enemy territory, the heaters were turned off. With the heat on, fumes might form if flak ruptured a gas line, and an explosion would follow. But the Norden should be kept warm. It must be kept warm.

Kneeling in one position for sixty minutes had caused Marshall's leg muscles to cramp. He stretched them out as far as he could, lifted his heavy boots with his hands and placed them where they wouldn't disturb the order of the stack of maps and instruments. He was careful not to jar the bombsight. Then he crossed his legs in front of him, Indian fashion, and leaned back against the bulkhead. He looked at his wristwatch. Still two minutes from the initial point, the I.P. a spot in space, the turning point before the last long seconds of the bomb-run. He did not move. The ability to sit still was not one of the many things that he'd been taught by the Air Corps. He'd learned that long before. Within the heavy gloves, his hands began to warm.

Emil Hyde's young palomino didn't like the strong odor of the piece of fresh hide, a musk gland cut from the leg of a buck deer. It was tied onto the bridle next to its broad nostrils, placed there to familiarize the horse with that scent, to teach it to tolerate that odor. The horse bucked, tried to free himself of the offensive scent, and of the rider. But Emil had ridden tougher horses and now cursed this one, his voice barely audible, almost as if he were swearing at himself, and it appeared to Marshall that Emil and the horse were one, inseparable now as the horse pivoted, his sharp hooves digging deep patterns in the moist dirt outside the barn. Backwards it moved, swiftly, then reared up, the muscles of its legs bulging like huge ropes, its ears flattened back tight against its head, but Emil controlled the horse, then trotted the palomino down the road in among the quaking aspens surrounding the two-story white ranch house. They all saw Emil jerk hard at a limb on the tree, break off a branch,

*and strip the yellow leaves from it. With it he stung the golden-brown flanks of
the rebellious horse.*

*Emil loped the palomino back towards them. White saliva stretched in a
long ribbon from its mouth, separated and dropped to the ground. The horse
snorted, shook its head from side to side, fought the shiny, wet bit pulled back
tightly in its mouth, but responded to the messages transmitted through reins
and Emil's knees and heels.*

*No one had moved. No one had said anything. It was Emil's business.
When it was all over, they followed him, guided their horses single file up a
dirt road towards the mountain.*

It's the same. Some high-ranking officer's making the decisions about
where to go and what to bomb, just as Emil ran the show on the cattle
ranch. And Frank and Gary must control the B-26, a stallion of airplanes,
with its 2000-horsepower engines suspended beneath each wing.

It was all preparation, for the next phase: The waiting and watching,
sitting in the nose of an airplane; the only difference is being behind a
bombsight instead of sitting hidden on a stand with a rifle. Even when
they were in training, the waiting to reach the target reminded him of the
hours he'd spent on a hunting stand, high in the Strawberry Mountains.

At first the noise of the engines had bothered him, but then he began to
realize that the constant, steady magnitude was not much different than
the complete enveloping silence of the mountains. Behind him now were
the roaring engines, the high-octane gasoline exploding without pause
within cylinders arranged in a circle around a shaft that spun into invisi-
bility two four-bladed propellers, pulling them, the fliers, forward, pushing air back across the curved wing surfaces, carrying six men at stations
within a fuselage, all of them surrounding the bomb bay with eight, five-
hundred-pounders hanging on shackles from vertical racks.

Dodge it! Run from it! Turn back from the sudden red flashes and the
black smoke and the ripping noise his mind said, pleaded, on that first
mission, while knowing full well there would be no turning back. Then
his mind capitulated, compromised with him and resolved, rationalized

that this was nothing more than a hunting trip. He was prepared. Emil and his dad had prepared him. Other bombardiers came from cities and brought no hunting memories. For them he felt sorry. Just as his little New Testament was camouflaged, so was Marshall's mind.

Rough air buffeted the B-26 as it flew through the prop wash of the flight ahead. Marshall glanced at the map in his hand, looked at his watch, then looked over his shoulder, twisted his body and pulled open the half-inch thick steel door. McAdam looked down at him over the top of the wheel, winked, and looked back at the instrument panel. Marshall could tell by the wrinkles at the corners of his eyes that he had smiled. A flak helmet like Marshall's reached almost down to his eyebrows and an oxygen mask fitted up tightly beneath his eyes.

"One minute to the I.P.," Marshall said. He swung the heavy door, latched it, then turned and looked back at the black puffs at eye level. McAdam is there alive, Marshall thought, helping Frank fly *DIANA*, all of them in this thing with me; like the hunters on the stands, each depending upon the other, yet functioning independently. Good old McAdam, he thought, riding like a spare tire on the family V-8. A piece of flak might puncture Mueller. Life would hiss out of him, as if he was a flat tire and the Ford had just run over a piece of sharp metal in the road. Put on the spare. Keep going. If another tire goes out? We've had it. And the others— Pop, the engineer, manning the waist guns, and the radio operator, Frantz, now in the turret, and John facing the rear, manning his machine guns. If we get it, there's another Marauder right behind to move into our position. Spike could take over the lead now. He's had four tough missions, been scared four times and returned matured each time.

Well, we'll call him Buck after a little mission to Lie`ge. Only guy in the outfit who ever admitted he hadn't shacked up. Took guts to be that honest and he'd take a lot of kidding about being a spike, but everyone liked him more for it.

Marshall squinted down at the terrain below. Far off to his right he could see the base of the great dark plume of smoke that extended into the sky a thousand feet above them. Small boxcars and tankers on threadlike tracks blazed at the base of the spiraling smoke column. From thirteen thousand, five hundred feet the yellow flames appeared no larger than the last flicker on a match after two cigarettes had been lit from it. Marshall leaned forward, over the round humps of the black bombsight. There it is! The roundhouse! Still intact. Why haven't they hit it? Lead bombardier must have a problem. They are drifting off our course too fast. The wind has changed. We'll have to take a longer run.

Marshall studied the roundhouse on the photo beside him, then looked back towards the target. *It is a button-mushroom pushing up through the moist earth after the rains, just before the germinating seeds send up their first tender green blades.* Forget your damn fields! Forget Chico and Tule Lake and the ranch, a voice commanded, not over the intercom, but from within. It is spring over Germany and the war is almost over.

Where in the hell is the I.P.? Back and forth Marshall glanced at the photos and then at the horizon and then across and over the bombsight, down at the earth. We're right on course. The Group lead bombardier must not have caught the wind change. We're on our own. Thirty seconds from the I.P. Trust me, Frank, Marshall thought.

White light reflected off spider-web like impurities in the Plexiglas nose extending in front of Marshall Sunder. Overhead the sun traveled its arc still higher, emphasizing against the dark blue sky the snowy vapor trails of their little friends, the P-38's and the P-47's watching over them, awaiting the Messerschmitts. Flying beneath their formation Marshall knew that more fighters would be seeking out the ack-ack emplacements, strafing them and dropping antipersonnel bombs on them when they could find them, discovering them despite the camouflage, hidden amongst the trees.

And crouched in the nose of a B-26 flying slightly behind and below him, a few yards away, was Spike, awaiting the opening of the bomb bay of Marshall's ship, while studying his own maps. Grouped tightly there followed three more B-26's with experienced, seasoned crews, all trained to clock-like efficiency. The bombardier-navigators who did not have

Norden bombsights had to toggle their loads at the first sight of a bomb appearing from the fuselage of the lead plane.

The earth patterns shifted from side to side, slowly, a motion like the swinging trunks of contented zoo elephants. Keep up the evasive action, Frank old buddy, Marshall thought. All it takes is fifteen lousy seconds for the krauts to track us, calculate our course and estimate our altitude, then send towards us at a thousand feet a second their little gift packages of jagged steel. Just keep changing course a little. Fifteen degrees right, twenty degrees right, now forty left, just as long as we get to the I.P. Now climb a little, dive a little. The bastards won't have us today!

Are they the hunters and we the pheasants, Marshall thought? Who are they down there, anyway? Young, blonde men with pale blue eyes and cruel mouths, clicking their polished black boots and loading those god-damn 88's. I wish I could see them, confront them. Why don't they give it up? They're whipped. If they're so damn smart, why don't they know that?

The roads! There are my roads. Marshall edged further forward, shaded his eyes, and studied the irregular, pie-shaped sections, pieces that formed the intersection. Fifteen seconds from the I.P.

Feverishly Marshall studied the panels of instruments on the panel beside him, looked at the compass, at the altimeter and at its barometric setting. He checked the trail setting and the disc speed on the Norden.

Shadows of the wings of a great Canada honker engulfed the transparent nose and Marshall instinctively dodged. Above the engine noise a roar reached his ears, penetrated the steel flak helmet and the leather helmet with its earphones. Red light filled the nose, reflected off of the glass face instruments around him. Blue sky reappeared, then the white hot spot of the sun. Marshall glanced behind him. The steel door was shut tight. It would keep flying steel fragments from reaching the legs and groin and belly and chest of McAdam.

"Everyone okay?" Frank asked.

"Okay up here," Marshall said. Four more okay's traveled the intercom system. Further conversation was pointless.

Now crouching over the bombsight, Marshall stared almost straight downward towards the earth, then pressed the switch at his side.

"Roll out and hold her close to two-sixty. We're over the I.P."

"Roger."

"Bomb bay doors open," Marshall said.

"Roger."

The damn smoke is drifting across the roundhouse. Have to take a long run. Forty seconds.

Orange flashes reflected off of the glass faces of the instruments followed by the instant wrapping of the feathery black wings of a nonexistent imaginary bird around the bomber's nose. Marshall heard the familiar ripping, screeching noise, as if a pointed rasp had been stuck through the side of a tin, five-gallon gasoline container.

A folded map was sucked into space by the drag of the still air outside the bomber, through a hole in the Plexiglas the size of a softball where the irregular shaped hunk of flak had exited. Above Marshall's head was a similar hole, but smaller. He stared at them, then held both hands in front of his face; suddenly afraid they might be gone, sucked away without his knowing it. Five seconds had elapsed.

With each brilliant flash of light the B-26 shuddered, vibrated like a car rumbling across a corduroy road, seemed to vacillate, to waver, as if unwilling to proceed through the turbulent air, beaten into ridges by the exploding shells.

Marshall pulled his maps away from the hole. He propped a clipboard against the bulkhead, trying to plug the hole. What good would a handless bombardier be? I've never known a left-handed bombardier. Probably regulations. Thank you, God, for not taking my hands. I'm still here, breathing oxygen and seeing in front and all around me the solid geese disintegrating into black smoke instead of feathers.

"Son of a bitch!" he said aloud, into the oxygen mask, knowing he'd said it only because he felt his lips move against the cold rubber. He would have to press the switch to hear his own voice.

Marshall discarded his gloves. With his left hand he grasped the round black bombsight head, and held the course-knob with his right hand.

"Breathe in slowly and deeply, Son. Raise the barrel up smoothly. Come on now, pull the stock back hard and tight against your shoulder. Good boy. When the bead on the front sight touches the bottom of the bull's- eye, hold your breath and pull the shot off steadily. Don't jerk the trigger. Squeeze with your whole hand."

"Okay dad. I understand. I can do it."

Marshall sighted over the cross-trail bar.

"Roll her out. Five right. Five more." Marshall spoke slowly, the hand switch depressed. He knew Frank would follow the compass, correct the course, coordinate each movement of pedal and wheel and throttle, blend them into one fluid motion. The medium bomber responded and was again flown straight and level. Marshall knew that behind them five more bombers copied each dip of *DIANA's* wings, keeping close so their bomb pattern would be tight.

Bet Spike's sweating this one, Marshall thought.

Grasping a knob atop the bombsight with his left hand, Marshall uncaged the gyroscope, glanced at the air bubbles of two glass vials, mounted at ninety degrees from each other, then bent forward from the waist and pressed his forehead and cheek down tight, staring with his right eye through the eye piece, compressing the black rubber eye-guard above the lens of the Norden bombsight.

The vertical cross hairs, framed within the circle, moved slowly from side to side with the roll of the ship, staying to the left of the tracks leading to the roundhouse. The lateral hair was in the center of the circle, moving across the terrain like the narrow blade of a squeegee being pushed upward instead of downward on a windowpane, representing the speeding approach of the bomber towards the target.

"Another five right," Marshall said. Frank responded. The vertical black line bisected the roundhouse, now barely visible at the top radius of the circle.

"Level, please," Marshall said. Quickly, he raised his head from the bombsight. He checked the positions of the bubbles in the glass tubes behind the small round window of the Norden and while Frank guided the bomber on as straight and level a course as possible, Marshall pressed with his finger tips inward first one knob and then the other, exerting a light turning motion.

"Level okay."

"Roger."

Again, Marshall thrust his head down upon the bombsight. Black shadows, the honkers and ducks, too, were all obstructing his line of sight. They disappeared, and more appeared and disappeared. Dense smoke momentarily hid the target, the flight of the aircraft remained steady, and the burning railroad yard revealed itself.

"Follow P.D.I.," Marshall said. He could feel moisture on his back and chest turning cold, the same coldness flowing from beneath his armpits, moving down his sides.

"Roger," Frank said. He now followed a single needle on his instrument panel, piloting the B-26 according to Marshall's electronically transmitted course-to-follow signals.

Within the scope the lateral hair reached the roundhouse, barely visible through the smoke of the burning boxcars. Marshall reached to the side of the bombsight, lifted a small switch and the black line began to move upward slowly. His fingers reached for a graduated drum, its diameter the size of a water glass. Slowly he revolved the drum on its axis away from him. The lateral cross hair stopped.

All of the calculators, the C-2's and E-6B's and steady fingers and practice, practice, practice with the same pilot and copilot and crew had combined with the mathematical, slide-rule mind of some men back home to bring into full synchronization the gears of the bombsight, blending flesh and formulas to bring them upon a nearly steady platform, shaped like a crucifix to a spot in space, the exact spot from which the bombs should drop.

Black smoke was dense, thick around the bomber. Hot, orange-red spots blinked outside the nose, and black smoke, not feathers, choked the air. Explosions sent hard vibrations through the bomber, jarred the rubber ring, and hurt Marshall's cheekbone. He pressed his face down harder. The cross hairs settled near the shoulders of a six-point buck. No! It's too damn mean to be a deer. It's a vicious, sheep-killing mountain lion!

"Kill clean, Son. Never hurry a shot. Pass up a shot if you have to, but try to never wound any game."

Perspiration emerged from Marshall's skin, soaked his face. He straightened, unbowed his torso, glanced away from the bombsight. His eyes flew across the rows of panels with their gleaming red beads.

Everything was set; the intravelometer knob, the bomb-panel switch up, now only something out of place, something wrong, would catch his eye.

Seven seconds! Marshall returned to the scope, saw the smoke and the target and heard her voice, not over the intercom, his mother's voice, reading it—Yea though I walk through the valley of the shadow of death…fear no evil—and he remembered, in a millionth of a second the touch of her hand folding his fingers around the small camouflaged book with the gold cross embossed on the cover.

Marshall looked through; past the black lines, the cross hairs, made a slight correction, and barely moved the drum of the Norden.

"Fucking cougar!" Marshall shouted into the oxygen mask, then forced upward a long black trigger, pushed a holding pin beneath it, checked the trigger to make certain it was locked in place, and saw on the curved surface of the Norden, beneath a glass cover, a small black indice, small enough to fit on the eraser of a pencil, gradually moving closer up the narrow curved glass of a window towards another indice the same size. Marshall flicked upward another switch. The bombs were armed.

The indices met, crossed. Marshall curved his body over the bombsight; peered through the optics and saw the cross hairs split the face of the screaming, white-fanged mountain lion. The black lines held steady, synchronized on the roundhouse.

"Bombs away," Marshall said, with the mike switched depressed. He next said, "Bomb bay doors closed." To the crew his voice revealed no excitement. It had always sounded the same, whether on a training mission or on a milk run.

In one motion Marshall retreated from the scope and checked the trigger. It had released. The brilliant red lights on the bomb panel darkened…NO, NO, all of them hadn't released, but the crew thought all of the bombs had fallen, felt the lurch upwards as three thousand pounds fell through open doors. Marshall knew it wasn't the four thousand pounds of eight five hundred pounders!

"Roger," Frank responded, and in the same instant Marshall pushed downward one of the polished metal knobs, caged the delicate gyroscope against a damaging tumble, and saw the horizon tip dizzily sidewards as Frank banked the bomber, dove away from the black bursts of flak, the explosions that sent dozens of ragged fragments of steel into the space around them.

Gravity forces pushed Marshall downward, an irresistible pressure, a weight compressing him into helplessness, sprawled across the bombsight over which he had leaned, hoping to see his bombs fall away, trying to keep in sight the roundhouse, but it slipped away, seeming to hang suspended on the tilted horizon.

He put his hands down to push away from the Norden and his right hand felt the air from outside the fuselage grab at his wrist, trying to suck his arm, all of him, out into the still air as it had the map.

Full, round and white tops of three parachutes, bright in the sunshine, like bloomers billowing on a clothesline, floated lazily downward, swinging fliers back and forth at the ends of taut silk shrouds.

The whiteness of the parachutes contrasted sharply against the dark brown smoke from the blazing, smoking target. They should hurry, Marshall thought, allowing a fleeting change of concentration. But how can they rush the descent of a parachute? Maybe trained paratroopers can slip the movement by maneuvering the shrouds, but that takes practice, is a different specialty. I hope the bastards don't shoot them in the air. They'll have a chance on the ground.

"Shack!" Pop shouted from his position at a waist gun. "The round-house is going up. It's on fire. Our flight hit it. Our flight!"

"Did you see those chutes?" Marshall spoke over the intercom.

"Number four is smoking," the tail gunner said. "Number three got it. Oh my God! It' spinning! It's going to spin in! I think that's where those chutes came from."

"Give me a heading," Frank ordered.

"Three forty. Possible bomb release malfunction," Marshall said.

Need for a tight wing tip to wing tip formation no longer existed and the medium bombers peeled off and away from one another, seeking a flak free route back to the base.

"Roger on the heading. Repeat message," Frank said.

"Possible bomb release malfunction," Marshall said. "I've got to check the bomb bay."

"Sit tight," Frank said. "Everyone okay?"

"Roger," was the response from each station.

"*DIANA* is a sieve," Frantz, the top turret gunner said.

"Pop, check the racks," Frank ordered.

"Christ, I can't stand up. Can you level off a second, Skipper?"

"Roger, we'll trim her up for you."

"Okay Pop. Give it a try."

Frank piloted the bomber in a reduced evasive action pattern, losing altitude, making it difficult for the antiaircraft guns to track them.

"Top two bombs, port side still on the racks," Pop said.

"I'm coming up to take a look," Marshall said. Before he unplugged his head set, John reported from the tail, "Number four still has a smoking engine and is heading for the deck."

Marshall removed his flak vest and steel flak helmet. Damn, he thought, the Spike is in number four.

McAdam slid the copilot's seat back. Marshall swung open the steel-plate door and folded the foot pedals aside and crawled through the space, careful not to snag a control with the straps of his chest-pack harness. Marshall struggled against the tug, the pull of gravity—the resistance to his crawling as Frank continued his evasive action, bracketing the heading Marshall had given him.

Marshall hurried through the navigation-radio compartment and viewed the two bombs still held by their shackles to the rack. Small wires were still in place so the tiny propellers could not function. The bombs were not armed. They were classified as "safe" until released from the shackles.

Marshall returned to the navigation department and plugged in his head set.

"Frank. The bombs are safe now, but I don't trust those shackles. Don't want them to release when we touch down."

"Roger. Can you find a target on the way home?"

"I'll find a bridge. Pop knows how to release the shackles with a screwdriver. We're well rehearsed."

"Who's going to tie me to the struts?" Pop asked.

"John, you'll have to help Pop. Hold onto him," Frank said.

"Roger," answered the tail gunner.

"I'm going back and set up the Norden for a ten-thousand-foot run," Marshall said. Again he crawled through the small space adjacent to McAdam and was relieved to see a flak free sky. Within a few minutes he was able to pinpoint their position over Bavaria. On his map, along a zigzag course route to and from the base to the primary target, Marshall had circled several potential targets-of-opportunity.

Any intersection of roads crossing a river or stream was a desirable target. The crews had been briefed by Intelligence: if a problem is encountered at the primary target, your priority is to disable the Germans' ability to move their tanks and trucks and men and ammunition. Don't bring back bombs.

"Eleven thousand," Frank said.

"Take a heading of twenty-eight," Marshall said, "That should bring us to Bad Scheidel in seven minutes. It's a few miles from that abandoned Luftwaffe base."

"Leveling off at ten thousand," Frank said. "Expect any eighty-eights on this run?"

"Should be a milk run," Marshall answered.

"Hooray," Pop said.

"Keep a sharp lookout for bandits. They can hear us all over Germany."

"The Norden is all set. I'm coming out again to review things with Pop," Marshall said.

"Any little friends out there, we might need you," Frank spoke into his mic, knowing his voice was being transmitted into space, beyond the confines of the ship he captained.

Marshall joined Pop in the bomb bay. Both plugged into speaker jacks. Marshall pointed to the A-11 shackle, a sturdy, sixteen-inch-long, stainless steel hourglass-shaped device with two levers fitting into slots on a release box. Marshall stretched to the limit of the cord to his headset, across one of the bombs and pointed to a slot on the shackle into which Pop would place the screwdriver blade, that with a twist would cause the shackles to open, releasing and arming the bomb.

"Bottom one first!" Marshall said. "You got that screwdriver and the piece of cord?"

"Okay, okay," Pop said, "I've got it. Christ it's cold!"

"Pop, you and John have got to wear your chest packs. Be damn sure that screwdriver is secured to your wrist. After you release the bottom bomb, repeat the top as quickly as you can. Okay?"

"Yes, yes, damn it! Already done that! On what command?"

"I'll say 'GO'! You say 'bombs away' IF they release. Got it?

"Roger."

"Good luck!"

Pop returned to his station at the waist guns, plugged in his headset and advised John of their assignment. Both snapped their chest packs onto the parachute harnesses.

As Marshall reached the pilot compartment, McAdam grabbed his shoulder before he could duck to crawl back into the nose. He pointed out of his window. Practically on their wingtip was a little friend, a P-38. The pilot waved at them. Lettered beneath him on the fuselage was written *Lucky Tim* atop a bright green shamrock.. Rows of little bombs were painted beneath the cockpit.

Off of Frank's wing tip was another P-38 escort.

"Got a problem, big friend?" one of the pilots said.

"Couple bombs hung up. We've got a bridge located. Thanks for showing up. Concerned about bandits."

"Hell, you guys blew up all of their gas stations. They're all through. We'll hang around till you get across the bomb line. Couple of our guys are guiding that smoking buddy from your flight on home."

"Thanks. Roger," Frank said.

He had to improvise! Marshall's mind took him to a hunting camp as he scanned the terrain for the sight of a road that passed through Bad Scheidel. There was nothing he could do to help the Spike or the other bomber. Again his mind brought up a memory, saw it like a home movie scene projected at an accelerated speed through his mind.

Marshall's dad and his uncle sat beside a small fire pit. Marshall stooped and warmed his hands.

"What is Uncle Bruce doing with his rifle?" Marshall asked.

"It won't fire," his dad said, "He thinks the stock got too wet and swelled up and has pinched the trigger mechanism. He recently added a trigger shoe to broaden the fingertip feel. It's locked on with little Allen screws and he doesn't have a wrench, so he's making one out of a nail. He can't get the action and barrel out of the stock with that little shoe on the trigger."

"Why doesn't he borrow your rifle? You've got your buck."

"*Combination of pride and stubbornness,*" *his dad said, then chuckled.* "*But he's innovative. The problem requires a little creative imagination, and your Uncle Bruce is a persistent one.*"

Marshall moved closer to his uncle and watched him file flats on the tip of the nail. "*I always forget to bring something,*" *Bruce said.* "*Who'd think I'd need an Allen wrench?*" *He placed the nail on a rock near the fire and turned it carefully, removing metal with the small file.* "*Think that might do it?*" *Bruce said, and looked at Marshall, who was engrossed by the task. Bruce then slipped the tiny six-sided nail tip into screw.* "*Fits pretty well, doesn't it,*" *he said.*

Marshall nodded and grinned.

"*Son,*" *Bruce said,* "*would you mind bringing me about a tablespoon of cooking oil in a cup.*"

"*Sure, Uncle Bruce.*" *Marshall went to the kitchen area of the campsite and returned with the oil.*

"*This is what's known as oil hardening,*" *Bruce said. He held the tip of the newly configured nail with a pair of pliers and placed it near the glowing coals and when it was red-hot he removed it and immersed it in the oil. A tiny puff of smoke emerged from the oil and Bruce held up the nail and examined it.*

"*Now that we've hardened it, we've got to temper it so it won't be brittle,*" *Bruce said.*

Marshall nodded, as if in agreement.

"*We'll just heat the rascal up again and let it cool down all by itself,*" *Bruce said.* "*Not many good elements in a nail, but good steel is like good people. When we call a man well tempered we mean he can take the heat, be tough and resilient and strong. Good steel has chromium and nickel and molybdenum mixed in with the iron, and a well-tempered man has character traits like honesty, and courage and patience and kindness. Like your pop.*"

"*I like that, Uncle Bruce,*" *Marshall said.*

Bruce fitted his new wrench into the opening of one of the Allen screws and removed it carefully

"*Wow,*" *Marshall said. Bruce laughed and winked at him*

Looking toward the earth over the dome of the bombsight, Marshall searched for landmarks, road crossings, patterns of forest areas, and he watched for the direction of drifting smoke. He was confident their improvised alternate plan would be successful. He too, could be inventive.

"Frank, I've time to take a drift reading. I'm coming out again."

"Roger."

Again, Marshall maneuvered his way out of the nose. In the navigator's department he used the optical drift meter, reached his conclusion and returned to the nose.

"I've got Bad Scheidel spotted," Marshall said. "See that road heading almost due north into the wooded area? A small river bisects the road. There's a village back in there and a bridge. That's our target."

"Roger. Give me a heading."

"Due north. That'll give us minimum drift."

"Roger."

"Pop, are you and John set?"

"Roger."

"Bomb bay doors open."

"Tracking well. Looking good," Marshall said.

"Ready for P.D.I."

"P.D.I. okay," Frank answered. "She's all yours."

Marshall scanned his panel, instinctively set his trigger, requested a leveling of the gyroscope, thrust his eye down upon the rubber ring of the optics, and began the synchronization that would finally stop the cross hairs upon his selected target. The indicies approached the point where they normally would trigger the electronic signal to the intervelometer to release the bombs. Frank followed the movements of the needle on the Pilot's Directional Indicator.

When the intersection of the cross hairs reached a spot approximately half the length of a football field, short of the edge of the bridge, Marshall said, "GO." He felt the upward lurch of the bomber and knew the bombs had fallen from the racks. He hoped the delay for his voice communication with Pop would be correct. And this time the lights on the panel went out.

"Bombs away!" Pop said.

"Bomb bay doors closed," Marshall said.

Without the menace of flak, Frank held the B-26 on course and Marshall leaned over the Norden Bombsight. Both bombs exploded at opposite ends of the bridge. Marshall was elated.

"Amazing! This is Tim Davis," one of the P-38 pilots spoke. "We'll escort you guys to the bomb line and then head for home. Well done. Man, that Norden is here to stay!"

The voice of Pop came though the intercom. "Need some help in the bomb bay."

"Roger. Be right there," Marshall said.

Quickly he exited the nose, stepped out of the cockpit area, and strode through the navigation and radio compartments into the dark bomb bay area.

"My god!" he said.

Pop was held so tightly by John that he could not move. John grasped a stanchion with one arm and his other was curled tightly beneath Pop's head, and around his neck. John's face was contorted into a teeth-revealing grimace, his eyes wide and staring.

"Slug him!" Pop yelled.

Marshall balanced on the narrow catwalk and put his hand on John's rigid arm, tried to grip his arm and pull it away.

"You'll be okay! You're safe! Let go of Pop! I'll help you back to the tail," Marshall yelled at John.

"Slug him damn it!" Pop gasped.

Again Marshall appealed to John. He stared blankly at Marshall.

Gripping a stanchion with his left hand Marshall pivoted his body and with force struck John on the side of his face with the palm of his right hand.

Stunned, John looked at Marshall, blinked his eyes, and shook his head. His lips closed and he looked at Pop.

"Oh shit, I'm so fucking scared," John yelled.

"Come on, let's get out of here. I'll help you back to the tail," Marshall shouted at him.

John released his grip on Pop and allowed Marshall to hold his arm as they tight-walked back into the tail section of the bomber. He kneeled down beside a waist gun and plugged in his head set. Marshall plugged in his on the opposite side.

"I'm sorry, sir," John said.

"Forget it. Everything's all right now," Marshall said. "You okay?"

"Yes, sir," John said. "I'm going on back to the stinger," and he returned to his station in the tail.

Pop had gone to the navigation department.

When Marshall reached him he asked, "You okay?" The engineer was untying the cord around his wrist that was tied to the screwdriver.

"Me okay? Damn near get choked to death by a tail gunner that's afraid of heights? Sure Lieutenant, I'm okay, okay, okay!"

"Well, Pop, your bombs took out the bridge."

"Big deal," Pop said. "Finally something to write home about it."

Marshall laughed, patted him on the shoulder and returned to the cockpit where he kneeled between the pilots.

"I didn't need a heading," Frank said. "We know the way home." Frank rested his arms on his chest as McAdam flew the bomber toward the base.

"But we're going down to take a look at the damage. Strafe that road a bit. Keep 'em nervous!" Gary said. "Hang on guys."

"What the hell happened back there?" Frank said.

Marshall and Frank communicated without using their throat mikes "Nothing real serious. John panicked when the bomb bay doors were open. He looked down and froze. Closing the bomb bay doors didn't help. I'll explain later, okay?" Marshall paused. Frank nodded, and Marshall continued, "How about relieving Frantz from the turret and let him ride on home with John?"

"Okay. Frantz, you can climb out of that glass house now. Check on John."

"Roger," Frantz replied. "Any chance of turning on the heaters, skipper?"

"Roger, you got it."

"Marsh. Our little friends took off. I don't know what happened to number four," Frank said.

Their conversation was again private. McAdam concentrated on piloting a bomber whose design was unforgiving of carelessness.

"Who are the pilots on number four?"

"Duffey and Sullivan."

"Well, the Spike is in good hands," Marshall said.

Marshall began to record his observations. He thought about the bomb run. Strange the group lead bombardier didn't pick up the wind change aloft. Dean was the best. Hope he wasn't wounded! He thought about their own bomb run. I hope we really did hit the roundhouse. The photos will be the final proof. Even if I dropped a little short the pattern of the flight would have scored. Maybe number three wouldn't have been hit if I'd taken a shorter run. Forty lousy seconds. I had no choice.

"How far to the bomb line?" Pop asked. He always wanted to know where they were. What difference did it make, Marshall wondered. What could he do about it to change anything? But if it made him feel better to know, that was enough of a reason.

"Should cross the Meuse River about 1318, Pop."

"How's *DIANA* look back there?" Frank said.

"Little lady's full of holes. A sieve," Pop answered. "Colder than a whore's heart back here. When we going down?"

"Few more minutes," Marshall said. "Christ, Spike's earning his goddamn air medal!"

"Hey skipper," the voice of Sgt. Frantz called, "how about a little music?"

"Roger," Frank said, and Marshall could hear the soft chuckle in Frank's voice before he released his mic switch.

"We got her whipped," Pop said. "Twenty-five more to GO and it's San FernanDO. HEY, I'm almost a poet, you guys."

Groans answered from each station.

"Keep your eyes open. They can still get a few fighters up," Frank said.

Marshall Sunder returned to his clipboard and continued to record his observation. Soon they'd be over the base and he'd close out the log, make a few last entries and turn it all over to someone in Intelligence to digest. That was the big difference, he thought. Just a few marks on paper and some photos of targets hit or not hit. Completely impersonal, not like hunting back home. An unsatisfactory ending, no culmination anyway you looked at it. *Intelligence will be surprised to learn of the destruction of the bridge at Bad Scheidel.*

Marshall's six-foot frame forced him to crouch in the nose of the B-26. The bulkhead above him was too low for him to sit erect. He unbuckled the parachute harness and pushed his hand through the zippered opening of his flight suit beyond the stiff leather holster containing his .45, and groped until he found the compact New Testament. He patted it. *Got us back again. Thanks, God.*

"Looks like a plume of black smoke on the horizon," Gary said.

"Oh?" Marshall replied.

Emil drove the old pickup fast, never having much regard for the mechanical values of any of his tractors or mowers or combines, not paying attention to the bumps in the dirt road. He was intent on looking out Marshall's window across the barbed wire fence.

When they were almost two miles from the ranch house he stopped. Marshall and Emil slid beneath the bottom strand of the fence, each stretching the wire upward for the other, then walked through the deep wet grass that cooled their feet inside their wet leather boots. Marshall carried the ax and had to jump ahead once in an awhile to keep up with the long strides taken by Emil.

"*Aspens won't do,*" Emil said. *They wouldn't burn, and neither would the pine when it was wet. Alder was just right. It would burn slowly and put out a good thick smoke, and besides, it imparted the best flavor.*

Finally they stopped at a thick clump of alders, their serrated leaves already fallen and lying wet moldy on the deep grass. Three trees, as thick as Emil's thigh, toppled before his ax. Marshall dragged them back towards the fence. Small branches were quickly trimmed.

Emil began to cut the long trunks into log-size pieces. "I'll spell you," Marshall said, wanting a chance to cut neat white chunks out of the trunks.

When they reached the smokehouse his dad and Percy were already hanging the red strips of venison. They pushed stiff steel wire through the top sections of venison and attached the ends of the wire to opposite sides of the smokehouse, pulling the wire tight and twisting the ends around nails. The meat had been soaked in brine for several hours to draw out the blood.

Marshall helped Emil build the fire in the lower part of the smokehouse. They closed the door tightly, but there were vents for some smoke to escape the house, drift upwards, carrying the pleasing fragrance of alder and venison. In a couple of days the smoked meat would be ready, still juicy, with a slight salt flavor, and saturated with the aroma of alder. It was the satisfying culmination of a good hunt.

In the distance Marshall could see the pattern of runways. At the end of them there arose the column of black smoke. There had been a crackup. He hoped it wasn't number four. Wounded hunters. I hope they all got out.

In his log he made his final entry, and once more swung open the heavy steel door. McAdam pushed his seat back as far as it would go and Marshall folded the foot pedals aside and squirmed past McAdam's knees, out of the nose of the B-26. It was good to see the unmasked faces of McAdam and Frank. The insulated boots felt heavy, but he'd soon be rid of them.

He remembered that first mission when he exited from the nose and looked at Gary and Frank. Later Frank had laughingly said, *"You looked like a startled fawn crawling out of there.*" Gary had swatted him on the buttocks with his open hand as he crawled passed him. Well, they'd all made it again. Twenty-five more missions and their tour would be completed and they'd be heading for the States. Marshall was willing to pass up the three-day pass just to more quickly get in some more missions, but understanding superstitions of fliers, he wasn't about to broach the subject with the other crew members.

Both Marshall and Frank had laughed when McAdam urged them to join him on the three-day pass. Their real hope was that the war would end any day. McAdam had added that he needed to taper off gradually. His prostate wouldn't be able to stand the withdrawal shock Stateside. Marshall smiled at the thought.

Contrary to regulations, he kneeled behind Frank and McAdam, and Pop was now behind them, too, studying the instruments. Their landing strip was ahead and it always felt as though they were diving towards the nearest edge of the surface of the long blacktop runway.

Rubber screeched as the tires of the B-26 met the runway. Frank lowered the nose wheel slowly until it touched the concrete strip. He guided the speeding bomber towards the source of the oily black smoke.

Firefighters were spewing white foam on the collapsed fuselage of the B-26. Marshall pushed open the canopy above the pilots and pulled himself upwards, outside the airplane. He sat and rode there, on the fuselage, his legs dangling inside the cockpit. The crisp air carried with it the odor of burning petroleum. Marshall watched the jeeps and ambulances rushing toward the burning bomber. Sirens screamed above the sounds of the twin engines, the huge, thirteen and a half foot blades now loafing, turning slowly, just fast enough for Frank to taxi toward their own squadron area.

From a distance, Marshall saw them lifting the charred, grotesque form of a flier, removing him from the wreckage, his parachute harness still clamped tightly to him, seeming to bow his body. The flier's head was twisted backwards, partially covered with the white foam.

"The dirty bastards," Marshall said. Frank guided *DIANA* past the smoldering, smoking wreckage. Marshall lowered himself back into the cockpit and stared ahead through the windshield. As Frank taxied, the bomber rocked, fore to aft, as a cradle rocks.

Marshall thought about the smoke and the flier with the white foam on his head and body. Suddenly he covered both eyes with his hands but the scene remained, as if he could see through his eyelids and through his hands. The crashed airplane became a shed, a smokehouse, and from it dark smoke rose slowly. *Venison hung in strips on wire and the smoke from the smoldering, slow burning alder would cure it.*

Marshall suddenly recalled the deer; a wounded spike that he and his dad had tracked, following the specks of blood and the drag mark in the dirt caused by a broken leg. Critically wounded, it had crawled into a clump of deep sage where its body had grown too stiff for it to rise and run when they approached. Through a few inches of snow they'd followed the crimson drops of blood. His dad had pointed out the drag marks in the dirt.

I've got to kill it, Son. When his dad raised his rifle the spike suddenly twisted and looked at them and Marshall jumped when he heard the loud retort of the rifle, and watched with dismay as the depth of the brown color of the deer's eyes retreated, became dull and lifeless and its neck and head slowly slumped to the ground.

"Son, I hope you'll never have to do this."

His dad had cursed the hunter who had wounded the young deer and failed to track it down. They had to find it, and put it out of its misery. Marshall remembered that his dad had comforted him, had supported his forehead when he became ill. He rested his arm across Marshall's shoulder before they returned to the tethered horses. His dad said, *"It's okay, Son. Decent hunters are sensitive about the death of any animal."* They turned and walked away from the dead spike. Emil would dress it out and take it to the ranch.

The wheels of the bomber stopped, and were blocked. All of the systems were shut down, the controls carefully checked. Marshall and the others lowered themselves through the nose wheel hatch and automatically touched the nose wheel of the bomber before proceeding further, assuring them that they'd be well clear of the propellers. He followed Frank and McAdam towards their squadron building. A group of mechanics stood watching an ambulance and a jeep near the burning B-26.

"Who got it?" McAdam asked.

"That young bombardier."

"Spike?"

"Yep. Heard someone call him that. Toggled his bombs, Then got it."

"Fifth mission."

"Lousy luck."

"Hydraulic system all shot to hell. Duffey had to bring it on its belly."

"Other guys got out okay."

"Piece of flak caught the kid right in the temple."

"Understand he did toggle his bombs."

"Yeahs, but Duffey had to close the bomb bay doors."

"Never knew what hit him."

"Hey, Marshall," Frank shouted, "Where're you going?"

Marshall trotted away from them towards the burning wreckage. Frank and McAdam ran after him. The three of them arrived beside the ambulance, as the medics prepared to open the doors.

"Where's the spike," Marshall shouted.

"What do you mean, sir?"

On the runway near the ambulance Marshall saw the body of the young bombardier, covered with a white tarp. Beside him the chaplain kneeled. Rising from beside the chaplain a medical officer turned and walked toward the ambulance. The chaplain pulled the tarp over the bombardier's face, and the edge of the tarp fluttered, moved by the breeze. Marshall ran to the body, pulled back the tarp and looked at Spike. He wiped white foam off of his face. His eyes were open.

"Hey! He's not dead! Spike, damn it, get up! He can't be dead. His eyes are open!"

Frank pulled at Marshall's shoulders, pulled him away from the prone body. But then Marshall recognized the disappearance of the blue color of Spike's eyes. They were blank, colorless, almost chalk white, like that deer's eyes. Then the medical officer returned and kneeled down and with his fingers closed the eyelids of the dead flier, and returned the tarp, covering Spike's head.

"I'm sorry, Lieutenant."

The medics lifted his body onto a stretcher and walked with it to the ambulance.

Frank grasped Marshall tightly with both arms, felt his body tremble. Then helped him stand. "Take it easy, buddy."

"You okay?" McAdam spoke directly into Marshall's face as Frank supported him.

"Jesus, I don't know! Jesus Christ, I just don't know!" Marshall said. "Get away, I'm going to puke."

Frank and McAdam stood aside. They waited for Marshall to wipe his face and mouth with a handkerchief.

"Can you handle debriefing?" Frank said.

"Yeah, I'm okay now." Marshall said, barely audible. "Why the Spike! I thought I saw his body jerk! I didn't think he was really dead! He was just a kid. Am I being too damn sensitive or something?"

"Hell no, and we're not insensitive either, Marsh. It's the God damn breaks!" Frank said.

"Come on, Marsh! Snap out of it! The poor kid is gone! He's not suffering now," Gary said.

"All right guys, let's get this goddamn debriefing out of the way," Frank said. The three fliers walked side by side, Marshall in the middle, towards their squadron building.

"Must be two o'clock," McAdam said, then forced a laugh, and he then began to laugh loudly, a forced, hollow laugh. He pointed to a group of people near the door they approached. "Good old Red Cross; packing up the donuts and coffee right on schedule! Their shift is over!"

"God, I could use a cup of coffee right now," Marshall said. "I've got the shakes."

"Damn good thing we've got a three day pass. Marsh," McAdam said. "Sunder, you're coming unglued."

"Knock it off, Gary!" Frank spoke sharply. McAdam looked surprised, nodded, then split off from Marshall and Frank and walking swiftly, approached one of the Red Cross women.

"Look honey," he said, "Can you unpack that gear long enough to get a cup of coffee for my buddy? His buddy just died in that bomber." Gary pointed to the smoldering wreckage.

"Oh, my God," she said, "a flier was killed? We thought someone was wounded, not killed. I'm so sorry! You fellows just landed? We thought all the bombers were back. Wait just a second. I'll fetch a few cups for you. Can't promise how hot it'll be."

"Thanks," McAdam said. He watched the sway of her hips, noticed the slim ankles below well-rounded calves, then waited and she returned with a cardboard box with six cups of coffee. Her smile encouraged him.

"Like to join me for a few days in Lie`ge?" McAdam said.

The Red Cross woman laughed. "Sorry, all booked up. Maybe another time?" Then the corners of her mouth dropped and she frowned. "And really, I'm very sorry for the crew of that bomber, Lieutenant. Really! None of us knew a flier was killed!"

"Sure, I understand," McAdam said. "And thanks for the coffee." He hurried to catch up with his crewmembers that were about to be debriefed.

During the debriefing they learned that the copilot of the Group Lead had been killed and the lead Bombardier, First Lieutenant Dean had caught a piece of flack, a flesh wound, just a slice on his forehead, but the blood had half-blinded him, which explained his bomb run. The navigator in the lead ship with Dean had helped identify the target, but couldn't stop Dean's bleeding.

Marshall discussed his selection of Bad Scheidel as a target of opportunity and described the help from Pop and John. Intelligence seemed pleased, looked at the map and the location of Bad Scheidel, but made no comments about his decision. Marshall decided not to mention the confrontation in the bomb bay. Might not look good in John's personnel file.

Before they departed, Major White, the flight operations officer, stopped them. "Understand you guys made a good hit on the primary. If the photos are as good as the reports you'll be hearing from me. Enjoy your pass. You deserve it."

"You see the entire report, sir?" Frank asked.

"There's more?"

"Two bombs hung up. Sunder found a bridge on the way home. With the help of Pop and John, our tail gunner, we took it out."

"Great. I'll review that report."

"Sir, I feel both Pop and John deserve bronze stars," Frank said.

"I'll take a close look at the report."

"Thank you, sir," Frank said, answering for the three of them. And he wondered if the medics or the Chaplain might say anything about Marshall's behavior. No one could hear Frank mutter to himself, " My whole damn crew is getting flak happy."

Pop joined the three officers as they walked towards trucks that would take the flight crews to their separate quarters.

"Lieutenant Sunder, I'm sorry that young friend of yours got it. The rest of the crew got out okay, except for Lieutenant Sullivan. Broke his arm," Pop said

"I just can't believe it. Spike didn't even shave, and this stupid war is days from ending!"

"I told them in debriefing how you had to save me from getting choked to death." Pop said.

Marshall glanced at Pop, but said nothing. Pop continued to walk with them.

"Well, gent's, you try to have a good time in Lie`ge, or where ever. See you all in a few days," Pop said, splitting off and headed towards a waiting six-by-six.

As the three officers prepared to climb up into the truck that would take them to their barracks, Marshall said, "I'm sorry guys, about my reaction out there. I'm just messed up."

"Come on!" Frank said, "You've got to forget it! It'll take time. You've got to shake it off! You're human. You're not a Norden bombsight." Frank smiled and gripped Marshall's shoulder firmly, shaking him lightly.

"Poor Wally. A broken arm! Two more lousy missions and he'd been out of here. Now he's grounded!" Gary said, then added, "But he is alive!'

CHAPTER 4

▼

THE OCCUPATION

As the Germans retreated into their own country, it was necessary for the Bombardment Group to leave Denain, to move to a different airport near Tegelen, Holland, which would enable the B-26's to penetrate further into Germany, and would also allow them to fly to Norway.

The entire crew, the six of them, wondered why the colonel would order them, just one crew, to report to headquarters. Frank and Marshall and Gary, the officers, were grouped together, separated by only a few steps, but apart from the three enlisted men. They all stood by the entrance to the squadron headquarters talking quietly. Its old stone walls were partly crumbled, but still formed a peak with heavy beams, blackened by smoke, holding apart the walls and now supporting a thick canvas that served as the roof of the building.

They met at the door. The First Sergeant said to wait here. They had come from opposite directions, the officers and enlisted men, from their tents erected amongst the short pines, which had been closely planted by the Germans to help camouflage the air base. Luftwaffe fighters had flown from the base early in the war, but then the Allies reached Belgium. The Germans evacuated, destroyed the buildings, bombed the runways, and then retreated.

When the Bomb Group arrived a few of the runways had been repaired, however, some were not sufficiently repaired to accommodate the weight of the twin-engine B-26's loaded with bombs, full fuel tanks, armor plate, a bomb sight, fifty caliber machine guns, radio sets, and flak suits. And men. No combat missions were flown from the new base, in Tegelen.

The surrender news reached the Squadron at night. The war ended in Europe.

I've made it! Marshall rejoiced. He said a prayer of thanks and took from his shirt pocket the small camouflaged New Testament with the gold cross embossed in the cover and laid it in the tray of his footlocker.

Nothing can happen now. I'm going home. I've escaped the flak and the fighters and the crash landings and exploding gas tanks. I'll not be trapped in the nose with dead pilots behind me, plunging downward, spinning, the earth rushing upward, forest patterns and lakes and autobahns growing larger, revolving beneath the glass nose. I'll never have to jump and hang from a parachute and stare down into hate-filled eyes of Germans, waiting with up raised pitchforks, poised like javelin throwers, waiting to puncture my skin and pierce my body. As this scenario flowed through Marshall's mind it occurred to him that he'd never seen a drop of enemy blood, and for that matter, anyone's blood. He'd stared at the dimming whiteness within Spikes eyes, but blood from the piece of flak that had pierced his temple had caused no bleeding visible to Marshall.

When they knew that it was official, the crews sang and whooped, and even those from the northern States screamed out at the top of their voices the Rebel yell. Some of the fliers ran to the parked airplanes. They fired the fifty caliber machine guns into the air. The guns roared and cracked the silence of the night. Hot orange tracers arched off into the darkness toward the Rhine River.

Marshall loaded his .45 and fired three shots into the sky. He held the gun too close to his head and the sharp reports made his right ear ache. It rang for days. Frank laughed and struck him on the back and told him not to worry about it. It was just the Liberty Bell being rung again.

Cognac and champagne and sparkling burgundy were plentiful. They drank too much. They laughed. No one went to bed. The sun came up. They wrote flowing, sentimental letters home. They played poker. Never before had the stakes been so high. They talked about what they would do when they got home. They drank. The sun went down. They laughed at one another getting sick and staggering away to puke, grasping the branches of the small pine trees for support, then returning to drink more. They climbed into the bombers and went to their stations and strapped on the oxygen masks and breathed deeply, hoping sobriety and fewer headaches would follow.

Gary, the copilot, emptied a full bottle of cognac. He aimlessly wandered off into the woods. Frank and Marshall tried to find him, but they were drunk too, and gave up. They found their way back to their tent and laughed. They slept, without undressing, on their cots. In the morning they found Gary still sleeping on the ground near where he'd been sick, huddled up on his side, his arms wrapped around his knees, his head resting on the empty cognac bottle. Together the three of them, pale, shaking, ill, walked in silence to their ship, the parked B-26. Even though the huge, windmill like propellers stood idle, useless without the roaring engines alive behind them, the fliers from long habit walked to the nose wheel of the aircraft, patted it, thus avoiding the guillotine-sharp edges of the propellers. Then they hoisted themselves into the cockpit through the wheel-well. They hooked on the rubber masks at their stations and breathed deeply of the sobering oxygen.

Each day a different rumor was considered. They would fly to the Pacific by way of Southern Asia and then help bomb for the invasion of Japan. They would go in trucks next week to a port in Belgium, board a Victory ship, cross the Atlantic, be discharged and arrive home within weeks. They would stay a few weeks at this base and train replacements for occupation duty.

Marshall had listened to all of the rumors. He'd lain on his cot and thought of home and the folks and imagined his dad writing up orders for merchandise for the empty shelves in the hardware store. They will want to know about the sixth Air Medal. Hell, we all got an extra one, our whole crew. It was a team effort. I was just lucky. Dad will be proud. I'll tell them I was lucky. Pop was the hero. He'd had to stand in the freezing cold, in the open bomb bay and release the two bombs hung up there, and John too was a real hero. No one knew John was afraid of heights. He'd never had to look down through an open space before. It was like climbing a ladder to a two-story window and then looking down and becoming terrified. But we got the bridge. That was the important thing. Wasted no bombs and slowed the krauts.

When the damn bombs wouldn't release it was time to select the target of opportunity and they'd followed Marshall's plan and succeeded in destroying the bridge. They could see that parts of it had collapsed. The retreating Germans were delayed. Damn, I didn't want to hit those houses. He remembered the little homes burning when they returned to strafe. The B-26 seemed to shudder, almost to stop in midair when the fifty-calibers beneath the wings roared. He saw the cobblestones spitting back dust at them. No people were in the streets.

Secretly, he was glad that there wasn't a machine gun in the nose that mission. Once he'd strafed a German ammunition train, and another time watched his fifty-calibers trail in a long curve behind a 109. It was gone before he could correct his lead a half rad. Fighter support, their little friends, got the 109. Seldom saw enemy fighter towards the end, but they never seemed to run out of ammo for the lousy 88's.

Then the miracle happened. VJ Day! The atomic bomb was dropped, twice, and the war was over and thoughts were suddenly about going home, about the assurance of staying alive, of seeing loved ones.

Now, as they all waited, he studied the debris around the squadron building and he thought of the burning houses and of the flames coming from them, and the color of the tracers.

"Tetch-hut!" Frank said sharply. The crew snapped to attention. Frank saluted.

"Rest," Colonel Schlosser said. He returned the salute. He walked a few yards away from the entrance to the squadron room and indicated for them to follow him. He was a Lt. Colonel, not a bird colonel, and he was twenty-eight. He'd been graduated from the Point, then earned his wings. Officers and enlisted men all liked him. When there was a rough mission scheduled, the colonel piloted the lead ship. If Intelligence said it would be a milk run, the colonel passed it up.

The colonel raised one foot up to a broken piece of stone wall, leaned and rested his arms on his knee. His hands hung relaxed. He looked at all of them without smiling, not with anger, or with an air of reprimand, but seriously.

"Normally, you men would get this information through your flight leaders. I'll make it short, if not sweet. Our group has been assigned occupation duty in Southern Germany. A mile from our base is the town of Bad Scheidel. Only a few in our squadron know that you men hit the bridge and a couple of houses there. I'll speak to the others personally, as I am doing to you. If word ever gets out that it was a ship from this Bomb Group, the occupation duty for our Squadron personnel could be a lot tougher. It might be dangerous for your crew, Frank, in particular. There's going to be a lot of hatred and revenge in the hearts of the Germans. For your safety, and for the well being of the rest of the outfit, you'd better forget that you ever heard the name Bad Scheidel. I know that I don't have to put this in the form of an order." He smiled, straightened up, then asked, "Any questions?"

They looked at each other, back and forth, probably thinking about the choice of that particular bridge. Marshall felt that they were all looking at him. He lowered his eyes and kicked at a loose piece of masonry on the ground by the broken wall.

"How long do you think we'll be assigned occupation duty, sir?" Frank asked.

"Probably six months, maybe more. Details of a point system are being ironed out now. You'll hear more about it soon." The colonel looked at them individually, openly, awaiting another question. "That it?" he said.

"Sir, why not keep it simple, and just ship our crew right on home now?" Pop said.

The colonel chuckled, "That was my first thought. But the higher ups are very concerned that the point system be followed to the tee. From headquarters' viewpoint you fellows are heroes. I want you all to recall that each of you received an Air Medal for that mission because destroying that Bad Scheidel bridge probably shortened the war, and especially saved, who knows how many, GI lives. You haven't heard the end of that mission, and I mean we're all proud of how your entire crew handled it, Frank."

"Any more questions?"

"A comment, Sir," Pop said, and all eyes again focused on him, "In the business world we had a saying regarding confidential matters. It was simply this—'there are no secrets in the industry!' and I for one think the same applies here and now."

"Your point is well taken, sergeant, and I bet you'd like to get back to that business world soon."

"Roger, sir!"

"Any more comments or questions?"

"One more, sir. I really don't understand the need for aircrews? What with the Japs out of it, isn't that a job for ground pounders, both here and in Japan?"

"Good question, Sergeant Skidmore. The German people were impressed with their own air supremacy for many years. They'll respect anyone associated with flying, especially for these occupation responsibilities.

We're needed, it's as simple as that. And remember, the point system is fair. You'll be on your way before long."

"Any more questions?"

Frank looked at his crewmembers, then said, "No sir."

The colonel saluted, turned and walked erect, swiftly back into the squadron headquarters.

Frank dropped his hand from his cap. He looked at the crew. They stood silently, exchanging glances.

Marshall looked at the ground.

"So, we knocked down a bridge," Pop said. Pop was the engineer. He was pushing thirty. The officers were barely over twenty. They considered Pop mature. He'd had a job before the war, was married and had a son. Sold paint. He'd been around. "Two months ago they were pinning medals on us for doing what we're trained to do. Now, they're telling us we're going to have to be quiet, to be careful. Hitler's ashes aren't even cold yet and we've got a big military secret to keep. Bull shit."

"It's our own safety the colonel's thinking of," Frank said.

"Hell, I could've picked a dozen towns and a dozen bridges. Why did it have to be Bad Scheidel?" Marshall said.

"You did what you were supposed to do, that's what! We all did. It was our crew, not just you, Marsh. Christ! Didn't you hear Schloss? Hell, we're heroes!" he followed his remarks by laughing loudly.

The other crewmembers joined in, all talking at once, reassuring Marshall, telling him not to be concerned about it; after all, they all got Air Medals because he hit that damn bridge.

CHAPTER 5

▼

BAD SCHEIDEL

Double paned windows with the space in between to keep out the cold and keep in the warmth were something new to Marshall. Some of the fliers had grown up in the snow country and had seen them before, but most of the Californians were impressed and curious and examined them carefully. Then they credited the inventive Germans with possessing great engineering genius.

The fliers from the snow country weren't sure who built the first double windows. They ungrudgingly did not dispute the credit allowed the Germans, and as the living victors still respected an enemy they never saw; still carried with them fresh memories of the too accurate antiaircraft guns harassing them, tracking them, leading them, sending the shells up to their exact altitude.

It was still fresh in their memories: how the shells exploded: the flash of yellow-orange when it was close, the black smoke being passed by and through. The ragged steel pieces ripped into the planes, bringing with it a sound like a pointed, round rasp being jammed through an empty five gallon gasoline can. The spinning chunks of jagged steel, cut control cables, shattered glass, ricocheted off of armor plate, and after severing the tightly woven threads of the cords sometimes stopped in a nest of soft white silk, deep in the bosom of a tightly packed parachute. Some of it stopped in the bodies of the fliers. Some of it mysteriously ripped on out of the airplanes, touching nothing but the paper-thin aluminum, leaving large holes, then dropping like heavy walnuts back to the German earth.

As the double windows insulated the buildings, so had each flier brought with him, not been issued by the Government, but possessed as a gift from home and family and taken with him into combat his own particular, individual insulator. Some fliers, thinking back, remembered now that they had been afraid, too afraid to go on a combat mission, they'd figured the odds; a thirteenth mission in a ship with a thirteen in the serial number, in January would be the thirteenth month, admitted being scared to themselves alone, but were too proud not to go on those missions, and now, being so alive generously allowed the vanquished the dubious credit for inventing double windows.

Spring and bird sounds similar to American birdcalls, and fragrances of blossoms no different from those at home welcomed them to their new living quarters a mile from Bad Scheidel. The move from the tents into the two-story, red brick buildings with showers and spacious rooms, the bar in the officers' club stocked with American whiskey, a piano and a clean dining room, made occupation duty seem less objectionable.

Four officers shared two rooms, one larger than the other. In the larger room was a table and extra chairs. Here the fliers gathered to play cards, read, and write letters.

And here too, began Marshall's love for Kristine. Its beginnings, the mysterious spawning of something more than platonic respect, started with a glance, a word, led to affection, then infatuation, and finally love. It began, if there could be a beginning, the day that she came to open the windows.

Six officers, still wearing their winter uniforms even though the days had begun to grow warmer, sat at a large table in the middle of the room, playing poker, smoking, talking, drinking Rhine wine from the tall, slim, tapered green bottles.

"Raise you ten."

"That's the last raise."

"Okay. Let's see what you've got."

"You lucky son of a bitch, drawing to an inside straight!"

The cigar smoke became thicker.

"Have you got your time in yet?"

"Yeah. Slept four hours in a DC-3 circling the field."

"Wish they'd get those damn points figured out. But, how about this? Old Sullivan got points for the Purple Heart and is shipping out tomorrow."

"So the ill wind did blow some good."

"Yes, in Wally's case, but back to the jokes, you guys know what alimony is?"

No one answered the flier. "It's the screwing you get for the screwing you got!"

All of them laughed at the joke. Marshall tried to think of any off-color joke in case everyone contributed, but nothing came to mind.

"Here's a definition my girl friend told me," a flier said. "You know what a perfect secretary is?" He paused for a second, then said, "One that works at MGM all day and Fox all night!"

Laughter and groans intermingled.

"Shuffle that goddamn deck!"

"Cut 'em and deal."

"Come on, pot stinks."

"Okay. Everybody's in. Deal 'em."

"And then this guy wakes up and here next to him is this good looking nigger babe, so he sneaks out and leaves five bucks on the dresser and these two nigger broads in the hall stop him and he says, 'I left something for her' and they say, 'but what about us bridesmaids?'"

Laughing loudly, blowing cigar smoke, they hardly heard the knock on the door.

"Come on in. It's open!"

Kristine Schuttenhelm walked past the table carrying a galvanized bucket containing soapy water. She held white rags, a squeegee and a chamois. They nodded. She walked past the table to the windows. They became silent. The flutter of the cards being shuffled seemed loud. The cards were dealt.

They talked in softer tones and made their bets. They exchanged suggestive glances, raised their eyebrows, grinned, and nodded towards Kristine. All of them turned when they heard the first squeaking noises.

"Check the ass on the Fraulein," the pilot from Texas drawled. They all leaned back in their chairs and looked at Kristine.

She reached out over the sill, briskly rubbing with the chamois the windows that had been pushed open. Her black dress was short and tight and her hips kept time with the oscillations of her hands moving back and forth, rubbing hard, polishing the glass. Her ankles were slim, and the fliers could see the white skin above the backs of her knees.

"Hey, Fraulein. How many candy bars for a night with old Tex?"

Kristine did not answer. All of them laughed and turned back to the card game.

"First queen bets," someone said.

But the pilot named Tex, encouraged by the laughs his comments had invoked, persisted, took a deep breath and launched once more into his solo harangue, drawling, combining American and German and French slang.

"Hey, Fraulein. Schlafen mit Tex? Be mine lieber. Was is los mit der Vaterland? Hitler is kaput. Alles kaput. Voulez-vous Couche avec Tex? Combien? You speak!" He laughed loudly and looked around the table. The fliers smiled and shifted uneasily, and stared at their cards. One of them coughed.

"Play cards."

"Come on."

"Pot stinks."

"Bet, or get out."

"Come on, Buzzard," Marshall said, his voice low, "let's get back to poker. Lay off for awhile. She didn't have any more to do with this mess than the rest of us."

"Who's giving out with the sermon, fella? You the chaplain around here?" Lieutenant Herbert Buzzard, known as Tex, answered. He stood up and threw his cards face down on the table. He glared at Marshall.

"He's right, loud mouth!" Frank said, his voice almost a whisper.

"You, Lieutenant Sunder, can go take a flying fuck at a rolling donut!"

Her voice was quiet, smooth, soft, and her enunciation perfect. "I am glad that there are some gentlemen amongst the Luftgangsters."

They turned in unison and stared at her. Her face was flushed. She stood with her chin up, shoulders back, holding a wet cloth in one hand, the chamois in the other. She looked straight at all of them, challenging them, taking them in as a group. She pushed a few fine strands of black hair away from her forehead.

"Well, gee ma'am, I'm real sorry," Tex stammered. "I didn't know. I mean. You see..." His voice trailed off.

"Why don't you just take that big Texas foot out of your mouth while you're still ahead," one of them said. The others laughed. Tex mumbled something under his breath, scooped his money into one hand from the tabletop, turned and left the room. They finished the game, watched Kristine scrub the windows and listened to the squeaking noise the chamois made. The fliers departed one at a time until there weren't enough for poker.

Marshall retreated to the adjoining room, his own room, closed the door behind him, and began to straighten the gear in his footlocker. He could hear the faint squeaking noise. He opened one of his windows, looked out, and saw her hand clutching the chamois, rubbing sideways across the glass and he thought of the motion of her hips. He stretched further, hoping to see her reflection in the glass. At the same instant, Kristine leaned out. Surprised, they looked at one another. They stared at each other through the windows. She smiled at him, and then they both laughed.

"The gentleman gangster?"

"Never been accused of being either one before," Marshall said.

"Your windows are next."

"Oh, they're okay."

"The captain says to clean windows. I clean windows."

"Captain?"

"The captain that does not wear wings," she said, nodding to those pinned above Marshall's shirt pocket. "I am now employed by the United States Luftwaffe." She disappeared.

Marshall heard the soft knock at his door, opened it, and she walked swiftly past him, her head reaching only to the top of his shoulder. She went straight to the windows. She began to unlatch them and push them outward. One would not open.

"I'll get it."

"I do not need your help."

Marshall ignored her comment, stepped by her, close to her and deep in his body sensed it: some communication, or attraction. He thought of the electricity in his wool sweater and how it crackled when he pulled it off over his head, and how it swung towards his body, charged with invisible magnetism, persistent, and he thought, hoped, for a fleeting second that the girl would be suddenly drawn close to him without his hands having to reach for her. She stepped out of his way. He pushed hard against the metal frame. The window flew open and struck the limb of a tree and white blossoms fell from it. Marshall slipped, lost his balance momentarily and she laughed. He turned around and laughed too.

"Clumsy Luftgangster," she said, smiling, "must you destroy even our apple trees?"

"Luftgangster? The war is over, you know."

"Really?" she teased, cocking her head sideways. "You have a name then, Mr. Gangster?"

Annoyed and flustered, Marshall did not answer. He pointed to his stenciled name on the open cover of his footlocker.

"Lieutenant Marshall Sunder," she read aloud. "Well, that is so appropriate. I will call you Lieutenant Sunder, if you please. And I am Kristine Schuttenhelm. Frau Schuttenhelm. And where in the world is Chico? Oh, I see it. Chico, California, I can read it now. What a strange name."

"Chico means little in Spanish," Marshall said. "My Uncle Bruce called me Chico Sunder when I was a kid, then just Chico. You know, nickname sort of thing."

He looked at her hands, expecting to shake hands with her. However, she raised her right hand. A narrow gold band was on her ring finger. "Frau, do you understand?"

"Certainly."

"I have two rings now. His was sent to me by a friend. From Stalingrad. But, still I am not sure."

"I'm sorry," Marshall said. He turned from her and knelt down by his open footlocker and moved his belongings aimlessly, from one divided section to another.

"You have a little Bible?" Kristine asked, looking across his shoulders. He looked up at her. She smiled, and asked. "May I read it? I wonder if it's the same as ours."

"Sure, sure," Marshall said. "New Testament." He stood quickly and handed it to her. "What did you mean, Lieutenant Sunder is so appropriate?"

Kristine stepped back from him after accepting the Bible. She looked up at him facetiously; her green eyes opened wide in mock surprise.

"Sunder? The translation you must know? It means sinner. Ha! Sinner and little boy are appropriate names for you, Mr. Luftgangster." Kristine said, and she laughed. "So? I may borrow your little Bible?"

"Why sure." Marshall said.

"For comparison." She smiled and departed.

Although Marshall visited almost daily with Kristine when she came to clean and dust the rooms, each maintained a discreet, business-like relationship. It was a few weeks later that Kristine brought her family Bible, as well as his, to Marshall's room. Side by side Kristine and Marshall sat upon chairs, without armrests, before a table in front of the open windows. Now, green apples half of their mature sizes were visible amongst the wide leaves of the tree beyond the double windows. Marshall looked away from the new fruit on the tree. He studied Kristine's profile as she read alternately from the Bibles. *Every feature is correct. Her nose is straight, her forehead high, her chin is strong but not in an aggressive way, her lips full. Yet, she seems so vulnerable.* He ventured to rest his hand upon hers. She glanced at him, smiled, and pulled her hand away, then turned back to the German Bible. She'd had his Bible for a long time, Marshall thought, and Marshall had looked at her big Bible, with names that he could read, but scrawled on pages printed in German.

Every day that she came to clean their rooms, she always stayed longer in his room and asked about his family and about California. She thought San Francisco was only a few kilometers from Hollywood. They both laughed when he told her how far it really was. He sketched a map of California and showed her where Chico was located, and Reno, and told her the High Sierra was much like the German Alps.

This day she stayed even longer. She sat down alone at his table. He hadn't asked her. She just did. She had her own Bible, and asked again for his and opened both of the Bibles, flipped from page to page and read aloud in German and then in English. After awhile, he pulled up a chair close to her and watched her and listened to her, then rested his hand upon hers. She did not move her own hand this time.

"Du sollst nicht toten," she read.

She studied the English Bible, slipped her hand from beneath his, and ran her slender, tapered finger swiftly beneath the words in his small Bible.

"Thou shalt not kill," she said. She looked at his questioningly.

"Did you think the Bibles would be different?" Marshall asked.

"How could your people read this book, believe this book, and then destroy us?"

"Aren't you forgetting who started it, Kristine?"

"Started it? Ha! I remember. I heard all about them, the Jews, taking our businesses and our money and our souls. My grandfather said it, and my father and mother, too. Gold is their only God!" Her mouth pulled downward at the edges.

"You're too young to remember anything like that."

"My father told me. Hitler told us. It's true."

"Then you really believe it." Marshall shook his head slowly from side to side and looked back at the tree. The sun was lowering and the fruit seemed to disappear amongst the dark shadows of the leaves and branches.

"You insult me," Kristine said. She pushed back her chair and arose.

"I'm sorry. Kristine, we're on different wavelengths. Sit down. Read again. Please."

"Wavelengths?"

"I guess our sources for truth are different. Please continue."

Kristine studied Marshall's face. He did not look away from her penetrating gaze. Then swiftly she turned the thin, gilt-edged pages of the large old German Bible. Her face was flushed, her lips pinched together into a thin line.

"And did you ever read your Bible?" she asked, her voice rising, small and hollow, but she looked straight into his eyes, her expression solemn, accusing. Her eyes are so green, so steady, so defiant, Marshall thought. They should be blue, pale blue and her hair blonde, not black. He lowered his eyes, looked at the pages of the Bible, but did not see the words.

"Come, come, my Chico Luftgangster. Did you read?"

"Yeah. Some." He studied her, wondered about her intentions, then stood, walked to the doorway and peered into the adjoining room. It was empty. Relieved, he returned. He sat beside her.

"Promised my mother," he cleared his throat, "before I went...came overseas," he hesitated again, "that I'd read the twenty third Psalm. And some other stuff."

Kristine turned the pages of her Bible.

"I will read in German. You will read from yours?"

Marshall stared at her.

"Can't you read English?" she teased.

He laughed, found his place and read aloud, "The Lord is my shepherd, I shall not want."

"Er weidet mich auf einer grunen Aue, und fuhrt mich zum frischen wasser."

"He maketh me to lie down in green pastures: He leadeth me beside the still waters."

"Er erquicket meine seele; er fuhrtmich auf erchter Strasse um seines Namesns willen."

"He restoreth my soul; He leadeth me in the paths of righteousness for his name's sake."

"Und ob ich schon wanderte im finstern that, furchte, ich keiin Ugluck; denn Du bist bei mir, Bein Stecken und Stab trosten mich."

"Yeah, though I walk through the valley of the shadow of death, I will fear no evil: for thou art with me; thy rod and thy staff they comfort me."

"Du hereitest vor mit einen Tishch gegen meine Seinde, Du salvest mein Haupt mit Del, und schenkst mir voll ein."

"Thou preparest a table before me in the presence of mine enemies; thou anointest my head with oil; my cup runneth over."

"Gues un Barmnerzigkeit werden mir folgen mein Leben leng, und ich werfde bleibein im Hause des herrn immerdar."

"Surely goodness and mercy shall follow me all the days of my life; and I will dwell in the house of the Lord for ever."

Marshall closed his Bible.

"German doesn't sound too bad when you speak it," Marshall said.

"It is pretty, especially in the words of the Bible."

"Even the words of a Jew?"

"David must have been a gentile."

Marshall laughed at her and shook his head again.

"What else did you read?"

"The Lord's Prayer."

"Let's read." She said, then turned the pages, stopped for a moment and began to read.

Marshall could not find the prayer.

"Ha!" Kristine chided, "Come on. I'll find it for you." She took his Bible and turned the pages, then set it in front of him. She put her finger on the page.

"Here. Matthew: Six," She said, and smiled sly, then began:

"Urser Vater in dem Huimmel. Dein name werde gehiligt."

"Our Father which art in heaven, Hallowed be thy name."

"Dein Reich Komme. Dein Wille geschehe auf Erden wie in Himmel."

"Thy kingdom come. Thy will be done on earth, as it is in heaven."

"Uknser taglich Brot gieb uns heute."

"Give us this day our daily bread. *No! This is what I prayed: Give us this day good weather and clear skies and no flak so we can have a smooth bomb run and a good level. I must have a good level. Level please. Level okay Bomb bay door open. Bombs away. Bomb bay doors closed. She's all yours, Frank. Over, Roger. Let's get the hell out of here. Did he hit it? Hell, yes we hit it; the whole flight hit it, great pattern, Marsh. Another bridge up the Fuhrer's ass! Come on; Pop, look for that train. There it is. Strafe the bastards. How do things look up above, Frantz? Just our little friends up high with the Forts. Bless 'em. Bless 'em! No bandits in sight. Yeah, Dover here we come.*"

"Come, come, Lieutenant Sunder, are you going to sleep?"

"What?" Marshall was vaguely aware that she'd read another sentence.

"Read here." Kristine tapped her finger on his Bible.

"And forgive us our debts, *Thou shalt not kill!* as we forgive our debtors."

"Und fuhe uns hicht in Verschung, sondern erlose uns von dem Uebel. Denn Dein is das Reich under die Kraft und die Herrlichkeit in Ewigkeit. Amen."

"And lead us not into temptation, but deliver us from evil; *if the primary target is clouded over, choose another. Don't bring back the bombs.* For thine is the kingdom, and the power, and the glory forever. Amen."

Marshall closed his Bible, turned and flipped it into his open footlocker. His mouth felt dry. He licked his lips and pushed his finger beneath his nose, pushing away the moisture. He sighed, then looked back out of the window, past the tree towards the red tile roofs in the distance, the roofs of Bad Scheidel. He hadn't been all the way to town, yet. *I'll have to go and look at the bridge,* he thought, *and at the houses we hit.*

"God." Marshall sighed, then let his head hang, his chin almost touching his chest. "I'm glad the damn war is over." He rested his hand again on Kristine's and they sat together, side by side, looking out at the fruit trees scattered across the slope that stretched to the road leading to Bad Scheidel.

Marshall raised his arm and rested it on the back Kristine's chair. He touched her shoulder with his fingertips. She did not draw away. He thought he felt her tremble.

Emboldened, he closed his hand on her shoulder gently, and moved closer to her. In the silent room the chattering skid of the chair on the hardwood floor seemed suddenly loud, and Marshall was afraid it would startle her and make her run. The few inches that he moved seemed like yards. With the back of his fingers he lifted a curl of fine black hair from her temple and with his cheek touched hers.

She did not draw away. The air outdoors breathed in on them warm and soft, its movement just enough to float the leaves of the apple tree a fraction, then release them to hang idle from their stems.

"Is it possible to love thine enemy?" Marshall whispered.

"Love?" she said. She shrugged her small shoulders. "Love? I've forgotten its meaning. In any of four languages I can speak it. German or French or Latin or English. How would you like to hear it?"

"You know that's not what I mean."

"I know. Like your friend. How much love for a chocolate bar or some good American tobacco or a package of coffee?"

Marshall released her shoulder, stood, walked to the other room, lit a cigarette, inhaled deeply then exhaled the smoke while he slowly turned the pages of a magazine on the table in the center of the room.

"Oh, I'm sorry, my Chico Luftgangster. You are a sensitive one," Kristine laughed and followed him, then took his hand and led him back into his own room. She pulled both of his hands behind her back and then raised hers and touched his cheeks and stood on her toes and kissed him. "So, like Uncle Bruce, you are just Chico to me!"

Marshall, with both hands on her small shoulders, pulled her close to him. He kissed her hard, then held her tightly. She's so frail, so light, like a bird, he thought. He released her and looked down at her. Her eyes were closed. She smiled. He pushed the door closed with his heel, then turned to Kristine again. She laughed at him, then walked from him across the room. He followed her quickly. They kissed again.

"Maybe I can again learn what the word means," she said.

"Kris! I love you."

"Ich liebe. Du liebst. Wir lieben!"

Kristine sat on the edge of the bed. She smiled up at him. "Can the widow still make love? Maybe: but please, Chico, don't ask this."

"Kris, if ever, it's got to be mutual."

"Danke.

CHAPTER 6

▼

POKER

Tex swore, slammed his cards down on the tabletop, then walked to the windows and looked out.

"Look at 'em," he snarled. "Goddamn kraut lover: bad as a nigger lover. Reading a book together. Bet that son-of-a-bitch's been shacking up with her."

"You playing poker or peeping tom, Tex?" Frank asked.

"Don't get wise."

"Are you in or aren't you, Buzzard?" another flier asked.

"Yeah, deal me in." He returned to the table, picked up his cards, looked at them, smiled and spoke again. "Guess you boys know 'ole Tex is the new Information Officer. Signed up for a year's duty. Get my silver bars in a month."

"Who in the hell are you going to inform?" a flier asked. Everyone at the table laughed except Tex.

"These fucking krauts, that's who. Two buses have been assigned to the squadron and I'm going to load 'em in and drive 'em out there. And the first load is going to have that little black haired bitch in it. I'll educate this whole goddamn town before I'm through!"

"You show 'em Tex," Frank said, the disgust in his voice evident to most of them. "That's what this world needs is more educators like you."

Frank, laid his cards down, retrieved his money, dropped out of the game and left the room, shaking his head.

"What's eating him?" Tex asked. He looked around the table. No one answered. He took a cigar from his shirt pocket, bit off the end, spit it on the floor, lit the cigar and blew a cloud of gray smoke across the table.

"Why don't you get a dictionary and look up the word uncouth, Tex," a flier said, laughing.

"Well, deal me out too, guys, I'm getting my final first-pilot check ride this afternoon." Gary said.

"Good luck!" Tex said, and the other fliers joined in with the well wishes.

The poker game continued. As one flier would drop out another would take his place at the table.

At dinner that night a jubilant Gary announced to Marshall and Frank that he was given the final 'up' on his check ride and was now officially a 'first pilot.'

"Congratulation Gary," Frank said, "and now all you need is an airplane of your own. Just what name from your harem will you put beneath the window?"

"Ha!" Marshall exclaimed, after also congratulating Gary. "Isn't that just the luck! You won't have to make that decision, unless Frank will let you paint over *DIANA*."

"Come on! Pop will find a ship without a name and I'll start with Abigail and work my way all the way to Zelma! I'll have to paint the names small though, to get them all in!" Gary declared.

X   X   X

Outside, beneath the double windows Marshall and Kristine had filled a bag with large, solid green apples. Marshall stood on the stout lower branches, twisted the apples off, wiped each one on his summer khaki trousers and then handed them to Kristine. She inspected each of them for wormholes. The good ones she placed in one bag, those rejected in another.

"It's funny," Marshall said, "I kept waiting for them to turn red." He held the apple that he'd picked up to his nose. It smelled good, the odor sharp and clean.

"Some are black inside. Worms, too. We waited too long."

"I hope there'll be enough good ones for you," Marshall said.

"There'll be enough, even on the ones that have started to rot. But I know a farmer on the outskirts, who will use them for his pigs." Kristine said, then continued. "Thank you for the flour." She glanced at the large paper bag leaning against the trunk of the tree. She walked to them and stooped to pick them up. Marshall dropped from the upper branch to the ground beside her.

"Let me carry the bags," he said, "I'll walk part way with you."

"No," Kristine said, "I'll carry them." She held a bag on each hip and supported them with her arms. She smiled up at him. "You've never walked all the way to the village with me. Are you ashamed of me?"

"For gosh sakes, Kris, of course not. I've just been flying a lot, you know, getting checked out in radar-navigation." He shrugged his shoulders and looked at the rejected apples on the ground, the ones with the wormholes and the scars on the green flesh, from rubbing against the branches.

"I just thought you would be curious. It is really a lovely little village. Except for our poor old bridge and some homes."

He walked beside her. In the distance he could hear the powerful roar of the engines on the B-26's being revved up, tested, and he knew that the airplane would be vibrating and trying to surge forward, the huge propellers spinning, invisible, and he knew that there would be the smell of high octane gasoline and men standing by with fire extinguishers and the pilot would be practically standing on the brakes and the engineer would be checking the magnetos. But here the sounds were different, strange sounds of grasshopper wings ratcheting as they flew a few feet and the hum of bees, and other insects and the high melodious song of a distant bird and the odors from the fields, the color of the soil, and the dust on the weeds, all of these were strange and unfamiliar, yet in their totality they reminded him of the fields around Chico.

They walked slowly along the edge of the paved road that led to Bad Scheidel. Marshall thought about the bridge. The colonel had warned them again never to discuss it. Marshall wanted to see it up close, just once. And the houses. He hoped they weren't seriously damaged.

In the field beside the road they watched a German man and his wife work together, one on either side of a low wagon drawn by an ox. The ox pulled the wagon across the rough plowed field, then paused.

They stopped and picked up brown stalks, like corn, and threw them on the flat bed of the wagon. The man touched the back of the ox with his switch, then applied the tip a little firmer. It strained, then moved forward. The woman stood erect and pulled her shoulders back, then rested both of her hands on her broad hips and watched the ox. As the farmer started by her he stopped, rubbed the small of her back with his hand, then walked to the wagon and threw more stalks on it. The woman went to the other side of the wagon and did the same work.

Thank God, Marshall thought, mother never had to do that sort of work. He could hear her voice. 'A woman's place is beside her man, plus keep a nice house for him.' His folks worked long hours at the store. He knew they'd borrowed up to the hilt, as Uncle Bruce had said, to go into business, and it had been prospering and then the Japs bombed Pearl Harbor and everyone's lives had changed overnight.

Marshall looked back at the farmer. The soil beneath his feet looked much the same as it had at home.

Only the people were different, he decided. Marshall glanced sideways at Kristine, carrying both bags. He wanted to help her. In his mind, it was difficult to associate her with the enemy that, in combat, he'd never seen, that from three miles down was trying to hit him, destroy the ship, and hit the crew. It had been too vague from the air. What is a German like, he used to think. It had been too impersonal. He wondered if any of the other fliers felt that way, not nurturing hate for Germans, not as a group, even finding themselves wanting the companionship of a single person, an insignificant, small, harmless one; having a Kristine of their own.

"Will your mother and dad be home?" Marshall asked. He tried to visualize an introduction and wondered if they would accept his hand, grasp it, shake it, release it and feel a truce.

"I have not told you," she answered. She stopped, kicked a small stone blackened with asphalt into the grass beside the road, then changed the bag of apples to her other arm. Marshall took the flour from her despite her objections. "Father is in a prison camp, in Holland, at a town called Ijumiden. We, grandmother and I—we are fortunate that he is alive. We are all that is left. Mother died the day that the bomber came. The baby died later."

"Your sister?" Marshall managed to say. He felt sick, as though he might vomit. It was hard to breathe. His mouth was dry.

"I have no sister. My baby. My baby died." She said. She stopped and turned and looked at him, her chin raised. Her voice quavered for an instant. She shifted the bag of apples, then looked up at him. "What is the matter Chico?" she asked. "Are you ill? You are pale."

Marshall inhaled deeply. He was stunned. He looked at Kristine, then said, "Come on, Kris let me help you with those apples."

She smiled at him and said, "No, really I'm fine."

Then, coming from behind them they heard the familiar motor noises of a jeep and they stepped off of the road into the grass. The jeep slowed and stopped beside them, close to them, startled them.

"Hey, kids. What 'ya doing walking when you can ride?"

"Hiya, Pop," Marshall answered, surprised to see him driving a jeep. He was suddenly relieved. There would be a change of subject. Marshall leaned into the jeep and shook hands vigorously with Pop.

"How'ya doing?"

"Great Son. Just great. The flowers are blooming, the bees are buzzing, the birds are singing and everyday in the Air Corps is just like Sunday down on the farm." He then laughed loudly and they laughed at him. "Climb aboard. Well, how 'bout an introduction? How come everybody in the outfit except old Pop knows you got yourself a steady?"

Marshall took the bags from Kristine. Pop extended his hand, which she took and climbed into the back seat of the jeep. Marshall put the bags at her feet, then sat beside Pop.

"Kristine, this is Sergeant Skidmore. We call him Pop."

"Sehr angenehm Fraulein," Pop said, he raised his overseas cap and grinned broadly.

"How do you do, sergeant." Kristine nodded. Folding her hands in her lap, she concealed her wedding ring. She did not shake hands with him. Pop drove towards Bad Scheidel.

"Son, you sure pick 'em," Pop struck Marshall lightly on the leg with the palm of his open hand, "Damn if that doesn't solve the language barrier. Just find one that speaks English." He laughed again, loudly, from deep in his chest, a contagious laugh, the catalyst that prompted them to laugh fully too. "Say honey, you gotta older sister running around loose?"

"Grandmother," she said. "For you I have a grandmother." She leaned forward from the back seat of the jeep, between them, looking from one to the other, smiling, almost giggling. In these few seconds, Marshall thought, with a few ridiculous phrases that the crew had heard over and over for two years, Pop could get them all laughing. The fliers, strangers, the officers, or the enlisted men, they all laughed. They all liked Pop. He spoke in clichés and had a collection of colloquialisms gathered in his business world that he delivered casually at those times he determined were appropriate.

Now, Kristine laughed too, appeared actually gay. "I think I like you, Pop," she continued. "But I don't understand. A Wehrmacht officer would never allow this, this Pop and Marsh…" She could not continue, so shrugged her shoulders, then moved one of her hands in a mixing, circular motion in the air between them.

"Don't fret little one. Old Pop will explain if I'm around long enough." He turned to Marshall. "Read the Stars and Stripes, Marsh? They're down to 65 points for GIs won't be long now." Then he again addressed Kristine. "I raised Marsh right these past few years, he'll explain this to you." Then he raised his own hand and duplicated her mixing motion. He laughed again.

"I think you are both crazy," she said. She pointed a finger at her own head.

"Where you kids want off?" Pop asked. The smooth paved road from the air base ended at the edge of Bad Scheidel and the jeep began to vibrate as the wheels hit the cobblestones. Marshall was conscious of the people looking at them, at Kristine sitting in the back seat, her dark hair blowing around her face, laughing and bouncing about and holding onto the back of their seats.

"Stop near the bridge, please," she asked.

"The bridge?" Pop repeated. He looked over his shoulder at her, then glanced at Marshall.

"Yes, anyplace along here now. We are close to grandmother's. My home is the one on the other side of the bridge." She picked up the bag of apples and the flour. "Right here, at grandmother's, or you'll pass it. Stop, please."

Pop pulled in quickly and she pointed to a small cottage between taller buildings.

"Oh my," she said. "Here comes grandmother now. I hope she hasn't seen us. Oh, it's too late. She does not want me to be with Americans."

They looked up the curved street into the sun. The slick cobblestones looked like the tops of loaves of bread. They saw the huge bundle first, then the old woman beneath it. Her shadow moved before her, was cast large and dark upon the stones and was shaped much like a black light bulb. She walked slowly. Wrapped around the four-foot-thick bundle of twigs and small branches was a thin blanket. It was tied with a heavy cord. She held onto the cord with one hand and reached behind her with the other to help balance the load.

Her dress was black, her stockings black, her shoes black, and so was the cloth wrapped around her head. White hair showed at her temples.

"Every day she goes to the forest," Kristine said. "We've had no coal for a long time, you know."

Marshall got out of the jeep and walked to the old woman. He smiled at her. She raised her eyes only, not her head, she didn't straighten. He pointed to the bundle and indicated by motions of his hand that he wanted to lift it from her back. She shook her head and looked back at the cobblestones, continuing to walk slowly.

Pop and Kristine followed him out of the jeep. They waited for the old woman.

"Leave her alone," Kristine said. Then she spoke softly a few German words. Her grandmother did not answer. Kristine pushed open a wooden gate for her. The old woman dumped the load by the front door, pulled the cloth loose, slowly folded it, and then neatly coiled the cord in her hand. She did not straighten or turn, but entered the house. The door closed.

"Her spine. Arthritis," said Kristine. She touched her own back with her hand. "She doesn't approve of me. All that had happened to us. And now she sees me with you. Can you blame her?" Kristine looked very sad, as if she might cry. Then she shrugged her shoulder and turned to the jeep. "Thank you for the apples and the flour. Tomorrow maybe Grandmother will like me after I fix a nice strudel." She walked almost to the door, then stopped and returned to where they stood leaning against the jeep.

"Would you do a favor for me, Lieutenant Sunder?"

"Sure Kris, anything."

"One moment then." She hurried into the house.

They waited in silence in front of the cottage. Men and women walked by them, looked at them, stoic, never changing expressions, revealing no emotion, wearing neither sneer nor scowl, nor smile. They looked first at the fliers, then at the house, then back the fliers. Two young, thin boys leaned against a broken wall and stared at them.

Marshall and Pop lit cigarettes, and then Pop took from his shirt pocket a sheet of paper, unfolded it and handed it to Marshall. "Read it," he said. "Boy, am I on top of the world! See right here, I'm getting the whole San Fernando Valley from Van Nuys to Tarzana, out where the movie stars live, a lot of them, on ranches, plus a raise. Start back at $300 per. Why, I can put the kid through SC with that, plus the commissions. And look here," he put his finger further down the sheet. "A new company car, a Ford, soon as they start making them again."

"That's great, Pop." Marshall said. He handed the sheet back to Pop. "You really got it made."

"You know it." He folded it and returned it to his shirt pocket.

Kristine came from the door and ran down the walk to the jeep. In her hand she held a small white piece of paper, folded once, a paper clip holding it closed. She handed it to Marshall. Between the folds was a small negative.

"It's the only picture ever taken of us," she said. "I've never seen the picture, only this. They could develop the film but there is no photographic paper. Can you have one made for me?"

"Sure, Kris. I'll ask the photo lab. I'm sure they can do it."

"Thank you." She turned, ran back to the doorway, stood there, she grinned at them.

"Happy to meet you, sister. Be good to my boy here," Pop said

"Good-bye, Luftgangsters!" she said, laughed, waved, then stopped suddenly and returned to the jeep and asked Marshall, " Is it possible for me to see the insides of one of your airplanes?"

Marshall turned to Pop. "Where's *DIANA* parked? Do you think we could do that?"

"No problem. Know what? I'll borrow one of Jim's flight suits. He's the smallest of the crew. I don't think she wants to climb up there wearing a dress, do you?"

"Roger."

"Well, how about after chow? There's still plenty of light."

"Well, Kristine, that's your answer. Can you meet us, say, near my barracks about six-thirty?"

"Would you get in trouble if we do this thing? It's just that I am so curious."

"Naw!" Pop said, "We'll pick you up and drive the jeep right up to *DIANA*, climb in, give you the tour, and drive you back home. Now wear something that will allow you to put on a man's flight suit."

"Why?"

"Just do it. You'll find out." Pop said and laughed.

"Roger," Kristine said, and turned and disappeared into the darkness of the room beyond the front door.

"Sweet kid," Pop said. "How do like that 'roger' with a German accent?"

"She's one of a kind, Pop. I really love that little Kraut," Marshall said.

"Come on, lieutenant," Pop said. "Cool that love nonsense!"

"You heard that bridge and house talk?" Marshall asked.

"Sure, I heard it. And you forget it." They looked at one another, then stepped aside for a man and a woman, allowing them to pass.

"Where you heading?" Marshall asked.

"Well now, Lieutenant, I just don't know that that's any of your business." Pop laughed, then climbed into the jeep.

"Didn't mean to be nosy. Thought I'd ride back to the base with you."

"As a matter of fact, I'm going the other way, but for an old washed up bombardier, I'll go outta my way."

"Heck no. Forget it, Pop, I'll walk."

"Naw. Come on. Climb aboard, Marsh. Only take a second. Then I gotta get out to see my little fraulein."

Pop turned the jeep in a circle and stopped suddenly near the two young German boys.

"Hey kinder krauts," he said. "Here's some Yankee smokes for you!" Pop tossed an almost full package of Luckies towards the boys and one caught the package, looked into it, showed his friend and they both yelled back, "Danke," and smiled.

"Might want to sell them some paint in a few years!"

"Yeah, and let's hope they're not some of those Hitler youth werewolves we've heard about." Marshall said, then laughed and said, " Oh hell, they're too young for that kind of crap. Wait a minute, Pop."

Then Marshall turned to the boys and said, " Hey, fellas. Do you want to work for cigarettes, or coffee, maybe even chocolate?"

They looked at one another, then cautiously approached the jeep.

"We will work," the older of the two said.

"If you want to polish shoes for cigarettes, come up to my barracks, it's D-6. I'll talk to my friends and we may be able to keep you busy. You understand?"

"Yes. When?"

"Any day, but the best time is around five o'clock, before we eat dinner."

"We will come today. Okay?"

"Roger." Marshall grinned. "I'll be waiting for you."

"Good idea," Pop said. "Send them over to my barracks, too, when you're through. I'll line up some work for them."

"So you think your points are going to be enough to send you home soon."

"Rumors. Always rumors. Are you anxious about getting home?"

"Pop, I might sign up for another year. I don't think the folks have enough stuff on the shelves yet to sell."

As they drove towards the officer's quarters, Pop said, "You know Marsh, if you're going to be involved with that store your folks own, you ought to read a book my boss gives to all of the salesmen. It's by Dale Carnegie."

"What's it about?"

"Understanding people. Getting along with them."

"I'll ask my mom to buy a copy and mail it to me."

"What the hell," Pop continued, "I'll just give you my copy. I've got it memorized anyway."

"By the way, Pop. Are you telling me you have a girl friend?" Marshall asked. He held himself down in the seat of the bouncing, speeding jeep with both hands. Pop drove fast through the narrow streets and honked at the Germans and laughed when they jumped and shook their umbrellas at them in anger.

"Gotta stay in practice, Son!" Pop laughed and pushed his cap down tight on his head. "Say, boy, how come you haven't liberated yourself a car by now?"

"Just don't think it's right, that's all. Aren't you happily married?"

Pop looked at him. He didn't laugh.

"Certainly. I'm happy at home! But I've one hell of an urge that needs slaking or I'll bust up something. It isn't love. Home is love. You're thinking is good on both counts, young man, sir, however, let old Pop know if you need transportation! Not liberate one. Just a good buy."

"Thanks, Pop, but Frank bought a car and Gary and I've used it."

Dust from the sudden stop in front of the officers' quarters clouded up over their shoulders. Pop looked at Marshall, expecting him to climb out, but he sat still.

"Pop, I understand you're flying crew, engineer, for the colonel."

"Right. And when my points are ready, I'll be the first NCO out of Europe." Pop laughed, then looked at his watch.

"You get to Paris don't you, on those hops?"

"Go into Villa Cloubeau every week. The colonel's sweet on a nurse there."

"Pop, will you take some of my cigarettes and some dough and buy some nice things, you know, silk stuff, perfume, lipstick, and all, for Kristine. You saw her size. She's little. Would that be too much trouble?"

"Glad to help. Go get the bartering stuff. I gotta get going, a corporal's trying to beat my time." Pop laughed and slapped Marshall on the shoulder. He let the jeep engine run.

In a few minutes Marshall returned with his bombardier's satchel stuffed too full. He couldn't completely zip it closed. He handed it to Pop, plus a roll of American bills.

"Christamighty. With this loot, I'll bring you a nice fat French girl. I hope you kept some weeds for those kraut kids," he said, laughed again, then turned the jeep in a tight arc and waved over his shoulder at Marshall. He drove towards Bad Scheidel. He yelled, "So long, Romeo. See you at six P.M."

CHAPTER 7

▼

KRISTINE TOURS A B-26

Kristine selected a pair of her husband's trousers hanging in the closet and slipped into them. Though Paul had been a very slim young man, it was necessary for her to find a belt and pull it up to the last hole, punched into the leather. She felt secure with the garb and had come to feel less threatened, and safe, in the presence of Marshall and now too, the flier Pop. Kristine rolled the trousers up above her knees, put on her raincoat, and walked to the officer's quarters. Neighbors would wonder about trousers, she knew.

Marshall sat with McAdam at the dinner table. They finished their dessert and were about to leave when Marshall put his hand on McAdam's arm.

"Gary. Want to have some fun?" Marshall asked.

"If it's fun, count me in."

"Pop and I are going to give Kristine a tour of *DIANA* after dinner. She's curious as hell to see our office. We're picking her up in a few minutes outside our barracks."

"Buddy, you've a weird idea about what's fun, but sure, I'd like to come along. Maybe that little kraut will show me a little more respect."

"I'll make sure that she understands that you are captain of the ship!" Marshall said. They both laughed. "Seriously, I know you're proud as hell of making first pilot."

"Yeah, I've already written to my folks and Sean."

They walked from the officers' dining room to the far end of their barracks and Pop was sitting in the jeep and Kristine was beside him now wearing Jim's flight suit over her husband's trousers.

"Hi Gary!" Pop said, "Heard you got checked out as a first pilot. Good going. Hi Marsh. Well, guess it's the back of the bus for you officers! Kris is my copilot."

Kristine moved out of the seat so that the two fliers could ride in the back seat. She climbed back in and looked towards Pop for reassurance. It was the first time Marshall had seen her grin like that. She giggled then, and turned around to speak to Marshall. "You like my uniform?" The sleeves of both arms had been rolled up, as well as the trouser cuffs.

"Real fashion model," Marshall laughed. "And did you know a couple of kids came up to the barracks and they've got more darn shoes to polish than they know what to do with. They'll be rich with cigarettes."

"You must not pay them until the job is perfect," Kristine said.

It was a short drive to the hard pan where the B-26's were parked. It was over a half-mile from the airplane to the tower. There were no guards on duty. Pop drove the jeep up to the nose of the B-26. When they were out of the jeep, Marshall guided Kristine to the port side of the airplane and nodded towards the window of the left-seat pilot. "That's where the first pilot sits and I believe you know that *DIANA* is the name of Frank's wife."

"I did not know that." Kristine said. "The airplane is so much bigger than I thought."

"Same with the Luftwaffe pilots, they put names on their planes, I believe," McAdam added.

"Come over here, Kristine, " Pop said. "See those big propellers? Well, the problem is you can't see them if they are spinning. So, it's a B-26 ritual with anyone entering the plane from the nose wheel opening. We always walk to the nose wheel before we climb into the cockpit area. Never take a short cut. So, my dear Fraulein, follow me now, and we'll all touch the nose wheel." Kristine followed Pop and touched the wheel, then waited as Marshall and McAdam did the same.

"Okay, little lady," Pop said, "I'm climbing up first, then one of those gents can give you a lift and I'll help you all the way in. Put your feet on the steps of that little ladder, and lift yourself."

"Now I understand the need for trousers!" Kristine said. " And remember, it is 'Frau', Herr Pop!"

Sergeant Skidmore laughed at Kristine. He hoisted himself up into the cockpit, then turned back and leaned down from above and said, "You ready? Let's go."

Marshall walked to Kristine and said, "I'm going to bend down now and put my hands together and hoist you up. There's two steps on that ladder, and some struts to hold onto, as you go up, then Pop will lift you on in." Marshall leaned over and Kristine placed a small foot into his grasped hands. McAdam stood near her and helped balance her as Marshall lifted her upwards.

Marshall and McAdam followed. "Sir?" Pop said, he paused and looked to Marshall, "Why don't you help her slide down into your office, then Gary can tell her about his office, and I'll show her the top turret, plus the stinger."

"Good idea, Sergeant Skidmore," Marshall said. He pushed back the copilot's seat as far as it would slide, then leaned down and folded the foot petals. "Follow me, Kris," he said, and then kneeled and crawled into the nose. "Okay, Kris, come on down." There wasn't a Norden bombsight, but a fifty-caliber machine gun was mounted to fire from the rounded cone shaped nose. The action rested against the side of the bulkhead. It was not loaded. No ammunition belt was present. The round black barrel extended beyond the nose.

She crawled on her hands and knees and found Marshall sitting with his legs crossed, Indian fashion. "My!" she said, "there is room for two."

"Well, it was kind of crowded when two big guys were in here. Sometime a navigator joins the bombardier to help find the target faster."

"So?" Kristine said. "It was from here that a Luftgangster found our little bridge?"

"For him, it was just another bridge in enemy territory, Kristine." Marshall said. "Just like your fliers, everyone had a job to do." Marshall avoided looking at her.

"It seems so ironic to me. We used to look up in the sky and we would see your airplanes and the profile of the wings and body formed a Christian cross."

"Never thought of it like that," Marshall said.

"So, how do you get out of here if the airplane is damaged, if it is on fire?"

"No escape hatch on a '26. We have to go back the way we came. So let's leave and you can see the pilot's office."

Kristine crawled out and stood up between the pilots' seats. McAdam sat in the first pilot's seat and smiled at her. "In *DIANA*, this is really Frank's position, or was, when the war was on. I'm now qualified to be in command of a ship, but now I won't have one of my own."

"My!" Kristine exclaimed. "Look at all of the dials and gadgets, at all of the instruments and handles and controls."

Gary slowly swept his hand across the instrument panel. "Altimeter, ball and compass, manifold pressure, oil pressure, cylinder temperature, cowl flaps, fuel gages, just lots of things, even a clock, and these handles control the temperature of the carburetor air, and these we push or pull for the power of the engines, and these we use to raise and lower the landing gear, and Pop is watching the tachs and listening to the engines. A good engineer will sense, will hear a poor engine! Right, Pop?"

"Right," Pop said, laughed, and continued, "you've impressed the little lady, now let me give her the rest of the tour. Come on, Kris, follow me and you duck your head when I do."

Marshall and Kris moved past a bulkhead, stepped down into a compartment behind the pilots, where the navigator's table was located, behind the copilot. On the opposite side were the radio and the radioman's seat, and desk. Pop then led Kristine through the bomb bay area, directly beneath the wings, and on to the top machine gun turret. "Climb up and look around, if you want, Kristine." Pop said, and the little German girl clambered up and seated herself so that she could look out at the sky and horizon.

"Kris," Pop said, " you fit pretty well. I had a heck of a time getting in and out of there so Frank had me man the waist guns. Any engine problems develop, then I could get to the cockpit quicker."

Kristine listened in silence, nodded, and climbed back down and stood next to him. "And back here is another set of fifty-caliber's and a nice chair for Jim." Kristine followed him, but didn't try to climb into the chair. "We call this the 'stinger' so if any bad guys tried to sneak up on us we could punish them!"

Kristine shook her head from side to side, and her eyes brimmed with tears. "And to think our boys were doing the same thing. How awful!"

"It's all over," Pop said, "You take it easy now, honey. Didn't know all this would upset you so!"

"I'm all right, Mr. Pop," Kristine said, then managed to grin. "But, what is it with you men?"

Pop shrugged his shoulders. They retraced their steps back into the pilots' compartment. Gary still sat in the pilot's seat and Marshall was in the copilot's seat.

Marshall turned in the chair and motioned for Kris to sit on his knees. He was pleased when she leaned against him. He rested his open hand on her waist, and she put one arm around his neck. Pop kneeled down and then sat on a ledge between the two pilots.

They were silent for awhile, then Pop asked, "Suppose we ought to climb out of here? I've got to take Kristine home. You can bring Jim's flight suit to work with you," He said, nodding to Kristine.

Marshall did not want to release Kris. Her body warmth melded with his, and she rested her head against his.

"Fellas," Marsh said, "I've got a great idea. Gary, you're the captain of this ship. Captains can conduct marriage ceremonies. You marry Kris and me and Pop can be the witness. How about it Kris?"

"I am already Frau Schuttenhelm!" She sat upright and stared into his face.

"Sure, sure. But this will be insurance, just in case, you know, but really because we are in love!" Marshall said "Right?"

"You are crazy, Chico!" Kristine laughed.

"Okay, you two," Gary said, "hold hands and I'll marry you." Gary raised himself out of his seat and stood in front of them. Marshall held one of Kristine's hands with both of his and Gary began an extemporaneous speech.

"We are gathered before you to join this man and woman in holy matrimony, providing Kristine will not be committing bigamy, and after that is determined, then this will be official, according to the power vested in me as captain of this ship."

Gary paused, looked at Marshall and Kristine. Marshall grinned, and Kristine stared at him, her eyes wide, a look of astonishment on her face. "Okay, you're both supposed to say, 'I do' now!"

"No, wait. I'm supposed to say 'will you take me as your lawful wedded husband, or something like that and she does the same."

"Well, do you, Marsh?"

"I do."

"What about it Kris?"

Kris laughed and looked at the three fliers. She shrugged her shoulders, "Oh, I guess I do."

"Any objection from the audience?" Gary looked at Pop.

"Okay, Pop, kiss the bride!" Pop stood up, leaned over and kissed Kristine on the cheek, then Gary shouldered Pop away and he leaned over and kissed her lips.

"Marshall. You may now kiss the bride!" Gary said.

"Luftgangsters! All of you are crazy!" Kristine said, giggling, then kissed Marshall before he could say anything. "But no honeymoon, you understand!" she added. She patted him on the cheek. Then all of them laughed.

The four of them climbed down out of the B-26, the fliers helping Kristine with her footing and balance, and then walked to the nose wheel, touched it, and went to the jeep.

The streets were dark by the time they reached the grandmother's house. Kristine jumped out of the jeep, turned. Laughed and waved to them and went into the house. Pop drove the jeep back to the Officers' Quarters.

"Thanks, Pop, it's been fun," Marshall said. Gary nodded agreement and they waved as

Pop turned and drove back towards Bad Scheidel.

Chapter 8

▼

Mail Call

Mail Call relinquished a few letters and Marshall was delighted to open the one from his Uncle Bruce.

"Here it is, you guys! A collection of my uncle's favorite jokes. Let me read from his letter," and Marshall began:

"Dear Marsh. Did you hear the story about the young man that was convicted of a crime and sent to jail? A few days into the routine of things he was befriended by a con and after their evening meal in a big mess hall, all of a sudden one of the prisoners stands up, looks around the room, laughs and loudly says, twenty-nine and the rest of the inmates all laugh heartily and the prisoner sits down, grinning.

"Well, the newcomer asks his friend what that was all about, and it was explained that they've all heard the same jokes hundreds of times, so they finally gave a number to a joke. So whoever wants to tell a joke, just stands up, calls out the number, and everyone enjoys it. A few days later, the new prisoner, anxious to get off on the right foot with his peers, asks the con if he can tell a joke. 'Sure', the guy says, ' and number seventeen is an all time favorite.' So the young man stands up, stares around the dining room, raises his voice and says seventeen. There is an embarrassing silence. He sits down, stunned. 'What did I do wrong? You said that number seventeen is a favorite.' 'Well, Son, the old con said, 'you see, some folks just can't tell a joke.'

Marshall looked at his roommates and they were chuckling. "Keep reading," Gary said, that wasn't too bad!"

Returning to the letter, Marshall read, "So, Marsh, there should be a point to every joke or anecdote you use. There are some tried and true ways to tell jokes, however let me share a few thoughts on the subject before you get to the attached list. First of all, try to remember the way the professional comedians tell stories. They precede and follow their jokes with smiles and laughter of their own. They don't wear Buster Keaton faces. And the best of them always make themselves the brunt of their jokes. They seldom ever are guilty of putting-down some poor soul to get a laugh. A good joke teller is generally a witty person, who sees humor or irony in every day predicaments. They kid politicians, they are fair game, and refer to current events and there are lots of jokes relating to baseball, football, golf and so on. My friends and I tell a lot of jokes, some pretty raw, however we don't tell dirty jokes around the ladies.

"Classifying jokes sometimes makes it easier for your own memory bank to come up with something both appropriate and funny. You can think of, say, animal jokes, then break it down to dog jokes, cat jokes, horses, cattle, elephants, and so on, and of course there are bird jokes. Sometimes you can tell a quick joke to ease some one's embarrassment.

"Now Marshall," Bruce continued, "I don't want you to hurry through this list trying to find what you think is the funniest. A joke should be pertinent, not just recited, hoping to get attention to yourself. Which reminds me of the story about the young bull and the old bull standing on a hillside near some big old valley oaks. All of a sudden the young bull looks into a pasture beneath them and sees a small herd of cows. He turns to the old bull and says, 'Lets run down there and screw a cow! He paws the ground, and the old bull looks at him and says 'Let's just walk down and screw them all!' So, perhaps that is pertinent to slowing down a bit. That's up to you to decide."

Marshall put the letter down and laughed and was joined by Gary and Frank. "Keep going," Gary said, "I can use both of those

Marshall enjoyed hearing Frank and Gary laugh at the letter. "This goes on for several pages," he said, "Tell me if you want me to stop."

"I can handle another right now," Gary said, " And I'd like to copy the whole letter if you'll let me."

"This is a refreshing change." Frank said, "Your Uncle Bruce is a sage of sorts, isn't he? "Read another, Marsh."

Marshall again read from the letter:

"Marshall, there's something else about telling jokes and that is being a good listener to your buddies' jokes. Laugh at them. Applaud them. And for goodness sake never say 'yes' if the guy all of a sudden stops and says, 'Have you already hear this one?' Say of course not, even if you've heard it a dozen times. Let the guy have the stage. Gosh knows we all need encouragement! But, back to the time and place for a joke."

Marshall looked away from the letter and both Frank and Gary seemed absorbed with its contents, so he continued:

"Son, there are dozens of jokes that take place in a bar setting. Here's one that I love, and I had to memorize it before I could tell it. Always goes over good at the Lodge if a new member is trying to get acquainted. So, first, I might introduce him to a little game of Boss Dice at the bar, then buy him a drink and finally dazzle him with this one:

'This funny looking old guy with a beaten up hat comes into the saloon, dragging a shotgun and he arrives at the bar, pounds on it, slams down a silver dollar, and hollers at the bartender,—'A bubble durbon please!' The bartender asks 'I beg your pardon, sir? A bubble durbon, damn it!' So the bartender quickly checks his book. No such a drink. He thinks maybe this guy wants a double bourbon, so he pours one and slides it to the man. He tosses it down and says 'Mighty good, barkeep, one more bubble durbon.' The bartender grins and says, 'one more bubble durbon coming up, then says to the guy, 'What's the shotgun for, partner?' The man stares at the barkeeper and says, 'I'm going on a shurkey toot!The bartender snickers and says, 'You're new around here, friend. Where are you from?' and the man says, 'I'm from Colder, Bolorado.' The bartender smiles, then walks to the other end of the bar and says to a friend standing there, 'Any time I hear something like that it just shickels the tit out of me!"

"But remember this, Marshall, you don't make jokes about a man's wife or friends or his possessions. For instance, if any one should try to make fun of Tara, you know, put her down, kid around about her retrieving ability, I would take quick and serious exception. So, when you make yourself the brunt of a joke, everyone loves it. But lay off of others!"

Marshall scanned ahead in the letter and chuckled, then said, "This just goes on and on."

"I've got to get out to the flight line. Thanks for sharing your letter," Frank said, still laughing. "I guess he's also telling us how NOT to tell a joke! See you guys later."

x   x   x

Time seemed to drag for the fliers, but the weeks and months of occupation duty extended through Thanksgiving Day and the cooks prepared sumptuous meals for both the enlisted men and the officers. Snow began to fall, but it did not hamper the flying schedules. Most of the flying involved ferrying selected pieces of furniture and file cabinets to someplace on the continent, and even to England, and occasionally a GI prisoner, under the escort of a couple of Military Police, were all flown to Paris where he'd be Court Marshaled. At each destination a different load of gear was loaded, generally office equipment, filing cabinets and typewriters and typist chairs, and desks.

A week before Christmas, large fir trees were delivered to both the non-coms' club and to the officers' club. Everyone contributed a variety of homemade ornaments to decorate the trees, and the brightly wrapped packages from the States were placed beneath the boughs. Every effort was made by the Commanding officer of the Bomb Group and by the Squadron Commanders to bring cheer to the holiday season. Again, the chefs prepared and served typical holiday meals.

But, it was bound to happen. They all felt it, sensed it, and tried to change the subject to keep them apart, at least Frank and Gary did when they were around. But it was inevitable. How the room adjoining Marshall's became the poker room no one knew. But they gathered there, a different group each day, depending on who was scheduled to fly. If Tex was there, Frank tried to keep him quiet, or sometimes he'd go along with him and kid him, ignore his bragging, or maybe try to bait him. The rest of them would silently laugh. Not that Tex was dumb. He was sharp; as competent a pilot as there was in the outfit. It was just his way.

"Humble them, that's what I say," Tex stated, "wipe their noses in it. Then they'll remember. They'll never start another one." Then he raised the bet; drew two, raised again, and finally won the pot.

"Hey, Tex," Gary said, pausing to laugh, "Did you hear the story about the cannibals discussing the best way to prepare their victims?"

Tex stared at him, smiled and said, "Go on."

"Well, this cannibal says, 'Those Americans are all different. Now take those from New England, well, we like to boil them. And then there are those Californians; we like to barbecue them. Those Great Lake folks, we roast them. Then one of the other cannibals said, "What do you do with Texans? And the guys answers, 'Hell, throw 'em away! Ever clean one?'"

Gary then guffawed and the other players joined in. All but Tex.

"Frank," Tex said, "How in the hell did a nice guy like you get stuck with McAdam and Sunder?"

"An old saying covers it, Tex, 'Birds of a feather flock together,' or better yet, 'fly together!'"

"Bull shit," Tex muttered.

Marshall laughed loudly, then said, "You know McAdam here has a Scottish name. Gary, do you know why those ancestors of yours, those Scottish shepherds, why they wear kilts?" Marshall again laughed, "Because sheep can hear a zipper from a hundred feet!" And the entire group laughed.

When the laughter subsided, Gary said. "I'm cashing in. I'm going to find Marsh's list of jokes and return with more money," He stuffed the bills and loose change into his pocket and departed. The game continued.

"Germans make good Americans," Marshall said, not directing his words to anyone in particular, but recalling the remarks made by Tex. He counted his marks, stacked the paper money evenly by the edges, then put some coins on it.

"You are the great German lover, aren't you. The good-German myth! Ugh! It gets me right here!" Tex grabbed his crotch.

"Just what the hell do you like?" Marshall said, his face reddening.

"Take it easy, Marsh," Frank said, almost whispered. He sat next to him at the table.

"Texas. What else, Kraut lover?" He laughed, arranged the cards in his hand, then continued, "Look me up when we get back to the States. I'll see to it that you get your luck changed: genuine black pussy. Not this Hun stuff."

Suddenly, Marshall stood up, his face livid. His chair toppled over behind him and banged the floor. He took large steps around the table, gripping the shoulders of the other fliers as he moved. Frank grabbed for him, and missed. Tex looked up in time to see Marshall and feel his hand jerk the back of his shirt and pull him over backward and upward. Tex dropped his cards, then twisted his body. Marshall's right fist struck him on the throat, below where he'd aimed. Tex sprawled on his back on the floor. He rolled and jumped to his feet, yelled something unintelligible, charged Marshall and tackled him, then Marshall felt the animal like growl, heard it emanate from his own throat. Furiously they struck at one another, rolling on the floor, each hearing the sound of their fists striking bone and flesh and being also struck, feeling the hot pain. Frank tried to pull Tex away from Marshall. He grabbed at his clothing.

None of them heard the first three knocks at the door. A flier heard the second series, pulled it open, glanced momentarily at the flier who knocked, quickly looked back at the combatants wrestling and cursing, then startled by his recognition, he stared again at the flier standing there, and then at the top of his voice called out, "Techhut!"

"What the hell's going on here?" Colonel Schlosser said. He glared at all of them. On his cheek and chin his beard showed dark. Beneath his eyes the skin was almost purple. Under his arm he held a package with brown string tied around it and letters scrawled on it.

"Just a little fun," Frank said. He stepped back, dropped Tex's leg and stood at attention.

"We'll discuss this later. I want to talk to you, and McAdam and Sunder." He nodded at Frank.

"Where's McAdam?"

"I'll get him, sir," a flier said. "He's down the hall."

The others took their money from the tabletop and left the room. Tex held his throat and followed them out. Gary rushed into the room, his eyes wide. His feet slid on the floor; he stopped, then stood at attention.

"Reports as ordered, sir," he said. He saluted.

"At ease, rest! Rest, damn it! Now, let's all just sit down, fellas. Close that damn door, McAdam."

"Yes, sir!"

All of them sat around the table with the package in the middle of it.

"That son-of-a-bitch Tex thinks even Albert Schweitzer is a Nazi!" Frank said. Marshall said nothing. He leaned backwards in the chair, his head tipped so that he looked at the ceiling, and with an olive drab handkerchief soaked up blood from his nose. The colonel looked around at all of them. He seemed to study their faces. Then he offered his cigarettes, pointing the open pack at each of them. All of them accepted his offer.

Frank held his lighter for the colonel and for Gary. He blew it out, annoyed by his own observance of the old superstition, re-lit it, held it for Marshall, then lit his own. They waited for the colonel to speak. Never saw him look so old, so tired, Marshall thought. He wished his nose would stop bleeding. He drew the smoke into his lungs, then folded the handkerchief, exhaled, and held it to his nose again.

"Pop is dead," the colonel said. "Damn! I'm sorry I have to tell you this."

They looked at one another. Marshall felt very cold. His body shook, shivered once all over, then stopped.

"What do you mean, sir?" Frank asked.

"That's it. He's dead. You all know Sergeant Skidmore has been my Flight Engineer. We flew up to Paris today. Then tonight, coming home, I started to taxi out, Pop stopped me. He said he had to go back to the ready-room for a package. I told him to hurry it up. He forgot to touch the nose wheel. Left prop got him. He never had a chance."

They sat and stared at one another. Through the walls they could hear music from a radio playing, but could not make out the tune. Laughter reached them from across the hall.

"Forgot to touch the lousy nose wheel?" Frank asked. He looked bewildered, Marshall thought. Suddenly Frank sobbed, tried to close his mouth to choke it silent. He stood up and walked to a corner of the room and they could hear him crying, quietly muffling the sounds he made, then take deep, loud, sucking breaths through his open mouth. Marshall looked at him. Frank blew his nose, wiped his face, then came back and sat down and lit another cigarette. Then he asked the colonel, "Where is he?"

"He'll be buried in the military cemetery in Paris. We'll fly up for the funeral."

"Dirty son-of-a-bitch!" McAdam said. He jammed his cigarette out, then lit another.

"I'll write to his wife," the colonel said. "I'll leave it to you fellows to send his personal belongings home." He sighed, looked around at all of them again. "If she wants him buried in the States, we'll tend to that later." He sighed. "I think all of us may have let down, relaxed too much, become forgetful, you know, now that combat has ended."

Frank nodded.

"We picked up the package. It's got your name on it, Sunder." He pointed to it, setting it on the table, amongst the playing cards still laying face down in groups of five.

Marshall picked up the package, looked at all of them. "Pop was such a well tempered man." Marshall said. He tried to remember the words his Uncle Bruce used, telling him about steel, having elements compared to honesty and loyalty and courage, but he couldn't bring it all together into anything that would make sense. He turned and walked into his own room and pulled the door closed behind him.

"After the funeral, you and the rest of the crew take a three day leave, whenever you want it," the colonel said to Frank. He gripped the back of the chair with both hands, stared at the floor.

"A few months ago, we expected this sort of thing. We were prepared for death. I think that's what makes it so much tougher now. I'm so damn sorry, fellas!"

Back in his room, still trying to stop the blood dripping from his nose, and choking back sobs, Marshall stared at the package.

Frank pushed open the door. "Gary and I are going over to the club and get a drink. Why don't you join us?"

"Alright," Marshall said, "and I need some ice for my damn nose."

News of Pop's death traveled quickly. At the bar, fliers nodded to them, held a drink aloft, wording out silently "To Pop." And they acknowledged by nodding and raising their own glasses. Several of the fliers walked by the three and put a hand on one of their shoulders or arms, patted, or squeezed but said nothing and did not attempt to join them.

"I'm heading back to the room," Marshall said.

"See you later," Frank said, "I'm going to chase down Frantz and Dublin. Want them to hear it from one of us, if they haven't already heard it."

"I'll join you, Frank," McAdam said.

Marshall returned to his room and sat in a chair by the table with the package. He turned out the light. In the blackness his mind kept repeating the words—*It is a cardinal sin to not touch the nose wheel!*

In the darkness he thought back to the early days of their training at Lake Charles. They pounded it into them. Marshall could hear the instructor saying it over and over. "On a B-26 with its tricycle landing gear, the space above the wheel is where you will enter the aircraft. Crewmembers entering the front section of the craft will lift yourselves. If you approach the nose wheel and touch the front of it you've automatically programmed a safe route to avoid the propellers, which, when spinning are invisible and are as deadly as a guillotine. Always do this, whether the props are turning or not. It must be an inbred habit that you'll never break. AND, touch it when you leave the airplane."

Marshall turned on a light and took the package and placed it in the back of his closet Marshall waited several days before opening the package. If only Pop hadn't gone back for the damn thing.

He helped Frank and Gary go through Pop's footlocker. They made sure everything personal would go to his wife, but nothing that would cause her any doubts

Gary found Pop's rabbit foot. He held it up for Frank and Marshall to see and raised his eyebrows.

"Deep six it," Frank said.

Gary tossed it into the wastebasket.

Frank opened the cover of a book. "Marsh, this is for you, from Pop."

Marshall accepted the book. "Pop said he was going to give me book. Thanks."

They didn't talk about Pop. Marshall explained about the package. They said they understood. Somehow, he wished they didn't understand.

It was his fault. He wished someone would say it, any of the crewmembers. They never did. Another inside voice told him it was just the fickle finger of fate: plain and simple bad luck.

Finally Marshall retrieved the package and opened it. It contained a black silk dressing gown and a woman's black panties, and a brassiere, also black, and three small bottles of perfume, two tubes of lipstick, and some sheer silk stockings

Marshall didn't tell Kristine about Pop forgetting the package and starting back for it. She couldn't believe it when he told her Pop was dead. Forget to touch the nose wheel? How could that cause him to die? He explained that they always touched the nose wheel, whether the props were turning or not, that way they would be certain to clear them. It was a necessary habit. Pop forgot. There was no point in telling her about the package, adding to her unhappiness. Maybe things from Paris will help her forget the faces in the picture.

In the negative that he'd held in front of the light, the faces were black and small. He was surprised when the photo officer gave him the prints.

"Blew one up so you could really see them," he said. He handed Marshall an enlargement, an eight by ten, and they both looked at the picture of the soldier and the girl and the baby. He hardly recognized Kristine. Her face was almost round. Maybe it was because she was smiling so broadly, yet her body was heavier, her arms and breasts and legs, all looked larger. The soldier was slim, not much taller than Kristine, and looked harmless in the Wehrmacht uniform. He'd never seen a picture of a German soldier with a woman and a child. This made him, the soldier, seem different, harmless. Marshall never thought about enemy soldiers having wives and children and mothers and fathers. It was obvious, of course, but not something he'd dwelled on. The negative was too grainy to make a real good print the photo officer said. Marshall thanked him for the favor. He didn't think Kristine would care about the graininess.

Marshall had seen Frank cry. McAdam clouded up, too, a little, when they started to go through Pop's footlocker. But Marshall's chest ached, his throat seemed taut and his voice was husky, yet he didn't cry. He almost did when they handed him the little book by Dale Carnegie. Pop had written a note in it, intending to give it to Marshall. But still he didn't cry.

Then he saw Kristine cry, but it wasn't about Pop.

When Kristine came to the room to clean that day he was standing looking at the trees. The good apples were all gone. The remaining had turned brown and mushy and had fallen to the ground.

The German maids picked up a few anyway and took them with them. They gathered the ripe fruit after they found out that the officers didn't care, and then they stripped all of the fruit trees on the air base. No one had thought to tell them it was okay to take the fruit. Then it was almost too late. Now the leaves were beginning to lose their fresh green color and were dusty and gray, some turning brown and beginning to shrivel.

"I am sorry that you are sad, about Sergeant Pop," Kristine whispered. She had put her arms around him from behind and he could feel her head resting on his back between his shoulder blades. Her breasts pushed softly against him. He raised his arms up high and turned, as if standing in a barrel, faced her with her arms still around him. He kissed her.

"I have something for you," he said. "Sort of a wedding present." He'd decided to give her the presents from Paris first.

"How did you ever get them?" she gasped, her eyes opened wide, with childlike wonderment lighting her face. She lifted a fold of the silk gown with the back of her hand and touched her cheek with it. She looked at the underclothes. "I didn't know you had such a talent for sizes," she said and laughed when he blushed. Kristine took the bottles of perfume from the package, put the top on it, hiding the black things in it, and then took each bottle, carefully twisted the glass stoppers loose and dabbed a spot of the liquid on the back of her hand. When she had opened the first one she drew her hand beneath her nostrils slowly, closed her eyes and said "Uhm," then sighed. She held her hand for Marshall to smell. She repeated the ritual with each bottle.

"Which do you like best?" she asked.

"I like them all. I'll wear them all at once." They both laughed. She leaned her forehead on his chest. Then she selected one and touched the glass stopper to her ear lobes.

"I never had French perfume before. How is the aroma? Does it excite you?"

"It's terrific! I want to buy lots of things for you Kris."

"We always heard about the rich Americans," she said. She tucked her fingers beneath his belt, then reached up and kissed him. "Now a lipstick!" she said, and selected a tube, turned it, stared at the pink substance, touched her upper lip three times, then joined both lips, spreading the pink coloring, and looked up at Marshall, seeking his approval.

"Real sexy, Chico Fraulein!" They kissed again, and Marshall held her close to him with both arms, feeling the warmth of her body. Then he looked across the room and saw the envelope in his open footlocker with the pictures. No use putting it off, he thought.

"Photo lab made the pictures for you." Marshall said. He released her and went to the footlocker. "I haven't seen them."

"So soon," she sighed, and Marshall thought there was disappointment, or anguish in the tone of her voice, "I thought it might take longer. The picture was taken almost two years ago, you know."

"No, I didn't know."

"I told you about my baby."

"You started to, you know, the day Pop picked us up in the jeep."

"Well, I'd better look at the picture, hadn't I?" She looked up at him, questioning him with her eyes, looking deep; he felt, searching, reaching for some wise answer that he couldn't give. Does she want me to tell her no, you shouldn't look, no you can't have the pictures?

"He said the film was grainy," Marshall said. He handed her the envelope. Kristine took it and sat on his bed and let the thin, slick photos slide into her hand. She looked at them. The picture was the same, but there were two that were smaller than the eight by ten. She studied all of them, as if they were different. Marshall lit a cigarette, turned and stared out of the window.

"I still have that dress. Wasn't I fat?" Kristine said, then continued. "Martin looks so young. He was seventeen. We went to school together. Got married. He left me pregnant. We only lived together three weeks, and then the Wehrmacht. He went away. He came back just once. He saw his baby, once. Then off to Stalingrad."

Marshall listened to her voice. He was surprised that it was so steady. The crying started without any sound at first. She didn't say anything more so he turned and she had slipped off of his bed and was bent over on the floor, her knees folded under her, her head hanging, the pictures gripped tightly in her hands on her lap, and he could see the tears dripping onto the eight by ten, running across the shiny surface, across Martin's face, the baby's face and across Kristine's, running off of the neat white picture edge onto her dress where it was absorbed into the black cloth. Marshall kneeled beside her. He didn't think she was breathing. Her face was distorted, her mouth open, pulled down, revealing her white teeth as if she were smiling instead of crying. Her eyes closed, but the tears flowed without stopping.

"Kris, Kris, honey!" Marshall said. He took her arm, shook her. "Take a deep breath, quick."

"Please leave me alone." She began to sob then, deeply, her body shaking, and she held the pictures to her breast and rocked back and forth and said over and over again, "My baby, my baby, my baby."

"Come on, honey," Marshall said. He took her arm. "Get up on the bed and lay still, rest. I'll be back in a little while." He unfolded an army blanket that was on the foot of the bed and covered her with it.

Marshall hurried down the hall. He found Frank in his room holding the same book by James. He was always reading. Marshall glanced at the cover, remembered the time he'd asked Frank if he could have the book next because he liked good westerns and especially the drawings, and Frank had raised his eyebrows and shook his head, and quietly said that this was a different James. Marshall avoided any comments about the book after that.

"Frank, when are you going to take your three days?" Marshall asked. He continued to walk across the room, picked up a chair by its back, turned it and sat on it, rested his arms on the top of it and waited for an answer.

"Haven't you time to say hello?" Frank said and grinned.

"Hello." Marshall said. He waited for an answer.

"I'm going to fly over to London. Valentine's Day is coming up and I want to get a nice card and present for Diana." Frank glanced at the page number, then closed his book and set it down beside him. "Would you like to join me? Have to have a navigator, you know."

"Thanks. Not this time. Any chances of borrowing your Mercedes?"

"Sure, but I've already promised it to Gary. Where you going?"

"I'm not sure right now. I'm going to take Kris some place and get married."

"Oh, for Christ's sake, Marsh! Have you lost your mind?" Frank said and stood up. He stared at Marshall.

"Damn it to hell! I'd give my left nut to have my Model A over here, Marshall growled, then stared at Frank. "Okay, okay, I'll get a car some place else," Marshall arose too, and walked brusquely toward the door.

"Hey, wait a minute my friend," Frank said. He grabbed Marshall's arm. "I just said you can borrow when Gary's through with it. What's this all about? You knock Kristine up?"

"No, I didn't knock her up!" Marshall answered and jerked his arm away from Frank's loose grasp.

"Now calm down, buddy," Frank said, "This isn't Tex you're talking to."

Marshall hesitated, then turned and sat down in the chair, gripped his hands together and told Frank about the bridge and Kristine's baby and her mother, about Kristine's home and about the enlargement. Frank watched Marshall's knuckles turn white as he gripped his hands.

"Listen to me, damn it! Use the damn car when Gary's through with it," Frank said, turning away from Marshall and shaking his head, "But don't do anything foolish like getting married. In the first place, you'd be court marshaled when the Air Corps found out. You can't marry a German. Hell, Now you'd need an act of Congress to marry a nurse or a WAC or a Red Cross girl. In fact, you'll be in a peck of trouble if you're even seen riding around together."

"I thought all I needed was God's permission to get married," Marshall answered, then immediately regretted his sarcastic tone. He stood, shifted awkwardly, sighed, looked at his feet and then back at Frank, "I'll take good care of the car, Frank, but someday I will marry Kris."

"All right now," Frank said. He spoke very softly, "As a friend, let me tell you, Marshall, you're going to have to whip this, this infatuation. Why don't you cool it for awhile? At least opt for a long engagement! Please think this over very carefully for a few days. Get together with Gary about the car. Okay?" Frank laughed and gripped Marshall's arm again.

"Thanks," Marshall said. He grabbed Frank's hand, shook it, then turned and rushed back to his own room. Kristine was gone. The package and the envelope and the pictures were gone too. Written on a piece of paper propped up on his dresser were the words, "Thank you." Beneath them were three small x's and Kristine's signature.

CHAPTER 9

▼

MUNICH

Four fliers who had grown up on farms got together and obtained saws and pruning shears and began to prune the apple trees. They agreed that the trees had been neglected for a few seasons and a proper trimming would increase the health of the trees and a better quality crop would be the result. The German maids watched with interest, and then volunteered to gather the bits of branches and limbs and stacked them so that they could be burned. Pieces that they could use in their own fireplaces were stacked in a separate pile and each maid would bundle up a share, tie it and take it with her after work.

Marshall and Frank stood watching the workers from Frank's room. Marshall persisted in asking to borrow Frank's car.

"Damn it to hell, Marshall," Frank said, "I told you that you could borrow it! However, this really is against my better judgment, but if you insist on taking that girl to Munich, for gosh sakes be discreet! Maybe this trip will help get her out of your system!"

"Thanks, buddy, and I'll do as you say."

For Marshall and Kristine to reach Munich and then go on to Garmisch-Partenkirchen they would first have to cross the bridge, go through Bad Scheidel and drive south a hundred or more kilometers.

At first Kristine refused to go with him, seemed shocked that he even asked. He told her it would help her to forget about the picture. She declined. Finally when he said that it would help him forget about Pop, she accepted. She had to find a maid that would do her cleaning chores at the air base. Then Kristine hesitated again and said she felt bad about lying to her grandmother. Finally she told the old woman that she was going with a girl friend to Munich to check on her father who was listed as missing by the Wehrmacht.

Marshall would pick her up after her grandmother had gone to the forest. He borrowed six cartons of cigarettes from Frank and Gary. He counted fifty dollars in American fives and tens that his dad had mailed to him. He zipped the side panels of the B-4 bag closed over the cartons of cigarettes. Maybe, he thought, he could find a minister or a priest or even a Burgermeister that would marry them. He hadn't yet told Kristine his plans to marry her.

The bridge was a logical spot to pick her up. It was far enough from her grandmother's house, yet not in the center of Bad Scheidel. Marshall saw Kristine standing alone, wearing a black coat over a faded blue dress. He stopped beside her. He wished he could have bought a new dress for her. She didn't fill out the dress. It seemed to sag, but it was clean and wool. Marshall jumped out of the car, took her bag and put it into the back seat of the car.

"All set?" he asked.

"Yes. I've been standing here soaking up the warm sun. I thought you'd be earlier? It is cold in the shadows." He stood beside her.

"Across the river," she pointed, "that is my home: the second one. We will repair it when father returns."

Marshall looked across the bridge. The first house was only a framework of bricks. Marshall started to walk towards the bridge. Kristine stood still. He turned to her.

"What's that old man doing, Kris?"

"Cleaning the bricks, of course," she said.

Marshall watched him take one brick at a time from a pile of rubble, examine it, and then with a small hammer chip away the bits of old mortar. When it was cleaned he stacked it next to another on a pallet. The stack was almost two feet tall. "Let's look at the river," he said. Kristine looked up and down the street, declined and said she would wait in the car if he wanted to look at it.

He left her and walked to the bridge and then along the walk beside the stone railing, waist high and a foot thick. He ran his hands over the stone, felt the cold hardness with his palms and fingertips. Before he reached the center of the bridge he came to the damaged section, repaired with rough wooden timbers. Two GIs clad in their winter olive drabs sat on a pine railing that replaced the stone one and looked down at the water nearly twenty feet below. They turned and smiled at him and started to get down to salute, but he said, "At ease" and nodded at them.

Marshall and Kristine looked back at the water. Three nuns walked toward them, staring straight ahead, their faces pale, without lines or wrinkles, expressionless faces dim in the shadow of their white hoods. Marshall felt they deliberately avoided eye contact. He walked to the other side of the bridge. A curved section of the stone jutted out and upon a statue of a man on one knee with his arms clasped behind him looking eastward at the horizon. Marshall couldn't read the inscription. He looked at the sky where the statue looked. A few white clouds moved slowly on the horizon. Must be seeking wisdom, Marshall thought: seemed Frank had quoted someone, or read something, about wisdom.

They must have flown *DIANA* off in that direction, after making the bomb run. The sun was at their backs, coming from the east. The bridge was bigger, thicker than it had seemed from the air. He remembered the vertical hair in the bombsight bisecting the bridge. The cross hair stopped short of the bridge on the roadway, synchronized, ready for the bomb release. He remembered seeing the black indices cross on the dial of the Norden; and Pop's immediate response to his "GO", the bombs fell, exploded, then they felt the buffeting from the turbulent air. While mangled beyond use, the bridge hadn't collapsed. The stone underpinning remained solid, and upon it had been built the temporary wooden section. He looked down at the thick wide planks where they joined the concrete of the bridge. There were spaces between the planks as wide as the side of his hand. Through some of them he could see the river. The first bomb hit here, he thought, the second one near the houses at the end of the bridge. A single, five hundred pounder can do a lot of damage, he judged. He turned and walked back towards the car.

He looked into the sky again. It was overcast the day that they had bombed it. Everything was gray except the flames on top of the houses. Now the red tiled roofs of the town seemed to loom over him, flame-like, to surround him. He walked back toward the wooden railing and looked down again at the river. It was clear and blue, reflecting a metallic color in the shade of the bridge, except where white foam splashed up and sloshed over rocks. The poplar trees that lined the banks of the stream had lost their leaves. Marshall walked back to the car quickly.

"My, what an inspection. Do you think it is safe enough?" Kristine said. Then she laughed and continued. "Your own army rebuilt it, you know."

"I thought it would be in worse shape." Marshall said.

"Why?"

"Oh," he stammered, "just from what you said about it."

"Well, it's a tough old bridge," she answered, "like our people."

He slowed the Mercedes when he approached the damaged homes. Two men squatted beside a pile of rubble and with their small picks knocked mortar off of the sound bricks. There were several neat, chest high stacks in the center of what had been the house.

"The second one is mine," Kristine said. It was a two-story brick house and the top fourth of the second floor was open like a stage set. Marshall could see the pattern of the brown wallpaper and there was a white wash basin attached to one wall.

"Your mother was in there?" Marshall asked. Moisture from his hands made the steering wheel wet and slick. He wiped his palms on his green wool trousers.

"No. Only an old woman in the first house was killed when the bomber came." She nodded toward the men cleaning the bricks. "Mother and I and the other strong women worked in the fields helping the farmers. When it happened we ran home. It was a long way. We could see our house was on fire. Mother tried to go into the house. They wouldn't let her. It was on fire," Kristine repeated. "She collapsed. Her heart. The running. The shock. She died that night."

"And the baby?" Marshall asked. He drove slowly. The car jostled them going across the cobblestones, but not like the hard jiggling of the jeep. He listened attentively.

"Grandmother took care of Maria when we worked. When the airplane came that day, after the bridge was struck and houses were on fire, Grandmother pushed the baby carriage to the bridge to see what had happened. She could not cross. It started to rain. Grandmother stayed there a long time. She shouldn't have. Maria caught cold, then pneumonia. There was no medicine, only aspirin."

"I'm sorry, Kris." Marshall said. He put his arm around her.

"I'm not going to cry again. Don't worry. I won't embarrass you," she said. She patted his leg, smiled up at him and he was sure that she would cry, but she didn't. "Now, let us enjoy our," she paused, "vacation." Her voice was husky.

"Sure," Marshall answered, then stopped the car and unfolded a map and began to study it.

"I checked with the Transportation Officer and he said that the road is good down through Stuttgart, then Ulm and then head sort of east to

Augsburg and then Munich. We'll just follow the map. How does that sound?"

"That sounds nice. But the autobahn is so fast." Kristine answered, "So, if you are to see the little villages and the farms and the countryside, we must take the old roads."

It was slower that way, but Marshall was glad they stayed off of the autobahn. Kristine pointed to a gray stone castle atop a distant hill. Most often she wanted him to slow the car so that they could look at the buildings.

Marshall pointed to one of the churches and said, "That has an interesting top on it."

"Zwiebel," Kristine said, and he stared at her. "Verstehen zwiebel? Ah, no, but you do understand onion shape?" Kristine smiled and held her palms open as if holding a large bowl, the then moving her hands upward, she allowed her fingers to curve inward and then part as they reached the imaginary point.

Marshall looked back at the onion shaped dome and nodded and laughed. " Okay, I verstehen."

"It is the inside that is beautiful, with religious paintings, and trimmings of gold, and colored glass windows." Kristine said. "Maybe we can visit one on the way back?"

"Roger."

They parked in front of many homes and admired the colorful Bible-scene paintings on the walls, and Marshall pointed up at the ornate yet delicate filigree that trimmed the homes and wondered how long it took the carpenters to cut them out and install them. Kristine said that each generation created a little more, and some of the houses were hundreds of years old.

When they reached Augsburg they parked and walked along the streets. In the shops there were framed oil paintings of the mountains and of the villages and there were woodcarvings and lace goods in the store windows. There were markets, but they were without food. At one window they stopped to look at round yellow cheeses, and at long reddish-brown sausages and fat bologna's and Marshall thought that they were real. It was difficult to believe that they had been carved from wood, then painted.

A tiny bell tingled when they pushed open the door of a small shop. Marshall selected a bracelet made of small metal squares, each one painted with a different bright colored enamel. The woman behind the counter looked at his leather jacket with the red devil and the bomb. He was glad that his bombardier wings were pinned on his shirt where she couldn't see them. He paid for the bracelet, then started to give her a package of cigarettes. Kristine took the package off of the counter before he could indicate that it was for the proprietress. Kristine smiled at the woman, opened the package and gave her six cigarettes. The woman thanked her and began to nod her head up and down. Kristine said something to her and she continued to nod. A tanned blonde man with a thick yellow mustache entered. He wore leather shorts and heavy shoes, like ski boots. He stared at Marshall and Kristine, hesitated, listened indifferently, then looked at the six cigarettes, turned and walked to the back of the store and sat down. The woman kept nodding. She and Kristine spoke. Marshall wished he could understand them. He wanted to give her more cigarettes to see if she would stop nodding her head. Marshall began to perspire. He looked at the man who sat staring at the cigarettes on the low counter. Marshall left the shop and waited on the sidewalk.

"What was that all about?" Marshall asked.

"I told her we were just married, secretly. I wanted to know the name of a hotel in Munich. It's a big city, you know."

"I was never over it," Marshall answered, then regretted his reference to the air and quickly said, "I didn't think they still wore those leather clothes. I thought that was from the old days."

"The lederhosen? Of course. They are very practical," she answered. "I gave her husband the rest of the cigarettes." Marshall was satisfied that he'd avoided a continuance of any conversation about flying. Someday, when they were married and had children of their own he might tell her about the bridge.

Shadows from the old wood fences lengthened across the narrow country roads. They rolled up the windows of the car. Marshall asked Kristine if she wanted the heater on and she said not yet. Kristine sat close to him and rested her hand on his leg.

They stopped at Odelzhausen, stretched their legs and looked in the windows of the stores, then decided that they had better hurry or it would be dark before they reached Munich. Marshall located the autobahn on the map and went the rest of the way on the broad concrete highway. As Marshall expected, it was wider. He remembered how they had used the autobahns for locating targets, how chalk-white they stood out as they curved through the dark green patterns of forests and the lighter green pastures and the plowed farmlands.

In Munich he turned on the car heater. The buildings were hollow and black. Rubble had been pushed back from the middle of the streets against the battered walls that still stood. Men and women methodically knocked mortar off of bricks and stacked them in tight square piles.

"I didn't think it would be this bad," Kristine said.

"It's awful. I wish we'd gone straight to Garmisch-Partenkirchen," Marshall answered. They rode in silence as Marshall slowly toured the city. Parts of it were undamaged. They stopped in front of the Hoffbraukeller and then Bergerbraukeller.

"That's where old Adolph got started," Marshall said.

"He was good for Germany."

"Come on, Kris! You call all of this good?"

"No! No, but you don't understand what it was like before Hitler. The Jews. Surely you understand?"

"No, I'm afraid I don't. I've read that they were sent to camps." He paused, did not wish to continue; to repeat what he had read.

"And we read that you put the Japanese Americans in camps and that you even tortured them," Kristine said, her eyes flashing as they had when she challenged Tex. "And we read at school that you did the same to the Indians."

"Propaganda," Marshall said.

"Who is telling the truth then?" Kristine asked. "Are the politicians all liars?"

"I don't know. At school I heard something about manifest destiny: the reason, or justification for putting the Indians on reservations. Let's forget it, okay?"

"My people could not torture anyone. No, and I do not feel yours could either. So, we will forget it." Kristine sighed deeply and rested her head against Marshall's shoulder. "It is all beyond my understanding."

"Let's find the hotel," Marshall said and began to look at street markers that meant nothing to him.

Amongst burned out buildings on both sides of the street in the same block, the hotel stood almost unmarred, narrow and five stories tall. Marshall parked in front of it and carried his B-4 bag and Kristine's small suitcase into the lobby, then set them down by the elevator. Kristine spoke to the manager. He frowned. She opened her purse and handed him a full package of cigarettes. He nodded. He looked at Marshall. He said something. Kristine walked over to where Marshall stood.

"Do you have any American dollars?"

"Sure." Marshall said and reached for his wallet and from it took out several bills. She took a five-dollar bill from him and returned to the manager.

On the way up in the elevator Marshall remembered Frank's car.

"I can't leave the car out there," he said to Kristine.

"Don't worry. The manager will take care of it. I told him there would be more cigarettes in the morning."

After the manager followed them into the room and raised the window a few inches and showed Kristine the closet and the bathroom, Marshall handed him another pack of cigarettes and smiled at him, winked and held up his hand, his thumb and middle finger touch, forming a circle. He'll understand that there's more where these came from, he thought. The manager said thanks in German. When the door clicked shut, Kristine frowned at him, "You are too generous," she said, then laughed and walked to him and he held her in his arms. She rested her head on his chest, felt the coolness of his leather jacket, then looked up at him and with her eyes flirted and teased him. She put her hands behind his neck.

"My big Luftgangster," she said, then laughed again. "You have looked worried or frightened all afternoon. What is the matter? Kristine won't let anything happen to you." She leaned back. He held her around the waist. She laughed again, then with her fingertip followed the bound edge of the leather squadron insignia. "This is you, my darling, riding downward, ever downward, with your horns and your forked tail, to the place where all sinners go." She laughed again, sighed, and then rested her head on his chest.

"If I could just speak a little German," Marshall started, "I hate to have you doing all of the arranging for the room and the car and all." And he remembered the store and wondered if that the big German might have been a former SS trooper.

"Darling," she answered and laughed again. "The manager can speak English. But he'll accept my lies and your cigarettes and tell no one. It is easier this way."

"Okay, Kris," Marshall answered. Then he began to laugh too. "You do the talking."

He walked to the window. Cold air carried the lace curtains up against him. He closed the window, shielded his eyes and looked through the glass. He turned back to Kristine.

"Now, tell me where we are going to eat in this dark city. Can't even see a single light bulb out there."

"Be patient, darling," Kristine said. She hung her coat up in the closet. Marshall took off his leather jacket and threw it into the center of the bed and watched it sink slowly into the thick down comforter covering the entire bed. Kristine walked to him, kissed him, then stood back and looked at the silver wings hooked to his wool shirt. She rubbed her fingertips across the wings.

"I wish you wouldn't wear these when you are with me. They are evil. A bomb on wings. Wings? I think of birds and their songs. Birds are so free and innocent. I think of angels, of doves. I don't like your wings."

"Okay, Mrs. Sunder. Off they come!" Marshall said flippantly. He unbuttoned his shirt and reached inside to unhook the spring clasp that held each end. He removed his hand and one wingtip dropped. Someone knocked at the door, tapped lightly.

Kristine opened the door and a young man, not yet of shaving age, pushed a cart into the room. He raised the silver cover of one plate and both of them looked at the steaming food.

"Grostl," Kristine said to Marshall. He shrugged his shoulders.

"Sliced veal and potatoes," she said. She looked at the food.

The young man pulled the table from the wall and set it with silver and white napkins and crystal glasses, both for wine and water. He put a tall, thick wine bottle on the table and prepared to open it.

"Wait," Marshall said. He picked up the bottle and acted as if he could read the German words printed on the label. "I ordered imported wine," he said to Kristine, sternly. "From California. None of this domestic stuff for our honeymoon."

Kristine, her eyes widened, looked shocked, then burst out laughing and spoke in German rapidly to the young man. He looked at both of them blankly. He stared at Marshall's shirt and at the silver wings hanging from one tip. Marshall laughed at him, then took a pack of cigarettes from his B-4 bag and threw them to the young man, who caught them with one hand, grinned, bowed and backed out of the room. He pulled the door closed.

"For your wedding present," Marshall said, "I'll remove them." He unhooked the other side of the wings and tossed them onto the dresser where they bounced and stopped next to an ashtray.

"Wedding present?" Kristine said. She stood and waited for him to pull the chair back for her.

"Tomorrow, we'll find someone to marry us. With your German and my cigarettes and Yankee dollars it ought to be a cinch." Marshall rested his hands on her shoulders and smiled down at her. "I'm serious."

"Darling, I'm a widow, I really believe that, or I wouldn't be here." Kristine raised her right hand and showed him her ring. "I still wear it. I don't know why. But I can't marry you."

"What about Stalingrad? You said your husband was killed. You were told he was killed."

"I believe that to be true, or I wouldn't be here. But, can you imagine what my father would say? How he would react. And, what if there was a mistake? What if someday Paul should come home? I must wait."

"I thought that you were sure!"

"That makes a difference to you?"

"Married, yes. Single, that's different." Marshall lit a cigarette and walked to the bed and leaned against it. It reached above his hips and he rested his elbows on the dark walnut footboard.

"Oh, I'm positive, Marshall, but before I could even consider marriage, I must wait a little while, until my father returns. Father used to say we live our lives by rationalization and self-justification. You understand, don't you?"

"That's one big mouthful."

Kristine raised her chin and laughed. "Many rehearsals by myself so that I could speak that in English."

Marshall laughed, "You are a strange little girl. But no, Kristine, I don't know what I understand anymore."

"Are you ordering me to marry you, not asking, nor speaking of love?"

"Oh, no, Kris," Marshall stammered. "What a clown. Do you want me to get down on my hands and knees? I will. I do love you!"

" I try to tease, but you do understand our nice dinner is getting cold?" Kristine stood up then, walked to him and took his hands and pulled him toward the table, "Come on darling. Remember, this is our weekend to forget."

"Kris, I took off my wings for you," he said, then he held her hands up in front of him. "In my country, the wedding ring goes on the left hand.

This weekend you are my wife. At least be my make believe wife. For now, you are Mrs. Sunder. Is it a deal?"

"My prerogative? Is that the correct word?"

Kristine held her hands up in front of her and looked at the backs of them. Then she turned the ring and squeezed it against her knuckle, the white flesh wrinkling in front of it, removed it and handed it to Marshall. He said nothing, accepted the ring and slipped it on the ring finger of her left hand. He held her hands in his. They were slim and tapered and small, but he could feel the roughness of her palms, and the whiteness of her skin, when viewed closely was not white, but as if burned. Her nails were short and clean and appeared to have been buffed. She looked up at him. He pulled her close to him and held her. They kissed.

"Too much soap," she said. She pulled away from him and studied her hands.

"In the kiss?" he said. They both laughed.

"Let's eat," Marshall then said and held a chair for her.

Even in the cold gray light of morning the warmth and weightlessness of the goose down comforter amazed Marshall. He faced the wall and stared at it. He had awakened in the night; warm but startled, thinking they were uncovered. Earlier Kristine had laughed at him when he asked where the blankets were hidden. He'd looked in the dresser drawers and in the closet, without finding them. But, they were warm without blankets. The comforter was like a warm floating cloud that barely touched them.

Marshall turned over and reached for her, then saw her form silhouetted in front of the window. She wore only the black dressing gown. A white lace window curtain was draped across each of her shoulders. She heard him and looked over her shoulder at him.

"The sun is coming up. It looks like a huge orange. I had a tangerine several years ago, from Spain, I believe. Come look at the sun now. It is so big, but it is struggling to get up out of the tangle of our broken city. That is the steel dome of the railroad station. Come quickly, darling, the sun is trapped in a bird cage."

Marshall sat up in bed. His trousers were on the other side of the room draped across the back of a chair. He pulled the bulky comforter around him and held it tight with his arms behind him and took a few steps to the window. He looked across Kristine's shoulder.

Behind the hollow curved framework of the top of the building, the sun slowly moved upward, its radius for a few minutes exactly that of a dome. The sun shrank as it slipped upward out of the grasp of the cage. The curved steel girders disappeared against the background of the ragged edges of buildings without roofs. The sun grew smaller, turned yellow, then white and they had to look away from it.

"What in the world are you doing?" Kristine asked, she laughed when she turned and saw Marshall still holding the comforter tightly around him.

"Come back to bed, Mrs. Sunder," Marshall whispered.

"Darling, you'll never see Garmisch-Partenkirchen," Kristine answered.

"Tired of me already?"

Kristine pushed him and he fell backward onto the bed and quickly covered himself with the comforter. The black gown dropped to the floor and she slid beneath the comforter, then poked her fingers against his ribs. Marshall squirmed, pushed at her hands, but she persisted and he laughed uncontrollably, then rolled off the bed and lay on the floor next to the wall. Kristine giggled and promised she wouldn't do it again. He climbed back into the bed. Lace filtered light filled the room. She closed her eyes, feigning sleep, her lips curved into a slight smile. The comforter was tucked beneath her chin and with her bare arms on top of the comforter she pressed it down tightly around her body. She began to hum a lullaby, then sang it.

"Guten Abend, gut Nacht, mit Rosen bedacht, mit Naglein besteckt, schlopf unter die Deck. Morgen fruh, wenn Gott will, wirst due wieden geweckt. Morgen froh, wenn Gott will, wirst du wieder geweckt."

Marshall leaned on his elbows and watched her sing, then rested his head next to hers on the pillow and listened to the words. She hummed again.

"That's beautiful," he said.

"You like Brahms?"

"If that's Brahms I like it. I'd like anything you sing."

"I do not understand you, Marshall." She opened her eyes. She held her arms down upon the comforter, outlining the shape of her body.

"Understand me?" Marshall asked. He raised his head, then kissed her mouth, her eyelids, her nose, her throat.

"Silly," she said, "You could have so many girls. Why me? I'm too thin. Oh, I was nice once. And someday I'll be plump again, for you."

"You're just right."

"Oh, how I do enjoy being loved." Kristine said. "Was it that first day, when I came to clean the windows? You were kind to me. Is that it? You feel sorry for the poor German maid. That's it, isn't it?"

"Don't tease, Kris. I love you. You know it. And someday we'll live in California and raise little Sunders and you'll forget all about the war. We'll bring your father and grandmother over too."

"You are crazy, Chico. You don't have enough cigarettes for that." They both laughed.

"Kris, I'm signing up for a year's occupation duty. By the end of my tour we'll be able to get married legally. Then you can go home with me, I'm sure of it."

"Go home," Kristine said. She closed her eyes. "First, I'll have to help father rebuild our house. That must come first."

"I'll help you."

"Ah, my kind luftgangster, you've done enough for me. You've become my mother and my baby and Paul, my substitutes, and now you are my Chico Marshall."

Marshall kissed her hard.

"Again, Kris?" he whispered.

"Darling, I've already seen Garmisch-Partenkirchen." She pulled her arms beneath the comforter and turned on her side facing him and smiling. They embraced, loved, and finally dozed off.

Marshall grunted, jerked his foot towards him and rubbed the bottom of it. He heard Kristine's soft laugh and rolled over in the bed and saw her walk away from it. She brushed her hair.

"Come on ticklish," she said, "It's time for lunch."

"Lunch? What happened to breakfast?" Marshall sat up, rubbed his eyes, stretched, yawned, felt the light beard stubble and then watched her as she continued to brush her hair. She stood in front of the dresser wearing the black panties and black brassiere that Pop had purchased in Paris.

"I'll fill them out better someday," she said into the mirror. She smiled and he grinned back at the reflection and yawned again. Well, he thought, now he knew what he'd been fighting for and he laughed out loud. Kristine turned and looked at him.

"Why did you laugh?"

"I feel like laughing when I'm with you. I'm just happy, that's all," Marshall replied.

"Maybe the whole world can be happy again. Starting right here with us, wouldn't that be nice? Happiness is like hate. It has to start someplace," Kristine said.

She continued to brush her hair, vigorously, and the fine hairs floated upward after the brush, attracted to it, unable to escape it.

Marshall sat and watched her. With her fingers Kristine pulled many strands of black hair from the bristles of the brush and placed them in the ashtray on the dresser. She picked up Marshall's cigarette lighter, lit it, and then held the nest of hair above the flame. It ignited, flared up and Kristine dropped it into the ashtray where it turned to ash. She resumed brushing her hair.

"Why'd you do that?" Marshall asked.

"I do not want to become pregnant."

"Boy, and I thought fliers were superstitious," he said. He got up and dressed. His wings were beside the ashtray with the burned hair. He looked at them, picked them up and seemed to weigh them, tossed them up and caught them, and then put them in his pocket.

After lunching in the dining room of the small hotel they left for Garmisch-Partenkirchen in Frank's newly washed Mercedes. Marshall gave the manager two packs of cigarettes and thanked him for his hospitality. The manager didn't answer in English. He looked at Kristine, bowed, then thanked them in German.

"You are much too generous with your tobacco," Kristine scolded.

"They only cost a nickel a pack at the P.X.," Marshall answered.

"I don't know about nickels," she said and nodded at the packs of cigarettes on the back seat of the car, "but each one of those is worth a sack of potatoes or several nice sausages or many loaves of bread."

"Okay, Mrs. Sunder, you can handle the finances as well as the language for us."

As they drove, the road twisted into the foothills and the dark woods grew thicker and closer to them, but the trees were so dense that they couldn't see far into them. Taller mountains, the Alps, Kristine said, showed in the distance behind the rolling hills. Snow was still on the peaks. The highest mountaintops pushed dents in the gray clouds that looked soft and light like the comforter.

Early in the afternoon they reached Garmisch-Partenkirchen. And as they had done in Munich, they again drove through the streets of the two small villages admiring the scenes painted on the walls of the homes. There were more soldiers than civilians in the twin towns Marshall thought. Third Army M.P.'s drove in jeeps and stopped soldiers and looked at their passes. There were other Air Corps fliers, a few escorting army nurses and one was with a Red Cross girl, but most of the men were in small groups and wandered about the streets looking into the shops. The German people didn't appear to be concerned about the Americans.

They hustled about their shops and seemed happy to sell their carvings and paintings.

"There is a nice view of the Zugspitze from in there," Kristine said. She pointed to a side street. Marshall turned, slowed the car and parked near a low rectangular concrete watering trough. A farmer led two brown oxen with horns. They pulled a wagon with wooden wheels. He let them drink at the trough, then splashed his face and ran his hand back through his hair. He led the oxen on down the street. In the center of the fountain stood a fifteen-foot Corinthian column. At the top there was a bronze figure holding a banner.

"That is St. Florian," Kristine volunteered, "He protects the villages from fire." She was silent for a moment, then added, "He should have been at Bad Scheidel."

"Yeah," Marshall answered. He started to drive further.

"Let's park here. Let's go across the street," she said. Marshall followed her, hesitated while looking at the statue.

"Our highest mountain," she said. She pointed to a peak that seemed lower than the others, but it was further away. Snow still rested along the cols, and was packed in the vertical crevices of the highest peaks. Dark clouds moved lower and concealed the tops of those furthest away.

"Father brought us here one time. We went up on the cable car: in a large gondola. I was a little girl and so frightened. Then I sat on father's lap. Would you like to go to the top?"

"Not if it would scare you."

"I'm not frightened when I'm with you. Let's hurry," she said. She took his hand and ran towards the car, pulling him after her.

It was too late when they reached the gondolas. Kristine spoke to the operator. He told her to come back tomorrow. Maybe the storm will blow over. They stood and looked up at the mountain tops and the gray clouds had moved further down towards them.

"It's getting very cold," Marshall said. "We'd better find a room."

But they could not find a place that would accept them. All of the rooms in the hotels and in the inns were reserved for military personnel on leave. There were no extra rooms, not even in a private home. Everything was taken. Well, maybe for the lieutenant, but not for her. The room might be checked. The military were very strict. The managers shook their heads sadly when Kristine mentioned the cigarettes and the American money.

The long drive back to Munich tired them. It began to rain. The narrow road was slippery. Marshall drove slowly. He didn't want to slide off into the ditch and bang up Frank's car.

Kristine rested her head on his shoulder, hummed the Brahms cradlesong, then dozed. Her head jostled loosely against him and he thought it might make her neck stiff, but he decided to let her sleep.

At the hotel in Munich it took four packs of cigarettes because the manager had already gone to bed. The desk clerk did not smile at them. For two more packs, he went out in the rain and parked the car. In the morning it was still raining. It rained on the way back to Bad Scheidel. Neither of them spoke. Marshall strained to see the highway through the swishing windshield wipers. Very often Kristine slept. He wished that he could hold her and rock her and protect her. It was afternoon when Marshall stopped at the bridge in Bad Scheidel.

"Don't get out, darling," Kristine said. "The water is deep."

"Let me drive to the house." Marshall said.

"Grandmother will be waiting," Kristine answered. She took a black cloth from her bag, put it over her head and tied it beneath her chin.

"I'd like to meet your grandmother. She'll see I'm not such a bad guy."

"No, not now. Sometime later."

"You'll get soaked," Marshall said.

"Please kiss me now," Kristine said. After their lips had parted, Kristine leaned back in the seat and studied her hands, then changed the wedding ring back to her right hand. Marshall stepped out of the car and into the water and walked around to her side. He wanted to share the misery of the rain as if it would lessen her discomfort. The rain drove into their faces, blurring their vision. He closed the door of Frank's car and watched her run to the side of the street and lean close to the buildings for protection. A jeep came towards her, slowed, and then stopped. He saw the door on the passenger side open. It closed. The jeep came on towards him. At first he didn't recognize the driver. In the passenger's seat, behind the arc of the moving windshield wiper, he saw Tex. Tex peered at him, glanced at the Mercedes, then grinned broadly. He thumbed his nose at Marshall as the jeep passed him and crossed the bridge. Wide, green army buses, two of them, followed the jeep.

Except for the drivers, they were empty. Muddy water from their wheels splashed up onto Marshall before he could close the door of the car. The dirty water sloshed up over the Mercedes. Marshall cursed. He drove to the barracks, parked and went to Frank's room. He tossed the keys to Frank, who raised his arm and caught them in his hand. Frank asked him about the trip.

"Everything was great until Tex and his new busses came by and splashed mud all over everything!" Marshall said. "Hell, I had that little buggy all washed up nice to return it. I'll wash it when this storm passes over."

CHAPTER 10

▼

SWITZERLAND

The wooden timbers and planks of the bridge in Bad Scheidel soaked up the water and the planks expanded and the edges began to turn black with mold. The rainy season that had begun in October continued through Christmas and the New year and into February, with snow falling when the temperature dropped.

They were becoming accustomed the crackling, intensely bright white flashes of lightening followed by great claps and booms of thunder. Both in the mornings and in the evenings they turned the lights on earlier. The maids and the kitchen-help walked home in the dark. Kristine would lag behind the others and Marshall would join her and walked with her until they could see her grandmother's house. The chilly rainstorms turned into snow.

In the beginning the silver dollar size flakes were pretty, floating downward unrushed, but they melted swiftly from the warmth of the ground. Sometimes Marshall awakened in the morning and several inches of snow had piled up on the boughs of the apple tree close to his window. The little bee-bee-sized droplets of snow must be colder, Marshall thought, because unlike the round flakes they didn't melt when they hit the ground, and the snow would grow deeper each storm. In their well insulated barracks the steam heat was kept too high most of the time. The double windows were now closed. Flying stopped. They were grounded. The fliers played cards and read and wrote letters.

It continued to rain in February. Most of the pruning had been accomplished on the apple trees. He wished he'd helped. Maybe it isn't too late, Marshall thought, he could still find a saw and help trim the branches of a few trees that hadn't been pruned, as he did at home. But he didn't pursue that idea, busying himself with letter writing, and playing various card games. He volunteered to accompany pilots that had just qualified to be left seat, or first pilots. A navigator had to accompany them even if it was just for training time with another first pilot. He contemplated asking the squadron chaplain about obtaining permission to marry Kristine, but both Frank and Gary dissuaded him.

"You're going to get your ass court marshaled if you don't quit sniffing around that little kraut broad, old buddy," Gary advised.

Frank agreed, but didn't express his view the same way, and Marshall was annoyed.

"You just don't understand." He said, addressing both of them, and both simultaneously shook their heads in disbelief.

In March Marshall was scheduled for a week's leave. Two choices were given the men who had flown combat missions: Switzerland or Scotland. Marshall chose Switzerland. He could not believe Kristine when she said it would be impossible for her to leave Germany. No, she couldn't cross the border anyplace. She could not be with him. He should go, she said. He should get away from the air base for a while.

The week in Switzerland was nice. Marshall was lucky. The military inspectors at the Swiss border only spot-checked the bags. His B-4 bag got by. It was nearly full of cigarettes. He traded all of them, and he traded his fountain pen and his colored glasses, his leather flight jacket and his camera for Swiss money.

The soldiers and fliers on leave rode everywhere on clean, silent electric trains with sparkling clean view-windows. It snowed. They told them not to drink milk because of undulant fever. They drank milk anyway. In Lucerne it snowed and he could not see the Alps. The cities were well stocked with food and watches and shoes. The shoes were as expensive as the watches. In Lucerne he selected a store with the most handsome facade and in it purchased a gold watch, its face not over the size of a dime, with a round black band. That was the new fashion, the girl said, a style not even yet seen in the United States.

Delicate scrolled carvings framed the face and microscopic initials had been stamped on the side and bottom of the watch. It had a thick crystal, almost as thick as the watch itself. The girl stretched it out gently in a long black velvet box with a black satin cover. She ran her fingers across it like she might stroke a reclining cat.

"It will make her very happy," the girl said. Marshall looked at her closely for the first time. She wore new clothes, fashionable and clean. She was plump. Her nails were long. Her hands were very white and very smooth. Marshall resented the smoothness. He thought about Kristine and her dark work clothes and her one good wool dress and her black underclothes. He remembered the texture of her hands; how they felt when he held them and when she'd rubbed his back.

"It's for my wife," he answered. Leaving the store, he stood in the snow and looked at the gray surface of Lake Lucerne, then went back to the hotel. It's no fun without her, he thought. He wrote a letter to his folks. He'd have to stay on another year, he told them. Politics and all, he knew they'd understand. He might be able to go to school in Heidelberg. He didn't mention Kristine. There would be time enough for that. They wouldn't understand that part. He bought a music box for his mother and a long curved pipe, and a wristwatch for his father.

In one store, a woman that reminded him of his mother stopped him, rested her gloved hand on his arm, and then shoved an envelope into his hand. "Please! Mail it for me in Germany: Not in Switzerland. Please," she said. Her English was broken, not crisp and perfect like Kristine's. Marshall hesitated.

"It is to my sister. We haven't heard from her in over two years. Here, I'll pay you," she said, her voice becoming panicky. She reached into her purse and grasped a smaller purse with paper money and coins which she started to empty into his hand. Marshall put his hand on her arm.

"No, no. That's okay, ma'am, I'll mail it for you."

"Danke! Danke! God bless you!" she said. She bit her bottom lip, cried, and walked out of the store. Marshall walked out after her. She was gone. In his face, the blowing snow felt clean and good.

He wished he could go back to Bad Scheidel. In Zurich, it snowed and it continued to snow when he reached Andermatt. The sun never came out. Finally, they returned to Basle and at last the train stopped at Bad Scheidel.

CHAPTER 11

▼

DACHAU

"Hi, men!" Marshall said. He laughed loudly as he stomped snow off of his shoes and he then walked further into the large room. He dropped his B-4 bag on the floor. He brushed powder snow off of his heavy beige coat, took it off and hung it on the doorknob.

"Howdy Marsh," a flier answered, then looked back at the cards in his hand.

Marshall slid the B-4 bag into his own room, then turned back to the fliers. They were playing blackjack.

"Hit me," a flier said.

The flier dealing the cards flipped a card to him.

"I'll stand."

The dealer looked at the next player.

"I'm pat," he said, nodding at the money lying across his cards.

"Splitting nines," the next flier said. "Hit me. Okay. Hit me. Hit me again. Okay."

Marshall stood in back of the dealer, pulled down his necktie, loosened his collar and unbuttoned his jacket. The dealer turned over his bottom card. It was a queen. A ten was up.

"Pay twenty-one," he said. He looked at their cards and dragged the money toward him.

"You lucky bastard. We oughta call this game Black Queen," a flier said.

"How was Switzerland?" the dealer asked. He shuffled the cards. He turned and looked at Marshall. The rest of the fliers looked up at him too. They said nothing.

"Great," he said. "Let me show you something." He reached into the inside pocket of his jacket, pulled out the package with the watch, unwrapped it and displayed it. "For Kris," he said. They all looked at it. No one said anything. "Well, isn't it a beaut?" Marshall asked. He looked at all of them. They lowered their eyes.

"Lot's happened since you left," the dealer said. "You'd better go see Frank. I think he's shipping out in the morning."

"Shipping out!" Marshall said. "What do you mean?" The fliers passed the watch around the table.

"Better see Frank, Marsh." the dealer said. "Okay, place your bets." He finished shuffling the cards, had the player next to him cut them, and then dealt. Marshall watched them, exasperated, annoyed that they would start to play cards again. He waited for a chance to question them again. He picked up the watch and put it back into his pocket.

"You bury a card?" a flier asked.

"Shit! No!" the dealer answered.

"Pay off."

"All right, all right!"

"What the hell's going on fellas? Is this one of your gags, or something?" Marshall asked.

"Goddamn it! Go see Frank!" the dealer growled. He turned in his chair and glared at Marshall. Then he stood up. "I'm sorry, Marsh. Just check in with Frank, will ya? He's up to his ass in problems."

When Marshall pushed open the door into Frank's room, he saw him kneeling beside his footlocker. He clamped a combination lock closed, spun the dial and turned and stood and stared at Marshall.

"They told you?" he said. He walked up to Marshall and shook his hand and then turned to his bed where his B-4 bag was laid out open with his uniforms hitched tightly by a cloth strap. It was ready to be folded closed.

"I just got in this minute, buddy. The guys said you've got a problem." He searched Frank's face for an answer.

"Sit down for a minute," Frank said. He offered Marshall a cigarette. They lit them and sat down beside the table.

"Red Cross contacted me. I received an emergency leave to go home. Funeral."

"Oh, no!" Marshall said. "Your mom? Your dad?"

"Diana."

"Diana?" Marshall exclaimed. "How could that be? A car wreck or something?"

"I really don't know what the hell happened. It's all happened so fast. If the Red Cross has any details, they've not given them to me. I'm pissed off about that, of course. But I'm not coming back. Schloss cut orders for me to report to a fighter outfit in Georgia. We're going to have to say our good-byes tonight or in the morning, Marshall."

"What about McAdam?"

"I guess you and McAdam are going to have to stick around until your points come up."

"Hell, I've already signed up for another year."

"Marsh, don't be surprised at anything that happens from now on in. I think Schloss figures our crew is jinxed, what with Pop getting it, and I'm sorry, but I've got to bring you up to date on what's been happening around here while you were in Switzerland."

"What could be more important than what happened to Diana?"

"Sit down," Frank said. "This is going to be hard for you to handle, but you've got to keep your cool."

"Like what?"

"Kristine's grandmother is dead. She hanged herself. She was buried the day before yesterday." Marshall lowered himself slowly back into the chair again and stared at Frank.

"Why?"

"Dachau, I guess," Frank answered. He stood up and walked to the windows.

"Look, Frank, I guess I'm pretty dense. Come on, give!"

"Tex took two bus loads of Bad Scheidel citizens over to Dachau. As I've heard it, he was pretty rough on all of them: mostly old people and the maids. That's about all there are around here. Anyway, he took them through the place. In this shower room deal he made them all look up at the nozzles, you know, the gas jets. Kristine's grandmother wouldn't look up. He pushed her, or something and Kristine slapped him. He grabbed her arm and shoved her, and yelled at her. That's the way I understand it."

"That dirty bastard!" Marshall said. He jumped up. "Is that all?"

"Not quite. On the way back he stopped the bus on the Bad Scheidel Bridge. He told them about us, my crew, all of us. About bombing the bridge. Then he told them that Kristine was your mistress."

Marshall groaned. He held his face in his hands, then turned and rushed from the room. Frank followed him.

"It's no use, Marsh. It's too late. There's nothing you can do!"

"I'll kill the son of a bitch!" Marshall yelled. He sprinted down the hall, through the room where the fliers played blackjack, into his own room. He opened his footlocker, dumped the top section and its contents on the floor, grabbed his .45 and shoved a full clip of bullets into it. He turned to leave the room.

Frank was in the doorway, walking toward him. He saw the .45 in Marshall's hand and struck Marshall's wrist with his right fist. The blasting roar of the exploding .45 gunshot and splintering crash of the glass of the double windows filled the room hurt their eardrums. Marshall dropped the .45 and stared at it on the floor. The smell of the powder was sharp in his nostrils. Fliers that had been playing cards crowded into Marshall's room, looked at the broken windows, at the gun and all of them began to ask questions at once. Outside they could see the branch of an apple tree that was splintered.

"Marshall dropped his gun. Accidental discharge," Frank said. "Leave us alone," Frank walked toward them and they retreated, their eyes wide. He closed the door, then turned to Marshall. "Tex is at the hospital undergoing psychiatric examination. He may be reassigned to another outfit. Schloss may ship him out, God knows where."

"I've got to see her," Marshall said. His hands trembled. He gripped the table edge to make them stop.

"You can't see Kristine. It's too late. It's over. Let it be. Put it to rest!"

"Oh yeah, and what if it was Diana? I'm going. Look out."

"Wait! Look buddy. It's all over. She's not the same. I know." Frank held Marshall by the arm. "Hell, she's in shock!"

"Not the same? Come off it, Frank. Please let loose of me. Don't you understand? Her grandmother couldn't look up. She had arthritis of the spine!"

"There's nothing you can do now! Marsh, this may be is our last chance to have a few belts together, with McAdam, and maybe we can have dinner."

"Look out," Marshall said. He walked past Frank. He stooped and picked up his .45 and tucked it beneath his belt.

"Goddamn it, Marsh! Leave that gun here! Shooting Tex won't solve anything and you'll be the one that hangs for it!"

"Okay! Okay! To hell with Tex. But I've got to see Kris. And I'm keeping my .45"

Frank stepped back as the angry Marshall pushed past him and strode out of the room.

Lights from the barracks windows framed bright paths across the snow to the road. Marshall hurried; tried to stay in the middle, on the high part of the road. The soles of his shoes squeaked against the frozen snow. He could see the dim lights of the first houses through the snowflakes. The air was cold. It hurt his chest. His exhalations fogged in front of his eyes. He paused a minute, looked back at the lights of the barracks and then at the lights in the town, orienting himself. He trotted; holding his hands high, his arms bent at the elbows like a distance runner. He slipped and fell backwards in the slush, got up, shook the icy water off of his hands, and walked.

A light was on in Kristine's grandmother's house. He leaned against the doorjamb, breathed deeply, slowly, then stood erect, pushed his hands through his wet hair, and knocked. He felt for the watch. It was in his inside pocket. He thought he heard footsteps. He knocked again, harder. The door opened, a few inches. He could smell the perfume and the warmth of the room and her body and smoke from a fire. He saw the chain across the opening.

"Lieutenant Sunder, I believe," she said. "I don't believe you had an appointment, now did you?"

"Don't kid me, Kris, let me in. I just got back."

"Go away, Lieutenant sinner!"

"Kris, stop it! Let me in."

"Yes, Sir. Whatever the American luftgangster says," she said. She unhooked the chain, opened the door for him, backed away from him, toward the small stove, its door open. He could not see her face clearly. Her body was silhouetted by the fire. The chunks of coal burned with an orange flame. She wore the black dressing gown he had given her.

"Why did you come here?"

"Kristine, you've got to forget all that has happened. God knows, I'm sorry about your grandmother and the bridge and everything. Christ, I love you! Our lives started when you came to clean windows, remember?"

"Remember, Ha! How I remember. I remember you looking at the bridge. Proud, so proud of your killing and your wings. Wear them forever!"

Marshall walked to her, but she backed away from him. He reached out for her arms.

"Don't touch me, baby killer!" she screamed at him. She stopped with her back against a bookshelf. He stared at her. He pushed his hands back through his hair again, trying to think, then remembered and reached into his jacket pocket. He found the case and opened it and stepped toward her again.

"Kris, I got this watch for you in Lucerne. It's the best there is. Look at it, please."

"I won't look at anything to do with you. You want to look at something. Look above you." She pointed to thick beams that crossed the room. A cord was tied to one of them, like the cord that bound the bundle of twigs. A short piece of it hung straight towards the floor. "Grandmother," she shouted, staring at him. "He showed us what we are: barbarians. That guide there, he showed us the scratches on the filthy walls the poor Jews, and God knows who else, made that weren't dead, that were still alive and piled on top of each other. He showed us barrels full of white human bones! It was horror!"

"Kris, stop it. This is nuts! I'm not Tex!" Marshall pleaded. "This is all insane. We're not responsible for all of the evil. You and I can start over: Start something good and clean."

"I laugh at you, Herr Luftgangster!" Kris snarled. Her lips were drawn back, revealing her teeth.

"Kris, remember the ring. We were going to be married."

She put her head back and laughed loudly.

"The ring!" She stopped suddenly and held her hands up in front of him.

"Do you see a ring? This hand? That hand? No? I am married all right." She walked to a pantry, opened it, and stood back. "See?" she said. "Fresh coffee! And cigarettes! Lots of chocolate: all in one day. Now a soldier who makes no pretenses has come to me with all of these treasures. Food and coal for affection. Yes, I am married. Married to that red devil you wear on your jacket."

A door on the opposite side of the room opened.

"Hey Fraulein, you comin' to bed, or ain't you?"

"Soon, lieber," Kristine said. The door closed. She turned back to Marshall. He put the case with the watch on the table, then closed the top. He stared at her.

"Don't go in there, Kris," he whispered, "Damn it to hell, just don't!"

"Get out!" Kristine screamed at him. She turned to the bookcase and picked up the book, the big old German Bible, threw it at him. It hit his arm and dropped open on the floor. Marshall stooped to pick it up. Kristine stepped to the table, grabbed the case with the watch and threw it at him. The case missed him, opened when it hit the wall. The thick round crystal rolled across the floor towards the stove, fell on its side, its polished surface reflecting the yellow light from the open door, like a tiny sun. He stared at it, then heard the muffled steps of her bare feet crossing the room, toward the door, and then the latch clicked. Marshall dropped the Bible.

Marshall roared, "No, goddamn it!" He ran to the door and grabbed Kristine by a slim arm, yanked her back and flung her across the room. "Get the hell out of here!" He again roared as he entered the bedroom.

"Who the fuck are you?" a voice yelled back.

"I'm her fuckin' husband! That's who! Now get your ass out of here before I blow your brains out!" Marshall pulled the .45 Colt from beneath his belt and pointed it at the soldier.

"Shit, fella, I didn't know she was married," the voice responded. "Hey buddy, take it easy! Put that goddam gun down! Let me get some clothes on and I'm out of here!"

Kristine sat on the floor resting her body against a solid upholstered chair. She gripped her knees with her arms and sobbed, her body shaking.

The young soldier strode past Marshall, pulling on a Eisenhower jacket, jerked open the door and walked out. He pulled the door closed behind him, slammed it. And Marshall turned to Kristine.

Marshall kneeled down beside her and attempted to wrap his arms around her but she rejected him.

"Do not touch me," she whispered.

"Did I hurt you?"

"Hurt? There's nothing left to hurt, Lieutenant sinner."

"Kristine," Marshall pleaded, "tomorrow we'll go talk with your pastor, or my squadron chaplain. One of them will be able to guide us out of this mess. Aren't we supposed to be Christians? Doesn't forgiveness have to start someplace?"

"It was you and Pop and Frank and Gary. Oh, my God," she moaned. "I cannot believe it."

"Jesus Christ, we were still at war. We were getting shot at. It just happened, like all of the other stupid things in war."

"You didn't have the character to tell me yourself."

"I admit that," Marshall said, "but after I got to know you, to love you, I was afraid to tell you. I thought some day in California, many years from now, we could talk about it."

"All I have left is hate, revulsion, and shame," Kristine said, then began to sob, her small body shaking.

Marshall again tried to comfort her, to put his arms around her, but again she pushed him away.

"Are you satisfied. You've shoved our faces into our own filth. We are barbarians. Animals would not do what we've done. They showed us the finger nail scratches of the Jews or whoever, on that cruddy, smelly wall.

Who could cremate a living human? And those barrels full of bits and pieces of white human bones! Oh, my God, I am so ashamed of being a German."

"No, no, no," Marshall pleaded and now moved closer and pulled her close to him despite her objections. "Only a handful of madmen caused all this. Look at our names, Kristine. Start with Eisenhower, and our own Colonel Schlosser, and Frank's last name is Mueller, and Frantz, and Klein and Klingenberg, all guys in my squadron. The Sunder name may be evil to you, but my father and grandparents aren't sinners. Where do you think so many of our grandparents originated?"

"I am too tired for your logic. Please go away. Just go away."

"Kristine." Marshall lifted her chin and tried to kiss her but she turned away. With his open palm he wiped away tears from her face. "Please look at me. I love you. I want to protect you. Promise me you won't allow any men in this house. None! Don't do that to yourself. We'll get help. Promise me that, then I'll leave."

"Help me up, please."

Marshall lifted Kristine, holding her beneath the armpits, attempted to hold her closely, but again she withdrew from him. Near her feet he saw the large Bible. As he bent over to pick it up the glow from the open door of the stove reflected off of the tiny watch crystal. Marshall placed the Bible on the table and then with his thumb and forefinger picked up the crystal, found the watch and case nearby, and placed them together beside the Bible. He sighed and turned again to Kristine.

"Promise, Kris?"

"I promise, I promise," Kristine whispered. "Now please leave me."

CHAPTER 12

▼

DESPAIR

Falling long and broken, Marshall's shadow stretched down the steps in irregular sections toward the gate where the exactness of its outline became diffused and blurred, finally disappearing in the darkness at the street's edge. Vaguely aware that he had stepped out onto her stone porch, he leaned against the doorjamb, stared at the white flakes brightening as they neared him. His eyes did not focus on one flake, or on a group, simply recorded their passing from dark to light to dark. Some flakes touched his cheeks and nose and chin. There they melted.

The open palms of his hands formed a nest and moved upward to catch his face. He heard the beginning of a groan, a dry sob, thought it came from the room, realized its source in the same instant, felt it forming within him. He rejected it. Dropping his hands to his sides, Marshall quickly stood very erect. He glanced toward the street. No one had seen him. As he started to move toward the street he heard the muffled sobbing beyond the door.

"No, no," Marshal moaned. He stepped forward, slipped on the glazed ice beneath the snow, fell down the steps, slid through snow on his hands and knees. He remained there, his hands spread out wide on the icy walk, supported by his stiff arms. His head hung downward like that of a junkman's horse. Pushing back away from the walk, Marshall sat up, and let his arms hang limp at his sides. His buttocks resting on his heels, he stared upward, his open palms up.

"Oh, Christ!" He shouted, "Oh, Jesus Christ!" He stared into the silent black void above him. The snowflakes had grown smaller and harder, pelting his upturned face. They bounced off of it, stinging it, not reposing gently to dissolve. Marshall grabbed handfuls of the snow at his sides, squeezed it into ice, dropped the cold molded pieces, then stood and walked, following his shadow to the center of the street.

Then he was running. He slipped, put out a hand, touched the ice and snow, recovered, ran. They teach you everything, his mind shouted, reprimanded him; how to bail out and how to put on a tourniquet and when to loosen it. You're in the Air Corps now, sonny. Just press a button, pull a lever, tuck your head, bend your knees, hold your breath: Name, rank and serial number. It's a fact; VD is higher in this town than any other in the country. Don't go off the base without a Pro-Kit. When a B-26 hits the water you have seven seconds to get out. The radioman goes first, then you put your right hand here, your left foot there, and the radioman will reach down to give you a lift up. What? The radioman is dead? Guess you're dead too, Lieutenant! Ha, ha, ha! Always touch rubber. Touch the nose wheel. Yeah, like a guillotine. Never trust your senses. Vertigo will get you. Nobody flies by the seat of his pants. Believe in your instruments. Have faith in your gauges, your dials. There's a switch for everything. Do as we say. Trust in solenoids, the instruments, the gauges, and the calculators. It's all been figured out for you.

Gasping for breath, Marshall slowed, walked, then stopped. His chest ached. He gulped for air. It knifed his throat and lungs and he could feel his heart pounding, pounding, pounding. He breathed in deeply, swallowed then turned, his hands clutching his hips. He looked back. Two hundred yards away he saw the opening in the building; the doorway, a rectangular glow, fuzzy at the edges, unblinking, a hole in the blackness like the opening at the end of a long tunnel. It disappeared then, the rectangle of light, and Marshall turned and once more ran towards the barracks. *Why did she open that damn door? To find me? To let in some son of a bitch. Oh shit!*

Beyond the apple tree with the splintered branch, beyond the broken window, Marshall saw a man moving about in his room. He slowed, then was close enough to recognize Frank. Marshall hesitated, stopped, turned his back to the window and leaned against a tree. His breath formed like puffs of fine dust before him.

Just like the dust kicked up by Emil's stallion. From the distance the faint high notes of the piano at the officers' club and singing voices reached him. Marshall walked toward the music. He tried to recall what his Uncle Bruce had described about character, about being well tempered, but hunting experiences had not prepared him for the joys and the anguish of love, just as cadet training had done nothing to prepare them for love, except scare the recruits with color slides of diseased women.

In front of the nine foot-carved oak doors, Marshall attempted to brush off the snow. He picked at the blobs of ice that stuck to his uniform. His trousers, already growing stiff, were soaked to the knees. In his cold shoes his feet were wet and clammy. His palms, cut by the ice and gravel when he fell, began to ache. He wrung his hands, flipped off the water, then put them in his pockets to warm.

Inside the club the hot air, rancid and bluish with cigar smoke, smelling of beer and bourbon, resisted him as if he were trying to walk through a piece of transparent silk sheeting. Eyes above open, moving mouths looked his way, the heads not turning, unconcerned, the mouths opening and closing, keeping time and in tune, singing on as the flier at the piano keys played from one song into the next without stopping. The eyes looked back to the sheet music.

"Lost a snowball fight tonight, sir?" the sergeant behind the bar asked. He grinned at Marshall, his chevroned arms relaxed and folded across his chest.

In the mirror behind the sergeant Marshall saw the reflection. His hair was matted and wet, his necktie soggy. Somewhere he had lost his hat. Marshall tried to smile, hesitated, stared down at the polished bar top.

"Scotch," he said. "Scotch. A double." Backing away from the bar, Marshall found his comb, forcing it back through his dark brown hair several times, then flipped the water into a corner behind a chair, spraying the wall. Taking his handkerchief from his pocket, he dried his face, wiped his hands again, and stared at the pink scratches on his palms, and then returned to the bar.

"Soda?"

"Please."

Marshall gulped down the drink, asked for a refill. Drank it fast. The sergeant turned to replace the bottle amongst the others on the shelf. Hearing the empty glass click against bar-top, the sergeant turned. He stood in front of Marshall and watched him wipe the excess from his lips with the back of his hand. Raising his eyebrows, the sergeant pursed his lips as if to whistle.

"Another please," Marshall said

"Drying out from the inside?" the sergeant said. He chuckled, and looked at Marshall who stared at the measuring glass being filled before him.

"No soda," Marshall said.

"Water?"

"Nothing."

"Single?"

"Double."

"None of my business, sir, but you're going to catch your death if you don't..."

"Forget it."

"Yes sir."

"No offense," Marshall murmured. The sergeant walked to the end of the bar where he began to dip glasses into soapy water.

Marshall shuddered. He began to shake. He shook his head back and forth fast when he thought about Kris, felt he might cry, clamped shut his jaw, ground his teeth, choked down the desire to weep, choked it until it settled deep into his chest, smothered and contained there by the taught muscles of his neck and throat. The fliers continued to sing. Two officers entered, stopped at the bar, had one drink and departed.

When Marshall had finished the third drink, he set the glass down carefully on the bar top. The strange new pain in his chest was dissolving in the scotch, he thought. Yes, sir, the Air Corps anticipated everything: even officers' clubs.

"Seargent?"

"Yes, sir?"

"One more time."

Marshall glanced up from the sergeant's hands and the bottle and the measuring glass, but the sergeant was looking down. Marshall looked at the hands again. They blurred. He cleared his throat, stood up straight.

"That it, sir?"

"Nope."

Shrugging his shoulders, the sergeant corked the bottle. He left it standing beside the drink he had poured.

"Goodbye, sweet world."

"Pardon?"

"Nothing, sir," said the sergeant, returning to the soiled glasses.

Marshall gripped the full glass, felt an urge to throw it at the mirror, but drank from it instead. Supporting himself at the bar with his elbow, he carefully lit and smoked a cigarette. When he had finished the drink he began to feel numbness in his lips and in his knees. Intending to set the empty glass down on the bar, he misjudged the distance and the glass bounced out of his hand, rolled away from him, off of the bar top, fell to the floor and shattered. Marshall rested both elbows on the edge of the bar and drew the forefinger of each hand down across his cheeks, poking and pulling at his face. He felt nothing. In front of him he sensed more than he saw the form of the sergeant picking up the pieces of glass.

"Shit. I am sorry about that, Sergeant." Marshall spoke, now slurring.

The wallet that he dug from his hip pocket was damp. He laid it on the bar top and pulled out bills, pushed a crisscross, irregular stack away from him.

"That enough?" Marshall said, slowly, carefully. "Damages and all?"

"Too much, sir," the sergeant answered, gathering four of the bills. He pushed the others back toward the open wallet. "I'll get your change. How about a nice big hamburger, sir? Might help soak up some of your problems?"

"Forget it," Marshall murmured, "You are a good guy. May I buy that bottle?"

"Yes, but…"

"I'll take it; help yourself to my money." Leaving the bills on the bar top, he struggled to get the wallet back into his hip pocket, gave up, then stuffed it into a side pocket. He turned and faced the door, squinted his eyes, focused upon it, leaned back against the bar, his elbows holding him erect, took a deep breath, pinched his shoulders back, held his head rigid, his chin tucked back tight against his Adam's apple and marched in a very direct, straight course to the door. He leaned against it, then gripped the knob with both hands, turned and pulled. When the door flew open Marshall's feet slid out from under him. Still gripping the doorknob, holding the bottle of scotch by its neck, he twisted his body and slipped into the opening before releasing his grip. On hands and knees crawled the few feet back to the knob, heard the laughter, then laughing too, smiling, he bowed at the waist, then stood erect and saluted and backed out of the club, still pulling the door closed after him. For a few minutes he sat on the steps. The cold sharpened his senses. He gulped cold air. He stood and walked unsteadily down the steps like a crippled old man.

"Gotta find Frank. I'll ride with him, wherever the hell he's going. Then say good-bye." Marshall murmured.

"Real clown!" Marshall said aloud, then laughed, cocking his head. Outside he wove his way through the trees to the barracks. He reached his door, turned the knob and kicked it open.

Except for Frank, the large room was empty. Pausing to check a page number, Frank put down the book he'd been reading, glanced at his wristwatch, stood and walked towards Marshall.

"Thought I'd have to go looking for you," Frank said, still not cognizant of the glazed look in Marshall's eyes.

"My B-4 bag is all packed and ready to go. Have a footlocker ready for shipment if you or Gary would help me out."

Maintaining his balance with one hand against the wall, he walked to the entrance of his room and stared at two bulging B-4 bags. The bags moved around the room, followed by a pair of twin footlockers, and the twin dressers, they too circled him. The tops of the desks were bare. Marshall gripped the doorjamb with one hand and put the other over one eye. Two B-4 bags became one and the footlockers and desks and dresser became single items and stopped the circling movement.

"I'm sorry," Frank began, "about you and Kris."

"Sorry?" Marshall repeated. He leaned back against the wall. "Sorry for your ole baby-killing bombardier?" He slurred 'bombardier', then sylabillized it, "bomb-bar-dear!" Laughing then, he lowered his head, his chin almost touching his chest and looked up at Frank. "Want to see my medals?"

"Cut it out!" Frank said.

"You, Frank, are the one I should be helping. So I bail out when you need me. What a fucking buddy, I am eh?" Marshall said.

"You're stoned," Frank said, as much to himself as to Marshall. "Better sleep it off."

"D'int you hear me, ole pilot, ole buddy? I'm a baby-killer. A Luftgangster!"

"You're no more to blame than me or Gary or the colonel."

"Thanks. Great philosopher that you are ole buddy, ole buddy. Got all the answers."

"All the world's a stage…" Frank started, noticeably deepening his voice.

"Bull shit!" Marshall said, louder than he had spoken before. "What book that come out of? Does your old buddy Shakespeare have the answers for this crap? I found the bridge. I hit the bridge. Killed a baby. Couple of old ladies too, you know: Bonus sort of thing. Want to see my air medal, ole buddy?"

"Shut up! You selfish drunken bastard!" Frank said. "Don't hoard the blame."

"Hoard the blame!" Marshall repeated. Through dulling eyes he stared at Frank's moving, livid, multiple faces, cocked his head thoughtfully and repeated the words very slowly, "Don't hoard the blame. Well now…"

"Come on, Marsh," Frank once more spoke softly, "let's hit the sack."

"Fuck the sack. Fuck it all!" Marshall said. "Here, have a swig!" He held the bottle of scotch up, then put it to his mouth and gulped from it.

"Okay, Marsh, okay" Frank answered patiently, taking Marshall's arm attempting to lead him into the bedroom.

"Lemme lone!" Marshall muttered, pulled away, lost his balance and fell backward against the wall. He slid down it and lay on his side, sighed and tucked a bent arm beneath his head. "Baby- killer," he whispered, then closed his eyes.

Frank tried to pull Marshall into a sitting position. He was unable to prop him so he dragged him, holding him beneath the arms, into the bedroom. Unable to arouse Marshall, Frank stood over him, cursed him, then shook his head and said, "You poor son of a bitch!" He left the room and returned with Gary, clad in his olive drab underwear.

"Ugh," Gary said, "What a stinking mess." The corners of his mouth pulled down, his nostrils narrowed. Gary turned his face, tried to protect himself from the odor. He looked back at Marshall. He gagged, then put his handkerchief over his nose.

From his mouth and nose brown liquid gushed onto the floor. His knees pulled upward towards his chest, pumped, then straightened and the flowing continued. He groaned. Water, perspiration, poured from his face and forehead and neck, tears flowed across his cheek and nose. He moaned. Tried to raise his head, regurgitated. His face was pale, bloodless, white.

"Goddamn it to hell!" Frank said. He turned and left the room and returned with a mop and a galvanized pail full of soapy hot water. They undressed Marshall and they washed him, dried him, and lifted his rubbery form into the bed where they covered him with blankets.

After they had mopped up the room, Frank took the clothes to the laundry room, washed and rinsed them, and hung them near the water heater.

Frank and Gary stood in the doorway looking at Marshall, his face white, large beads of perspiration still oozing up through his skin to form curved pools on his face, then run down his chin and loose mouth to his neck.

"What a beaut he's going to have," Gary said, then laughed.

Through the broken windows small flakes of snow drifted in. Some of it melted as soon as it touched the warm furniture, but near the window a small mound formed that didn't melt. With the wind there came a faint, high, sorrowful whistle, probably caused by the broken and jagged pieces of glass over which it passed.

CHAPTER 13

▼

FRANKFURT

In the morning the pain in his head was intense, pounding, throbbing, and when Marshall moved it seemed as if a solid steel ball slammed from one side of his temples to the other. Unable to eat breakfast, even to think of food, he had brushed a clear spot on the steps in the snow as he sat near the door of the officers' club, his back resting against the cold stone walls. Frank and Gary had helped him dress and encouraged him to join them, to eat some toast. He managed to locate the wristwatch he'd purchased for his dad and put it in his pocket. But he couldn't go farther. He stopped there at the door, too ill to go in and faintly conscious of the shoes moving by him, scraping off the snow, going into the mess hall, returning, of laughs and snickers, but it didn't matter to him.

He was alone again, and getting colder. It was better, the humiliation, the shame, the waves of nausea, the childish desire to weep, the bitter cold in his bones, all of these things were better than the nagging deep voice within him crying out, demanding, beseeching, pleading then snarling at him... *Go to her, it directed, "Go back to her! She needs you. And still another voice saying No. A voice not quite a part of the suffering, painful body sitting on the steps, but one of those fighting-within voices never before heard by the hung-over Marshall, then compromising itself, remembering the light from her open door. It isn't true. She wouldn't do that. She couldn't.*

Why did she learn of the bombs? Oh, God, I do love her. I love her! So, if you love her go back to her. The voices in his head resounded: She is frightened and hurt and she too is sick, but not with liquor, sick with sorrow and remorse and disbelief. I can't go back. Tex was right; all of the damn Germans are evil. Frank was right. There was no chance for us. No! No! She's a victim! She's the one that didn't have a chance. Pulling his legs up toward his chest, Marshall held them with his arms, forehead on his knees.

A man paused beside him. Marshall looked down at the pair of highly polished brown shoes, so slick with wax that droplets of water formed atop them. The wetness of the snow hadn't been able to penetrate the leather.

"Mind if I sit with you?"

Marshall looked up, was surprised.

"Oh hello," Marshall said, his voice quavering, "Frank's leaving."

"Yes, I had a chance to say good-bye last night. Understand you and Gary are going to ride up to Frankfurt with him."

"I pretty well screwed up my good-bye scene with him last night. We'll give it another try today."

Chaplain Waldron leaned over and brushed snow off the step beside Marshall and sat down.

"Remember when you guys would come to the old mess hall back in Denain? We'd all shoot the bull for awhile, I'd read a bit from the good book and then say a little prayer and you'd all head out to those bombers like you didn't have a care in the world?"

By the slight movement of his head, lowering it and raising it slowly, Marshall acknowledged remembrance, but said nothing.

"Strange isn't it, I felt, I really knew, that I was helping in some way to make your missions easier. Oh, not just you, Marsh, but all of the fliers who stopped by on those black, early, cold mornings. I tried to meet the challenge of doing right by all of you. The Catholics and the Jews; all of you in the outfit."

"We appreciated it, Captain Waldron."

"That's not why I stopped. Marshall, you need me now, or I should say you need my commanding officer, Jesus, more than you did even in combat. It's not too late for you and your girl friend. Schloss filled me in on what's been happening. I'll personally do all that I can for her, and of course you. I'll contact her pastor or priest and I feel together we can help." The chaplain sighed and put his hand on Marshall's shoulder. "I'll go see her this morning."

Marshall did not reply.

"That trip to Dachau, her grandmother's suicide, well, all of the things that have happened to her combined to shock her, just as soldiers and fliers experience shell shock. It's not just the terrible noise of exploding shells, and barrages, the sight of death, the loss of friends, terrible destruction. It's trauma. She's had to withdraw. She's withdrawn; she's retreated from reality. Whatever God's servants or the medics call it, we know she's temporarily another person. She has built a facade to protect herself from more injury."

"And if that holy, holy, Bible-quoting Tex, our squadron foul mouth, hadn't hauled all of those people out to Dachau, none of this would have happened." Marshall lifted his head and stared at the chaplain. Thank you for talking to me Captain Waldron, but when I find Tex, I'm going to beat him to death!"

"Marsh, forget about Tex. He's like a lot of mixed-up people who think they are being Christians by playing St. Peter. None of this kind of thinking will roll back the calendar. Violence and revenge will reduce you to his plane. Believe me. I'll go see Kristine."

"All I wanted to do was marry Kris sometime. All I wanted to do was love her and be good to her and take her home with me. Did you know her mother and little girl also died after that mission?"

"The world hasn't ended!" The chaplain tightened his grip on Marshall's shoulder. "You're both going to have to be respectful of these occupation rules. Don't flaunt your disdain for rules. But first you must forgive yourself and if you feel you really love this girl, you have to understand she's probably in shock and won't even remember the last few days."

"Sir, Kris and I had a terrible argument last night. There was a G.I. in her bedroom. I chased him out. She promised she wouldn't see another soldier. Would you go see her and talk to her? I don't think she'd talk with you if I was along. Gary and I want to see Frank off. We'll be back on the base tonight, and I'll check in with you."

"I'll go see her this morning." The chaplain said. "Now let's get out of this cold for a few minutes. My old bones are stiffening up. We'll find a private corner and I want to share a reading of first Corinthians, thirteen, with you."

"Whatever you say," Marshall said, arose and brushed snow off of his trousers. He held the door for the chaplain and followed him into the officers' club.

Marshall listened to the words being read from the Bible and wondered if anyone could really feel that way.

The chaplain shook his hand. "I'm going to see Kristine as soon as possible."

"She's a Lutheran," Marshall said.

Marshall returned to the steps outside the officers' club and sat on the cold steps. His head throbbed. The thought of toast, of food, made him gag. He closed his eyes and rested his back against the cold, stone wall.

Beneath his armpits he felt a gentle lifting, the pressure of their hands and looked up at them, at Frank and Gary, as they raised him to his feet. Together they walked. He was steadied by them when necessary, en route to the area where the six-by-six truck was parked.

"The colonel's coming to say good-bye," Frank said.

"I'd feel bad if he didn't," Gary said.

"That must be him," Frank said, and pointed to a jeep being driven in the direction of the six by six truck towards which they walked. The jeep stopped. The truck driver stepped down from the cab and two men climbed out of the canvas covered truck and stood at attention and saluted, then relaxed and one of them pointed in the direction of the trio walking slowly towards the truck.

Walking towards them alone they recognized the build of the colonel, tall and broad shouldered, stepping through the six inches of snow carefully and deliberately.

"Shape up, Marsh," Frank whispered.

"Sure," Marshall said and took several deep breaths and hoped that the cold air would clear his head.

The colonel returned their salutes. Unsmiling, he shook hands firmly, nodded to each, and seemed to be stalling, seeking time to select the correct word?

Try again to perform it: the last, and an appropriate farewell to extend to a civilian officer. As a "Point Man", I'm a professional soldier, aviator, and as conscious of the difference between civilian officers as the civilian officer is aware of his distance from the civilian enlisted man. All of us in the squadron had been as one, all equal he felt, in the air, as fliers, and deep within all of us was the feeling of our sameness. A healthy amalgamation bonded solidly once the propellers of our airplanes began to turn, then, for the first time in military history, ours was fluid-integration of humans, all of us stationed within a flying machine, free of earth. A group of men flying winged devices constructed of aluminum and wire and gasoline and Plexiglas. All of the component parts of this were blended into a common purpose, and no doubt some of my civilian warriors wondered if they were indeed flying the machines or whether the machines were flying them. And now I must allow this good leader, Frank, to return to a disastrous situation. I could forewarn him of flak, but not for what is in store for him. I can't tell his crew members, yet. And I can't allow him to return to my outfit.

The colonel looked from one to the other of the three fliers standing at attention in front of him. "All right fellows. Rest."

They stood, because there was nothing for them to sit down on or lean against.

"Well, Frank, you headed up one damn fine crew and I'm sorry you fellows didn't finish your tour and all go home together. Also sorry you have to ride out of here in a 6x6, but the guys at weather say we're grounded. I spoke with the meteorologist myself before coming here. So, with Gary and Marshall wanting to go along for the ride and the other passengers we can use just one vehicle."

"It's only a couple of hours to Frankfurt," Frank said.

"Lieutenant Mueller, I'm trying to figure a way to get the rest of your crew out of here, regardless of points, especially now that the locals know you took out the bridge. You guys are heroes, remember that, and be sure that the enlisted men know that." He turned to Gary, "It's up to you and Marshall now, Gary, to get that message across."

Desperate to sit down, nauseated and feeling faint from his hangover, Marshall struggled with his uniform, finally took a cigarette from his pocket, lit it, inhaled deeply and offered the pack to the others.

"A classmate of mine is C.O. at your new base in Georgia, Frank. I've already written him, recommending you for anything you want to fly from B-29's to jets to helicopters."

"Thank you, sir."

"At our meeting back in Tegelen," Frank began, "you advised us, sir, of the situation we were likely to be in, if word ever got out, about bombing the bridge, and again the meeting the night 'Pop' got it. Now this, my emergency leave. It's all the breaks, I'd say, sir."

"Decisions and breaks," the colonel answered. "Why I didn't transfer your crew to another base before we moved to Bad Scheidel, I'll never know. But the fact is, I didn't. And the breaks? Coincidence? The analytical boys back at the Pentagon don't allow for coincidence. It's against the odds. Illogical and impractical." The colonel cleared his throat and took from his jacket pocket a cigarette, and lit it, inhaled deeply, then exhaled.

"Let me add," he paused, cleared his throat and studied their faces, "I try to know what is going on with all of the men in our outfit, with the Germans in town, the enlisted men, officers, everyone. With your crew especially, Frank. I know about Marshall and his girl friend. How I must perform as your C.O. is one thing, Marshall. What I feel for you and for the German girl is another thing. If it is any small comfort to you, I can tell you this. I've learned that her father will be home soon. Her grandmother's home, where she is living, is now off-limits except for the chaplain. He's already on his way to talk with her.

"For any of you to leave my command, feeling that your missions, your devotion to your assignments, well, that it hasn't been worthwhile...." The colonel drew deeply from his cigarette, glanced at the truck and at the three men standing beside it, then scanned the dark, clouded sky, and turned back to them.

"When I was in school, back before the Academy, I can remember that it struck me that much of the emphasis of our history studies, relative to the wars we were involved in, was devoted to the persecuted. Wars are fought for the underdogs in society. Back then it seemed to me that there should be a double awareness. True, slavery was an evil thing, and a civil war was fought, but too little was written about the fact that white men decided to fight their own kind. We remember the evil deed and forget that someone did something about it. All of the writing was about the injustice to the Negroes: All that is true. It is history. But as white men we did some pretty profound things about ending slavery. So there have been other wars—twice against the Germans. Damn! It doesn't seem right that you are leaving my command on a truck." The colonel pressed his cigarette against the bottom of his raised foot, then began to field strip it. "What are you going to remember? What are you going to carry home? I wish I had a beautifully worded speech mimeographed that I could read to you. I don't have. What you've done has been for a just cause. Those who suffered, and who were persecuted, will eventually heal and forget their wounds. Historians, maybe even some politicians, will remember individuals, like you fellows who answered the call for help. Your records show that you all volunteered." The colonel flicked the tiny ball of paper aside, watched it disappear into the mud. Snowflakes began to float down quietly and drift amongst them. Stubs were all that remained of their cigarettes. Frank field—stripped his cigarette. Marshall and Gary followed his example. They all looked upward simultaneously at the sky, at the gray clouds, and exchanged glances again.

"Really socked-in," Gary said.

"Yep," the colonel said, then sighed, "Well, I guess I haven't anything profound to add."

Saying nothing more, Colonel Schlosser turned and walked towards the six by six truck. They followed him, and he stopped and turned to Frank, Marshall and Gary, shook hands with each, saluted, said "Good luck!" then turned and strode on briskly to his waiting jeep. Marshall thought that he saw a dampening around the colonel's eyes, but figured it must have been caused by the cold air. Steam from the hot breath of the jeep engine obliterated it from their sight.

They climbed into the back of the truck, nodded to four other fliers from a different squadron. A sergeant asked, "Is the driver alone?"

No one knew, so he climbed out of the truck, then returned and said, "I'll keep him company." He disappeared again and they heard the door slam. The truck lurched forward towards Frankfurt.

Within the truck Marshall tried to close his eyes. He rested his head back against the canvas top but the truck bounced and with each jolting, twisting lunge the tight canvas snapped his head forward, his eyes opened and recorded the blank stares of Frank and Gary bouncing on the opposite side of the truck, near him, their knees almost touching his, swaying and bracing and lurching sideways and backwards and forwards like helpless dolls in a runaway toy baby carriage. Gripping the wooden seat he tried to hold himself still.

Behind the truck, houses swept by them, slowed as the street narrowed. Details of the houses were blurred by the finely ground snow dust sucked backwards and upwards into the opening of the truck. They rumbled across the bridge at Bad Scheidel. He saw Kristine's house and then it disappeared and Marshall leaned out across the tailgate, slipped down on his knees and heaved green bile and sour juices out onto the ground and the swirling, dirty, ground-up, dusty snow cooled his hot face. He rested his head on his arms, but the tailgate smacked his arms and jolted him. His chest ached.

"You're just fucking pitiful," Gary said. He chuckled.

"Here," Frank said. Marshall felt a hand on his shoulder.

Marshall turned and Frank was leaning over him with an army blanket in one hand, grasping one of the curved steel struts that supported the canvas for balance. "Sit up," Frank said.

Marshall pulled himself up onto the seat. Frank folded the blanket and then spread it out on the truck bed, motioned for Marshall to lay down. Marshall collapsed on the blanket, felt another blanket thrown over him, then pulled his knees up close toward his chest, folded his arm beneath his head and slept.

I am dead and I have been buried face down. But I am not sightless. I can see the roots of the trees. They are very naked and they stretch in all directions especially downward. Down deeper and deeper into the earth. Then they become slim, slimmer than a pencil, as slim as the pencil lead, and fragile looking, but they are gripping the soil and sucking life from it. I deserve to be dead and buried here in the earth, but not face down. Why didn't they put me in a box with an American flag over it and lower me so my back could rest and I could see through the lid and view the red and white stripes and field of blue with white stars, see upward through the new, loosely compacted dirt, all the way to the sky. Why is the earth gray, and where are the rocks and ledges and the white-bone remains of other creatures like me? The earth and the roots are still surrounding me, fine and lace like and swaying in the mud, vacuuming it, trying, like me to find an anchor hold.

"Feel better?"

Marshall blinked. Laying flat on his back, looking upward, he turned his head from the canvas opening of the truck, stared at the tops of the swaying, leafless trees, and looked up at Frank and Gary.

"Yeah," Marshall answered. Again he looked back at the tops of the leafless trees moving by the truck. It had all really happened, he thought. It wasn't a nightmare, not a dream. He'd seen Kris and gotten drunk and the colonel had said good-bye and now they were on the way to Frankfurt. Closing his eyes again, Marshall wished that he were buried alive. His chest ached and his throat tightened when he thought of Kris. The pain would not leave, nor would the visions of her face when he closed his eyes, or the sound of her voice. He resented Kristine's complete hold on his mind, a domination he would not have believed possible, and knew that his focus now should be on the departure of one of his best, closest friends. My priorities are all fucked up, he concluded. At least I grabbed that wristwatch.

"Hey Marsh," Gary said, chuckling, "You old bastard, are you going to sleep the whole trip? Look here, buddy, what I brought. A little hair of the dog that bit'cha."

"Leave him alone," Frank said.

"He's been laying there snoring for an hour."

"Leave him alone."

"I'm okay," Marshall said. He sat upright, then pulled himself up on the seat. He rubbed the back of his neck with both hands.

"What a send off. Geez, I'm sorry Frank."

"Here, have a belt of this," Gary said, reaching out with a pint of Cognac. "Can't hurt, might help."

Gary was holding a bottle of cognac by the neck and sloshing it back and forth in front of Marshall's face. Marshall looked at it and suddenly felt his stomach retreat back from his rib cage. But he took the bottle, uncorked it, stared back at Frank's steady gaze, then took a gulp, swallowed, shuddered and wiped his mouth on his sleeve.

"Christ Marshall, you must be suicidal!" Frank said, shaking his head.

"I can't feel any worse. It might really help. They say it does." He tossed the bottle back to Gary.

From one of the other passengers a voice broke in. "Lieutenant, if that pair of clowns are your friends, you sure as hell don't need any enemies!" All of the passengers in the back of the bouncing truck laughed.

"Well," Frank said, joining in the laughter, "I'll be in Kansas tomorrow and they'll be stuck with each other back at Bad Scheidel. Seriously though, we were one hell of a team awhile back."

"What did you fly?"

"Twenty-sixes."

"The flying coffin. The B dash crash?"

"Yep. It's got a lot of nicknames. Mostly undeserved," Frank said, nodding and smiling.

The truck driver pulled up at the front entrance to the Frankfurt officers' club. He dropped the tailgate and all except one of the passengers jumped down to the ground, where they were handed their B-4 bags by the remaining passenger, a buck sergeant who stayed in the truck to be taken to the enlisted mans' club.

"They've a good menu in there, I've heard, sir, and they'll fix you up with quarters." The driver nodded towards Gary and Marshall. "I'll drop off the others, get some chow and gas up and if you two want to ride back with me, I'll pick you up about 1330. Okay?"

"Roger," Gary said, "we'll be ready."

The three fliers went to a desk near the door of the club. Marshall and Gary stayed back as Frank spoke to the sergeant. He accepted a room key, then slid his B-4 bag to the wall behind the desk.

"It'll be safe here," they overheard, and the sergeant pointed to a doorway leading to the bar and dining area.

The three fliers were led to a round table with a linen cloth, similar cloth napkins and water glasses. They seated themselves and the sergeant asked if they'd like coffee and they answered, "Yes, please." The dining room was otherwise empty.

"You fellows are kind of between breakfast and lunch. Which menu would you like to see?"

"Lunch okay with you guys?" Frank asked, and they both nodded affirmatively.

"Well, we've not a lot of time for lengthy good-byes, and I think it's best that way," Frank said.

"We're going to have to have regular reunions when we all get home and settled in," McAdam said.

"We've got plenty of room in Chico for everyone, and I can take you guys into the Sierra to some fabulous trout fishing spots," Marshall said.

"Assume John and Jim will want to get together," Frank said.

"Like I said, we've got room for nearly everyone at my place, and if not at our house, I've got my Uncle Bruce in town, plus very friendly neighbors."

"What's the future hold for you guys?" Frank asked.

"I think my dad's expecting us, Sean, my twin and me, to join him in the construction business. But I don't know. Not a big business. Might be only one of us could fit in. Chicago I wouldn't miss, especially now that I've seen a little bit of the country. California looked awful good to me when I was in Santa Ana. That's my idea of winter weather!"

"Like McAdam, I guess the folks are expecting me to be interested in our mercantile business."

"And you, Frank?"

"Jesus Christ! I really wish I knew! I can't believe Diana is gone!" Frank sighed, revealing a sudden irritation, then stopped abruptly. He pushed his coffee cup away from him, then slowly brought it back. He paused and slowly sipped from the coffee cup. "I've got to get through these next few days. Have to find out what the hell happened."

"Of course," Marshall stammered. "I'm sorry, Frank. That was a stupid question."

McAdam spoke, "You know, Frank, that Marsh and I would like to be going with you now, to be at your side."

"Hell, relax, guys," Frank said. "This is such a screwed up situation, trying to say good-byes under these conditions. I'll have to sort everything out when I get home. God, imagine what Diana's dad and mom must be going through, and I'm not there to help them. But I will be in a matter of hours. The Red Cross didn't tell me a damn thing. Just that she died. Schloss said my folks would be notified when I'm expected in."

The fliers accepted a warm-up in their coffee mugs and ordered their lunch. The waiter volunteered that the hamburgers were big and juicy, and the three fliers accepted his advice. None were interested in studying a menu.

"Listen Marsh, your question wasn't out of line," Frank said, "My mind has been going a thousand miles a minute since Schloss called me in to talk to the Red Cross people. I never really thought beyond Diana and me being married, going back to college, and raising a family. She supports, she did support, I mean, my desire to get a college education. Maybe I'll stay in the Air Corps awhile."

"Frank, I've got a little going away present for you." McAdam said. From his shirt pocket he pulled out a small container. "I've got a WAC typist friend in personnel. I know your 'first' is coming up. Orders are already cut."

"You and your harem. Aren't you something!" Frank, said, shaking his head in mock disbelief.

Frank opened the package containing the silver bars of a first lieutenant. "Well, that is real thoughtful, McAdam!" Frank said and laughed quietly, then extended his hand. "Hope you're right!"

"Sterling." Gary McAdam said, "And my source is impeccable."

Marshall applauded, then reached to the inside of his jacket. "Me too, Frank." Marshall said. "Traded a few cigarettes for this little guy when I was in Switzerland." He handed him a narrow leather case, one of the gifts he'd intended for his father.

Frank opened the case and took out the Omega watch and attempted to put it around his wrist but, the leather band was too stiff and had to be massaged a bit. "This is really handsome, Marsh. Wow, this really is too much," Frank said. "More than a few packs of cigarettes crossed the counter!"

"Remember what Pop used to say, 'It's as important to be a gracious receiver as it is a generous giver'," Marshall said.

"Yep, old Pop came through with some good ones, didn't he? You guys have outdone yourselves and these will be treasures for me. Especially this little get together. Eventually, we all ought to try and see Pop's wife and their little boy."

Marshall raised his arm and looked at his watch. "Well, that 6 x 6 will be showing up soon."

"I'm going to try to sack out for a few hours. I understand there's a flight at ten hundred hours, ETD. Fly all night, on a C-47, into Washington, DC, then a DC 3 to Kansas City. All routine flights that Schloss and the Red Cross lined up for me."

"Marsh and I'll get a check in the mail for the Mercedes. It should be grabbed up soon at that price," Gary said.

"Fine." Frank said, "Yep. Ought to be able to unload it in a hurry. Hell of a car." He reached for the lunch tab and paid for it over the objections of Gary and Marshall. "Suppose I can get serious with you guys for a second?"

"You still occupy the left seat, skipper," Gary said.

"For your own good, Gary, why don't you try to limit your lovemaking to the allies, the WACS, the nurses and Red Cross girls. Maybe even throttle back a little. Save yourself for the States."

"Well Frank, not because you're going to a 'first' soon, and not because you're such a damn puritan, but only because you are my senior by eight months, I will do my best. Honest injun!"

"I'm glad you have some respect for your seniors," Frank said, and laughed.

"And me, skipper?" Marshall asked.

"You know, buddy, you're great with a Norden, and we trust your navigation, but you've sure as hell painted yourself into a corner with Kristine. I hope you find another girlfriend somewhere. Gary can line you up with one of his WAC friends. All the cards are stacked against you and Kris. And, seriously, buddy, trust me, this goddamn booze thing with you lately; it's just a crutch. Kick it! It'll make matters worse."

Marshall nodded, "Thanks, Frank. The chaplain has already talked to me and says he'll help Kristine, too."

The fliers had slowly walked towards the front desk. They stopped there and Frank was given a key to a room, plus directions and he asked to be awakened at nineteen hundred hours.

"Yes, sir, I'll have someone knock on your door and wait until you open it. It's about ten minutes to the flight line. Can we pack you a little dinner box to take aboard?"

"Very thoughtful, yes, I'd appreciate that."

"Well, see you guys around," Frank said.

They shook hands and Frank turned and walked alone down a hallway. Marshall and Gary walked back to the lobby and stood there awaiting the appearance of the truck that would take them back to Bad Scheidel.

A buck sergeant kept the driver company. Marshall and Gary had the truck interior to themselves.

"Somebody was mighty thoughtful to equip this rig with blankets," Gary said. He folded one army blanket and sat on it, then draped another around his shoulders. Marshall did the same and they sat near the tailgate.

"This son of a bitch must not have any shocks," Gary said.

"Probably less bounce closer to the cab. But I need the cold air," Marshall said.

"Isn't this a kick in the ass!" Gary said, "We can check out a fucking bomber and fly to England or the French Riviera or to Paris, otherwise we're reduced to this. Might as well be in a cattle car!"

"This is what they mean about being an officer and gentleman."

"Well said, Marsh," Gary laughed, "you must be getting well."

"You know, Gary, I've nothing to compare this mess with; I mean that I'm in. I keep trying to apply some hunting or fishing experience that I had with dad and my uncle. It worked when we were getting shot at, but I'm drawing a blank."

"Well, I'm not big on religion, on praying and such, but if the chaplain can help Kris, maybe he can bail you out."

"You're a Christian, aren't you, Gary?"

"Know what I believe buddy, "Gary spoke, "I believe in Jesus because He believed He was the Son of God. I mean He REALLY believed it! I think He preached a lot of truth. So, I can believe what He tried to tell us because He was so convinced and then took the rap for it. Believed it enough to go that horrible death on the cross. I believe because He believed, and for the all of the rest of religion, I think the preachers, the rabbis, the priests, the pastors and even the lawyers all got a hold of a good thing and now you can get as many interpretations as you want. I believe what He said and taught. Just keep it simple. Because he believed, I can believe. That's it."

Marshall studied the serious face of Gary. "This is about as deep a bull session we've had since I've known you, Gary."

"Come on, face it. The excitement is over, gone and done with. We're now obsolete. Hell, there must be thousands of pilots and bombardiers and navigators, to say nothing of the engineers and radiomen and gunners. So now we can all sit around and try to figure out what civilian life will hold. Now we can drink, read, write letters: go to museums that haven't been blown up. The guys that prayed before a mission ought to keep praying. And we can make love."

"Funny, isn't it. For nearly a year and a half everything has revolved around dropping bombs, then this stupid occupation duty caught up with us. And you, Gary, you continue to be the great Don Juan of the entire squadron." He laughed, and Gary joined him, "I remember Pop saying 'you're so horny you'd screw a snake!'"

"Come on, Pop was no saint! And I've no qualms about making love to every nationality that will invite me into bed. I have no prejudices."

"Just a perpetual hard on," Marshall said and laughed. "But what about some moral code?"

"Oh, morals my ass. I'm not married. The difference between us is that I simply enjoy the hell out of shacking up and you want to make it holy, or to the other extreme, evil or sinful or something. You know the saying, 'a stiff dick has no conscience', and I'm not ready for a long-term commitment! And none of my girl friends are either. We screw for the sheer enjoyment of it. For them it's no big deal, no more important than getting their hair done. Something natural and fun."

"Hell Gary, I've had my share of adventures with some really beautiful dolls in France and Belgium, with you pointing the way. Those few days in Lie`ge with Ginger and her mom: man that was incredible. But this deal with Kris: there was nothing planned. It just happened. It's real"

"Now seriously, don't you really think that being sorry for her and those awful things that happened to her mother and grandmother and child, all of that kind of triggered the whole thing?"

Marshall was silent. "I really don't know," he said, finally, and moved his head from side to side, "Why can't it be called love?" They became silent, looking out of the back of the truck at the leafless trees continuing to form a narrow tunnel behind them.

As they approached Bad Scheidel, Marshall wondered if the chaplain had spoken to Kristine. He wanted to see her and hold her in his arms and reassure her that they'd be able to resolve their problems. Maybe it's too soon. I'll try to find the chaplain when we get to the base and find out what went on.

Both Marshall and McAdam stared, silently at the Bad Scheidel Bridge as they crossed it.

"Well, buddy, we can't un-bomb the son of a bitch," Gary said.

"Back to the fickle finger of fate, eh?" Marshall said.

The truck stopped at the guardhouse and the sergeant in the front seat jumped out and came to the back of the truck. "Would you guys like to get dropped off at the officers' club?"

"Roger," both responded simultaneously.

Within a few minutes, the truck came to a stop and the sergeant came to the back and lowered the tailgate.

"Well, thanks for the buggy ride," Gary and Marshall returned a salute from the driver.

"Hey, sir?" the driver said, "Any chance of getting a ride some time? Just to say I flew in a twenty-six?"

"No problem. Just give us your name and how to reach you. Put it in an envelope and tack it to our bulletin board. I'm McAdam, and he's Sunder. Either one of us can set up something."

"Thanks a lot. See ya!" The driver saluted and turned and walked away without waiting to receive the acknowledging return from Gary and Marshall.

"I'm going to try to find the chaplain," Marshall said. "Want to have chow together later?"

"Sure," Gary said. "And I've got to take inventory of my little reward packages. If you want to get rid of any cigarettes, let me know."

"A fraulein?"

"How'd you guess?" Gary said, laughed and struck Marshall on the arm.

Chaplain Waldron was in his office, responded to the knock on his door and asked Marshall to sit down.

"Well, we got Frank to the airport at Frankfurt. He'll be on his way in a few hours."

"I'm glad you and McAdam accompanied him."

"Sorry about my condition, sir: out on the steps. Promised Frank I'd go on the wagon. Well, almost. I am going to knock off the cigarettes too. Darn things make me feel lousy."

"Glad to hear that, of course. Well, things are looking up, Lieutenant Sunder. I drove down to see Kristine. Poor kid had dumped some chocolate and coffee packages right outside her door in the snow and had thrown chunks of coal out, too. Well, I picked up as much of it as I could, but she wouldn't even look at it so I put it in the jeep. Funny thing, I had a big bag of coal for her, and she was willing to accept it."

"Well thank God she's not obligated to anyone. Except you, of course."

"I told her it was a down payment on work I need done. That got her interest. Of course she advised me that she was working already, as a maid. I think some of the town's people saw me, and it made her nervous. They all need coal, you know."

"Did my name come up?"

"Oh, eventually, but I didn't want to stir that pot."

"Do you really have another job for her?"

"Talked it over with Colonel Schlosser. Going to create a library in one of the rooms in the officers'club, for use of everyone, of course, and we'll have a selection of German books, too."

"And Kristine will be involved?"

"I've already given her some material to study. You know, the Dewey Decimal System. She's a sharp little lady. She really perked up. She'll be doing most of the work. The correspondence and then arranging the material when it starts coming in. She can type."

"Did she mention me?"

"She was very upset when she heard about Miller's wife. She volunteered that you and McAdam would be upset."

"Upset? Certainly," Marshall said. "And Frank is devastated and doesn't know what happened."

"Oh," the chaplain said, "I assumed," Then he hesitated.

"Do you know any details?"

"I thought Frank knew. Assumed you knew. Diana died during an abortion, Marshall."

"Oh my God!" Marshal said, and stood up, "The poor bastard. The poor girl!"

CHAPTER 14

▼

METAMORPHOSIS

Marshall was virtually speechless when he left the chaplain's office. At the bar he found Gary, but said nothing to him about Diana until they had finished their dinner and then went to Marshall's room.

Gary became quiet and morose as Marshall told him the news about Frank's wife.

"I just can't believe she could have done that to Frank; to herself. God, that's so depressing."

"I wonder why in the hell she didn't just write him a 'Dear John' letter?" Marshall said.

"Who knows? I'd guess her lover told her to have it done? Her parents? Frank's parents? Her pastor? Her doctor." Gary sighed, "Probably some damn quack; you know, in secret."

"God, I hope Frank doesn't do something stupid!" Marshall exclaimed.

A knock on Marshall's door interrupted them.

"It's open. Come on in." Marshall said, raising his voice.

The pilot named Tex entered.

Both Marshall and Gary stared at him in silence.

"Can I speak to you guys for a couple of minutes?" Tex asked. "I brought a jug of J&B, if you'll join me?"

"Oh?" Marshall exclaimed.

"Just what the hell is on your mind, Tex?" Gary asked, anger revealed in his tone.

Tex, his head hanging, stared at the floor, then stammered, "I want to apologize, to both of you, but to you especially, Marsh."

Neither Gary nor Marshall spoke.

"Can I sit down?"

"There's a chair," Gary said.

"Awhile back I told you guys I was sorry about Pop, and I meant it, and I'm telling you now that I'm real shook up, like everybody else is about Frank."

"So?" Gary said.

"And Marshall, you've got to believe I am as sincere as I know how to be when I tell you that I realize my actions brought, well, caused the agony for Kristine. And to you, obviously."

Marshall said nothing. He looked, unblinking at Tex, stifled the rage in his chest, and attempted to control his emotions.

"I suppose that makes you feel better?" Gary said.

"Damn it to hell, Gary, I don't even know what I know anymore! Hell, I think Schloss feels I'm a damn psycho. I even talked to the Group Psychiatrist," Tex whispered. "You guys know I'm a good pilot. I never screwed up anyplace until we got to this godforsaken place!" Tex said. His hands and chin were shaking. "Would you guys join me in a shot of scotch?"

"Break bread?" Marshall said. He snickered. "You got a lot of guts!"

"Ease up, Marsh," Gary said, "I'll get some glasses," and he pushed his chair back and went to the bathroom. He returned with three drinking glasses, which were plentiful in the poker playing room. "Here you go, Tex. You pour."

Tex poured three ounces into each glass. He raised his glass and Gary touched his glass against Tex's. Marshall did not touch his glass.

"I told Frank I'd go on the wagon," Marshall said, and looked away from Tex. He felt revulsion, but the man had apologized.

"Gary, you remember when we exchanged visits with the ground pounders in Belgium." Tex said.

Gary nodded. Marshall stared into space.

"Well, I volunteered for that. Thought I would be spending a couple of days with some engineers, bridge builders, you know, but several of us were put in a six by six and hauled right out to a village, Malme`dy, and in this area, smaller than a football field, partially covered with snow, were over eighty of our GI's, artillery men, all dead. They had been machine-gunned to death by the SS: a massacre! Our guys were prisoners of war! Unarmed! They'd surrendered before the Battle of the Bulge!" Tex began to sob, he put his head down on the table and his body shook. "I have these goddamn nightmares. I wake up yelling and shivering and I see our men wedging those guys' mouths open. Jesus! They'd crack their teeth off. Then they clamped their jaws shut to hold in their dog tags. They tried to close their eyes. Their eyes were frozen open. And the stench was so awful. The poor guys had dirtied themselves." Tex's torso shook, throbbed violently, caused by his deep sobbing. "I got so sick, and I couldn't stop throwing up."

Marshall stood up, shook his head from side to side, and went to Tex and put both hands on his shoulders, "Good God. Come on Tex, it's okay now. Talk it out."

"Schloss says I'm paranoid about Germans. He sent me to the chaplain, too. Waldron said to share this with my peers. Jesus, guys, I keep dreaming about it!"

Tex sat back upright. Tears flowed from his eyes. He blew his nose loudly on his green handkerchief. "Talk about being fucked up, that's me."

"Guess we can understand a little better how you feel. How you acted." Gary said. He lit a cigarette and pushed his pack and matches toward Tex.

"Thanks," Tex said. He took a cigarette, lit it, sucked in the smoke, and then exhaled. "Shit, all I want to do is fly. I'm a pilot. Marsh, I never wanted to get involved in punishing anybody, but I started wanting revenge for those poor damn kids at Malme`dy, so I got messed up in that fucking Dachau tour thing. You know. And there's more, if you can tolerate me awhile longer."

Marshall listened in disbelief, then took his drinking glass and touched it up against that of Tex. "Drink up, fella," he murmured.

"I'm no more a Texan than the man in the moon."

"What in the hell do you mean by that?" Gary said, shaking his head, and Marshall stared at both of them in disbelief.

"Marsh, I'm from California. From Bakersfield."

"Well, why all of this Tex stuff?" Marshall blurted out and leaned forward, staring into the wet and swollen eyes of a flier he'd grown to despise.

"Hell, Bakersfield IS Texas; and Oklahoma, all rolled into one. It's cotton pickers and oil riggers. They all moved there during the Depression. You can't tell a Bakersfield Okie-Texan from the real McCoy."

"So why fake it?"

"I can tell that you guys come from nice families. It shows." He looked at them through wet swollen eyes. "My folks are just plain old white trash. I'm from so fucking far on the wrong side of the tracks, well, you'd never even find the dump. I never want to see any of my kin again. I'm so ashamed."

Then Tex laughed, nervously, "You think I'm a crude son of a bitch. Shit, I'm couth compared to my old lady and dad. They kicked me out when I was fifteen. A nice old guy in town felt sorry for me. He owned a gas station so I pumped gas and cleaned up around the garage, and his wife, a kind woman, fed me and allowed me to wash my clothes in her sink, use her clothes line and iron. I had a cot in the garage. I picked cotton. Worked out at Kettleman and then the riggers started calling me Tex because I was too ashamed to tell them my name."

Gary poured more scotch from the bottle of J&B. Marshall went to the bathroom and returned with a glass of water and diluted his drink, leaving the glass of water in the middle of the table. Gary and Tex ignored it. They all lifted their glasses and Gary and Marshall sat, staring at Tex.

"The army set up a recruiting office in town. I signed up when I was seventeen. They sent me to the Air Corps gunnery school at Lowry Field, and I told my classmates I was from San Antonio. Got a book out of the library and read Texas history. Lots of things to be proud of, being a Texan, I thought. And I heard them call California guys prune pickers. Jesus, I wanted to be something, to be somebody, to be respected. A gunner sergeant encouraged me to go to the library and learn something about math, you know algebra, calculus, and I studied physics, too. They had courses for anyone interested in learning. I signed up for everything! I studied English, and composition, and got to where I could write a decent paragraph.

"This sergeant was like a big brother, or maybe even a father. Dixie Webb was his name. 'You got a head on you shoulder, kid' he told me. He encouraged me to spend all of my free time in the library, to stay away from bars. Then one day he took me aside and said he'd set things up for me to take a test to see if I could qualify for cadets. And I made it."

"So why'd you keep the Tex moniker?" Marshall asked.

"Hell, I don't know. After CTD, I was sent to SAAC, and every time I'd get some leave I'd go visit the historic places in San Antonio, like the Alamo, and, man, those Texans were heroic figures. Davy Crockett, Jim Bowie, and men like Austin and Sam Houston. And who isn't impressed with the Texas Rangers? It got to where I knew more about Texas history than most Texans."

"So why are you telling us all this stuff?" Marshall asked.

"I guess because the chaplain said to tell a couple of friends about it. He said you'd understand." Tex hesitated and studied the still bewildered countenances of Gary and Marshall. "And before we got to Bad Scheidel, you were my friends. Remember, weren't you?"

"Oh shit, we are still your friends!" Gary said. He stood up abruptly and walked around the room, then returned and sat down again. "But man, you put a load on us, I mean especially on Marshall."

"What would you say if we started calling you Cal, instead of Tex?" Marshall asked.

"God, Marsh, I'd love it!" Tex said.

"Okay, from now on, you are Cal, and if anyone calls you a prune picker refer them to me!" Marshall said.

"Once a guy in a bar called me a loud mouth Texan, and everyone laughed, and I guess I loud-mouthed myself into that kind of character. I'm going to look up every Texan in the squadron and apologize for disgracing our," he paused, "their state."

Marshall cleared his throat and said, "Cal, the day after tomorrow Gary and I are going to take a bunch of ground pounders on a little tour around Germany, to show them the ruins, the Rhine River, and a couple of bright spots. Providing Gary hasn't selected someone else already, would you like to take the right seat?"

Cal looked toward Gary.

Gary raised his fist with a thumbs-up gesture, and said "Meet us at the flight line about nine. Bring your engineer, too, if you like," He patted Cal on the shoulder. "You must feel pretty wrung out, fella?"

"If you guys are willing to trust me, maybe Schloss will change his mind. All I want to do is stay in the Air Corps. It's the only home I have!"

Suddenly Marshall laughed. "Talk about names, look at that bottle, will you. Justerini and Brooks. Can you imagine a Scot named Justerini? I hope his nickname is Scotty!"

CHAPTER 15

▼

SIGHT SEEING FLIGHT

McAdam, and the pilot who underwent the emotional metamorphosis, formerly known as Tex, now answering to Cal, together arranged to check out a B-26 that had been stripped of armament and equipped with seats behind the bomb bay near the top turret. Cal's engineer, Barney, agreed to accompany them on the sight-seeing mission. Because a navigator was mandatory, and Marshall had originally agreed to help set up the trip, the crew was complete.

Four enlisted men had been selected from a dozen potential passengers who had expressed a desire to go on such a flight. Referred to as guests, they were advised to contact the medical officer who provided them with a small dosage of scopolamine, with advice on when and how much of the medication to take to help prevent airsickness.

Much to Marshall's delight, from another navigator he learned that the Special Services Officer had available a suggested flight plan, plus a printed text with information about interesting sights to view from the air, including the widespread devastation from months of bombing.

To his surprise, the briefing officer took him to a wall map and showed him a curving black line across which he should not navigate. It was the Russian Occupation Zone.

"I thought we were supposed to be allies?" Marshall asked.

"Buddy, the soldiers have turned this mess over to the politicians. I understand the Russians fired a few warning shots across the bow of a B-17, near Berlin, carrying a load of sightseers! So, Lieutenant, this is a serious warning. You don't want to get shot down this late in the game!"

"Well, I'll be damned!" Marshall said, "So what happened to all of the Lend-Lease stuff?"

"My friend, you're talking to a soldier that's chomping at the bit to become a civilian. That's too complicated for me to even comment on, but back to your little sight- seeing mission, you won't miss a thing. Ruins, that's all that's left of the fatherland from Bremen to Munich, from Cologne to Dresden. But seriously, there are some interesting castles and things left standing. Now, look at this map," the officer emphasized, "stay away from Erfurt, from Chemnitz, from Dresden and further north, avoid Gottingen, that's right on the border, and anything northeast of there. You must not go to Leipzig, and especially stay away from Berlin. Study that map. Don't get careless and cross over that line or some crazy Russian just might shoot you down."

"Wow, Dresden is practically to the Poland border. Do you remember that afternoon, back in Denain, when the sky was full, from horizon to horizon, with British bombers, on their way to Dresden? It was Valentine's Day and we all thought 'what a hell of a present.'"

"Yeah, I remember, and I understand that over 50,000 civilians died. Most of them smothered to death down in the subways when the fire burned up all of the oxygen."

"Awful way to go!" Marshall said.

"Yeah, and the war was just a few weeks from being over."

"Why was that mission necessary?"

"Politics, I've heard. Number one, we didn't want a nice old, clean, prosperous city like Dresden falling into the hands of the Russkies, and then jolly old England could do without a competitor. You know, fine china. Ha! How's that grab you?"

"Where'd you hear all of that?

"Folks send me a lot of clippings. Ever hear of Westbrook Pegler?"

"No. I do read *The Stars and Stripes*. I read Ernie Pyle, and Bill Mauldin. They're about my speed."

"Well, you know where not to fly, and you have some recommendations about where to go, and that poop sheet from the Special Services Officer is good stuff. He seems to know his history. You're supposed to fly at even numbered altitudes heading north, and odd heading south. Really be alert for other aircraft out there now. Fliers seem to be wandering all over the sky."

"Thanks, we'll try to stay out of trouble!"

By the time Marshall reached the flight line, McAdam and Cal had obtained the chest-pack parachutes for each of the guests, and in case of an emergency, gave them some quick basics on where and how to exit the airplane, how many numbers to count, and that each number should be preceded by saying ten thousand, until it was time to pull the rip cord.

Over and over again they were instructed to touch the nose wheel prior to climbing into the airplane and after exiting to touch it again. They all had headsets, throat mics, and wore warm clothing. As advised by Marshall, each brought a rolled up towel.

They had waited before boarding the B-26 to allow Marshall to brief them all on the trip. When he arrived, McAdam said "Hi," then turned to the guests. "Meet Lieutenant Sunder. We flew a lot of missions together and I guarantee he's the best navigator in our outfit."

"Hi," Marshall said, and grinned at them. "McAdam's a BS artist! We're lucky, real CAVU day. Anyway, here's what we've got planned. We're going to take a kind of a circular route. I was checked out very carefully about where we can't go. The Russians don't want us snooping around in the northeastern part of Germany that they are occupying, but we've plenty to see. We'll be doing as much straight and level flying as possible for your benefit, and we'll do 360's now and then so each of you will get as good a view as possible. I've flown this tour once, but I've some fresh material, so I'll be reading from the text over the intercom.

"We'll be flying at various altitudes, according to what the pilots feel safe. No buzz jobs or acrobatics. McAdam and Cal can do all that stuff, but not today. Our engineer, Barney, has the reputation of being a real perfectionist, and when he says these big engines are okay, that's the final word before taking off.

"Let me give you a quick outline of where we are going and what we expect to see. Crowd around and take a look at my map." Marshall held the map up against the fuselage beneath the pilot's window. "I need a couple more hands to hold this flat." Two of the guests stepped forward and each held a side of the map.

"Okay, here we are at Bad Scheidel. We're going to fly southeast, over Stuttgart, then down near Ulm, and then we're going to fly as close as possible to the base of Germany's highest mountain, the Zugspitze. Don't know if we'll be able see the top of it or not. Supposed to be some of the best skiing in the world. Couple of little villages at the base are untouched by the war, Garmisch Partenkirchen. It's one word that covers both of them. Anyway, if you want to see a bit of Germany like it was before the war, it's good place to take a leave."

Marshall pointed to the map, "Heck, I'm telling you the stuff I'm going to read. But anyway, we're going to circle around and then see a couple of incredible castles."

The curious and adventurous ground pounders all listened carefully, Marshall observed.

"We're not going to bother with Munich. From the air you can't see much now, but it's worth taking a couple of days to make a trip to see the Carillon in the Clock Tower. It wasn't working when I saw it a few weeks ago, but I understand it is now. Most of the old Roman walled city is intact. We won't fly over Dachau, either. Nothing to see from the air. But it is an awful place. You guys owe it to yourselves to go tour it. You'll certainly understand why we got into this mess.

"Anyway, follow my pen and after the castles you'll see, we're going to fly almost due west until we reach the Rhine River, then we'll follow it west all the way up to the Ruhr Valley, then we'll head back southeast towards Frankfurt, to Nuremberg, down to the Eagle's Nest, then finally back to Bad Scheidel. You'll notice there's not a damn bridge standing across the Rhine, and a lot of that thanks to our outfit. Now, see that curved line? That's the part of Germany we can't fly into. That's the Russian Occupation Zone and it's off limits for us. Don't ask why. I was told 'politics'."

"Thank you, sir," a corporal said, "and, I don't know what CAVU means, sir."

"Sorry about that. It means ceiling, altitude, and visibility unlimited. In other words, good flying conditions!"

"Thanks again."

"You're welcome. Now let's climb aboard. I'll show you where you are going to sit for take off and landing, and I'll show you the jacks for your headsets and throat mics."

Marshall evaluated the guests by height and weight. Two of the shorter, slender men were selected to crawl into the nose after they were airborne. The smallest of all of the men was selected to occupy the seat in the stinger. The other man seemed agile and was advised to occupy the top turret. The two men selected to go into the nose were seated in the navigation—radio department, and told to swing the backs of the tall seats toward the nose for both take off and landing. The other men were shown where to sit and advised to use the seat belts. While dangerous, both Marshall and Barney had been accustomed to kneeling in a small area, shoulder to shoulder, behind the pilots, during take off and landing.

It was time to start the engines. Hundreds of times Marshall had observed Frank and Gary participate in a ritual that prepared the B-26 for flight. When satisfied in the performance of both engines, a pilot would give the ground crew the thumbs-up signal to remove the restraining blocks from in front of the wheels. Then they'd taxi out to the designated runway for the take-off.

Once, with a friend, Marshall attended a Roman Catholic funeral. He was fascinated by the timing, the flow, of the liturgy, and it reminded him of the oft-rehearsed procedure of the pilots.

Gary now sat in the first-pilot's seat, and Cal, a qualified first pilot with his own crew, had eagerly agreed to sit in as copilot. Barney, his flight engineer, had joined them.

Whatever idiosyncrasies these two men had were now shed, Marshall observed, when they slid into the pilots' seats. Gary was wild and exuberant, a fun loving flier, but once seated behind the wheel, his demeanor was that of a serious, intent, skilled bomber pilot.

Marshall had never flown with Cal, but his reputation as a competent B-26 pilot overcame the roughneck, boisterous, loudmouth Texan image he'd created. Now his own professionalism quickly revealed itself as he and Gary set about their task. Still, Marshall was both skeptical and apprehensive about Cal's sudden personality transformation.

Satisfied that the purring of the huge engines was satisfactory, Gary taxied out towards the runway upon which they would take off. Cal began to go through their checklist, checking the magnetos, power from each Pratt and Whitney, the propeller pitch governors, position of the cowl flaps, and Gary double-checked the movement of all of the controls. Marshall never tired of watching the team procedure of the pilot and copilot.

They spoke quietly, not needing the intercom, nodded, glanced at one another, and continued to study all of the gauges before them.

To Marshall, it was like two men playing a huge organ, their hands rhythmically moving, checking the fuel booster switch, and then the rudder and then the wing flaps, which were set to desired degrees. Finally satisfied, Gary turned onto the runway, moved the throttles forward and the B-26 with its load of guests began its journey. Gradually the pilots nurtured the speed of the ship from fifty miles per hour to eighty and finally at 130 miles per hour the ship was willing to leave earth. Gary pulled back the wheel and the bomber escaped the bumps of the runway, and when satisfied that the spinning, invisible props were well clear of the earth, Gary signaled with a lift of his hand and Cal retracted the wheels.

Barney and Marshall looked at one another and smiled. The engines were spinning the great propellers and the wind traversed the wings, creating the necessary lift to give them flight.

After the nose wheel and landing gear had been raised and they had flown to two thousand feet and leveled off, Marshall went to the navigator's and radioman's compartment. "Okay fellows, you can unbuckle and follow me. They stood up and smiled at Marshall. "Wow," one of them exclaimed, "That was some steep take-off!"

"Roger," Marshall laughed, "wait until you see our final approach. Now, you guys are going to have to squeeze by Barney and me, so let's head for the nose." Marshall tapped Cal on the shoulder and he nodded and pushed back his copilots seat.

"Kneel down now, pull back his foot pedals and crawl on into the nose. Plenty of room enough for both of you. The ground crew took out the Norden and the fifty-caliber machine gun. When you get in, push the pedals back for Cal." Marshall said to the second man crawling into the nose.

"Okay, Gary, Cal," Marshall said, "Those guys are all set. I'll go back and settle the other fellows."

"Roger," Gary said, " How about a heading?"

"180 to Stuttgart, it's only a few minutes, then take 120 degrees to Ulm. Hell, Gary, you remember Ulm: where the damn bombs hung up."

"Roger," Gary answered. He shook his head and laughed, "Well, go on, get to the back of the bus and get those guys seated. If you're not back in a half hour, both Cal and I will come looking for you."

Cal laughed, and Barney looked back and forth at them, shook his head, then smiled. Barney was still not used to his pilot being referred to as Cal. He'd known him as Tex for almost two years. Marshall walked back through the compartment, then along the walkway through the bomb bay, until he reached the other two passengers, still strapped into the newly installed seats. Quickly he instructed them how to relocate themselves comfortably. The man that climbed into the top turret was a maintenance mechanic and he understood the use of the controls to revolve the turret.

The guest for the tail gunner's position—the stinger—was also familiar with the seating. "Hope you like seeing where you've been. You've a lot of windows back here." Marshall said, and patted him on the shoulder.

"Always wanted to go on a mission, sir, and handle these guns. This is next best."

"Okay. Plug in your headsets and throat mics. I'm heading back to the cockpit." Marshall said, then gave each a casual salute and returned to the pilot's compartment.

Marshall spoke over the intercom, "You guys' in the nose are number one and two, the turret is three and the stinger four. Now, Just say your station number and 'Roger,' and we'll know we're all hooked up."

The stations each answered as directed.

"Where are we?" Marshall asked, as he kneeled between the pilots.

"Passed over Stuttgart and we're on that 120 heading."

Marshall turned to Cal, "Were you on any of those missions to Ulm?"

"Yep. Hate to tell you, Marsh, I was in a flight next to yours that day your bombs got hung up. Strange day for all of us, right?"

"Roger," Marshall answered. "Stay on this heading and we'll end up pretty close to the Zugspitze. Won't be any trouble spotting it in this weather. You guys decide how close you want to get. Might be some strong winds around that mountain."

The mountain rose steeply above the twin villages of Garmisch Partenkirchen. They flew close enough to clearly see the big gondolas, half the size of a boxcar, that were carried along the steel cables between tall towers, stopping at a lodge high on the mountain.

"I'm going to do a shallow 360 so everyone can see the mountain and the villages," Gary said, over the intercom.

"That mountain is about 9000', not high by California standards, but mighty elegant," Marshall said.

"Great view, " Marshall said, "now roll her out to about 280 and take her in as low as you feel safe." Over the intercom he said, "In a few minutes we're going to get a view of two incredible castles, built right on these craggy mountainsides and tops. The quaint one is the Neuschwanstein Castle and building started back in 1869, by King Ludwig II, and it says here he was considered the Mad King, and that the word in English means Swan Rock. Many don't feel he was 'mad', but simply eccentric and very creative for his time. Apparently he just about put Bavaria into bankruptcy building castles, and finally died very mysteriously. You guys be the judge about how mad he was to create and build it.

"Across the canyon is the Hohenschwangau Castle, and my notes call it a more lived-in castle, with colorful paintings and frescoes, and beautiful furnishings. It goes on to say that the Mad King grew up in this castle.

"We're trying to give the guys a good look at those places. We're doing another 360 for them, then we'll need a new heading, Marsh," Gary said.

"Roger." Marshall glanced at his map and continued, "Well, just go east, 90 degrees, if you can get down on the deck, we'll see the little village of Oberammergau. Every ten years the citizens, children, business people, old timers, all get together and perform The Passion Play. Supposed to be a very moving event."

"My notes don't tell me what happens during a war. It falls on even years, like 1930, 1940, 1950, and so on. Started back in the mid sixteen hundreds after a plague wiped out part of the village's population. The residents promised God to put on a Passion Play if they'd be spared another devastating plague.

"We're as low as we dare get without scaring every dog, cat, duck and chicken in town. To heck with the krauts though!" Gary said. " I understand that now we're heading west until we reach the Rhine. What say, Navigator?"

"Roger it is!"

Cal opened his mic, "How are you guys doing? Anything you want to see, we'll turn this baby around and do it again. Just depress that little hand switch and each of you give your station and answer Roger, if you feel okay."

Four okay's came back from the guests.

"I'll point out a few castles as we head up the Rhine. Mostly, what you are really going to see is a terrible honeycomb of bombed out buildings, mile after mile. Cal and Gary will maintain an altitude that is safe, and where you can see something. So, we're heading northwest towards Strasbourg, which is right on the Rhine River, however it is in France. So we follow the river to Speyer, where you'll see the Reichburg Castle, and I'll ask Gary to do a 360 so all of you can get a good look. These castles date back to medieval times and it's hard to imagine how they built them."

As the pilots circled, they also scanned the horizon for other sightseeing flights. Satisfied, Marshall gave them a NE heading and within a few minutes they were over Heidelberg. "My script tells us that this is a thirteenth century castle, and has been a political, intellectual and cultural center. Look at those red tile roofs! Here's where our river at Bad Scheidel, the Neckar, flows into the Rhine. I don't know how close the pilots can get to the river, but watch for the little legendary rock with the girl on it, the *Lorelei Rock*. The myth is she had seven sisters and they were naughty and got turned into boulders in the river which is dangerous to navigation, so beware, *Lorelei* is still there enticing sailors to come close, and of course, crash on the rocks!

"Please circle it guys, then back down the river to Boppard where you'll get another view of one of those ancient castle, and this one is called Marksburg. Guess you've seen all of the pontoon bridges before. If we didn't blow up their bridges, the krauts did it for us as they retreated," Marshall said.

"And now Koblenz and yet another famous fortress, named, wow, Ehrenbreitstein!" Marshall said, "Enough for castles and fortresses. Gary, see if you can spot the Remagen Bridge. Yeah, there it is! What's left of it. Would you guys believe that we tried to knock it down and our bombs kept straddling it, and then finally that's where our troops crossed the Rhine? Only damn bridge we didn't knock down in Germany! It finally collapsed after our guys crossed the Rhine." Marshall laughed and Gary and Cal joined over the intercom.

"We're passing Bonn and then we'll cruise around the Cologne Cathedral so that everyone gets a good view. My notes tell us that it is Gothic, stands 500 feet above the Rhine, and they spent 600 years building it, starting in 1248. You can see the rubble around it, but it's still standing.

"Fellas, I know I'm throwing a lot of facts and stuff at you. I'm going to be quiet while we fly around the Ruhr valley. Cities like Solingen, Dusseldorf, Essen, all of them flattened. There's a town down there called Wuppertal, and one day Gary and I took a jeep from Tegelen and went looking for souvenirs and we saw a fantastic monorail. Naturally it wasn't working, but what a great idea!

"Guys, we aren't going any further north. Assume you've seen enough rubble, so we'll head south to a little village that we can buzz without the town's people being too angry. It's Rothenburg, on the Tauber, a little river. The town is west of Nuremberg, and we'll head over there in a few minutes. My poop sheet tells us that this was a historic town, going back to the time of the Romans, and the town encompasses an old walled city.

"Seems Patton's Third Army guys arrived here and were about to announce their arrival with tanks blasting, cannons roaring, mortars shelling it, all that kind of stuff, when General Patton says, 'Stop this nonsense.' And I'm certain he isn't being quoted verbatim, but anyway, he decided that the town had no military significance, and shouldn't be destroyed.

"I guess the Third Army just rumbled on by, so a very historic old city, surrounding an inner city built by the Romans was left intact, thanks to a General that has a little heart!"

"Nice speech, Marsh," Gary said, "So we'll just circle it, then do a 360, and circle it again so every one can get a good view of one we didn't bomb."

"Roger. Now head due east and in a few minutes we'll see what's left of Nuremberg. There's one huge stadium and I think the field is long enough to land this B-26 in, and my notes say the Nazis used to fill the thing up with thousands of troops and citizens all giving the infamous Hitler salute. Looks like you could fit four football fields into it. Some stadium. Everyone get a good look? We can circle it a couple of times, too." Marshall spoke, referring to the printed sheet he read from, ad-libbing as he went along. "I'm sure all of you guys have kept your subscription to The Stars and Strips paid up, so you know this is where they plan to have the trials."

Marshall was kneeling next to Barney behind the pilots as he read from his notes and occasionally offered a new heading for Gary. As they finished the tour of Nuremberg, and turned south, awaiting a new heading, the pilots and Marshall and Barney heard the chilling cough, the rough sputter of the right engine.

Barney said, "Tex! Cal! That right engine oil temp is going up and the oil pressure is dropping. We're losing power in that engine!"

McAdam glanced at Cal, "Let's cut the engine and feather the prop. What say?"

"Roger! Give that other engine full power first!"

"Roger." McAdam said, "Cal, I've never landed a single-engine. What's your experience?"

"Three times."

"Take over," McAdam said. "You're the captain."

"Roger," Cal said. "Let's get as much air under us fast as that port engine can handle. Full power! Let's see if we can get up to six thousand feet. Marsh, give me a heading to Bad Scheidel."

"255 degrees."

"Barney, how's that good engine sound. Are the readings good?"

"They look good and it sounds good."

"Gary, call the tower. We want a straight-in approach. No traffic patterns. Need the longest runway. Tell them to clear all other traffic. We can't do any evasive action!"

"Sunder. We're going to try to reach five or six thousand feet, and hope to maintain 150 miles per hour. How about an ETA?"

Marshall grabbed his E6B computer, spun it, and then said, "1420 hours, Cal."

"Give that ETA to the tower, Gary."

"Roger."

"Sunder. Better get those guests into their landing positions. Listen close now. They can't hear me. If this baby won't hold altitude at 3000 feet, you all have the option to bail out. What's our true altitude?"

"Terrain varies from 1000 to 1300 feet here on in."

"Barney, how's that engine sound?"

"Everything looks good and sounds good."

"Okay, we're leveling off at 5500 feet. I'm going to throttle back and see how we do. How's it look, Gary?"

"2,600 rpm and 42 inches. Man, this yaw is something else! Want some more trim?"

"Roger," Cal said, and smiled. "You take over while I slide back and let these guys out."

"Roger," Gary said.

"Marsh," Cal said, "we don't want to scare these fellows. If they panic, no telling what they might do, especially here in the cockpit."

"Roger," Marshall responded. In the fraternity of B-26 crews, it was simply a fact. A single-engine could mean they were just one cough from death if the good, remaining engine failed. If the port engine failed, their glide pattern towards the earth would be like a falling boulder, with little chance of escape.

Over the intercom Marshall advised the two men in the nose to crawl out of the nose and to be careful not to touch any of the controls. They moved swiftly and carefully, their eyes wide. Marshall crouched down and snapped the foot pedals back into position for Cal.

"What's going on?" They stared across Cal and out his window and saw the unmoving, feathered blades of the right engine.

"Routine single-engine procedure," Marshall said. "Plenty of power in the other one to get us back safely. Now, I'm going to ask you guys to return to the navigation department and sit just as you did on take off. Fasten your seat belts."

"We aren't going to crash, are we, sir?" the smaller of the two asked.

"No. No. Now just sit down and relax. I'm going back and talk to the others. Understand?"

Both of the passengers nodded. Marshall then walked back through the bomb bay and spoke to the man who had already climbed down from the top turret.

"Lost an engine, eh?" he said. "So *Lorelei* is still doing her dirty work, even up here?"

"Yes. We're doing great with the port engine, as for *Lorelei,* screw her! This ship is in good hands, and, yes, we'll be landing before long, so we want you to get seated, just as you were for take-off."

"Roger, but what if that engine can't do the job?"

"You've flown in 26's before?"

"Yes sir."

"The pilot says if she won't hold at 3000 feet we all have the option to bail out."

"What's down below us, between here and the base?"

"Fields and some forest. Terrain is about 1200 feet."

"Let me know if and when we get to 2700 feet. Below that and I'm bailing out"

"Roger. You're sure you know to use a chest pack?"

"Yes sir."

Marshall then reached the man in the stinger. He was oblivious to the fact that one engine had failed and had been feathered. He turned when Marshall patted his shoulder, then moved out of the stinger, stood up and faced Marshall. Quickly he was advised of the situation and his options. He responded quickly, "No way will I jump out of this airplane! I'll take my chances on you guys landing it."

"I understand," Marshall said. "It's time for you to get into the same position that you were in on take-off. Use that seat belt. We'll be landing in a few minutes. See you on the ground!" Marshall patted the young man on the shoulder and smiled.

Upon returning to the cockpit Marshall paused and spoke reassuringly to the two men seated in the chairs. "Put those seat belts on, fellows," he said." He decided to check the altitude before saying anything about bailing out. He stepped up into the cockpit area and glanced at the altimeter. They were at 3300'.

Marshall put his hand on McAdam's shoulder. Gary turned, smiled, and said, "She's holding. The base is expecting us."

"Gary," Cal said, " I'm going to have my hands full with the wheel and throttle. Procedure is to crank out the trim when we are on the final, and that will be soon. I can see the runway from here."

"Roger."

"Okay, Barney, that port engine has to get us home!" Cal said.

"Prepare for landing," Cal now spoke over the intercom so that the passengers could be advised. It was time to land. The wheels were lowered and locked. The fast, steep descent always excited Marshall. The final approach reminded him of a ride on a roller coaster, when the string of cars creaked up the tracks to the apex, then paused before plunging almost straight down, inspiring screams and yells from the kids. Then suddenly the roller coaster leveled off and started another climb, but with the B-26 the bottom of the descent arrived when the wheels touched down. Marshall heard the tires screech, gave a sigh of relief, and the bomber sped along the runway, until the nose wheel was lowered to the surface of the runway.

Cal leaned back, turned his head and smiled, "Turning this ship back to you, Gary." He said.

"Hell of a landing Cal. I'm proud to fly with you!" Gary said, then taxied the bomber towards one of the maintenance hangers.

Gary cut the good engine and watched as the propeller slowed and stopped turning. "Guess you'd better get our guests out of here," he said.

The two men in the navigation-radio compartment had unbuckled their seat belts and now stood peering into the cockpit. "All right fellows, lower yourselves down to good old mother earth, touch the nose wheel and I'll catch up with you later." As they lowered themselves, the other two passengers arrived from the aft section of the plane and prepared to lower themselves to the ground.

"So much for sight-seeing!" Said the sergeant who had ridden in the top turret. He then looked at Gary and Cal, raised the thumb of his right hand and said, "Nice landing!"

Finally the young man from the stinger lowered himself to the ground. Marshall climbed down just in time to see the top-turret passenger kneel down on his hands and knees and lower his head and kissed the tarmac. When he stood up, he walked to the nose wheel, patted it, and joined the others he said, "You know, luckily, you guys aren't even aware of what a close call that was!"

"You mean 'ignorance is bliss'?" the smallest of them asked.

"You got it, pal!" He said, then continued, "That crate wasn't designed to fly on one engine!"

Marshall then joined them. The top-turret passenger walked up to Marshall and quietly said, "Sir, I see the plane doesn't have a name. My old man's a Greek. Told us kid's, my brother and sisters and me a lot of stories about the myths. You ever heard of *Nausicaa*?

"No," Marshall said, shaking his head, and he became attentive.

"Seems this babe, *Nausicaa* saved Odysseus's butt, you know, helped him. You can read up on it, sir, if you're interested."

"Yea, I'm interested, but go ahead. Repeat those name for me, though"

"O dee see us…and naw see ca."

"I'll try to remember them."

"Before I was drafted I was studying to be a illustrator, you know, magazine covers and such, and well, I'd like to put the pilot's name beneath the window and *Miss Nausicaa* on the fuselage. I know that was done back in combat. And I know, too, those pilots did one hell of a job getting us down in one piece, despite *Lorelei*."

Marshall grinned and laughed. "Well, Gary has had a lot of girl friends, but none called *Nausicca*, but sure, by all means. Do it. Terrific idea!

Marshall pointed to Gary and said, "Lieutenant Gary McAdam was in the left seat. Man, would he be proud!" Marshall then spelled Gary's name aloud for the passenger. "If you accomplish it, let the photo lab know and they can fix all of us up with a shot of the plane."

"Consider it done, sir." He nodded, and rejoined his friends

A ground crew sergeant climbed into the cockpit to join the pilots and Barney. There would be lots of discussions about engine maintenance.

Marshall spoke to the passengers. "I'm going to fix up maps for each of you and attach copies of the little spiel I read. We'd planned on going on down to The Eagle's Nest at Berchtesgaden, but you can do that on another sight-seeing tour. Glad to see none of you had to use those towels!"

"I was too damn scared to get sick, sir!" the top-turret man said, then laughed, and they all joined in the laughter." And then he added, "I saw more sky than anything else. One sight-seeing tour is enough!"

"Well, I'll see you guys later. I've got to file a report," Marshall said.

"So long, sir," the smallest one said, "and thanks!" He saluted, and the other three followed his lead. Marshall returned the salute and departed.

X   X   X

Within the hour, after the fliers had returned to the Officers Quarters, Marshall responded to a knock on his door.

"Lieutenant Sunder?" a corporal asked. They exchanged salutes.

"That's me."

"Colonel Schlosser has requested your presence. I've already advised Lieutenants McAdam and Buzzard, and Sergeant Barnaby."

"When?"

"Well, sir, he didn't stipulate, but I kind of think it's S.A.P."

"Thank you Corporal," Marshall said and each saluted.

Marshall put on a necktie and his Eisenhower jacket and went to Gary's room. He was ready to go, and Cal was waiting. Cal decided to put on a tie, and when he saw Marshall and Gary, he put on his own jacket.

"What's up?" Marshall asked.

"Probably something to do with today's little adventure," Gary said, and Cal nodded agreement. The three fliers reported to the colonel's office and Barney was already there.

"The colonel will see you now," a staff sergeant seated at a desk outside of the colonel's office said, "just go on in."

The four fliers entered the office and the colonel stood up and smiled. "Reports as ordered," Gary said, and the men saluted. The salutes were returned. "At rest, fellows, and grab a seat." The men settled into chairs and waited.

"I want to ask a few questions about your flight today, and that emergency landing. Gary, you're first."

"Sir, we had four enlisted men aboard, ground pounders, who had asked to go on one of the sight-seeing trips. Everything checked out real well before take off, and went well until we were out at Nuremberg, and we lost our starboard engine. Feathered it, and went into single-engine procedure."

"Tex, or I guess it's Cal now. Seems you've a new moniker." The colonel smiled, then continued, "You were flying right seat?"

"Yes sir."

"From the report I just read, you took over and landed. Why?"

"May I answer that, sir?" Gary said.

"Go ahead."

"I've only assisted in one single-engine. That was with Frank back at Lake Charles in O.T.U. I asked Cal how many he'd performed and he said three, so I felt his experience dictated turning over command to him."

"All right, good decision."

Colonel Schlosser then turned to the flight engineer. "You were apparently satisfied with the engine's performance or you'd have recommended aborting the trip?"

"Yes sir," the sergeant said. "Everything checked out perfect. It was very sudden, losing that engine. Thankfully the port engine got us back."

"Lieutenant Sunder, any comments?"

"When we lost the engine I took care of advising the passengers what to do, keeping things calm. Cal told me that if the ship wouldn't hold altitude at 3000 feet, we'd have the option to bail out. I told the men in the top turret and in the stinger. One wanted to jump if we got to 2700 feet; the other wanted to stay aboard, regardless. By the time I got back to the cockpit I learned she was holding at 3300 feet, and we were heading for a runway, I didn't say anything to the other two passengers. Cal told everyone to fasten their seat belts on final."

"Very good." The colonel said, then looked at each one of them. "Now, I want each of you to think carefully before you answer." He paused again. "Do you feel our maintenance is up to standard? In other words, perfection. Go ahead, Gary."

"Well sir, we're not getting in all that much flight time now. Gosh, going back to combat, Frank and I depended so much on Pop's knowledge and his ear. The three of us more or less, double-checked everything. As you know, with engines, Pop was a perfectionist. There are just so many things you can check. I don't feel there's a difference."

"And you, Cal?"

"Pretty much the same, and I don't think there is an engineer in the outfit that can top Barney's professionalism."

"How about you, Marshall?"

"Sir, I've not the ear for the engines, or the depth of knowledge about the Pratt and Whitney's, that the others have. I've just assumed that the maintenance guys would be conscientious. Our lives depend on them."

"Right," the colonel said. "Sergeant Barnaby, what are your feelings?"

"Well, sir, this is going to come as a shock to the others because I haven't had a chance to speak to them. After everyone left the line, except me, the ground crew engineers couldn't start up that port engine. Why, I don't know why. But I'm going to try to find out."

Almost in unison, Gary, Cal and Marshall gasped. They stared at Barney. Then Sergeant Barnaby continued. "Obviously we just missed ending up in the morgue. Frankly sir, I feel there is a laxness that wasn't there when we were in combat. There was never a real load on those engines. Of course, when we lost the one, the other had to really put out. But we didn't have any armament or a bomb load. No sir. I don't feel comfortable. Someplace along the line, those defects should have been caught. And, sir, I'm going to request that I be taken off of flight status. I trust Tex—I mean Cal—but I no longer trust the Pratt and Whitney's."

"Wow!" Colonel Schlosser said, "I appreciate your frankness, sergeant, and I want you to report back to me with any information you learn about those engines. I hope you know that I won't stand for mediocrity in maintenance, or any place else in this squadron."

"Yes sir. Thank you, sir."

"Thanks, gentlemen, for your cooperation. I want to compliment all of you on your teamwork. It got you and your guests back safely," He smiled at them, then added, "Lieutenant Buzzard, Cal that is, I want you to stick around. The rest of you are excused."

The fliers stood, saluted, the colonel returned the salute and they departed.

"Well, Cal, I'm going to level with you. First of all, I am amazed that you and Sunder have buried the hatchet, at least on the surface. And I like the way you and Gary handled that single-engine."

"Well, Gary and I didn't have a lot of choice. We just teamed up and got the job done. As far as Sunder and I are concerned, Captain Waldron paved the way. He says we aren't stuck with our personalities, that we can change. I really think I'm getting my life back to straight and level, sir. I feel the hatchet has been buried. Hope Sunder does."

"That's great. Now Cal, do you know what your AGCT is?"

"All I know is I tested high enough to get into cadets."

"Well, it's 138, and while that's not genius, it's the kind of IQ the Air Corps is going to need."

"Sir, the Air Corps is the only home I have."

"What about your family?"

Cal began to perspire. He ran a finger beneath his collar.

"Go ahead and loosen your tie, Cal. It's hot in here, isn't it."

"Sir, I unloaded on Gary and Marshall. They listened me out. I ran away from home when I was fifteen. I joined the army when I was seventeen. Thank God, a guy from the south, Dixie Webb, took me under arm. He was like a big brother. He introduced me to the library, told me what to read and how to study and concentrate. I quit going to the bars and getting into fights. It was the first time anyone ever gave a damn about me. He told me to apply for cadets, and I made it."

"Relax, Cal. I'm trying to reassure you that the Air Corps needs men like you."

"Sir, I'm so embarrassed about my last name. You see, I was kidded and taunted so much, that I decided to tell people just to call me Tex, and then I had an identity. I became a Texan, sort of."

"Cal, if you don't like your surname you can change it. Lots of people do. Lots of names were spelled incorrectly when people went through immigration. Instead of Buzzard, let's say your name is Bussard. Pronounce it like it's French. Boo-sard. How's that sound?"

"Better, I guess. How could anyone like Herbert Buzzard? But you know, sir, as a kid I thought how great it would have been to have a name like eagle, or hawk."

"Yes, I kind of like Lieutenant Hawk."

"Sir, would the Air Corps allow me to change my name?"

"Probably require a little red tape, but anything is possible. If it's that important to you, I'll send a memo to Personnel and you'll hear from them."

"Colonel Schlosser," Cal said, hesitating, "you know, when you told me to stay, I thought you were going to ship me out someplace."

"No. No. Cal, I'm pleased with the way you handled that single-engine. That's the main reason I wanted you to stay, and also, if you put in a request to make the Air Corps a career, I'll recommend you. I also feel you've made a lot of progress with some of your personal problems. Just let Captain Waldron take over where Dixie Webb left off."

"Yes sir."

"And keep me posted on that name change request."

"Yes sir," Cal said. He stood, came to attention, saluted, and after the colonel returned his salute, he executed a military about-face and strode from the office, erect, his shoulders back and his chin up.

CHAPTER 16

▼

A BULL SESSION

Often in the early evening after dinner, many of the fliers congregated in a lounge adjoining the main living room area, not far from the bar, where they smoked cigarettes and cigars, and a few smoked pipes. In the lounge was a piano and generally there was one of the fliers who could sit down and play by ear. A sing-along of popular songs would occur, and sometimes the flier might play a classical composition. Sometimes Gershwin or Irving Berlin, or Hoagie Carmichael tunes were requested, or the pianist might play one of his own favorites, quite often going from song to song without interruption. Others might go to one of the small desks and write a letter, desiring the presence of others in the room, rather than retreating alone to their rooms.

Several fliers congregated in a large booth, with a high, padded back and an oblong table in front of it. Eight fliers could comfortably sit there. They drank beer and talked about what they were going to do when their points came up. Only a few had indicated a desire to pursue a military career. They talked of baseball and football and of their conquests with women. Because most wanted to avoid controversy, politics and religion were avoided, but sometimes that was unavoidable, and if the arguments and beliefs became heated, many of the fliers would leave the table.

All of them seemed to like the taste of the German beer that was now available, and they drank it from large glass steins.

"Hey, Gary," a flier said, "hear you pulled off a good single-engine with a load of tourists."

Another added, "Come on! Any single-engine you can talk about was a good one!"

A pilot at the table raised his stein and said, "Hear, hear!" and his toast was followed by all of those at all of the tables!

Marshall was interested to see how Gary would respond, and he was pleased when Gary said, "Hell, I just helped! Cal, here," and he nodded to Cal, " he took over. I asked him to. He's had a lot more experience with single-engines. The credit goes to Cal!"

"Well, nice going Tex, or Cal, or whatever you're going by these days!" A flier said, raising his glass. "But, friend, I'm still not used to this 'Cal' moniker yet!"

"Team effort," Cal responded. " Only way we could have lightened our load was to ask Marsh and our guests to bail out!"

"Hell," Another flier exclaimed, " Marsh would have been easy to replace, but I don't know about those ground pounders."

"No way," Cal said, "His heading were right on the button. And Marsh had our guests convinced we enjoyed flying single-engine!"

Marshall smiled, nodded, then looked at the group of officers, searching faces, then said, "Hey Jackson, weren't you a high school teacher?

Jackson smiled at Marshall, "Still am, Marsh, They are keeping my job open for me. Why?

"Ever hear of Odysseus and a girl named Nausicaa ?" I think I pronounced them right."

"At Madison High, Homer's, *The Iliad and The Odyssey*, were required reading."

"Not at Chico," Marshall laughed, "But what about them, Jackson?"

"Well, you ought to read the books, Marsh, but as I recall Odysseus, after wrecking his raft, survived drowning and this pretty girl helped him, then nursed him back to health before he completed his Odyssey, as Homer called his adventure."

"Thanks, Jackson," Marshall said and raised his stein. Jackson acknowledged and raised his. Marshall wondered if the illustrator would really paint McAdams name on a B-26. He turned back to the on going conversation about the single-engine procedure.

A pilot got up and went to the bar and returned with two large, full pitchers of beer. "This round's on me, Cal."

"Thank you, partner," Cal said and grinned at those around the table. They were silent for a few awhile, then one asked, "Are these ships getting weary, getting too much flight time on them, or are the ground crews getting bored, you know, slackening off a bit on maintenance? Those Pratt and Whitney's need a lot of tender love and care."

"I think we're all getting bored as hell, waiting for our points to come up, unless a guy is making the military a career. Most of us want to go home and get on with our lives," a pilot named Sol Schneider said.

"So what does the future hold for you, Sol?"

"My folks own a little furniture store in L.A.. I'd like to expand it. Get into the furniture manufacturing business, you know, dining room sets, living room furniture, couches and chairs, that kind of stuff. That G.I. loan sounds interesting."

"Lots of Jewish families are in the furniture business in Chicago, Sol," Gary said. " You move to Chicago and Sean and I will build you a nice big brick building. You put it out to bid, get three bids, then let me see them, and I'll guarantee we'll be lowest!"

Sol said, laughing, "You guys come on out to L.A. and we've got a deal! And no lousy snowstorms to fuss with in the winter! Can you handle seventy-degree weather in the middle of January?"

"You know, by God!" Gary said, "That's not such a bad idea. I bet my brother Sean would go for it. We could get the folks out of Chicago, hell, they're in their fifties. Winters are getting rough on them. Time to slow down and warm up."

"Talk about building something. What the devil is going to happen here in Germany?" Marshall said. "Why, you could fill Death Valley with just the ruins we saw today. There must be a circle, a hundred miles across, of just rubble, just ruins!"

"Hell, give the Krauts twenty-five years and they'll have the whole damn world involved in another war. That's all they understand! Clean up, tool up, and fight someone, all for the Deutchsland!" a pilot said.

"Sure," another said. "And we'll back them, and the Jews will loan them the money at high interest rates. What about that, Sol?"

Sol laughed, "Probably a lot of truth in what you say. But if any of these horror stories we're beginning to hear are true, well, I have my doubts."

"Jesus, I think Sol has got to be right. I got stuck with the job of taking the local people over to Dachau. Pretty horrible. They say it couldn't be true, but I've heard there are more places like that. I don't know what the hell to think. It made me sick, and I did some dumb things." Cal glanced at Marshall, then continued, "Now, I honestly don't think these Bad Scheidel people were aware of anything like that going on; most of them anyway."

"You know what baffles me?" a pilot spoke up, " Why in the hell didn't some of these so-called good Germans get together and knock off that bastard Hitler before he led them into this chaos?"

"I've read that several groups of high-up officers tried, but the fucking Gestapo, and the SS infiltrated everything. The rebels, just anyone that tried to object, ended up getting shot or hanged. The Gestapo had it all wired! Wasn't religion forbidden?"

"Sure it was forbidden, and I remember those Newsreel shots of them burning books. That's scary. That kind of control."

Another pilot left the large table and returned with two more pitchers of beer. "I think it's a lot of horse shit to even think that all of these so-called good Germans didn't know exactly what was going on. They just wore blinders, or didn't give a damn!"

"I guess I just don't want to believe that's possible," Marshall stammered.

"Darn it, Sol, " a flier asked, "speaking of religion, when are you Jews going to give Jesus some recognition?"

"Recognition? Respect? We admire him, but Jews don't believe he's the Messiah. Come on, you don't think Jews are sensitive about Jesus? Ever know a Jew named Judas?"

Then a pilot spoke, "Hey wait a minute, just look at the mess that Jewish carpenter got himself into." Then he continued, "Darn it, Sol. Jews refuse to recognize a Messiah even when he does show up. God has already sent Jesus, Ghandi, Lincoln and now Einstein."

"Einstein?" Marshall asked. "What do you mean by that?"

"The atomic bomb! What else?" The pilot said, " The Jews are still waiting for the first coming, the Christians are waiting for the Second Coming, but here he is! Right on earth now. He's solved mankind's dilemma. We can now blow the entire world into oblivion. He's given us that power! We now possess the power, the heat of the very sun. We own fire! I wonder if we can handle it?"

"Scary thought," Gary said.

"No," The pilot shook his head and continued. "We'll either get along with one another or blow up the whole damn world!" He sipped the beer from his stein.

"God must have had an off-day if he created man in his own image. Wow, look at what mankind has done to his creation!"

"You know," a pilot offered, "I think God realized he screwed up, so he sent us Jesus to bail us out!"

"Guess you're going to have to shape up, Gary. Judgment Day might be near!" a flier said, and laughter followed.

"It has always amazed me," a pilot said, "how this one little man, a nice-guy Jew, preached a lot of wisdom, got picked on, gets himself crucified, forgives everyone while they are killing him, then appears from the grave, then disappears. Now a whole lot of people had to believe all of that stuff really happened for the world to change the calendar!"

"So, you believe in the Bible. It's that simple. It's called faith." a bombardier-navigator volunteered.

"Hey, I think the Bible is a great book, but it was humans, like you and me, that wrote it. I never have understood why some insist that there had to be a first chapter and a last chapter. What editor was around to wrap it all up and say, 'Okay boys, that's it. Put it to bed!'"

"Don't be sacrilegious."

"Hey, my friend, I don't want to offend anyone, however, you explain, or rationalize, why the Mormons can't write another chapter, or the Christian Scientists. Hey, Sol? Does your Bible have a New Testament attached to it?"

"Come on, lighten up you guys, and enjoy this brew," a pilot said.

"Okay, and I'll shut up after I propose that from here on we change the calendar again. Last year they dropped the big bomb, so let's call this Einstein Two! Or, if you prefer, we can call this year, Atom Two."

"I like that!" Cal said, "and I bet it'll be Atom Three before your points come up. Come on, get the cards out. How about some poker or bridge or black jack?'

Then Sol said, "Count me out fellows. I'm going to my room and study the New Testament."

"New testament?" Marshall said. "What do you mean by that, Sol?"

"I was afraid no one would ask!" Sol said, laughing, "Didn't any of you jocks wonder why I always went to Captain Waldron before a mission?"

"He took care of all of us," a pilot said.

"And none of you ever noticed I didn't wear a yarmulke?"

"That little skull cap? Come on, Sol, what are you trying to tell us?"

Sol laughed, "Cal, I'm a Christian. It's as simple as that."

"You've got to be joking."

"Not about something as serious as my religious belief. I was born a Jew. I was raised a Jew. I had to experience a Bar Mitzvah, but down deep I was never really convinced that all of those Jewish disciples, you know, the apostles, that believed in Jesus, could be all that wrong. And I don't believe in the 'eye for an eye' way of solving things. So, back in college, I fell in love with a Christian. Now, I've a choice. Break my mother's heart or break Laura's mother heart. So I broke my mother's heart, but when we have children she'll forgive me. Dad said he understood my feelings, that Jewish men have to take a lot more shit in society than Jewish women."

"I never heard of a Jew becoming a Christian before," Cal said.

"Come on, Cal! Jesus was a Jew! Paul was a Jew. Lots of people change their thinking," Sol said. "I bet there are Protestants right here who were raised Roman Catholic, and vice versa. I know a Christian who is seriously studying Zen Buddhism. And there's another thing. Even in L.A., which isn't exactly a melting pot, I got tired of being called a kike, a yid, a dirty Jew, and so on. So my kids won't have to go through that crap. I believe there's hope for this dumb world through Christianity. Judaism is too passive, and so is Buddhism. Muslim is scary. My decision wasn't a hasty decision!"

"I just don't see how you can change your religion," a pilot said. "How can you justify it?

"Don't you think you inherit your religion?" Sol asked and looked around at the silent group of fliers. "How many of you fellows took a part in making a decision to be a Protestant or a Roman Catholic or a Baptist or Presbyterian? You became what your parents are.

"I'm a Jew by inheritance. As for justification, why you can turn to the Bible and justify a time for anything, from war and killing, to making peace. Through the Bible you can justify anything! And then the Preachers and Rabbis and Priests set about trying to explain the mystery of it to us. If you aren't familiar with Ecclesiastes, go read it, especially Chapter three. It's in the Old Testament. You see, I decided that there was a time to embrace, so I embraced Jesus. This Sol joined the other Saul, S-a-u-l," he spelled out the name, "who became Paul: my decision. Okay?" Sol slid his chair back from the table, arose and began to walk towards the door.

"Hey Sol, are you going to change your name?" a flier asked, "like the movie stars?"

"How does Patrick Schneider sound?" Sol said, smiling. "That could pass for an Irish-German, couldn't it?" He laughed again and said, "You guys get on with your card game!"

"I think Sol is one of the few around here who is without prejudice," a navigator said.

"Everyone is prejudiced, and I guess, some in a mean, crude sort of way," a pilot said.

"Why do you feel that way?" Marshall asked. "Little town I grew up in had all races and colors and creeds and we all got along fine. Only meanness I saw was when some bullies beat up on this poor kid because he was a queer."

"You want to know about prejudice?" a pilot spoke. "You guys know I'm from Brooklyn. Red Hook area, and we've every nationality in the world there. We leave each other alone pretty much of the time, but how do you like this? For the senior prom, I asked this girl, who was mostly Negro, I guess, dark skin, curly, but not real kinky hair, really pretty, nice build and her voice was so pretty, larks would fly in from Jersey just to hear her sing." He sighed, "So my folks really objected! Just because she was a Negro. I told them I'd make my own decisions about who I dated. Golly, I thought I'd be disowned. But, when I went to her house to see if she'd be my date, and to find out what kind of a corsage she'd like, her old man wouldn't even let me in the house! So she cried, and her mother was embarrassed, and the next day at school she apologized and said her father felt the colored community would hold it against him, if he allowed their daughter to go out with a white guy!"

"So what did you do?"

"I went alone and we danced together and none of the kids thought a thing about it, even her escort, a nice colored guy didn't object. But later,

I guess my mom thought she was educating me or something, she sat down next to me with a foot high stack of National Geographic magazines. 'Son,' she said, 'many nationalities are noted for their contributions to civilization, or culture. In these magazines we can see pictures of the Parthenon in Athens, and read what the Greek scholars thought, and the Egyptians built huge pyramids, and the Chinese built the famous wall, and beautiful temples, as did the Japanese, and both created languages, and of course the Romans—well, where do you start or stop with their creations? The Germans and Austrians are noted for their great music, languages, and the French, they created the model of our Statue of Liberty, and the Eiffel Tower, and produced so many writers, and artists. And in India there's the Taj Mahal. The same for Spain and Mexico. But not Africa.'"

"Stupid me." the pilot said. "So what are you trying to prove, mom? And she replied, 'Son, so far, none of these kinds of contributions, these creations, have been unearthed in Africa. Your father and I just feel they are, well, that the Negro people are sort of still evolving in those areas. In time, they'll catch up, you know, but it'll take time. Honestly, Son, we don't dislike the colored people. We're just not comfortable around them."

A pilot chimed in; "Those Africans didn't live on a damn rock pile like the Greeks, or in a desert like the Egyptians. They had all of the food they wanted for the taking, fruit or fowl, fish or antelope, buffalo, anything they needed for food and clothing. They hunted and harvested. The Greeks and the Egyptians sat around starving, drinking wine and thinking big thoughts. The Negroes weren't put into that position."

"So?" a flier said.

"So, a Negro in the good environment we have will flourish. Look at Booker T. Washington, one of the first to get some recognition for his gray matter. Or take music: start with Nat King Cole, for real pleasure, or Louie Armstrong, or look to the high brow stuff with Paul Robeson. You've got to be intelligent to be musical. Get it?"

Another flier spoke, "Come on, who gives a damn. As far as Negroes go, I'll make my judgment according to character, just like I do with a Mexican or a Chinaman. And I'd love to fly along side any of those Tuscaloosa pilots."

"Ha!" a pilot grunted, "Those guys just might reject you."

"Touché! They damn well might."

"Relax! Let's not get upset. Come on, someone play that friggin piano, or get the cards out," a navigator urged.

Marshall spoke, "Hey Sol, I'll bet you a beer that both of the families involved with that senior dance fiasco were nice Christian families!"

Sol stood up. "Good night, fellows, I really am going to study my New Testament."

"This is getting too damn serious for me, "Gary said. "See you all later, I've got to pick up my laundry."

"Laundry hell. You know what that guy is after!" a pilot said, grinning.

"Deal me in for whatever we're playing." Marshall said. "Goodnight Gary."

"Sunder," a flier volunteered, "that damn pilot of yours is a walking hard-on!"

Six fliers remained to play poker. The others either stayed to read, or visit with a friend, or write letters.

"Goodnight Sol!" Cal said, then looked back to the card players and added, "That Jew is really a good Christian!" They all chuckled.

A flier picked up the deck of cards and said, "Okay, I'll shuffle the damn deck. Cut them, first ace deals. Dealer put in six chips. Let's play!"

CHAPTER 17

▼

MORALE

Colonel Schlosser stood erect, and while his bearing was relaxed, his stature commanded respect. He glanced around the room at the gathering of officers he'd called together. They sat at a long table facing each other. Most of them had been with him, under his command, for well over a year. A few of them had signed up for additional duty, but that wasn't a true indication that they wanted to make the military a lifetime career. For the most part they were ground pounders, as the fliers called them, and thus hadn't earned enough points to return to the States. The married officers had been promised that if they'd sign up for an additional year, their spouses would be moved to Bad Scheidel. They sat and chatted, smoked cigarettes, and a few had brought hot coffee in white mugs. A few brought lined note pads and pencils which they placed in front of them on the long table.

"Gentlemen," the colonel said, "the general has asked the squadron commanders to discuss with their staffs the subject of morale. Before coming to this meeting I asked each of you to be prepared to comment on the subject. So, Captain Waldron, Martin, why don't you get the ball rolling."

The chaplain started to rise, and the colonel said, "Relax Martin, let's keep it informal."

"Yes sir, Colonel and Officers," the chaplain said, and sat back down. He began to pass out sheets of paper with typed information. "What I'm going to discuss is covered here," and he held up one sheet. "First of all you'll be pleased to know that our squadron choir is growing and while we are losing a few voices as men are shipped out, we are inviting the new arrivals to join us. The other squadrons are doing the same and Father O'Donnell and I are already working on plans for a Christmas and an Easter program, combining all groups. We're encouraging a couple of WACS and nurses, so we want a real variety of voices. If you haven't had a chance to hear the barber shop quartet you are really missing some fun. They appear at announced gatherings and they'll be joining the visiting entertainers such as the Glenn Miller Band. "Very good, Martin," the colonel said. "Anything else?"

"Probably should have mentioned this first. We are having Bible study groups, and we'll cover the Old Testament as well as the New. We've already got quite a few men signed up. And, progress with the library is excellent. We've hired local talent, in this case one of the maids, Frau Schuttenhelm, and she is a competent, hard worker. Books should be coming in from all over the world very soon." The chaplain looked around the table and back at Colonel Schlosser. "That's about it, sir."

"Excellent, Captain Waldron," the colonel said, smiled and added, "It's important to hire as many of the German people from the community as possible. However, make certain that Intelligence, G2, checks them out thoroughly. We won't hire any former Gestapo or SS members.

"Okay, let's hear from our Special Services Officer, Captain Parks."

"May I stand, Colonel?"

"Certainly. Proceed."

"Well, guys, we've got quite a contingent of jocks right here in our own squadron and when you combine all of the squadrons, we can field a hell of a football team, or a track and field team. I understand there's going to be planned competitions all over the American Occupation Zone.

"Okay, one of you guys, imagine you're going down for a long one! Here it comes!" He then gazed at an imaginary football player sprinting down the sidelines, and he leaned back, coiled, then threw an imaginary football into space. "Stretch for it! Wow, he caught it. Touch down!" He turned to the colonel who was laughing aloud. Then Captain Parks looked at his smiling audience; "Okay guys, get the picture?" He then slapped his fist into the open palm of the other hand, "Would you believe we've got a former baseball big leaguer right here in the squadron, Don Russell, and he's volunteered to coach baseball." The captain then swung an imaginary baseball bat, said "Smack! Look at that ball go. A home run for sure."

The captain again studied the smiling group of officers. "You know what?" he started, "Why right out there in a flat field near the runways we're grading a nice banked 440 track around a football or soccer field. And a local Kraut just got out of the Wehrmacht and he turns out to be a member of a championship soccer team, back before the shooting started, and he's eager to teach our guys soccer. I hope he gets a clearance from Intelligence. And we're setting up posts with backboards and nets on one of the unused taxiing strips." He then stood back, twirled an imaginary basketball in his hands, paused and deftly threw the imaginary ball, and watched it arch upward and descent through the net. He made a loud swishing sound, turned to the colonel and said, "I was always good with free throws!"

"Well, Captain Parks, at least you are getting a workout. Your morale must be good. Anything else?"

"As a matter of fact we have located a former pro golfer. He ran the shop at a big country club in Florida, had a stable of caddies, and is eager to teach. He's got his own set of clubs, believe it or not, and says he can get a load of clubs from the States if we give the okay" Captain Parks turned, addressed an imaginary golf ball, his arms extended downward, gripping his hands together and then performed a graceful golf swing back and down and through, ending up with his hands high and his weight balanced on the toe of his right foot. "How about that? You guys ever witness a hole in one before?"

"You're too much, Parks. That it?" the colonel, asked, while most of the audience laughed.

"Just one more thing, sir. This winter a lot of the guys took off and went down towards Austria to a quaint little Bavarian village. Two towns, actually, and called Garmisch-Partenkirchen. Fabulous skiing and skating and, a bonus, lots of nurses love the place. As a matter of fact there is a former Luftwaffe pilot giving skiing lessons. Graduation is a trip down the Zugspitze, one steep mountain. It's still not too late to take advantage of it. Probably like Germany was before the war."

"Thanks, Captain Parks. Your enthusiasm is contagious. And seriously, a word to all of you and to your men, we've all got to get onto an exercise routine." He looked around the room.

"Okay, how about some words of wisdom from the Finance Officer. Captain Aftuck, it's all yours." He looked at the heavy, over-weight officer, who was nearly bald. His large, mostly red nose always inspired stories about his binges.

"Yes sir. As you know, I've been concerned ever since we left England about the money exchange travesty that is going on. When we were in France and in Holland, the men have been paid with American dollars and the first time they get a leave they head for Brussels or Li`ege or Paris and find the illegal money-traders. They take a couple of hundred dollars with them and come back to my office and deposit five hundred or more in their account depending, on the exchange rate. It's still going on. It's a form of stealing!"

"So, now what do you recommend, having covered this subject with you several times!" the colonel said.

"Okay, okay, " the captain said, shaking his head, revealing his frustration. "I realize we can't have every man trailed by an intelligence officer, but with all of this expensive investment in keeping up morale there ought to be more emphasis on morals."

"Captain, I'm going to leave the morals equation to the squadron chaplains, however, I want everyone here to know that while we don't condone this money exchange situation, our own G2 has their eyes on really large swindlers. You may not know that a couple of Supply Department men lined up a boxcar full of butter, in Sweden, imagine, and tried to sell it on the black market for something like fifty thousand dollars. I've heard of large deals in precious gems being thwarted. So, on the large scale, something is being done. Anything else, Captain Aftuck?"

"Since you asked, yes sir." The captain seemed to swell up, then proceeded, "Seems to me we're spending a lot of the American tax dollars on this so-called morale problem. Aren't these men supposed to be soldiers, as well as fliers? I say they need to be marched and drilled and involved in strenuous exercise, calisthenics. Wear 'em out, and they won't need to be pampered. Then they'll sleep well, and they won't get into mischief. I don't think we should be spending American dollars building a country club for them. I, for one, am unimpressed by the sophmoronic antics of Captain Parks."

"Well, I did ask for your opinion, didn't I. Thanks." the colonel said, unsmiling, looking at the faces around the table. Most of them looked down at their scratch pads and a two of them noticeable shook their heads as if in disagreement. "And Captain Aftuck, my earlier comment about exercise includes everyone in the Finance Office."

Captain Aftuck stared at the colonel. Suddenly the Special Services officer, Captain Parks, jumped up, and pointed at the Finance Officer, "Know what, Aftuck, we're looking for a guy for our track and field team to catch the javelin. Why don't you come out and see if you can qualify?" Captain Parks then posed with an imaginary javelin took a couple of steps toward

Captain Aftuck and went through the motions of heaving a heavy object over Captain Aftuck's head into space. Laughter filled the small room.

"Knock it off, Parks," the colonel said. "Anyone ever order you to do laps around a track?'

"Yes sir, sorry sir," the captain grinned. "Way back in O.C.S., and I had to carry a damn M-1 over my head while I was running! Terrible punishment. Terrible. I do apologize."

"Okay, back to reality. Lieutenant Wilson. Stand up, please, Robert. Have you built that little red school house yet?" The colonel nodded to another officer.

"Well, sir, believe it or not I've already located three officers, and one enlisted man who have high school teaching credentials. We're setting up a Three R's program, and we are going to be able to teach beginning French. Most of the fliers have a background in math, however we've quite a few enlisted men who couldn't qualify for cadets because of their eyesight or some other physical requirement, and they are eager for the math, algebra, and geometry we're offering: And how about this? I've a Lieutenant Rowe who taught history and is writing a book about why the Germans are such a war-oriented nationality."

"Really?" the colonel said, evidencing surprise. "Anything you can enlighten us on at this stage?"

"Well," Lieutenant Wilson started, then took a deep breath, "Very briefly, and you understand this is coming from Lieutenant Rowe." He paused and again looked at the colonel.

"Proceed, Robert."

"He believes that over a period of several hundred years, every hostile raiding party from the Vikings, to the Celts, the Romans and the Spaniards, from the Greeks to the Turks, just everyone moving into Germany and Austria, and even what is now the Russian Zone, well, they all used the Rhine River whether coming or going. And these tribes were all skilled warriors, fighting and killing and raping the fair maidens. And with them they brought all of the highly skilled craftsmen needed to equip the warriors to fight and rob and steal and pillage and loot. They had their metal-smiths and carpenters and riggers for their ships, and they had their own blacksmiths and cooks and for entertainment they brought along their storytellers, the poets and troubadours, musicians, you know, I mean every one that tagged along was the best in his specialty. So, all of these conqueror genes were spread around Germany especially, resulting in a species, that's what Rowe calls them, that has resulted in these obedient, intelligent, and dedicated fighting men and women." He paused, looked around the room and back at the colonel, "So, that's how the modern German evolved, according to Rowe."

"I'd like to see a copy of his book. Then I might be able to explain to my grandparents why we Schlossers are such trouble makers." The colonel laughed. "Anything to add?"

"Nope, sir, that's about it. And I'll tell Rowe."

"Gentlemen, I've already had a meeting with Maintenance, and as you might imagine the emphasis was on keeping up the same high standards we had during combat. So, now I know we'd all like to welcome our Flight Surgeon, Captain Courtright." The colonel nodded toward the medical officer.

"Colonel, and Officers," Captain Courtright began, "Thank God we're not having to patch up these kids, digging flak out of them, and trying to sew them back together after crashes and tending to burns. I think you all know about those castrations, and we've learned G2 apprehended a couple of former SS troopers. In fact, we think a man that was hanged out at that farm, the pig farm, well, they don't know yet if it was suicide or murder. The farmer led the M.P.'s to the scene. God knows we don't want another castration in our surgical department.

"Presently, we still have the problem of venereal disease and I do recommend that every person on this base be ordered to review the films on VD. Yes, I know they are repugnant, but it may keep some of these kids from catching something, and of course, passing it around. The policy of no one, regardless of rank, leaving this base without a supply of condoms and pro kits, should be enforced. I've three cases of gonorrhea we're treating with sulfa, and a case of syphilis that we're trying to control with gold shots, but we're sending this man home for treatment. Two tragedies: Another man walked into a spinning propeller, and there's been a suicide." The medical officer paused and looked towards the colonel. "Schloss and I have been having some bull sessions of our own about this morale thing. Do you want me to hit on some of it?"

"Please continue."

From the audience a question was asked, " Hey Doc, is that object we're to take with us the same as a cundrum?"

There was quiet laughter and another officer spoke up. "Murphy is from Boston, doctor, and when he drove his yellar caw taking his date to down to the sea showa, he stopped first at the drug stowa and went up to the druggists winder and asked for a rubba."

More laugher followed and then Lieutenant Murphy stood up and said, " Like hell, I asked for a dozen *Sheiks!*"

"Sure Murphy, and you wear your orange sweater to the St. Patrick's Day Parade!"

"Okay, okay you fellows," Captain Courtright said, also laughing, "I don't give a damn what you call them, but take them and use them!"

"You started to say…" Colonel Schlosser said, looking at Captain Courtright.

"Yes sir, back to reality, personally, I feel we're on the right path with the programs covered by Captain Parks, plus the school house and the chaplain's music and Bible study. Schloss has been very emphatic, or maybe I should say understanding, about the fact that he understands completely that these men in the Bomb Group are basically civilians. They are not career soldiers. Some were drafted, some volunteered, but it makes no difference. They've served their country and they have little patience with the delay in getting back home, whether to a wife and family, a business or college, or whatever. As I hear it from those who come into my office, they've had it up to here with politicians who are suggesting priority for the commercial use for the fleet of Victory Ships and Liberty Ships, rather than sending our troops back to the States. I've heard that the Canadian veterans in England are really getting restless: even rioting. Can you imagine being away from home eight years: I mean if you're not a career soldier or sailor?" Captain Courtright paused and again looked towards Colonel Schlosser.

He continued. "Oh, hell, we can beat this subject of morale to death, however, I feel we owe it to these young men to keep their morale up, regardless of the expense. And, incidentally, I'd like to see a show of hands indicating how many of you are making the military a career. I'll start. I'm going home to the practice my good father is maintaining for us in Mattoon, Illinois, just as soon as I've enough points." None of the officers raised a hand to indicate a desire to make a career of the military. It was obvious that Colonel Schlosser, a West Pointer, was a professional soldier.

"Thank you, doctor and professional civilians. I appreciate your time and your reports, which I'll pass on to the general. In the meantime, please remember and emphasize to those in your charge, fraternization is still a no-no. And one more thing, I'm very nervous about the civilian attitude that is beginning to show. While the official shooting has stopped and these civilian-minded fellows are willing to meld back into a peacetime existence, it can be dangerous. Some of these local frauleins are pretty enough and have been starved, not only for affection but also for our luxuries, meaning coffee, chocolate and tobacco. So our civilian minded boys are vulnerable.

"To give you an example, a couple of fliers took off on their bikes to take pictures and explore the countryside. I'm not saying they were looking for female companionship, but what did happen is this. They found an abandoned farm and went into the barn to look around for souvenirs. Typical curious Americans. So one of them noticed an oil can with a long spout and a plunger handle. Naturally he depressed the handle, and it was a booby trap left by the Nazis, or by one of those SS bums we've yet to capture, that were stopped back when the bridge was bombed. So the kid lost his right hand and his right eye. Please pass this fact around to everyone. It can be very hazardous off of this base. It's only been a couple of weeks since a couple of Non-Com's got in their cups and took a jeep out for joy ride. Unfortunately they didn't drive one with the steel pole welded in front of the bumper, and I guess it's common knowledge that a taut piano wire across the road they chose, damn near beheaded both of them. They died. So, occupation duty means to stay alert!" A hush fell over the room and the officers squirmed in their chairs.

"Any questions?" The colonel asked. No one spoke. "Okay then, I'll buy you all a round at the club. See you there."

CHAPTER 18

▼

CASTRATION

Frau Greta Klistoff was a widow. Her husband had been killed early in the war. About a fourth of a mile from the Neckar River, her small home was set back thirty feet from a cobblestone lane joining the main highway crossing the Bad Scheidel Bridge. As a war widow, Frau Klistoff received a meager stipend from the Nazi Government. To supplement her income she washed and ironed and mended the clothes of the American soldiers and airmen.

She had a few fruit trees, but they were now dormant and the earth was nearly frozen, still too cold to plant a garden. She was appreciative of the payment arrangement with the Americans. The German mark was worthless. If they paid her with American dollars she was satisfied because the money was negotiable with the merchants in Bad Scheidel. Though she never suggested it, she was delighted when one of the Americans brought coffee, sugar, and cigarettes or candy bars. These she could use to barter for coal and flour and cheese and potatoes and even sausage. She kept some of the coffee and sugar, her only luxury.

The young flier, a customer, reminded Greta of her husband. His laugh and bravado made her think of Karl, and was a reminder of her loneliness. This evening she invited the flier to sit beside her at the wooden table, where they both sipped hot coffee. He tried to communicate, using an English-to-German translation booklet. He didn't realize how fluent she really was with the English language, however she felt he might stay longer if she listened to his efforts. She'd nod and say yes, then smile, when he read and then he would laugh and again look up for her approval.

The four burly men did not bother to knock on Frau Klistoff's door. They entered as an implosion, the cold winter air blasting in behind them, surprising and bewildering the flier and Greta. The men were dressed in the dark, well-worn clothes of farmers. About them was an obnoxious body odor, as if they'd not bathed in weeks.

"What do you mean by this! It's not what you think! What do you want!" Greta screamed at the men. The largest of the men sneered at them and then with his burly arm swept the tea cups and sugar bowl off of the table. The cups and saucers clattered, broke and the man walked across them cracking and smashing them as he reached for the woman.

"My God," she screamed, "My china, my cups! My sugar! Are you crazy? What is the meaning of this?"

"Grab that bastard," one of the men yelled and two of them reached out for the flier, but he dodged and struck out, swung madly with both arms, directing his clenched fists, smashing them into the jaw and face of one and then the other, as they roared in anger, feeling the pain and frustrated that they could not deter him. A third tried to tackle the flier, but he kicked him solidly in the face and the man growled in pain and again attempted to tackle him as he flailed away with both fists, jabbing and fighting as he'd been taught, striking them, and kicking at the other. The fury of the resistance of the flier stunned the men momentarily.

"Get that whore first," the big man yelled and the flier looked away from his opponents and with that distraction the man trying to grab his legs, stood and jumped on the flier from behind, just as the flier yelled, "Leave her alone you pigs!"

The man forced his forearm up beneath the fliers chin, choking him, and another moved behind and grabbed one arm attempting to pull it behind him, but the flier suddenly lunged, throwing his weight forward and downward, he bent his knees and the man behind him floundered, flew over his back landing on the floor, cursing and lashing out again with his legs and feet at the flier, who kicked back as vigorously, as all of them roared vulgar oaths.

Greta ran to her bedroom and attempted to slam the door behind her, but the man followed her. She glanced up above her bed at the carved wooden figure of Jesus on the cross and muttered a prayer and crossed herself. She was yanked off her feet when he grabbed a handful of her hair and then the man returned to the living room dragging her, still grasping her hair, as she struggled, screaming, and kicking at him. With his other hand the man reached into his pocket and brought out a switchblade knife which he opened with a quick touch and immediately held the point in front of Greta's eyes.

"Leave her alone you yellow fucking coward!" the flier roared, and again distracted from his fight was grasped from behind, his arms pinned down by the strongest of the men.

"Tie his hands behind him, and his legs, quickly, stupid," the man with the switchblade knife yelled. A man took a length of twine from his pocket and with the help of another tied the flier's legs at the ankles, and tied the arms of the exhausted flier behind his back.

"Sleep with the Americans." The man hissed, "No more will you wash and iron for these swine." He pulled her head back, her long white neck arched and as he reached further upward with the point of the knife touched her throat, Greta fainted, falling limply at his feet, and the man pulled the knife away from her.

"Yellow fucking coward!" the flier again screamed.

The man, snarling, yelled back, "Shut up! You will regret those words."

He turned to the other men. "One of you! My God, does it require three of you to hold that stupid flier? One of you help me, quickly." Two of the men held the flier, his hands and feet tied together, while the other joined the man with the knife.

"Lift her," he ordered, "Now lay her across that table, on her back. Put her arms out straight. All but her elbows. Elbows on the table, not over the edge. There. Good. Now break her arms."

"What? You are crazy. What is the good of it?"

"A lesson to all German women. We will not tolerate whoring with Americans!"

"You do it then. I think you have a sickness of the mind," he said and backed away.

The man with the knife snorted, glared at the other, and closed the blade of his knife, pocketed it, then looked back at the unconscious figure of the German woman sprawled atop her table. He walked to the table, pushed down on Greta's right arm above the elbow with one hand, then swung his own forearm down swiftly and snapped her arm, breaking the bones between her wrist and elbow. He then broke her left arm.

The man who refused to help flinched, turned his head and walked further away when he heard the crunching of the breaking bones. He said to the man with the knife, "Thank God she was unconscious. I am through with you. You are a sick man. " He turned to the others; "I will not betray you. I will keep silent. But this is not war." He shook his head from side to side, lowered his chin, his shoulders slumped and he turned and walked through the doorway into the cold darkness. "I am ashamed," they heard him mutter.

"I'll take care of that whiner later," the man snarled. "Now, let's get on with this American."

The flier had witnessed the breaking of the arms of the German woman and became nauseated, was sick to his stomach. He began to heave, then spew coffee and bile.

"Get the tool," the German commanded. "Take him out into the yard and put those lights from the car on him."

The exhausted flier was thrown to the ground, on his back, his hands tied behind him. One German sat on his chest, facing him, while another untied the cord around his ankles. His belt was quickly unloosed. He thrashed his legs about, kicking at them, but the men were too strong. His shoes were yanked off, and his trousers were then pulled off of his legs. His shorts were ripped off of his body and then two of the men forced his legs apart. "Take his handkerchief, there. It's in his hip pocket. Tie it in his mouth behind his head. Quickly." A man said.

And then the third, the leader, the largest, leaned over him and said, "Vulgar American, you are about to lose you goddamn balls!"

He held the tool with its wooden handles, almost like pruning shears, in front of the flier's face, "Raise him, get him up high, onto his shoulders, higher! Good." Then he lowered the tool and quickly castrated the flier. The flier fainted.

"That is good! No more evil sperm from him. Leave his balls for the dogs! Let him spill some blood then pull his trousers back up! Dress him, and we'll deliver him to his comrades so that they too will learn a lesson. Don't put his shoes back on. Keep them! Heil Hitler!"

x   x   x

The road leading from Bad Scheidel to the air base was intersected by another road and at that intersection was the small, white guardhouse, occupied by an Air Corps sergeant assigned to guard duty. Every vehicle entering the air base was stopped and the passengers checked for identification.

On a moonless, ink-black night, from the direction of Bad Scheidel, a dark Mercedes sedan without its headlights shining, screeched to a sliding stop, raising a cloud of dust, and a back car door was thrown open and a body was dumped out onto the macadam near the door of the guardhouse. A sergeant stepped out into the darkness with a flashlight in one hand, a whistle in his mouth and a .45 in his other hand. There was no time to comprehend what was happening.

The sergeant ran to the body, the Mercedes spun in a tight circle, gravel flying from its tires, and sped off down the dark road. More concerned with the body than shooting at a car, the sergeant rolled the man over and saw a white cotton gag pulled tightly around the man's head. He quickly removed it and saw the gold bars of the lieutenant and the pilot's wings, and the arms tied behind the officer. His trousers were bloody below his belt. The pilot attempted to roll over and sit up.

Instantly the sergeant reentered the guard shack and over the telephone yelled, "Get the medics out to the gate in a hurry. I've an injured flier here on the ground." Without waiting for an answer he returned to the flier, and the flier groaned and said, "Oh sweet Jesus, help me!"

The sergeant untied the rope holding his arms and pushed the flier down.

"Lay real still, sir," he said, "the medics are on the way." The flier fainted.

Within minutes the medics arrived, their siren wailing, the red lights flashing. A medic clad in a white uniform jumped from the vehicle before it skidded to a halt.

The Guard Duty Sergeant returned to the shack and over his phone said, "Notify the Officer of the Day to come to the Guard House. It's an emergency."

The medic kneeled down beside the groaning flier, who had regained consciousness. One glance at the blood in the groin area of the flier and the medic knew what had happened. It was the third time while he'd been on duty, and again he was sickened. From his medic's valise he obtained a syringe, held it aloft and stared at the needle, viewing the point, lighted by the headlights, then lowered it and injected the fluid into the flier's arm. Shortly the morphine would act.

The medic looked up at the Guard Duty Sergeant. "The fucking werewolves castrated another one!"

"My God! Let's get him to the hospital." The kneeling medic spoke to the driver of the ambulance. "You got the stretcher. Is he bleeding?"

"Yep. Bleeding pretty bad. Hard to tell. Don't want to touch him out here. Let's get going."

Before they could depart for the hospital a jeep skidded to a stop beside the guardhouse.

A pilot, a first lieutenant, wearing an armband with the letters O.D., jumped out of the jeep. Before the medics could close the doors of the ambulance the officer ran to the stretcher, now in the ambulance. He could see the flier's white face, his eyes now closed.

"Good God! What happened?" he yelled, as he pulled back from the ambulance. "Is he alive?"

"Yes, sir."

"Get going. I'll follow in a minute."

The ambulance sped off, its siren blaring.

"What the hell happened?" the O.D. asked, turning to the Guard Duty Sergeant.

The sergeant told the Officer of the Day all of the details.

"I'm going to the hospital," the O.D. said. "We'll have to write this all up, you know. And call the squadron C.O., Colonel Schlosser, and inform him."

"Yes sir. Did you recognize the guy?"

"Yes. He flew a couple of missions as my copilot. Name's McAdam."

At the base hospital the ambulance stopped and the medics quickly removed Gary McAdam and wheeled him into the emergency area. A flight surgeon was on duty, along with a nurse. McAdam was taken into the operating room where his clothing was cut from him and the nurse began to wash his body. They'd been informed by telephone and had already washed and prepared for emergency surgery if necessary.

"Not much bleeding, now," the nurse said.

"No, Ellen. The bastards used an emasculator. Crimps the wound. Not a lot of bleeding. But he's now a gelding."

"The poor kid," the nurse said, staring at McAdam's groin.

"Big of them to leave his penis," the surgeon said.

McAdam moaned, "Where am I?" he asked. "They broke both her arms. Mrs. Klistoff. She needs help."

"For Christ sake! You heard him? We'll have to get the M.P.'s."

"Help her," McAdam whispered.

"We will. You're in good hands now, Son," the flight surgeon said, "You're going to be okay."

"Better give him another sedative, Lieutenant," the surgeon said. The nurse nodded, obtained a syringe and injected the medication.

"He must have put up quite a fight. Look at his knuckles. They're bruised and bleeding."

"His eyes will be blackened, for sure; and maybe a broken nose. Cut lips. Get some ice on all those areas after you've got him cleaned up. And we'll have to do some stitching," the surgeon said. He sighed, went to a cabinet and returned with surgical instruments.

"At least we can reset his nose." With the nurse assisting, first the flight surgeon stitched the wounded groin area, then placed small wood sticks on each side of McAdam's nose and taped them tightly across his cheeks, straightening and aligning the cartilage and shattered bones.

As the flight surgeon began to remove his white mask and cap and rubber gloves, the squadron C.O., Colonel Ted Schlosser, and the Officer of the Day were led into the operating room by a medic.

The surgeon and the C.O. had been friends for over a year. At the cessation of combat they'd seen less and less of one another.

"Is he going to make it, Owen?" the colonel asked, having been briefed by the Officer of the Day.

"Hi, Schloss. Oh yeah, he'll survive okay physically. How he'll handle being a eunuch is another matter."

"God, I wish we could catch those bastards that did this!"

"Come over here," the surgeon said. "Take a look at his knuckles. He put up a hell of a fight."

"We'll round up every goddamn man and boy in this area and check their faces for bruises, and their hands!"

"I'm going back to the guardhouse," the OD said.

"Thanks for the ride," the colonel said. The OD departed and Colonel Schlosser turned his attention again to the flight surgeon.

"His face is swollen," the surgeon pointed out. "Did he have a straight nose?"

"Yes," the colonel nodded. "Good-looking kid. Or was."

"That much we tried to fix."

"I hate to even ask you about testicles?"

"Nothing we can do about that."

"Well, construct him a new set."

"What! Why? Cosmetics? We can't make him fertile, Schloss?"

"Can you imagine what he'll feel like in a shower if there are other men? Like at a country club, after a game of golf, or after a workout at a gym? Or with a woman?"

"You're asking us to try to make him look like a man?"

"Precisely. That kid, for Christ sake, he's just another of our typical born-civilians that fight these wars. He came to my outfit with a set of balls and I want to send him home that way, fertile or not!"

"You may be asking for more than we can provide. Plastic surgery is still fairly new. I'm really not qualified, but there may be one of the other surgeons who've had some training. If any had experience with the Shriner hospitals, well, they've done amazing things with crippled children. But, believe me, Schloss, he is sterile and there's not a damn thing we can do about that now."

"Owen, that I understand." The colonel rested his right hand on the surgeon's shoulder, "Nevertheless, would you do me a favor and check with the other MD's in the Group, or other outfits around here, and see if a surgeon can fix this kid up with a new pair of testicles, a scrotum, whatever?"

"Okay, Schloss, yes, I'll check around. You know we had a similar case last month and the kid got a hold of a .45 and put it in his mouth. Ended it. So, I feel you'd better get the chaplain involved. Handling depression is going to be toughest. I'll contact the group psychiatrist. And this kid's own crew members could be a real support."

"Okay. What's left of them! And you will get back to me on the other?" His thoughts went to Pop, so recently killed by the spinning, invisible propeller blades.

"Certainly. And I hope your M.P.'s can find the bastards, so I don't see another man like this in here."

"May turn this over to the Third Army. Patton's guys are smart and tough." The colonel rested his hand on McAdam's arm, but the flier was unconscious.

He turned to the nurse, felt guilty suddenly about his profanity, quickly decided it would be worse to apologize than ignore it, then spoke, "And thank you too, for your help nurse." He raised his hand and saluted, without assuming any sort of military stance, which was accepted by the nurse as a gesture of respect.

She nodded, rather than making any gesture to salute, still wearing one bloody glove, and as she removed it, she forced a smile and nodded to him. She had performed her cleanup tasks, obtained ice, which she was placing into towels, arranging them on McAdam's wounded body. She had listened, unobtrusively but intently to the surgeon and squadron flight commander. The colonel departed.

"Doctor?" the nurse said.

"Yes," the MD answered and leaned back against a desk.

"I overheard part of your conversation." She sighed and seemed to look for encouragement.

"Of course. Well, go ahead, Lieutenant. What's up?"

"I've become acquainted with some of the nuns in Bad Scheidel. Some are trained nurses. They speak rather secretively of a doctor who has done a lot of reconstructive surgery, putting children and adults, war victims, back together. He apparently does this on the Q.T. at some little out-of-the way -church, his own secret clinic in Bavaria. The German higher-ups, the SS, the Gestapo, seem to be oblivious to his existence. Or at this stage simply don't care."

"That's great! Good. Well, find him. Locate him. Get his name and bring it to me as soon as possible."

"I don't want to violate the trust I have with the nuns, with the church." She sighed. "It might cost him his life."

"Oh Christ almighty!" The flight surgeon raised his voice and turned his back, then slammed his open palm down on the desk. It made a loud retort, startling the nurse. He stared at her, then took a deep breath. She appeared to be on the verge of tears.

"Ellen," he spoke softly, "I'm sorry to startle you. I think I understand. Our oaths as medical people, and the oaths God's people take and live by, their ethics and our own ethics, and I don't want this to sound sarcastic or melodramatic, but what I do want you to do, right now, is think about what you'd say to that pilot's parents, to the mother and father of that young man you're icing down?"

Both were conscious of the clatter made by the surgical tools being placed into a container to be sterilized. They breathed the aroma of disinfectants, of the alcohol and iodine. The nurse did not respond. She switched off the white glaring overhead light that illuminated McAdam. As she slowly moved from one station to another in the room the rustle of her starched nurse's uniform was noticeable to both of them, seemed loud. Each could hear the other breathing, and were now aware of the clicking of the minute hand moving on the face of the clock.

The surgeon paused, the quietly said, "Personally, Ellen, it's just that I'm a whole lot more concerned about putting this kid back together, than the trust you've established with the nuns. That may be unfair, but, I want you to know I do respect your viewpoint."

"I'll find out his name and where we can locate him," the nurse said, and turned and began again to care for McAdam. "I'll put him in a private room for now."

"Thank you, Lieutenant," the flight surgeon said. "I'd better try to reach the chaplain and the psychiatrist tonight. God, it'll be good to get home again some day, won't it?"

"Roger."

CHAPTER 19

▼

DOCTOR ERNEST FRIEMUTH

Doctor Ernst Friemuth was located at a small Catholic Church constructed of round river stones. The small building was deep in the woods, surrounded by dark fir trees, near the village of St. Blasien. Atop the church was a cross, displaying the figure of the crucified Christ. A nun answered the knock on the thick oak door and led the two Americans through the church to a private room. With an interpreter to assist him, the flight surgeon introduced himself and asked for a few minutes of Doctor Friemuth's time.

"I am Doctor Owen Courtright, Captain Courtright, from the air base at Bad Scheidel, doctor."

"How did you know I was here? That I am a physician?" He responded to the words of the interpreter in excellent English.

"I can't answer those questions as yet, sir. However I've some questions for you, and I'd appreciate some straight answers," Captain Courtright said.

The assistance of the interpreter was quickly ignored.

"And why should I be interrogated? Why do you feel you have the right to question me? I'm a professional man. I'm a medical man. I am not a Nazi! I'm a neutral." Doctor Friemuth was slim, less than six foot tall and wore a neatly trimmed dark brown mustache and beard. "I resent your belligerence."

"Let's cut the bullshit in a hurry! You are subject to the rules, the laws, and the regulations of the Allied Army of Occupation! And, Herr doctor, the Nazi party happened to consider you a member!" the flight surgeon responded. "Now, may I suggest, as one physician to another that we sit down someplace where we can speak privately, just you and me."

There was a pause, as the corners of his mouth sagged. Dr. Friemuth hesitated, then he sighed, as if in resignation, and said, "follow me."

The flight surgeon nodded to the interpreter to remain where he was.

They went to a small library, paneled in dark wood, appearing to Owen Courtright to be polished, hand rubbed walnut. A large table was in the middle of the room with several solid, ladder back chairs.

"Thank you, Doctor Friemuth." The flight surgeon pulled one of the chairs across the room and placed it beside Doctor Friemuth, not across from him. Owen Courtright remembered the Human Relations course he had to take at the University and believed the professor when he told his students to avoid a face to face seating whenever endeavoring to convince someone of your viewpoint. Side by side was disarmament, a subtle position of a shoulder to shoulder approach in which the participants were involved in looking over common horizons.

Doctor Friemuth seemed to be slightly annoyed; however, he pushed his own chair back slightly, sat sideways and stared at Doctor Courtright.

"From our G2, our intelligence officers, I've learned a few things about you that might be of interest."

"Your Gestapo?"

"God, I hope not. But tell me this. Is it correct that you visited the U.S. in 1936?"

"True."

"Why?"

"You don't know?" Doctor Friemuth laughed. "Some intelligence!"

"You studied at the Graduate School of the University of Minnesota, at Mayo Clinic, in Rochester. Your specialty was reconstructive surgery."

"The brothers, the doctors Mayo were incredible men. In 1936 I met them, Charles and William, at a reception. They were kind to me. They did not know how to be condescending! Men of such fine character. Brilliant, humble, modest. Something to emulate. I'm sorry I could not have stayed in the United States. Yes, I spent two years studying, practicing at Mayo Clinic."

"Go ahead."

"After my studies, my wife and I and our children returned to Germany late in 1939. Two sad things. Both of the Mayo brothers died, and it was then I realized, could see, what was happening in Germany. I wanted to take all of my family out of Germany. The mad man was in complete control, had complete power, but it was impossible for a doctor to leave Germany, and my family didn't want to go without me."

"You are a member of the Nazi party?"

"Of course. You, sir, you register as a democrat or a republican or socialist. We had one choice! Finally, it became that you must join, you must register, or, especially if a professional man, you risk death. I had to live, to practice. I had to provide for my family. I didn't have to believe, but survival is important."

"Did you practice at Schonbrunn Sanitarium?"

"Yes."

"How long?"

"Almost a year."

"What about Eglfing-Haar, the so-called healing center?"

"I am ashamed to say that I heard things about it. No, I was never there. I managed to leave Schonbrunn by volunteering to go to the front. I did, but before I left I was able to hide my family. Now, thankfully, my wife, our children, my mother and father are still alive. I managed to get them out of Germany. My wife's parents live not far from them. My mother-in-law is a Jew. All are in a very remote location. Secluded."

"I'm happy to say that all checks out."

"Am I to be put under arrest...?"

"Good God, no!"

"Then why are you interrogating me?"

"I've heard that you are serving as a clandestine surgeon here in your own clinic."

"Clandestine, ha!" Doctor Friemuth put his head back and guffawed. He then turned to the flight surgeon and said, "Come, Doctor, I'll show you."

"Wait a minute, Doctor Friemuth. Did you ever develop a taste for bourbon? I mean when you were in Minnesota?"

"Of course, but I always preferred scotch!"

"Let me talk to my interpreter before I get the tour."

"Oh?"

The flight surgeon walked from the room to where the interpreter waited and spoke to him. He left the church and quickly returned with a paper bag that was stowed with others behind the passenger seat.

"How about this?" the flight surgeon exclaimed, "Johnny Walker Red an unopened fifth. Can a priest or a nun come up with some glasses and water and ice?"

"Now the bribery begins?"

"Ha, no. Let's just have a little restorative before I see your operating room. Those damn jeeps have lousy shocks."

Doctor Friemuth went to a doorway and spoke in German and a nun appeared with two glasses and a pitcher of water.

"No ice. Sorry, Captain."

The American MD opened the scotch and poured liberally into each glass. He poured some water into one of the glasses and looked to Dr. Friemuth for advice. "A touch will be just fine."

"To your health," the captain said.

"And to yours! It's been a long time. I don't think the Scots consider themselves British. Perhaps that's why this fine concoction is possible."

The doctors touched glasses and sipped the scotch whiskey.

"I take it you don't care for the British?"

"By comparison, we Germans are civilized."

"I'm not going to pursue that!"

"It seems to me that physicians and musicians and mathematicians all desire neutrality," Dr. Friemuth said.

"So how do the madmen take charge of the world?"

"Complacency, naiveté, ignorance, selfishness, greed?"

The doctors sipped their drinks without speaking; each seemed to be lost in his own meditation.

"Where does that put mathematicians like Von Braun?" Captain Courtright asked. "I don't want to describe the expression on a child's face, for that matter, on any one's face, when the engine of one of those V Bombs cut off!"

"I think you are correct. Maybe it's the engineers? But, let's forget the mathematicians, and substitute poets. My, my, perhaps we Germans have become a nation of sociopaths? Could such a thing be possible?"

"God, I hope not. I'm signing up for a year of occupation duty. It'll give me a chance to locate the home of my great-grandfather. His name was Hans Schadel."

"So the Germans come back to the fatherland to fight the Germans." Doctor Friemuth chuckled. "Well, if you desire to see my little clinic, please follow me."

The captain followed Doctor Friemuth along an arched tunnel, constructed of the same river rock, the passageway dark and cool, faintly illuminated by low wattage bulbs, and he felt as if he was walking slightly downhill. He estimated they'd traveled about twenty yards when they arrived at an oak door that reached to the ceiling, approximately eight feet.

"After you," Doctor Friemuth said, pushing the door open ahead of them. They entered what appeared to be a small waiting room, with a desk, behind which sat a woman in the garb of a Catholic nun.

After speaking to the woman, Doctor Friemuth opened the next door and led the flight surgeon into a large, paneled room, painted glossy white. A large operating room light was in the ceiling over an operating table. There were white enameled cabinets, a stove, and three separate wash basin sinks. Two doors at the far end of the room were also painted white.

"I was able to build this shortly after the invasion. The other doctors and I worked for days without sleep trying to save the lives of our own young men, and of English and Americans and Scots, the Canadians and Australians. It was carnage! And even then it was obvious to anyone with any brains that we had lost the war. I suppose I am classified a deserter. All I wanted to do was mend broken bones, to heal the sick and wounded. I didn't care who they were. I tended to German soldiers, so sick they'd have died if they'd remained with their units, and they'd be shot, as traitors, if they tried to leave. The frustration could drive you to madness!"

He studied the captain's face. "So, I deserted and came here. And yes, with what I learned at Mayo, I have repaired and mended anyone who needed me. And, God knows, not with the approval of the Catholics, here I've helped girls abort their unwanted pregnancies. Some were raped, others were foolish—said they'd fallen in love with an American Indian boy, who of course was a Negro. They tell the girls they are American Indians, ha! And you'd be amazed at how many Jewish boys and girls came to me with the typical Arab nose and they departed looking like gentiles. But I could do nothing about their genes."

"And then?"

"Oh, I've two small recovery rooms. It is naturally cool in here. I believe there are probably icy streams traversing our property, I mean the property of this church. I believe some of this construction dates back to the Romans. And we can create a draft with opening and closing doors so there are no medical odors. The nuns take excellent care of any patient. I told them about the Protestant doctors Mayo, both Masons, who work so closely with the Catholic St. Mary's Hospital. If the Americans can perform as Christians, why can't we? And I feel we have."

"Are you Catholic?"

"You're Intelligence missed that?"

"You are a Lutheran."

"Amazing. Why are you trying to trap me in a falsehood?"

"That wasn't fair of me. I apologize. What happens to your patients?"

"Now that the war has ended they can meld back into society. Before that, as you Americans did with the Negro slaves, we had our underground railway of sorts. My patients could walk to Switzerland, with help, of course. We had very secret paths always washed by streams from the glaciers and snow banks, so even the bloodhounds could not track them if there was suspicion. Our isolation was perfect for escape. But that's a thing of the past."

"So why are you still hiding out like this?"

"Am I hiding?" The doctor asked of himself. "I guess I am. You know the name, Dietrich Bonhoeffer?"

"No."

"He was my close friend. Dietrich organized an underground theological school. He was a leader in the anti-Nazi movement and was accused of plotting to kill Hitler. The Gestapo hanged him. It is known that we were friends. I am now still afraid that I am on the Gestapo wanted list. They are the bastards of German society and most of them are vengeful and persistent. My family needs me alive, and I feel that I can soon join them. Escape this madness. Do you understand? We hear rumors about your trials? When that is over, I can rejoin society."

"I think I understand. Let's go get another little shot or two of that Johnny Red to warm us up."

"Ha! You are plying me, Captain."

The doctors returned to the library and Dr. Courtright again poured liberally of the whiskey.

"As you have observed, we've no ice. It's a luxury."

"Doctor Friemuth, I've a favor to ask, and with a serious proposition thrown in?"

"I suspected such."

"Have you ever created a scrotum? A pair of testicles?"

"Ha. That is the last thing I expected!" Doctor Friemuth sipped the scotch. "Surprisingly enough there were bizarre, incredible accidents on the farms in and around Minnesota. The corn pickers were treacherous, rendering such mangled bodies." He moved his head slowly side to side.

"And the balers and rakes and tedders and combines and sickle bars, those are the names as I remember. And too, the hunters were shooting at pheasant and stags and hitting one another. Every kind of mutilation you can imagine!"

"Testicles?"

"One poor man was brought in and his son brought in the penis and the scrotum and the testes all in a container with ice. Believe it or not, we sewed back his penis, but that was the best we could do. He was sterile of course."

"Can you create testicles for one of our fliers?"

"Create a scrotum? It is possible. But why?"

"I supposed that's in Freud's field, however the boy's Squadron Commander, Colonel Schlosser, seems to be obsessed with the notion that this flier from his outfit should once again, well, can at least look like a man, perhaps feel like a man. Go home with testicles, as useless as they may be. He still has his penis. I guess its sort of a paternalistic attitude on the part of his squadron leader."

"What kind of accident?"

"Did you ever hear of Nazi werewolves? Possibly Hitler youth gangs."

"Oh, my God! Dumm!"

"So, we're asking you to create a set of balls for this kid."

"You Americans always surprise me," Doctor Friemuth said, and from a drawer in the desk where again they sat side by side, he removed a pad of paper and pencil and began to sketch.

"I believe we could slice, maybe eight or ten millimeter wide, strips from his thighs, below his penis and make a basket, a scrotum. The ends would, of course, be reattached to his thighs. The spaces between the strips would be close enough for quick healing of the thigh wounds. It would be painful, but he would heal quickly if he is in otherwise good health. With the woven flesh basket, a new scrotum is created, which might tend to grow together quickly, a problem we could solve, of course, and we will have to use something heavy enough to sag, but not too heavy, and I repeat, we must not let the basket itself grow together. Make small testes, egg-shapes from plastic? What do you think?"

"You've got the podium, doctor."

"At Mayo we saved the curled lengths of stainless steel, from the lathes. One surgeon experimented with reconstructing a breast. If you could obtain stainless steel wool, perhaps that might do?"

"Hell, I can get one of our tool and die makers to make us up a sample."

"Doctor, you know, I'm sure, that there are many types of stainless? I've seen stainless steel impervious to everything except water. Acid won't touch some stainless steel, yet it will rust!"

The captain chuckled. "How about another little shot of old Red label, Doctor Friemuth?"

The German doctor smiled and pushed his glass toward the captain.

"How soon will it be convenient for you to come to the air base hospital and perform the surgery?"

"So that is the favor. You mentioned a proposition?"

"How would you like to have your family move intact from Lucerne to the United States. You could join them after the surgery?"

"So you know they are near Lucerne? All of this for a useless set of testicles."

"No. I'm afraid not. Unfortunately all musicians and mathematicians and physicians, even poets, are not idealistic neutrals. Our Intelligence feels that your decisions to avoid going to Eglfing-Haar separates you from some German doctors who did practice there. Some of the horror stories that happened to children, well, I'm not going to repeat them."

"And so?"

"Your passports, even with new names if you wish, will be available if you will provide us with as many names as you can of doctors who practiced at Eglfing-Haar. Most of the records at Schonbrunn Sanitarium were destroyed, however the administrators will probably be defendants at worst, or witnesses at best at the Nuremberg Trials. We can assure you that you will not be called as a witness, providing you cooperate. It would only be a matter of hours to fly your family in a C-47, or a B-29 to the United States and safety."

"Some doctors may have been coerced."

"But you made the right decision. You refused to go there."

"I honestly don't know what happened there."

"Would you like to see photos? Of the children? And of Dachau, also?"

Doctor Friemuth shook his head from side to side. "No, I don't need the repugnance. You leave me little choice. I must choose America."

"Congratulations. This is a decision you'll never regret." The captain said. He poured again from the bottle of Scotch.

"However, Captain, I want you and your authorities to know that I will not be available for surgery, or questions, until I receive a letter, or a telegram, from Rochester from my wife advising that all of the family is there safe. Understood?"

"Doctor Friemuth, I would have been disappointed in anything less! But I would suggest that you begin compiling a list of physicians who knowingly violated the Hippocratic Oath. I know my superiors are going to want to see some names before your family departs from Switzerland."

"I understand."

"Can you contact your wife safely?"

"It will take a few days."

"If you would be comfortable with writing a letter to her, it can be delivered tomorrow."

"You are even more urgent than I."

"Frankly, Dr. Friemuth, our Intelligence people don't care about the kid that was castrated. They want names for the Nuremberg Trials. That is the urgency."

"The list will have to be from my recollection. I've no documents. Do you want it now, Doctor Courtright?"

"If I can return to the base with a list of names above your signature, everything else will fall into place with amazing speed and coordination. Your family will have homes to move into, with German-speaking Americans if desired, where they'll await your arrival. Employment for you will be arranged."

"At Mayo?"

"I don't know, but if that is important to you, I'll pursue it."

"There really is life after death!" Doctor Friemuth exclaimed. For the first time during their meeting he smiled, then laughed aloud. "I'll have a list ready for you within a few minutes. Perhaps more later, if I recall." He sat back in the chair and with his long slender fingers stroked his beard carefully.

"And the letter to your wife."

"Of course. That would be most expeditious."

"I'll return as soon as things are in motion, okay?"

"Yes. Return with a message from my wife, please."

Captain Courtright arose, turned and extended his hand, which Doctor Friemuth accepted and shook vigorously. As the captain started to leave the library, Doctor Friemuth said, "Wait. Your scotch."

The captain stopped and looked back and laughed, "Not much left. Keep it, compliments of the Ninth."

Doctor Friemuth laughed, then suddenly said, "Ach! Where is my brain? Captain, Doctor Courtright. It's too simple! We remove some body fat, from near his waistline; he has to have some fat. We'll create two eggs sized blobs, and use gut, you know, like cat gut, shape them, tie them and they will be supported nicely in the new basket we'll construct. Yah? Okay? And one more item. In the States I used a product called KIP. A healing, soothing burn ointment. Please obtain several, ah, containers, tubs, for our patient's recovery. All right?"

"Brilliant, Doctor. But, if you don't mind I'm going to go ahead with the stainless steel thought, and have a machinist turn it down into a wool—like consistency. We'll check it in water and blood to see if it changes. And I'm certain we can obtain the KIP. Now you enjoy your scotch!"

"Ah, yes," Doctor Friemuth said. "Thank you so much for the restorative. Ha! And, Doctor Courtright. You are probably on the right track. With out a blood supply, a circulation of blood, the fat might deteriorate."

x   x   x

Doctor Friemuth was astonished at the rapidity, the coordination of the timing, rendered by the U.S. military establishment. What he had been promised had transpired. Within a few days of his meeting with Doctor Courtright his entire family had been moved to Minnesota. Even much of their treasures, their oil paintings and crystal and large pieces of furniture were shipped and Doctor Friemuth was delighted to learn that they were comfortable in their new home near Mayo Clinic, on the outskirts of Rochester.

Captain Courtright, the flight surgeon, drove alone to the small chapel in the wooded forest of green darkness in Bavaria. He was greeted by a nun and guided to the paneled office of Doctor Friemuth. The men shook hands and both grinned and allowed a chuckle as they thought of the recent events, not having to vocalize their thoughts.

"Out of respect, our Intelligence people didn't try to break the secret code of Doctor and Mrs. Friemuth." Both of the doctors laughed aloud. "I'm glad you are satisfied we lived up to all of our promises, and now we can go ahead with the surgery on Lieutenant McAdam."

"Yes, of course," Doctor Friemuth said, then paused, lowered his palms to the top of his desk and stared at his hands for a few seconds. "I've still some of that good scotch that you left with me. "

He crossed the room, opened the heavy door and spoke in German to one of the nuns. He returned to his desk and removed the bottle of scotch from a drawer. The nun knocked, then entered with two glasses and a pitcher of water. Doctor Friemuth poured two ounces of the whiskey in each glass and poured a splash of water into his and pushed the pitcher toward his companion, who did the same.

"I've a feeling there is to be some more negotiating," Doctor Courtright said.

"I am hopeful that you will understand that while I feel I am not cowardly, I've reason to believe that some of the people in Bad Scheidel are knowledgeable of my plans to come to your hospital, and these could well be former Gestapo and SS members. And if they were evil once, they'll probably always be of the same demented mentality. There is no doubt in my mind that they would risk their own lives to destroy me. That is my problem."

"Well, secrecy will have to be a priority," Captain Courtright said. "Give me a couple of days. I'll be back personally, AND good Doctor, I'll replenish the scotch."

"You see," Doctor Friemuth continued, "Bad Scheidel was once a small but favorite health resort in that part of Germany, and of course the high ranking officers, and the Nazi politicians too, visited the baths frequently."

"Back to the surgery," Captain Courtright said, "Do you have a time of day that you prefer?"

"The earlier the better. Six in the morning for this procedure, there are some unknowns, so we should allow perhaps three hours. I assume you will be assisting me?"

"Of course, I'd be delighted, and hope I'll never have to do another!"

Captain Courtright arose and Dr. Friemuth came from behind the desk and together they walked along the corridor to the chapel. "Perhaps I can arrive in darkness and depart in darkness?"

"Certainly." Captain Courtright extended his hand and Doctor Friemuth grasped it, shook vigorously.

"It is difficult for me to express my thanks. You must know how relieved I am to know my family is safe, and with the grace of God, I'll soon be with them." Then he laughed, and added, "Are you the least bit curious about our secret code, that my wife used in the telegram when she felt secure and became settled a bit with the family?"

"Of course, but it was your personal code. We didn't attempt, didn't try to decipher it. We did what we said we'd do."

"Ah, yes, but you understood my apprehension?"

"Certainly. And I still do. And, yes, I am very curious."

"So then, we used two words, canju luta, and these I learned when I was at Mayo Clinic. A young, very proud and handsome Sioux cowboy was hurt trying to ride one of those huge bulls at a local rodeo. Broke his arm and badly dislocated his right shoulder. He said he was a Lakota, which I presume is part of the Sioux nation. We became friends and he taught me several words or expressions. My, he had a tremendous pain shield. Disdained pain pills. And I think this is interesting: He said the white man would never make slaves of the Indians as they do with the Negroes. He would tease me. 'You white men beat the Indian because we refuse to be slaves and you beat the Negro because he's a willing slave.' It makes me wonder why the intelligent Jews can be so easily enslaved?"

"Good question. So, what do the words mean?"

"Symbolic: it has to do with the Indian search for a meaningful life. Canju luta."

"That is interesting. Sounds like you are about to resume a meaningful life, doctor. Now, you keep the faith! I'll see you in a few days." Captain Courtright said, then turned and strode to his jeep, waved at Doctor Friemuth and drove through the dark green corridor of evergreens.

x   x   x

Two days later Captain Courtright arrived at the small chapel in the woods and outlined the plan to which the base group commander had given his approval, as had the squadron commander, Colonel Schlosser.

"We'll pick you up just after dark in a Mercedes and drive you to Freiberg where a AT 17 airplane will be waiting. Squadron Commander Colonel Schlosser and Major Wilson will fly us directly to Bad Scheidel, and again we will be picked up in a Mercedes and we'll be driven directly to the officer's quarters. That evening you will have an opportunity to meet other physicians and nurses and examine our operating room. How does that sound, so far?"

"You are making me feel very secure."

"After the early morning surgery, again we'll drive in a civilian car to our airport and fly up to London, where you'll then fly to Washington, DC, then catch another plane to Rochester, Minnesota. Okay?"

"A list of names deserves all of this?

"Your list allowed Intelligence to expand their lists," Captain Courtright said, then sighed, and continued in a slow, serious tone. "It's a damn shame that men like you are leaving Germany."

"I'm not political. I can support the decent Germans with my contributions from America. You'll see. Do you know what I intend to do? To the friends I have left here I will mail copies of your Constitution and Bill of Rights. Germany will rebuild. As the saying goes, 'The cream will rise to the top.' Good, intelligent Germans will respond."

"Well, Doctor, isolated like this, you probably haven't seen what's happened to your country. What a task is ahead, but, anyway, back to the plan, we will be double -checking for any unidentified observers at all stops. Any strange activities and we'll postpone the whole scenario. Oh, I almost forgot, our medical facility will be closed during the day of your surgery, for security purposes, and for your safety. We are setting up a separate first aid station at the base morgue. Our medics will know about it, so any accidents, any emergencies, with our own personnel, will be treated there."

"And what is the mental attitude of the patient?"

"Thankfully he's a tough rascal. Wants to meet you before the surgery. I've described the procedure and explained all of the ramifications. He knows he'll be sterile, and he seems to be able to cope."

"Did you explain to him the use of the testosterone supplement, shots?"

"No," Captain Courtright said, and sighed," I don't want to give him any false hopes. It's not always a sure thing."

"It's peculiar. We had a little Dachshund. All he wanted to do was propagate the species. We had him neutered, and he didn't slow down. It must be partially in the mind, right?"

"Well, that will be a plus for this flier. I understand he was quite a cocksman."

"A what!"

"You know, like your dog!"

"Ha, ha," Doctor Friemuth put his head back and laughed loudly. "We'll wish him luck then!

" We need a date, Doctor."

"I'm ready!"

"Wednesday evening then, the day after tomorrow."

"I'll be ready. Ah, I wish I had a replacement for this little clinic. I hate to say good-bye to these fine people. These are the Germans that will rebuild."

"I hope you're right. And, incidentally, doctor?" Captain Courtright said," I brought another fifth of Red Label."

The doctor laughed heartily, "I'll call a nun! " And doctor Friemuth arose and went to the door and placed his order for glasses and water.

▼

CHAPTER 20

MARSHALL ORDERED HOME

Kristine Schuttenhelm went to the chaplain's office when she had completed her maid chores. Chaplain Waldron provided a list of names and addresses of likely contributors for the library he was starting. It would be situated in one of the rooms in the officers' club. Her typing speed was improving and as she completed one list, she asked for another. She was not interested in taking a rest-break, which was suggested by the chaplain.

Marshall went to chaplain's office hoping to see Kristine. Attempts by Marshall to start a conversation with her were fruitless. She rebuffed him. "I am too busy to speak with you, Lieutenant Sunder," she said, when he spoke her name. He hadn't talked with her since the night he went to her grandmother's home, after his return from Switzerland. After Tex had told her that Marshall bombed the Bad Scheidel Bridge. Marshall could understand her attitude, but hoped she would eventually understand.

As Marshall turned to go to the bar he was intercepted by a sergeant. "Lieutenant Sunder?" Marshall returned the salute.

"Colonel Schlosser would like to see you."

"Really? Well thank you. I'll go right over," Again they exchanged salutes.

A WAC corporal occupied a desk in a small office that fronted the office of the squadron commander, Lieutenant Colonel Ted Schlosser.

"I understand the colonel wants to see me," Marshall said.

"Yes sir. I'll tell him you are here."

The colonel's swivel chair had been turned so that it faced the window and Marshall could see his back. He appeared to be looking at something, but turned when the WAC entered and spoke to him. He stood and smiled and waved for Marshall to enter.

"Reports as ordered, sir." Marshall said, and saluted.

"At rest," the colonel said then stepped from behind his large mahogany desk. He walked to Marshall and extended his hand, which Marshall grasped and shook.

"Sit down. I've some good news for you," he said, still smiling. "Orders have been cut for you to ship out. Your friend, Tex, or Cal, or whatever you're now calling him, will pick you up early tomorrow morning. He'll fly you Le Havre, and they'll process your orders to board the first available Victory Ship. Destination New York, then a DC 3 or 4 to the West Coast. How does that sound?"

"Home?" Gosh sir, I signed up for another year, besides, I don't think I have enough points to go home," Marshall said.

"Sunder, for your own good, I turned down your application. And I took care of the points. One of my classmates at West Point is in charge of priorities, you know, for things like emergencies. I told him this is an emergency."

"Really! Wow, I've got some packing to do. As for Cal, God knows we've buried the hatchet. But, sir, how do I rate being considered as an emergency?"

"Lieutenant, I'm just trying to keep one member of Frank's crew intact. The enlisted men, Sergeant Dublin, and Sergeant Frantz, are now on their way home. I don't want you to go through what happened to McAdam.

We're not sure we caught all of the gang that worked him over. The M.P.'s arrested a couple of SS guys hiding out on a hog farm. It's common knowledge in the village that you were the bombardier that caused a little havoc around here. Understand? And it's no military secret that you and Kristine were friendly. I'm doing you a favor, Sunder."

Marshall stared at the colonel, then nodded his head affirmatively "I see," Marshall said." Sir, I'll have to say good-bye to McAdam. I understand he's getting around pretty well now."

"Okay, you can go see him. Now, Lieutenant, keep this absolutely confidential. He's going to be operated on tomorrow morning by a German surgeon. The doctor studied reconstructive surgery at Mayo Clinic a few years ago, back before the war. He and Doctor Courtright are going to create a scrotum with testicles, of sorts."

"No kidding! What's Mayo Clinic?" Marshall asked.

"It's up in Rochester, Minnesota, actually it's a group of clinics and hospitals and is quite large and it's also quite famous around the world."

"Will McAdam be able," Marshall stammered, "you know, to do it again."

"As I understand it, they can give him shots. I really don't know much beyond that. They are calling it cosmetic surgery. A sex life? For his sake, we can hope."

"How does McAdam feel about the surgery?"

"You know him. He's eager to get on with it."

"I wish I could be around a few more days to see how he gets along."

"Sorry Marsh, for your own good, I want you out of here." The colonel stood up. "Your orders are in the outer office."

"Sir, I understand that Kristine's home was off limits. I'd like to stop by on the way to the plane, just to say good bye."

"No, damn it, Lieutenant Sunder! It's still off-limits. And, according to Captain Waldron, she has no interest in you anymore."

"I really don't believe that, sir. I really wanted to marry her. Legally.I still do! And take her back to the States. That's why I signed up for another year."

"The answer is no!" the colonel said, raising his voice. "Are you some kind of a damn masochist or something? As a matter of fact, if your combat record hadn't been excellent, I had seriously considered court marshaling you for taking that girl to Munich!"

"You knew about that?"

"Come on, Sunder, this probably sounds like a damn cliché, but it really is my job to know what's going on in this squadron. Now, I want to shake your hand and wish you well."

"Thank you, sir. I guess I'm still in a state of shock about getting to go home. I thank you, Colonel." Marshall started to turn away, then stopped and faced the colonel. "If you don't mind me saying so, Schloss, you're one hell of a pilot and a great leader!"

The colonel put his head back and laughed loudly, "Okay Lieutenant, out of here and good luck."

Marshall stood at attention and saluted. The colonel returned the salute. He turned then, and stared out of the window. Earlier in the day, he had received notice from Headquarters that all of the B-26's in the entire Bomb Group were to be destroyed.

Marshall stopped at the WAC's desk. "Here are your orders, sir," she said.

Marshall opened the envelope and studied the orders. He put them in the inside pocket of his flight jacket and decided to first find Cal and confirm the plans. *Going home! Unbelievable. But now, all of a sudden-like, Cal is now supposed to be a friend. Tex or Cal, either way, I'm still not used to it. Oh well, if the colonel wants him to fly me up there, I can handle it. Maybe the poor guy really has changed. Yeah, he's already changing for the better. And who am I to judge?*

Marshall went to the barracks. Cal wasn't in his room. He told his roommate he needed to see him as soon as possible, then continued on to his own room. Immediately he began to sort his belongings. One pile was of things he didn't want, but one of the other guys might like or need. When the footlocker was as full as he could get it he locked it, spun the combination, and then began to pack his B-4 bag with the changes of clothes, T-shirts and shorts and pajamas and uniforms he determined he'd need to arrive in Chico dressed in a clean outfit. His shaving gear, and his shower clogs and the books from the pastor and from Pop, he packed in his B-4 bag. All of his navigation tools, his E-6B, and his bombardier charts and computers were placed in a brief case and packed in his B-4 bag. He'd never need them again, he knew, but he now considered them as souvenirs. In a barracks bag he packed clothes and shoes, wash cloths and a couple of towels that he felt he might need. It was light enough to fling over his shoulder. He'd carry the B-4 in one hand. He placed his .45 Colt in its shoulder holster deep inside the B-4 bag.

Cal walked through the open door into Marshall's room. "Howdy, partner," he said. "You happy about going home?"

"Hi Cal," Marshall replied, "I asked to stick around for a few more days to look in on Gary, but Schloss vetoed that. It's happened so quick, but sure, naturally I want to see my folks and my Uncle Bruce. And, man, it'll be fun to rev up my Model A!"

"Good for you," Cal said. "You know, I think I'm getting off of Schloss's shit list. He's giving me more assignments, you know, involving responsibility."

"That's great. And I think you ought to kind of stick close to Captain Waldron, for advice and stuff."

"You're right, Marsh," Cal said. "You know, I quit praying when the shooting stopped. Kind of hypocritical, I guess. Yeah, I think I will see the chaplain now and then. Boy, I need all of the help I can get!"

"Cal, I'm pretty well packed. Can I ask a favor? Would you mind getting my footlocker shipped home?"

"Sure thing. Anything else?"

"What's our ETD?"

"Nothing written in stone. Schloss said early morning. How about chow at 5:30 and go to the strip at 6:00."

"Roger. See you in the mess hall at 5:30."

"Marsh, I'm very happy that Schloss selected me to fly you up to Le Havre."

"Yeah, me too," Marshall said. "Well, I'm heading down to the infirmary to say good-bye to McAdam."

"I imagine you want to do that alone. So, I'll see you in the MORNING" and Cal left the room.

Marshall thought about McAdam. *I don't have a darn thing to give him. I don't want to bring up any thoughts about Frank or Pop. Hell, even in his condition he's probably already made a pass at a nurse. I'll take him some good booze. Even if he can't drink it he can be a host of sorts.*

Marshall left his room and walked directly to the officers' club where he went to the bar and caught the eye of the bartender.

"Is it possible to buy a full bottle of bourbon or scotch or something?"

"Back in the States I'd say no, most places anyway. But here, name your poison, sir"

"I'd like to take a bottle to my copilot, Gary McAdam. He's laid up in the infirmary."

"That's pretty easy, sir. With a name like McAdam, take him scotch."

"Okay, pick one out for me, please."

"Sir, we've a hell of a good procurement officer. He came up with a case of Glenlivet twelve-year-old pure single malt scotch whiskey. Even here, it's a tad more expensive than Johnny Walker and some of the ones we know so well in the States."

"Hell, wrap it up in something nice, if you can, it's a gift." Marshall said.

"I'll try, Lieutenant. Have you any silk from a parachute ?"

Marshall laughed, "You're a real comedian, Sergeant. I'll take what ever you give me."

"Yep, I was kidding, sir. Actually it comes in a nice box, and I'll put a little white tissue paper around it. Best I can do."

The cost was higher than Marshall anticipated, but he paid for it without question, thinking a few cartons of cigarettes would cover it. "Thanks, sergeant, I appreciate your help."

Marshall walked to the infirmary, the hospital, where Gary was recovering from his wound. The nurse at the reception desk quizzed Marshall, and upon learning that he was one of Gary's crew members advised him the location of the room. Marshall peeked through the partially open door. Gary was on his back, with the bed elevated. Instinctively, Gary turned his head to see who was at the door.

"Hey, Marsh!" Gary called out. "Come on in, the water's fine, you old bastard!" He then laughed, and sat up.

"I expected to find a nurse in bed with you!" Marshall exclaimed.

"That's after they turn out the lights" Gary laughed, "A modest group here."

Marshall walked to the bed. Gary flung back the lightweight blankets and swung his legs around. They shook hands.

"Hear you're getting a new set of balls in the morning, buddy. And I'm heading home early tomorrow." He paused when he saw the surprise in Gary's eyes. "So I won't be around to pick on you."

"Well, lucky you! Guess you know Schloss and Captain Courtright located some Kraut surgeon who did this sort of thing back in the States a few years ago." Gary and Marshall seemed to stare at one another for a moment, then Gary again spoke. "Hell, what choices have I? It's a gamble I want to take."

"Understand he studied at Mayo Clinic. They're world famous, you know."

"I trust Schloss and Doctor Courtright, that's all that counts."

"You know they are looking out for you, and I guess me, too."

"So you're really heading home?"

"I tried to get Schloss to postpone it a week or more so I could be here to check up on you, Gary. He's says it's locked in." Marshall sighed. "I think he's more stubborn that these real Germans."

"Marsh, I've got something for you," Gary said. "Go to that dresser, buddy, and find a large envelope with a couple of photos." Marshall found the envelope. "Remember that guy that rode in the top turret on our little sight-seeing adventure?"

Marshall nodded, and slid the 8 x 10 glossy enlargements out of the envelope. He studied the photo and then turned to Gary and smiled broadly.

"He brought me a couple of these and said he had one for each of the passengers." It was a photo of a B-26, with *Miss Nausicaa* in eighteen inch high letters scrolled across the nose of the bomber and beneath the first pilot's window the name Gary McAdam. "That guy that rode in the turret did this for us, and told me about this guy Odysseus being taken care of by Miss Nausicaa. This copy is for you, Marsh."

"That's really keen, Gary! Thank you! Some day we'll make contact with Frank. You'll have to get another copy. He'd love to hear about that flight!"

"Oh, I do have a copy for him. Right! He'll love it! Something else I want to share with you," Gary added, "You know, when I came to, after being attacked, and realized what had happened, I well, I wanted someone to bring me my .45. But Captain Waldron and that psychiatrist, Doctor Bershadsky, both worked me over pretty good. I calmed down a bit, and then Jim Frantz came in to say good-bye. He and Dublin are both out of here, on their way home, with enough points, I guess. But anyway, Jim comes up close to me and opens his shirt a bit, then pulls this chain up over his head. Hell, I thought he was going to show me his dog tags, and then he gives me his Saint Christopher medal. Well, I held it and looked at it, and then he says 'Put it on, sir. Saint Christopher got all of us through combat, you know.' Well Marsh, I'll have to admit I was touched.

Then Jim whispers, 'You must have faith, Lieutenant McAdam, and Saint Christopher will help you through all this.'"

"That's really nice. See how many people are thinking about you, and pulling for you?"

"I am amazed, Marsh, Gary said. I Understand they caught a couple of the bastards that did this."

"Headquarters has kept the whole thing kind of hush-hush. My guess is they didn't get the whole gang. I've heard they weren't kids. They were SS shit heads that didn't get past Bad Scheidel!"

"God knows I want revenge, Marsh, but first I've got to get through this surgery and see what happens from there."

"Forget the revenge Gary. Just get well and get your skinny ass back to the States. You've got that family business waiting for you, plus your brother and your folks. That's what is important."

"Okay, navigator. If that's the course you've plotted." Gary laughed, "Guess the same applies to you, eh?"

"Roger. And in the meantime, I've got a little medication for you. I'm sure your favorite nurse will let you know when you can have some. Good scotch whiskey. Pure malt scotch, according to the barkeeper," Marshall said.

Gary accepted the package and removed the white paper. "Hey, some fancy box! Really must be good stuff. Thanks, buddy!"

"Well, Gary, I'm off now. You've got my address. Will you drop me a line and let me know how you're doing?"

"Sure, pal. So, I guess this is 'roger, wilco, over, and out,'" Gary smiled. He extended his hand and they shook, both hesitating to release the handshake.

Marshall departed. A nurse had been waiting outside the door, observing their farewell.

"Take good care of him, ma'am," Marshall said, very quietly.

"Ha!" the nurse said, then laughed, "He's been trying to get me into that bed since he got here." She patted Marshall on the arm. "He'll be okay."

Marshall laughed. He then went back to the barracks to check up on any final packing decisions and was satisfied that he'd done as much as possible to prepare to leave. Marshall stopped by the bar at the officers' club, had a scotch and soda, and then went to the dining room. Three other fliers came to the table where he dined and told him good-bye and good luck. The word got around fast when someone was going to leave. He did not seek fellowship, and didn't want to visit again with Cal. Marshall went to his room and wrote a short letter to his mother and father. He told them he'd probably arrive at Camp Beale before they got the letter and would telephone them from there. Marshall opened his B-4 bag and found his copy of the book by H. E. Fosdick. He decided it was a book to study, rather than to browse through, and began to understand that Captain Waldron apparently had a good reason to select it for him.

Marshall set his alarm for five o'clock. He showered and scrubbed his teeth, then turned off the light and climbed into his bed. In the dark he thought about home, but his mind kept coming back to Kristine. Surely she wouldn't carry her grudge towards him much longer.

The clanging bell on the alarm shattered the morning silence. Marshall jumped up. He quickly dressed. He re-read the letter to his folks, then sealed it. He would drop it off at the box in the dining room. Cal was waiting for him, his hands surrounding a mug of coffee, warming them.

The fliers ate a light breakfast, then loaded Marshall's gear into the jeep and headed for the flight line. The road to the airport passed by Kristine's home.

"Cal, I want you to stop for a second at Kristine's place. Don't even turn off the engine. I just want to say good-bye to her."

"Isn't that a no, no?

"I don't want you involved. You just slow down, but keep rolling, I'll jump out and catch up to you a block down the street. It'll be quick. I don't want you involved."

"Okay, damn it, but make it fast. That lil 'ole L-5 is going to be purring and ready to take off."

In the early morning they drove down the cobble stone road. The flashing lights of the ambulance and those of the M.P.'s jeep startled both of them.

"What in the hell is going on, Cal!" Marshall shouted.

Damned if I know, but it's bad news as far as I'm concerned. Let's get the hell out of here."

"No! No! It's Kristine's house. Damn it! I've got to find out what's going on. Slow down! Please!" Marshall shouted.

CHAPTER 21

▼

KRISTINE SHOT

Kristine Schuttenhelm was comfortable with her two jobs at the air base. The challenge to create a library was accepted with enthusiasm and curiosity. Under the supervision of Chaplain Waldron, she began typing letters, and mailing them to a list of possible donors. Within weeks, boxes of books began to arrive from colleges and universities in the United States, and from private collections.

This responsibility merited a higher respect among her own peer group. Although she also continued with her maid duties, her new capacity earned a reputation of being a perfectionist, and of being remarkably persistent. Quickly she understood the Dewey Decimal System, and was arranging books on the shelves and typing up cards for the reference files.

It was common knowledge in Bad Scheidel that she was also being treated as a privileged person. While her neighbors knew that she was employed at the air base, they also were aware that other German maids were not chosen to receive the supply of coal and flour and sugar and coffee that was being provided by the chaplain. On various occasions when a maid's work was outstanding, the chaplain did have a sergeant make a coal-drop, as he called it, or he personally presented them with a container of coffee or sugar. Often this bonus was based on need, from confidential information that he gleaned from his association with the local Lutheran Pastor.

The neighbors rationalized that as a man of God; Captain Waldron must be motivated by empathy and compassion towards Kristine, who had suffered the loss of so many family members. Some were also aware that the flier, the man who bombed their bridge, no longer visited Kristine.

Kristine was conscious of the feelings of her neighbors and did her best to share chunks of coal and a few cups full of flour and even sugar. In her own mind she began to feel worthy again, and a bit special. She worked hard for every dollar and gift, and her feeling of self-esteem began to grow.

Still, a certain tension existed when she went home in the evening, because she knew that her home was a restricted area. She had no desire for companionship with any of the fliers, and there were no German men in the village that had ever approached her. She was known to her neighbors as Frau Schuttenhelm, and she wanted it that way.

After work one evening when she arrived at her grandmother's home, she saw in the shadows across the street, the figure of a man leaning against a building. The bright glow of a cigarette being inhaled startled her. She could not make out any of his features, but she was certain he was not wearing an Air Corps or Third Army uniform. She felt the man was watching her. A delivery of coal had been made to her home earlier in the day. Thieves were known to be in the area. Her coal was valuable. Too, in her own mind she was not positive that all of the men who had maimed Lieutenant McAdam had been apprehended. She overheard Colonel Schlosser and Captain Waldron discussing that he was to be operated on in a few days. When they saw her and thought she might have overheard them, both admonished her to utter not a word about it. Knowledge of it might be a risk to his life. She wished that she had heard nothing.

Kristine fixed a meal of toasted bread and boiled potatoes and cabbage. She added flour and salt to thicken it. She ate slowly, then cleaned her kitchen. She fixed a cup of her one great luxury-coffee, with a teaspoon of sugar, then sat in her chair a few feet from the glowing iron stove. Thank God for the chaplain, she thought, and then she heard a faint noise at her door. Someone attempted to turn the doorknob. She jumped up and ran to the door, hesitated a moment, and called out, "Who is it?"

"Paul! Let me in!"

Kristine unlocked the door and opened it and her husband stumbled, and nearly collapsed in her arms. In disbelief, she grabbed his weaving form, and he rested his hands on her shoulders and stared at her.

"My God! You are alive! Oh, my God, Paul, you are so thin. You are so frail! I was told that you died near Stalingrad!" Kristine hugged the decimated young soldier, held him tightly close to her. "Here, my darling, come to the table. I have hot soup and bread and coffee for you!"

Paul walked very slowly to the table and sat with his arms resting on it, his head hanging, and his body began to shudder. "Christ, I am cold! My God, Kristine, I never thought I'd see you again. I don't know who told you that I was dead. But, I'm not surprised. There were so many corpses, so many of my friends dead and dying, and starving, and freezing. It would be easy to believe that I, too, was killed."

"A soldier brought your ring to me and said you wished me to have it. He said you knew you would be killed. I don't even know who he was or where he was from. He said he'd been in Russia with you. My God! Are you still in the Wehrmacht?"

"Kristine, I deserted my outfit months ago. A messenger named Fred Glesener was sent to a command center, told to request help. I asked him to take it to you, to give my ring to you. We knew he wasn't going to return to our outfit.

"Kris, I'm a deserter. Do you understand! If the SS or the Gestapo find me I'll be executed."

"No! No! They are all through. All finished."

"Those swine consider me a traitor. I witnessed an SS officer kill our captain because he said the Fuhrer was a madman. Then our sergeant garroted the SS officer. The sergeant was now the first in command, and he ordered us to retreat. And we all did!"

"So, you didn't desert. You were ordered. Understand?" Kristine said, in a pleading voice, then continued, "My darling! Have you the strength to wash your hands and face? I'll fix a bowl of warm water for you. I have soap. "

"All I understand is fatigue. I am too tired to think."

Kristine obtained the bowl and a bar of soap plus a wash cloth and began to clean his face. His brown hair was matted, but she dampened it and pulled a comb back through it. His hands were thin and bruised and she held them tenderly in her own as she washed them.

"Paul dear, my prayers are answered. You've come back to me! God spared you! Now rest on the couch and I'll fix your food." Kristine warmed the potato soup, toasted slices of bread, and poured coffee into a mug. She stirred in a tablespoon of sugar. She helped him up from the couch, then hugged him, pressing her breasts against his chest, wrapping her arms around him tightly. "I cannot yet comprehend that you are here with me! This is unbelievable!"

"God, this is good. Real food! Thank you, Kristine. Thank you. It seems like two months, maybe more, that I've been walking and crawling, always at night. I've stolen eggs and turnips and potatoes, and even caught a few little fish. I swam across a couple of rivers and streams. That's the only bath I've had! I managed to keep my matches dry. Once I found a cave. I built a little fire and cooked the fish, and later I shot a hare, and cooked it. I kept my little Walther and a pocket full of bullets. I threw away my Mauser rifle. It was too damn heavy." Paul walked to the table with her beside him, holding him with one arm.

"Why didn't someone help you? Why weren't you helped?" Kristine asked, then held a chair and he sat at the table.

"Who could help? The peasants? The Americans? I would immediately become a prisoner of war, if not first shot! Who knows whom to trust? The Russians would make short work of any of us stragglers." Carl sighed. "God this tastes so good. Where did you get it?"

"I've two jobs at the American Air Base. It's part of my pay."

"I'm afraid to ask about our families?"

"It'll wait until the morning," Kristine said.

"I need to know."

" Really." Kristine sighed and shook her head. "Paul, it is the two of us, here, and my father."

"Our baby?"

Her voice barely audible, Kristine said, "Gone."

Paul shook his head in disbelief, and stared at Kristine blankly, "Your mother, grandmother?"

"Gone. Paul, I haven't been able to go to Kitzengen to find out about your parents. I can only hope that they are all right, and the mail is useless."

Paul dropped his face into his hands and sobbed, his body shook, then he sat back up, stared at her and asked, "What are we going to do? Where is your father?"

Now crying, tears flowing down her cheeks, Kristine whispered, "He lives at his home, alone. He is crippled, and in pain. He stepped on a land mine in Holland. He has, well; it's like a peg leg. The American doctors at the hospital, here at the air base, they are helping heal the wound. I've been living in grandmother's house because it is closer to work. And I don't want people to think it's abandoned."

"God, I'm so sorry. Why isn't your father in a prison camp?"

"The Canadians took over the submarine pens at Ijmuiden when the war ended. He was in the hospital, and he says they were willing when he asked to go home. No internment. I don't know why. Maybe because he is older, crippled, frail, and he looks so harmless. They gave him a supply of medication and bandages, and a crutch and he managed to get rides all the way home. The Americans have given him a job. Who can make sense of any of this?"

"Should I surrender to the Americans?"

"My darling, I don't know. I'll ask Captain Waldron. He is a chaplain. I trust him." Kristine said, "But now I'm going to bathe you. I'll wash your clothes. What I feel is that you would be safe with the Americans. Tomorrow I will talk with the chaplain. He is a Lutheran minister. He'll advise me."

"Jesus Christ, Kristine, I really can't go much further."

"I'll put on some more coal. You get out of those clothes. I will bathe you, Paul. But now you must undress. I'll wash everything and hang it up and it will be dry by morning. Tomorrow I will trade for eggs and carrots and a big piece of pork and we'll have father join us here for dinner. Does that sound good?"

"Oh, yes, but I just want to lie down on a bed. Oh, for a down comforter and some sleep. Put my gun where it will be close to me."

"Paul, my darling, I will soon be your comforter," Kristine said, as she helped him remove his soiled uniform and underwear, his boots and stockings. "Put this blanket around your shoulders and go to the bed. I'll heat the water and wash everything. You go to bed and pull our comforter over you. I'll be along soon. I hope the need for guns has ended."

"Thank God you are here and you are well," Paul murmured.

Kristine scrubbed all of Paul's clothes in a large metal tub, rinsed them several times, wrung them out by hand, and then hung them on a line stretched tightly between rafters near the iron stove. She sighed, then made a small pot of coffee. After it had brewed, she held a cup of it in her hands and sat staring at the glowing stove. She finished the coffee and walked to the bedroom and pushed open the door. Paul's snoring reminded Kristine of the purring of a cat. She pulled the door closed. Kristine once more cleaned her kitchen, then went to the bedroom, removed her clothing and crawled slowly into the bed, behind Paul, and quietly maneuvered her body up very close to him.

In the night he awakened and the hunger, the craving, of each for the other was gratified. They both slept embraced, facing one another, their arms entwined, peacefully, until Kristine awakened, arose quietly and prepared a breakfast of porridge and toasted bread and coffee. While he slept she mended the holes in his heavy woolen stockings. His trousers and shirt and jacket were not quite dry but Kristine heated an iron with a curved handle of hardwood, resting it on the hot stove, and then pressed the clothes and hung them up again. She gave him one of her grandmother's robes, and although it was too small for his frame, he wore it while he ate his breakfast.

"Two hot meals in a row. I can't believe I'm home." Paul said.

"Don't leave the house, Paul," Kristine said, "I'm nervous about a stranger watching the house. I'm sure he is not one of the Americans. The military police from the air base drive by here regularly. Some awful things have happened and I'll tell you about them later." Kristine spoke softly, as if afraid she might be overheard. "I'll locate father for supper. He will be amazed. He believed you had been killed. And I will ask the chaplain for advice."

"Christ, Kris, I hope the war is really over!" he said.

"God has returned you to me."

Before the time scheduled to begin her chores as a maid, Kristine waited in the hall outside of the office of Captain Waldron. A punctual officer, he arrived promptly at 8:00 a.m.

"My! Frau Schuttenhelm, what brings you here so early?"

"May I confide, sir?"

"Confide?" Captain Waldron said. He unlocked his office door and indicated with his hand for her to proceed into the office ahead of him. "So, what's so serious with you this bright morning, Kristine?"

"My Paul is alive. My husband. He has escaped the Russians. He is home, at my grandmother's house. I told him to stay in the house. Not go out.""

"Your husband Paul!" the chaplain exclaimed. "That is incredible. Didn't someone tell you he'd been killed?"

"Yes. A soldier. It was a mistake because of our wedding ring. He gave it to a friend, who was killed. But it was to be given to him to indicate to me that he was alive. But that boy was killed and passed it along to another. By the time it exchanged hands, between soldiers, the story I was told was that he was dying and wanted me to have it! Crazy! Crazy! Can you believe it?"

"Kristine, after the last couple of years, I can believe anything. I'm so happy for you."

"I need your wisdom," She said.

"Oh?"

"Should Paul surrender to the Americans?" Kristine asked. "He has only his military uniform. But no one, no military authority, so far, has ever questioned my father or made him a prisoner of war. Is it because he is disabled? I don't know what to tell Paul."

"Wow!" the chaplain exclaimed. "I'll have to check with Colonel Schlosser, Kris, or the adjutant. Yes, I would think he should turn himself in to the M.P.'s, but let me make a couple of calls. I don't know about your father, but I'd say just leave it alone. A military inconsistency."

"May I ask a favor, sir?"

"Certainly."

"May I trade some coal for some eggs, some carrots, a portion of pork or beef?" Kristine asked. "I don't think Paul has eaten much for several weeks."

"Sure. We'll go over to mess hall before you close the library."

"May I leave early today? I must locate my father to tell him."

"Sure, Kristine." The captain said, "What are you going to do next?"

"I've the rooms and hallways to clean."

"Okay. On your mid-day break, meet me here at my office and we'll go see the mess sergeant and fix you up with some supplies."

"Thank you. And about Paul?"

"I'll have an answer for you at noon."

"Thank you, pastor, oh, I mean Captain Waldron."

Captain Waldron laughed. "Haven't been called that since I left home. Has a nice sound. See you later, Kristine."

Kristine departed. Her cleaning supplies were in a large closet. Other maids were arriving and they greeted one another, selected the items they needed and went their separate ways.

At noon Kristine returned to Captain Waldron's office. She stood outside of his open door. Captain Waldron was speaking on the telephone when he saw her and he motioned with one hand for her to enter and be seated.

"Hi Kristine," the chaplain said. "We'll head over to the mess hall in a little while and fix you up with stuff for a good supper."

"This will come from my pay, yes?"

"That's right," the chaplain said, "Now for the important thing. I've spoken with Colonel Schlosser and he checked with the military police, Intelligence, everyone concerned. The best thing for Paul to do is simply surrender. He suggested tomorrow morning. The colonel is going to be busy the rest of the day and evening with a V.I.P., so he won't be involved, but I'll come to your home early in the morning with the M.P.'s, if that's okay."

"I'm sure Paul will be anxious to get on with it, but, V. I. P.? I don't understand."

"Very important person," the captain replied, laughing. "Now, Frau Schuttenhelm, there's something else I want you to know. Lieutenant Sunder is shipping out in the morning. The colonel doesn't want something happening to him, like happened to Lieutenant McAdam. I know that at one time you and Marshall were friends. But Colonel Schlosser has also ordered him not to see you. He won't be able to say good-bye."

"I do not wish ever to see him. You know, sir, that he was the one who bombed our bridge," Kristine said.

"Come on now, Kristine, I believe we've already covered the subject of a soldier's duty, or a flier's duty. Marshall, the entire crew, they did what they were ordered to do, but certainly not with the intention of harming you."

"Yes, I understand. And I wish him no harm. I simply do not want to see him," Kristine said, with finality.

"Well, the colonel has already taken care of that. So," he paused, looked at his wristwatch, and continued. "What say we go to the mess hall, to the kitchen rather, and see what we can select?"

"I will work extra hours," Kristine said.

"I'll keep you very busy," Captain Waldron said, and laughed. "Now, I know where your father is working. We can stop on the way to the kitchen. Let's go."

Kristine walked at the side of chaplain as they went from his office to one of the buildings where the fliers and other officers were billeted. The odor of wet paint greeted them when they entered the building. Captain Waldron and Kristine walked along the hallway, finally stopping at one of the rooms. Drop cloths were scattered around, covering the furniture. He was busy painting and didn't hear them. Kristine's father stood balanced on one leg, leaning against a wall as he slowly moved his tapered brush along the edge of the wood trim next to a pane of glass.

In German Kristine said, " Father. Excuse me. I have news."

Her father turned to her slowly. He glanced at Captain Waldron and nodded. He removed excess paint from the brush and laid the brush across the top of the container. Captain Waldron suspected that he could speak English, but the conversation proceeded in German.

"News?"

"Paul has returned. He's at grandma's house. He's weary. Please join us for supper tonight after your work."

"Paul! My God! Alive? Home?"

"Yes, father. There's much to tell. He will surrender to the Americans tomorrow."

"That's good! That's good! Oh! Thank God! I can't believe it, Kristine. It's a miracle!"

"Please tell no one, father. No one. We will see you tonight."

"Of course. But he must surrender only to the Americans. You understand? You must obtain a guarantee that he will not be turned over to the Russians or the British!"

"Yes."

Her father reached for the paintbrush and dipped it into the container. He began to paint, then turned to Kristine and Captain Waldron and whispered, "Look at my hands shake. Finally some good news!"

Kristine then walked to him and put her hand on his arm and leaned close and kissed him on the cheek.

"Thank you, my little girl," he said. Captain Waldron and Kristine departed.

"Well, Kris," the captain said, looking down at her, "I got the gist of most of that. Now let's see if we can load you up with some goodies!"

"Father is concerned that Paul might be turned over to the Russians or the British."

"Why? For what reason? I can't believe that would happen. What is his military rank?"

"A corporal."

"Then I don't think there will be any problem, but I'll make sure. I'll speak to Colonel Schlosser this afternoon."

"Despite the V. I. P.?"

The captain laughed, "No problem. I shouldn't have even mentioned it. Come on, let's get you some supplies for that dinner."

They walked briskly to the officer's mess hall, then to the kitchen where the First Sergeant, a highly trained chef, was located at his desk. The captain introduced Kristine and explained that she was heading up the new library, and that she was eager to fix a substantial meal for her father and husband. The cost of supplies would be deducted from her pay.

The First Sergeant shook Kristine's hand and smiled down at her. "So what have you in mind for this feast?"

"If it is possible, I would like to prepare for them some beef or pork. I have potatoes, cabbage, and bread. I have coffee, too, and sugar and flour. A few fresh eggs would be wonderful. I don't have time to trade my coal for eggs in the village."

"Well, let's take a look in the meat locker," the first sergeant said, and she followed him to a vault-like refrigerator. When he opened it, the cold air wafted out over them, and then Kristine looked in and gasped as she saw the slabs of beef and lamb and pork held by hooks.

"I have never before seen that much meat!" she said.

"It is amazing isn't it. With these new refrigerated air cargo planes, it's almost like the States."

"Just enough for two men, really, that's all I need," Kristine stammered. Her eyes were wide.

"Well, little lady, you mentioned pork. I've a boneless top loin roast all ready for the oven. How does that sound?"

Kristine looked towards Captain Waldron; "Can I afford so much."

"Let me worry about that Frau Schuttenhelm. I told you I have loads of work for you," The captain said. He then looked to the first sergeant and nodded, "That's just fine, sergeant, and thank you very much."

"Well now, what would you say to a nice bunch of carrots? And we just got in some terrific MacIntosh Red apples, crisp and sweet! I'll throw in a head of lettuce and some navel oranges and you've got the makings for a fruit salad, or whatever. Do you have oil and vinegar, or any bleu cheese? I don't want to split up a carton, so we have a dozen eggs for your package."

"No sir," Kristine said, "No oil or vinegar or cheese." and tears began to form.

"Well now, I'll put our selection in a bag for you, but one thing," the first sergeant said, appearing to become stern. "One thing now, Frau, I shall expect to find some of the latest cook books in that library of yours very soon."

"Yes sir," Kristine said, nodding, looking up at the man, her voice quavering.

A stout brown bag, filled with supplies, was handed to Kristine. She thanked the sergeant, and followed Captain Waldron out of the kitchen and the mess hall.

"Okay, Kris. Why don't you head on home and get your dinner prepared. I know things will go well for all of you. I'll be coming to your grandmother's house early in the morning to meet Paul. We'll look after him."

"Thank you very much, Captain. Lately, I don't feel like the enemy."

"Come on now, Kris. We're liberators, you know, not conquerors."

"Good evening," Kristine said, and nodded. She balanced her load on one hip and turned to walk towards her home.

"Wait a minute, Frau Schuttenhelm. That's too heavy. I'll give you a lift in my jeep." The chaplain said, then took the package from her.

"You won't get in trouble?"

"Naw. The colonel respects my big boss. He out-ranks everyone."

Kristine laughed at him and followed him towards the vehicle parking area.

When they arrived at her grandmother's house, Kristine scurried out of the jeep, balancing her package on her hip and knocked. Paul opened the door a crack, saw her, then opened it further in time to see the chaplain drive off. He accepted the package from her and leaned over and kissed her. She put her hand behind his head and kept her lips close to his.

"My, what is all of this?" Paul asked, peeking into the top of the package.

"A fine supper for you and father, that's what." Kristine said. She put her arms around him and hugged him. "You smell better, my soldier boy! Your uniform dried, I see."

"And I used your good soap to scrub my head twice. God, it feels so good to be clean again!"

"I found father. He was painting window frames. He was stunned when I told him you'd come home."

"And he is free to move about. I don't understand."

"I don't either. You must understand though, the Americans are strange."

"I'll find out soon enough."

"Look at this food! All I do is clean and type letters and mail them and they allow me to select food that would now cost a fortune. There just isn't any food like this available to us. You see, I'm a V.I.P.!"

"I don't understand?"

"Today I learned that these letters mean 'very important person.'"

"With no obligations?"

"None. Just work. And I am lucky that I speak English and know how to type. That's the difference."

"I've used a little of the coal. What can I do to help you?"

"Just relax, my sweetheart. Have you changed much since you left me?"

"Kristine. I can't tell you what I've seen and done. And today I re-read some of *Mein Kampf.* I feel deceived. We were all deceived."

"Yes! Destroy that book!" Kristine said. "Use it as fuel with the coal. Yes. We were deceived!"

Without hesitation Paul walked to an end table beside the couch, picked up the book and opened the door of the stove and threw it into the opening. "I'll add a little more coal," he said. I'm relieved you feel the same as I. What about your father?"

"We've never talked about it. I don't know. He still seems dazed. I don't know how he copes without mother. He does find a little schnapps some-place, amongst his friends. It's a day at a time now, you know."

"My God, would you look at that pork! Are you going to roast it?'

"Yes. And look! Carrots, apples, oranges and even a head of lettuce. Even some oil and vinegar and rarest of all, some bleu cheese. For one meal, at least, we are rich!"

"Ah, for some beer!"

"You'd better relax. There are texts from the library. You must improve your English. These Americans speak only English, and I feel they may be around for quite awhile."

"So, again, another defeat, and again we'll be punished?"

"Politicians will decide our fate. Not the chaplains, I'm afraid."

"Kristine. It was so incredible when we awakened last night. Is there time before your father arrives, while the supper cooks?"

"Off to the bedroom with you, my sweet!" Kristine said and laughed. "Now, give me a few minutes to get the roast in the oven!"

"And I bathed again during the day, Kris. I am a clean husband now!" Paul said, and Kristine was delighted to once again hear the sparkle in his voice.

Later, as they were sitting on the couch looking at pictures in a scrapbook, they heard the knock at the door. She jumped at the sound, and was relieved when she opened the door and let her father enter. Before she closed the door she looked across the street, but saw no one. A jeep slowly drove past her house, a soldier raised his arm and waved at her and grinned, and she had grown accustomed to its schedule. She waved back.

While she hesitated at the door, her father, balancing with his crutch beneath one arm, embraced Paul.

"I never thought we'd see you again, Paul," her father said. Kristine was surprised to see tears stream down his face. He'd always been so stoic. He hadn't reacted that emotionally when he had returned and learned of the death of his wife and grandchild and of the suicide of Kristine's maternal grandmother. By then, they had assumed that Paul, too, was dead.

"My God, this house smells of wholesome food!" the father said.

"We have a home-coming feast tonight," Kristine said.

"I am sorry about your leg," Paul said.

"Maybe it is a blessing. I don't know what they did with my comrades. The Canadians treated me kindly enough. I think I was more trouble than I was worth. You know, to haul around and stumble over."

"Father. You are doing fine now."

"Kristine. Did I tell you the Americans are going to fix me up with a prosthesis, they call it, and help me learn to walk with it." Her father said, " I may not even need a crutch. At least that's what the doctor has said."

"Well, our own doctors can do that when they start to practice again," Kristine said. She tilted her chin upwards.

"Of course, if ever," the father nodded, "But now, I've a little surprise for you! My neighbor saved some schnapps in his basement. For little odd jobs the fliers pay me with cigarettes. Eight cigarettes and we have a flask full, so each of us will have a generous swallow or two!" The father displayed a small flask and handed it over to Kristine. Both she and Paul joined him as he laughed heartily.

"Let's save it for after supper to sip before the stove," Kristine said, and the two men nodded in agreement.

Kristine then told them to take their places at the table and she served the food she had prepared. At each place she placed a small salad with lettuce. She cut pieces of the apples and divided sections of the oranges and mixed them in with the lettuce leaves. "I have both the oil and vinegar or I have this bleu cheese that you can crumble into the salad. Whatever you wish."

"Shall we hold hands, children?" the father asked. They did, as they lowered their heads, and the father spoke quietly, "Bless this food to our use and us to thy service, in Christ's name. Ah men."

Kristine and Paul and her father took small portions and ate slowly, quietly. Her father looked at Kristine and nodded, "Excellent pork. You fixed it perfectly."

"I'd forgotten what good food tastes like," Paul said. "You must be a very good worker!"

"What is the saying, 'even the darkest cloud has a silver lining.'"

"And, 'it is darkest before dawn.'" her father added.

"And now, my dear ones," Kristine said, "I too have a surprise. An extra apple and an orange for each of us for dessert! You may eat them here at the table, save them for later, or go to the couch and the big chair and enjoy them. But no dripping of orange juice, understand," she said, laughing. "I will do the dishes and you men relax."

"I will eat mine now, and I will be careful," Paul said. He walked to the couch and took with him a dishcloth. "An orange is so rare. It will have to follow the apple."

"Paul, I have an American cigarette for you. Actually, I have two. Kristine would you like to have a cigarette?"

"Come now father. Not for me. You and Paul enjoy them!" Kristine said, laughing.

"And then the schnapps."

"And some more coal for the fire," Kristine said.

A rare feeling of content engulfed the Schuttenhelm family. It had been over two years since the three of them had been together. Each felt the absence of the mother, the grandmother and the baby, but none wished to break their reverie by bringing up the names of the deceased. There would be time for remorse and grieving.

"So, you experienced the war's brutality," Kristine said. She did not address either man, simply made the statement as she stared at the flames beyond the open door.

"I've had so many nightmares," Paul finally offered. "I am haunted by the faces. They were so close to us. We were shooting point blank at the Russian boys and they were dying and shooting back and running and screaming and our men were doing the same. Men slaughtering men! Why, for God's sake?"

"Stupidity! We humans are simply stupid!" The father said. "At Ijmuiden, twice we knew they were coming, the Americans, in the same airplanes that are here. They came across the English Channel, not far above the wave tops, and we lowered our 88's and blew them apart. A few boys somehow survived the crashes, the others we buried. Many were trapped as the airplanes sank. Why they didn't learn the first time, God only knows? How could such ignorance have finally beaten us?"

"Father, so that you will know, Paul and I burned *Mein Kampf*." Kristine said, hesitantly, apprehensive about his reply.

"Sehr Gut!" he said, raising his voice, and they thought he would stand for emphasis. His eyes opened wide and his mouth quivered. "Now listen carefully, Kristine, Paul," he whispered, and leaned towards them gripping his hands together. "It is my generation, your mother even, but especially me, that allowed ourselves to be deceived by that puny bastard. We were greedy. We were ambitious, we wanted better things for Germany, and we turned our backs on the Holy Bible. We permitted this horrible thing to happen to our homeland. Blame me. Oh, do not burden yourselves with this catastrophe. You were young and innocent. I did not seek the truth when the Rappaport family disappeared. It was me that looked the other way. I'm afraid now to even ask about them! God forgive me!" He unclenched his fists and rested his face in his hands, and they watched his body shudder over and over, and heard him sob.

Paul and Kristine both walked to him and rested their hands on his thin shoulders. Kristine rubbed the base of his neck. He sighed deeply, sat back upright and said, "I am sorry to be so emotional in front of you. Remember children," he said, pacing his words slowly and deliberately, "you must disdain blind obedience!"

"We will, we will father," Kristine said, " And, I know this is a bad time to tell you this, but the violence hasn't ended," Kristine said. "Right here in Bad Scheidel, American fliers have been caught with German girls and castrated. It's horrible."

"So, the German girls are guilty, too, then?" The father said.

"That is such an ugly thing to do!" Paul said. "Does a sane life begin for me tomorrow? I hope your chaplain can be trusted. And father, I want you to have my Walther. Here are extra cartridges and it is loaded. I don't want to have it with me when the Americans arrive."

"I trust Captain Waldron," Kristine said.

"Well, I hope you know him well," Paul yawned and stood up. "It's to bed with me, dear family. Pray tomorrow will be better. Goodnight."

"Wait, Paul, Kristine, listen carefully now," the father said. He had dried his cheeks with his open palms. "Kristine, I want you to find a needle. Paul, you take off your shirt." Kristine returned from her sewing basket and handed a slim, polished needle, one and a half inches in length, to her father. He studied it. "Just right. Now, Kristine, conceal it, hide it in his collar, along the line of the sewn edge, right at the front there. Yes, very good."

"What's that for" Paul asked, as he watched Kristine push the needle into his shirt along the edge of the collar.

"If things don't go too well, for whatever reason. You ask for an American doctor and tell him of the very great pain in your kidney area. I know the Americans. They will want to give you a physical. When it is time to provide a sample of your urine, use that needle to punch the tip of your finger and put several drops of your blood in with the urine. They will order bed rest. Then you can collect your wits and determine your next move. You will be fed well, and the rest will do you good!"

"Where did you hear of such a thing?" Kristine asked.

"A friend, in Holland. He was so exhausted, we thought he would die. Another soldier loaned him the needle. It worked, and he rested and was finally strong enough to return to duty."

"Thank you, father," Paul said. He arose from the couch and went to the bedroom. Kristine's father struggled with his crutch, then lifted himself out of the chair and turned to Kristine to say goodnight.

"Father, it is cold and very slick outside. I want you to curl up on the couch and I'll get blankets for you. If you want to undress, we have several of grandmother's robes to cover yourself."

"Really? I must be up early for work, you know?"

"Ha! That's both of us, father, and the captain will be here early for Paul. I'll awaken early."

"Thank you, Kristine. You are a very caring daughter."

"I'm throwing on a couple more chunks of coal so you'll sleep warmly."

Kristine found a bathrobe, the longest of her grandmother's and gave it to her father. As he took it she realized he wasn't much taller than her grandmother.

"Where is the little pistol?" he asked. "I will keep it with me." The gun was where Paul had laid it and Kristine found it and gave it to her father. He put it in a pocket of the robe.

"Really no need for that," Kristine said.

"I know, my dear. I just don't want it sitting around."

"Goodnight, father," Kristine said. They embraced and touched their cheeks together.

They slept soundly until the quietness of the house was violated when the front door was kicked. It resisted and was kicked twice more and the inside latch was broken away from the molding. The father rolled off of the couch and turned onto his knees and tried to lift himself to where he could reach his crutch. He was pushed back to the floor by a large man who bent over him and said, "Where is the American? Where is the flier? So, he's in the bedroom with that whore?"

"Get out of here! There is no American here! Take your coal or whatever you're after and leave!"

Blue light from the early dawn made the few objects in the living room visible. Only a few coals glowed in the stove.

Kristine opened the bedroom door, clad in a light dressing gown. "What is this? Out with you, thief! The M.P.'s are near!"

"Where's that American, you whore!"

"Stupid! Stupid! My husband is with me!" Kristine screamed at the intruder.

"Husband shit! I'll cut his balls out now, like the others!" He pushed Kristine aside and started for the door to the bedroom.

"My God! You are insane!"

At that instant, Paul, with only his military trousers on, his chest bare, rushed out of the bed room.

"Who do you think you are, you stupid pig? I am a German soldier!"

"You lie!" The intruder yelled. He reached into his pocket and brought out a switch blade knife, touching the button and the blade snapped open, the blue morning light reflecting off of the razor-edge knife.

The father had recovered. He stood leaning on his crutch, his eyes wide, and watched as the intruder approached Paul. Kristine screamed and jumped on his back. He turned to throw her aside. She fell heavily to the floor, and Paul ran forward and grabbed the intruder by the throat with both hands, and raised his knee as hard as he could into the man's groin. The man cursed, and pushed one large hand into Paul's face and broke free. He then swung his fist, still holding the knife in his other hand, and caught Paul on the point of his chin. Paul collapsed, his head struck the floor hard, and the man bent over the unconscious form, and struggled to pull down his trousers.

Holding the small end of his crutch, the father balanced himself and swung the top of the crutch in a great arc, and it broke and splintered as it struck the back of the intruder's head. The intruder fell, then yelled "Traitors! Traitors of the Fatherland." The father struck him again, but he arose and with one swing of a heavy, muscular arm sent the father crashing across the room, knocking over a chair. The intruder put a hand to his head. He had dropped his knife and looked on the floor for it. Kristine, now on her knees, saw it and grabbed it before he could reach for it; she flung it across the room away from them.

The morning had brightened, the reddish-white arc of the sun moved above the rooftops, and the furniture in the room was now visible. Kristine knew it would not be long before the M.P.'s would cruise by her door.

The intruder stood and looked around the room for the knife. He could not locate it, then yelled, "This is not over, traitors!"

In her fury, once more Kristine flung herself onto his back as he moved towards the front door. Her father was able to sit up and crawled to the overturned chair. From the robe pocket he took the Walther and yelled, "Kristine, get away from him. I will shoot him!"

As with a wounded grizzly bear, the man raged and growled, and turned as he attempted to shake Kristine off. He could not free himself and tried to loosen her hold by backing against the doorframe. She fell then, and her father fired when she was out of his sight, but the chair was unsteady and the bullet ricocheted off of one of the stones around the doorframe. The bullet struck Kristine. The stranger saw her gasp and grab her side. He swung one fist and caught her on the temple and she collapsed. In quick succession the father fired twice more and heard the thud of the small bullets striking the stranger. The father did not know where the bullets had hit, but the man stumbled, then stood up and looked back at Kristine, blood now forming on her gown, he grimaced. He yelled, "Whore!" then tried to run, began to hobble, limping hurriedly in the direction of the bridge.

The sun had pushed half way up the roof tops and the shots from the small pistol were faint, but the M.P. riding in the passenger side of the patrol jeep thought he heard shots. "Better cruise by that German woman's place," he said.

"Little early, isn't it?" the driver asked.

"I though I heard some shots. Like firecrackers."

"The driver made a U-turn with his jeep and quickly arrived at the grandmother's house.

"Wow! What happened to the front door?"

"The father was standing over the still form of Kristine, balanced on his good leg, when he looked up and saw the M.P.'s

"Help! Help!" he yelled, in English, and waved for them to come to the door.

Both of them jumped from the jeep and raced to the door. "Holy mackerel, that little German woman is bleeding like a stuck pig!"

"Call the medics, quick." The sergeant responded and used his walkie-talkie.

"Where's your crutch, Pop?"

"It is broken. A thief attacked us." Again he spoke in English.

"Tell the medics to bring a crutch."

"Roger. I've made contact. They're on the way."

"Jesus, what can we do for the girl?"

"Get a towel," the father said. He nodded to the living room. The M.P. returned quickly and the father kneeled and pulled the gown open. Blood trickled from a tiny hole just beneath the rib cage. He pressed the towel against the opening. Kristine did not move.

With the sirens blaring, the medics arrived at the grandmother's home.

The medics pushed through the gathering crowd of Germans to the side of Kristine. Her face was white. The medic felt her pulse. "She's got a good pulse, but she's either in, or approaching, shock. We've got to get her to the morgue in a hurry."

"What are you saying! Kristine is not dead!" her father shouted.

"Take it easy mister! The first aid station is temporarily at the morgue. Come on along if you want, and we've got a couple of crutches for you. You just hang on, stand there for a second, damn it, and I'll fetch a crutch for you," the medic said.

"Her husband is unconscious in the front room." the father said. "I shot a burglar. I hit him twice. He ran towards the bridge."

A gurney was brought to the doorway. Several German women and a few elderly men had congregated there. They pushed and shoved one another, gawking, trying to see what was happening. The two boys who polished shoes for the fliers arrived, on their way to school, and crowded around the front door. Kristine was carefully lifted and placed on the gurney. A sheet was thrown across her and it flipped up, covering her head. Blood from her gown stained the sheet quickly, and blood continued to flow slowly. The father, using the crutches, went to the ambulance and climbed into it.

"Get her into the ambulance and get a I.V. going, use that Ringers solution," one of the medics shouted.

"Roger. I'll be ready for her," the other medic replied.

Then Cal and Marshall arrived at the scene.

"What the hell is going on!" Marshall shouted. "Let me out. Stop here! Cal, stop! I've got see what's going on."

He jumped from the slowing jeep and ran towards the gathering at the front door. The medics were wheeling the gurney towards their ambulance.

"It is Frau Schuttenhelm," housewife said. "She's been shot. She's dying!" Another housewife yelled. Another cried out, "She's dead, that one!"

Marshall ran towards the ambulance, pushing people aside, shoving them violently, yelling, shouting at the top of his voice, "Kristine, Kristine!" Again and again he yelled her name. "Kristine!" He tried to elbow his way to the ambulance but was pushed back by irate Germans.

"Get that guy out of here," one of the medics yelled. "We've got to head for the morgue!"

"Oh, my God, my God," Marshall screamed at them. " Wait. She can't be dead!"

"Hey, Sarge," one of the medics yelled at the M.P. standing beside the front door. "Clear this damn crowd out of here. We've got to get to the morgue!"

"Marsh, for Christ sake, get hold of yourself," Cal said, gathering his breath. He had parked along the street, several houses away, ran back, and tried to restrain him.

The M.P. grabbed Marshall's arm. "Quiet down, sir, or you're going to cause a riot. These Germans are pissed off with us enough as it is!"

Marshall shoved the sergeant, pushed him away. "Damn it, sir, I'm going to have to arrest you if you don't calm down."

"Go fuck yourself!" Marshall yelled, struggled, then swung his arm, his fist clinched, at the sergeant, who ducked, grabbed Marshall and spun him, and then with his billy club, the M.P. struck Marshall on the back of his head and he collapsed on the cobblestone street. The M.P. saw Cal rushing toward him. "Sorry, sir, but I had no choice," he shouted.

Two German women began to kick Marshall. They kicked his chest and kicked his head. He was unconscious. Cal tried to reach him through the crowd.

"Stop that you pigs!" one of the small boys yelled, and with the help of his friend, dragged Marshall away from the angry women. "He is our friend! We work for him!" Cal arrived at Marshall's side. He thanked the boys. "Now please help me get him into my jeep," Cal said.

The boys helped Cal carry Marshall's limp form to the jeep, where the three of them managed to get him into the front seat. He fell forward from the waist, head resting on the dashboard. His hair was bloody above his neck.

"Wait, mister, I'll be right back." The boy said, and he raced into the grandmother's house, found a towel and as he returned he stopped at a snow bank and scooped up snow onto the towel, then folded it and ran back to the jeep. "This will help his headache," the boy said, then he and his friend stood back, their eyes wide, as Cal drove towards the flight line.

The M.P.'s looked on in amazement. The ambulance drove away, with its sirens again blaring.

As the ambulance disappeared, another vehicle approached. It was a staff car, driven by a M.P. with another in the front seat. In the back seat sat Captain Waldron. He saw the crowd as it began to thin and slowly wander off, the women talking excitedly with each other, pointing back at the house.

He was stunned to see the M.P. standing at the door. The other M.P. was in the house trying to arouse Paul. The sergeant had seen the small boy obtain the snow, and he did the same. He held the chilled cloth to the back of Paul's neck.

"I'll get out here, please," Captain Waldron said. "When you are parked come on back."

"Yes sir," the driver said, "and First Sergeant Kelleher can accompany you."

"May I also?"

"Oh, certainly, come right ahead, sergeant."

At the doorway, Captain Waldron asked the M.P. what had happened. "From what we can gather, some guy broke in and tried to rob them. I guess they all put up a whale of a fight. The young lady was wounded and the medics have taken her to first aid, along with her old man. He said he shot the burglar a couple of times, and we'll look into that later. There is a young fellow in there that my partner is trying to revive. Guess he was knocked cold. Wouldn't you believe it? Now the damn Germans are fighting each other!"

"Great Scott! Well, let's take a look." First Sergeant Kelleher followed the chaplain into the house.

As they entered, the M.P. was trying to help Paul sit up. He looked around the room. His eyes were still glazed, but he tried to stand up.

"Just sit still for a little while, fellow," The M.P. said and then arose and saluted Captain Waldron. "I'm surprised to see you here, chaplain."

Captain Waldron returned the salute. "The kid is really out of it, isn't he?"

Paul then struggled to his feet and raised both arms over his head and said, "I surrender."

"Okay, Paul, you can lower your arms. I'm Captain Waldron, the squadron Chaplain. Kristine said you wanted to surrender to Americans. Here they are," and he turned to First Sergeant Kelleher.

"Skinny kid, isn't he," the sergeant said and laughed. "Well, come along Son, we'll fatten you up."

"Yes sir," Paul stammered..

"Why don't you put on the rest of your uniform." The chaplain suggested. "Then tell us what happened. I understand that Kristine has been taken to first aid, and that her father accompanied her."

"What happened to my wife? I was unconscious. And to father?"

"I'm not really certain, Son, but she's in good hands. In a few minutes we'll try to contact the first aid station."

As they waited, the chaplain began to pick up the broken pieces of the crutch. When the chaplain and Sergeant Kelleher righted the overstuffed chair, they saw the open switch-blade knife. The captain and the sergeant looked at the open front door. The sun was higher and the room was brighter. The hinges were intact, and except for the broken latch, the door was in otherwise good condition. As they started to close the door, they heard the engine of a small airplane. Cal flew low over the house, dipped his wings, then turned, gained altitude and headed west towards Paris, and eventually Le Havre.

"That must have been Cal and Marshall," the captain said.

While they were busy with Paul, the M.P. at the door walked back into the room and picked up both the switch blade knife and the Walther pistol and put him in his own jacket. Then he approached Captain Waldron.

"Sir, I'm Sergeant Jesus Chavez. A couple of fliers stopped by here just about the time all hell was breaking loose. One of them was really hysterical, yelling 'Kristine', and when I tried to calm him down he took a swing at me, so I had to cold-cock him. I hated to hit him, sir, but we were afraid of these Germans rioting. I'll put it all in my report, sir."

"Incredible!" the captain said, shaking his head.

When Paul dressed, he made certain the needle was secure in the front edge of his shirt collar. "Okay, we're off to headquarters," Sergeant Kelleher said, then continued, "Relax Son, you're in good hands. Nothing to worry about."

"Captain Waldron, sir?" one of the M.P.'s with whom he'd arrived at the house called out.

"Right here, sergeant. What is it?"

"Learned from first aid that the little German woman is going to be okay. The bullet didn't hit anything vital. They've got her stabilized. Her dad is with her."

"That's great. Thank you."

"You hear that, young man?" Sergeant Kelleher asked. "The wife is okay."

"Thank you," Paul said. He was pale and shaken as he was guided out of the house.

"Everything is going to be fine," Sergeant Kelleher said. He had six gold bars sewed on his sleeve, indicating three years overseas, and the rockers beneath his three top stripes indicated he was a first sergeant.

"Sure thing," the M.P. at the door said, snickering, as they walked past him. The three stripes on his arm indicated that he was a buck sergeant, "He'll have a choice of a black blindfold or a cigarette." He laughed aloud, then, as he saw Paul turn and stare at him.

"Pardon me a minute, chaplain," First Sergeant Kelleher said. He walked back towards the door.

"Hey! Geronimo!" Sergeant Kelleher addressed the M.P., "Do you think you can track down that Nazi bastard that caused all this trouble?"

"So what's in it for me? The war is over. Remember?"

"Chavez," Sergeant Kelleher said, "if you can find that guy and get him back here alive, I'll personally recommend you for a Bronze Star."

"More pay for the medal?"

"Of course. Plus points."

"How about just a scalp?"

"No more damn scalps! Maybe a rocker, if you bring him back alive."

"Hmmm. Staff Sergeant Jesus Chavez. That has a nice ring to it, Meeester Kelleher!" The sergeant looked down at his sleeve with the three stripes and with his fingertip drew an imaginary curved rocker.

"Come on, Chavez, get a couple of guys to help you and knock off that Tijuana lingo."

"Okay, okay, Meeester sergeant, I will capture you a Nazi bastard. Hey man, you know, seriously, someday back in the States, you must come to L.A., I'll introduce you to my seeester. We're important Mexicanos. We've a raveeene named after us!" He put his head back and laughed, his dark brown eyes sparkled, his grin revealed straight white teeth, and his black hair was straight and trimmed neatly. He spoke loudly enough to be sure the chaplain heard him.

"Get going, Geronimo!" Sergeant Kelleher said, "And take some back-up. We want that hombre back alive."

"Vereee good Spanish!" Sergeant Chavez said, and laughed. He looked around at the other M.P.'s, "Any of you Gringos want to give me a hand?"

"Sure, I'll join you, Poncho. You got more guts than brains," A corporal said, laughing, and then another corporal walked over and said, "Climb into my jeep, Sergeant Chavez, I'm at your service."

"My, you've quite a group of characters, sergeant," Captain Waldron said.

"All darn good men, sir, and we're running a little loose now that the war is over."

"I understand. But what was all that nonsense about a scalp?"

"That's true, sir. Chavez was with the 3rd Army before they transferred him over to us. I think it happened someplace in Belgium. A family, an old man and his wife and a couple of grandkids were hiding some American fliers, and an SS trooper discovered them. He took his burp gun and just cut them all in half, killed them all, all six of them, and then our guys showed up and Chavez arrived first, and kind of went nuts. He flipped. He shot the SS guy, then honest to God, he scalped him, then walked into the headquarters tent, and dumped the damn thing on the platoon lieutenant's desk and said, "Long live the Apaches!""

"Absolutely amazing!"

"Well, they made him a buck sergeant, and gave him a week's pass, but the guys in his outfit were leery of him, didn't know how to cope with him. He is a real character! So they transferred him to us. Hell, he's really quite a bright guy. Went to college in L.A. and has had some bit parts in the movies. Handsome kid, isn't he?"

"Certainly. But do you think he'll find the intruder?"

"Sure. You know, he's told me about how he's helped his cousins hide, then helps them cross the border from Mexico into California. Any Mexican, he considers a cousin."

"I never cease to be amazed. I realize I'm naive, Sergeant Kelleher. I admit it. So, now, before your Maker, are you putting me on?"

"Chaplain, if you want me to say all this on the Good Book, I'll do it!"

Sergeant Chavez rode on the passenger side of the jeep with one of the corporals riding in the back seat.

"Drive very, very slowly," Sergeant Chavez cautioned. "I need a scuff mark, a drop of blood." He leaned out of the jeep and scanned the roadside as they barely moved. "Stop and I'll get out here. If he's like my cousins, he'll be hiding up in the guts of the old bridge. Yep! He's dragging a leg. No blood, though."

The driver stopped the jeep at the edge of the road. Sergeant Chavez spoke quietly, "Okay. I hope you guys are good shots. One of you go to other end of the bridge, and I'm going to climb beneath it. I want the sun at my back." He nodded to the other M.P. sitting in the back seat. "You watch from the other side. Now remember, you guys yell 'halt' if you see him make a run for it. If he doesn't halt, aim for his knees, and if you miss, aim for the middle of his back. Understand?"

"Yell 'halt' once?"

"He'll understand. Once is enough! Okay?" Sergeant Chavez said, "I'm going to try to talk him out of there. I want that damn medal, or the promotion, or both, understand?"

"What if we hear a shot?"

"I hope he's not carrying a P 38, or a Luger, but I've my .45 is right here," and he patted his hip: "plus I have the old man's twenty two-pistol, and I know how to use that bastard's switchblade better than he does! If he makes a run for it, shoot him! If he drops into the river, follow him along the bank, downstream of course, and shoot the bastard! And, for Christ's sake, watch out for each other! Don't shoot each other! You got it?"

Both of the M.P.'s nodded and began to cautiously walk towards their stations. Sergeant Chavez waited a few minutes, was satisfied that the two men stopped where he had advised. Then he too, cautiously began to lower himself down the embankment where the bridge joined the cobblestone roadway. *Just like the border. Good place to wait until dark.* He leaned against a thick post and waited until his eyes had become accustomed to the darkness. Cross-braces and beams supported the new planks installed by the Army Corps of Engineers.

"Hello, my friend!" he hollered. "Make it easy for me, and come out with your hands up, okay?"

There was no response.

"I am a very patient Indian. Apache ancestors. Ever hear of Geronimo? He was my great, great third or fourth uncle, I theeenk. Do you speak Apache, or Mexican or a leeetle Spanish," Sergeant Chavez spoke loudly, in a singsong melodious tone. "I know you are under here. I can smell you!" He laughed loudly. He sat down for a few minutes and listened for any sound of movement or of breathing. All he could hear was the gurgling of the river. "Now I am going to sharpen your switchblade on my leather boot. When I am through, I'll be able to shave with it. Can you see me? A leeetle speeet on the leather, and then I sharpen the blade in a circular motion. Ah, pretty good steel. I am patient." He sharpened the tip of the blade, then called out "I'll wait just a leeetle bit longer!"

As the sergeant chattered he scanned the area, looking into every dark corner, he then began to move very slowly, watching for any movement. "Hey, hombre, do you know that we Mexicans and Negroes are making love to your widows and your sweethearts? You are too pure, you Aryans, but we will improve your bloodlines! A leeetle Jesse Owens blood and you can really run and retreat much faster! My Apache blood will help, too. Indians don't need to beat up leeetle girls, and old, one-legged men! Aha! Maybe you are one of those tough SS gringos, eh?" Sergeant Chavez raised his voice, "Come on Deutscheclown, surrender! I smell you, and now I can hear you breathe!"

Sergeant Chavez was quiet then, and crawled beside a beam very slowly. He deliberately kicked loose a stone and it clattered down the bank to the water. "I'm getting closer!"

"Schweinehund!" The voice came from the darkness further back beneath the planks.

"My sharp shooters are at both ends of the bridge. They won't understand the words 'I surrender' in case you choose the river! Verstehen Dummkopf!"

There was no answer.

"Hey, Heinie, I have the old man's leeetle pistol. You can't have much of a bullet in you! And I have my American .45, which makes a nickel size hole going in and a saucer size hole coming out. Verstehen saucer? Big fucking hole right in the middle of your back. Or skull!" Sergeant Chavez now shouted his words. "So, if you don't start sliding down from there with your hands over your head very queeekly, I am coming in and I will shoot you full of beeeg holes, and when you fall into that nice warm creek, my men will shoot more big holes into you!"

"Ach! I surrender! Schweinhund!"

"Okay, Mister. About damn time! Good! Now kneel or slide or crawl, or walk, if you can, but keep your hands over your head or I'll shoot you!" Sergeant Chavez hissed his commands. "I hate to tell you this, you big ugly bastard, but you'll probably live a long time if you don't fuck with me now! So get going! Man, you steeenk like a hog farm. You need a bath!"

The man was over six foot tall, with broad shoulders and thick arms, his clothes dirty, and he slipped and fell and struggled towards Sergeant Chavez, with his hands over his head, swaying side to side to keep his balance, as he limped at every step.

"Well, well," Sergeant Chavez exclaimed, "You are the first blond German I've ever seen, and I've been here for over a year! If Hitler could only see you now."

The German turned and spat at Sergeant Chavez and in English, yelled, "Shut up!"

"Do that once more and I'll cut your tongue out and throw it to the fish!" Sergeant Chavez said. They worked their way up the embankment until he could see along the length of the old bridge.

"Hey corporal!" Sergeant Chavez yelled, "Please come over here! Keep your .45 handy. We've superman on our hands." The M.P. ran to the edge of the bridge and looked down at them.

"Now, careful there! Don't help the bastard up that bank! If he gets a hand on you he'll drag you down it and I'll have to shoot the both of you. Let the girl-beater crawl!"

The German stumbled to his knees, rested, then with his hands clasped behind his head, managed to reach the cobblestone road. The other M.P. saw them, and ran the length of the bridge. He held his .45 in one hand and panted. "Jesus!" he exclaimed," you caught the guy!" The German struggled to his feet, spread them wide and stared from one to the other.

Sergeant Chavez laughed, then said, "Where'd you learn my name?"

The M.P. didn't answer. He stared at the German, then at Chavez.

"Okay, fella, you put your peashooter away and we'll keep our guns on superman while you handcuff him. Get his hands behind his back now! Damn, he must live with hogs!"

"Yes sir!" the M.P. said.

"Well done. Now you guys are going to help hoist him into the front seat, and you'll ride in the back. I'll drive."

Several German men and women had stopped to observe the arrest. They watched, but remained silent. Sergeant Chavez made a U turn with the jeep. Then he slowed and stopped the jeep beside an elderly man. "Sir?" Sergeant Chavez asked, "I admire your hat. That little green feather and all. Would you part with it for some cigarettes? Four packs of Luckies?

The man grinned broadly, handed over his hat and accepted the cigarettes that Sergeant Chavez had in his jacket.

"Shutzstaffe," Sergeant Chavez said, nodding to the handcuffed German beside him.

"Ubelater!" The man said and looked at the prisoner and scowled, then turned and walked away from the jeep, back onto the sidewalk. He put two full packs into each of the side pockets of his coat. He ran his hands through his gray hair, turned and smiled at Sergeant Chavez.

Sergeant Chavez plopped the hat atop the prisoner's head. "Pretty good fit," he said and laughed.

"Why in the hell did you buy that hat?" One of the M.P.'s asked.

"For Sergeant Kelleher's benefit. You'll see!"

They slowly drove to the M.P. Headquarters. The German shook his head, trying to dislodge the hat. Sergeant Chavez reached over with one hand and pushed it down tight. He pulled the jeep up close to the steps leading up to the office where First Sergeant Kelleher was located.

"Okay guys, out with you, and in a minute, I want you to escort this Aryan son of a bitch into Kelleher's office and watch the expression on his face." He then walked around the jeep and said, "Look at me, you yellow bastard!" The German turned and faced Sergeant Chavez, who jerked the hat off of his head. "Okay, fellows. Each of you grab one of his ears and hang on tight."

"What the hell are you going to do?"

"Don't panic. I'm just going give him a little warning not to smack little women around!" Sergeant Chavez said, then he took out the knife and touched the button and the blade flew open and stopped with a snap. He turned to the German, " I don't scalp cowards, you Nazi ass hole, but a leeetle slice will give you the idea of what we do to warriors." Then suddenly he drew the tip of the blade deeply across the man's forehead, from ear to ear, just below the hairline. The German struggled and screamed, "No!" but just as suddenly Sergeant Chavez closed the knife blade. The slice was only an eighth of an inch deep, but blood began to stream down across the German's face. The sergeant pulled the hat down tightly so that the cut didn't show. "Okay, now guide him into Kelleher's office and tell him Geronimo is outside with a scalp!"

They each took one of the German's arms and guided him up the few steps to the office.

Sergeant Chavez waited beside the jeep. The door of the office flew open and first sergeant stood with his arms on his hips and bellowed, "Jesus Chavez, what in the hell have you done!"

"Why Meeester Kelleher, didn't you take the prisoner's hat off?"

"What! What the hell do you mean?" He turned and went back into his office and removed the hat from the German and saw the full head of hair. "My God. He didn't really do it." He looked at the blood flowing from the slice. "Clean this punk's face up and lock him up. If he keeps bleeding, call a medic."

He turned back to the door and shouted, "Chavez, get your ass up here!"

Sergeant Chavez walked up the stairs and into the office. "Here's your smoking gun, Sarge." He tossed the switch blade knife to Sergeant Kelleher.

"Didn't you pick up that little pistol?"

"Yep, and you know what. In the awful struggle with my prisoner, it fell out of my pocket into the river." Sergeant Chavez grinned broadly.

"Sir?" One of the corporals interrupted. "I think this guy has been shot in the leg or the rear end or both. He's bleeding a little."

"Good!" Sergeant Kelleher exclaimed.

Blood was still flowing down both sides of the German's nose, across his cheeks, and dripping onto his soiled shirt.

"Mop his ugly face for him, corporal," Sergeant Kelleher said, then turned back to Chavez.

"Meeester Kelleher," Sergeant Chavez, said, "let's go over to the club. I'll buy you a drink and explain how you should compose your report about my brave, daring and heroic deed!"

Sergeant Kelleher said, "Shut up for a minute, Geronimo! I guess the old man was a better shot than we thought. Hell, take this bum over to the medics, and keep those handcuffs on him. I'll inform Intelligence."

The German prisoner scowled, looked at them, from one to the other, but said nothing. Blood continued to trickle down his cheeks, on both sides of his nose.

Sergeant Chavez walked up closely and put his face close to the face of the prisoner, and then whispered to the German, "Scared the shit out of you, didn't I? They let you loose, and next time it's for real!" He laughed, and added, "Senor Kelleher, I theeenk you owe me both a medal and a promotion!"

"Jesus Chavez," Kelleher said, "and if you'll knock off that corny lingo I'll buy you a drink. Anything but tequila."

"Yes sir! You got a deal!"

One week later Sergeant Chavez received word that First Sergeant Kelleher wanted to see him. He reported to the office.

"Reports as ordered," Sergeant Chavez said in mock seriousness as reached the desk of First Sergeant Kelleher. He clicked his heels together, then stood at a very correct military attention, his shoulders back, heels together, his shoes formed a forty-five degree angle. He saluted smartly and awaited a response from First Sergeant Kelleher.

"What the hell do you think you are doing? Trying out for a part in one of those B movies?"

"I try so hard to please you, sir."

"Okay. Stand there. Stand still. Keep your damn chin up! I've got a medal for you." To the surprise of Sergeant Chavez, the sergeant opened his desk and took out a box, then approached him and before Sergeant Chavez could see the medal, Sergeant Kelleher pinned it on his uniform. He then stepped back and smartly saluted Sergeant Chavez, who returned the salute, then looked down and recognized a German iron cross."

"Why you son of a bitch, sir, that's a real Got-cha!"

Putting his head back, Kelleher roared with laughter. "That, Sergeant Jesus, is for that false scalping prank!" Then he said, "Okay, sit down and relax and I'll tell you about your prisoner. And you can keep the medal. Put it with that little pistol in your souvenir collection!"

"Still no respect!"

"Well, as of today you are officially Staff Sergeant Chavez. And truthfully, I recommended you for a Bronze Star, but it'll be months before that's processed. So don't hold your breath."

"Thanks, Kelleher," Sergeant Chavez said, "and I really mean it."

"Back to that kraut. To make a long story short, he's one of a few SS troopers who got stopped here, but wasn't captured, back when that bridge was bombed. Intelligence finally got it out of one of his buddies that they caught awhile back, that he was in on that castration job on one of our fliers. They're now trying to prove he killed one of his own SS buddies."

"So, I should have scalped him!"

"Naw. He'll probably end up in jail for a few years. Wish they'd let us hang him. Scalping is too good for that bastard."

"By God you're right, Kelleher. That should have been my line."

"Let's head for the club, staff sergeant! And I'll buy the first one!"

CHAPTER 22

▼

LE HAVRE

Soon after Cal had taken off, Marshall regained consciousness. He sat upright, felt the back of his head, which was wet from his blood and the melted snow. The collar of his flight jacket felt wet. He looked down and saw that his seat belt was snug. He glanced at Cal, who turned and smiled.

"Think you'll make it?"

"What the hell happened, Cal?"

"Well, Sunder, you took a hefty swing at a M.P. and he flattened you with his billy club. A couple of German kids helped me get you into the jeep. It was those boys you hired to polish shoes. They saved your ass, pal. I think those German women would have kicked you to death!"

"My God." Marshall exclaimed and stared at Cal, "What happened to Kris?"

"Why, you heard them! Hell, you must have heard them? Twice I heard the Medics yell, 'Get her to the morgue.' There was a bloody sheet covering her. I think her old man shot her, and they were taking him to the morgue, too. I heard one of those ladies say 'shot himself'! So, he may have committed suicide. I really don't know for sure, it was in German, but I do know they were both in the ambulance on the way to the morgue."

"Kristine dead!" Marshall leaned forward and turned towards Cal. His facial expression revealed his incredulity.

"Marshall, I had to get you away from there before a damn riot broke out. The guys at the flight line thought I should haul you over to First Aid, but your head wasn't bleeding too bad. We all looked at the wound. Hell of a bump and a scrape. Nothing deep. Mainly just a bump and the size of a goose egg. And, damn it, Schloss ordered me to fly you up to Le Havre early in the morning. So here we are. We passed Saarbrucken and are now heading towards Paris. Charts are folded up between our seats if you decide to do a little navigating."

"Yeah," Marshall murmured. "Okay. Let me see a map. My God, I can't believe Kristine is dead!" Marshall added. He felt the knob on the back of his head and then looked out at the horizon.

Marshall then turned to Cal. "Why don't we do a 180 and go on back and really find out if there was some kind of a mistake about Kris."

"Pal, if you think I'd take you back to Bad Scheidel, you've taken too hard a hit to the head! I'm telling you, Marsh, Schloss ordered me to fly you to Le Havre, and that's exactly what I'm doing. Now if you can figure out how to get a ride back with someone else up there, that's up to you. I'm really sorry, Marsh. But, damn it, I'm obeying orders."

"Christ, my head is killing me."

"We'll go to the medics as soon as we land."

Marshall studied the charts. He selected the one that showed most of France. It was almost a due west course all the way to Le Havre. He looked out ahead at the terrain, then at the map, and back again. He placed his finger on a spot on the map and held it up for Cal.

"We're making pretty good time," Cal said, after glancing at the map. "I'm not going to try to return today. We'll go to the medics and get you checked out; then we can stay in the B.O.Q tonight. Maybe even have time to start getting your orders processed this afternoon."

"Christ, this just can't be happening." Marshall said, and he dropped his face into the palms of his hands. "Yes, yes, Cal, you're right, I heard them. I really did hear them say they were taking Kris to the morgue. I just don't want to believe it!"

"Christ-a-mighty. I understand! Why don't you push your seat back? It'll lean back a little. Close your eyes. If I need any help I'll wake you up when we are beyond Paris."

"Thanks, but I sure as hell can't sleep."

The terrain continued to move beneath them. There were patches of snow on the hills and higher elevations, and from the air the French countryside and the villages appeared to be unharmed by the war. Marshall moved his finger along the chart and when they were a few miles from Le Havre he put the chart in front of Cal and pointed to their position.

Cal called the tower, identified himself and received permission to land, and a runway was designated. The little L-5 airplane sat down softly and Cal taxied towards a group of Quonset huts. A ground crew man walked out and with flags directed Cal to a spot where they could park the aircraft.

Both fliers climbed out of the airplane. Cal helped Marshall with his B-4 bag and barracks bag.

"Sergeant," Cal spoke to a man starting to tie down the little craft, "I'm going to spend the night. Would appreciate it if you could have someone top-off that gas tank."

"Roger," the man answered. "Operations office is that second hut." He casually pointed to a building.

"Thanks. Is First Aid anywhere near here."

"Operation officer can tell you. Just a block or so. They'll fix you up with a jeep. Bachelor Officers Quarters are near the First Aid building, too."

"Thanks again."

Numbly Marshall listened to the exchange. He carried his barracks bag and Cal took the B-4 bag and carried a slim briefcase. They entered the Quonset hut and a lieutenant greeted them. "Colonel Schlosser ordered us up here from Bad Scheidel. My buddy here, fell and smacked his head pretty bad, just as we were leaving. Said he felt okay, so we came on. Like to obtain some transportation, a jeep or any car. Want to go to First Aid and then to the B.O.Q. He's supposed to ship out from here."

"No problem," the lieutenant said. "Let me see your orders, Lieutenant." He addressed Marshall, "then I'll be able to direct you to the right office."

Marshall handed him the envelope with two sheets of paper, which he quickly scanned. "Looks like you are on a priority list to ship out, so you'd better report to the Administration Office, after you get your head looked at. It's building number 17, and it's right next to the B.O.Q. I'll give you a little map of the layout."

"Thank you," Marshall said. "How late is that office open?"

"Oh, there'll be someone there until six this evening," The officer said. "Here are keys to a jeep. Pick it up behind this building. Motor Pool non-com will show you the one. Here's a map of the layout. Turn the keys back in right here."

"Is there a PX available? And a laundry or a dry-cleaning facility available. My shirt and jacket are really foul," Marshall said.

"Yep. It's all on that little map, or directory."

"And a finance office?"

"Yep, just look at your directory." The officer laughed. "Now ask me something that isn't on your directory and surprise me!"

"You mean we're supposed to be able to read?" Marshall said, trying to laugh. "But thanks, and we'll get out of your hair now. Let's go, Cal!"

Cal found the First Aid Station and accompanied Marshall to the desk. Marshall was questioned, and he explained that he'd fallen and banged up his head. Cal followed Marshall into an emergency room. A nurse asked him routine questions, checked his pulse and blood pressure and recorded them on a clip board, and with soap and water and a wash cloth cleaned the back of his head, and rinsed blood from his hair. Then a MD entered, wearing the two silver bars of a captain. He read the report, and told Marshall to sit on a table, where he examined his head.

"That sharp impact wound looks like some one hit you with a baseball bat."

"It was a billy club, sir," Marshall said without emotion. "I got out of line. My girl friend was shot and killed. I guess I kind of went berserk, and one of our M.P.'s had to quiet me down."

"My God! Well! I am sorry about your girl friend," the doctor said. "Now, Lieutenant, about all I can do for you is to recommend ice-pack applications. Try fifteen minutes every hour. The nurse will tell you where to get ice, and you can use a towel to hold it. We'll fix you up with bottle of aspirin. You can take a couple at a time, up to ten of them before midnight. Should feel better in the morning. Continue with the ice tomorrow, and try to stay at around ten tablets a day of the aspirin for the pain. Don't take the aspirin on an empty stomach. If the aspirin doesn't handle it, come on back and I can prescribe something stronger."

"Thanks, sir," Marshall said. He started to slide off of the table.

"Wait a minute. I want to check your eyes."

"Watch the tip." The doctor held up a tongue depressor and moved it back and forth, from side to side, up and down. Marshall's eyes followed.

"Good. No signs of a concussion."

"That's a relief," Marshall said, and climbed down.

"Young man. In case no one told you, we have an excellent laundry and dry cleaning establishment right here on the base. Guys going home want to look their best, you know."

"Thanks for checking me over, doctor," Marshall said. "I think the laundry is on a little map we were given down at the flight line." He turned to Cal, "Guess I'm going to live. Let's find the B.O.Q."

Following the simple map they found the Bachelor Officers' Quarters, were assigned a large room with single beds, two chairs and a desk, plus a bathroom with a shower.

"Cal, I'm going to take a shower and put on a clean shirt, then find the Administration Office and check in. Looks like a short walk from here and I need the fresh air. I should be back soon, then maybe we can find the officers' mess and get a couple drinks, and some chow. What say?"

"Roger. Just don't use all of the hot water," Cal answered, and laughed.

Marshall found building 17. A WAC corporal smiled as he walked to her desk. "Help you, sir?"

"My C.O. is getting rid of me. I checked in at the B.O.Q. So, would you like to look at my orders?"

She smiled again and accepted the envelope. "Hum? I don't see many like this. Priority. So, you will leap frog a few hundred others. I wonder why?"

With a straight face Marshall said, "I'm a music teacher, you know, piano and voice. President Truman has requested my presence."

The corporal stared at him. "My God, another funny flier to deal with." She shook her head and laughed, then added, "You know, sir, the last pilot through here thoroughly convinced me that the Pope has become a Protestant."

Marshall chuckled, then recalled some of the advice from his Uncle Bruce. He smiled and said, " I guess you really have to put up with a lot of BS?"

"Oh, it's kind of fun, Lieutenant," the young girl said.

"Would you believe me if I told you I'm running from the SS?"

"Well, honestly I suspect you didn't use your oxygen enough at high altitude, but sir, my assignment is to get you safely onto a ship. I've heard all sort of weird, imaginative tales right here at this desk. I'm going to write a book about them!"

"Do you date?"

"Only men with the rank of first sergeant or second lieutenant. Higher ranking men are bores."

"How about dinner with my buddy, Cal, a Texan, and me tonight?"

"Three of you?"

"Oh?" Marshall grinned, "No. You see, Cal is a Texan."

"I'm off duty at 1700 hours. Incidentally, I can't take you to the Non-Coms dining room, but I can go with you to the officers' club."

"You're kidding!"

"No sir. That goes back to George Washington."

"Okay, another flier is had!"

"Is this outfit okay?"

"Stunning. We'll pick you up at 1700."

"See you then. My name is Lorene, if you are interested."

"Wow, sorry I didn't ask sooner, Lorene. In the meantime, can you shed some light on what my future holds?"

"Yes sir, you will be boarding the Victory Ship, Laconia, in four days. Depending on the tides, you'll depart within the week. Another five days, to a week, and you'll arrive in New York City, depending on storms, icebergs, and stuff like that. You'll be able to stay in the B.O.Q. We'll keep you informed on the bulletin board, and we'll have someone personally chase you down when the boarding date is near."

"That's it?"

"Yes sir. We'll keep you posted and you'll go to the ship on a bus and meet a few hundred other guys enroute to the States!"

"Thank you, corporal. Cal and I will see you at five P.M, or seventeen hundred hours, if you prefer."

Marshall returned to the B.O.Q. *This is going to work out fine. Cal will jump at a chance for a date and I can have some privacy while he's gone, and I hope it'll be for all night.*

Cal had showered and was sitting in a chair reading the Stars and Stripes. "Well, that didn't take long. What's up?"

"This is where I'll stay for a few days, then I'll board a Victory ship and be on my way home." Marshall said, "Gosh, that sounds strange, doesn't it? Home."

"I envy you having a home to go to, but I'm getting good vibes from Schloss. He said a career for me in the Air Corps is now a possibility. ."

"Cal, I've invited a sweet little corporal WAC to have dinner with us at five o'clock .She can go to the officers' club with us. We're going to pick her up at the Administration Building. I know you'll like her."

"Ha, another first! No one, I mean nobody ever fixed me up with a date! By God, Marsh, if you say she's cute, that's good enough for me."

"Cal, I've got time to run over to the P.X. Need a couple of shirts. Join me if you want."

"Think I'll read."

It was a short walk to the Post Exchange. Marshall was astonished at the size. The interior was as big as a basketball arena, and there were dozens of booths up and down the many aisles. Marshall found the clothing department and bought two tan shirts. While he was paying for them the clerk said, "Sir, we've got a hell of a deal on genuine leather flight jackets. Fifty bucks, and if you've got a day or two we can emboss your silver wings. Here, try one of these on, sir. Size forty about right?" Marshall nodded. It seemed like a long time ago that he'd used his own leather jacket for barter with a Swiss merchant to buy gifts for his folks and Kristine.

"Damn, that does feel good," Marshall said. It settled comfortably on his shoulders. The leather had a nice odor, and suddenly memories of the deer hunting trips with his dad and uncle Bruce. "If you can put bombardier wings on it I'll take it."

"You'll be real pleased, sir. Just letter out your name, rank, bombardier wings, and serial number and you can pay for it when you pick it up."

Marshall wandered through the store. He didn't want to carry anything more in his B-4 bag and duffel bag. He stopped in the jewelry section.

"Anything I can help you with, sir?"

"What would a watch, for a teen age boy, cost? Not fancy, just accurate."

"Well sir, our prices here are probably two thirds less than you'll pay for a Swiss watch in the States. Let me show you a great watch for a young man. Nice leather band, it's got a thick, rugged crystal and a round face with easy to read numbers. Omega is a big name in Europe, but not too well known in the States."

"And the price?"

"Twenty-five dollars."

"Okay, wrap up a couple of them, please."

Marshall paid for the watches and returned to the B.O.Q. Cal was still reading. He looked up and asked, "How'd you make out?"

"Fine, Cal, but I'm kind of sick to my stomach. My head is killing me again. I've six aspirin left of my allotment. I'm going to find that ice and lay down and chill my damn brains!"

"What about our date?"

"You go, Cal. Really, she's a sweet kid: nice set of boobs. Her name is Lorene. You just identify yourself as Cal. I told her that you are a Texan. She's a witty girl. Tell her I'm sorry to have pooped out, please. But my head is really throbbing."

"A blind date. I'll be damned. Okay, buddy, I'm on my way!"

Marshall went to his B-4 bag and obtained the book, *On Being a Real Person*, which the chaplain had given him. In the index he found "death" and read each reference, and felt comfortable with the voice and approach of the author, and tried to relate his wisdom to the death of Kristine. Marshall began to realize there would be no easy formula. He could take data from pages of Air Corps manuals and set up a Norden Bombsight. If a certain amount of things were true and adhered to by the pilot, he could place a bomb near the bull's eye from 11,000 feet, but there was no such formula that he could find to explain his grief for Kristine. There was no satisfactory answer.

Marshall left the room and located the supply of crushed ice, and carried enough back in a towel to make a pack. There was a rectangular rubber bath mat in front of the shower. Marshall placed the mat on top of the bedspread that covered the pillows. He lay on the bed and rested his head on the towel holding the ice atop the rubber mat. Marshall dozed, but never actually slept, and finally after an hour had passed he arose and decided to go to the mess hall, feeling sure that if Cal and Lorene had gone there to eat, they'd be finished and gone.

Before he stepped all the way into the room, he glanced at all of the tables and was relieved to see that they were not there. From the specials, he ordered spaghetti and meatballs, plus a small salad. The waiter suggested a glass of red wine, and Marshall nodded. The meal was hot and tasty. Marshall then ordered black coffee, and was negative towards a suggestion that a serving of spumoni would go well. When he received his bill for a dollar and a half he was amazed, suspecting it would be much higher.

The amount was similar to the prices at the Pepper Tree Inn at home. Cigarette tips weren't in vogue at the officers' club, so he left one dollar, feeling that was more than ample. He could remember his dad leaving a quarter tip if the service was excellent for the three of them.

Marshall returned to his room and read some more in the book given to him by Chaplain Waldron. It felt good to be alone. He was trying very hard to eliminate from his memory all of the irritating deeds of the man they'd known as Tex, and who was now called Cal. He was still trying to forgive him, to understand him, but his vexations had been cruel, had hurt Kristine.

Marshall needed the solitude. The prose and the wisdom of Doctor Fosdick calmed him. Finally Marshall dumped what was left of the ice into the sink, wrung out the towel, replaced the bath mat and turned back the covers of the single bed. He poured a glass of water and washed down two aspirin, put on his pajamas and after turning off the lights, climbed into bed, and immediately fell asleep.

When Marshall heard the doorknob turn and the door was pushed open, he quietly asked, "Cal?"

"Roger." Cal spoke very softly, "Tried not to wake you up."

"Turn on a light. It won't bother me."

"Christ Marsh! What a night! Man, I have to thank you for one hellova time!"

"I'm glad. I gather you liked Lorene."

"You know, pal, I'm trying to avoid being so damn uncouth, so let me just say that tonight we enjoyed terrific, exhilarating sexual intercourse! Why, that little lady is a very ambitious girl. Did you know she's saving for a college education? I almost had to twist her arm to accept fifty bucks towards her college fund. She was reluctant. Jesus! Maybe I'll have to stay another day, just to make sure that airplane is air-worthy!"

"You mean contribute another fifty towards her education?" Marshall chuckled.

"Come on, Marsh, don't try to make something tawdry out of it. I could fall in love with Lorene and take her back to meet Colonel Schlosser."

"What the hell time is it?"

"About three thirty, civilian time. Do you want it in military time?"

"Did you have a few belts before dinner?"

"Sure. Scotch for me and we split a bottle of French wine. She has a nice little apartment all of her own. Says permanent party gets treated royally here. Plus she had a record player with a collection of Tommy Dorsey, Glenn Miller and Harry James albums. What a night!"

"Cal, you are something else! Well, it's time for my double aspirin treatment, then I'm going back to sleep while you enjoy your exhilarating memories. Okay?"

"Sure. Shake me when you get up. I'll join you for breakfast."

In the B.O.Q., the army officers awaiting orders to board the Laconia Victory were left to their own routines as far as getting up and going to bed. Most had seen combat, regardless of the particular corps in which they served. There were no assignments. They would be notified when it was time to board the ship.

Marshall arose, took a shower, dressed and went to the table and found stationery and envelopes. He stared at the blank sheet, then wrote:

Dear Gary, I write with mixed emotions. First of all, I'm happy that you've been repaired, so to speak, and as I understand it from Schloss, you can still have an active sex life. On the other hand, the awful thing that happened to cause it is just so damn monstrous it's difficult to say anything at all. I hope you'll come out to California when you've recovered. You always raved about how you liked Santa Ana. But, I'd like to show you the really great part of the state- Northern California!

The enclosed money is for some sort of a memorial for Kristine. As far as I'm concerned, she was my wife, although I know our little wedding ceremony in the '26 was for fun. You married us, Ship Captain! The morning you were being operated on Cal and I drove by her place on the way to the airport. I just wanted to say good-bye. We got there in time to see her on a gurney, covered with a bloody sheet, and they were taking her to the morgue. I wanted to see her body, her face, struggled to do so, but some jackass M.P. knocked me out and I woke up with Cal flying enroute to Le Havre.

As I write this I'm thinking of your misery, and I too, selfishly perhaps, am engulfed in my own sorrow. I cannot believe Kris is gone! I know you and Frank felt I was all screwed up about my feelings for her, but I believe both of us felt more than infatuation, as Frank called it.

Gary, I don't know that I comprehend just what love is. Your track record as far as lovemaking is away beyond mine, but I know my feelings towards Kris were genuine, not just a casual fling in the sack. So, I'm sick. I'm nauseated. You cope better with your trauma than I do with my loss.

Schloss is sending me home to save my ass and I wonder if it's worth saving. I'm being denied the chance to say goodbye to Kris. I can't drop a single flower on her tiny body, or upon a casket. Can you understand I want to put my lips to hers, no matter how cold they are? Gary, I am nauseated by my own confusion. I want to return to Bad Scheidel and hold Kristine. I want to put warmth into her body with mine, to bring her back to life. It's not to be.

Am I supposed to turn off my head and heart and forget her because she was a German? And I'm torn because I can only imagine the hatred for Germans that must fill your heart. Are all men evil? Have the Germans and the Japs and the Italians a corner on the evil market? Are we all evil? Schloss tried to tell us we did the right thing, I mean being civilians and volunteering and flying combat. Just seeing that awful stinking mess at Dachau was enough to convince anyone we tried to do the right thing. Correct?

Gary, I tried to get Schloss to let me stay until you were out of surgery so I could be there to offer whatever support you might want from a close friend. But he turned me down.

Well buddy, I didn't mean to ramble on like this but I had to talk to someone. I guess we have to move forward. As an incentive for you to get busy on some project, I'd like for you to select a little marble cross or something appropriate and put Kristine's name on it. No doubt, there is a stone cutter, or whatever they call them in town, and probably Chaplain Waldron could help. He seems to get along with the German Lutheran pastor there. If it costs more than the enclosed two hundred dollars, drop me a line. You've got my home address. And when you do get home, let's see if we can put together a reunion with Frank

Your buddy, Marshall.

He put two, one hundred-dollar bills in the envelope with the letter and sealed it, and wrote Gary's name on the front.

The officers' mess was open twenty four hours a day, which was a rarity. Marshall and Cal strolled into the mess hall at eight o'clock. They could choose the cafeteria-style served from hot plates, or sit down and their order would be taken. They chose to select their own. Fruit juice and a bowl of oatmeal plus toast satisfied Marshall. Cal selected ham and scrambled eggs, fried potatoes, and toast. Both took a mug of coffee with them on their trays and sat at a table near the door.

"Still in love?" Marshall asked.

"Yep," Cal answered. "And how come you told Lorene I'm from Texas?"

Marshall chuckled, "Well, some girls are listeners and some you can't shut up. I figured if she was the listening type, you could talk for hours about your adopted state."

"Well, I educated her about Texas all right, but boy, did she ever educate me about between the sheets action!"

"You going to stay another night? Donate again to her educational fund?"

"Come on Marsh, what are you suggesting?"

"I was just kidding. But, seriously, when does Schloss expect you back?"

"Oh Yeah. I've got to get back today!" Cal said, "But I'm going to take my next leave, and check in right here and pursue things with Lorene. I could get serious about that little WAC."

"Cal," Marshall spoke, "I'd appreciate it if you'd do me a couple of small favors when you get back to Bad Scheidel." Marshall took the two watches from his pocket. He opened one of the boxes and showed the watch to Cal. "Would you give these to those two kids that helped you when I was out of it? These aren't expensive, but they are of good quality. You know those boys."

"Why sure, Marsh." Cal said, "The little krauts really did help me get you out of that mess."

"You know?" Marsh said, "My cheek bone and jaw both ache." He put his hand against the right side of his face. "Must have been those hausfraus working me over?"

"That was pure bedlam."

"Next, would you drop by and see Gary when he can have visitors and give him this letter, please?"

"Of course, Marsh. Why, you and Gary were the guys I came to when I was drowning in frustration and my own self-pity. This probably sounds corny as hell, but my mind, my soul, everything, in me, was writhing in agony. You guys gave me a chance to survive, to change, and God knows I'm really trying."

"Hell, don't change too much. You won't be any fun. Keep that sense of humor and you've got it made," Marshall said. "And you know, you might like to read the letter from my Uncle Bruce about how to tell a joke, plus he lists a lot of really good ones. Gary copied the letter word for word. Why don't you ask to see it?"

"I'll do just that." Cal said, "Marshall, do you know the words I'd most like to hear someday. I mean about myself?"

"Shoot."

"Cal was a good guy. And thanks, Marsh, for, you know, for allowing me a second chance."

"Roger," Marshall grinned. "And, let's settle for the present tense and say, 'Cal IS a good guy'!" He pushed back from the table, stood, and said "I'm heading over to the finance office to close my bank account and get everything in American money."

"Watch out for those big poker game sharks on that ship!" Cal said, then laughed loudly. "Marsh, I don't want to get maudlin about how you and Gary treated me one night, so I'm going to head for the flight line now, and say good-bye. My shaving kit is by the door. I'll grab it. I'm going to check out and head east. I'll leave my key on the dresser. So long, my friend."

Gary grasped Marshall's hand and they shook vigorously, and then went their separate ways.

Ice treatments reduced the size of the knob on the back of Marshall's head, and fewer doses of aspirin were needed to stop the pain. He was surprised to see his right eye blacken, apparently from being kicked on the cheek. He applied ice to his cheek and chin and the pain diminished.

He was pleased that the dry cleaning establishment was able to remove the bloodstains and other soil from his Eisenhower jacket. He reattached his wings and ribbons, and felt that he was again presentable in the officer's mess and lounge. The P.X. did an excellent job embossing his wings on the new leather jacket, and from then on he wore it when he left his room to dine. The P.X. had a newsstand and he bought copies of *The New York Times* and *The San Francisco Chronicle* and devoured the information. He was lonely for the camaraderie of the men in his squadron back at Bad Scheidel. It was the first time in over two years that he felt alone, isolated, and he had no desire to strike up a conversation with another officer.

He sat in the comfortable chair in his room reading a newspaper when someone knocked on his door. "Come on in!" he said, loudly, but there was no response, only another series of knocks.

Marshall opened the door and a buck sergeant stood there. He saluted Marshall, who returned it and said, "What's up? Time to head for the big boat?"

"Just about, sir," the sergeant said. "Think it will be tomorrow. But my assignment is to ask for you to turn in any Government Issue side arms, your .45 for example."

"You mean you don't want my Norden Bombsight?" Marshall said, laughing.

The sergeant laughed, too, and said, "I can't imagine what they're going to do with them! We've got hundreds of .45's stacked up in a supply room. I suppose we'll have to melt them down or something."

"Okay. Let me dig into my barracks bag. Hell, I thought that was one thing I could take home!"

"Sorry sir, I'm just following orders."

"Okay, I understand. Just give me a receipt. I don't want to go through this again." Marshall dug into the bag and found the .45. He checked to see if it was loaded, then replaced it in its chest harness and handed it to the sergeant.

"Thank you, sir. I'll just need your name, rank serial number and the serial number off of your .45." He handed Marshall a clipboard with a form that he filled out. He'd never looked for the serial number before, but found it and recorded it, and signed the form. Then the sergeant signed it and gave Marshall a copy. "I'd suggest you take a look at the bulletin board outside of the officers' club. Probably have an update on your departure date."

"Do you know how many passengers a Victory ship holds?"

"Not exactly, but several hundred, I suppose. I'm really not sure. I do know that the higher your rank the higher up your quarters are. So, a buck-ass-private is in the bilge! The real brass get flown back, so a lieutenant might even have a porthole above the water line. How about that, sir!"

"I don't care as long as the damn thing sails west."

The sergeant smiled and said; "Have a nice trip." They exchanged salutes and Marshall put on his new leather jacket and headed for the officers' club. Somehow he had expected to be notified in person about his departure, but luckily he listened to the sergeant who took his gun. On the bulletin board he found the Orders to Board the Laconia Victory Ship, and after searching through several pages he arrived at the letter S and finally found Sunder, Marshall, second lieutenant. A bus would pick him up outside the B.O.Q. at 1400 hours, tomorrow, and take the departing group of officers to the ship.

"Wow," he said. *That information from Lorene wasn't exactly correct. Oh well, she's probably busy earning money for her college education!*

Most of the officers that awaited the bus didn't have two pieces of baggage. Marshall balanced the barracks bag on one shoulder and carried his B-4 bag with the other hand. A stranger helped him with his bag as he boarded the bus. He stowed his atop all of the other bags and sat in the only seat available, next to another flier, and both knew why the seats were vacant as the rear wheels over which they sat jolted against every bump in the road enroute to the Laconia.

The boarding was swift and well organized. There were ample bulletin boards and Marshall was pleased to find his room was mid-ship and well above the water line. Somehow, the thought of being below the water line bothered him. He loved the mountains and endless vistas and enjoyed flying. If they weren't being shot at, 'the best seat in the house' as he called it, was in the nose of the bomber.

Marshall arrived first in the room and immediately took possession of the top bunk. He'd heard all of the stories about the man in the top bunk being seasick, to the detriment of the man below.

It was a wise choice. His roommate, Tom Ferguson, was a first lieutenant Combat Engineer, and was seasick in varying degrees from the time they were towed into the channel until the tugs slowed them and guided them in a berth in New York. Marshall felt sorry for the man.

Anticipating wisely, the crew had placed small galvanized pails along the corridors. Tom kept one beside his bed. He apologized about his condition and cleaned up his messes, but the odor forced Marshall to spend many hours on the deck, shivering, and staring at the gray ocean and the mountainous waves. They passed small icebergs, but seldom saw another ship. Seagulls finally disappeared, but soon a new flock appeared. A Flight officer, a pilot, was constantly taking pictures. He showed Marshall his Leica and explained that he had a wide assortment of lenses. With a tele-photo lens he took pictures of the seagulls, and told Marshall he was going to find out if his wife could tell the difference between a French seagull and a American seagull, then he guffawed, so Marshall joined him and laughed too.

Finally Marshall convinced Lieutenant Ferguson that he'd have to go the dining room and at least try to stuff some bread down his gullet, or the dry heaves would kill him. Tom took the advice, and his regurgitating became less frequent and less painful and finally he could sleep.

"Can you imagine a couple of hundred guys feeling like you?" Marshall asked, when Tom was calm.

"Couple hundred, my ass!" Tom replied," Where did you come up with that number?"

"Oh, the sergeant who was collecting the .45's said several hundred."

"Collecting .45's?" Tom exclaimed, " You didn't fall for that?"

"What do you mean?" Marshall said. "He gave me a receipt."

"Well, friend, you've been duped. Your .45 is now on the French black market, and the guy you gave it to probably got ten bucks for it."

"No shit!"

"Hell, Lieutenant, the army has literally thousands of .45's floating around and doesn't have the faintest idea where they are!" Tom Ferguson said, and shook his head.

"It seemed so official. I have a signed receipt."

"Oh, don't worry about it, you'll be able to buy them at the surplus stores, if you really want one," Tom said, "and incidentally, if it matters, they can put over 2000 of us on this tub and have room left over. Did you see that little blurb on the bulletin board? This ship is named after a Laconia Cruise Ship that the Germans torpedoed."

"No, Tom," Marshall sighed, "I've been kind of out of it these past few days."

"That black eye says something, but I'm not going to ask."

"Thanks," Marshall said. "See you later, Tom."

Marshall visited the library. He grinned at the sight of men taking a book from a shelf and then going to a long table to sit with others to read and suddenly all of the books not hand held would slide across the table top and there would be a mad scramble as readers tried to recover theirs. Just as he arrived at the information desk a major placed a book down on the counter and said, "Well, I'm through with this classic. Do you want it for your library?"

The librarian, a first sergeant, picked it up, looked at the title and said, "Well, I've already read it, but the government says it's not to be on our shelves. I guess it's still banned in the States."

"Then toss it in the circular file."

"Hey, wait a minute," Marshall said, "If it's banned it must be good. Care if I have it?"

"Your welcome to it Lieutenant," the major said, grinning, "but it is a wee bit racy."

"Just what I need," Marshall laughed, and accepted the book. He read the title, *Lady Chatterley's Lover*, by D. H. Lawrence. "Who's Lady Chatterley?" Marshall asked.

"Ha," the major said, "you'll soon find out!" The officer laughed again and patted Marshall on the shoulder. "Better fasten your seat belt for this one!"

Selecting a heavy, comfortable chair, Marshall sat down and began to read the book. When he left the library, the librarian saw him and smiled, "Well, how do you like it?"

"Great change of pace!" Marshall said, and raised the book and saluted. The first sergeant smiled.

Back in their room Marshall looked at the gray features of his roommate. "Tom," Marshall said, "You'd better join me and try to get something into your belly. Have you asked the medics for anything?"

"Yeah, Marshall. They gave me some benedryl, but said I should have started taking it before I boarded. So now they tell me! Typical damn army! But, I really do think I'm going to live."

"Okay, spruce up and we'll go up on deck and get some fresh air. Just to see how you feel."

"How do you fliers reply? Roger?"

"You got it. Roger!" Marshall put on his new leather jacket and enjoyed the feel of the leather.

When they reached fresh air, Marshall suggested that they walk to a position directly below the pilothouse. "Tom, stand here and focus your eyes on the horizon. Try to forget the motion of the ship. Just look at that straight line, the horizon. Maybe your inner ears will get the message. Might work."

"This cold, salty air breathes good," Tom inhaled deeply.

"Come on, Tom, concentrate," Marshall chided, "I saw you start to look at those icebergs!"

"A couple of days ago I wished we'd hit a big one!"

Again the food was served cafeteria style in the officers' mess. Marshall and Tom both ate lightly. They accepted thin slices of roast beef and mashed potatoes with gravy, and string beans. They both took two hard rolls and mugs of coffee. Dessert didn't sound good, although they had a choice of apple pie or tapioca.

"Couple more days and we'll be back to good old terra firma," Marshall said.

"You know, Lieutenant, I never dreamed I'd be sea sick. I rowed shell for Harvard, back before this mess, and I was flown over in a B-17 and that was terrific, but this tub rolls and dips and twists and pitches, Christ, it's awful."

"Harvard? Wow!" Marshall said.

"Okay," Tom turned to him and laughed, "Go ahead, say it!"

Marshall was bewildered, "Say what, Tom?"

"Christ, that's refreshing. You must be from the so-called 'coast.'"

"Yep, northern California. Chico. That's where the term, 'from the sticks' originated."

"Well, Marshall," Tom said grinning, "Among my Ivy League snobs, the response you were expected to make was—'Well, you can always tell a Harvard man, but you can't tell him much!'"

They both laughed, and they sat silently sipping on the black coffee.

"I guess some of my buddies that made it on athletic scholarships to U.S.C. and Stanford would probably have responded differently."

"Did you get a chance to go to college?"

"Only college I've had has been in the service schools in the cadet program. But I was accepted at Cal," Marshall answered. "Are you going back to Harvard?"

"Probably."

"What were you studying to be?"

"Oh, hell, I don't really know. I liked crew and Wellesley girls. I guess it's time to get serious. They say you go to college to find out what you don't want to do with your life. Now I do know I'm not cut out for politics."

"Well, then I for one, envy you," Marshall said. "I haven't the faintest idea about what I don't want to do or be! So, I guess I'll go to the library and do some more reading." He stood up and turned and said, "Tom, why don't you try that pilot house routine again, and stare at the horizon for awhile."

"Roger, Marsh," Tom said, "I honest to God think that helps. See you in the morning."

Marshall read a several chapters of *Lady Chatterley's Lover*, then quietly slipped into the room he shared with Tom. He was snoring, and Marshall took that for a good sign. Four days of vomiting had to wear out the poor guy.

Marshall opened his eyes the following morning and saw Tom looking out of the porthole.

"Glad to see you're on the vertical!" Marshall said.

"Hi, sleeping beauty!" Tom answered. "Man, you were noisy last night!"

"Really?" Marshall said, but he wasn't aware that his dreams caused him to be vocal.

"Yeah! What the hell were you doing? Did you get into Lady Chatterley's pants?"

"Hey come on, Tom! So I had a nice dream!"

"Was that a N.E.A or a N.E.A.U?"

"I haven't the faintest idea what you're talking about," Marshall said. He climbed down from the upper bunk. "That lady was awful, talking about her passion being in her bowels. But she did like to screw!"

Tom laughed loudly. "Back to your moans! Damn it to hell, we ground pounders refer to a nocturnal emission as either assisted or non-assisted. Now, what in the hell does the Air Corps call a wet dream?"

"Christ, Tom," Marshall said and grinned, "the fair sex took care of us. We have to fight them off. What makes you think I had, what the hell did you call it, a N.E.A or N.E.A.U?"

"The groans, buddy, the little laugh, those happy groans and then finally that deep sigh. That book must have really rattled your gonads!"

"Didn't you ground pounders have enough to do without analyzing wet dreams?"

"Hell, my outfit was getting shot up so bad we had to have diversions. We'd make bets on whether some sleeping beauty would offer a little assist. If we decided he'd assisted things along, we'd try to convince him that masturbation would put him in the insane asylum. And there was the standing gag about the guy whose mom found his *Police Gazette* under his mattress and told her son if he masturbated he'd eventually go blind, and so he really tried to stop, but finally told his mother he'd stop when he had to wear bifocals!"

"That's awful!" Marshall said, laughing, "And to think I used to hold you Harvard guys in such high esteem!"

"Marshall, I have a good buddy who's already back in the Harvard Med school. Before the war, when studies got too difficult, we'd relax and discuss absurd things like the superstitions about masturbation; some really weird beliefs. Those Med school people concluded it was natural as hell, and for women too!"

Marshall shook his head from side to side, evidencing disbelief. "Women? Really? You know what baffles me is that I never set eyes on the girl I dreamed about."

"Speaking of books, if we were, have you read *Brave New World*, by Huxley?"

"Nope."

"Amazing book," Tom said and continued, "There was a guy at Med School, Gordon Bassett, well, he was fascinated by the book and decided that to solve the world's problems he'd have to figure out how to alter the sex drive of homo sapiens, you know, genetically. He compared us, man, to the white tail deer. Women and white tail does weigh about the same, as do bucks and men. But the doe comes into heat once a year, and the bucks respond and mate and they have their little fawns. But we humans are always in heat! A woman is producing her eggs every damn month and there is a man eager to mate every damn hour of every day of the month! He figured that the way we're going, we'll have filled up every edge of the world with kids we can't feed, by the year 2000. He figured that a worldwide plague, or more wars, would be the only way to solve mass starvation. Bassett felt we're going to screw our-selves into oblivion."

"Wow," Marshall said. "So is he back working on it?"

"No. He was a medic. Got it on D-Day. Drowned."

"That's awful," Marshall said. He moved his slowly side to side.

As they neared the East Coast of the United States the seas began to calm, and Marshall and Tom walked along the deck and watched the other officers busy themselves. The flight officer pilot was busy taking pictures of the white caps, of valves, of other officers, and of the lifeboats and of coiled line.

Marshall smiled at him and asked, "How are the New York seagulls doing?"

"Believe me, we are hours from docking. I can feel it. I can smell it. Look at those gulls. See the difference?"

"I'll take your word for it, buddy!"

After days on the Victory Ship, the suddenness of entering New York harbor startled most of the passengers who were able to line the decks. They were quiet, almost reverent, as the Statue of Liberty came into view, and then the fireboats appeared, shooting massive sprays of white water skyward. Tugboats maneuvered the Laconia Victory into a berth and Marshall and Tom watched from the deck as an ambulance parked beside the ship. Two passengers were taken on gurneys to the ambulance.

"Wonder what happened to them?" Marshall said. A major standing next to Tom replied. "I understand a heart attack took one, and the other was shot during a poker game. Caught cheating."

Finally they left the ship and soon they were sorting through the stacks of luggage, placed in large bins identified alphabetically.

Marshall finally found his barracks bag, balanced it on his left shoulder and carried his B-4 bag in his right hand. He worked his way through the crowd of soldiers and fliers and finally spotted Tom Ferguson.

"Hi Marshall!" He said, "I see you've got your gear. Me too. Christ, I can't believe it. I'll be in Boston tonight, if I can catch the train!"

"Just wanted to shake hands and wish you luck," Marshall said. "I'm scheduled for a flight to the coast in the morning."

"Hey, would you look at that guy!" Tom said.

Marshall turned and a first sergeant was dragging two heavy barracks bags to the edge of the dock. He opened one, and took from it what appeared to be a shaving kit, then let out a yell, an announcement, "I've been carrying these sons of bitches around for three fucking years, now Davy Jones, put 'em in your locker, take em, they are all yours!" And he placed his foot up against one, pushed it off of the dock into the East River, and then did the same with the other. "Brooklyn, here I come!" he shouted, and walked away without looking back.

"Jesus! What a finale!" Tom said, "Well, friend, good luck. I'm heading for Grand Central. I report in again in Boston, then I'm a civilian forever!" They shook hands. "Nice meeting you, Marsh."

"The same," Marshall answered.

Marshall located a bus that would take him to the airport in Newark, New Jersey. Several other fliers were already on the bus, but he recognized no one. Again a stranger helped him with his barracks bag, and he swung his B-4 bag onto the top of the other luggage.

Now it was happening quickly. They unloaded at the air base. Marshall studied the bulletin board and found that he'd depart on a DC-4 early the next morning. At the officers' club, a quick dinner was followed by a shower, and a clean bed in the B.O.Q. It was a relief to learn that he'd be awakened by an orderly in time for breakfast, and then a ride to the flight line.

CHAPTER 23

▼

THE FAIRMONT HOTEL

Upon arriving at Camp Beale, sixty miles east of Sacramento, Marshall was processed for an honorable discharge and provided thirty-two days of leave, plus two travel-days, before officially becoming a civilian. Without ceremony regarding his status as a returning combat veteran from the E.T.O, he was also advised that it was simply Air Corps procedure for him to retain his commission and be placed in the U.S. Army Air Corps inactive reserve. So, with a total of two months pay, Marshall pocketed his six hundred and fifty dollars, decided to drink to his new status, and asked for the location of the officers' club.

Virtually empty, the club had a scattering of round tables with brown leather tops flawed with white ring-blemishes and cigarette burns, and empty ashtrays. There were upholstered chairs, with solid oak arms and curved oak backs. On the walls were black and white enlargements of military aircraft. Marshall studied the photos as he slowly walked in the direction of the bar. He stopped and stared at the enlargement of a B-26 Martin Marauder and a mixed flood of memories engulfed him. Abruptly he turned and walked to the end of the bar farthest from the entrance to the room.

As he waited for the bartender, he thought about going home to Chico, a three-hour journey by car or maybe four by bus or train. It was also a three -hour journey to San Francisco, and about the same to Reno. *Why am I putting off going home when that's all we talked about for two years?*

"What's your pleasure, sir?" the bartender said.

"Oh, a boiler-maker, I guess," Marshall said.

"A brand preference?"

"A what?"

"Well, sir, we're pretty well stocked now. I can offer you Jack Daniels, Old Granddad, Old Forester, some nice blends like Canadian Club or V.O., or our whiskey from the well."

"Oh hell," Marshall stammered, "I don't care. Anything you pour is okay. I'm just thirsty."

"Yes sir." The bartender put a shot glass in front of Marshall, filled it to the brim with whiskey from a bottle beneath the bar-top. Beside it he placed a full glass of tap beer drawn from a spout mounted near the center portion of the bar.

"Thanks," Marshall said. Gripping the small glass with two fingers and thumb, he gulped the whiskey in one movement and followed it with a sip of beer. He repeated his order.

"Just get in?" the bartender asked.

Marshall chuckled. "Just got in and just getting out."

"Well, the bombardier wings are obvious enough, and I can read ribbons," the bartender said. "E.T.O., flew out of England and France. Enough clusters on that Air Medal to have finished a combat tour. Presidential Citation. Not enough points to come home: Occupation duty. How's that fit?

"That's what I'd call a shack. You can also add navigator to that listing, but we didn't finish our missions. Our C.O. threw in an extra Air Medal, for a little side job we did, but I didn't complete fifty missions. In fact, about that time they were deciding sixty-five would be a tour. War ended. Maybe I should say both wars ended, and, you are correct, not enough points to come home."

"So the military isn't for you?"

"Who needs bombardiers? Or navigators? Radar is already taking over. No, I'm really a civilian at heart."

"That's kinda par for the course. Most fliers coming through here are headed back to civilian life."

"You making the military a career, Sergeant?"

"Yes sir."

"You get overseas?"

"Yes sir."

"Which theater?"

"Also the E.T.O. I was a paratrooper and that jump into southern France ended my fighting days. We've a good hospital here and they take care of my aching back." Then he held up both arms in front of him and his sleeves slid down to his elbows. "See these ugly little black and blue spots. Well, the damn kraut shrapnel keeps growing out, so now and then the medics slice my skin open and pull a piece out and give me a dose of sulfa."

"Geez. That's really the shits," Marshall said, staring at the bartender's arms.

"Naw." He paused, "I got it made. I'm assigned to the Supply Department. I play the piano. Got a little combo. We keep busy between the officers' club and the NCO club, plus weddings. I'll get in my twenty years, retire with a disability pension, get married and have a couple of kids and sell real estate for the rest of my life."

"Sergeant," Marshall asked the bartender, "If you wanted to go to San Francisco, how would you go about it?"

"No problem, Lieutenant. Two buses a day will take you right to the Ferry Building. One at eight, one at noon. Return the same. They also stop at the train station if you are heading down the coast, and they unload at the Greyhound Bus station. You can catch a cab at any of them, and there are buses going all over the city, plus the cable cars, of course. Our buses stop at both clubs."

"Thanks, and what do you recommend for heading north?"

"How far north? Portland, Seattle?"

"No, just to Chico."

"Where in the hell is Chico, sir?"

"Up towards Redding and Red Bluff, a little east, up towards Mount Shasta."

"Well, I think the same trains originating out of Emeryville, I think they stop in Sacramento, you know, the ones heading up to Portland or Seattle. They probably stop in that part of the country. I can check it out for you by phone real quick."

"Thanks, but never mind," Marshall said. "The Greyhound still goes through, I imagine." He drained the beer from his glass and ordered another boilermaker. "It'll be San Francisco."

"Frisco is a great town," the bartender said. "Any preference on bourbon? No extra charge."

"What do you recommend?"

"There are a few good ones. Old Forester is one of the best. It's smooth. Been in the barrel a long time," the bartender said. "Look at this, Lieutenant." He took a bottle of Old Forester from the back bar and holding it in front of Marshall, shook it back and forth vigorously. "Look at the bead on that stuff, sir. See all them little soapy looking bubbles? They aren't popping. Last a long time. Staying nice and firm. That's an indication of good, honest aging. Now here's some rotgut. Now watch." He shook the next bottle vigorously. "Now look at them little bubbles, tiny and popping and disappearing real fast. Got it?"

"Yes. And does that same theory apply to scotch?"

"Yes sir. From my years of experience behind a lot of bars, the more the bubbles the better the booze and especially if they last a long time."

"Okay, how about an Old Forester boiler maker?"

"Coming up, sir," the bartender said, "and, you know, sir, this stuff is so good I'd recommend a splash of water with it and forget those beer chasers."

Marshall chuckled. "You remind me of our flight engineer," Marshall said. "He was always giving the rest of the crew his big-brotherly advice. "Okay, cancel the beer," Marshall laughed, "Think I'm taking on too much high-octane fuel?"

"No sir, no sir," the bartender said. "But, I did neglect to tell you that this Old Forester I served you is bottled in bond, meaning it's one hundred proof. See this little green sticker across the cap?" He held the bottle in front of Marshall. Then he held up another bottle of bourbon and showed him a red sticker across the cap. "This is good stuff, too, but it's eighty six-proof. Not as potent."

"I can stand some education on alcoholic beverages. Drank my share of three-two beer at the officers' clubs, and we'd get a few ounces of some kind of whiskey for every mission. We'd save it up for awhile, then guzzle it down and chase it with beer and get smashed pretty fast."

"Ever eighty-sixed, Lieutenant?"

"I don't know what you mean."

"Well, I'm sure it won't happen to you, sir. It's when a man can't handle his whiskey, especially if it's a hundred proof, and has to be cut off for his own good. A bartender has to eighty-six him, or he should. In other words, for his own protection we downgrade a guy's alcoholic intake. We eighty-six him. Most whiskey is eighty-six proof, or forty three percent alcohol. Another good reason to know whether you're being served bottled in bond stuff or eighty six proof: if you get in a drinking match and you're drinking hundred proof and your buddies eighty-six, you're getting an extra jolt every time! Comes out to fourteen percent more."

"Well," Marshall said, and suddenly realized he was speaking slower and that it was an effort to enunciate, "I do appreciate knowing this, and I bet you're thinking you'll have to eighty-six me if I order another."

"Naw," the bartender laughed, "it's quiet in here now and I get lonely and just like to shoot the breeze. That's all."

"Sarge, another question for you. Where can I store my barracks bag? I'll hang on to my B-4 bag."

"We got a room to store gear. Just be sure your name is stenciled on the bags. You'll pass it on the way to the officers' quarters. Look for the Laundry sign. Ask for Sergeant Nakamoto."

"Nakamoto?"

"Yeah. You know, that 'Go For Broke' outfit. American Japs."

"Oh."

"And sir, you won't take offense if I make a suggestion?" The bartender vigorously wiped the surface of the mahogany bar until it gleamed.

"Hell no."

"Well, we do provide fast service on both laundry and dry cleaning, if you know what I mean."

Marshall laughed. "Yeah, I did sleep in this uniform." He looked down at his Eisenhower jacket and pink slacks. "All the way across the country in a DC-4. Bucket seats. Dirty damn plane, they must have been hauling pigs in it. I really did start out clean! Just point me in the direction of the cleaning establishment.

"Seargent Nakamoto will help you." Then he leaned across the bar and asked in a hushed voice. "Sir, did you keep your .45?"

"Nope, turned it in at Le Havre."

"Well, a bunch of them are lying around here that officers turned in, that they could've kept, if they'd wanted them. Like a souvenir, you know. Just in case you are interested, we can fix you up with one: receipt and all. Twenty-five bucks. Goes into the welfare fund. Cash money, you understand."

"Whose welfare?"

"NCO club."

"Oh."

"And this Japanese guy is handling the forty-fives, too?"

"Yep."

"Wow, my dad would love a .45! Do they have holsters?"

"Yep."

"Seems strange, buying a .45 from a Jap."

"Sam was one of those 442nd guys. Got all shot up in Italy. Transferred to the Air Corps. Now a career man. Plus he's trying to set his folks back up in the nursery business. Trees and roses, flowers and stuff like that. His father and mother and a couple of sisters spent their time down at Manzanar, in one of those detention camps while he was overseas. Lost their business. How do you like that?"

"Weird."

"Anyway, we're throwing a dinner dance to raise some money in a couple of weeks for the cause. But, one more thing, sir. If you're going into Frisco, be sure you have your ID."

Marshall paused at the bar and looked at him inquisitively.

"They're starting to get tough all of a sudden, on sailors and GIs who are under twenty-one ordering booze. You're obviously over twenty-one, but in some of them darkly lit places, well, you know, they could lose their liquor license if they serve hard stuff to anyone under twenty-one."

Marshall laughed and said, "I don't know whether this is a briefing or a debriefing session, but thanks. I'm wearing my dog tags. That ought to do it."

"Well, sir, I'd suggest taking your old driver's license if you have it, or something with your day of birth. Incidentally, neither my dog tags or my social security card shows my date of birth, for what it's worth."

"Well I'll be darned. I haven't looked at them for years. Just assumed, I guess. Well, more thanks to you. Haven't had to concern myself about my age for a few years, but I will be able to vote next time around!"

Marshall signed in for a room in the bachelor officers' quarters, then took a load of soiled clothes, plus his pink trousers and Eisenhower jacket to the laundry. He stored his gear and the sergeant sold him the .45, which he put in his barracks bag.

He looked at the sergeant, as he tied and knotted the white ropes on his bag.

"It'll be safe here, sir," Sergeant Nakamoto said, smiling.

At the officer's mess he was surprised at the selections from the menu. From behind a round ebony face the waiter's mouth smiled and revealed the largest, whitest teeth Marshall had ever seen. He looked into the black eyes, and the whites of the eyes contrasted against the black skin of the waiter.

"What looks good to you, sir?"

"Any recommendations?"

"Can't go wrong with our prime rib, sir."

"Prime rib it'll be."

"And how would you like it, sir?"

"Again, what do you recommend?"

"Well, sir, most folks out west here seem to prefer their meat, beef especially, on the medium-rare side. Matter of taste, you know."

"How do you like yours?" Marshall asked.

"Tell you the truth, sir, I'm coming around from well done to medium. Down south we sort of cremated all our meat. 'Ceptin fish, of course."

"Really," Marshall said. "Why's that?"

"Now, according to the chef, it just custom. He says southerners, as a whole, didn't have the ice to keep meat cold. So we cooked it a lot longer," he said, and grinned broadly, then continued, "Your dinner comes with soup and salad and coffee," the waiter said.

"Let's go for the prime rib, medium rare," Marshall said, and returned the menu to the waiter.

"Would you like to see our wine list, sir?"

"Why not," Marshall said, paused, then asked, "What is your rank?"

"Buck sergeant, sir."

The waiter departed and in a few minutes returned with a wine list. Marshall studied the list, then turned to the waiter. "You know, sergeant, I'm getting a drinking lesson starting today, after three years away from home. In England and France and Belgium, Holland and Germany, and I stuck with beer. I know nothing about stronger alcoholic drinks!" Marshall chuckled, returned the list to the waiter. "The last wine I drank was from a Jerry can that my copilot scrounged someplace in Germany. It was good, but I don't know what the hell it was."

"Well, with your permission, sir, I'd recommend a nice hearty Burgundy to go with that prime rib. Might try a glass, rather than a bottle, just to see how it goes down."

"You're on," Marshall said, laughed loudly and raised his right arm, his thumb upright above his clinched fingers. "Roger!" he exclaimed.

Giddy from the boilermakers, Marshall thought, *If I don't get some food into me it's going to be Roger, over, and out, for me.*

Marshall devoured every course of his dinner beneath the watchful eyes of the smiling waiter, and followed up with black coffee, including a couple of refills.

Before leaving the officers' dining room, Marshall returned to the bar. "Tell me something, Sergeant," he said, "What's the deal here on tipping?"

"Well, assuming you had good service, the going rate is fifteen percent. Maybe twenty percent if it's really outstanding. But it isn't really required here. Even expected."

"Thanks. And I did speak to Sergeant Nakamoto. Still kind of surprised to see a Jap stationed here. Strange damn war. Well, goodnight, Sergeant."

"Roger," the bartender said. "Night Sir, he nodded and smiled.

Marshall returned to the dining room and placed a one-dollar tip at the table where he'd been served.

Rested after the all-day flight across the United States in a DC-4, followed by the day and evening at the Separation Center, Marshall dressed in his freshly cleaned uniform, attached the two rows of ribbons beneath his silver bombardier wings, pinned the Bomb Group Presidential Citation award on the other side. He then found the bus stop. With him he carried his B-4 bag.

Marshall's breath clouded in the March air. The morning was crisp, the sky cloudless. Marshall sat by a window on the G.I. bus. Winter rains and warm sunshine had germinated the wild grass, and the almost treeless, rolling hills were knee-deep with the lush green growth. The tall grass moved, seem to breathe in and out, swelling, then retreating from the breeze. It reminded him of rippling green satin. The tops shimmered when the sun reflected off of the long shoots. An occasional sturdy White Oak leaned across the hillside, twisted and bent down by the decades of wind pressure, following the contour of the hillside.

Marshall remembered the last time he saw the hills and the oaks. It was summer and the wild grass was a khaki color, and he commented to his dad that the hills looked sort of feminine to him. And his dad asked, "Why's that Son?" and he said, "Well, look at them: nothing sharp or rugged. They seem to be soft, with lots of gentle curves that sort of roll from one ridge to another. They sort of undulate, if that's the right word."

"Interesting observation," his dad said. "Maybe that's how the expression 'mother earth' came about." And they drove on, following the winding two-lane highway towards the bay area. Marshall stared at the hills and could imagine breasts and buttocks. What Marshall didn't tell his dad was that he thought some of the hills looked like reclining women, and that the ridges often came together as a V shape, like legs joining, and at the bottom of the V a clump of oaks made him think it might be like a woman's pubic hair. The thought embarrassed him and he looked skyward, wondering if his dad imagined such things.

Marshall remembered and chuckled aloud as he now viewed the green goddesses of the hillsides and the green leaves of the oaks gathered at the crotch of the hills. On the flat lands were acres and acres of walnut trees, and the newly plowed fields revealed endless rows of turned earth that disappeared into infinity as if railroad tracks.

A few flat-backed Herefords grazed, and hawks floated on the wind, their beaks always pointed earthward, diving suddenly towards some prey in the deep, lush grass.

Finally the bus followed the curve around the North Bay, beneath the Berkeley Hills, and Marshall spotted the Golden Gate Bridge and he marveled at the long sweeping lines of curved steel cables attached to the rugged towers supporting the roadway.

It had been over three years since he'd seen it. And he suddenly recalled the sight-seeing flight, taking the ground pounders aloft, and the single-engine procedure. He remembered that not a single of the original bridges that spanned the Rhine River were intact. He was glad the Golden Gate Bridge still stood so tall and magnificent.

The incline up the ramp of the Oakland Bay Bridge was gradual. Marshall had always felt that he could have duplicated the structure, the abrupt, stiff angles of the bridges connecting Yerba Buena Island and Oakland to San Francisco, with his tinker-toy set. But the grace of Golden Gate Bridge could not be duplicated and its beauty mesmerized and captivated him.

"Thank God it wasn't bombed," Marshall said, quietly, and the solider next to him said, "I beg your pardon?"

"Oh, I'm sorry. I was just thinking aloud. About how beautiful the Golden Gate Bridge is."

" March is a good time of year to visit the city. Gets all fogged in during the summer."

Marshall turned to the soldier and asked, "Where would you go? Like, to what building, you know, for the best view of the bridge and the bay?"

"Top of the Fairmont. No question about it."

"The Fairmont is a hotel, right?"

"Right you are: on top of Nob Hill. The best."

"Real expensive?"

"Well, sir, that's all relative. If I want to impress my girl friend, that's where I take her. Know what I mean?"

"Roger," Marshall said, and laughed.

From the Ferry Building Marshall took a taxi directly to the Fairmont Hotel. The cab turned into a curved drive and an attendant opened the cab door. Marshall felt he ought to salute when he saw the attendant's dark uniform, with gold trim and epaulets. He paid the driver and followed the attendant through the doors. "We'll bring your bag when you know your room number, sir," the attendant said.

"Oh, yeah. Sure," Marshall said. He scanned the faces behind the long registration counter and walked to the position where a young Chinese girl stood.

"You have a reservation, sir?"

"No, ma'am," he said. "I just want to stay a couple nights before I go home."

"Fine. Where's home?"

"You probably never heard of it. Chico," he said, then added, "It's been three years."

"Sure, I've heard of Chico and Red Bluff and Redding. But I'm going to have to speak to the manager about a room." She turned from her station and walked to a man at the other end of the counter. He returned with her.

"Hello, Lieutenant. Gather that you're getting home from someplace?" he said.

"Yes sir. Left Germany about ten days ago. Flew up to Le Havre, then onto the Laconia Victory ship, then a DC-4 up to Beale, and now I've got to buy some civilian clothes and presents for my folks."

"Well, we saved a room for you. Not the most deluxe, but from the window you can see part of the Golden Gate Bridge. Miss Fung will take care of you."

"Well thanks. That's just great!"

Marshall filled out the form placed before him, and the girl signaled to the bell man who took two keys and, carrying Marshall's B-4 bag, said, "Follow me, sir."

"Man, this place is plush," Marshall said.

"First time here, eh?"

"Oh, I've been to San Francisco before, but not here. After I graduated from high school. We all stayed with friends down the peninsula."

"Well, you can see the curve of the earth from the top of the Fairmont," the bellman said, then chuckled.

"Sure you can," Marshall answered and laughed.

The bell man opened the room, asked Marshall to enter, followed, and placed the B-4 bag on a luggage rack. He showed Marshall the bathroom and pulled back the drapes and Marshall could make out the Golden Gate Bridge where it touched Marin County.

"Anything else I can do for you, Lieutenant?" The position of the bellman's hand was not subtle and Marshall took a dollar bill from his wallet and gave it to him.

"Thank you, sir," he said and pulled the door closed as he departed.

Marshall unpacked his few items from his B-4 bag, hanging up a pair of dark green trousers and two newly laundered shirts. His clean underwear he left in a side pocket of the B-4 bag, and put his shaving kit in the white-tiled bathroom. He laughed as he examined two pro-kits he hadn't discarded on his journey home. He remembered the explicit and nauseating movies of venereal diseases they'd shown them in cadet training, and how even Pop had admonished the crewmembers to use the kits if they fooled around.

Considering walking up the stairs, but not sure of just how many flights to the top of the hotel, Marshall pressed the UP button and waited for the elevator.

"Floor, sir?" the elevator operator asked.

"Top of the Fairmont," Marshall said. "I've been told that's the best view of the whole Bay Area."

"The Crown Room. Yes sir, it really is."

"That's the name of the room?"

"Yes sir, and here we are. Enjoy your stay, sir."

Everyone is sure well mannered in this place, Marshall thought. He walked towards the brightness and entered a room with tall windows, broad and sparkling clean, with an elevated, horseshoe shaped bar in the center. Rows of small tables were in front of the windows. He walked to the bar.

"All right to sit at those tables by the windows?"

"Absolutely, Lieutenant," the bartender smiled. "First time in the Crown Room?"

"Yep. But I've heard about it for years."

"On your way home?"

"Yes sir."

"Well, we don't see quite as many guys in uniform up here as we used to."

"I got stuck with some occupation duty."

"The first drink is on the house for returning servicemen."

"No kidding. That's real generous."

"So what'll it be?"

"Old Forester and water, please."

"Good call. You go find yourself a table over there that you like and one of the cocktail waitresses will bring your drink."

"Thanks very much."

"Relax Lieutenant," The bartender grinned broadly, "You just sit where you want. All of us here welcome you home!"

Seems sincere, Marshall thought. From the table Marshall selected, he could view the entire length of the Golden Gate Bridge, Alcatraz Island, and the length of San Pablo Bay.

The Coit Tower dominated the foreground, and if he looked to his right out other windows he could see part of the stiff angles of the Oakland Bay Bridge and a portion of Treasure Island. As with the Golden Gate Bridge, the bridge from Treasure Island to the city was graceful. He wondered if it had a name of its own.

The waitress brought his drink with a bowl of peanuts and a napkin. She placed a tab with the drink, but smiled and said, "No charge for this one. Welcome home." As he looked up to thank her eye caught the slim figure of a blonde girl seating herself at a table three removed from his. The waitress went to the girl and took her order, and when she departed Marshall looked squarely into her eyes, nodded and smiled. The girl looked away, towards the scenery, unsmiling, expressionless, Marshall thought. Probably married, he concluded.

By the time Marshall had consumed most of his drink, the Crown Room began to fill with customers. The waitress appeared. "Another of the same?" she said, and he replied, "Sure." The waitress approached the blonde girl, and she looked away from the view of the Golden Gate Bridge long enough to smile and nod affirmatively.

When the waitress returned with the second drink, she asked, "We're getting short of tables and wondered if you would mind sharing yours?"

"That'd be okay," Marshall said. He watched the waitress approach the blonde girl, speak to her, point to people waiting for tables and then looked toward Marshall. To his surprise, the waitress picked up the blonde's drink and they both walked to his table.

Marshall arose as the girl stood by the chair opposite him, staring at him, he felt. Marshall stood up and stepped around the edge of the table and reached for the top of the chair and pushed it back to enable the girl to be seated. She stared, expressionless, into his eyes for a moment then sat down and accepted her cocktail from the waitress.

"I'm Marshall Sunder," he said and extended his hand. "Eileen O'Ryan," she replied, touched but did not grasp his hand and immediately turned and stared out of the window.

Both watched ships entering and exiting beneath the bridge. The hum of the people chatting in the Crown Room, the sound of glasses touching in toasts of happiness, the fragrance of pipe and cigarette smoke, filled the void between the young strangers.

Marshall gazed at the Golden Gate Bridge, then muttered, "Bridges that stand." His remark was followed by silence, as he sipped his drink and ate a few peanuts.

"What did you mean by that?" Eileen said and for the first time looked at him, seemed to make eye contact that evidenced recognition, studied his wings and ribbons beneath them, and seemed to be aware of his presence.

To Marshall, her light blue eyes and blonde hair reminded him of the image of what he'd envisioned as a typical German. Yet he saw no blondes in Germany, and for that matter could recall none anyplace in Europe. He wondered too, if the darkness beneath her eyes was make up, and if her hair was bleached.

"What did I mean? You mean about the bridges?" and Eileen nodded, and Marshall felt as if she, too, was studying his features. It was early that morning when he shaved, but his afternoon chin growth was never as dark as his hair.

"Well, my outfit was known as The Bridge Smashers. It was our job to knock down all of the bridges we could to stop the krauts from moving their troops, tanks, supplies and trucks and stuff. I was a bombardier-navigator. I was just thinking, thank God the Japs didn't destroy our Golden Gate Bridge. Our bridges are still standing. Saw some beauties from the Victory ship in New York harbor."

"Oh," she said, then looked out of the window at the bridge. "I understand, sort of. My husband was a P-38 pilot. I suppose he had something to do with destroying bridges. Maybe protecting our bombers. It doesn't matter, and I really didn't look closely at your wings."

"We flew in mediums. B-26's. You said your husband was a pilot. What's he do now? Back in civvies?"

"He's gone: even Bill's C.O. lied to me. You see, for over nine months I've felt it was something more than just missing in action. They should have told me the truth when they knew he was killed. They think they are doing us a kindness to postpone the truth. When I learned that his squadron, his C.O. and some buddies would be coming home through San Francisco, I invited myself up to speak firsthand with some of Bill's friends. I didn't want to wait forever to know the truth." Then quite suddenly, she paused and stared out of the window, "Of course, I should have been wiser, should have been better prepared, so, finally, I am no longer Mrs. Bill O'Ryan, I am not the wife of Captain O'Ryan, fighter pilot. I am now widow O'Ryan."

"Gosh, I'm sorry!" Marshall said and looked into his glass.

"Sorry?" she paused, then said, "My God, I guess that does wrap it up. It's strange, I didn't think I'd ever be able to speak of it, and now I'm blabbering to you. A Fly Boy I don't even know."

"Well, I am a good listener, it that's any comfort. Like a lot of us, I got stuck with the duty of writing to the folks of a few friends that got it. As far as I'm concerned, my buddies and I figured that living or dying in the war was just a matter of the fickle finger of fate; just good or bad luck. There was nothing I could ever come up with that I felt could make sense to a mother and father or a wife. The chaplain had a book of sayings, but generally I relied on the 23rd psalm, and added a few things about bravery, and stuff. Anyone that got shot at prayed, on both sides, and we all prayed to a God, probably the same God."

"Thanks, I think," Eileen said. "It wasn't until I got here and heard first hand that Billy and a Zero pilot collided in mid air. Neither got out of their planes. That was it. Final! And for over nine months all I've heard is missing in action. And I still haven't heard anything different officially. Just what his friends saw."

"Yes. Knowing for sure is bad enough, but missing in action, well, I guess that gives you hope. False hope sometimes."

"Well, I've got to face up to my new status, I suppose."

"Where's home?"

"L.A."

"You heading back to L.A.?"

"Yes. Classes await."

"High school?"

"My, that was sweet. No. U.S.C."

"Great track teams, and football, of course: baseball, too."

"And law school, and medicine, philosophy, history, business, dentistry, even cinema photography."

"Are you going to be a teacher?"

"Ha! Typical male. All women should be nurses, or teach, and if real lucky marry and raise babies."

Marshall squirmed in his chair. "My mom helps run our family mercantile store. Does the books. Really does everything and anything. Puts away inventory, fills orders, delivers fence posts and barbed wire, sweeps up and also cooks for my dad and me, plus keeps us in clean clothes. She went to teachers college a couple of years before getting married. I think my mother would have made an excellent teacher."

"Sounds like a very competent woman," Eileen said.

"So what are you studying to be?" Marshall asked.

"You really want to know? Really give a darn?"

"Look Eileen, that's if it's okay to call you by your first name, I wouldn't ask if I didn't mean it. I'm not the enemy."

"Okay, Fly-Boy. You actually do seem sincere. Let's finish our drinks and go down to the lobby and I'll show you what I want to be."

She actually smiled a little, Marshall thought, then he signaled to the cocktail waitress and paid for the drinks. He left a dollar tip and they went to the elevator together.

"Thanks. I didn't expect you to pay for my cocktail," Eileen said.

"You're welcome. That's the first drink I've bought for anyone since I got home. My first one was on the house."

When they reached the ground level, Eileen led the way down a long hall, its walls covered with old photos of the San Francisco earthquake and fire, then turned into the large lobby where she asked Marshall to sit beside her on a couch that overlooked the expanse of the room.

"Well, what do you think? What do you feel when you look at this room?"

"Very handsome. It's beautiful. The pillars or columns, just everything. The color, the ceiling."

"I don't suppose you'd have any reason to know who designed it?"

"Not in the least. Some guy from SC?"

"This is considered one of the most beautiful hotel lobbies in the entire world, and the architect was Julia Morgan."

"No kidding."

"And that, Lieutenant, is what I'm studying to be. An architect!"

"Well, I'm impressed."

"You've heard of William Randolph Hearst, the publisher?"

"Yep, I've heard of him, and the *Examiner.* Sometimes I delivered it on my bike."

"Well, he travels all over the world buying up ceilings, statues and entire buildings, all kinds of art work, and he has it all shipped to San Simeon where Julia Morgan puts it all together for him at his castle, the Hearst Castle. She's his own private architect."

"I guess I just never thought about women being architects, but more power to you!"

"You don't think that is unfeminine?"

"Hey look, I grew up with folks that said you can do anything you can visualize, you can be anything you want, if you are willing to work at it. If you are persistent."

"Hmmm. I could get to like you, or maybe your parents," Eileen said. For the first time since they'd met, she laughed aloud. "So now it's your turn. What are you going to do, or be?"

"Jeez, I really don't know. My mom and dad assume I want to eventually take over the family business. I'll have to sort it all out. That's why I delayed going home for a few more days."

"Childhood sweetheart waiting for you?"

"No." Marshall's mind was suddenly engulfed with mixed signals. He thought of Emil's daughter, up in Oregon. A friend, not a sweetheart. But he could not erase his memories of Kris and the tragedy of her death. It had been several months since he'd been with Kris in Munich. After the Dachau trip she wouldn't have anything to do with him. Learning that his crew had bombed the bridge changed everything. He still couldn't envision Kris as being anything but perky and smart, alert and soft, but frail, when he held her in his arms.

"There's the G.I. Bill, if you want to go to college."

"I was accepted at Cal, after high school, but about that time I was needed in the store, and then Pearl Harbor happened, so like all my buddies, I joined up. I bounced around from one army school to another and finally decided I wanted to be a pilot. I was accepted in cadets, and that meant another long wait while going to various colleges. Finally the Air Corps decided they needed a big batch of bombardier-navigators, and all of us that expected to go to pilot training, found ourselves in the noses of AT-11's. Then it was overseas training, forming our crews, and finally it was off to the E.T.O. in B-26's to participate in the invasion, then we moved into France and bombed Germany from there."

"The war's been over awhile."

"I got stuck with occupation duty. Not quite enough points to come home. Officers had to have a few more points than enlisted men for some reason."

"What was that like? Occupation duty?"

"Oh, I had my ups and downs, like everyone." Marshall sighed deeply. "Don't think I was cut out to be a conqueror."

"A girl?"

"What are you, a mind reader or something?" Marshall glanced at Eileen, unsmiling. Then Marshall was startled, almost jumped when he felt Eileen's hand brush his, and he was surprised when she allowed it to rest lightly atop his. He felt the slight twinge, almost electrical, in his groin. He wondered if the bodies of other men reacted as he did, even when he studied the well formed hips and breasts on any woman, there was that mild jolt.

"Why don't you buy me a drink, Marshall?" She studied his face, then thought, *I've actually touched another man.*

"Hey, you called me Marshall," he replied, and laughed and stood up, took both of her extended hands and helped her up from the couch. He was suddenly more aware of her figure, and although slim, her breasts pushed against her dress which clung nicely around her hips.

"Back to the Crown Room?"

"Let's find a quiet little pub or something."

They walked to the doors and Marshall looked around at the lobby.

"Boy, this is really some lobby, Miss Architect," he said.

Eileen grasped his arm, her head reached to his shoulders, and she stood closely at his side.

He looked down at her, "You know, I've got to confess. I don't know a damn thing about San Francisco."

"Let's ask the concierge for a recommendation."

"Sure, Eileen, and where do I find him?"

"Oh come on, Fly-Boy, follow me!" Eileen walked to the Information Desk. "Ask away."

Marshall felt the blood rush to his cheeks, felt unsure of himself, but lately he had reminisced, remembered his combat experiences and, knowing he'd faced plenty of flak, and while admittedly scared as hell, he had performed his tasks, he should now be able to cope with anything civilian life offered. Two uniformed men stood behind a desk and one looked up as they approached.

"May I be of assistance, sir?"

"Would you recommend a nice, quiet place where we can have a cocktail and dinner tonight."

Eileen was surprised and pleased to hear him mention dinner.

"We've several nice dining rooms right here in the hotel, sir."

"Well, we'd like to get some fresh air, and then kind of go someplace where local people like to go."

"If you lean to the elegant, I can recommend Ernie's, or the Blue Fox, however if you want something that's fun, a little less formal, and where you can't beat the food, try New Joe's."

"How does any of that sound to you, Eileen?"

"Let's go to New Joe's." She gripped his arm and smiled up at him.

"I'll be happy to call and reserve a table for you."

"That would be great. Let's see," Marshall glanced at his wrist watch, "It's five thirty, how about six thirty?"

"You are guests of the hotel?" Marshall nodded affirmatively, then took his room key from his pocket and showed it. The concierge glanced at Marshall's shoulders, "So, that will be Lieutenant and Mrs.?"

"Sunder," Marshall said, then spelled it out.

The concierge picked up the desk phone and made the reservation.

Marshall removed a dollar bill from his wallet and tucked it in the man's hand.

"That's not necessary, sir, but thank you."

"I've a question," Eileen said. "Is there a drug store in the hotel?"

"Down one floor. Take the elevator and turn right when you exit. It's open until eight p.m."

"Thank you," Marshall said, then added, "They do serve cocktails at New Joe's, don't they?"

"Yes sir, plus excellent wines. And I'd recommend a cab. It's a steep walk, and too, Ma'am, there'll be a chill in the air."

"I want to go to the drug store, Marshall, and then I'll go to the suite and put on something a bit warmer," Eileen said.

"Me too. Let's go," and they walked to the elevator.

The small brightly-lit drug store seemed to be divided according to male and female clientele, with the cosmetics on the left side and newspapers, tobacco, magazines and shaving supplies on the right. The cash register was partially concealed by a rack of merchandise. A man with gray hair and horn rimmed glasses waited behind the cash register and smiled when Marshall approached.

"Help you, soldier?" he asked.

"You have Sen Sen?"

"Select your flavor. They're in that rack with the Life Savers."

Marshall selected a small package, then leaned over the tray that contained packages of cigarettes, and whispered, "And a package of *Sheiks*."

Smiling, the man whispered back, "Three, a dozen, or a gross?"

"Dozen, please," Marshall said, and handed the clerk a ten-dollar bill, accepted his change and the small white paper bag. Marshall felt grateful that the man kept his voice low.

Marshall strolled to the magazine rack, thumbed through the pages of a *Saturday Evening Post* while awaiting Eileen. She made her purchases and she walked to Marshall and rested her hand on his arm. He replaced the magazine, looked down into her face and realized that she was indeed very pretty. She smiled up at him, eyes wide, "Getting hungry, Fly-Boy?" she said, then added, "Let's go to my room. I want to get my coat. And a special bonus: I've some Canadian Club. Daddy insisted I bring it along. We can order up some ice and still have time for that drink."

"Lead on, Miss Architect!" Marshall said, laughing.

Eileen handed her room key to Marshall. He unlocked the door and followed her into the room.

"Wow," Marshall said. "Pretty fancy. Your view is of Oakland, and look at that wrought iron railing. Just like New Orleans."

"Daddy made my reservation. Felt I should have a small suite. He isn't handling Billy's missing in action situation very well," Eileen said. She dialed room service and ordered a bucket of ice. "I told father there would be some other fliers' wives. I really thought there would be."

"What does your father do?"

"Stock market. He was one of the founders of the Pacific Coast Stock Exchange. Survived the crash, and has rebuilt a little empire all of his own. Smart, and unlike most of his golfing and drinking buddies, he spends some time with mom and me. He's been a fortress for me since Billy turned up missing. He has a law degree, too."

"Well, our mercantile store will provide the family with a good living, but it's sure as hell no empire!"

"There's the ice," Eileen said, responding to a knock at the door. "Have you another dollar bill?"

To Marshall's surprise, a waiter wheeled in a small tray table with a white cloth, cloth napkins, a silver plated ice bucket, a selection of different sized glasses, and two bowls, one with mixed nuts and the other with small crackers, and small bottles of soda water and ginger ale.

Marshall thanked the man and handed him the folded dollar bill, which was accepted with a retreating slight bow at the waist.

"Thank you, sir," he said, "and will you be having dinner in your room this evening?"

"No, no. That's all for tonight."

Eileen appeared from the bedroom with an unopened fifth of Canadian Club, and handed it to Marshall. Studying the label, Marshall said, "This is one of the brands the sergeant at the officers' club recommended."

"I'll have water with mine," Eileen said, as she sampled the nuts.

Selecting one of the shorter glasses, Marshall held it up to eye level. "Say when," and began to pour slowly into the glass. "Stop!" Eileen yelped. "Do you want to have to carry me to dinner?" Both of them laughed, as Marshall measured out a similar level for himself, and added some ice cubes and water.

"A toast is in order, Fly-Boy, but I hope you can stand, well, some honesty, I've really got Billy on my mind, and I raise my glass to him."

"Hell, I'll go along with that, if you'll allow me to include a little kraut girl named Kris."

They touched glasses, stared at each other briefly, unsmiling, and tears began to swell in Eileen's eyes, and then simultaneously they turned and stared out of the view windows, across the wrought iron railings towards Oakland and the hills beyond.

"That goes down pretty smoothly," Marshall said. "Handle one more?"

"One more and I might not make it to New Joe's. Very light for me."

"You can lean on me."

"If I accidentally call you Billy, will you forgive me?"

"Of course. Is that why you keep calling me Fly-Boy? Anyway, you're just getting half a shot or I'll have to eighty-six you. Drink up. Then we're off to dinner. Okay?"

"Okay Billy boy," Eileen said, then sighed. Well, I guess I call you Fly-Boy because I'm afraid that Marshall is personal. You are Air Corps. Billy is Air Corps. Fly-Boy is Air Corps, but impersonal, or something. Hell, I don't know. Does calling you that annoy you?"

"No. At first I thought it was kind of a put down, but now I think of it as a friendly nickname."

"Oh, Marsh, I intended respect, and now affection!"

"Well there's that old gag about 'you can call me anything but be sure to call me for dinner.'"

Eileen laughed and she walked to Marshall, took his hand and together they walked to the door. Marshall and Eileen stopped in the lobby of the Fairmont Hotel and unselfconsciously turned, arms clasped, and admired in silence the beauty of the room. Yellow cabs were lined up in front of the hotel and quickly they were deposited at the front door of New Joe's restaurant.

"Yes, sir, we've a table for you, or if you prefer we've two seats at the counter."

"The counter?" Marshall repeated.

Both he and Eileen looked towards the counter, behind which chefs with their appropriate tall white-starched hats were busy preparing food.

"That would be different," Eileen said.

"I feel you'll enjoy it," the maitre d' said.

"Sounds great," Marshall said, laughing, "the counter it will be."

"This is fascinating," Eileen said. "Watch him! He throws those vegetables practically to the ceiling!"

One of the chefs poured olive oil into a large frying pan, stirred in a selection of lima beans and green beans and small bits of carrots, tiny tomatoes, diced potatoes, a green vegetable, and cauliflower, stirred the whole concoction vigorously and then with athletic coordination, flung the entire contents upwards, watched it reach its peak, then return en masse into the awaiting skillet, which in turn was placed over the flaming grill.

A waiter in a tux with a black bow tie leaned across their shoulders and made his recommendation, "The Petrale sole for the lady with a small tossed green salad, and a New York, yes, medium rare, for the Lieutenant. And yes, the house wines are from Almaden, a glass of Chablis for the lady and a Pinot Noir for the Lieutenant," and quietly, "I know you won't mind showing me some ID."

Oh, Christ, Marshall thought, I didn't even think about Eileen's age, but she presented a driver's license, and before he could reach for his own wallet, the tuxedoed waiter simply patted him on the shoulder, saying, "It's okay, sir, if you tell me you're twenty-one."

"Roger!" Marshall said.

"Enjoy your dinner."

"Gosh," Marshall said, "I think we're lucky to be sitting here. It's a real show, watching them prepare all of the dishes!"

"Look, he's pushing his thumb down on top of each of those steaks," Eileen said.

The chef overheard her, turned and said, "We know by feel. Rare is very soft. Medium is a bit of resistance, well done, it's stiff to the touch. But who would order a steak well done?" He grinned and raised a finger to his tall, white starched hat, nodded, and returned to the grill.

When the waiter presented the check, Marshall asked, "Their hats are different, why?"

"Different chef schools, just like nurses' caps, you know?"

"No, I didn't know, but thanks and the dinner was great." Marshall tipped more generously than a dollar.

A cab appeared, slowed and stopped at the curb, and they quickly jumped in. They journeyed up the hill to the Fairmont.

At the Fairmont, Marshall accompanied Eileen to her room and Marshall again accepted the key. He opened the door for her, prepared to say goodnight, but Eileen said, "Let's check out the view, the lights across the bay are so pretty."

Marshall walked past the serving table and scooped up a dozen peanuts. Eileen did the same, then raised the top of the ice bucket. "Still plenty of ice, if you'd like a night cap, Marsh?"

"Great. Same as before?"

"Just don't knock me out."

Marshall fixed the highballs and this time raised his glass, "How about a toast to us, Eileen. Don't we deserve something as survivors?"

"To us, yes. I'll toast to that. You realize we've only known each other, how long, since mid day?"

"It's past midnight," Eileen said.

"Our engineer, Pop, came up with this saying, "Hickory, dickory, dock, two mice ran up the clock, the clock struck one, and the other got away!"

"You are a funny guy."

"The last few days have been interesting. Enlightening," Marshall said. "What I know most, now, is that I'm simply a country hick, uncomfortable out of my bomber, and not sure what the hell to do next. This half a day with you has been a great bonus."

"Feeling sorry for yourself?"

"Oh hell no. I'm lucky: just so lucky to be alive. It's luck that I met you today. You're pretty. You're educated. You're ambitious, you have goals, a future. I think it's kind of the opposite of feeling sorry for myself. It's more of a 'why me' kind of thing, like being grateful: but to whom? To God? God didn't look after a lot of really great guys, like your husband, I'm sure. Sorry? Hell, Eileen, I am so sorry, really sorry for you, but I can't express my feelings, can't seem to put them into words. This God deal confuses the hell out of me. We thank God when something good happens, but we don't blame him for the tragedies!"

Eileen placed her drink on a table and walked to Marshall and lifted both of her arms, encircling his neck and pulled his head down towards hers and kissed him fully on the lips. She stepped back and began to untie his necktie.

"What the heck are you doing, Eileen?"

"Come on Mr. flier. Let's go to bed."

"Holy Jesus Christ!" Marshall stammered. In one motion he bent over and swept Eileen into his arms and carried her, giggling, towards the bedroom.

"Let me down, you big oaf," Eileen laughed. "You want to wrinkle my dress?"

Marshall lowered her slowly, "This isn't that Canadian Club talking, is it?"

"You are now the passion of my life," Eileen whispered. She retreated to the bathroom and when she returned she stood at the closet opening and began to undress and carefully hung her dress on a hanger as Marshall stared.

He watched her pull her hands up behind her, her elbows bent, and unsnap the hooks and pull the brassiere upward and he stared at the fullness of her breasts, realizing that the brassiere was a cover only, not a support, and looked away suddenly, feeling for a fleeting second that he'd been doing something sneaky, forbidden, peeking-tom-like, but then with a paced, controlled nonchalance began to remove his own clothes, and too, hung them carefully.

Eileen, naked, extinguished the overhead lights, turned back the bed and turned on the lamp beside the bed, slipped beneath the sheets and sat up with her back against a pillow propped against the bedstead, the sheet and blanket folded neatly beneath her exposed breasts.

Marshall went to the bathroom, selected a medium size towel and returned with it wrapped around his waist.

"Why've you got that towel around you?" Eileen asked, laughing.

"Didn't want to scare you," Marshall said, startled by his own comment.

"God, you are a cute one," Eileen said.

Marshall approached the bed lamp and extinguished it.

"Turn that back on," Eileen said.

"Really?"

"I'm not afraid of you. I'm afraid of the dark," Eileen whispered, as Marshall turned the lamp on, and in turn entered the bed with Eileen.

"I have these," Marshall stammered, "To protect you." He revealed one of the condoms held in the palm of his hand.

"So confident you'd get me into bed?" Eileen said, laughing, "And I thought you were so shy!"

"Hell no. I really didn't expect to. I hoped, of course. But I was a Boy Scout."

"Helped little old ladies across Main Street in Chico?"

"How'd you know Chico has a Main Street?"

"Come on, Marshall, ever hear of a town that didn't have a Main Street?"

"We don't have enough cars in Chico to pose a threat to little old ladies." Marshall said, and discarded his towel.

They laughed together, and Marshall leaned across the bed, kissed Eileen, and then lowered his head to kiss her breasts.

"When you come up for air, let me tell you that you won't need those, unless you're afraid you'll catch something." It was too personal a subject, Eileen thought, to tell him she'd not menstruated in over nine months, but Doctor Hart said it was natural after trauma and nature would take care of it.

Marshall responded, "Hell no! It's you I was thinking of."

"Let's not ruin this with a lot of chatter."

"Roger," Marshall said. He wrapped his arms around Eileen. Completely engulfed in the grasp of Marshall's arms, held very tightly, closely, Eileen said, "It's been an eternity. Wow, doll, I can't breathe, you're holding me too tightly."

Their caresses were urgent and bold, their hands exploring swiftly, yet mutually satisfying. Eileen opened and was joined, they melded, their bodies moving rhythmically instinctively in the silence invaded finally by the oh's and ah's of Marshall.

"Slowly," Eileen whispered, "we're not rabbits," and Marshall laughed, "Christ. I can't hold it any longer," and Eileen said, "Oh, wow. Thank you, Marsh. This hasn't happened in such a long time. Hold me closely, quietly."

"Know what?" Marshall said.

"What?"

"You didn't call me Billy and I didn't call you Kris."

"So, we've fallen in passion…"

"Passion or lust or love. Whatever we've done has been terrific. Now I know what I was fighting for."

"I honestly didn't imagine this happening."

"With a country hick from Chico?"

"Don't put yourself down," Eileen scolded. "That's annoying; unbecoming; unnecessary; and untrue."

"Okay. Can you handle another Canadian Club?"

"Yes. Would you be offended if I accidentally called you Billy?"

"I think I understand," Marshall whispered, then asked, "Want to do it again, Kris?"

"What do you think?" Eileen said, and laughed, successfully accomplishing a mood of seductiveness in the timbre of her voice.

Marshall returned to the bed and handed one of the glasses to Eileen.

"What's your opinion of me, now, Marshall?" Eileen said. She sipped from the glass.

"I said it once. I'll say it a thousand times. You're pretty, you're ambitious, intelligent, plus you are just terrific in bed!"

"Plus I'm an easy lay?"

"I figured maybe tomorrow night, if I was persistent. And irresistible!"

Marshall and Eileen resumed their love making, climaxing simultaneously, then finally rested, lying back, exhausted, stretched out naked, side by side on the bed, their heads on pillows, still embraced.

"Good God, Marshall," Eileen said, "I must be really hard up. I seldom had two orgasms in one encounter with my Billy." Eileen reached across Marshall's chest and wiped perspiration from his brow. "How are you holding up, Fly-Boy?" With one finger she wound hairs on his chest into curls.

"Ha," Marshall laughed, "I've had two for each of yours." but hesitated to tell her he'd never heard a woman use that word, orgasm, unless a French girl or a Belgian had said it and he didn't realize it, didn't comprehend the word, the language, although there had been ample ohs and ahs during the encounters.

"Ha, yourself! Two for one! Don't kid me," Eileen said, then punched her small fist against his chest. Marshall grunted, laughed, then said, "Come on, cut it out," as Eileen walked her fingers across his abdomen. His muscles rippled, cramped, and he pushed her hand away. "Stop it! I'm ticklish." But Eileen lowered her hand and touched his flaccid penis.

"The little devil is starting to grow again, Marsh," Eileen whispered. She raised herself, resting on her elbows, her firm breasts pushing against his chest. "Okay, Lieutenant, now it's my turn to ask the question. Again?"

"Roger. And how! Over, Wilco and out, I mean in, or something. Over you, I mean you roll over, and I'll soon be in!" Marshall laughed at his own attempt at jest, and Eileen joined him in laughter.

Again they made love and again collapsed, side by side, Eileen's head resting on Marshall's shoulder and arm.

"You make noises like a train engine chugging and puffing up a hill." Eileen whispered, her mouth close to Marshall's ear. Then she nibbled his ear lobe.

"Cut it out wench!" Marshall said, "You aren't exactly quiet."

"I know I'm not ladylike enough for you."

"Believe me. You are the epitome of femininity!"

"Thank you. I can't believe this has happened."

"That is all well and good, but I'd better go to my own room before the sun comes up."

"Why?"

"Shaving gear is there. Tooth brush. Clean underwear, you know."

"Come on Fly-Boy. What you need is some sleep. I'll close those drapes, turn out the light and you hold me close and promise not to snore. Besides, you haven't had your clothes on long enough today to soil them!"

Marshall laughed, guffawed, and asked, "Am I supposed to be your obedient servant?"

"Let's just get some sleep. I want you fresh for tomorrow!"

"Tomorrow I've got to buy my mom a present. And, my sweet thing, I've got to check out of here. I can't go home broke."

"I'll help you shop. And you can move in with me." Eileen walked naked across the room and pulled closed the drapes. As she climbed back into the bed, and turned off the bedside lamp, Marshall said, "What's this deal about being afraid of the dark?"

"I just like to screw with the lights on."

"Aw, Geez! Don't use that word," Marshall said.

"Screw?"

"Takes the romance out of lovemaking. Talking like that will ruin it."

"Okay, my darling. You can wash my mouth out with soap when we wake up. Goodnight. Now hold me closely. And shut up."

In their slumber they turned and moved and finally Marshall was huddled with his chest close to Eileen's back. He breathed the fragrance of her hair, of her lightly perfumed neck and shoulders and he pondered what had happened so quickly in the short day and evening in San Francisco. If he'd been in Belgium or France, he'd have used a pro kit. But he didn't with Kris. He'd felt safe that time, and she now was in his mind, the little German girl, not the beautiful blonde he barely knew, and now he felt simply wearied by exertion and confusion. It had only been a few days since he'd been rushed out of Germany to France and then across the Atlantic, a quick flight in a DC-4 across the United States, and all of a sudden shacked up in a famous hotel with a confused, emotional, sex-starved war widow. Marshall fell into a sound sleep.

Reveille, faintly but distinctly was being whistled near Marshall's ear.

Opening his eyes suddenly he stared into Eileen's pale blue eyes, now twinkling, mischievously, as she continued to faintly whistle the military wake-up call. The drapes had been pulled back and sunlight poured into the room, shadows from the wrought iron on the terrace outside the room repeated the configuration on the white carpet.

A pink silk dressing gown clung to Eileen's figure, tantalizing, revealing just a little, seeming to promise a sudden view of more of her body as she slowly walked around the bed.

"I've showered and ordered up some coffee, sweet rolls, and fresh fruit."

"What the hell time is it?" Marshall said, sitting up in bed and pulling the sheets around him.

"Oh, it's about eight-thirty; plenty of time to get that present for your mom. What about your dad?"

"Would you believe I bought a .45 Colt at Beale for him? I turned mine in back in France before we got on the Victory Ship."

"Bet that will please him."

"Yeah. Too bad it isn't my own."

"You'll tell him that it was yours, of course. That it was strapped to your hip on every mission."

"We used a chest holster. But I wouldn't want to deceive him."

"Oh, my God, Marshall!" Eileen said, raising her voice, "Haven't you ever heard of a little white lie? Can't you imagine how proud he'd be. How he'd feel," and she emphasized feel, "If he knew that that particular gun accompanied you on your missions. Give him a chance to be a part of your combat, of your missions. Are those guns all that different, one from the other?"

"No," Marshall said. He grinned and let his head hang self-consciously, "They're all the same. They made forty-fives by the thousands."

"Okay, your dad is all set. And you're going to tell him it is yours? Right?"

"Yeah, I suppose. I guess I see your point. Okay Eileen, It's my forty-five."

"Speaking of deception, Marshall, I hope I haven't deceived you. I'm selfish. Somehow you don't really exist. You're my Bill."

"Come on, Eileen, your needle is stuck. So, you are a girl named Kristine. Fair enough?"

"I guess that equals things out."

"We've just fallen in lust, not love, just plain old lust!" Marshall said.

"Afraid of falling in love?"

"Doesn't that lead to marriage? Vows and stuff?"

"As far as I'm concerned, we're just doing what comes natural."

"You mean I don't have to marry you?!"

"God," Eileen exclaimed, "you are funny! Guess I've already called you cute."

"Forget cute. That's not me."

"Then let's talk about your mom. Seriously, didn't you send anything home? Weren't you overseas a year or more?"

"Sure. I sent her a little music box, some handkerchiefs and perfume and a couple of nice prints of scenery that I bought in Paris," Marshall said. "I just want to show up at home with something special in hand."

"We'll find something nice for her, now take your shower like a good boy," Eileen said. "Breakfast will be here soon."

In the bathroom Marshall glanced at the bathtub and thought it was twice the size of any he'd ever seen. The white tiled shower was roomy, too, with an overhead light, and the white bath towels were longer and wider and thicker than any he'd ever used. He held one of the towels up beneath his chin and it almost touched the tile floor. It sucked up the water from his body, became heavy and after he returned the towel to the bar he saw reflected in the mirror, hanging on the back of the bathroom door, the white terry cloth bathrobe.

Wondering if his own bathroom was so equipped, Marshall put on the robe and pulled up firmly the tie around his waist. On the sink, Marshall saw Eileen's tube of toothpaste. He squeezed some of it onto the dampened end of a white washcloth and scrubbed his teeth.

Only thing missing is a razor, Marshall thought, and rubbed the stubble, the growth on his chin and cheeks. Marshall ran his fingers back through his brown wet hair, and began to wonder what the day ahead held in store.

Clad in the full-length white terry cloth bathrobe, Marshall, barefooted, walked into the spacious room. Eileen had partially straightened out the bed covers and fluffed the pillows. She looked down at his bare feet.

"Gave my clogs to a French guy at Le Havre. He was cleaning my room. Probably used them for fuel."

"Well, we can include slippers in our shopping spree. There's the morning *Chronicle,* if you're interested."

"Where'd you get the paper?"

"They leave them at the door. Complimentary."

"That's funny. All I've read for a couple of years has been *The Stars and Stripes.* I used to be able to hit everyone's front porch with a rolled-up *Chronicle* or *Examiner.*"

"And I bet you toted one of those darling little white bags around with the *Saturday Evening Post?*"

"Nope. I sold *Liberty.* And do you know it was the first magazine in the U.S. to actually print the word 'sex.' They made a big deal out of it. My mom was mortified."

"I'll have to tuck away that little fact for trivia time at the sorority."

"So you're a joiner," Marshall said, not waiting for an answer, and followed with "Man, I could sure stand a cup of hot black coffee."

"It'll be here any minute. Have you any spare dollar bills?"

"Oh, sure." Marshall went to the closet and from his wallet brought three one-dollar bills.

"One is enough. Don't want to spoil them."

"We used to give the waiters two cigarettes if they were really good."

"Really? Now you are doing the kidding."

"No, seriously. You know the war couldn't function without cigarettes, coffee, and chocolate. That's all we needed to live first class."

"There's the door." Eileen said.

"I'll get it. Come on. Cover up, Eileen!" Marshall said, and glanced at her revealing dressing gown. She'd make a heck of a model for Mr. Petty, Marshall thought.

"Okay, Fly-Boy. You're beginning to sound like a husband."

Adjusting to what he felt was now becoming a routine, Marshall greeted the waiter, tipped him, and advised that nothing further was required. The man bowed, and backed out of the room studying the young couple.

Eileen's figure was silhouetted, leaving little to the imagination, as the bright white sunlight filled the room. Marshall could understand the stares of the waiter.

"Daddy always puts a little brandy or Canadian Club in his coffee on Sundays," Eileen said. She brought the bottle to the table and poured liberally of the liquor into each cup of coffee, filling a third of the space. "He calls it 'a little lacing' says it is good for your veins, or arteries or something, opens them up so the blood can pump through easier."

"I think it affects your inhibitions."

"Mine, or yours."

"Oh, probably both," Marshall said, and laughed. "As a matter of fact I don't think you have any inhibitions."

"Gee, I don't know whether to be flattered or insulted," Eileen said, and feigned a pout.

"You mentioned your sorority, about the time the waiter showed up."

"Kappa Kappa Gamma."

"Only one I ever heard of was I Felta Thigh."

"God, that is really corny," Eileen said, and joined Marshall in laughter.

"Well, my sorority sisters feel strongly that we girls should be able to enjoy sex, to talk openly about our bodies, about men and women relationships, and we feel that most men are sex-ignoramuses."

"Talking about it doesn't make it any better, any more fun."

"Well, I mean we don't feel men in general even think that we should admit enjoying sexual intercourse. What's fine and natural and normal for you is naughty or evil or shouldn't be talked about openly for us. We're compiling a list of your disrespectful slang remarks and descriptions."

"Like what?"

"Whim, wham, thank you ma'am, for instance."

"That's just supposed to be funny, that's all."

"Then how about referring to a girl as 'a good piece of ass', or 'she's built like a brick shit house'. Or, 'I bet she's a good lay'."

"Tell you what, Eileen, I really do hate to hear you, or any girl, any woman use four letter words like that!"

"And, Fly-Boy," Eileen continued, speaking flippantly, "have you ever said, or heard one of your buddies say, 'find 'em, feel 'em, fuck 'em, and forget 'em'?"

"Like I said, I think it is stupid and offensive and vulgar for any woman to use the four letter words you've spilled out. I think there ought to be more important things for your sorority sisters to involve yourselves in…like wanting to become a great architect."

"Sorry to offend you, Marsh," Eileen said. She poured coffee into one of the small cups and walked to Marshall and handed it to him.

"Thanks," Marshall said, "I'll for damn sure be careful about what I say about the fair sex," placing a sarcastic emphasis on the word, 'fair'.

"Okay, but while I'm at it, let me ask you what you know about a girl's anatomy?" Eileen retreated to a long couch and stretched out on it, leaning back against a thick pillow, her legs bare, slim and curvaceous.

"More Kappa Kappa whatever stuff?"

"Yes, as a matter of fact," Eileen said. Marshall sat down at the table and stared across the top of his coffee cup at Eileen reclining on the couch.

He looked at her carefully, quizzically. Her gown opened beneath her throat, the nipples of her breasts pushed against the gown and Marshall felt the jab, the sensation in his groin, and wished he could deny the stimulation, but could not. He sensed an air of mischievousness.

"A couple of the girls have brothers, ex-servicemen, who have, I'll have to admit, somewhat reluctantly contributed to our research. And I think they are kind of ashamed of themselves, are embarrassed, but we've coerced them, but they tell us that this kind of talk is common in YOUR world."

"The guys I pal around with say a lot of things, but not in front of girls."

"That's refreshing, but, be truthful now, how many girls' cherries have you broken?"

"Well, I grew up thinking virginity was supposed to be important. Something to do with marriage vows. Ha, maybe I ought to wash out your mouth with soap. How'd you like that?"

"You sound like my dad! I do like your idealism. And Billy married a virgin, if it matters, I mean if you care."

"If I were Billy, I'd have cared a lot. So go on," Marshall said, but he began to feel uncomfortable, began to recall his B-26 outfit and the crew members, and the image of the young bombardier nicknamed Spike suddenly filled his mind, and the thought of Spike's death caused his chest to suddenly ache.

"I think I really am embarrassing you. But I honestly don't want it to affect our new friendship."

"God," Marshall stammered, "I guess I'm a prude. I'll admit it upsets me to hear stuff like that from you."

"Oh, come on now, remember, what I say is not how I speak, and we don't refer to you guys in slang ways, at least my girl friends and I don't, but what irritates us is what we've learned about how you guys talk about us."

"That was a mouth full. Go on."

"You've used, or heard the words, 'cunt, box, slit, pussy, snatch, boobs and tits'?"

"Let's just say that I've heard about every goddamn expression uttered about women during three years in the service!" Marshall pushed away the plate with the partially eaten Danish roll, and leaned back in the chair. He felt the perspiration on his face, on his chest, even on his forearms, and felt a little light headed. He wondered if the whisky in the coffee was getting to him. Then, before him was the vision of the twisted body of the virgin bombardier, Spike, dead, yet his eyes open, covered with foam, and his body and parachute harness blackened by the fire.

"Are you all right!" Eileen asked, and stood up and walked quickly, quietly, to his side. "Why, you're perspiring!"

"Yeah," Marshall whispered softly. "I'm fine. I'm going to my room and put on some clean clothes." He stood and started towards the closet where his uniform hung.

"Good lord, Marshall," Eileen said, "Did my jabbering upset you that much?"

"Eileen, I've got to tell you I have never ever heard a girl, a woman, use the words you used. Yes, it upsets me. I realize you're being scholarly or sophisticated, or some damn thing, being so objective and all. We got exposed to a little psychology and even psychiatry during cadets. But, well, I'm not prepared for this challenge right now. I'll take off for a bit. Then maybe we can go shopping. Okay?"

Stunned, Eileen stood unmoving in the room and watched him discard the terry cloth robe and put on his under clothes and uniform. He pulled on his dark green socks and tied his shoe and didn't bother to tie his necktie, but draped it on his shoulders, and carried his jacket. He strode towards the door.

Suddenly, Eileen moaned. The sound shocked Marshall, chilled him. He'd heard hounds howl, heard their eerie moan, their groan, and the sound was similar to the wail of a cougar at night in the mountains, and the groan, the wail was coming from Eileen.

"You're not coming back! I know it. Just like Billy. Oh, Jesus Christ!" Eileen stood in the middle of the white room, her back arched, her shoulders back, her head tilted, her eyes staring at the ceiling, with both of her arms raised and her hands across her ears, sobbing. The sobs made her small body shake.

Marshall strode to her and held her in his arms tightly. "Hey! Come on. Take it easy, Eileen! I'm just going to my room to freshen up. Come on. My God! Calm down! Cut it out now!"

Eileen began to sob uncontrollably, her body shuddered, and her arms hung limply at her sides. Marshall held her closely, thought she might faint. Thought too, for a second that she might be faking, then his own instincts told him she couldn't be acting.

"My dear God, what have I done? What have we done?" Eileen said haltingly.

"Hey, come on. Snap out of it. We've done nothing wrong! We've made love. We've shared our passions. We've hurt no one. That's all. But, honey, you're going to have to go on with your life and your education. And I've got to go home to Chico and help with the family business. This little sortie of ours has been fun but it's got to end."

"Please, please don't leave me just yet, Marsh."

"All right, all right." Marshall pushed her away from his chest far enough to raise her chin and kiss her. Her mouth was wet and salty. He used his finger to rub tears away from her cheeks and ran his hand through her blonde hair. "Shall we warm up that laced coffee and eat some fruit?"

"You aren't going to leave me then?"

"No, Eileen. I'm not going to leave."

"I can't believe what I said could have upset you so," Eileen said and studied his face as she sipped on the coffee. Tears continued to flow down her cheeks. "I was just trying to have some fun with you. You know, get your goat."

"Well," Marshall stammered, "I've never talked to anyone about an incident that happened towards the end of the war." Marshall hesitated. The clink of the spoon on Eileen's coffee cup was the catalyst for him to resume. "This cherry talk, this virgin subject. It's just, well, there are some sorry memories about a young guy, and I feel like I might somehow dishonor his character, the memory that a few of us have for the kid, a bombardier, if I talk about it."

"Please tell me," Eileen said very softly.

Marshall looked into her eyes, still wet, brimmed with tears, and thought, she's sincere, and fragile despite her frankness that made him uneasy, nervous, agitated.

"Well, this kid had joined our outfit. He was really innocent. I guess naive would be the way to put it. He openly admitted that he'd never been to bed with a girl. He was a virgin. No one, I mean no guy would ever admit to that, not a guy that any of us had ever known. So, I nicknamed him Spike."

"Spike? Why Spike?"

"I used to go deer hunting with my dad and my uncle. A buck deer that has little nubs, or pointed horns that aren't divided, not split into vees, is considered too young to mate, so we protect them. We wouldn't shoot one, even though it's legal. In another year they'll be fair game when the rut sets in. Their horns will have divided. They've sort of reached manhood, but a spike is a virgin."

"So?"

"Well, after his fifth mission Spike would receive a weekend pass and a couple of us intended to take him into Lie`ge or Brussels and introduce him to some of the girls we knew. It'd be up to him then."

"Were they prostitutes?"

"Hell no!" Marshall said, anger showing in his voice. "There weren't many Belgian or Frenchmen around. Damn near all of them were in the service. Christ, they were just nice, working gals, nurses and clerks and typists, secretaries, and widows, that were lonely and scared and the damn war left all of those people deprived of the just plain necessities of life.

"Our cigarettes and chocolate would buy us all a nice dinner, complete with wine and fantastic desserts. We'd go to a dance. If something developed, well, you know."

"So Spike was fulfilled."

"No. Spike was killed on his fifth mission."

"Oh my God. I'm so sorry," Eileen said.

They sat silently. The sound of Eileen's teaspoon touching her coffee cup again startled Marshall.

"So my remarks triggered your thoughts of that boy?"

"Hell, Eileen, I don't know. We were all shook up at the time. It was just a few weeks before the war ended. I think he was just barely eighteen, if that. I think he lied about his age to get in. It just seemed so damned unfair. Our flight surgeon gave all of us that knew Spike an extra ration of whiskey. The chaplain and our C.O. acknowledged his death, sent a letter and an air medal to his folks. That was it. I got stuck with sending home the stuff in his footlocker."

"Couldn't he have parachuted out or something?"

"There's no escape hatch in the nose of a B-26." Marshall said, "I think, kind of hope, that he was already dead when they dragged him out of the burning plane. I heard a tiny piece of flak caught him in the temple. But, who knows?"

"I somehow feel selfish about my own grief," Eileen said.

"Why? Grief is normal, and I've heard my mom say it's a necessary part of healing. Like when there's a death in the family. All of the things the loved ones have to do, getting involved with the undertaker, the casket, the burial, buying the flowers, and the support of friends, all of the food and hugs and tears and handshakes, and dealing with the banks, and lawyers and the state. That period of busyness keeps the body and soul intact for awhile, mom says, but then the grief sets in."

Again they both sat in silence. The shadow of the cast iron railing retreated, but the room was still bright.

Eileen broke the silence. "Marshall, can I ask you a question dealing with love making? No four- letter words: You won't be angry?"

"Guess I come across as a snob, don't I?" Marshall said, then laughed, "Ask away."

"Assuming you have an orgasm," Eileen said, she paused and studied his face, "how do you feel afterwards?"

"You know, Eileen, that's another word I never heard a girl say, until you used it earlier, and I do know it is something natural, something important to both men and women," Marshall said, then continued. "I guess it untangles things. Tension. Feelings of violence or hate or frustration sort of subside. You know what a tangled up bowl of cooked spaghetti looks like? Well, after the climax, it's as if all of the strands are laid out neatly in rows, like they came out of the package. The mind kind of straightens itself out," he laughed, embarrassed, felt the warmth in his cheeks, "and what about you?"

"At first, I associated it only with love for another person. Now I'm beginning to believe it's therapeutic. That's what some of my sorority friends believe. But, if and when it happens, I just feel at peace with myself, at peace with Billy, and now with you. And, believe me Marshall, there's been no one else: just you two boys. I enjoy the penetration, the fullness, being held by strong arms, but I'm happy whether or not I have an orgasm. But it does seem to be very important to some of the girls at school."

"Christ, this is getting to be like an air medal mission! When are we going shopping?"

"Would you do me a favor before we go shopping?"

"Sure."

"Let's go to bed awhile. I'll untangle your spaghetti!"

"Wow," Marshall said, then laughed. "This making up is fun, and I want you to know I've never made love in the daylight."

"Blush away, Fly-Boy," Eileen said, and giggled.

Again they removed their clothes.

"Better make sure that 'Do Not Disturb' sign is hanging on the door-knob," Eileen said.

Marshall pulled the terry cloth robe over his shoulders. He put the sign on the outside of the door. He felt like he ought to prop the back of the chair against the inside knob, hesitated, then dismissed the idea and returned to the bed.

"It's my fantasy time again, Fly-Boy," Eileen said. She sat upright in the bed, her breasts exposed, her shoulders slightly back as if to lift her breasts higher, "Would you mind massaging my breasts with this baby oil?" Eileen said, "I rubbed some on the other night and it felt so good to me, even with me doing it, I began to imagine Billy doing it, liking it."

"Glad to oblige. God, you and your fantasies are going to be the death of me. You're bringing up the whim, wham thoughts and I can't hold on forever!"

"Oh, that feels so delightful. You're hands are so gentle. Strong, but gentle. Be a little patient with me, Marshall, and oh, yes, I am ready."

"I can't help those choo choo train sounds, Eileen."

"I love them. I love you. How do you like love making in the daytime?"

"I love it anytime of the day or night. I think my wartime education is beginning to round out nicely, right here in San Francisco."

"After we shower, let's go shopping. Okay?"

"I can't believe it! No more fantasies?"

"I didn't say that."

"Shower and shop. That's priority!"

Before entering the shower, Marshall and Eileen embraced, hugged and he kissed her lips. She opened her mouth, pushed her tongue against his mouth, against his teeth, touched his tongue and accepted his, and their tongues stroked and explored. "You set the temperature," Marshall said, "and, boy, is that shower cap ever becoming!"

"Just tend to the washing," Eileen said. "Wow, you're ready again."

"Nothing a cold wash cloth can't handle," Marshall said and laughed. "Our scout leader believed in cold showers for growing boys."

"No cold wash cloths in this shower," Eileen said, and lowered her head, the water splashing, splattering noisily off of the top of her shower cap, and suddenly her mouth, her lips embraced Marshall's erect muscle and with one hand she stroked up and down slowly and then it was over as she retreated, the semen gushing as he groaned, consumed by an ecstasy that caused his entire body to shudder.

"Is that the way the French girls treated you?" Eileen said, giggling, resting her head against his chest and hugging him with both arms, the shower pummeling both of them.

"Wow," Marshall said, then sighed, holding her closely, the water still showering down across both of them. "Nothing like that happened in France or Belgium or Holland or Germany.... and I'll throw in England for good measure."

Eileen laughed, "I was saving that for Billy."

Marshall pushed back the shower curtain. "Okay, sweetie pie," Marshall said, turning her so that she faced him, "Turn about is fair play." He placed both of his hands beneath her arms pits and lifted her upward, then sat her on the tile wash stand. He spread her legs quickly and lowered his head and she reached down and held the back of his head and allowed a soft, long "ooh" to escape her lips as his mouth smothered her labia, his fingers gently parted and stroked the lip-like folds and his tongue moved constantly touching her clitoris, as it had caressed her own tongue.

"Enough, enough," Eileen whispered. "That, too, is a first and I can't describe the joy. My God, it's almost excruciating! It's like electricity in my brain and it rushes down across my breasts and between my legs."

Marshall stood up and stared into her eyes. Eileen's eyelids had lowered and she stared at him as if in disbelief.

"I'm going to clean up this saying I've heard in the barracks, you know, for your sorority sisters' collection. 'Show me a guy who won't, ahem, kiss his girl friend there, and I'll steal his girl from him'."

"I'm actually shocked, delighted, really, but this tile is cold on my bottom. Help me down, Fly Boy."

"And now can we go shopping?" He helped her off of the sink and he felt the coldness of her buttocks. "That tile was cold, wasn't it?"

Eileen laughed, "That's not what I'll remember."

They returned to the shower, soaped one another and rinsed, then dried one another with the large towels. "You've got a couple of cute little dimples right at the base of your spine," Marshall said. "Know that?" He patted her buttocks.

"Nope, I didn't know that," Eileen lied. Billy, too, had observed the dimples and commented about them. She whispered into his ear, "This afternoon you're going to get an anatomy lesson. But no four letter words, I promise."

"Fine, but now, little blondie, listen carefully, I don't want any hysterics when I go to my own room for a few minutes."

Eileen pulled closed the long terry cloth bathrobe and watched Marshall put on his uniform, and again felt queasy at the thought of him leaving.

"You will hurry back?"

"Ten or fifteen minutes at the most. Then it's time for lunch, okay?"

"Roger. Is that the correct response?"

As Marshall departed, he stopped at the door where he glanced at the 'Do Not Disturb' sign, considered changing it, then left it where it was. He winked at Eileen and pulled closed the door.

Eileen returned to the bed and fluffed the pillows and pulled the sheet and blanket up, smoothing the bed. She returned to the table, poured some coffee into a cup from the heavy, silver plated container, then poured an ounce of Canadian Club into the cup. She sat in a wicker rocker near the window and stared across the wrought iron railings, across the bay towards Oakland.

Aloud, she whispered, "I shouldn't have said 'I love you'. Billy is the only man I'll ever love."

Eileen finished her coffee and went to the closet and selected a dress.

The morning *Chronicle* lay flat in front of Marshall's door. He picked it up, fumbled with the key and finally pushed open the heavy door. The bedside lamp was on, the bed covers turned down partially and a small foil-wrapped mint chocolate was on his pillow. Marshall picked it up, unwrapped it and tossed the morsel into his mouth. He then fluffed and pounded both pillows and grabbed the sheets and covers and caused them to be disheveled.

In the bathroom Marshall observed that he indeed had a bathrobe and very large white towels. Quickly he lathered and shaved and cleaned his safety razor. He wished he'd taken time to buy some skin bracer, but that could wait. Marshall took the pro kit out of the shaving kit, studied it for a second, *too damn late now*, and tossed it back into his kit.

Marshall put on a clean pair of olive drab shorts and a tee shirt of the same hue, a clean starched tan shirt, his beige tie, his pink trousers and dark green Eisenhower jacket. He packed his other belongings in his B-4 bag, looked at his shoes, and recalled that he'd seen a special polishing cloth in the bathroom, so with his foot on the bathtub edge he polished a shoe, then the other, and felt that was as good as he could do to be his most presentable.

Man, Marshall thought, *"I need some time to let my batteries get charged up! That babe is wearing me out. Screwing? I never thought I'd get caught up!"*

Debating whether to go to the desk and check out before returning to Eileen's room, Marshall decided he'd better drop off his B-4 bag with Eileen, then check out later. For damn sure he didn't want to be exposed to any more hysterics.

A few light taps with his knuckles on Eileen's door and it opened and she stood before him, elegantly dressed in a brown dress, faintly patterned with dark green and she held a waist length black jacket. She smiled, and Marshall found himself staring at her, her beauty, her smooth complexion, her perfectly spaced white teeth, her reddened lips parted, her pale blue eyes studying him.

"Mac Arthur and me," Marshall said, and laughed.

"Mac Arthur?"

"I shall return."

"Ha! Of course. But I knew you'd return!"

"So, how's the appetite?" Marshall asked.

"I'm starved. Ever been to Fisherman's Wharf?"

"When I was a kid. Before the war," Marshall said. He entered the room and placed the B-4 bag in the closet.

"Let's take a cable car to the wharf!"

"Ha! I'm going to fill you up with oysters," Eileen said, giggled and grasped his arm as they left the room and headed for the elevator.

"Know what?" Marshall said, not waiting for an answer. "I'd better check out now or they'll get me for another day."

"I'll wait for you at our couch in the lobby."

Marshall paid his bill and murmured something about having already checked his bag and would pick it up later which the clerk ignored.

"Hope your stay was enjoyable," the clerk said, not making eye contact with Marshall.

Marshall turned and saw Eileen across the mammoth lobby, a tiny figure engulfed by the pillows, fragile, yet forceful he felt, awaiting him as she sat alone on the couch.

He sat beside her. "I'll have to say I agree with you one hundred percent, little architect," Marshall exclaimed. "This truly is a beautiful lobby."

"I hope I can design something as grand," Eileen said.

"Why not? I really believe you will."

"Thanks, I appreciate you saying that."

"So, how do we get to the cable car that goes to Fisherman's Wharf?"

"That's why they have the concierge."

Marshall and Eileen approached the station and the concierge looked up and smiled. Another man was with him in the U shaped station.

"Did you try New Joe's?"

"Yes. You remembered! It was delightful," Eileen said.

"And now where?"

"Can we get to Fisherman's Wharf using the cable car?" Marshall asked.

"That's easy. Take the elevator down a flight, take the exit out to the street and jump on a cable car that has Fisherman's Wharf on the front. All of the cars stop at Powell and California, right where you'll be standing."

"Any restaurant you'd recommend?"

"If it's got an Italian name it'll be good," he said laughing.

Marshall and Eileen both laughed, thanked him and walked towards the elevator.

Then Eileen stopped and went back to the concierge alone. "I'll be back in a second. Another question." She looked up at Marshall and smiled.

"What store do you recommend for a nice gift to take home to a mother?"

"Well, we do have a great gift store here in the hotel," he said and nodded across the lobby, "and of course Gump's is one of the finest in the city, and Chinatown is fun and there are some excellent quality items at very reasonable prices."

"Thank you very much," Eileen said, smiling at both of the men at the concierge station.

"They've got 'just married' written all over them," he said, grinning, to the man beside him.

The brightly painted cable car they wanted was clearly marked. Marshall helped Eileen jump aboard and together they entered the enclosed area. Marshall marveled at the strength of the brakeman as he maneuvered the heavy pole-like gripping device that clamped onto the endless cable. The bell clanged loudly and an atmosphere of merriment, of gaiety prevailed. Some of the passengers preferred to stand on the steps, hanging on with a one-armed daredevil stance. The air was cool and salty in the nostrils. Marshall reached for his coins when the conductor approached.

"Been home long, Lieutenant?" he asked.

"Few days."

"Put your money away, sir."

"Gee, thank you," Marshall said, and smiled at Eileen.

"They'll get it later," she said, laughing.

"Boy are you cynical."

"Just kidding, Marsh."

They disembarked and walked to the wharf and scanned the signs.

Marshall pointed to one. "Tony is about as Italian as any of them."

"It looks like they have a second floor with a view of the harbor. Let's try it." Eileen said.

Greeted by the maitre d', Marshall expressed their desire for a window table and Eileen followed the man to a table where he seated her. Marshall seated himself, and thought that Eileen was very quick to follow the maitre'd, allowing him to trail the short procession.

"You sure tagged after that guy in a hurry," Marshall said. "I wanted to seat you."

"Silly boy," Eileen said and tilted her chin, smiling her prettiest. "That was the first thing daddy taught me at the Jonathan Club. But mother and I will always resent having to ride in a separate elevator!"

"Come on, you're kidding me again."

"Darling, I don't think that you've even begun to realize it's a man's world."

"I'm beginning to understand where you and your sorority sisters are coming from."

Waiting for their conversation to ebb, a waiter in a dark suit with a starched white shirt and black bow tie hovered nearby.

He approached the table and asked, "Cocktails before lunch?"

Eileen looked questioningly at Marshall.

"What's your favorite?" Marshall asked.

"Well, daddy said that San Francisco is the best place in the world for a very dry martini."

"Let's do it," Marshall said and nodded to the waiter.

"Would you like to know our specials?"

Marshall nodded.

"The Chinook salmon are in, and our serving is broiled. Very delicious. As are the sand dabs, and our Petrale sole is a delicacy. For an appetizer, I'd recommend our Oysters Rockefeller, or a baby shrimp cocktail, and the larger prawns are crisp, or we've a nice tossed green salad."

"Marshall, may I recommend an order of the oysters?" Eileen said.

"Bring 'em on," Marshall laughed, understanding her hint.

"I'll have the small salad with oil and vinegar, and the sand dabs, please." Eileen said.

"I highly recommend the salmon, sir."

"That'll be fine. But, where are they allowed to catch salmon this time of year?"

"Horse Mountain, north of Shelter Cove. Humboldt County, so I'm told."

"Interesting," Marshall said, raising his eyebrows.

"Would you like to see the wine list?"

"What say, Eileen?"

"Let's see how the martinis go down."

The waiter departed and quickly returned with the martinis served in chilled long stem glasses, each with a green olive.

Marshall held his glass aloft and they reached across the small table and there was a slight clink as the edges of thin glass met. "To our honeymoon," Marshall said.

"To us," Eileen responded. "And how do you like your martini?"

"You can tell your dad that this drink reminds me of some of the spillage I got when I siphoned gas for my model A!"

"That's great!" Eileen said, and laughed, "I'm not big on martinis either. But, you know, it's sort of the in thing."

"Honey, you come visit me in Chico. The in thing is a boilermaker! Sophisticated we're not!"

Eileen sipped slowly from the glass, then looked across the linen-topped table at Marshall. "Do you think I'm going to tell daddy about you. About us?"

"Geeze, that just sort of slipped out, about the gasoline flavor," Marshall said. "But back to us. No, Eileen, I realize I don't really exist, that I'm a strange, weird sort of substitute for the husband in your life. As a matter of fact, I think I'm beginning to resent playing the part. And no, of course I don't think for a minute you'd tell your folks about meeting me."

"Marshall, that's a sad thing to say. There'll be no more mention of Billy. I'm sorry. God, I'm so screwed up. I adore you. I know that, for sure. And I'm sorry. And I really will tell my dad about you, but just that we're friends. I hope we can continue our friendship. Maybe you could learn the stock market business?"

"Well, there's also Sierra Mercantile."

The waiter returned with Oysters Rockefeller and the salad. "How'd you like those martinis?" he asked, smiling at them, back and forth from one to the other.

"As martinis go, these were terrific," Marshall said, feeling that would end the subject and not be too untruthful.

"Good. Because the bartender spotted you folks, the uniform, you know, and told me to serve you again, compliments of good old Tony."

Marshall and Eileen looked at each other and both laughed. "Thank Tony for us!" Marshall said, and scooted his chair around attempting to see the bartender. He raised his arm and waved his hand in case the bartender could see them.

Again they touched glasses and sipped the cocktail. "This second is either smoother or I'm getting used to them."

"Pardon me for mentioning my father so often, but he said if you could drink two martinis you'd be hooked forever!"

"Well, maybe I will meet him some day."

"I bet you are already thinking about when you'll come down to see me."

"Darn right," Marshall said. They looked at each other, each seeming to ponder the seriousness of their remarks, then they simultaneously stared out the window across the bay towards Alcatraz. There were a few small sailboats, and a tanker appeared that moved slowly, dwarfing the sailboats.

"Wouldn't it be great to see a big aircraft carrier come beneath the Golden Gate Bridge." Marshall said, "My copilot has an identical twin in the Navy, on a carrier. Their folks didn't want them to be in the same branch for some reason."

"I wonder why," Eileen said.

"Maybe they think the survival odds are better or something. Who understands parents? I hope I can handle the folks and all of the questions mine are apt to ask," Marshall said, then sipped again from the martini glass.

"Why, they'll be so happy and proud to have you home they'll be bursting at the seams. Why'd you say that?"

"Oh, it's too long a story, Eileen. Our crew got so messed up during the occupation, hell, combat was a cinch."

"Want to talk about it?"

"Nope."

"Better dig into those oysters."

"Share with me, okay!"

"Thank you, no. Better eat up. You might need them."

"Man, I never had anything so tasty. Really, Eileen, try one. Just pass your salad plate to me."

"Well okay, thanks," Eileen said, and scooped one onto her plate with a tiny fork and said, "My, I think they're better than the J.C."

"Boy, this French bread is good!" Marshall said, "Never had any bread this good in France!"

"Remind me to buy a loaf to take home. That was my mother's last words to me at the train station."

"You're taking a loaf of bread home?"

"Dear boy, San Francisco sourdough French bread is world famous."

"What a couple of days! I'm getting educated in beef, wine, booze, love making, French bread and Martinis and you know what, Eileen?"

"What?" Eileen asked, hoping, expecting some remark concerning romance or affection or even love.

"My lips are getting numb." Marshall said and laughed as he touched his upper lip with a fingertip.

The waiter presented their entrees and asked, "Any decision about the wine?"

"Do you like Chardonnay?" Eileen asked Marshall.

"My favorite," Marshall said. He laughed aloud. "Please bring a bottle and it'd better be California!"

"What's tickling your funny bone?"

"Oh, nothing much. As I told the bartender back at Beale, the last wine I had in Europe was out of a big jerry can that one of our guys filled up at some local wine maker's farm."

"If I could get you down to L.A., daddy and I could polish you up a bit," Eileen said. "Might even make you an apprentice at his brokerage house." Eileen took the olive from her martini, nibbled on it and pushed the glass away from her.

"You can keep L.A., sweetie." Again Marshall chuckled, feeling the effects of the second martini. "Now what I'd prefer is taking you out to the Sacramento River for the fall run, and helping you hook up with a thirty-pound king salmon, or we could drive up into the Sierra, into the high country, then backpack to some trout- filled creeks and tiny little clear lakes, bluer than your eyes. You know, the valley can be hotter than hell, but when you get to about five thousand feet it's spring again and the Lupine and Indian paint brush and a jillion other colorful little flowers are blooming, and different kinds of ferns, and birds, tiny chipmunks, and squirrels." He paused for a second. "I could teach you how to fly fish, build a campfire and make a bed out of pine boughs. We could stare up at the Milky Way and count falling stars. Then we could climb on up above the timberline, that's where the mountains are really beautiful; ever hear of the Bristle Cone Pines?"

"No, and what would your mom say about taking me on a backpacking trip?"

"Oh Christ!" Marshall grinned. "I'd have to marry you first!"

"Is that a proposal?"

"Hey! We fell in lust," Marshall said. "Remember?"

"I forget easily," Eileen smiled. "But now I feel I'm beginning to dislike the word lust. Let's call our friendship love!"

The waiter poured a splash of wine in Marshall's glass, then waited. "Are you going to taste it, dear, or do you want me to?" Eileen said very quietly.

"Oops!" Marshall said and laughed, vaguely remembering the ceremony from a dinner in France, when he and Frank had gone to Paris for a few days leave. They visited the Louvre, saw the Mona Lisa and Winged Freedom, the Eiffel tower and climbed part way up, as far as they'd let them go, and saw the original model of the Statue of Liberty, and Napoleon's tomb. A couple packs of cigarettes bought them a full course meal in a fancy restaurant, and he remembered that Frank sipped the little sampling of wine before the waiter poured it. Marshall tasted the wine and nodded to the waiter, ignored the cork, and watched as he partially filled both glasses.

"This may be a two-aspirin lunch," Marshall said.

Eileen laughed and said, "Is the salmon as good as I'm going to catch someday?"

"Yep. It's really better than I anticipated. And how are those little fellows?"

"As good as the J.C." Eileen said, smiling at Marshall. "We've got to find that present soon, before I get you back in bed."

"Man alive, you are so damn subtle!" Marshall laughed each time he spoke. "How about another order of those oysters?"

"You're going to need then," she said.

"Eileen, you are beginning to scare me, to say nothing of wearing me out!"

Annoyed by his lightheadedness, Marshall took a large section of the French bread, buttered it liberally and hoped that it would soak up some of the gin.

"Think you can finish off my martini? I didn't think he'd pour the wine until we finished these!" Eileen said, raising her chin, lowering her eyelids and smiling so that her perfectly spaced white teeth glistened. She pushed the glass toward him.

"That sounds like a challenge. I'll try, but you may have to carry me to the cable car." Marshall said and laughed loudly. He sipped the martini from her glass. "I'm damn near ready for surgery!"

"Marshall, you think I'm a nymphomaniac, don't you!" Eileen suddenly blurted out, staring into his eyes, unblinking.

"Geez Eileen, what a thing to say! I never gave it a thought," Marshall said and looked back squarely into her eyes, then laughed and said, "Hell, I think these martinis and the wine are affecting you, too." Marshall said, looking away and again chuckling. "You know what my copilot, the poor bastard, said? He used to say when he got home he was going to try to marry a deaf and dumb nymphomaniac whose old man owned a liquor store." Marshall chuckled, but then wondered how McAdam was getting along.

"Very funny," Eileen said. "But what about it? What about me?"

"What in the heck is with you, Eileen?" Marshall said. "Just let me be a happy drunk. You know, there were guys in our outfit who'd get real surly after a couple of drinks. Does gin affect you that way? What a subject to bring up!"

In silence they stared at each other.

"I thought we covered all of the bases about our relationship, early on." Marshall said, gruffly, "And no. I don't think you're a nympho. I do think you're a hard up, beautiful war widow and somehow or other I'm the lucky guy." Marshall finished off the rest of Eileen's martini. "Why me? That sky

room, the Crown Room, whatever the hell they call it, that room was full
of men. Naval aviators, Air Corps pilots with ribbons and brass galore:
Marines, prosperous looking civilians: why me?"

"Thanks, I think," Eileen whispered, "And a fair question," Eileen
sighed, looked into her wineglass. "No, I really don't consider myself a
nympho. I guess it's just referring to our, what do I want to call it, a friendship maybe, but you're always referring to it as lust. And lust just has such
a ring of, well, of our little fun and games thing being so immoral," Eileen
said. She paused and sipped her wine. "I prefer the word infatuation. Can't
we be infatuated without being evil?" She leaned back in her chair, glanced
towards Alcatraz, then back at Marshall.

"Why you?" She shrugged her small shoulders. "Because out of the
dozen or so men in the room, you were the only one who didn't make an
obvious pass at me. Even a couple of Billy's buddies, earlier, had hinted
around about 'my needs', and one, not so subtly, let his hand pass across
my buttocks and linger a bit too long, and finally when I arrived at your
table and you were nice enough to stand up, and I looked into your big,
brown, sad eyes, honest and almost innocent, and you just seemed safe
and well, decent. I guess I've been so damn lonely, so starved for some
affection, and believing, for nearly a year, that Billy was alive, I just
selected you. I'll admit. I needed masculine love: to be in bed with a man:
A good man."

"Oh," Marshall stared into his martini glass. "Maybe my luck is changing," Marshall said in a very hushed voice. "I sure as hell am not making
any moral judgments. I remember Frank saying, nothing is right or
wrong, only thinking makes it so, and I don't think it was original with
him, but it makes sense."

"Sure it wasn't 'good or bad'?"

"Might have been. Same thing, eh?"

Then Marshall caught the eye of the waiter and ordered another serving
of Oysters Rockefeller. "These will be our dessert," he said.

Marshall consumed several more slices of the sourdough French bread liberally buttered and began to feel more in control of his senses.

The waiter returned to the table and filled Eileen's glass with wine. "No more for me," Marshall said.

Together, they shared the oysters at Marshall's suggestion, and when the bill was presented, Marshall studied it, then added fifteen percent and placed the money, including change on the platter. Eileen was amused that he'd counted out the exact amount, and felt a respect for his apparent perfectionism. Marshall stood and circled the table to assist Eileen and stumbled a bit as her reached for her chair.

"Vertigo," Marshall said, laughing at himself.

"Thank you," Eileen said as he helped her with the chair. Arm in arm they descended the stairs, departed Tony's, walking to the street level where they paused.

"A little stroll in this cool air is going to feel good," Marshall said. They walked to the wharf area and watched a few of the busy crews of the fishing boats that had returned from the ocean. They were scrubbing the decks and hosing them down and stowing their gear.

"So where are all the fish?"

"Probably all cleaned and stored someplace."

"What say we take a cab back and buy that present for your mom?"

"Good idea," Marshall said. "I spotted some cabs parked over near where the cable car turned around." It was a short walk and they found a cab quickly.

"Where to, Lieutenant?" The cab driver was stout, swarthy, and wearing a dark blue wool turtleneck sweater. He smiled and spoke loudly.

"Gump's," Eileen said.

"Gump's it is. Trust you brought the family jewels," Again he laughed loudly as he walked to the rear cab door and held it open for Eileen.

"What's with Gump's?" Marshall said, looking at Eileen.

"Let's find out, sweetie."

The cab driver looked into the back seat and studied Marshall's ribbons and wings. "You kids ever been down Lombard Street?"

Marshall looked at Eileen questioningly and she shook her head negatively. "No sir," Marshall said.

"Home long?" the cab driver asked.

"Couple days."

"Well, then this ride is on Yellow Cab, so hang on." The cab driver drove up Hyde Street, past Russian Hill, to the top, then paused and advised them to enjoy the view, waited a few seconds then turned and drove slowly down the series of S curves. "Only street like it in the world," he said, over his shoulder and chuckled. "So now you can tell the folks you've been down Lombard Street!"

"Thank you," Eileen said, "That was fun and so unique and all of the flowers along the way were so lush and colorful."

"Okay, kids, we're off to Gump's and after I drop you off I'll circle around the block for a few minutes and meet you out front."

"Really?" Marshall said, "Why?"

"You'll see. I may be wrong. But I'll tour around awhile and if I spot you coming out, I'll stop. Okay?"

"Sure," Marshall said, then thought, *I don't get it.* The cab stopped in front of Gump's. The driver slid out of the driver's seat and opened the door for Marshall and Eileen.

Immediately Marshall was impressed, awed by the displays of a variety of merchandise, the endless shelves of sparkling crystal, the paintings, the figurines, and bits of sculpture. Eileen led the way as they began to walk through the open, spacious aisles. A young Chinese girl approached them.

"May I help you?"

Marshall studied a tall porcelain pitcher, lifted it by its gracefully curved handle, admired it and finally looked at the price tag on the bottom. He studied it, wondering if the decimal point was in the correct place.

"Eileen," Marshall said, "I'm afraid this place is a little too rich for my blood."

"What a beautiful store," Eileen said. The Chinese girl nodded and smiled.

"But thank you for your time," Eileen said, "I think we'll just keep shopping."

"Any particular type of item that you have in mind?"

"Something for a mother," Eileen said.

"You like oriental. Chinese?"

"Oh yes," Eileen answered.

The Chinese girl glanced around the store, then surreptitiously slid a small business card into Eileen's hand.

"Excellent quality. Fair prices for GIs. You understand?"

"Thank you," Eileen whispered. Marshall had observed, but not heard the communication between the women.

They departed the store and stood hesitantly at the curb. Eileen studied the card. At that moment a yellow cab stopped beside them. The driver exited and came around and said, "Hi kids! I should've made a bet with you Lieutenant." He laughed and raised his arms to push wavy gray hair back from his forehead.

"That's one bet I'd for damn sure lost. What are you, psychic or something?"

"Nope, I'm a native. Okay kids, want another free ride on Yellow Cab?"

"How about Chinatown?" Eileen asked.

"Climb in."

Within a few minutes the cab stopped at Grant Street, at the entrance leading into Chinatown, where they were again helped from the cab and the driver advised them it was more fun to walk its length, than ride. "It's only a couple of blocks long. And remember kids, some of them chinks like to dicker, like the Mexicans. It's a game. They expect you to Jew them down!" he laughed loudly.

"Thank you sir, for the rides," Marshall said and extended his hand, which was accepted and clasped strongly and shaken vigorously.

"Have fun," the cab driver said, grinning broadly as he drove away.

"What now?" Marshall said, looking down at Eileen.

"Well, let's see if we can locate Chang's. That's the name of the store on the card given to me by the girl at Gump's."

"I wondered what the two of you were up to."

"I imagine Gump's would fire her on the spot for that, but I really believe it's your uniform."

Jostled and bumped by Chinese and by tourists and a variety of Caucasian business people, Marshall and Eileen found Chang's. Eileen spoke quietly to a middle-aged Chinese woman, clad in a formfitting, emerald green silk dress, and showed her the card and the lady looked at Marshall and nodded. She asked Eileen and Marshall to follow her. Then she showed them a variety of vases and bowls, explaining the age and origin of each.

"Antiques, " Eileen said, to an inquisitive Marshall.

"Let's keep in mind that the Air Corps gave me two month's pay and all I want is something nice. Just nice. Not a collector's item," Marshall said, then added, "And I'm not into dickering around about price."

"Okay, then how does thirty dollars sound for an antique tea pot that'll probably be worth four times that amount in a few years?"

"That's in my range," Marshall said, relieved. "You pick out a nice one, okay?"

Eileen continued to look closely at each item the lady brought to her and selected a small teapot.

"Marshall, dear, pay attention a minute. I think this color will go with anything, and it's sweet, and beautiful and probably very valuable. I really believe she's trying to do us a favor."

"Just fine," Marshall said, growing anxious to leave the shop, annoyed by the confinement. "Does it come with cups?"

"No, dear, it doesn't come with cups, but she will wrap it so it'll get to your mother safely."

"Fine. Now I'd like for you to pick out something for yourself, from me."

Surprised and pleased, Eileen began to browse while the teapot was being wrapped. She paused at a counter displaying a large selection of brass and bronze items. From the inventory she selected a brass candle-holder. She held it up and found that around the center post the other four holders revolved, separating so that two candles would be opposite each other, surrounding the center candle.

"Like that?" Marshall asked.

"Love it," Eileen said and turned to the Chinese lady to ask the price.

"Don't ask," Marshall interrupted. He turned and said, "We'll take it," and nodded back to her as she smiled and lowered her head.

"White candles? Red candles? Yellow candles?" the Chinese lady asked, looking at Eileen.

"White would be nice. Thank you." The candles were wrapped carefully, individually.

Marshall paid for the two gifts, feeling that the cost was certainly reasonable compared to the one price he'd seen on the bottom of the vase at Gump's.

"Could you tell us the best way to get to the Fairmont Hotel?" Eileen asked.

She walked them to the front of Chang's and told them to walk along the street and they would come to the cable car tracks and the cable car would go right up the hill. To Marshall's surprise, she extended her hand to him to shake, which he grasped lightly.

Within a few minutes they arrived at the stop and again enjoyed a quick, breezy, cool and clanging ride to the spot where earlier they'd departed from the Fairmont. It was early afternoon when they reached Eileen's room. Marshall's B-4 bag was where he had placed it just inside the door. He picked it up and placed it inside the closet door. Eileen watched him, then opened both sets of drapes, the sheer as well as heavier ones and together they looked out across the east bay towards Oakland and Berkeley.

"This would be some view in a storm," Marshall said.

Eileen walked up beside him, put one arm around his waist and said, "You are now my storm. My lightning and thunder and hail and rain and wind and whatever else goes with it."

Marshall was startled by reference to lightening, thinking of the nickname for the P-38, but did not allow his mind to pursue the thought, hoping he wouldn't become involved in any display of hysterics. For the first time in months he was feeling an urge to return to Chico, to see his mother and father and to get his Model-A down off the blocks and fire it up.

"Okay, off comes the necktie!" Eileen said, and she stepped in front of him and began to loosen the knot.

"So it's lovemaking time with a hangover to boot!" Marshall said, laughing, as Eileen began to unbutton his shirt.

"Marshall, how many parts can you name on that bombsight you used." As she spoke she completely unbuttoned his shirt and started to unbuckle his belt and search for the buttons on his trousers.

"Damn it, Eileen, I can undress myself."

"You old prude. Don't you understand that you excite me?"

"Well, dearie, you excite the hell out of me, too, and I'm even getting used to doing it in broad daylight," Marshall said and laughed and began to undress.

"What's with the Norden bombsight?"

"It's not secret, is it?"

"Not anymore."

"Can you name the parts?"

"Hell, there's a jillion of them, but I can start with the gyroscope and the levels and its leveling knobs and go into the disc and the optics and all of the settings and the synchronizing knobs and the trigger and the indicies and on and on…" Marshall said.

"And I suppose there are parts on your Model A that you can identify?"

"Where do you want to start? Transmission, gears, cylinders, rings, fuel pump, carburetor, valves, brakes, battery, fuel tank, instruments, window wipers, oil dip-stick. Hell, Eileen, that's easy. Why?"

Eileen had disrobed and turned back the bed, throwing off the blanket so that only the top sheet and the pillows remained. "Climb into my chamber, into my net if you like, and quiz time will begin."

"Quiz time?"

Disrobed, too, Marshall climbed into the bed, pulled the sheet over both of them, and curled his elbow beneath his head as he rested on a pillow and marveled at the marble-like whiteness of Eileen's body.

"Let me have your hand," Eileen said, and he volunteered one hand as he moved closely to her body, stimulated by the touch of her flesh, excited, already rigid, delighted just to be near her and see her naked body beside his. Marshall had never envisioned such excruciatingly intense stimulation, had never experienced such physical excitement. Eileen lowered his hand until it reached between her thighs.

Marshall instinctively placed the palm of his hand where her legs joined and began to explore with his fingertips.

"Name my parts," Eileen whispered.

"What?"

"What are you touching, feeling?"

"Your personals."

"Oh come on, now. You can name all of the parts of a bombsight and all of the parts on a car and you can't name any of mine? What kind of husband would you be? What kind of lover?"

"Come on Eileen, I don't need a course in physiology to know you excite me."

"But I know scrotum and testes and penis and buttocks and chest."

"Okay. Breasts and nipples and buttocks and lips and tongue and, oh hell, this is like dissecting a frog in a biology class."

Eileen laughed, then spoke quietly, "If you have any respect for any woman you should know that you are touching my vulva. And these mounds are called labia, both major and minor, and the key to our excitement, and I mean all women, is our clitoris and that spot seems to be what you somehow instinctively want to fondle."

"Okay teacher, I confess my ignorance but now guide my finger tip to that spot of your own passionate desire and tell me what to do."

"Right here, and be gentle, lover boy, remember gently, just massage ever so gently, slowly, carefully."

"Is that where I kissed you?" Marshall laughed, then leaned over Eileen and held between his lips the nipple of her left breast, sucked on it, nibbled at it.

"Ouch, hey, your teeth are sharp: not my nipples: golly, I'm tender there, sweetheart."

"Oh, I'm sorry. I'll be careful. But, have I found the key to your ignition system yet?"

"God, I'm ignited. I'm ready. I'm ready."

More vigorously, with abandon they joined their bodies, bouncing together and apart and slamming the torso of each against the other, Eileen wrapped her legs across Marshall's back and groaned, gasping for air. Marshall began to feel as if a roar would erupt from his chest and mouth and he forced himself to stifle the violence of his utterances as they groaned together deliriously, sensing the climax, each of the other. Eileen gasped, "How animal," then seemed to wilt. Marshall lowered his body close to hers, supporting his weight with his elbows. "Don't want to crush you, little lady."

"Off now, just roll off. But hold me closely," Eileen whispered.

"This must be the ecstasy I've heard about," Marshall whispered, his mouth close to Eileen's ear.

Eileen began to hum.

"What's that?"

"You must have seen the Wizard of Oz? Remember 'Over the Rainbow'?"

"Oh, yeah."

"Ready for one more of my fantasies, Marshall?"

"I may have to go back to the wharf for an order of oysters!"

Eileen laughed. "This will be just some clean innocent fun. Hate to tell you, but I'd planned some of it for Billy."

"Well, I hope he's not watching from that big hangar in the sky."

"Don't be sacrilegious!"

Eileen slid from beneath the sheets and walked to the telephone. She dialed and waited. "Room service? Good. Please send up a bottle of champagne in a bucket of ice and a couple of glasses, of course, and a selection of hors d'oeuvres. Yes, domestic will be fine." She gave the room number and turned back to Marshall. He was asleep.

"Forgive me Billy. I did it for us," she murmured as she walked to the bathroom. When room service arrived with a cart holding the bucket with the champagne and the hors d'oeuvres, Marshall was still asleep and Eileen, clad in a white bathrobe, accepted the bill, signed it, and tipped the waiter.

Eileen scooped some cream cheese onto a cracker and sat in a chair overlooking the Oakland hills. *It simply amazes me, how men can go to sleep so quickly. Billy could. And dad can sit back in a chair, place his feet on a footrest and drop off while I am visiting with him. I wonder if they'll add much to the room charge because of Marshall? Maybe they won't even know. But it has to be obvious. Two cocktail glasses. Two of everything being used. Oh well, daddy can afford it. I'll have to tell him it was another war widow if he asks. The lies just pile up. I'll make it right, somehow. I wonder if my lover would conk out until tomorrow morning if I didn't awaken him. I'll give him another half-hour. I've got to think about the train, about mother, about school. Hell, I wish I didn't take after my mother…*

Eileen read the *Chronicle* for awhile, worked on the crossword puzzle, laughed at Herb Caen, was amused by the comic strips but preferred the single cartoon drawings, feeling they were wittier. Finally, she went to the dresser drawer, opened it and took the Gideon Bible from it and turned to the psalms and read the 91st, which was supposed to bring Billy back alive. She held the Bible in her lap and stared out of the window, viewing only the emptiness of pale blue of the sky. Eileen shrugged her shoulders and returned the Bible to its drawer.

Entering the bathroom, Eileen studied the huge bathtub, then giggled. There was a broad level space at the end opposite the controls. Eileen turned on the water, favoring the hot control. Hope they've got a big water heater, she mused.

She returned to the large room with the bed containing the sleeping, snoring Marshall. Eileen unwrapped the gift from Marshall. She held aloft the candleholder and revolved the holders, rubbed the metal with a cloth napkin, and then carefully fitted into the round bases the thick ends of the white candles. She carried it to the bathroom and sat it on the ledge at the end of the tub. She put her fingers into the rising water and turned down the valve controls a bit. The water barely flowed.

Eileen took one of the glass drinking glasses and returned to the other room where she scooped some ice from the bucket, then found the almost empty bottle of Canadian Club and poured two ounces into the glass, returned to the bathroom and filled the glass with water. When the level of the water in the tub was correct, she closed the valves and returned to the chair and sipped the drink.

While Marshall slept, Eileen allowed her mind to roam, to explore her thoughts at random, to wonder and she phrased sentences, composed paragraphs of her thoughts and feelings, created questions and reached conclusions in her mind. *If I could get him down to L.A. we could teach him to play golf. Daddy was disappointed that Billy didn't care anything about golf. Tennis was his sport. Get a good workout and get on with it. Why waste four hours on a golf course. He'd have to get a degree in economics or business administration to get ahead. First, I'd put him in a dark blue suit, a white shirt and a maroon and blue striped tie.*

"I think I'll wake him and give him the best screwing he'll ever get. I've probably already ruined him for the next woman in his life!" Eileen laughed aloud. *"God, am I just plain evil? What a bitch! Maybe I really am a god-damn nympho, or just a slut? No, as Marshall put it, I'm just a hard up war widow. Ha! A year of wondering and waiting; never allowing myself to believe the worst. I am so loathsome! So now I'm taking out all of my frustrations on this poor flier. Oh, bullshit, Eileen, you're doing him a favor. He loves it!*

Eileen permitted the bulky white bathrobe to fall to the floor as she stood by the bed. She carefully pulled the sheet back then climbed into the bed and snuggled up against Marshall. She began to gently massage his chest. He grunted, but didn't awaken. Eileen continued to massage him and enjoyed entwining her fingers in the hair on his chest. She lowered her hand gradually, continuing to massage Marshall's torso. She massaged between his legs and his arousal was immediate.

Eileen laughed softly and thought, he isn't even fully awake! She giggled aloud, and lifted one leg over his legs and sitting astride him leaned over and kissed him fully on the lips. His eyes popped open and when he started to say something Eileen pushed her tongue past his lips and teeth and touched his tongue with hers, then moved further up atop him before he could speak and pushed the nipple of her right breast into his mouth. "Watch those sharp teeth," she whispered. "My other one is sore!" He reacted as she expected and continued to mouth her nipple but didn't bite, and with both hands reached for her buttocks, and lifted her, then lowered her and they were melded. She sat upright then and squirmed against him and he lifted his arms and massaged both of her breasts with his hands.

Eileen smiled down at Marshall. "It feels like it's almost up to here," she said, drawing a line with her fingernail below her navel, across her abdomen.

"So it's fantasy time again?" Marshall said. "You know, Eileen, you are too damn beautiful, too sexy for your own good! Men kill for this!" She lifted her chin and looked upward, moved her hips slowly, and Marshall studied the shape of her chin and marveled that even her nostrils were perfect and small and narrow. Marshall quickly reached a climax, but Eileen was content to rest while lying atop him.

"Know what?" she asked.

"What?"

"The champagne is chilled. Shall we aim the cork right out into the bay?"

"Why not?" Marshall said, "If that'll keep you happy, let's do it. Hey, that food looks pretty good. And I don't even have a headache anymore."

"I think you transferred it to me."

Marshall took the champagne bottle out of the ice and began to untwist the wire, as he walked towards the windows. "Slide one back, honey, and I'll see if my thumbs are strong enough to uncork this thing."

The afternoon air was cold and it swished the curtains and chilled their faces, but flushed with passion and desire they stood side by side, both naked, and Eileen gently massaged Marshall's back near the base of his spine as Marshall pushed and finally the cork exploded out into space and the champagne began to bubble out before he could straighten the bottle.

"Bring on the glasses!" Marshall said, as both of them laughed loudly, their joy erupting from their throats as the champagne bubbled from the neck of the bottle.

"Here they are," Eileen said. She pointed to the table where the glasses stood. "Now excuse me for a second. I'm drawing our bath!"

"You're what?"

"Another treat in store for you," Eileen giggled, "Follow me."

She walked to the bathroom, picking up a tray of hors d'ouvres as she walked towards the bathroom. She sat the tray down on the ledge at the end of the long, deep tub, then turned the hot water on full, and said, "Get ready to climb in," Marshall, naked, his arms hanging at his sides, stood staring at the bath tub, the candle holder, and the hors d'oeuvres. As Eileen walked past him she slapped him on the buttocks with the palm of her hand. He jumped, said, "Ouch!" then laughed. Eileen returned with a book of matches, lit the candles, then turned off the lights in the bathroom and in the candle light, her flesh glowed with a warm, pink tint. Eileen departed and returned from the bedroom carrying one of the chairs into the bathroom, departed and again, returned with the ice bucket and the filled glasses of champagne, setting them on the chair. "Okay lover boy, into the tub for you!"

"Yee gods, Eileen, you must have really flipped this time!"

"Help me in, this tub is slippery." Eileen sat in the tub, the water reaching almost to her breasts.

"And you want me to get in there with you?" an incredulous Marshall asked.

"Chicken?"

"Okay doll, but remember, we've got to get out!"

Marshall cautiously stepped into the tub.

"Good boy! Very good. Now let's sit face to face and I'll wrap my legs around you." Eileen moved closely to Marshall, who was more intrigued than excited.

"Now we sip from the champagne and if you're up to it we'll do it the oriental way. Oh, you are a good boy. Oh my God, isn't this divine?"

Eileen reached, stretched one arm across his back, poked her solid breasts into his chest and returned with a half of a sliced turkey-breast sandwich, its crust removed, and told Marshall to open his mouth and she held the small sandwich for him to eat.

Almost speechless, Marshall had to laugh. He took a bite of the sandwich. "Who can I tell about this?" he said, his mouth partially filled with pieces of the sandwich.

"Only me. You'd better not blabber a word about this little tryst to another living soul!"

Eileen leaned close to Marshall and wrapped both arms around him. "Oh, golly, Marshall. It's happening. Just sit still now and hold me closely. Oh, thank you, thank you."

"Godamighty, Eileen. That was something! I'm too exhausted to climb out of this damn tub."

"Then rest and have some crackers and cheese and fill those glasses again."

As they ate and drank, sitting in the tub of hot water, they looked into each other's eyes and both laughed. "Christ, I don't think I'm even self-conscious anymore!" Marshall said.

"You like me better with my clothes on or off?"

"Believe it or not Eileen, that almost see-through gown you had on yesterday damn near drove me crazy. I can understand your pride in your body, your nakedness, but honest to God, you are just plain beautiful in or out of anything!"

"What a lucky choice I made," Eileen whispered. "But really Marsh, I couldn't plan all of this. It just sort of unfolded. Fate took me to your table in the Crown Room."

"Well honey, I think fate is telling us to get out of this thing if we can, the water's cooling off."

Marshall grasped the side of the tub and lifted himself, then stepped out of the tub, still holding the edge.

"Next."

"Don't let me slip."

"When I get home I'm going to buy a couple of these monstrous towels, just to remember you by."

"I'll do the same. Promise me you'll think of me when you use one?"

"I promise."

"God, Eileen, do you know what I'd really like now?"

"More loving?"

"Have mercy. I'm drained! No, I'd like a nice big juicy hamburger and a glass of milk and then a big pot of black coffee."

"You're easy." Eileen said. She pulled a white bathrobe around her and tied it, and found the telephone. She ordered the same for herself and added an order of cheesecake.

"I'd be real content now if we could just lay down close to one another and rest," Eileen said.

"You won't let me go to sleep will you. I'm beginning to think my body is still on ETO time!"

Eileen returned from the closet with two extra pillows. Both clad in the big bathrobes, they rested with two pillows each, the sheet, and a light blanket pulled over them.

"Back at Tony's you said something about your copilot being a poor bastard. What did you mean?"

"You mentioned fate, well fate just seemed to have it in for our crew." Marshall said, then sighed deeply.

"Like what?"

"You see, when we all met at Lake Charles, down in Louisiana, we just blended into a compatible crew. No jealousies or personality conflicts. Some new crews had to be broken up and switched around because of tempers and such. Everyone knew his job and did it and when we finally got into combat we functioned just as we'd been trained. No big deal."

"So?"

"By coincidence, our base in Bavaria after the war, during the occupation, was right near a little town our crew had bombed. We took out the bridge there. I think we felt a little guilty or something about it when we moved to a base right next to the town. You know, we met the people, the Germans, face to face. Saw what we'd done to civilians. Hell, I don't know. Maybe it was just me."

"Go on."

"Well, there was a little maid I kind of took a liking to. Oh hell, Eileen, let's forget this war stuff!" Marshall said.

"Kris?"

"Yeah."

"And?"

"Well, her old man, he got out of a prisoner-of- war camp, all shot up, and one-legged and he comes home to a busted up town, his wife, mother and grandchild are all dead. I don't think he ever found out about Kris and me. She learned that I was the bombardier, the luftgangster, that selected that damn bridge. She wouldn't talk to me after that. But I tried to stop and say good-bye to her when I was ordered to come home." Marshall sighed.

"When we got to her house all hell had broken loose. I honestly don't know what happened. I heard some German woman say that her dad shot her and himself. The last I saw of her, the medics had a bloody sheet completely covering her on a gurney and were wheeling her away. The last thing I remember before getting knocked out was a Medic saying, 'Take her to the morgue!' I couldn't even get close. Germans were all over the place trying to find out what happened. And the M.P.'s were everywhere." Marshall ran the fingers of both of his hands back through his hair, searching for the bruise.

"Terrible things were happening to our crew. To Pop and McAdam and even Frank!" Marshall raised his voice, angrily. "Everyone thought our crew was jinxed, after bombing that damn bridge. My C.O. figured he'd be doing me a favor to ship me out of there, I guess."

"It might be good if you could sort of unload some of this on me," Eileen said. She rested her head on his chest.

"Our engineer, Pop, was like a big brother to all of us on the crew. He was a damn good engineer: knew his stuff. The colonel asked Pop to fly with him on a simple little flight to Paris, after combat, you know, but when they landed back at Bad Scheidel, he'd forgotten some stuff I'd asked him to buy, and he went back to the plane and didn't touch the nose wheel. Ground crew had the engines still going, and props were still spinning. Didn't see them. Killed him."

"That's awful."

"About McAdam? Think you want to hear more?"

"Go on."

"The fucking Hitler Youth, their idea of Boy Scouts, and they were called werewolves, they caught him with a German girl and castrated him!

They didn't know who did it, for sure, who really did it; maybe some SS bums," Then Marshall lowered his head. "Please forgive me, Eileen, I've never used that word in front of a girl."

"Oh, Marshall, you may need professional help handling this sort of thing, sorting it all out."

"Hell, there's more: and Frank: our fine, decent, educated, talented pilot. Never cheated. Said if a priest could remain celibate his whole life, he could handle it for a year or so. Know what?"

"This is too tragic. The bad luck has to stop somewhere!" Eileen said.

"Oh yeah? Well, the Red Cross showed up at headquarters one day and the colonel called Frank in. Had to tell him his wife had died. Gave him an emergency leave to go home for the funeral."

"How sad."

"Yeah, especially because she died during an abortion. Three months pregnant."

"And you were overseas, too long?"

"You figured it," Marshall said. "And I'll never tell anyone else what I've told you."

"You must have a confidant at home. That scout leader, a priest. A pastor or minister or someone?"

"It's too personal, Eileen, and I feel what I've said to you is sacred."

"Of course."

"What happened to Frank?"

"He never came back to Germany. Schloss transferred him to a fighter base in Georgia. When I get home I'll write to his home address. Everything happened so fast I didn't write to him, or hear from him."

The knock on the door startled them.

"Took a long time for hamburgers, didn't it? I'll need some change if your supply is handy." Eileen said.

Both arose and pulled the white robes tightly around them. Marshall located his wallet and took some dollar bills from it and handed them to Eileen as she crossed the room.

Eileen advised the waiter where to place the cart, signed a tab, tipped him and as soon as he had departed she removed the polished round metal lids and both of them admired the large hamburgers, surrounded by potato chips and sliced fruit with one large kosher pickle.

"I'd forgotten how good milk tasted." Marshall said, tipping the glass and drinking half of the contents.

Eileen took the food from the tray and arranged it on a table. "I forgot to blow out those candles," she said, then went to the bathroom and returned with the candleholder, walking slowly, protecting the flames with one hand. She sat it down in the middle of the table. "Might even be some cold champagne left," Eileen said, as she went back to the bathroom, and returned holding the bottle in one hand, a tray with the glasses, and a few little sandwiches in the other.

"Eileen, I'm going on the wagon! That damn champagne gives me a headache!"

"Okay, I'll take champagne over milk any day. How about a trade?"

Marshall had already finished drinking his glass of milk.

"It's a deal," Marshall said. "I've spilled out my tale of woe. It's your turn."

"Hey, I leveled with you when we met. Billy will be in my memory forever. But I've got to start a new life, which is what I'm doing at SC. I know these couple of days will be a precious memory, but that's all."

"Brother? Sister?"

"Spoiled only child."

"Your father sounds like a great guy. You haven't said much about your mother."

"Hate to say this, but my mother is a very ambitious woman." Eileen sighed, "If their marriage lasts, it'll be a miracle."

"You're not serious."

"Ha, I wish it could be different. My father's a great provider. We want for nothing. Mom drives around in her fancy Rolls Royce, and even if I say it, she's a handsome woman. No, I should honestly say a beautiful woman. But she isn't even subtle about wanting to get her hands on a multimillionaire oilman that lives in Beverly Hills. Owns a huge yacht, and an airplane and pilots them himself.

"He's a widower and mom scares me. She'll dump dad and set her hooks into that guy when the timing is right. I can just sense it. And I'll loathe her, but I won't have the guts to turn my back on her. That makes me the sick one, eh?"

"Hells bells, " Marshall muttered. "I think you're the one who is going to need a good old fashioned Girl Scout leader! Does your dad suspect?"

"Marshall, it's beneath his dignity to even acknowledge what is going on. I think he'd give mom a divorce without a whimper. He's busy with the stock exchange, with golf and all of his wild dreams."

"Wild dreams?"

"He's convinced that LA will be nothing more than another big Middle West hick town if it doesn't have water around it. I mean lots of water!"

"Water?"

"He says any great city, like New York, and San Francisco, and Chicago, for instance, all are looking at a large body of water. A lake, an ocean, even a river like in Paris. So he says if we could dig the Panama Canal we could dredge out all of the little dumpy towns like Culver City and Palms and Inglewood, everything all the way up to and around the coliseum. Then there could be parks and pleasure craft, shops, you know, just like here in San Francisco. It would be wide and deep and there would be fishing and sailing, you know, and trees and flowers, it could really be quite beautiful.

"What chance has he of selling that idea?"

"Zero. He says that himself. But that doesn't mean he won't keep trying. He's ahead of his time, I think."

Eileen poured coffee for Marshall.

"Thanks. You said dreams. Plural."

"How about gouging out a huge gorge right in the middle of the San Gabriel mountain range? Those mountains surround LA, and the area all around the basin from Long Beach to Santa Monica and well, they are like the broken off edge of a cup. The sea breezes come into this big basin, off of the Pacific but are trapped."

"So?"

"Oranges and lemons and grapefruit and tangerines, citrus, they are what make southern California prosperous. And every year the growers light up their smudge pots and burn mountainous stacks of old tires, and oil sludge, to keep the fruit from freezing and all of that rotten, black smoke is trapped. So daddy feels a huge canyon could be created, again like the Panama Canal project, and all of that lousy air would be drafted away when the sea breezes move in. He says they'd employ thousands of people, on both projects, too."

"And your mother would leave him for a millionaire."

"Come on, sweetie, I'm talking multimillionaire, a mansion, society status, like I mean rich!"

"Could you choose sides?"

"I hope I'm out of SC with a masters in architecture and maybe married to some nice guy before it happens. I love them both. I refuse to take sides. As for me, I want it all. Career plus kids."

"I'm glad we're not rich. My folks."

"I feel you are, in a different way," Eileen said. "Look Marshall, the candles are melting down onto the sides of the brass. I'll blow them out now."

"Well, baby, you've blown me out, too. I gotta get some shut eye."

"Will the light by the bed bother you if I read?"

"Just no more fantasies."

"Tomorrow I'll have some surprises for you."

Marshall began to snore. Eileen wondered if he even heard her.

Eileen looked at the cover photograph and read the copy in a LIFE magazine, but soon her eyelids were heavy. She tossed the magazine onto the floor, turned off the light and pulled her small frame close to Marshall's backside. Her head ached and she blamed the champagne, as had Marshall.

Eileen slept fitfully, turning away from Marshall, she faced the edge of the bed, tucked her forearm close to her body and rested her face on her palm and stared into the darkness, and tried to get comfortable.

I've won. I've drained you, Marshall. I am superior. Women are superior to men! But, damn, damn, damn, there is no winning. I still need your seeds, your sperm. Without your seeds I am barren and desolate and worthless! God is our tormentor! He gave me the ability to genuinely love, to love you, Billy my fine man, and God, who is supposed to be aware of the death of a sparrow, allows you to be destroyed. Forgive me, Bill, but now I need Marshall. He needs me, too, honestly. Oh God, You ignored Bill. You let him die! You ignored my prayers for him."

Eileen dozed, then was awakened by the noises emanating from Marshall. For awhile Eileen was amused at the various sounds of Marshall's snoring, but finally became agitated She arose and found her small travel clock and walked to the bathroom to check the time. She took two aspirin. It was past midnight. She returned to bed and dozed. Eileen was awakened by the warm trickle between her legs, felt the liquid with a finger tip and was startled, frightened for an instant, then arose and went to the bathroom, turning on the light and pulling closed the door.

Eileen suddenly realized what was happening and laughed aloud, then whispered, *"Oh, thank you dear Jesus. I really am a woman."* With a makeshift hand towel and the tie from the white robe, Eileen carried one of the large bath towels with her back to the suite and draped it over the floor lamp to shield it as much as possible, then picked up the telephone.

"Room service? I want to speak with a lady," Eileen waited, and a girl's voice then asked if she could be of service. "Yes, I came unprepared. I need some small sanitary napkins and a belt as soon as possible. You can? Oh, thank you," Eileen gave her name and room number and sat in the semi-darkness and smiled. She recalled that Marshall's wallet was atop the dresser. She opened it, thumbed through the bills and took a five-dollar bill from it.

There was a light tapping at the door and Eileen opened it. A petite Chinese girl handed her a package and Eileen pushed the bill into her hand. She made an effort to decline, but Eileen smiled, held a finger up to her own lips, and the girl nodded and departed.

Clad in the bathrobe, Eileen soon returned to the bed, quietly, carefully lifting the sheet and blanket and rested, but did not sleep.

It was barely light when Eileen arose, showered, and dressed. She packed her few things, including her candleholder and then ordered coffee and apple juice and Danish from room service. The delivery was made and Marshall snored but slept soundly.

Eileen made three phone calls. Scanned the Chronicle and finally walked to the end of the bed and lifted the sheet and blanket and tickled Marshall's feet.

"What the hell!" he exclaimed, jerked his legs and sat up in the bed and stared at Eileen, at the cart with the food and the coffee. The drapes were open and again the wrought iron railing shadows were on the carpet.

"What time is it? Why, you're already dressed," Marshall exclaimed. Eileen wore the same dress she had on when he first saw her in the Crown Room.

"The bellhop will be here in about twenty minutes," Eileen said. "I'm catching the Daylight to LA Haven't a whole lot of time."

Eileen carried a cup of hot coffee to Marshall, and handed it to him.

"No, take it back, please," Marshall said.

Eileen accepted the cup, placed it on the table and Marshall tossed back the covers, stood and reached for Eileen. She laughed, then puckered her lips slightly and stood on her toes to kiss him. Her lips were warm, soft, and barely parted.

"What's this all about?"

"I promised to call home, and well, some of what I told you about is beginning to happen. I'm honestly sorry, Marshall."

"Well gee, you've got to do what is right. I was hoping we could have a nice calm day. Back before the war my folks and I visited Golden Gate

Park. I wanted to take you there, and back to the Crown Room, you know, and Fisherman's Wharf and stuff."

"You don't have to check out. The bill is all taken care of. Daddy established credit and will be billed."

"Come on! I want to pay my share of this room."

"Sweetie, it would complicate things, really, just let it be."

Marshall shrugged his shoulders, frowned and said, "I'll shave and shower and be dressed by the time the guy gets here."

Dressed, Marshall returned to the cart. "That's good coffee."

"You've time to sit down and have some juice and a sweet roll and relax with a cup of coffee."

"Eileen," Marshall said. "You're a surprise a minute. I'm so stunned I haven't had time to get angry."

"My sweet aviator. It had to happen, even if unplanned. We've got to remain friends, haven't we?" Eileen said. "And here's the C.C., at least some of it. Put it in your bag."

"I can remember Pop saying he could handle his enemies, it was his friends that fouled him up." Marshall accepted the partially consumed fifth and put it into one of the B-4 bag pockets.

The bellhop tapped at the door and Eileen opened it. She pointed to her bag and to Marshall's B-4 bag. "We're all checked out. We can meet you at the cabstand, or just leave them there. We'll be right along."

Marshall crossed the room and gave the bellhop three one dollar bills.

"Thank you, sir." He said and started to leave.

"What time does the Crown Room open?" Marshall asked.

"Opens at eleven sharp, sir," he answered, and he could see Marshall mouth the words, "damn it to hell."

"See you in the lobby," Eileen said.

The bellhop left the room and they followed. Marshall said, "Nuts, I could've carried that little bit of stuff downstairs."

Eileen did not respond, stifling a comment that would have come across as both condescending and sarcastic, about not carrying your own luggage in and out of the Fairmont. She did think, *wait until I get you to LA, we'll polish off those rough edges.*

When they walked the length of the long hall and turned into the expanse of the lobby, Marshall and Eileen both stopped. Across the room she saw the bellhop speaking to someone at the front desk, he nodded towards them, then proceeded with the bags to the hotel entrance.

"Marshall, let's say our good-byes right here," she nodded towards the couch where earlier they had sat. "I'm taking a cab to the station and unfortunately haven't much time."

Marshall watched her seat herself, but instead of joining her walked to a desk, took a sheet of paper from the drawer and using a hotel pen wrote a few lines, then returned and dropped heavily beside her. He handed her the sheet of paper. "Both home and business addresses, and our phone numbers."

"Mine are right here in my purse," Eileen said, and brought forth a folded piece of paper. "Home and sorority house, plus the phones, and while you were sleeping I borrowed five dollars for more tip money here and at the station. I'll mail it to you."

"Hell! That doesn't even deserve a response."

"Marshall, I know this is abrupt and I hope you aren't angry. Didn't we both go into our little escapade with our eyes wide open? After all, you did tell me about Kris."

"Eileen, yes, but I guess I'm still a little old fashioned." Marshall stammered, searched for words, and Eileen hoped he was going to become chivalrous, had anticipated something more than a handshake good-bye from him. "As you, and your well informed sorority sisters know, virility and fertility are two separate things. I don't know if I'm fertile. I hope so of course. But I'm assuming you could get pregnant."

Eileen was delighted, but spoke gravely, "That would be my problem, not yours. I'm a big girl now." *But I will let him worry a little bit.* She rested a small white hand upon his. "We'll just stay in touch. Just in case. Okay?" She leaned towards him and puckered her lips and accepted a light kiss from Marshall. "Goodbye, and I want to walk to the curb alone. No awkward good-byes out there."

"Roger," Marshall said. He stood and extended both hands to assist Eileen. "One more thing, Eileen," Marshall reached up to his chest and unbuttoned his Eisenhower jacket, reached inside and quickly removed the clips from his wings, then handed them to Eileen. "Something to remember me by."

"Oh, Marsh," she gasped, "why I'll treasure them always. Thank you, thank you." She stood on her toes and put one hand behind his neck and kissed him hard. "I love you." She said, then tears began to fill her eyes and she turned quickly, patted him on the arm and walked towards the hotel entrance.

"Eileen," Marshall spoke just loudly enough for her to hear. She stopped, turned and smiled at him. "Don't forget the sourdough bread," Eileen laughed, blew a kiss to him and turned again and walked out of the lobby.

Marshall sat back down on the couch and thought about Eileen and Los Angeles, then his mind turned to home and his mother and father, and his uncle. Especially he thought of his Model A, propped up on blocks for over three years. He walked to the front of the hotel, spotted his B-4 bag and nodded and said thanks as the doorman waved a yellow cab to the curb.

"Ferry Building, please," Marshall said.

CHAPTER 24

▼

CHICO

Marshall boarded the practically empty military bus parked near the Ferry Building and was grateful that no one had selected the long back seat. He exchanged howdy's with a couple of other passengers and went to the back and stretched out on the seat. Marshall loosened his necktie, and rested his head on his folded right arm and his back fit snugly against the seat. Immediately he fell into a sound sleep.

"Sir?" a voice said, "The driver wants to know if you want off at the officers' quarters or the officers' club?"

"What, what?" Marshall stammered and sat up quickly, "Wow, I really passed out. Back already? Yes, the officers' club, please."

The bus slowed to a stop. "Well, thanks for the ride, Marshall said, "I really conked out!" He grasped the handle of his B-4 bag and looked through the windshield.

"Here you are, sir, and watch the steps."

Dropping his B-4 bag inside the door of the club, Marshall proceeded to the bar.

"Hi Sergeant!" he said. "Don't you ever have a day off?"

"Well, Lieutenant, welcome back. How was Frisco? And what will be your pleasure?"

"Draft beer, please."

"Foggy over there?"

"Perfect. C.A.V.U. and I was treated royally by everyone. Hell, I felt like a hero for once." Marshall chuckled, "And where do you go when you get a leave?"

"Reno, sir." the bartender said. " I love to gamble. I've a little system that works pretty well on the crap tables, that is if I don't get greedy. And there are a few small bands at the casinos that allow me to sit-in. I play the piano, you know."

"I remember you told me you have your own band, for weddings and dances. Right?"

"Correct sir, and are you Lieutenant Sunder by chance?" the bartender asked.

"Roger. That's me," Marshall answered. "What's up?"

"Major Crandall is looking for you. He asked if I knew you. He put a notice on the bulletin board out in the lobby, and at the Officers' Quarters."

"So he's probably at the administration office?"

"Yes sir. And it's just across from the P.X., in case you need another set of wings" The bartender winked and nodded towards Marshall's uniform and then chuckled. "So, someone clipped your wings."

"Very observant!" Marshall laughed and looked down at his chest.

"Well, Major Crandall is a nice guy and probably wouldn't say you were out of uniform, but there are some barracks lawyers around here that might embarrass you, if they knew you were a flier."

"I'm much obliged, and I'm heading for the P.X., right now, then on to see the good major. Wonder what in the hell he wants? I'm damn near a civilian!"

In the P.X. Marshall was able to buy a set of bombardier-navigator wings and pinned them above the two rows of ribbons. Before reporting to Major Crandall, Marshall decided to purchase another Army Colt .45 for his Uncle Bruce. He'd tell him it belonged to a buddy that didn't want it. Now that Eileen had encouraged his little white lie approach, another wouldn't hurt and would please his uncle. Sergeant Nakamoto helped him select a nice clean weapon. He stuffed it into his barracks bag, and stored it. He then departed and found the administration office and quickly located the office of Major Crandall.

A WAC corporal sat at a desk, behind which was a closed door with a glass window bearing the name of the major.

"Hi, Corporal," Marshall said. "Understand Major Crandall is looking for me. My name is Sunder."

"I'll tell him you are here, sir," she said and walked to the door, knocked, and they both heard a cheery "Come on in!"

The corporal returned to her desk and asked Marshall to go right in. Major Crandall grinned and walked around from behind his desk, extended his hand and vigorously shook Marshall's .The major was an inch or two beneath six feet, trim, solid shoulders, and was grinning so widely that his mouth seemed to be full of strong evenly spaced teeth.

"Reports as ordered, sir," Marshall said. He raised his arm to salute.

"Hey, relax Lieutenant Sunder. Have a seat. I don't get to meet up with many real live heroes anymore."

"You must have the wrong Sunder, Major," Marshall said, laughing

"Seriously," the major spoke a little more softly, "I've got a lot of good news for you. Important, but not the most important news is that your 'first' came through, so we'll have to replace those gold bars with some silver. I'd be honored if you'd accept an old set of mine. They're sterling and will polish up nicely!"

"Well I'll be darned! "Marshall exclaimed. "I knew my pilot got his 'first', but I thought it was because he's staying in."

"Well, part of my duties are to give men like you a little pep talk about making the military a career. There are some great opportunities at famous colleges around the world. The University of Paris, the Sorbonne, you know, right in Paris, and Oxford in England, Heidelberg in Germany, just to name a few. Looks like we're going to be in the occupation business for quite awhile in both theaters. We'll need good administrators."

"Thank you very much for these bars," Marshall said. "Lots to think about before going back to active duty though, but thanks," then continued. " Maybe I can buy you a drink at the club, to celebrate, you know." Marshall observed the pilot wings and the single row of ribbons worn by the major, "And what did you fly, Major?"

"Roger on that drink! I flew B-29's, but now for the REAL news!" The major spoke excitedly, "Look here at what I have for you Sunder!" He walked from behind his desk and stood in front of Marshall. The major held a small rectangular box in his hand He flipped open the lid and extended his arms and hands towards Marshall.

"Is that a DFC?" Marshall asked, his voice hushed.

"And this is why I called you a real live hero."

"Hell, I didn't do anything to earn a DFC!"

"Well, I can read all of this aloud, or can boil it down and you can study it later," the major said, returning to his desk where he held up a sheet of official letterhead for Marshall to see. He then dragged a chair closer to Marshall, sat down and pointed to another chair. "Grab a chair and relax, Sunder," he said. "As I understand this citation, the flight you were leading hit a marshaling yard in Ulm, then you discovered you had a couple of bombs hung up. Sound familiar?"

"Hell, that was no big deal. That's what we're trained to do. God, that was ages ago!"

"So you dropped a couple of bombs on a bridge at a place called Bad Scheidel? Pretty well wrecked it."

"Right. Just a small village with some hot springs, near an abandoned Luftwaffe base."

"Do you recall Malm`edy? The massacre at Malm`edy? What those German SS bastards did?" The major asked.

"Yes sir. I know about that."

"You were awarded this medal because a whole damn contingent of SS troops were stalled at the bridge at Bad Scheidel, which allowed our guys to catch up with them. Killed a bunch, a few escaped, and they arrested a handful. They were on their way to Berchtesgaden, you know, for a last stand for old Adolf!"

"Why that's incredible!" Marshall exclaimed. "Just pure henhouse luck to choose that bridge."

"Ha!" the major exclaimed, "I think I could like you, Lieutenant! You're my kind of hero!"

Marshall grinned broadly. He looked at the medal. "Wow, I assume each of the crew also got one."

"Seems the others of the crew got bronze stars. You were the decision maker and that's the difference."

"Hell, without my pilots and our engineer, Pop, what could I have accomplished?"

"Being a pilot, I'll have to agree! You couldn't accomplish a whole heck of a lot," the major said, then guffawed, "Hope you know I'm joshing. Come on, Mr. First Lieutenant Sunder, I'll buy you a drink. And let's have no false modesty. You earned that medal, now enjoy it."

"Yes sir!" Marshall replied, trying to duplicate the major's enthusiasm and vigor.

"Stand up and let me see if I can squeeze this little DFC ribbon in next to the air medal. Have to move things around a bit." The major removed some of the ribbons, then rearranged them. "There, that ought to do until you can buy a holder at the PX and slide some of those plastic covered ones onto it. My, your folks are going to be mighty proud."

The major and Marshall departed and the corporal was advised that they were going to the officers' club.

In the club they walked directly to the bar and the sergeant looked up and greeted them. "Welcome Major Crandall, Lieutenant Sunder. You gentlemen do look thirsty. What can I fix you?"

"Beefeater on the rocks with a twist," the Major said.

"Last time I had one of those both of my lips got numb. How about Old Forester and water?"

"Coming up," the bartender said. He winked at Marshall and nodded his head slightly. He walked to where he was opposite Marshall and studied his uniform for a minute.

"Congratulations, sir, on getting your first. And if I can trust my eyes, I'd swear there's a new ribbon tucked in there. Like maybe someone got a DFC?"

"Boy, you sure don't miss a trick, do you,?"

"Again, my congratulation, sir!" the bartender said, and he reached across the bar top and shook Marshall's hand. "And because I'm in charge here, the drinks are on Uncle Sam. Right, Major Crandall?" The bartender poured plain water into a glass and the three of them raised their glasses and touched them, then put them to their lips and drank.

"Want to tell me what you did to earn that medal?"

Marshall laughed. "Well, there we were at ten thousand feet hanging by our throat mics, surrounded by ME 109's and walls of flak, you know, that kind of stuff." Marshall laughed again. "Seriously, there was no big deal. We knocked down a little old bridge, and I just now learned that it happened to interfere with some fucking SS bastards trying to get to Bertchesgaden. That's about it."

"Where are you off to from here, Sunder?" Major Crandall asked.

"Home. Chico. North of here a few hours."

"Have a job waiting for you?"

"Well, I'll probably go by the employment office to pick up extra jobs, but my folks own a hardware store; farm and ranch supplies, that sort of thing. Carry about everything you'd need to run a ranch. They call it Sierra Mercantile. Probably spend most of my time there. But, the last letter from home said their inventories were almost depleted. The war effort, you know."

"Interesting."

"You a career man, sir?"

"Haven't really decided yet. If I could keep flying, I'd be interested, but I think the powers that be want to anchor me to a desk."

The bartender approached and asked if they'd like another round. They nodded and added please.

Major Crandall continued, "It was funny. Back when we graduated and learned that we were going to advanced training in B-29's, the C.O. had us all gathered together in a auditorium and he called out each flier's name, and the guy was supposed to stand and call out his age. Most were about twenty-one or two, and then he called out Crandall and I stood up and loudly and clearly said thirty-four. I sat down, and the C.O. corrected my answer and said Lieutenant Crandall erred, he meant twenty-four. So, I stood up again and loudly and clearly said, Lt. Crandall, age thirty-four. And everyone in the class laughed and even applauded." The major laughed heartily. "So, by Air Corps standards, I'm an old pilot, pushing 40. But I do manage to get in my four hours a month."

"Wow, that is funny. Heck, we called our engineer 'Pop' and he was about twenty-seven."

"So, Sunder, what if there isn't enough to keep you busy at the store?" Major Crandall turned on his stool and looked directly at Marshall.

"Really won't know for awhile."

"Let me be serious with you about re-enlisting for a couple of years. The first year, maybe more, you'd be studying accounting, purchasing, inventory control, marketing—which would include advertising and salesmanship. You'd come home really prepared to run that store."

"Well Major, you get your flying time in as a pilot. What about me, a bombardier-navigator? That would make a big difference in pay."

"I'm fairly sure you could fly as a navigator from the closest air base. But that's a good question and I'll check it out."

"How urgent is it to make a decision?"

"Well, you are automatically in the inactive reserve until you relinquish your commission. So there's no big rush, but those good schools may fill up fast." The major swirled the martini around in the glass, sipped it, then said, "How are you getting home?"

"Train or Greyhound, I suppose."

"Care to ride up in a Piper Cub? I've been renting one, with the option to buy."

"Hey, that would really be fun. And fast. I'll buy the gas if you're really willing?"

"Hell, Sunder, it was my idea, and don't worry about the gas. Cubs aren't '26's you know!"

"I remember there used to be a little air strip at the edge of town. I could call the folks to meet us. I could show you the store and my '31 Model A. It's been up on blocks since I left home. It's a real beaut. White side walls, a rumble seat, even a squirrel's tail attached to the hood ornament."

"Well, why don't you get on the phone and see what would be a good time for them to meet us. I'm assuming that strip is still there. They can tell you. If we can arrive there about noon, that'll give me a chance to check out the plane, get your gear loaded, and we can do a little sight seeing on the way, too."

"Roger, Major, I'll put in a call right away," Marshall said, revealing his delight with a big smile.

"I've scheduled a photo session for you to attend this afternoon." Major Crandall said, "We've a visiting fireman looking over the base. A brigadier, General Brogan. I'm sure he'd be delighted to have his picture taken presenting the DFC to you. Then I'll have publicity mail it up to your local paper, assuming you have one in Chico. So be at my office at 1400 hours."

"Yes sir," Marshall answered, "Our paper is *The Union*."

"And damn it, Sunder, quit calling me sir. My first name is John, or just call me Crandall."

Marshall almost said, "Yes sir", but halted and said, "Okay."

That afternoon the base photographer spoke to his subjects briefly, then posed the general draping the long ribbons of the Distinguished Flying Cross so that it rested on Marshall's chest, displaying the medal and with his other hand shaking Marshall's hand, while grinning at the 4x5 Speed Graphic. He took three photos using flash bulbs to fill in the shadows beneath their brimmed hats.

The general shook Marshall's hand, and said "Congratulations, young man," saluted and turned and walked to a waiting staff car.

x   x   x

Major Crandall arrived, driving a jeep, at the Officers Quarters at 10:00 a.m. and found Marshall waiting for him in the lobby. The major carried Marshall's B-4 bag and Marshall swung his barracks bag up onto his shoulder, grunted under the load. It held souvenirs packed in the center, surrounded by heavy clothing.

"The L-4 is in Marysville," Major Crandall said. "Only a few minutes from here. I looked over the charts. You can navigate. It's a short ride, even by Piper Cub standards. I'm glad you are wearing your Eisenhower jacket with all of the ribbons. That'll be a thrill for your folks."

"Talked to my dad. He was really excited. That's the only reason I got all dressed up."

"Might as well alert you right now, Marsh, when you hang up that jacket and start wearing civilian clothes, it'll be a different world. No saluting, damn little respect from anyone but your kin. So, consider yourself forewarned."

"Guess that's to be expected," Marshall said, not dwelling on it, and then added, "I'll be happy to give you headings to Chico, or you can follow highway 70 right into town. Or if you want to head a little north west, we can follow the Sacramento River, and I can tell you when to head east. The old Bidwell Mansion is a good landmark right in the middle of town and the airstrip is three or four miles north of it. And, as the Limies used to say, 'You caw'nt miss it, yank.'"

The airport at Marysville consisted of a couple of small hangars, Quonset type, a gas pump, and a windsock. Marshall followed the major into a small office papered with navigational wall charts, plus a clock and a barometer. The proprietor smiled as they entered.

"Howdy John, understand you're doing a little chauffeuring this afternoon. Better file a flight plan."

"Roger," Major Crandall said, "just going to drop Lieutenant Sunder off up at Chico. Family will be waiting for him, then I'll head on back. I've got charts."

"Just getting home, Lieutenant?"

"Yes sir," Marshall answered, smiling. "Had some occupation duty in Germany."

"Bet the major is trying to woo you back into active duty."

"Hey, there are better deals for a young man now than there's ever been. And no one shooting at you!" Major Crandall said. "Well, let's get going. You know how to crank the prop on these little fellows?"

Marshall's B-4 bag and barracks bag were placed behind the seats of the Piper Cub. He said, "Better give me a quick lesson on pulling that prop," Marshall said. The major explained and after a brief cockpit check, Major Crandall called out "switch on" nodded to Marshall and a quick pull of the propeller started the engine. Marshall avoided the spinning propeller, climbed in behind Major Crandall and slammed the door behind him.

Within minutes they were airborne and heading north towards Chico.

"Let's follow the Sacramento River," Major Crandall said, raising his voice over the sound of the engine. "Here's the chart. How's your pilotage?"

"Don't think I'll need a map for this leg," Marshall laughed, but took the chart. They flew westward for several minutes and reached the river, then followed it north. "I'm amazed at the way it twists and curves. I'm not aware of that when we fish it from shore, or even from a boat. Only cover a few miles at a time, of course."

"What's that group of hills called?" Major Crandall asked, pointing to the east.

"Sutter Buttes," Marshall answered. "Bunch of us scouts hiked in to a little camp area, called Peace Valley, back before the war. I think our scoutmaster had to get permission from the folks that own the whole darn mountain. We hiked all the way up to North Butte, almost 2000 feet."

"Interesting formation," Major Crandall said. "Lots of wide open country up this way."

"You like to hunt or fish, Major?"

"Oh yeah, and I intend to resume when my hitch is up."

"I just assumed you were a career man."

"No, like I said, military seems to think I'm too old for jets."

"Lots of other planes to fly."

"To be quite honest, Lieutenant, my eyes can't handle the higher speeds very well, so I realize I'll have a little problem with all of the faster equipment that's out there and getting faster, so, it's just as well."

Major Crandall scanned the horizon, then tipped the wing of the Piper Cub and asked Marshall, "Know what that little burg might be?"

"Just east of the river? That's got to be Butte City. We're about halfway there already!"

"Well, this isn't a '26, but it beats the Greyhound!"

"Next intersection of any consequence will be Hamilton City. Take about twenty five or thirty minutes, and then we'll head due east, fly a bit north of the Bidwell Mansion, and the strip ought to be in sight."

"Sunder, you want to fly this thing for awhile?"

"Roger. I had a little time in Cubs during cadets."

The major sat back and folded his arms and Marshall flew the Piper Cub, checking the air speed regularly. He looked down at the scenery, at the curving Sacramento River nearly beneath them.

"Getting pretty excited about getting home?"

"Been three years. Got home a couple of times. Wonder how my folks have changed?"

"You're the one that's changed, Lieutenant. Your folks will be just like they were the last time you saw them."

Marshall weighed that statement, and continued to fly the small airplane. The weather was perfect. Now and then the small airplane hopped about, bounced, when the air currents changed as a body of water was crossed.

"I think we're coming up on Hamilton, Major. I'll take an easterly heading now. We'll be there in a few minutes. That's Mount Shasta, due north. Lassen to the east. Beautiful, eh?"

"Roger. Fantastic, and look at all of that snow still on them!" the major answered. "When you spot that landmark, the Bidwell Mansion I believe you called it, I'll take over and see if I can contact their tower, assuming they have one. Take her on down to three thousand feet."

"There it is, the mansion, sticking out like a sore thumb."

The major then took control and flew the Piper Cub. He contacted the tower, and asked for permission to land, which he received. They gave him the barometric setting, and the wind speed, however he quickly spotted the crisscrossing landing strips, saw the wind sock and made his approach on the final leg.

Marshall peered through his window. "I can see a couple of pickup trucks and cars. And hey! I think that must be my Uncle Bruce's Lab, Tara, down there with him! That's got to be my folks next to Uncle Bruce!"

"That's just great, Sunder. I'm going to taxi right up to them. You wait until I tell you it's okay to get out! I want that prop dead still. Understand?"

"Roger," Marshall answered. *Christ, at last I'm getting pumped up about getting home!*

The major slowly taxied the small airplane towards the parked pickup trucks, then turned so that the dust blew away from the awaiting family.

He turned off the ignition, allowed the small propeller to stop, then," said, "Okay, go get 'em, kid!"

Marshall opened the door and started to reach behind him for his gear. "I'll get that stuff out of here. You go see your mom and dad."

"Thanks. There's some fragile stuff in my barracks bag."

"I'll be careful," the major said, laughing aloud.

Wishing that he had something in his hands, Marshall walked casually towards his mother when suddenly Tara, the Black Labrador, ran towards him and Marshall recalled the command that Bruce had taught her and he yelled "Chest high Tara!" and the dog leaped as she was almost upon him, twisting her body in mid air, landing solidly against his chest with the flat side of her body. Marshall had to take a step backward to maintain his balance, holding the solid dog, cradled in his arms. Tara squirmed, turning her head so that she could lick his face.

"Tara, come!" his Uncle Bruce called out and Marshall released her, dropped her and the Lab immediately ran to Bruce and sat beside him, her tail wagging and her long pink tongue hung from her mouth. Then his mother was in his arms hugging him. Tears streamed down her cheeks. She said nothing, then stepped aside and Marshall accepted the handshake of his father, noticing that tears were in his eyes. He too stepped aside, and Bruce stepped forward, gripped his hand, shook it vigorously, and said, "The band couldn't make it," and then they all laughed. "Quite a display of ribbons there, Marshall!" Bruce added.

"I think Tara has put on a little weight since I last saw her, Uncle Bruce."

"Oh, she's a healthy little lady. You know, in dog years, it's been twenty-one since she saw you. She remembered. She's only eight. Right in her prime. Probably sixty pounds now, but fit."

His mother removed her glasses and with a white handkerchief dabbed at her eyes.

The major exited from the airport office and slowly approached the group. Marshall saw him and said, "Major Crandall, please come over and meet the folks!"

Major Crandall smiled and joined the group. He said "How do you do, Mrs. Sunder," then heard the names, Newell and Bruce, shook the hands of each of the men with vigor and each said "Howdy." He then walked towards the airplane and said, "Better get your gear. It's by the plane." Marshall followed him and took the B-4 bag and Major Crandall carried the heavy barracks bag. Newell and Bruce walked towards them, and attempted to assist them, but the fliers continued walking towards the trucks.

"I'll put the gear in the back of the folks' pickup," Marshall said, and located the truck, lowered the gate, and placed his baggage there, slammed the gate closed and latched it.

"Dad, before Major Crandall heads back to Marysville, I'd like him to see the store. And my Model A."

"That'll be fine, as far as it goes, Son," Newell said, hesitating then, dropping his head and looked at the ground for a second. He kicked a small stone aside, then looked to Bruce, " Why don't you take the major with you and we'll meet you at the store."

"I don't want to interfere with this homecoming," Major Crandall said, "I'm all cleared to take off."

"Only take a few minutes," Newell said, "And we'd love to have you join us for some refreshments at the house. Martha fixed a nice lunch."

"Climb aboard, Major," Bruce said. "Tara will ride in the back."

"Well, just to see the store." Major Crandall said. He followed Bruce to his truck. Bruce lowered the tailgate, signaled to the dog, and Tara jumped into the back of the truck. "I trust the little lady," Bruce said, "however, I've got a little harness device that I rigged up that I attach to her collar, so she can move to either side of the truck to look out, but there's no way she could jump or fall out. That plywood on the bed keeps the temperature of the truck bed comfortable for her."

The men climbed into the truck, pulled the heavy doors closed and Bruce drove towards the Sierra Mercantile store.

"Mighty nice of you to fly the boy up here. We could have driven down, but he didn't want us to. My wife and I never had children and he's kind of like a son to me."

"He's an outstanding young man. I've been trying to convince him to stay in the Air Corps. We need his type."

"He's going to be in for a shock, Major, when he gets to his house."

"Oh?"

"Damn, I tried to convince Newell to tell him: to write to him awhile back. You see, they sold his Model A to a collector down in Frisco, but Newell couldn't face up to writing to him about it and my sister just doesn't think it's all that important."

"Wow. He was anxious to show me his car. I realize it's none of my business why they sold it." The major looked at Bruce questioningly.

"Wasn't for the money. Hell, Martha put that in a savings account for him where it'll earn some interest. I'm sure you know that all hardware stores, since the war, are just about empty. The owner of a big industrial supply house bought it. His salesmen told Newell and Martha they would get favored deliveries. God, I do hope so!"

"Well, Mr. Kane, after the tour of the store, I'd appreciate if you'd take me back to the airport."

"I understand," Bruce said. "Well, here we are."

Several diagonal lines were in front of the store and Bruce pulled up a few spaces from the front door. The building was approximately sixty feet across, the exterior plastered, and painted white. A double door, with glass mounted within heavy wood frames, was in the middle of the building. Two large plate glass windows stood on opposite sides of the doors. Merchandise was displayed behind them. Above the doors within a frame, black, foot high letters on a pale green background, spelled out Sierra Mercantile. Three steps led up to a six-foot deep porch area, where they displayed lawn mowers, lawn tables and chairs, and barbecue equipment during business hours. At the left end of the building a small pool hall occupied a space on the same deck level.

"I've a set of keys," Bruce said. "They ought to be right behind us. I wonder if Newell told Marshall about that damn car?" He walked to the side of the truck and unhooked Tara's collar, then went to the back of the truck and lowered the gate. "She could jump over the side, but no use risking a bad landing. Right?"

"Makes sense to me," Major Crandall said, grinning. The dog came to his side and he reached down and patted her. "My pooch had to be put down."

"Sorry to hear that. Well, here are the rest of them," Bruce said, nodding to the truck pulling up into a space in front of the store.

Marshall assisted his mother from the cab and the three of them followed Bruce and Major Crandall up the three steps to the front door, which Bruce was unlocking. The men followed Martha into the store, but Bruce touched Newell's arm before they entered and whispered, "Tell him about the car yet?"

"I'll tell him when we get home."

"The major is going back to the airport from here."

"Just as well," Newell said, and they entered the store.

They overheard Marshall, "You know, mom, the store doesn't seem as big. Outside or inside. Isn't that funny?"

"Well, when you left we had a lot more inventory than we do now," she said. "Why don't you men show the major the store and I'll check over some items in the home section."

Major Crandall was led from one department to another, and finally to the loading area, at the back of the store, that was high enough to allow a pickup truck to back in so that its bed was level with the deck.

"We don't have much thievery in these parts, thank goodness," Newell said, "so we can leave these barrels of creosote, and fuel oil, and these crates of wheel barrows, shovel and picks, stuff like that, out here and not worry too much about someone backing in and helping themselves."

"I'd love to live in such an environment," Major Crandall said.

"Are you a career man?" Bruce asked.

"It hasn't worked out that way."

"What's the future hold?"

"Not sure. My eyes are okay by any standards, other than by the Air Corps' Flight Surgeon. I've been grounded for most of the newer military aircraft. I'm just not the desk jockey type, so I'm going to take my time and look around before making any quick decisions. I'm a little old to be going back to school," the major said, then added, "This is awfully nice country up here, what I've seen of it from the air."

"You into fishing and hunting?"

"You bet."

"Well, you'll have to join our group, if you'd like."

"Just might take you up on that, Mr. Kane."

"Call me Bruce."

"Okay Bruce," Major Crandall said, laughing, "if you'll just call me John!"

"Yes sir," Bruce grinned, "John it is!"

"Let's lock this place up and go get some refreshments," Newell said.

"We'd love to have you join us, Major," Martha added.

"Thanks, folks, but I've got to get that little plane back to Marysville. Besides, you've got a lot of family reunion business to get on with. I've enjoyed meeting you folks and seeing your store. Keep in touch, Lieutenant Sunder, and good luck. Bruce and Tara are driving me over to the airport."

"Thanks again, Major, for flying up here!"

"After you leave the airport, come on by the house for some lunch, Bruce," Newell said.

"Goodbye, Major," Martha said, smiled and waved as he and Bruce departed with Tara in the truck

It was a short drive back to the airport and Bruce spoke, " Newell's really slowing down. Got really sick last year. Doc Keith said it was rheumatic fever and there wasn't much he could do for him. Apparently fouled up a valve in his heart."

"Will he be able to handle the work at the store?"

"So far, so good. I've been helping out with some of the heavy stuff, like kegs of nails and nuts and bolts. That's where Marshall fits in. After the car, learning about his dad will be the next thing he learns."

"Well, there's the tower, Bruce, and my little yellow friend is all gassed up. I want you to know I appreciate your hospitality. But I don't want to be around when that kid learns he doesn't own a Model A!"

Bruce shook his head. "Martha just can't comprehend the importance of some of the toys we men get to love."

Bruce parked and joined Major Crandall, watching as he completed his paper work for his flight back to Marysville.

The major shook Bruce's hand and said, "Next time up I'll take you for a sight -seeing ride. Okay?"

"I'd love it! Can Tara join us?"

"I'll have to mull that over. Think you can fashion a seat harness for her?" the major asked, chuckling.

When Newell drove the truck into the curved driveway, Marshall looked from his window, and just as he had felt at the store, somehow his home also seemed smaller than he remembered. Four-inch lapped red-wood siding, painted white, covered most of the exterior, except for a section on the north side of the house where a stone chimney, ten foot at its base, tapered as it extended above the roofline. Several round posts, sixteen inches in diameter, rested on a thick concrete porch, and supported the overhanging roof, creating a deep, cool shade. Within the extra wide oak front door was an oval shaped section of heavy plate glass with a beveled edge. Engraved on an eight-inch long brass plate was the name Sunder. The brass door handle curved below the shiny knob, and beneath the nameplate was a solid brass knocker. The glass in the door gleamed. It was spotless. A lawn swing was on one side of the door, and on the other side were two white, wood, reclining chairs with wide arm tops. A detached two-car garage sat at the end of a driveway that extended from one side of the curved driveway. Small grape-size pieces of gravel covered the entire surface of both the curved section and the extension.

"It's so great to be home!" Marshall said, gazing at the house.

"I've your favorite potato salad all chilled waiting for you. Let's get out of this truck." Martha said.

"I'll get your gear for you, Marsh. You go on in with your mom."

"No way, dad," Marshall said. "I'll take that big duffel bag and you can have the B-4 bag. I'm anxious to unpack. I've some little remembrances for you and mom, and Uncle Bruce, too."

The three of them entered the house and Marshall and his dad carried the gear to Marshall's room.

"Everything is just the way I left it!" Marshall exclaimed. He was anxious to go the garage, but thought-*first things first.*

They walked to the kitchen. "Boy, a nice glass of good old high Sierra water will hit the spot," Marshall said. He opened a cupboard, took a glass, filled it and gulped the water.

"Martha," Newell said, "it's time to tell Marshall what we've done."

"What do you mean?" Marshall refilled his glass and looked at his father.

"Son, it was against your dad's wishes. I want you to know that. Marshall, please understand that this store is our future, our retirement, and eventually it will be yours. The thought of being a burden to you, or ending up in the poorhouse, that is just unbearable for your dad and me." Martha fanned her face with her dishcloth.

"Now Martha," Newell stammered.

"Heck, I understand that. Well, come on. Out with it, Mom. What's the big secret?"

"Son, I sold your car, and I'll explain why now..." Martha's voice trailed off.

"You what!" Marshall, interrupted, raised his voice, nearly shouted. "You sold my Model A? I don't believe you! Is this some kind of a joke?"

His voice quavered. Marshall stood looking at his mother and father, an expression of incredulity on his face.

"We were offered an incredibly high price from a collector and we put your money into a savings account for you," Martha said. She walked to him, extended her arm and intended to place her hand on his arm, but he withdrew from her and walked away, across the kitchen and stared at them.

"You had no right to sell my car!"

"You're right," Martha said, nodding, a note of pleading entering her voice. "I've been so worried that we'd go under, lose the store. The owner of Torburn and Fox collects cars. First we said no, but then he told his salesman to tell us that if he'd sell it to him, we'd get preferential treatment on merchandise for the store."

"Oh nuts," Marshall said, "I don't believe this. I'm going for a walk. I'll be back in a little while. I've got to think."

"I just didn't understand that the car was so important to you," Martha said. Tears flowed and she blew her nose on her handkerchief. She picked up a cloth napkin from the kitchen table and opened it and fanned her face.

"Come on, don't cry. It's okay, mother. I understand. You had to sell it. The store and all. I'll be back in a little while."

As Marshall walked towards the front door, Newell stepped close to him and put his hand on his arm. "Want some company Son?" he asked

"Thanks, no, Dad. I'm just kind of surprised, that's all. It's okay. I just want to take a little walk over to the park."

Marshall left the house, walked down the steps and crossed the gravel driveway, then a portion of the mowed lawn and stopped at the sidewalk. He took two deep breaths, then walked in the direction of a small park. Ten minutes later he reached the park, and selected one of the benches. From it he watched two small boys throwing a ball for a cocker spaniel. A stooped man with a cane walked towards him. Marshall hoped he wouldn't sit next to him. The man nodded, said, "Good afternoon, soldier," and continued on.

"Good afternoon my ass!" Marshall hissed, when the man was out of sight. He slammed the open palm of his right hand down on the seat of the bench, and his hand stung. *I guess this is what they mean about crying over spilled milk. In his mind he began to formulate comparisons. Compared to Spike, this is nothing. Compared to Pop this is nothing. Compared to McAdam this is nothing. Compared to Eileen's husband this is nothing. And God knows, nothing compares to Kristine's death.*

Several yards away on a sidewalk three little girls, down on their hands and knees, played jacks. They laughed and giggled and tossed the ball high sometimes, and low sometimes and grabbed for the jacks before the ball bounced twice. Their play made no impression on Marshall until one of the girls stood up and pointed at the smallest of the three and said, "You cheat. You cheat. You always grab jacks after the ball bounces twice!" and the accused girl arose and said, "I don't, either. I don't cheat. You can't even count!" Then she turned and ran crying across the grass area of the park. The other two girls resumed the game.

Marshall rested his head in the palms of his hands. *There's got to be an answer to this mess. What was that line from the Bible that Chaplain Waldron read to me back at Bad Scheidel? ... "When I was a child—something or other, then—I thought as a child, I think that's the way it went, then the important part,—but when I became a man, I put away childish things."* That will have to do, Marshall thought, he sat upright, sighed deeply, and looked back across the park at the children still throwing a ball for their dog. *Okay, so I'm not a child. He sighed again. I do feel sorry for mom and dad, to have gotten themselves into such a position with that damn store.* He stood, glanced at the two remaining children playing jacks. *I've got to get out of this uniform.* He loosened his tie and removed his Eisenhower jacket, carrying it over one arm.

Marshall unhurriedly walked back to his home. He'd been gone a half-hour. Bruce's car was in the driveway. When he entered the living room he saw beyond the dining room into the kitchen where his mother and dad and Bruce sat at the breakfast table. His mother held a cup with coffee and the two men had mugs. They looked up at him as he entered, solemnly, their mouths drooping.

"Hey, this looks like a wake!" Marshall said, then forced a laugh. "Okay, mom, dad, its history. You did the right thing. Sorry. I was a little surprised and upset at first. Come on now, mom, where's that potato salad?"

Marshall walked to each of them and patted their shoulders. They began to relax and move about the kitchen area. Martha went to the refrigerator and returned with a round bowl. Wax paper covered the contents. Newell began to select plates from the cupboard and Bruce said, "That Major Crandall, John, he's is a nice chap. I asked him to join us for some fishing and hunting, Newell."

"Really? Well, he did seem like a friendly sort."

"I'm going to my room to get some things. Will be back shortly. Any chance of getting a glass of lemonade or some iced tea?"

"Coming right up," Newell said. He walked to Martha and put his arms around her. "See. Everything is all right."

"I know him. I doubt if he'll ever forgive me."

"Come on Sis, you know better than that!" Bruce said.

"Oh, I'll make it up somehow." Martha said. She set the bowl of potato salad in the middle of the table, then placed slices of ham and beef and chicken on another platter. Mayonnaise and mustard and catsup were still in jars on the table. Paper napkins were beside each plate.

In his room Marshall quickly unlaced the cords of the barracks bag and soon found both of the Colt .45's, and the thickly padded, carefully wrapped gift for his mother that Eileen had helped him select.

Hurriedly he removed his uniform and in the closet found a pair of Levi's and a white T-shirt. He hung up his uniform, dressed, and took the presents with him to the kitchen.

"Mostly sentimental value, dad, Uncle Bruce. I didn't try to gift wrap them." He handed a .45 to his dad. "This was my .45, and Uncle Bruce, this is identical and it belonged to a good buddy who just didn't like guns. I told him it was for you. I traded our chest holsters for side holsters for you guys. Okay?"

Both of the men studied the guns, weighed them, then removed the clips and checked the chamber of the guns. Almost simultaneously they turned in their chairs and extended their arms, holding the pistols in their right hand, and supporting their right arm with the left hand. They peered across the iron sights, lining up the front and back, then lowered the guns.

"Son, that pipe you mailed was such a thoughtful gift. And this really tops it all! You can't believe how much this means to me," Newell said, and Bruce nodded, and quipped, "Two presents that both smoke, how about that!"

Bruce then added, "If you weren't so darn homely I'd up and kiss you. I'll treasure this! We'll have to go out to the range soon."

Laughter followed, and then Marshall handed the gift to his mother and said, "Bought this in San Francisco's China town. The Chinese lady said the color would go well with anything. I was led to believe it's an antique, of sorts."

"Newell, will you help me with this wrapping? We'll need a knife or scissors, I think."

Almost the size of a basketball, the package was tightly crisscrossed with tape. Newell's pocket knife blade cut through the layers of tape and bulky protective padding material until he finally arrived at the gift wrapped box, a third the size of the original package.

"Do you want me to cut the ribbon?" Newell questioned Martha.

"Thanks, dear. I'll take over now," Martha said. She turned to Marshall, smiling, and said, "This must really be fragile." With her fingers she was able to slip the ribbon off of the container, then set it aside. "I'll save it," She said, quietly. There was still more packing around the teapot, and inside of it. The lid was packed separately. She took the final wrapping off of the teapot and held it up for everyone to see, turning it, looking at the sides and at the bottom. "I just love it! It is so dainty, so beautiful. It's too precious to brew tea in, of course. I'll find a special place to display it." She unwrapped the lid and carefully set it atop the teapot. "What a thoughtful gift! I love it Marshall. Thank you so much. Can I give you a kiss?"

Marshall walked to his mother's side and leaned over and accepted her kiss and hug.

"You've outdone yourself, Son. You sent us so many nice things from Europe. We've shown them off to our friends. I love my little music box so much! And this is really so special," Martha said, looking from Marshall to Newell to Bruce.

"Time to dig into this food," Bruce said and they began to sit down, except for Newell.

"Folks, I've a little surprise for this occasion!" Newell said. He went to the refrigerator and from it brought forth a bottle of champagne. "Picked this up over at O'Toole's place. He said to chill it down good. So, have we some champagne glasses around here someplace, Martha?"

"Well, wine glasses are close enough, I hope," she said, arose and went to a cupboard.

"Bruce, you've got strong thumbs. How about pushing that cork off?"

"Remember the corks flying when Nedra and I were married?" Bruce said. "Golly, I wish she was here to join in on this little celebration."

"We like to think she is watching," Martha said.

Bruce unwound the wire and looked around for a place to aim the cork. "Heck. I'm going out on the back porch. I don't want to put a hole in a wall!"

He departed and shortly they heard the loud retort and Bruce hurried in and went to the kitchen sink with the overflowing champagne bottle. Then he filled each of the wineglasses, and when through, held his aloft and looked towards Newell. "Let's go into the living room and sit down and enjoy this champagne." They followed Martha and sat down, then Newell held his champagne glass up and said, "Just welcome home Son! That about wraps up in a couple of words a jillion prayers all of us have made over the past three years for your safekeeping. We thank the good Lord for bringing you back in one piece."

"Amen to that!" Bruce said.

"We were confident that Jesus would look after you," Martha said.

Marshall felt he should tell them that he was simply lucky, but he was grateful for their concern. So, he said, "I'm certain your prayers helped get me through. But a lot of great guys, well, they were not so fortunate."

"Son, your letter telling us you were on the way home only arrived a few days ago. When you called from Camp Beale, we were astonished," Newell said.

"Yes. Happened pretty fast. Got some good news when I got to Beale. Don't know whether you noticed, but my bars are silver now. I'm a first lieutenant in the inactive reserve. And what really came as a surprise, well," Marshall cleared his throat and continued, "Just a second, I'll get it for you."

Marshall went to the bedroom and returned with the award box containing his DFC. He handed it to his mother. She opened it and looked at the medal, then held it aloft for Newell and Bruce to see. Finally she handed it to Newell. He studied it, then passed it onto Bruce.

"It's the Distinguished Flying Cross. Really came as a surprise. The notification orders must have come by plane, certainly not on a tub like that Victory Ship! Major Crandall advised me of it. The rest of the crewmembers received a Bronze Star. posthumously for Pop. I told you in a letter about his death."

"Well, tell us about that DFC, Marsh. That's quite an honor," Newell said.

"I've a copy of the paperwork in my B-4 bag. On a mission, we had a couple of bombs hang up after leaving our primary target, so we found what's known as a target of opportunity. You never want to bring bombs back. Anyway, we pretty well knocked out a small bridge, and it turns out that our troops were able to catch up with a contingent of SS troops responsible for the Malm`edy Massacre." Marshall paused and looked at them, "You know, about the time of the Battle of the Bulge."

The three nodded. "Heard about it on the radio," Bruce said, softly.

"How'd the other crew members happen to get the Bronze Star. It's a lesser award, isn't?" Newell asked.

"Oh, just because it was my responsibility to find a target, I guess. You see, we didn't want to take bombs back to our base with us. Our priority was to destroy something like a bridge if possible, you know, if we had a malfunction like that, and we didn't want to land with those bombs in the bomb bay. Pretty dangerous."

"So you had to find this bridge, then using that Norden bombsight, you hit the bridge with the two bombs that were left over," Newell said.

"Yes, dad. That's it."

"Okay, back to the dining room folks," Newell said. "Glad you enjoyed the champagne"

As they returned to the kitchen and dining room area, Martha said, "There's so much we want to ask you. We can get the photos you sent and go over each and every one and you can fill us in."

"Yeah. Sometime," Marshall answered. "And you've got to bring me up to date on all of the Chico gossip."

Each filled their plates, sat at the dining room table and the men listened as Martha talked about the church activities.

"That was a lot of lunch, Martha," Newell said, "I think I'll stretch out and take a little snooze."

"You into naps now, dad?" Marshall said, "I'm surprised."

"Well Marsh, I suppose I ought to fill you in on a little health problem that's slowing me down just a wee bit," Newell said. "Last fall I came down with a cold I couldn't quite lick. Doctor Keith first thought I had pneumonia. Then he decided it was rheumatic fever. Apparently there is no medicine to cure it. I guess it's an infection of the blood. Anyway I finally got well, but my blood pressure went wacky. They finally decided that a valve in my heart was altered. You know, like an exhaust valve on an engine. When they get burned they have to be reground or replaced or you lose pressure. Same with the heart." Newell cleared his throat and continued. "Doc Keith says I'll probably live forever. Lots of people are so afflicted, but I won't have quite the stamina is all, and he suggests a nap once in awhile."

"Geez, Dad, I'm sorry," Marshall said. "Why didn't you write me?"

"We didn't want to upset you, Son," Martha said. "Nothing you could do."

"I guess you're right," Marshall said, and in his mind began to feel childish about his reaction to the selling of the Model A.

"I'm heading home," Bruce said, "Have some chores to get caught up on. Want to oil up that gift, too."

"Dad, I'd like to borrow the pickup and take a little ride around Chico, just to see if much has changed."

"If you'll put out any dirty clothes, I'll laundry them for you," Martha said.

"Thanks, Mom," Marshall said. "Appreciate that. I've got to buy a new pair of tennis shoes, too. Maybe do that while I'm out."

"Tonight we're going to have fried chicken, mashed potatoes and cream gravy, green beans and salad, and I baked an apple pie," Martha said, "And Bruce, you're invited, of course."

"Well, I'm going to take off," Marshall said. "Uncle Bruce, I might stop by your place if it's okay. I'd like to play ball with Tara."

"We'll be expecting you."

"The keys are in the truck.."

"Thanks. See you this evening. Have a good nap, Dad. Bye Mom," Marshall said, then took the truck and drove to the center of Chico. He parked on Main Street and strolled along the sidewalk, looking at merchandise in the stores. He noticed his reflection, realized he was stooping, so put his shoulders back.

He saw the SHAPIROS sign extending from the building above the shoe store. He wondered if Mr. Shapiro would look at his feet before he looked into his eyes. Marshall entered the store, said "Hi, Shap. Remember me?"

Mr. Shapiro approached him, smiling, looked downward at Marshall's shoes, and said, "Welcome back to civilization, Marshall Sunder."

He then looked into Marshall's face, and Marshall saw his sad, brown eyes, dark circles beneath them, and felt sorry for the little man. "Are you feeling okay, Shap?" Marshall knew that he and Mrs. Shapiro didn't have children.

"Marshall, I'm sad for the young men who are never coming back to my store. Back to Chico. Too many, too many casualities."

"Some of us were just lucky."

"So, your GI shoes need replacing?"

"Just want to get a pair of tennis shoes right now. Dress shoes later."

"Keds, then. Your size?"

"Shap. Take a look at the bottoms of these shoes. See where they have cracked? Well. The Air Corps says I wear a size nine-and-a-half."

"Awful, awful, that can't be correct. Here, stand up on this sizing bar. Two measurements are needed. This one to the ball of the foot, where the big toe attaches, this bulge, right here, feel that?"

"Marshall looked down and said, "Yes, sir."

"That measurement is the important one. It says size ten-and-a-half. Now the length. Should be at least a ten. I recommend ten-and-a-half because of the other measurement to the ball area. You understand?"

"Sure do. Heck, Shap, I grew an inch during the last three years!"

Mr. Shapiro went to his stock and returned with the shoes. He laced one and asked Marshall to lace the other. "You want a couple of pair of nice white athletic socks?"

"Roger."

Mr. Shapiro obtained the correct size from a rack and Marshall slipped them on. "You fliers and this 'roger' talk. It took us awhile to understand it," he said, then using a shoe horn, helped Marshall with the shoes, instructing him to wear them both to see how they felt. Marshall walked around on the carpet, walked to a full-length mirror and approved.

"My feet feel better already, Shap," Marshall said, laughing. "I'll take them and wear them, and if you've a trash can, I'll throw these old ones into it."

"I'll dispose of them. But remember, Marshall, constant wearing of tennis shoes isn't good for foot health. You should have quality leather, too," Mr. Shapiro said.

"You've a better inventory than we have over at Sierra Mercantile."

"Canvas and rubber and leather are more plentiful than steel, I'd guess."

"So how much do I owe you, Shap?"

"Three dollars for the Keds, the stockings are a gift from Mrs. Shapiro and me. And no charge for the sizing advice," he laughed.

"Come on, Shap. I'll pay for the socks, too."

"Accept them in good health, please."

"Well, thank you sir, and I'll be by next week to get some advice on dress shoes. And tell Mrs. Shapiro thanks, too. Is she okay, Shap?"

"No, not too good, Marshall. You see, her parents are still in Germany. We write, but the mail never even comes back. We send letters by Registered Mail. We receive no replies. Now we are going through the State Department, but it is very frustrating, very futile. We cannot believe some of the things we've read and have seen on the newsreel." He moved his head slowly from side to side.

"Gee, I'm sorry to hear that," Marshall said. "There's a good possibility I may go back on active duty and go to school in Germany. If I do, I'll come by for some addresses. Maybe I can find out something."

"Thank you, young man. You are very kind. Say hello to Newell and your mother."

"See you soon, Shap," Marshall said. He walked out wearing his new tennis shoes, a pair of Levi's and a white T-shirt with a round neckline.

Marshall walked further along Main Street until he reached the Chico Emporium, pushed open the full-length glass doors and entered.

"Can I be of any help?" a girl asked. Looks over eighteen, Marshall thought, as he quickly scanned her physique. He liked slim ankles, a full bosom, and a slim waist above plump hips, all of which the girl possessed, besides having a pleasing smile, a soft voice and wavy brown hair. Then he noticed a wedding ring on the finger of her left hand.

"Need some help with a couple of short-sleeved sports shirts. Been wearing a uniform for three years, so I don't know what's popular now."

"Oh, I don't think men's styles change much when it comes to sports shirts. We've short sleeve in solid colors, mixed patterns, stripes, with a pocket for your cigarettes, some with two pockets.

"May I try on a large, any color, however I like red."

"We keep a good inventory for our Mexican customers. I think it's their favorite, too."

The girl slipped a red shirt from its paper cover, and pointed to a changing room. Marshall slipped it over his head, studied the mirror, and was satisfied.

"I'll just keep it on. And I'd like a pale blue, and a tan, all plain, please."

"If you're going to get dressed up, you know, for church or a wedding or something, I'd like to make a suggestion."

"Shoot."

"These Arrow Dale and Dart models are very popular. Let me measure your sleeve length."

The girl used a tape measure and asked Marshall to raise his right arm. The tab beneath his armpit tickled and he laughed. She then told him to lower his arm and she walked behind him, leaned against his back and he felt the solid push of her breasts against him as she placed the tab at the base of his neck, then stepped to his side and measured the length of his arm.

She then approached him from the front and said, "How about a neck measurement?"

Marshall was delighted to be standing close to a girl and he fleetingly thought he'd ask if he could take her measurements, but the wedding ring vetoed the idea. The faint aroma of perfume excited him, and thoughts of both Kristine and Eileen mingled, melded into one remembrance of love-making.

"In Germany the girls wear their wedding rings on their right hand." Marshall said.

"That's interesting. Why? "

"Something to do with the way blood flows to the heart, I think, but I wasn't paying too much attention when this girl told me," Marshall said, " Was your husband in the service?"

"Yes. A pilot. He's with the Sheriffs Department now. He went from first lieutenant to sergeant and no flight pay, or overseas pay. So we both work. I'm Patricia Barta. Where do you work? Here in town?"

"Ever hear of Sierra Mercantile? Hardware and supplies for farms and ranches. What did your husband fly?"

"He flew the B-17's. And, yes, I know where the store is located."

"Well, you and Sgt. Barta drop by some time and I'll give you the tour."

"Do you have drawings, or prints, you know, for making furniture? A play pen, to be specific."

"For furniture plans you're probably better off over at Skeggs Lumber yard. But we've all kinds of nails and rulers, and screws and nuts and bolts, hammers, screwdrivers, and paint. So come on over."

"Fine. Mr...?" She hesitated.

"Marshall Sunder. Call me Marsh."

"We've had to buy uniforms for my husband's new job. But I've also fixed him up with a nice blue blazer, some gray slacks, white shirts like you are going to buy, I guess, and you're going to need a necktie or two."

"You don't think khaki ties are the in thing?" Marshall said, grinning broadly.

"Assuming you have a gray suit, or a blue suit in the closet at home, you can borrow one of your dad's ties, of course. But I'd recommend a maroon tie and a nice paisley-pattern."

"Pat, just select a couple for me, and I'll be back soon for help with a civilian wardrobe."

"Why don't you open a charge account. We'll bill you monthly. No carrying charges."

"Sign me up!" Marshall said. "I've money in my savings account, but always seem to be short on cash."

Patricia put the application form in front of him and Marshall filled it out. "What branch of the service were you in?"

"Ninth Air Corps. Bombardier Navigator on mediums. E.T.O. Ended up with occupation duty down in Germany."

"I don't see a wedding ring."

"Nope, still free, white and a bit over twenty-one."

"If you want to go out, like on a double date, I've some nice girl friends and I could arrange something; picnic, a weenie bake, a show at the drive-in, a dance, bowling, or roller skating."

"That sounds like fun," Marshall said. He signed his tab and said, "Thanks for the suggestions. I'll be back for the slacks and blazer so I can be presentable. Hope you have a twin sister!"

Patricia smiled as he left the store. In her mind she had just the girl for Marshall.

Marshall returned to the pickup truck and decided to go to the home of one of his high school friends. Within ten minutes he'd crossed town. He drove up in front of the home of Al Rodriquez, and parked at the curb. As he got of the truck and started up the steps to the front porch, in a window by the front door hung a flag with a gold star. A sudden chill gripped Marshall, and he hesitated, thought perhaps he should telephone first before coming for a visit. But Mrs. Rodriquez appeared behind the glass in the front door, recognized him, opened the door, and said, " Marsh, Marsh, come in, it's been years since we've seen you."

She spread open her arms and he returned her hug. Marshall liked the aroma of their home. It was different than his home. He liked the Mexican food that she prepared. It was more spicy, and flavored with a hint of garlic, and all of the large family would tease him and urge him to eat some tiny little-yellow-green peppers. He soon learned he couldn't handle the peppers, but he loved the tortillas and enchiladas and the tacos and the refried beans. And he asked Mrs. Rodriquez one time why they refry the beans, and she laughed loudly and said, "You don't expect us Mexicans to do it right the first time, do you, Marsh?"

"I'm surprised you aren't driving that cute little car with the rumble seat you kids had so much fun in. Now you sit there on the couch. I'm going to get us both a little glass of red wine."

She disappeared into the kitchen and returned with two water glasses of red wine. "Marshall, you are going to love this wine. The boys have become quite the vintners. May get a Veterans' G.I. Loan, and build a little winery. They say that California wines are finally getting the respect they deserve!"

She placed the glasses on a coffee table in front of the couch and then settled in next to him. "How are your folks? Are you going to be working with them at the store?"

"They're fine Mrs. Rodriquez, but first, well, I'm shocked to see that star in your window. No one forewarned me."

"It was Al, Marsh," she said very quietly.

"Oh no!" Marshall moaned. "I didn't know. I'm devastated. My folks didn't tell me!"

"Now, now, Marsh." Mrs. Rodriquez whispered, "I understand. We go to different churches, shop at different stores, travel with different friends, and it was happening so often. There was a short piece in the paper. He was a Marine, you know. He was a first sergeant when it happened at Iwo Jima. We heard from both the Navy and the Marine Corps. They told of his bravery. He was really very heroic. They awarded him a Silver Star and a Purple Heart."

"Jesus, not Al. We were such good buddies."

"We pray for his soul to be in heaven, not purgatory. In a letter he told us he'd violated a commandment,—thou shalt not kill,—but Father O'Donnell assures us he is forgiven and is already in heaven."

"Of course he is in heaven! God, we used to do everything together. Coming to your home for dinner, and being with Hector and Carmine and Mike and Mr. Rodriquez and he came to our house. He was as close to a brother as I would ever have."

Marshall stared into space, sipped some red wine, and continued, "You know, in '41 our football team beat Red Bluff, Redding, Oroville and Marysville before Yuba City knocked us off."

"You kids were a bunch of tough little fighters."

Suddenly Marshall slowly leaned, almost fell sideways and dropped his head into the lap of Mrs. Rodriquez and sobbed, and his body shuddered.

Mrs. Rodriquez held him, patted his shoulders, pulled his head close to her soft bosom and said very quietly, "Just let it out. Just let go. Al was not the lucky one in our family. I'm honored to know you feel so deeply about him."

Marshall sat up then, wiped the moisture from his face with the palms of his hands, and then managed to retrieve a handkerchief from his back pocket, wiped away the moisture flowing from his eyes. "You folks always made me feel like part of your family," he whispered. He sipped some more of the wine, then sighed, and said, "So Hector and Mike are going to grow grapes and make wine. This is delicious, but I'm sure not an authority on wines."

"They've a friend down in Sacramento. Mr. Ashley. A winemaking expert they say, but it's a hobby with him. He's willing to tell them how to go about making fine quality wine, the blending, and all of the different grapes. And he's told them to come up with a good name. Not Rodriquez, of course."

"Why not?"

"Now come on, Marshall. " She laughed and patted his leg. "A smooth Pinot Noir under the name Rodriquez of Chico, California? No, maybe Tequila, but not a quality wine."

"I see what you mean. There are a lot of nice sounding French names. I was stationed near a little town called Denain, but it wasn't in the wine country."

"It has a nice ring, though. And what average American customer would know where Denain might be, or care."

"Well, I can bring over a map of France and the guys can have a great selection of names. How about Cannes, down on the French Riviera?"

Mrs. Rodriquez put her head back, laughed and said, "If you can stand a pun, it sounds too tinny to me, Marsh." She patted his leg, and continued, "It'll only take me a minute to fix you a taco. Would you like that?"

"Wow, that would be terrific. Like old times, eh? Are you sure you've the time?"

"Come now, Marsh," Mrs. Rodriquez answered. "We'll enjoy our wine, and we'll break bread together. Come help me in the kitchen, or just watch, and tell me about your plans."

Marshall explained to Mrs. Rodriquez that even though his dad wasn't in the best of health, he didn't figure that there would be enough income to enable his folks to pay him a salary. "I really want to get some education," he said. "In the Air Corps, a chaplain gave me a book to read and the author is always quoting these famous writers and poets, statesmen and philosophers, and of course, the Bible, and I am so ignorant in those areas. I'd just like to go to school. After high school I was accepted down at Cal, but then Pearl came along and changed everything for all of us. I could probably go on the GI Bill."

Mrs. Rodriquez placed two beef tacos on the kitchen table. "I'll join you dear, one won't spoil dinner for either of us."

"This is nice and crisp and the flavor is terrific. Sure haven't lost the touch, have you?"

"Thank you. And I, too, honestly believe that education is the only way we can get ahead in this world. Carmine is going to night school learning to be a secretary, you know, typing and dictation and using the switchboard. And Hector and Mike are both working and going to night school, and they are writing away for everything they can learn about the wine business."

Marshall finished his taco, used the napkin and said, "If you hadn't come to the door, Mrs. Rodriquez, I don't know what I'd have done, when I found out that it was Al."

"Marshall, I talk to the Virgin Mary every night, and she gives me peace in her answers that only I hear, of course."

"It's going to take me awhile to get it all sorted out in my mind. This dying for our country thing."

"That's where education comes in. You should go to school, Marshall."

"Well, thank you. Say hi to the family. I'll get back to see all of them in a few days." Marshall said, "And you know, Mrs. Rodriquez, that Tequila distilled by the Rodriquez Brothers in Chico, California, does have a nice ring to it."

"Off with you now, and my best to your folks."

Marshall kissed Mrs. Rodriquez, walked to his truck and drove directly to the home of his Uncle Bruce.

Bruce was standing on the front porch, his muscular forearms crossed, and the lowering sun cast a shadow across his face. His nose had been broken slightly in an altercation with a mule's hoof he said, and he said it added to his handsomeness. Anyone can have a straight nose, he joked.

"Well, young man, Tara and I about gave up on you."

"Gee, Uncle Bruce, I'm sorry. I stopped by the Rodriquez's. I didn't know Al got it. Had a long visit with his mom."

"Imagine they're taking it pretty badly, like all parents."

"Of course, but they seem to get support from their priest."

"All kinds of sayings to make life bearable. What's that one, 'Man can't live by bread alone,' it's something like that?"

"I guess."

"Come on in. We'll have a little shot of JD. Tara can wait for the ball game."

"You kind of dropped out of the church when Aunt Nedra died, Uncle Bruce."

Bruce took glasses from the cupboard, put ice cubes in each, poured two ounces of the bourbon and sat down at the kitchen table and nodded for Marshall to join him. " I don't think your mom can understand my feelings regarding Nedra. None of the cliché's, none of the Bible passages made me feel anything but more bitter. Take the 23rd Psalm, Bruce paused, sighed deeply, then continued, "The morticians print it out by the dozens on those little forms, and then fill it in with a born and died date and pass it out at the service. It didn't cut it for me."

"Uncle Bruce, do you believe in God?"

Bruce stood and walked around the table, then very quietly said, "I believe there is an order to the universe: has to be: must be some universal truth. Yes, I believe there's a God, but I feel He is very indifferent to the human race. We're just a small part of the equation. I simply don't think He'd hear me, or pay any attention, if I got down on my hands and knees and prayed. As a matter of fact I did. But it didn't help Nedra." Bruce sighed. "You know, Marshall, I work at being optimistic about life. Cynicism, pessimism, they are our enemies. That attitude ruins any chance for a healthy frame of mind. I feel we must choose optimism. It's sometimes a tough choice, but it does create possibilities, you know, to keep on living and not burden others with your problems." Again Bruce sat down opposite Marshall.

"We never talked like this before, Uncle Bruce," Marshall said. He emptied his glass. "Time for another belt of old JD?"

"Hell yes." Bruce said, and stood up, selected some ice cubes and for the first time used a one-ounce jigger to measure the bourbon. He splashed water over the contents and returned with the glasses and sat down and glanced at Marshall.

"Son, you seem to hold this stuff pretty well, but you've got to learn to pace yourself."

"Yeah, Uncle Bruce, since I got home I realize I've got a lot to learn about a lot of stuff." He touched his glass to that of his uncle. They both laughed quietly.

"While we're in such deep thinking, let me tell you about your Granddad and Grandmother Kane; about how your grandma thought. It was on a Fourth of July and your mom and I and our parents had finished dinner and were sitting out on their porch, just relaxing. Conversation got around to how lucky we were to just being born white in the United States. Dad kind of nodded his head, like he was tipping his hat, towards the flagpole on the porch, stares at it a bit, and then continues, and says 'And thanks to our Lord. It's to Him we owe our good fortune.'

"I was pretty young. Maybe sixteen. So I asked your grandmother where they got their religious beliefs, and she said they were handed down from one generation to the next, and I said, 'Well, don't you ever question what people tell you, like preachers and such?'

"Your grandmother said, 'I have faith. I have faith in God and in Jesus.'

"Well, I persisted, and said, 'mom, describe faith. What is faith?'

"It got very quiet. I remember that so well. Then a slight breeze came up and the flag fluttered, moved away from the flagpole.

"'Son, I've faith that a breeze moved that flag of ours, but I can't see the breeze. I can wet my finger and hold it up and feel the coolness and know its direction, but I can't see it or touch it or feel it, or hear it. I just know it's there. I can see it move leaves and make the windmill wheel spin, and I know it can cause white caps on the lake. I can hear it howl, but that's because something is resisting it. I understand barometric pressure and storm fronts and all of those scientific things we hear about on the radio, but I don't need to complicate my feelings about faith in God and Jesus. My eyes don't have to see something, or I don't have to touch something, to have faith. And that's as good as I can do to answer your question. I have faith that a breeze is moving that flag.'"

"'Thanks, mother,' your mom said, and I nodded and said, 'Yeah. Me too.'"

"So you've got faith, Uncle Bruce?"

"Oh, of sorts. Like I said, I believe there is some order in the universe, and to me, order means intelligence, and I might as well call intelligence God as anything else."

The men sat, silently, and sipped from their glasses of bourbon. Marshall cleared his throat and spoke. "When are you going over to Red Bluff for that redwood?"

"No big rush. But I want to get that deck down before the rainy season. Why, you getting horny?"

Marshall laughed, "Hell, Uncle Bruce, I'm always horny."

"Hey, Tara, get off that couch. You need some exercise," Bruce said, standing up.

The Black Lab jumped down off the couch, immediately found a tennis ball and dropped it at Marshall's feet, where it bounced and she caught it before Marshall could grab it.

"Okay, outside you two. No roughhousing in my mansion," Bruce said.

"Can we go down to the pond, Uncle Bruce?" Marshall asked, "She's so beautiful when she leaps into the water."

"Of course. Hell, she thinks she's a seal, anyway."

Marshall grabbed the tennis ball away from her successfully and ran down a dry, straw-colored grass slope towards a half-acre pond. There were bass and catfish in it, but the water temperature was too warm for trout. Marshall threw the ball high in the air. Tara watched it, and then ran towards the bank and launched herself into the air, stretching, her front legs tucked, and her back legs already paddling before she hit the water and submerged in a white splash. She surfaced, swam directly to the ball, grabbed it in her jaws, and swiftly swam back towards shore. Marshall accepted the ball, now willingly dropped at his feet, and they repeated the exercise several times. Marshall made an errant toss and the ball landed in a clump of dry branches.

"She can't get that, Uncle Bruce. She'll cut her self all up fighting those branches."

"She'll know when to back off," Bruce said, laughing.

"Like hell!" Marshall yelled, also laughing. He pulled his red shirt and T shirt over his head, kicked off his Keds, took off his trousers, and in his shorts, dove into the pond. He swam to the area where Tara was struggling and pulled her away from the branches. She swam in circles then, and Marshall struggled with the branches, separating them, and finally was able to reach the ball. Tara was swimming towards him, so he tossed it over her head towards shore and followed her towards the bank.

"Wow, Uncle Bruce. I'm winded as hell. Boy, am I in lousy shape."

"Okay, you dogs, out of my pond," Bruce laughed. "You're coughing up more water than you did when the good Reverend Harms baptized you a few years ago."

"You know, Uncle Bruce, that clown didn't even tell me I could hold my nose. I about drowned."

"But he saved your soul, young man. That's what counts."

"If you say so, Uncle Bruce, " Marshall said, then added, "how about a towel?" as they walked towards the house.

"Sure, and when you're dried off, use the rest of it on Tara. Time is moving along. Your mom and dad will be expecting us."

"Man, I feel better. Playing with Tara is good medicine."

Marshall dried off. He put his wet shorts in a paper bag to take home. He dressed, rubbed Tara down, then she ran out to the dry grass in the yard and scrunched along on both sides until she was satisfied. She jumped into the back of the pickup truck and Bruce adjusted her harness.

Bruce drove toward the Sunder residence. " Uncle Bruce, I enjoyed our little bull session. I guess I'm still so shook up, learning about Al Rodriquez. He was one of my best friends."

"I didn't know all of your buddies, Marsh. Losing a single one is awful," Bruce said very softly.

When they all reconvened that evening at the Sunder home, they were subdued, all of them, and spoke quietly to one another. The dinner and dessert that Martha prepared was praised. After the dishes were cleared and washed they sat in the living room and listened to music from the radio.

Marshall broke the silence when he said, "dad, did you and mom know that there's a gold star in Mrs. Rodriquez's window. That Al was killed on Iwo?"

"Why yes, Marsh , we read about it in *The Union*."

"I don't understand why you didn't tell me?"

"We just didn't want to upset you when you were overseas, I guess, and you've found out now, before we could tell you."

Marshall had a difficult time comprehending that his folks knew about Al Rodriquez, and never told him. Indignant, he decided to try to forget it. He would go visit the Rodriquez family in a few days.

"I'm going over to see all of them in a few days. Like for you to accompany me, if you want to."

"I'll join you any old time," Bruce said. "Thanks for the dinner, Sis. I'm on my way." Bruce arose and turned towards the front door. He paused when Martha spoke.

"They live in a different part of town," his mother said, glancing at him with what he determined was a critical gaze.

"What's that supposed to mean?" Marshall asked. He abruptly stood up, shook hands with Bruce, which surprised Bruce, looked at his dad for a slit second, hesitated, started to walk towards his bedroom, then turned, looked at his mother. He selected a chair furthest from his parents and again sat down. He sighed and slumped in the chair. "It's been a busy day. Right? Thanks for the swim, Uncle Bruce. Maybe there'll be some good news on the radio."

"Why in God's name did I say that?" Martha whispered, looking at Newell.

"Let's try to forget today and start over tomorrow. Okay?" Newell said, arose and went to Martha and bent over and kissed her. Again Newell sat down, and both of them turned back to and looked towards the radio, as Bruce looked on. He stood up then and turned towards the front door.

"Good night, Bruce," Newell said.

"Well, good night, folks." Bruce sighed, and departed, slowly moving his head from side to side.

He pulled the heavy front door with the oval glass closed behind him. They expected to hear his steps moving across the porch, but there was a pause and door reopened and Bruce poked his head in and said, "It was still on the porch." He lifted his arm and continued, "I'm delivering *The Union* to you personally, and wait until you see who made the front page!"

Marshall and his father and mother hadn't moved from their chairs, sitting and seeming to stare at the radio, listening to the music. They simultaneously turned to Bruce.

"Will you look at this," Bruce said, grinning broadly. "Picture of our very own hero right here on the front page with some General pinning that medal on your chest, Marsh!"

Newell jumped up from his chair and strode across the room and accepted the newspaper from Bruce.

"Hot damn!" he said. "Look here, Son, Martha, isn't this just great!"

On the lower section of the front page was a photo of General Brogan shaking hands with Marshall, with the Distinguished Flying Cross resting on his chest, held by a ribbon tied behind his neck. Marshall stood at attention, erect, his shoulders back, and was unsmiling.

"My goodness!" Martha exclaimed. "We'll have to buy several copies and mail them to all of our relatives!"

"They must be hard up for news to put that on the front page," Marshall said. He looked at the photo and estimated it to be about four inches by five inches in size. He handed the paper back to his father. "That General was just passing through. Likes publicity."

"By golly, everybody in town will see this. Our Boy!" Newell said, looking at Bruce and Martha.

"See, if you just wait long enough, something good is bound to happen," Bruce said. "We're all proud as heck of you, Marsh, whether you like it or not. Come on, darn it, smile!"

"Thanks a lot, Uncle Bruce," he grinned then and noticeably began to relax. "I think I'll take the sports section and read it in the kitchen." Bruce and Newell and Martha studied the front page.

Newell opened the paper and handed the sports section to Marshall. He nodded to all of them, smiled, and went to the kitchen table and began to scan the page.

CHAPTER 25

▼

ADJUSTING

In the spring, thousands of acres on the flat valley floors north of Sacramento are diked and flooded to grow rice. As the green shoots of rice appear above the water, so too, emerge the blossoms of the fruit trees.

The variety and purity of the colors excited Marshall: the white blossoms of the cherries, presenting an entire orchard of thick white clouds, and it is the same with the blossoms of the plums, and of the apples, with shades of pink, and the pears and the almonds. Along the highways and in the foothills grow the wild scotch broom, with yellow blossoms, and there were clumps of red bud, wearing a rich lavender hue.

As the days grew into weeks Marshall was aware that his parents, especially Martha, seemed to assume that he had made a commitment of some sort to the business. He resented this attitude, yet found he was slipping into the role of the obedient son, not wishing to alienate either parent. Deliberately he found a way to separate himself from their routine and went to the State Department of Employment and found work in the orchards and packinghouses. He explained that there wasn't enough to do at the store to keep him busy, plus it was a way to earn extra cash.

In the morning, when going to work at Sierra Mercantile, Marshall rode in the truck with Newell and Martha. Sitting in the middle, Martha was constantly directing their vision out of one side of the windows or the other. "Look at that row of forsythia. It's as bright and cheery as the Scotch broom." And she would advise Newell to slow the truck as they approached a home where several dogwood trees were loaded with white or pink blossoms. At another curve in the road she'd point out the pink and white azaleas and admired the landscaping of homes that included rhododendrons, heavy with lavender blossoms. Another morning she would ask Newell to drive a different route so she could show them a whole hillside of the butter-yellow Emperor daffodils. "And if you'll go by the Scroggins, you'll see the most magnificent assortment of tulips. They simply plant every color imaginable, and you know how expensive tulip bulbs are. My, I wish I had time to garden," Martha said.

As the joyous spring colors fade, the fruit sets and matures. In the region north of Sacramento, as far north as Red Bluff and Redding, peaches and plums, walnuts and almonds, and plump grapes are gathered from the trees and vines and trucked to the long wood sheds, sorted, graded, packed, iced down and shipped to the eastern cities

During the spring, Marshall worked in the orchards, as well as in the store, and later, in the summer, worked in the packinghouses. His muscles responded and became hard and very little body fat was on his torso.

There was one particular girl that seemed to always be on the edge of his vision at the packinghouse. She smiled at him and he smiled back, assuming they must have been in high school at the same time. Yet he could not help glance at her bust line, accentuated by the tight cotton blouse that clung to her, wet from perspiration: eagerly noticing that her nipples noticeably pushed at the fabric of her blouse. She had to be about his age. People seemed to be in a holding pattern, from their mid-thirties to sixty-five, But, with memories of Kristine foremost in his mind, he forced himself to ignore the urge to speak to the girl.

How long must I mourn? Ha! Mourn! One look at Eileen and you quit mourning! Maybe you just mourn for yourself? Is that it?

The peak of harvesting passed and the housewives, students and transient farm workers vacated the orchards, vineyards, groves and the packinghouses and sheds. He heard several people say, "Money earned will help at Thanksgiving and Christmas it will go a long way towards college tuition."

Now, as before the war, Marshall understood that the transients were mostly the leftovers from the dust bowl, some still saving their cotton-picking sacks, as they follow the maturing of the crops. A few of the more industrious would accumulate enough money to buy a car, and become permanently located somewhere in the long valley, where their new harvest would be opportunity: an opportunity for a better life in California. Others moved on, followed the harvesting of different crops, as they matured in some other region up and down the fifteen hundred miles of the state.

From the exhausting work, Marshall generally slept well. Occasionally he dreamed of the figure of Kristine covered by a bloody sheet, and would sit up in bed, staring at the dark wall, and perspiring. Time seemed to drag, and Marshall was surprised when Newell and Martha and Bruce invited him to join them for the Fourth of July parade and the fireworks display at the fairgrounds. When they returned home they shared a watermelon, eating it on the porch in the warm evening. He thought, *maybe I ought to go down to Berkeley and see if I can get into Cal.*

Marshall had forgotten how hot the summers were in Chico. Shimmering heat waves rise in continuous vertical ripples from the Sacramento and San Joaquin valleys, from Redding in the north to Bakersfield in the south. Heat reflects off of the white concrete highways, and black macadam roads, and off of the gravel roads and dusty dirt roads. The one and two story buildings, the churches and the city hall of the small towns seem whiter, glaring in the late summer. Even the sky seems to lose its cool blue to the still, hot whiteness that rests heavily on the resident's shoulders.

Uncultivated fields and the rolling foothills are knee-deep with sun-toasted, golden, khaki-colored wild grasses. Clumps of massive white oaks dot the valley floor. As the hills begin to rise both in the east and west towards the higher elevations, the variety of trees render a compatible mixture: the live oak and scrub oak, the digger pines and the manzanita, and appearing at three thousand feet the ponderosa pines proliferate, becoming the dominate species of a forest of sugar and ponderosa pines and fir and cedar.

Had the air not been so dry, the humidity so low, and the living so slowly paced, the heat would be unbearable. It is a stiff, crackling heat melded with the relentless brightness of the sun, filling the three-hundred-mile long valley as does heat from the furnace of a blacksmith furnace. Faces of both young and old are toasted brown and wrinkle too soon. Shiny mirage-lakes are so commonplace they are ignored.

There was still employment in the packinghouse, so Marshall worked there as well as at the store. But what consciously bothered Marshall most was his inability to escape his anger, his frustration about the sale of his Model A. Outwardly he displayed a facade of indifference. *The damn car was just a piece of cold machinery, and God knows the store needs merchandise. If you'd only asked me! Oh, bull shit, I'd probably have said okay. But it was MY car! You should have found another way to get the damn merchandise!* So, inwardly he seethed, while making an effort to find some answers to his frustration in the book given to him by the chaplain.

One morning after breakfast he decided he didn't want to go to the store. It was boring. It was their store, not his.

"Well, boys," Martha said after cleaning the breakfast dishes. "Time to put away some of that nice big shipment from Torburn and Fox."

"Dad, I've got some personal business. I'll come in a little later," Marshall said, and thought, *Screw Torburn and Fox!*

"Fine."

"What kind of business?" Martha asked.

"He said personal, Martha," Newell said, brusquely. Marshall was both surprised and pleased.

"Oh," Martha said, and brushed her wavy hair away from her glasses. She fanned her face with her apron, then removed it and hung it on the doorknob.

When they departed, Marshall walked behind the house to the garage. He swung open the doors, but it was dark.

He peered into the darkness and finally his eyes became adjusted and he saw the four blocks, ten-inch by six-inch, stacked against the wall, that had held his Model A car up off of the floor. Until now, he had avoided going into the garage. He picked up a small stone and threw it against the back wall of the garage. The thud reverberated, then the sound diminished. Marshall saw his old bicycle standing near the blocks. He guided it into the bright sunlight outside the garage. It was clean and apparently was occasionally being used. The tires were firm.

Marshall guided the bicycle around to the front of the house, and went to his bedroom. In his dresser he found his bankbook and shoved it in his shirt pocket. In a kitchen drawer he found some stout rubber bands, and returned to the bicycle. Able to expand the rubber, he pulled them over his right shoe, folded the trouser tightly around his ankle and calf and the rubber bands held the cloth in place.

Marshall mounted the bicycle and pedaled towards the edge of Chico where Bowman Ford was situated. He'd seen a few used cars on the lot adjacent to the showroom. He parked the bicycle at the front door, entered and looked around the showroom.

"Can I help you?" a salesman asked.

"Yep. Is Mr. Bowman around?"

"In the office over there," the salesman said, pointing to a row of glass-enclosed offices. "Follow me. How about a cup of java?"

"Sounds good to me." Marshall accepted the coffee in a large mug, then followed the young man, who paused and knocked at the door of one of the offices. Mr. Bowman looked up, then stood up and said, "Come on in, Marshall Sunder! Damn, kid, you look just great. Saw that picture of you in *The Union*, and your dad told me you've been helping out at Sierra."

"Yes sir," Marshall grinned, transferred his cup of coffee to his left hand, and accepted the hand of the owner of the Ford agency. "Sure great to be back. I haven't seen Bud since I got home."

"Well, Bud stayed in Marine Corps. He's a Captain now, and says he'll stay in for twenty years, and if we still own this agency, he'll put me out to pasture and take over."

Marshall gazed around the showroom floor. There were two 1941 sedans with white side walls. "Guess the new cars will be showing up soon?"

"Damn few, and I've got dozens of people waiting. The cars are the same models as before the war, only new. No time for tool and die work yet."

"So what can I do about getting some wheels? Any old pickup truck will do, a half-ton would be great. Nothing all gussied up. I just need something to get to work, and out to the river when the salmon run starts."

"Well, I'm going to ask Don Hernrich here, my sales manager, to show you what we've got. He was a flier, too."

"Hi Don," Marshall said, extending his hand, "Air Corps?"

"Naval aviator. Graduated down at Corpus Christi in Texas, and then shipped back to California. Taught cadets down at Livermore."

"Hell, teaching cadets! Now that was dangerous!" They both laughed. They sipped coffee as they looked at the few cars on the lot.

"Well, friend, I'm not sure how much you want to invest, but we've got a $250.00 price tag on a nineteen thirty-two Ford half-ton pickup. It needs a paint job, but otherwise it will do what you spoke about with Mr.

Bowman. Straight six. Lot of torque if you want to haul a fishing boat behind it."

Marshall followed the salesman to the car. Walked around it, then climbed in and Don said, "Start her up," which Marshall did. He revved up the engine, held it there, listening to the sound, and then gradually let it slow to an idle.

"Tires are pretty good. Transmission and rear end are okay. We put new brakes on all of our used cars. Want to take a spin? New paint job will run you another fifty bucks. Your choice of color."

"Nope. Engine sounds smooth enough. I can spray paint it. I'll take it as is."

"Let's go see Mr. Bowman."

"Well, that didn't take long, fellows. See anything out there you like, Marshall?"

"He likes our little half ton-pickup, sir," Don said.

"Well, that's been sitting there quite awhile. How about two hundred bucks and a full tank of gas?"

"Hey, I'm not here to chisel you, Mr. Bowman."

"If you want it, take it. However, I would appreciate you selling it back to me or trading it in here, when you want a later model."

"Of course," Marshall said. "I've got to ride on over to the bank and get some cash. They ought to be open by now." He started to walk to the parked bicycle. "Will be back in a little while."

"Hey, throw that bike in the back of the truck. Come on back at your leisure."

"Thanks a lot, Mr. Bowman, and thank you, too, Don, for the coffee." Marshall drove away in the truck.

Mr. Bowman spoke to the salesman. "Wish I could do better for these vets. He's another of a friend's sons, Newell Sunder, a business man here in town. And, Don, your commission will be on the two hundred and fifty figure."

"Well, thank you sir. And that truck was under priced as it was. I think you should have asked $300.00 for it"

"What the hell!" Mr. Bowman exclaimed and laughed, "What's the old saying? We only go this way once. Don, I know about car dealers' reputations, but, if you screw a veteran, well, that I just can't do. Understand?"

"I guess," Don said. He shrugged his shoulders and refilled his coffee cup.

Marshall drove to his home in his half ton-pickup. His dad and Uncle Bruce felt Mr. Bowman had done him a favor, and his mother asked him not to park it in front of the house.

"Wait until I get about five coats of candy apple red on this little baby and you'll beg me to park it in front of the house!" Marshall said, and even his mother joined in the laughter.

The late-summer evenings were warm, and often Marshall sat on the porch with his parents and Uncle Bruce.

"Think I'll wander into town and see if I can run across any of my old high school friends." Marshall said.

"Have you been over to Gus Harmon's place, the *Shuffle-em?*" Bruce asked. "He's got pool tables, couple of card tables for the cribbage and pinochle players, a dance floor and a nickelodeon, and he's pretty strict about who he serves alcohol to."

"You seem to know all about the place," Martha said.

"You know, sis, it might be fun for Newell and you to go over and maybe dance a little," Bruce said. "How about it? Why don't you get out of the house?"

"Newell and I are going to listen to the radio."

"Want to join me, Uncle Bruce?" Marshall asked.

"No, Marsh. Thanks. I'm heading up to Red Bluff in a few minutes, and when that moon gets up high, I won't even need my headlights. I'm taking Tara with me."

Marshall stood up and said, "Well, I'm taking off. See you all in the morning." He exited through the back porch door and they heard his engine and the gravel crunching in the driveway as he backed out.

"That kid's gotta have some company his own age," Bruce said.

"He used to be a good mixer. Seems awful tense since he got home," Newell said.

"If we could get him over to the church, there are really some nice young girls he could meet."

"Forget the matchmaking for awhile, Sis. Leave him alone. Let him come around at his own pace!" Bruce said, then stood up. "So, it's good evening, folks. Thanks as usual for the hospitality. See you in a couple of days."

"I think Bruce is right," Newell said. "Come on Martha, let's just enjoy the fresh air. Sit next to me in the swing for awhile. Full moon is coming up. It'll light things up real nice in a little while."

It was almost dark when Marshall parked in a space in front of the tavern. He turned off his headlights, took his keys from the ignition and stepped down out of his truck. *I'd be flattered if someone wanted to steal this rig!* In the east he could see the white roundness of the top edge of the moon.

Marshall had been in *The Shuffle-Em* with his dad and Uncle Bruce before the war. The owner, Gus Harmon, sponsored the Pop Warner football and the American Legion baseball teams, coaching both off and on, and appeared at many of the high school football games to watch his cheerleader daughter.

Marshall remembered his dad telling him that Mr. Harmon really went by the book. Unless with a parent, he didn't allow anyone under twenty-one in his establishment. Marshall had asked, why?

"A liquor license is hard to come by. Only so many of them, and lots of politics involved now to get one. If he sold an alcoholic beverage to a minor, they'd close him down and he'd never get another. The pool table and the cards and the dance floor would be left, but a lot of folks like to have a beer or some highballs when they go out."

Curious if he'd remember anything about the place, Marshall decided to go in and have a beer or two. He looked around the large room with a high ceiling and huge beams supporting the roof. He remembered the large framed picture depicting Custer's Last Stand, and there were paintings of horses and cowboys and a several black and white enlargements of scenes of Yosemite. Mounted trophy heads of deer, pronghorn antelope, a cougar, were high on the walls, and a head mount of a black bear gazed down at the patrons. They'd been given to Gus by hunters who had them mounted and then found they had no space to display them. The mahogany bar was fifteen feet long, and behind it was a polished mirror the same length. Individual stools lined the front of the bar, and a brass rail was available for a customer's feet. He recalled the words of his Uncle Bruce; "Gus won't have brass spittoons in his place. He won't use one, clean one, or ask anyone else to do such a menial task."

From the nickelodeon the music of *I'll be Seeing You* played softly enough for two couples to dance in the privacy of the dim lights. Marshall could hear the clicking of the ceramic balls at the far end of the room. Two men played pool and another watched from an elevated wicker chair. The card tables were empty. If anyone played poker, money had to be out of sight. Gambling was illegal.

Marshall walked to the bar and was surprised when Mr. Harmon greeted him. Over six feet, he was solid, and above a grinning face he had a shock of brown wavy hair, graying at the temples. He wore a white apron. The collar of his white shirt was open and tufts of graying hair were visible. "Welcome home, Marshall Sunder. About time you came by to see old Gus!" He extended his arm and hand across the bar and Marshall shook it and Gus responded with a firm grip.

"Let me buy you a drink! I saw that picture of you in *The Union* with that general pinning a medal on you. We're all proud of you. Your dad and Uncle Bruce drop in once in awhile. They kept me posted about your whereabouts during the war. Hell, I think the last time I saw you was when Chico played Redding in thirty-eight. You kids waxed those lumber men!"

"What a memory, Mr. Harmon," Marshall said, laughing, delighted to be recognized. "Any good draft beer?"

"Coming up. Pabst okay?"

"Heck, anything is fine by me, and thank you."

Marshall sat on the barstool, sipped the beer from a frosted stein, and looked along the length of the bar wondering if he'd recognize anyone. Beyond two men, a brunette leaned forward against the bar, peeked out in front of the men. She smiled and said, "Hi Marshall! Remember me?" She giggled, then said, "American History, Miss Dunlap? Does that ring a bell?"

"Gosh yes! Demonico, isn't it? Carla?"

"Yep! Go to the head of the class! Bet you remember my nickname too. I hated it then, Now I don't give a damn." Again she giggled.

"Let me think."

"T.H. Carla! Top Heavy? And they didn't mean my brains!" She tipped her head back and laughed, straightened her back, and her breasts pushed tightly against her blouse. Bet you remember me now!'

"Heck, Carla, I remember you for your nice laugh," Marshall said, and did recall that she had flaunted her attributes and that the undeveloped girls in his class made jokes about her.

"You married, Carla?"

The two men at the bar sitting between them, turned their heads back and forth, smiling as they listened to the exchange. They had leaned backwards a little to let Marshall and Carla talk. They finished their drinks, then pushed their empty glasses back, away from them, and departed, and one grinned and said, "Now you can have some privacy."

Three other men entered and sat on the stools. One man, not with the pair, sat at the far end of the bar, near the entrance. Marshall thought he recognized him. His profile was familiar, but the light in the room was dim. He would investigate later. Marshall moved to the stool beside Carla.

"You asked me if I'm married? Nope! But I was, honey, and once was enough. Do you remember Doug Lewis? His idea of being tough was to beat me up. He fell in love with my measurements, but really, he got married to avoid the draft. I divorced him, but the draft board never caught up with him. He's selling war surplus now. He is a cruel son of a bitch, Marsh."

I'm sorry, Carla," Marshall said. "I suppose the war brought out the worst in some guys."

"Marsh?" Carla inquired, "I think I seen you out at the packing house. You follow the crops?"

"Not really. I work at Sierra Mercantile. When things are slow, I pick up jobs anyplace I can find them. But yes, I am working at the packing-house part time. And I do think I saw you the other day, too, but I didn't think about our school connection."

"Well, I do follow the crops and the money beats the hell out of baby-sitting and it seems that's about all I'm good for," Carla said, then looked towards Gus. "Want to draw me another, honey?"

"Put it on your tab?"

"I'll settle everything up tonight, before I leave," Carla said, then stared into her beer stein.

"Living with the folks?" Marshall asked.

"Yep. With my mom when I'm in Chico. I managed to get my name changed back, too. My dad tried to warn me about Doug, but would I listen? Ha! Cute guy, Doug. Dimples and cleft chin, blond wavy hair, cute little nose, everything a girl dreams of. But, boy, was he stuck on himself! For him, I was just a good lay. Thank God, no kids." Carla sipped from the beer stein, then said, " Know what, Marsh, I'm going to night school learning to type and take shorthand and operate a switch-board. The lady at the state employment office said I should take a course in English and quit my cussing. She says I butcher the king's English. She also says she won't give me a referral slip to a good job the way I talk. Isn't that a bitch!"

"I understand. My pop got on my case about swearing, especially in front of my mom. Got to be a habit while I was in the service, I guess. And more school for me? You bet I am going back. Education is the only chance people like us have, Carla."

"I was my own worst enemy, Marsh. High school was a lark. I belonged to a girl's club, we jitter-bugged, joined the Frank Sinatra fan club, dated, sang, skinny-dipped, stayed out late, but they still gave me a diploma, which don't mean much. Guess I should have studied more."

"Come on, Carla, don't put yourself down!"

"Ha, I think I averaged straight D's!" She snickered. "Want to play Liars Dice for another beer?"

"Maybe later, but listen, Carla, you talk like your life is behind you. It's ahead of you, but you've got to do something about it."

"'Preacher Sunder', that would be a good nickname for you!" She smiled slyly. "Come on, let's roll for one." She shook one of the thick round leather dice boxes, held the box to her ear, rattled the dice, laughed and rolled the dice out atop the bar. "My smile and you know what, get me what I want," she laughed loudly and winked at Marshall. "Your roll, honey. Beat that," she said, looking back to the dice on the bar top.

They played one game, Marshall lost, paid for a round of beers, then they quit and both sat and stared at their steins.

On the dance floor one of the couples stopped and walked to the nickelodeon and put several quarters into it and made their selections. One of the men that had entered earlier sat next to Carla. He wore a white T shirt and had rolled the sleeves up high, almost under his armpits, into little scrolls. A pack of cigarettes was held beneath one of the scrolls. Both of his thick arms were tattooed. His Levi trousers were worn very low, and supported by a wide leather belt with a heavy cast metal buckle. His hair was cut in the 'butch' style.

The other man was slim, needed a shave, and hung his head, rested his elbows on the bar, seemed to stare at it, then at his drink and nodded once in awhile, as the larger man talked incessantly.

From the nickelodeon the notes from the selection, *Deep Purple*, were heard.

The man next to Carla turned to her. "How about a spin around the floor, babe?"

"No thanks," she said, and turned back towards Marshall. But the man persisted and stood up, and from behind her placed his hands beneath her armpits and attempted to lift her off of the barstool.

"Come on honey, I won't bite," the man whispered.

"NO! Leave me alone," she said, jamming her elbows back against him. She turned to Marshall, "Isn't that the number you asked me to save for you?" She stood up then and stepped towards Marshall.

"By golly, that IS our song," he said and led her to the dance floor. He smiled at the man.

Skeptical, the man glowered, then stood aside and watched them dance.

"You know that guy, Carla?"

"Never saw him before. He smells bad! He's got BO. Needs a bath."

"When we go back to the bar, you sit on the other side of me, away from him."

"I think he's an odd-ball!"

Deep Purple ended, and then another tune, *The Last Time I saw Paris*, followed and they continued to dance. At first Carla kept a slight space between them, and seemed frightened from the encounter, but with his hand in the small of her back Marshall pulled her close to him. She relaxed then, and they danced smoothly. *My God, that nickname really fits. She's a brunette Ginger!* Carla danced almost on her toes so that she could touch her cheek to Marshall's. He was delighted when she began to hum, then quietly sang the words of the song.

After the third number they returned to the bar. "Do you come here often, Carla?"

"Oh, not really. If there's work in town. Usually after night school, or a picture show. Seen both movies. And Gus lets me run a tab. It don't amount to much, but I don't like to carry any money around, to speak of."

Gus approached them and asked, "Those beers warm up? I can toss them. You want to start over?"

"Yes, thanks, Gus," Marshall said. "Maybe you ought to start a tab for me."

Gus took their steins and as he did the man who had asked Carla to dance, approached her, and slid a shoulder into the space between Marshall and Carla, resting his elbow on the bar top.

"Hey, babe," he said, "here's a handful of quarters. Let's go pick out some nice slow tunes."

"Fella!" Marshall raised his voice and made eye contact, as the man turned, "You don't seem to understand. She doesn't care to dance with you."

"Butt out! I'm asking the lady!"

Gus returned with two steins of beer. He overheard part of the conversation. "Hey!" Gus said. "Something troubling you, fellow?"

"I just want to dance. You got a nice dance floor. Any problem with that?"

"It becomes a problem when the lady says no!" Gus said, "Isn't that simple enough for you?"

"Okay, okay..........where's the john?"

"Men's room is down that hall," Gus said and nodded his head.

When the man returned he stopped very close to Marshall, his shoulder brushed Marshall.

"You a vet?" he grunted.

"Yep. Air Corps. You?"

"Infantry. We did all the dirty work for you guys while you rode around bombing us."

"We made a few mistakes."

"You a pilot?"

"Nose gunner."

"Shit!"

"Look silver tongue, why don't you and your buddy there just leave us young lovers alone?"

"I get it. You're a lover, not a fighter!"

Again Gus approached and overheard part of the conversation.

"Okay bud, you're eighty-sixed. You and your friend take off."

"Relax boss. I just don't like these stuck-up Air Corps ass holes."

Suddenly Marshall jumped off of his barstool, but Gus reached across the bar and shoved him down, "Cool it, Marsh!"

"Come on lover boy, why don't you step outside and we'll just have at it."

"Get the hell out of here!" Gus shouted. "There's the exit," and he pointed to the door. "Understand?"

"Got the guts to come outside, lover boy?" The man again addressed Marshall.

Marshall stepped towards the man and reached for the collar of his T shirt. The man stepped back and nodded to his friend.

"He's pissed. Let's see if he's got any guts!"

Again Gus grabbed Marshall from across the bar, and nearly jerked him off his feet. He put his face and mouth close to Marshall, lowered his voice and hissed his words.

"Now listen! Damn it to hell! They'll gang up on you. I've heard about that big bastard. He'll whip you with that belt. That buckle can kill you. I don't want a brawl in my place, but here, put these rolls of nickels in your pocket. If it gets to a fistfight, grip them in your hands. If he goes for that belt grab it and jerk him off his feet. But don't go out that front door. Hear me! Now I'm calling the sheriff!" Gus walked towards the telephone at the end of the bar. "Damned full moon," they heard him murmur.

Marshall stared at the two men. The smaller man worried him most. He was wiry and revealed no emotion. He stared at Marshall.

"Marsh, you sit down! You know they are baiting you!" Carla said.

"Well, honey, the Air Corps taught us a couple of dirty tricks. If I have to, I have to," Marshall said.

Abruptly Marshall then stood and with quick strides walked towards the large man, who was startled, and Marshall pushed him backwards, off balance. He turned to the other man and said, "Get your ass out of here, now! This is between me and this fat prick!"

Marshall turned away and out of his eye saw the big man start to slide the belt out of his Levi's, but his friend hadn't taken a step towards the door. Marshall turned quickly, lunged and grabbed the loosened belt, stepped back, and jerked the buckle free from the Levi's and the man lost his balance and fell forward, striking Marshall in the face with his fist as he fell. Marshall flung the belt across the dance floor. The heavy buckle banged against the leg of a card table and the belt curled around the leg.

Surprised, the patrons became motionless, staring at the scene. Then just as the slim man started to run towards the belt, Marshall heard a glass bottle shatter.

The man nearest the door had smashed off the base of a beer bottle against the edge of the bar. Holding the neck, he held the jagged edges upright, and yelled, "Hey gringo! Yeah, you! Forget that belt. Stop right there! Now get your skinny butt out of here or I'll spill your belly! Pronto!" The thin man retreated, backed out of the front door, holding his hands up, his eyes now open wide.

Marshall stared at the man holding the broken beer bottle, then shouted, "Mike! Mike Rodriquez!" And in the same instant spun back to the larger man who had risen, and now with his arms stretched out in front of him, his hands spread open, charged towards Marshall. With the exception of Mike Rodriquez, the rest of the patrons stood transfixed. Gus had phoned the sheriff, and Carla moved behind the bar and stood beside

Gus, her eyes wide, staring, her mouth agape. The Andrews Sisters were singing *Apple Blossom Time*.

Now it was the Air Corps cadet training, not lessons from his dad or his Uncle Bruce, plus a surge of adrenaline that equipped Marshall to fight. The instant the man's hands reached Marshall's throat, he joined both of his hands together tightly, then flung both of his arms upward, and then smashed them down and his gripped fists struck the bridge of the nose of his tormentor, and simultaneously, and with vigor, raised his right knee into the groin of the man. The instigator roared in pain and fell towards Marshall, again driving a fist into Marshall's face. Together they fell to the floor. Marshall was dazed and the large man stood up, looked at Marshall, flat on his back and ran towards him. And again Marshall remembered, they had practiced it by the hour. Quickly he pulled backwards the toes of his left foot, clamping it behind the man's calf, and pulled it forward as he slammed the bottom of his right foot just below the knee of the big man, who groaned, cursed and fell backwards.

Marshall jumped to his feet and the large man was rising too, exclaiming, "I'm going to kill you!"

In an instant, from his pockets, Marshall retrieved the rolls of nickels, gripped the solid roundness in each hand and as the man lunged towards him Marshall swung his right arm upward, an uppercut motion, and his knuckles stung as his fist crunched the man's jaw. Marshall stepped forward and with a left cross, smashed the side of the face of the man. The two blows staggered him, and he looked for help, but his friend was gone. Then he stood upright and roared and again strode towards Marshall, and this time Marshall struck him flush on his jaw with a right cross, and the man fell to his knees.

Behind the bar, Carla cringed each time she heard the crunching, hard sound of Marshall's fists striking bone. Her eyes wide, she gasped, and held her hands to her mouth. Gus was moving out from behind the bar, watching the fight.

Marshall stood over the man, still on his hands and knees, then he jammed a knee into his ribs, pushed him, and the man collapsed onto his back. Marshall jumped astride him and placed both of his knees on the elbows of the man's turned-back arms. Gasping for breath, Marshall leaned over the face of the man and allowed blood from his nose to drip onto the face of his tormentor.

"I give. I give!" the man shouted, spitting blood, trying to turn his face away from the red drops of Marshall's blood. The drops filled his eyes. He felt the hot liquid dripping on to his lips, and again he shouted, "I give!"

"Give shit!" Marshall hissed. "Okay fuck head. Recite your serial number! What outfit were you in? What was your rank? Speak, or I'll smash your nose all over your ugly face!"

The man stared upward, blinking, turned his head from side to side trying to dodge the hot blood dripping from Marshall's nose. He coughed and tried to turn his head away from the flowing blood.

"You never got out of the States, did you? Come on, out with your serial number!"

"I don't remember. I give!"

"You never forget your serial number! Never! You were a fucking draft dodger. Right!"

"No! I tried to enlist. I'm 4F. I got flat feet," he growled, shaking his head from side to side. "I'm a four-effer! God damn it! Get the fuck off me!"

"You are a liar! Now tell all these nice folks, loud and clear, 'I am a liar.'"

"Oh shit! Let me up! Yeah, I'm a liar! Now get off me!"

Marshall was startled to hear the quiet, firm command, "Okay Sunder, that's it. Let him up," Gus spoke quietly, as he patted Marshall's shoulder.

Marshall crawled off of the large man, stood up and swayed over him, and Gus grabbed his arm and steadied him. Another man stood beside Gus.

"Carla has some ice for you. Go on over to the bar."

Immediately Carla placed a wet towel with ice onto Marshall's bloody face.

Gus turned to the sheriff, "Well, Captain Holcomb, it was nice that you could arrive for the main event."

"I'll haul them in if you'll file charges."

"Naw. I think you probably know the Sunders. This bloody one here is their little boy. We'll ice him down good and he can tell the folks about the door he walked into! Do what you want with this bum and his buddy outside." The sheriff nodded, then looked towards the bar.

"Well, guess I'd better say hello, Sunder. I didn't recognize you," Captain Holcomb said. He nodded his head and then advised the man to get in the car and with his friend, leave town. "Don't want to see either of you in Chico again. Understand!"

The big man nodded and outside the door, found his companion waiting. He spoke, and the small man listened, then turned an entered the bar, found the belt and backed out of the tavern with it in his hands. Together they walked across the parking lot in the bright evening. The full moon illuminated the area, as if a huge klieg light was flooding the town in a clean whiteness, creating sharp contrasting scenes of blacks and whites. The slim man helped the other into a sedan and they drove off.

With his fingers, Marshall had to squeeze the rolled coins out of his hands. His fingers and knuckles ached. He tossed the rolls to Gus and said, "Thanks Gus, using those, that was something new, for me."

"An equalizer. Brass knuckles are illegal. If you'd gone outside, that other punk probably had a couple of beer can openers in his pocket. They use 'em to rip a guy's cheeks open. And some of those punks have bicycle chains to whip you with."

"So, I'm lucky! Thanks coach!"

Marshall walked to the end of the bar. Mike Rodriquez had picked up shards of glass and placed them on top of the bar. "You got a broom back there, Mr. Harmon?"

"Relax, Mike. I'll sweep up."

"Hey Sunder! You fight dirty." He laughed and walked to Marshall, opening his arms and then drew Marshall up close to him and hugged him. "Mom said you came by."

"Yeah, Mike. Jesus, about Al, I'm so sorry," Suddenly Marshall sobbed.

"Come on, relax, buddy. Clean up and get some more ice on that face! The family is handling our loss, Marsh."

Carla walked around the end of the bar carrying a wet towel. She continued to wash away the blood from his face. He winced.

"Your whole body is shaking, Marsh! Gus crushed some more ice. We'll hold it on your nose and cheeks. Are you hurt bad?"

One of the men who had been dancing before the fight walked up to Marshall. He rested his hand on Marshall's shoulder and looked into his face, and said, "I was with Patton. I'm sure you know we had a great respect for you fliers."

"Well thanks. Mutual, of course!"

"Glad you beat the shit out of that punk."

"Man, I'm about fought out. Combat was never this tough! Think I'll have a boiler maker," Marshall said, turning to Gus. He took a seat at the bar and Carla sat beside him. He opened and closed his hands.

"Same for me, please," Carla said.

Gus delivered the drinks, then leaned across the bar and at the same time placed a half dozen quarters on the bar top in front of Carla. "Honey," he said, "Get that nickelodeon going. Everyone is still in shock."

She did as he requested and when the first number began to play, Gus raised his voice. "Okay folks, the floor show is over and the bar is open!"

Couples again began to dance. Carla returned to the barstool next to Marshall. She picked up the towel with the crushed ice and held it up to one cheek. "A few minutes on each side, and on your nose, ought to help a little." Both of them grimaced when they gulped the bourbon from the shot glass. They chased it with a sip of beer, then turned with their backs to the bar and watched the couples dancing.

"Guess my damn nose has finally stopped bleeding. You let me know when you feel like dancing."

"Are you kidding, sweetheart? I wasn't in a fight! You tell me when you want to dance. I'm always ready!"

"Then let's have at it," Marshall said, and guided her to the dance floor.

Before he pulled her close to him he glanced down. Her blouse was low cut. *Top heavy is right. Thank God my eyes and my balls are okay! I hope that bastard suffers! Damn, I hope I crushed his nuts!* Marshall and Carla finished the dance, returned to their stools, and drank from the steins, then returned to the dance floor for the next selection.

"Carla," Marshall whispered, "you mentioned that you've skinny dipped. My Uncle is out of town and he's got a great little pond, nice clear water; not too cold now; grassy area to sit on. Lots of privacy. What say?"

"Sure. Might even get a chance to reward you for protecting me!" Carla winked at him.

Marshall laughed and guided her back to the bar. He caught Gus' eye, "Mind running a tab for me? We're taking off."

"Okay," Gus smiled, "I've another bowl of crushed ice. Take it, with that towel, and keep it on your face till it's all melted. Better soak those hands in the ice water, too. This is coach Harmon talking."

"Roger," Marshall said, nodding his head.

"Gus, it's time for me to settle up. Don't want to get obligated," Carla said, she smiled, and flirted with him.

Gus walked to the cash register and flipped through a dozen small tabs, "Eight bucks and we're square."

Carla turned away from Marshall and opened her small purse. She peeled off nine individual one-dollar bills from a small roll, and placed them on the counter. Gus took the money, counted it and said, "One too many," and pushed a dollar bill back to her.

"That's a tip, handsome." She pushed the dollar back and patted his hand.

"Thanks sweetheart. I'll start a new tab."

"Just never let me get into you for over ten bucks, Gus. That's a lot of dough."

He nodded, grinned and wiped the bar top with a clean white towel.

As they walked towards the door, Marshall stopped when he reached Mike. "Good luck with the winery, and hey buddy, where in the hell did you learn how to break a beer bottle like that, you know, and not cut yourself. The Marines?"

Mike grinned. "Naw. The movies. John Wayne!" He nodded at Carla, smiled, and said, "Hi T.H."

Marshall and Carla stepped out into the bright evening and he escorted her towards his truck. "Your chariot awaits," He opened the door for her and helped her climb into the truck.

"Well, that's a first!" Carla said, she immediately slid across the seat and was close to Marshall when he climbed in behind the steering wheel.

"A first?"

"Come on, Marsh. I open and close my own doors!"

"I'm going by my house for a minute to grab a couple of towels. Okay?"

"Well hurry up. I'm getting anxious!"

"Marshall laughed, "You know how to shift gears?"

"Certainly."

"Then I can hold onto something soft while I steer and use the clutch. I'll tell you when to shift."

Marshall started the truck, backed out and drove towards his home. Then he put his right arm around her shoulders and cupped her breast with his hand. When he put in the clutch and said shift, he squeezed her breast, and she put the lever in the wrong place and the loud metallic growl caused him to release his hold and reach for the gearshift.

They both laughed. Marshall parked on the street in front of his house, let the engine idle, and entered quietly. In the bathroom cupboard he retrieved two large bath towels, and from his dresser a clean shirt, and in his dresser found a Pro Kit. He stripped the top blanket off of his bed; tiptoed across the floor and cautiously pulled the front door closed behind him.

Relieved that no one heard him, he trotted back to the truck, jumped in and drove to his Uncle Bruce's house. He parked in the back, away from the street. The light from the moon was so bright he didn't need a flashlight.

"Heck of a time to ask you, Carla, but can you swim?"

"That's one thing I'm good at. My pop threw me in over my head when I was a kid and my mom screamed, and then I remember him saying, 'She's too tough to drown. Nature will teach her to swim,' but I do remember him jumping in and helping me and how later he really taught me. I loved my dad."

"I got a blanket for us to sit on, and a couple of towels. I even brought a clean shirt. I'm getting rid of this bloody thing right now, and he pulled it over his head, and threw it toward Bruce's porch.

"Gosh, it's like daylight out here, but the water looks black." Carla walked up to Marshall and ran her fingers through the wiry hair on his chest. "Nobody ever stood up for me before, Marsh." She paused, then added, "I mean like that." He put his arms around her and held her for closely. She continued, "Do you hear that bullfrog?" He listened to the deep ba-roomp sound. "Do they bite or sting?"

"Sure, but I'll protect you! Come on. Last one in is a nigger baby!" Marshall shouted, laughed, stepped back, took off his tennis shoes and white sweat socks then pulled down his trousers, tossed them aside, removed his underwear, and ran towards the pond and dove into it. Against the blackness of the water, the white spray of the splash was a brilliant, chalky white and the gem droplets glistened in the dark, suspended in space, before disappearing.

Turning away from Marshall's vision, Carla stood on the blanket and removed her dress, folded it carefully, placed it on the edge of the blanket, then removed her bra and underpants, folded them, too, and placed them beside her dress. She kicked off her shoes and then ran, as had Marshall, and dove headfirst into the pond.

Marshall swam to her. "I think we can stand up here," he said. She pushed her wet hair back from her face, smiled and slowly stepped across the soft muddy bottom and then reached up and put her hands behind his neck and parted her lips. His hands first cupped her buttocks, then hurriedly he moved them up the curve of her back, and allowed her to move away a bit as he sought her breasts. They kissed. He gasped when he began to caress, to fondle her breasts, realizing now that they were indeed large, firm, and perfectly formed.

She pulled his head back and continued to kiss him. She lowered her hand and touched him, then pulled away and laughed, and said, "I suppose you want to do it to me now."

"Not to you, sweetheart, with you!"

Carla laughed, and said, "Another first. I'm used to this 'we' stuff."

"Come on, Carla, making love has got to be as much fun for you as for me."

She smiled and moved close to him and accepted his caresses. "You're cute, Marsh." They kissed again. "The bottom of this pond is kind of muddy. I can feel it oozing up between my toes."

"Yep," Marshall murmured.

"Want to try it right here?" she asked. "If you can lift me, Marsh, I'll wrap my legs around you. Think you can hold me?"

Marshall immediately responded, lifted her, and together they accomplished the joining of their bodies. "God, Carla, you're so warm in there." Marshall whispered. He supported her by gripping her buttocks and again their mouths were joined in a wet kiss. Her firm breasts pushed against his chest, but he was afraid to release his support, holding her gyrating buttocks, as she simultaneously pushed her abdomen into his, while he still wished to touch her breasts.

"Wow," Marshall groaned, "I'm entering heaven!"

"I'm happy. That's your reward for sticking up for me," Carla whispered, then sought his lips again.

"How about you? Did it happen?"

"I'm a slow poke, Marshall. When you rest, will you do it to me again?" She giggled, then added "You know you, Marsh, we were keeping time with that big old bull frog's voice."

"Ha!" Marshall exclaimed and then laughed, "Let's swim a little. Then I want to admire your nakedness in this moonlight. What do you think?"

"Why not? Marshall, I'm not used to guys being nice to me. They just want me to lay down spread my legs, climb on, bang me, groan and moan, slap my butt, kiss my boobs, then go to sleep," Carla said. She pushed away from him, then slowly backstroked around the pond. "Look Marshall, the man in the moon is staring at us. Do you think he's blushing? What happened to the stars? I don't see any?"

"I bet the man in the moon is just laughing, and because he's so bright, the stars don't have a chance."

"I never heard crickets so loud, Marsh," Carla said, "they make more noise than those old frogs."

"Just be happy there's enough of a breeze to keep the mosquitoes away." Marshall swam too. He gulped water and spat it out. The cool water felt good on his sore, burning cheeks and nose. His knuckles ached. Marshall lowered his mouth into the water and roared and shook his head, blowing both air and water loudly through his lips. Then he swam close to the bank and climbed out of the pond, pushed his hands through his hair and walked to the blanket and began to dry himself.

Carla finished swimming, and as she walked naked towards him he marveled at the fullness of her breasts. Equally well formed were her hips and slim legs. The brightness of the full moon bathed her in white light and to Marshall she seemed to be a moving, living, marble statue.

"So you don't remember the girl called 'top heavy'?" Carla asked, observing his stare.

"Well, I guess high school kids wouldn't have said 'well endowed' now would they?"

"Nope. I know. To you guys, big boobs mean sex. To me, it means my back hurts holding the damn things up!"

"And I haven't even had a chance to kiss them!" Marshall exclaimed. He finished drying and threw the towel onto the blanket. Carla dried her body, then tried to dry her hair, and flung the wet strands about, shaking her head from side to side.

"Well, Marshall, if you want to kiss my boobs," she paused and laughed, "you'd better get started. There's a lot of me!" They both dropped to the blanket and Marshall rested beside her and he grasped one of her breasts in each hand and began to kiss them. He held her protruded nipples in his lips. "What a shame," he whispered, "only one mouth!" He dropped his hand down between her thighs and began to gently massage her.

Carla whispered, "What are you doing, Marshall? Why are you touching me there, like that?"

"Christ, my lovely, it's supposed to feel good. Doesn't it?"

"I just don't know. I guess so, but I'm supposed to slap you. My mother told me to never touch myself there, or allow a man to touch me there. 'Play with yourself and you end up in the insane asylum', she told me."

Whispering too, Marsh said, "Well, she's wrong. Our scoutmaster explained all that stuff. You know, take cold showers or go run around the track a few times, but jacking off sure as heck didn't send you to the nut house. Carla, you know I prefer to make love over talking about it, and from a very good source, I learned that the key to a girl's joy, is right there," and Marshall again manipulated his fingers gently.

"It tickles. Oh, my, that really is beginning to excite me! God, Marsh, I'd love to have an organism!"

"A what?"

"You know, like you men have."

Marshall stifled a desire to laugh. *God, that would be cruel!* "Well, honey, you just lay back and let me continue, and believe me, this is what God created us for. We were designed for this!"

Carla began to relax, and Marshall thought he heard her sob. He was able to continue with his fingertips and still lean over her and kiss her breasts. *Magnificent! I can't believe this is happening.*

"Carla, I'm about to burst. Are you ready for some lovemaking?"

"What in the hell have we been doing?" She laughed. "My God, I do love this 'we' approach! It's me and you, baby. You tell me what to do, Marsh."

"Let's face each other and see if we can get joined up. Kind of slide our bodies together."

"Wow, that's different. I'm so happy I feel sinful!"

"Well, don't bounce around too much or it'll be over for me. Slowly, slowly."

"You wouldn't dare end this! Oh, please, please, hug me tight!" Carla moaned. "Oh, gosh, Marsh, it's happening. Oh, my, my, just keep doing that slowly." She dropped her head towards her chest; her body shuddered, and then sensing that Marshall was spent, she leaned backwards, away from him, then raised herself and lay down on top of him and sought his mouth with her lips.

"I actually had an a organism, Marsh. Thanks to you."

"So honey, now you understand what this 'we' approach is all about."

"Now I know what some of my girl friends mean, the excitement, the .. oh, hell, I don't know how to say it."

"Carla, I won't ruin it for you if I say something about the expression you used, describing it?"

"All my husband ever said was, 'kiss me quick I'm coming!' That sounds so corny."

"No, I mean the word you used is pronounced orgasm, not organism. Let me hear you say it once."

"Orgasm?" she whispered.

"That's it. No big deal, just thought you might like to know, what with taking English lessons and stuff."

"Honey," Carla giggled, "I don't care what the hell you call it, I just want more of this 'we' stuff that causes it. Hell, I thought I'd do you a favor and it's turned out the other way around! But, Marshall, then what does organism mean?"

"Oh, I think it covers living things, like us, or that big old bullfrog, or mushrooms. Stuff like that. Living things."

"Hmmm," Carla said, then sat up and began to pull a comb through her damp hair. She shook her head from side to side and the water jewels sparkled in the moonlight.

"So where did you get so smart about girls?"

"Oh, a college girl I met."

"Guess I'm a real dummy, Marsh, not getting that word right."

"Oh no, Carla, not at all. Talk about getting words fouled up, I'm the dummy! My pilot, Frank, went to college before signing up and he was always straightening me out. One time I asked him, 'What the hell does pot-pour-e mean Frank,' and he explained, and then said you pronounce it 'pooh-puree, or something close, and then another time I said some occurrence was the real eppa-tome, and then he said "You're right Marsh, but you pronounce it eh-pit-o-me."

"That woman at the employment office told me to buy a dictionary and learn how to use it," Carla said.

"Good, and don't believe that stuff about going insane. That's a lot of nonsense. I think our folks must have told us things like that to keep us out of trouble," Marsh said.

"Oh BS, my mom is just plain ignorant. I sure hope I take after my dad. He was the smart one in my family. He tried to advise me. Didn't want me to marry that jackass." Carla sighed, "Well, at least I didn't get knocked up, so I suppose I can't."

Marshall thought, that's a relief, then spoke. "Guess it's time to fold our tent and head for home. I've got to show up at work at seven. It must be about two, now," Marshall said.

"Can't we just lay on our backs for a couple of minutes and get moon tanned?"

"Ha! Where did you come up with that? Sure, tan yourself Carla. You know, it's so bright we could read a paper." Then Marshall rested on the blanket next to Carla. She began to hum.

"That's nice. What is it?

"It goes, 'When you wish upon a star, makes no difference who you are', and so on. So now we can make our wishes to the man in the moon! God, what an evening! What a morning!

Carla rolled on to her elbows and looked directly at Marshall. "You know, Marsh, you really scared me when you were fighting that guy.

"Oh? How's that?"

"You made sort of growling sounds, like an animal, you know, like when a couple of big dogs are fighting. But ever since then, when we danced and made love, well, you've been polite and even gentle."

"That's funny, isn't it. You know, I honestly feel do I could have killed the bastard. I never felt that kind of rage or hate during combat. I guess it was 'cause he was pestering you."

"He was a mean son of a bitch and I'm glad you beat him up," Carla said, then sighed and added, "Time to get my clothes on and go home. Well, I live over by the high school. I have to get up early, too. And, I have to go see what kind of jobs are available. Today, or rather yesterday, was my last at the packinghouse. Have to pick up my check, too."

"I guess this has to end," Marshall said. "Carla, I really wish I could paint or draw, or take artistic type photos, then I'd record your beauty forever. You know you are something special."

"How sweet. Since you aren't an artist, guess you'll have to settle for being a lover," Carla said, then giggled. "Marsh, one of the girls at the cannery saw your picture in the paper getting a medal. Were you wounded?"

"Hell no. Only blood I saw was my own when I got in a fight with a pilot. Of course I got sheet burns on my elbows and knees a couple of times."

"Carla giggled, then said, " Marshall Sunder you are impossible!"

Marshall chuckled, then stood up and began to dress. "Carla, I've kind of a stupid question to ask you?

"Oh?"

"Another girl called me cute. Now, for damn sure, that's something I'm not. What do you mean when you say that?"

"Cute?" Carla sat naked in the bright moonlight, her legs crossed Indian fashion and combed her hair. "I guess it has to do with respect. Better than nice. Kind of sexy. Respectful. That kind of thing."

"Thanks, I think," Marshall said. "Well, I hope you find work in town, Carla. Now that I know you like to swim." Both of them laughed. Carla began to dress, turning her back to him.

They returned to the car. And Marshall drove towards her home. Carla leaned against him, rested her head on his shoulder and placed her left hand on his thigh. She hummed *Deep Purple*.

"Your folks apt to be awake?" Marshall asked.

"Mom's a sound sleeper. Works hard out at the cannery. My dad got killed a couple of years ago over at that lumber mill at Eureka, just after he'd been promoted to supervisor. Big old redwood logs rolled over on him. It was awful. Poor guy."

"Geez. I'm sorry."

"Yeah," Carla sighed, "thanks."

He located her home, parked and climbed out of his truck, walked to the passenger side and opened the door for her.

"Bye," she said, and kissed him, then walked swiftly to the front door. The moon was still bright. It had almost completely traversed the sky from the High Sierra towards the Pacific Ocean. Carla stopped at the front door and turned and waved.

Marshall drove back to Bruce's house, found the key to the front door beneath a large rock, and entered the house. He went directly to the bathroom and applied the medication from the pro kit, found the alarm clock, set it and flopped down on the guest bed.

He groaned when the alarm awakened him. Marshall went out of the house, looked around, found his discarded bloody shirt, the towels and blanket and rolled them up and tossed them into the back of his pickup. He stopped at the Gold Nugget Diner for a quick breakfast.

In the darkness of the shaded packinghouse the banging of hammers, nailing the tops onto the wooden crates, and the rumbling of the conveyors rendered a din that protected Marshall from idle, unwanted conversation. Marshall looked for Carla, but could not find her. Finally, exasperated, he went to the foreman during his lunch break.

"Sid, I haven't seen Carla around this morning. Have you?"

"Christ! What the hell happened to you?"

"I walked smack into that damn forklift last night after work. Somebody didn't lower those arms. What about Carla?"

"Oh yeah, her friend, Carmen, checked in early and said Carla joined a couple of car loads of workers heading down to Salinas. They got artichokes and lettuce, plus the canneries at Monterey to keep them busy. Carmen will mail her final check to her. Why?"

"Oh, I just wanted to tell her about a book I read."

"Hell, I didn't know she could read!" Sid said, and laughed loudly, then patted Marshall on the shoulder.

"I really think she's trying, Sid. Making an effort. Did you know she's been going to night school here in Chico?"

"News to me," he said, winked at Marsh and continued, "Man, that girl is built like a brick shit house. With that body she don't have to be smart, but I'll have to say this, Carla's a hard worker."

"Well, I'll get her address from Carmen. Thanks. And, Sid, will you give me a medical slip so I can visit Doc Keith. My vision is still kind of blurred."

"Sure, kid. You look like hell! And say, I think you know this job is closing down at the end of the week."

"Yep. It's been fun!"

"Fun? Ha fella, you are a real clown!" Sid said, shook his head and walked away. "Ain't you glad the company has insurance!"

Doctor Keith examined Marshall's vision and said it was all right. "You can get aspirin at the drug store for the pain. So you walked into one of those big steel arms on a forklift?"

"Yes sir."

"And when you fell, you hit the concrete floor with the knuckles of both hands?"

"Yes sir."

"Tell me, Marsh, what does the other guy look like?"

"Come on, Doctor Keith, would I try to kid you?"

"Certainly. But you'd better come up with a better story for your mom!"

"I'll think of something. Can you bill the packinghouse for this examination, Doc?"

"For what? Helping you create a fib?" They both laughed.

"Doctor Keith, while I'm here. How's my dad doing?"

"He'll be okay, if he takes it easy. That distorted aortic valve makes his heart pump a bit harder. Sorry we can't do anything to help him. There's no cure. And, Marsh, when your folks see you, just remember that little saying on my wall." The doctor grinned and nodded across his office, and a framed slogan read, *"When in doubt, tell the truth"* Mark Twain.

CHAPTER 26

▼

THE LETTERS

Major Crandall was right when he said there would be a profound difference when Marshall put on civilian clothes, Marshall mused. In the Air Corps, he'd become accustomed to the respect that came with the wings and the decorations, and while he didn't expect anyone to notice him, the act of being saluted when approached by an enlisted man was a sort of payment for all of the rigors of cadet training, plus getting shot at in Europe.

Now he blended into the northern California scenery, feeling not unlike any fenced pasture or tree or distant mountain. He was a part of the hot summer breeze and of the cloudless sky. And he understood and accepted the fact that only his immediate family really cared whether or not he existed.

Kristine still dominated his memory: the timbre of her voice, its resonance, the fragrance of her hair and body, the softness of her breasts, her laughter, and her eyes, seeming to look deeply into his, to question him, his motives, to search and penetrate, sometimes suspicious, most often sparkling, and finally evidencing a renewed hope for the future. She was bright and feisty and he liked that. Then all of that had been destroyed. He longed for the touch of her lips upon his closed eyelids. Any attempt to forget her was rejected. Suggesting that he erase her from his memory was a desecration of their friendship, of their love. He felt as though he was in love with a ghost.

The noise, the clangor was his sanctuary. The steady, rumbling noise of the machinery, the conveyors and the hammering created insulation. He was surprised that when they were outside of the sheds, just a backfire of any engine startled him, actually made him jump once, and he looked around, hoping none of the other workers noticed.

In his B-26 home, a cough of one of the big Pratt and Whitney engines could mean losing the engine, and a single-engine on a B-26 could mean sudden death. Marshall mulled over his thoughts, and began to become annoyed with them and wondered if other fliers had more easily forgotten such trivia.

When thoughts of the encounter with Eileen interrupted his memories of Kristine, he felt he had violated his love for Kristine, yet he would grin. In San Francisco, those couple of days had been an unexpected, unplanned sexual experience, a relief valve of sorts for both of them, Marshall thought. What kind of a jerk would turn down the love offerings of a beautiful woman? It had been fun and exciting and when his mind would contemplate a journey to Los Angeles to see her, he would again feel guilt stricken, simply because of the memory of Kristine. Her tragic ending seemed to engulf him, to hang over him, still filling him with remorse and with guilt feelings because he'd selected that idiotic little bridge at Bad Scheidel. *It was the damn Germans! It was the Nazis that invited even the destruction of a small bridge. Maybe I ought to join the American Legion. Might find some old friend there from high school days that served in the ETO.* But Marshall did not join the Legion, and began to withdraw more within him as he worked long hours in the sheds and at the hardware store.

At times he felt a little guilty about his one-night-stand with Carla. *What a piece! What a body! Hope she gets back in town soon. Hell, maybe I ought to go to Salinas.* He laughed aloud when he recalled her saying she wanted an organism, but then he felt ashamed that he'd laugh at another person's ignorance, and tried to save face by admitting his own ignorance of word pronunciation.

With his thoughts now again on Carla, Marshall drove into town and sought the help of the woman clerk at the bookstore and purchased two selections. He wrote a note, put it with the slim, compact books which they wrapped for mailing.

Dear Carla, You got out of town before I could give you these. The lady at the bookstore recommended them. I admire you for going back to school and hope that's what you are continuing to do down at Salinas. You know, my mother does tutoring for some Mexican people who are having a difficult time learning English. They want to become citizens.

I bet you could find someone like that, which would give you a head start, so to speak. You know, and I hope this won't hurt your feelings, but this is something my mom drilled into me back in high school days. Never use the word 'seen', unless you put the word 'have' in front of it. I have seen it, instead of I seen it. Another one that mom drilled into me was never to start a sentence with 'me,' for instance I wouldn't say, me and Carla went dancing. I'd say— 'Carla and I' went dancing,' or 'we' went dancing. You do like that word ' we' don't you! I feel sure you know you shouldn't say ain't. That is covered in one of these little books. You're about three words from being acceptable to that lady at the employment office. I'm sorry about your dad. If you ever feel the need of some fatherly advice, go see my dad or my Uncle Bruce. Bruce Kane. Give me a buzz when you return to Chico. Good luck. Your new-old-friend, Marsh.

The post office was still open and Marshall mailed his package. He felt a bit self-righteous, and he remembered the guidance he'd received from the squadron chaplain. *You don't have to be* a *chaplain to want to help a friend!* Contemplating whether to return to his uncle's place, or to go home, Marshall decided that he might as well face whatever his mother might have to say. Back in his truck he tilted the rear view mirror and looked into it. His eyes were getting blacker and he realized it would be several days before they returned to normal.

After driving to the rear of his home, Marshall retrieved the blanket and towels and his shirt. He folded the blanket neatly, and carried the towels and shirt loosely. The back door slapped the framework behind him, making a muffled noise, as he walked directly to the back porch and put his shirt and the towels in the clothes hamper. He'd wash them later.

With the blanket under his arm, he started towards his bedroom. Newell and Martha sat at the breakfast table reading the *Union*.

"Hi Dad, Mom," he said, and quickly continued, "Got in a fight over at *Shuffle-Em*. Couple of out-of-towners insulted a girl. I knew her in high school. Sheriff Holcomb showed up and told them to get out of Chico and stay out. Mr. Harmon and the sheriff supported my part in the ruckus."

Without waiting for an answer or a comment, Marshall hurried to his bedroom with his blanket under his arm. He placed it back on his bed. In the bathroom he washed his face and hands and wetted his hair, then combed it. He glanced in the mirror and grimaced.

Marshall returned to the kitchen and said, "Saw Doctor Keith for a few minutes. He asked to be remembered. Said you are doing great, dad."

"Are you sure that you're okay?" Newell asked.

"Yes, dad, I'm fine. Frankly, I was going to try to come up with a story about walking into the arms of a forklift. The doc saw through it. Said you and mom would, too." He grinned sheepishly.

"My God, Marshall, " Martha said, raising her voice, "you are hardly home and you're into a fight! I can't believe you! Have you no respect for us: for your father: for me: or the business! I don't want you in my store looking like that. What will customers think?"

Marshall turned angrily, and started to stalk out of the room. "Hold on, Son!" Newell said. He then looked at Martha.

"Martha, you calm down too!" Newell said, with authority, raising his voice, and speaking with a belligerence Marshall had never before heard.

"Son," Newell continued, " you cool it, also." He then looked towards Martha, "As for the store, it's our store, Martha, not your store, if your memory needs refreshing!"

"I didn't mean my store," she stammered.

"Son, listen to me. You are welcome in OUR store! Whether there will be anything worth inheriting, I don't know, but Sierra Mercantile is as much yours as it is ours!" He then looked directly at Martha, "I don't like to ever raise my voice, but I'm telling you this as a fact, Mrs. Sunder, on this subject, I'm not seeking your opinion, or your approval! Our boy is welcome there!"

"Good lord, Newell, Marshall," Martha whispered, "I don't know what came over me. I'm so sorry," She began to sob and reached for one of her small handkerchiefs.

Marshall heard the clicking of the clock on the kitchen wall, and finally said, "Excuse me. I'm going to walk over to the park." Then he paused in the doorway, "I'm sorry to be a problem to you folks. I love you both. I'm going to find a room someplace else."

Newell spoke again, "Son, you take your walk. Please understand that we are all very human. We have our little disagreements. Your mom and I'll take a little stroll, too. We want you to come on home and have dinner with us. Right, Martha?" Newell hesitated, again glanced ant Martha, then continued, "And please don't even consider not staying here. This is your home!"

"Forgive what I said, Marshall," Martha murmured, "Please come for dinner with us."

"Yeah," Marshall whispered, "I guess so. See you later."

X   X   X

Towards the end of summer the heat recedes and the people, dogs, and cats, all of the domesticated animals, and the sheep and horses, the milk cows and cattle, and the wild animals: the quail and pheasants, the ravens, and the magpies and the red-winged black birds, the eagles and hawks and turkey buzzards, the little wrens and the titmouse, and the hummingbirds and the mockingbirds, the robins and the blue jays, the stellar jays, and the crows, the jackrabbits and the cottontails, the blacktail deer, the mule deer, the pronghorn antelope, the black bear, the skunks and the beaver and possum and badger, and the coyotes, all the residents of the upper Sacramento valley, seem to share a common sigh of relief when coolness arrives. Marshall and his dad delighted in spotting and identifying the animals and birds, just as Martha was joyful identifying the flowers.

Fall comes to the California valleys, not in the raucous colors of the eastern seaboard, but it is felt with the first slight drop in the temperature. Men who hunt feel it. Their body-barometer tells them it is time to hunt. Through narrowed nostrils they breathe the change, seem to sniff out a slight variation in the temperature, and as the barometer falls, the middle-aged men suffer the arthritic pain and stiffness in their elbow and knee joints. The older men talk about it, but the aches and pains that result from a low-pressure area arriving, have been accepted as another part of growing old. Men who hunt acknowledge it. Within them grows a desire to get out their rifles and shotguns. They clean them and sight along the barrels at imaginary targets, swinging through the tail feathers of a ring neck pheasant, passing the beak and still moving the barrel before they pull off a shot. And their wives chuckle when they hear their men let out with a "pow-pow" utterance as they swing their shotguns through the targets.

Before the hunters depart for the fields and the mountains, many of the women gather to make quilts. They talk about their men and the preparations for the hunting season.

"They've still got a lot of the little boy in them," one will offer and they'll all nod and smile.

Among the hunters are those who know that they hunt, not for need, knowing as they've always known that there exists no genuine necessity for them to stalk, to pursue game, in order to fill the winter lockers and freezers. It's not that they can't ignore the urge, rather they choose to respond to the call from deep within, a beckoning emanating from long corridors of inherited genes, now prodding them, urging them to partake in the harvest, a Neanderthal or Cro-Magnon, primeval voice commanding acknowledgment that winter is approaching, that they should collect and store food for their families.

Also are those who question their urge, who debate with their friends, with themselves, with their wives and children the rightness and the wrongs of hunting pheasant, and quail and deer. There are others who give no thought to the puzzle of their urge and eagerly pursue a tradition, a ritual inherited from parents and grandparents. For them, men who do not hunt evidence unmanliness, and "have a little of the bitch in them," they are apt to joke.

A common awareness among the hunters, both the thinking and feeling, the dull and thoughtless, nevertheless quickly bonds them into a singular fraternity. It happens when the air chills the valleys and the first frost whitens the fields.

Though most of the leaves have fallen, it is not yet time for the winter pruning. For the men, it is the season for sharpening the eyes at the skeet range, a time to shoot trap, a time to talk of loads, and chokes, or the merits of a side by side compared to a superimposed. They discuss stock lengths and trigger pulls, and the advantages of vented rib barrels, which allow the heat waves from a hot barrel to dissipate and not disturb the vision of the shooter.

It is a time to oil saddles and boots, to sharpen knives and axes and to exercise the retrievers. For the women it is a time for canning, and if lucky, their spouse will help them.

After the clouds of the first rain storm in the valley dissipate, there is revealed a white dusting of snow in the foothills. The radio reports a foot of new snow in the Sierra, east of Chico, as well as far to the west in the Trinity Alps, the range west of Red Bluff and Redding.

As the men go about the business of making a living, their minds possess visions of the ring necks, the quail and doves, and squirrels, the large mule deer up high in the mountains, and black bear who have feasted during the summer and now are prepared for the cold and darkness ahead. A few with their trained hunting dogs will pursue the cougars.

Involuntarily their heads turn skyward, and without forethought, their eyes search the graying skies, their ears strain for the distant honking of the snow geese and Canada honkers, the muffled clapping of thousands of southbound wings, the first sight of the pointed-trowel shapes plowing the sky. While Marshall loved to watch the graceful honkers, who reminded him of the high altitude flying B-17's and B-24's, it was the speedy mallards with their tireless wings flapping at a blurred speed that fascinated him. They were indefatigable, as were the beautifully colored little wood ducks. Sometimes the flight patterns of the geese seemed bewildered, as if the leader was indecisive, but the ducks flew as if their destination was plotted on map with a straight edge, unwavering, straight away. They were the P-38's and Jugs and Me 109's. Their downfall was their descent into ponds where hunters awaited. His dad had accidentally killed a little drake wood duck. "Drat it," he said, "I was aiming at a mallard and this little guy just got in the way." His dad felt so badly about it he had it mounted and it was displayed in the store on a shelf behind the cash register.

Marshall was aware of the rituals of the coming hunting season and enjoyed the changes of temperature and the changes in the colors of the leaves of the trees and bushes, yet he still felt estranged, somehow left out of it all. Being away from it all for three years had diluted his enthusiasm. He hoped he could soon establish a career flight plan of his own. Doubts about a future in the supply business were already forming. Marshall did not seek the companionship of anyone, but occasionally he would stop at *Shuffle Em* and have a beer and listen to the conversations. Gus Harmon said nothing about the fight. Marshall remembered Carla and her dollar limit, and advised Gus to tell him when his tab reached ten dollars.

It was against the nature of Marshall's father, Newell, to ask questions about his son's war experiences. His mother, inquisitive about everything whether it involved her son, her husband, or the family business, also followed the example of Marshall's dad, whether by agreement or coincidence, it didn't matter to Marshall. But he was relieved. No one quizzed him.

He realized they were sincerely interested in his wartime experiences, but he couldn't bring himself to sit down and start talking, as if there were numbered chapters to open up, and he was to reveal the contents of the pages one by one.

Marshall was slowly recovering from the shock of his Model A being sold by his mother. The edge in their voices, the abruptness in their conversations had slackened, had eased off, mostly because his dad had consoled him, and his Uncle Bruce had also tried to explain to him how his mother's mind would logically conclude that if selling the Model A to the president of the largest wholesaler in the bay area, Torburn and Fox, if that would give them preference in purchasing, and in the delivery of all of the scarce items needed to restock their store, then to her way of thinking that was just common sense. Damn! he thought, *if she'd just asked him first. That would have made a difference.* Depositing the money for the car in a savings account in his name simply irritated Marshall.

Uncle Bruce was a widower. Had been for nearly eight years. Cancer had taken his wife, Nedra, and for a year he was inconsolable, but his construction business kept him busy.

Marshall's mother said that he'd probably lost his mind if he hadn't been able to work hard. To stay busy, he'd build anything from a house to a garage to a chicken pen, a warehouse to a corral, and he needed the income. With the Cal Vet Loan in place he was able to start construction on new homes for returning veterans.

Bruce regularly stopped by to see Newell and Martha, especially since Newell had suffered with the rheumatic fever attack. It was Bruce who could best communicate with Newell. He always had the latest joke, and often would wait until Martha was well out of earshot before telling it to Newell, and Marshall listened and laughed loudly, observing that Bruce always laughed loudly at the end of his story, just as he'd advised Marshall. Bruce knew when Newell was down, when he was feeling sorry for himself about the effects on his heart.

Bruce could somehow tease Newell, say insulting or challenging things to his dad, but within the comment there was always a hidden, subtle, veiled, compliment, or word of encouragement, and Newell was cheered.

Bruce could tease his sister, too. When she'd start lecturing about the evils of alcohol and gambling, he'd interrupt her, "Come on, Sis, get off your high horse!" he'd tell her, and she'd laugh, and just shake her head. Marshall didn't recall his father ever speaking to his mother that way. He enjoyed having Bruce visit them, and he often stopped by to have dessert and coffee in the evening.

Marshall recognized the sound of Bruce's truck as it turned into the curved driveway of their home. It was a Saturday and they'd planned on listening to the radio together.

"Am I too late for whatever sweet stuff you're serving tonight?" he said, laughing as he entered through the front door. He'd knocked, but hadn't waited for anyone to come to the door. He stopped when he saw Marshall. "Wow, Marsh, what a couple of shiners!" He laughed again, "Guess I'd better not get smart and call you Chico Sunder! Right? Those are beauts though, kiddo! Hope your mom put a slab of beefsteak across them! Now, tell me the same little white lie you told the folks!"

"Check it out with Mr. Harmon, Uncle Bruce, if you really want to know."

"Well, just make yourself at home," Marshall's mother said, "and, dear bother, Marshall explained to Newell and me that he was being chivalrous."

"Hey. Give with the details." Bruce joked, then became aware of the uncomfortable silence, of the chill in the exchanges.

All of them then went to the dining room table and Martha served each a section of pineapple upside-down cake and mugs of coffee. She sipped her own coffee from a small, delicate cup, with a saucer. " My Limoges," she'd say, if anyone admired the cup.

"Newell, why don't you and Marsh and I climb in my truck tomorrow afternoon and we'll go up to that little rifle range we built last year at Musty Buck Ridge. We could zero in the scope on that Mauser, check out the Winchester and the other rifles and maybe toss some clay pigeons around?"

"Am I a free man tomorrow afternoon?" Newell said, looking towards Martha.

"I think it would do you good," she said. She lifted her apron and fanned her face.

"Count me in," Marshall said.

"Sis, why don't you join us. You were always the best shot with that little twenty-two. We can take it and find some tin cans to plunk at."

"Thanks, but no thanks," she said, and Marshall was relieved. He looked forward to being with his dad and uncle for a few hours.

"That cake was terrific," Bruce said. "I thank you, and now I'll leave you to your radio. See you after church. All right?"

"Certainly, and plan on having lunch with us. Then we can head up to the range," Newell said.

"You going to church with the folks?" Bruce said, looking toward Marshall.

"No. I've a great book my squadron chaplain gave me. What this minister writes makes sense to me."

"Well, I'll ask Reverend Harms what he knows about him," his mother said.

"Too bad Harms wasn't in the ETO or the Pacific doing his preaching."

"You know he's a pacifist."

"Chaplain Waldron was a pacifist. He just tried to help out the guys doing the dirty work."

"Well, I for one am going to try to stay out of harms way. " Bruce said, and laughed. " Get it, Sis?"

"I got it, and you git!" She smiled as he departed.

Newell went to the living room and busied himself trying to tune in the station they desired.

x   x   x

Marshall's father and mother returned from church and Bruce arrived almost simultaneously. Marshall had just returned from the Sierra Mercantile store, and was lacing his ankle-high leather boots, when his mother said, "Reverend Harms sends his regards. He'd like you to join us some Sunday."

"Thanks mom," he said, looking up at her, "but I'm really enjoying the book by Doctor Fosdick. Boy, that sure is a pretty dress. Like that hat, too. Dad's a lucky guy."

"Thank you. That's real sweet of you. By the way, I asked Reverend Harms if he'd ever heard of your book. He seems to think that man Fosdick is some kind of a liberal, not really following the teachings of the good book."

Marshall felt the sudden warmth in his neck, and refrained from a desire to tell his mother and Harms to mind their own damn business, and instead said, "If you'd like to borrow my book and read it and decide for yourself, Mother, you're welcome to."

Bruce strode into the room, smiled broadly and said, "Well howdy, all you good Christians. I hope you put in a good word for your big brother, Sis."

"Well, you need someone to pray for you. Excuse me while I change clothes," Martha said. She returned in a few minutes wearing a house-dress, low shoes, and putting on an apron that she tied behind her.

"Yes, Bruce, Reverend Harms sent his regards. It wouldn't hurt you to show up some Sunday. Lots of nice people attend. Some very attractive single women, too."

"Sometime, Sis," Bruce said, but Martha also knew he'd never attended church after Nedra died. No loving God would have allowed her to suffer and to die so young, Bruce had told her many years ago. He wasn't likely to change his mind, she also knew.

"I've thrown together a quickie lunch for you boys," Martha said, nodding to the round table in the kitchen. She'd already poured milk into their glasses from a large white pitcher with a curved handle, and upon plates in front of three chairs were meat loaf sandwiches on thick slices of bread she'd baked the day before. Other clear glass plates, salad-plate size, held slices of oranges and apples and pears.

In a wicker basket were apples and pears and oranges, plums and Thompson seedless grapes. A folded paper napkin was at each place. There was a large glass bowl holding olives, almost the size of a banty chicken egg. A small empty bowl was at each table setting. The men munched the olives and put the pits into the small bowls. A platter held dozens of peanut butter cookies.

"Sis," Bruce said, "You sure know how to spoil us!"

"Honey?" Newell asked, "any chance of a thermos of black coffee?"

"Coming up," Martha said. She walked to the back of chair and placed her hands on his shoulder and felt the strong throbbing pulse. She worried about him. The doctor said he'd live a long, normal life. His aortic valve had been distorted from that rheumatic fever attack, and his heart beat harder, enough to shake the bed. Martha couldn't bring herself to telling him she had a difficult time sleeping. She knew she'd have to bring up the subject of twin beds soon.

"Sis, I'm going to give you one more chance to join us. Why don't you dig out that twenty-two? You were always the best shot in the clan. We can throw in some tin cans, or bottles."

"Thanks Bruce. I honestly think you mean it. I've got some bookkeeping to do, and I just want to rest and listen to the radio. Okay?"

"Whatever is important," Bruce chided, "but no bookkeeping on the Lord's day, now. And thank you for the delicious grub!"

"Oh, take your rifles and stuff and get out of here," she said, laughing.

"Fellows," Bruce said, "I cleaned out the box behind the cab and I've put in my guns, and those little sand bags. I brought a roll of white wrapping paper, a can of black paint and a little brush. You've got that contraption to throw some clay pigeons and I brought a full case."

Marshall and his dad looked at Bruce, waiting for him to continue. "Our stuff is laid out. The spotting scope is there, and I bought a tripod for it, and also some binoculars, a wad of cotton for our ears, and yes, both shotgun shells and 30-06 and 270 ammo. I've thrown in a couple of police whistles. What are we missing?"

"We'll need a stapler and a piece of plywood to tack that paper to," Marshall said, "Unless you want to build a frame?"

"Right," Newell said. "I've some pieces of three-quarter plywood in the back of the garage.

"Throw one in and something on top of it. Don't want it to blow out. So, I guess we're about set. Toss in a roll of that black electric tape, too."

The bench seat of the three-quarter ton truck was wide enough for three men to sit comfortably. Marshall was in the middle.

"Watch your knees, kid," Bruce said. He placed the gearshift in the low position and they drove out of the curved driveway onto the black macadam road, heading northeast out toward the foothills. Bruce shifted the gears, managing not to bump Marshall.

"We should've thrown in our fly rods. Used to be some beautiful ponds along Big Chico Creek," Marshall said, "but I haven't even bought a license this year."

"Maybe next Sunday, Newell said. "I imagine Bruce would be available."

"Hell, Newell, I'm always available for anything, anytime, any place, " Bruce said, "But I don't want to horn in on you guys."

"You've got to be kidding, Uncle Bruce," Marshall said. "You know some of those things you and dad told me, and showed me up at the hunting camp in Izee, well they came in handy on missions."

"Like what?"

"Oh, like when you are on a stand. How important it was to sit real still, not move, but stay alert, ignore distractions, like flak, " Marshall said. "That kind of thing."

"Oh?" Bruce said, but hesitated to pursue the subject. He and Newell had agreed they weren't going to pry. When Marshall wanted to talk about the war, they'd be an eager audience.

"Son, I don't think you've had much of a chance to see that rifle we had made into a .270. A GI managed to ship home a few unfired Mausers, 8mm, which is too slow a caliber for deer hunting. The gunsmith put a new barrel on it, reworked and jeweled the action and the bolt, and we had a nice new Fajen stock fitted. It's a beauty. I got my hands on the last of the four- power Redfield scopes from our supplier and it's all mounted. This will be the first time it's been fired. Want you to have the honor, test it out, you know, and zero it in. The German Mauser actions are supposed to be the best."

"Thanks, dad," Marshall said. "That will be fun."

"Son, since your last trip to the range, we've improved it a bit. Rolled in a few logs and stacked them so we have a pretty good, solid bench-rest," Newell said. "Nailed some planks on top, too. And we paced off a hundred yards to the embankment, and below it there's a little gully to get into so a bullet can't ricochet into that area. You'll see."

The narrow, two-lane road followed the gentle dips and rises of the terrain, gaining a few hundred feet elevation. Thick chaparral grew close to the roadside and spread thickly across the hills. Manzanita, with the large twisted trunks with shiny areas of maroon on many of the branches, grew in clumps, mingling in with the scrub oak as it began to appear and there was a scattering of White Oaks and of the huge Valley Oaks with trunks eight foot in diameter supporting thick, solid branches that spread into a wide circle. The oak trees were two and three stories tall, and were circled at their bases by deep shadows. The wild grasses were dry and the color of crisp brown wheat. Marshall counted seventeen white-faced Herefords with nice flat-ledge backs that meant they were expensive, good stock. He forgot who had told him that, but he'd always looked at cattle more carefully since then. Some were built that way, and some had backs that sagged, so in his mind the flat ones automatically were better. Then he recalled the German farmers with those oxen that always looked weary as they pulled the plows through the black German soil adjacent to Kristine's home. *Well, ours are going to end up at the packing house whether they are flat or sagged, and those German oxen will pull until they die in their tracks,* then Marshall sighed so deeply, so audibly, that both Newell and Bruce were startled and looked at him.

"Anything wrong, Son?" Newell asked.

"No. Guess I was just daydreaming."

"There's the turnoff, Bruce," Newell said.

They'd traveled northeast on the blacktop for about twenty miles, then turned west onto a gravel road. A dust cloud began to form behind them. Newell glanced through the cab window behind Marshall, "Better slow her down a bit, partner. We're sucking in a lot of that dust."

"Righto, well, it's only a few miles to that turnoff," Bruce said. He leaned forward and rested his muscular forearms on the steering wheel, and began to concentrate on the tree trunks as they drove along the bumpy, dusty road.

"Look for one of those digger pines. I carved a blaze about head-high on it."

"I bet those digger pines will be the last surviving thing, when the world comes to an end," Newell said.

"How's that, dad?"

"They're good for nothing. I mean, man doesn't want them for firewood, or fence posts, and they are too brittle and too crooked to make a telephone pole out of, or to use for a log cabin. So they're safe. Nobody wants the damn things."

"Mom likes their pine cones. Decorates with them at Christmas."

Bruce laughed. "Great! What she really likes are those huge cones from the sugar pines. You guys can gather up an assortment to take home with us."

"Look. There's my blaze," Bruce said. They saw the twelve-inch long, six-inch wide area where he'd removed the bark. Bruce slowed the truck, then turned off of the gravel road and drove the heavy vehicle back through the manzanita where he found a place to park, concealed from the primary road.

Each of the men took a load of material from the truck and walked fifty yards further to a clearing where logs had been placed so that a bench was formed with a relatively flat area six foot long, and two feet deep which allowed two of them to place their sandbags so that both the butt and the stock of the rifle could be supported as the shooter leaned across the bench and aimed through either a scope, or through iron sights. It was much more sophisticated than Marshall imagined. His Uncle Bruce was an exacting builder, even for something like this, stuck out in the woods, and his dad seemed to understate everything.

"Anyone anxious to take the first shot?" Bruce asked.

"I'll take the plywood and target stuff out to the hillside," Marshall said.

"Well, paint on a couple of saucer size spots and we'll have your pop go first. He'll take six shots at each target, and there'll be a delay after each shot as we pick out the holes with his spotting scope. Take that whistle and give it a good blow when you are down in that gully. We'll answer and then start. Okay? And watch out for rattlers."

"Roger, Uncle Bruce, "Marshall said, and departed with the material for the hillside.

Following a faint trail, Marshall inhaled the fragrance from the con-glomeration of trees and bushes and marveled at the color of the clean red-dish-brown earth. He'd forgotten how red it was.

A Steller's Jay scolded him, and a California ground squirrel scooted through the underbrush, and tiny chipmunks studied his approach, nervously twitching their tails. Above the treetops the sky was blue and Marshall was pleased to see the contrast of the flat bottom clouds with their cauliflower-shaped tops floating eastward. Above the treetops a large hawk glided, so large that Marshall wondered if it might be a Golden Eagle.

The narrow path led to the open area where a tall muddy bank was the obvious place to put the target. Marshall stapled a piece of the white paper onto the plywood, then painted two black orbs on either side of the sheet. A flat area, a shelf, existed where he balanced the plywood. He found two dead branches and propped them up on either edge to hold it steady, then climbed back down and sat in the area where he'd be protected from a ricochet. Putting the whistle to his lips, Marshall blew loudly and almost immediately heard the answering shrillness of the other whistle.

Marshall was startled by the loud thud the bullet made as it penetrated the plywood and buried itself in the red earth, as simultaneously the roar of the 30-06 shattered the silence. Marshall had forgotten to take some of the cotton and place in his ears. Another loud slamming into the hillside of a bullet, along with the roar of the rifle disrupted the silence of the forest, and a third shot and the loud thud of the bullet penetrating the plywood and digging into the hillside followed, and suddenly Marshall put his hands over his ears and lowered his head.

"Let's take her down and strafe that goddamn bridge!" Gary said, "We'll put the fear of God into any krauts hanging around."

My God, Marshall thought, is that what it must have sounded like when those fifty-caliber's dug into the surface of the bridge at Bad Scheidel? "Oh shit," he said, "what does a poor goddamn deer think or feel if the fucking shot misses him. The noise is enough to kill it." Marshall looked up at the sky, "Christ, now I'm talking to myself."

Marshall began to perspire and suddenly felt disoriented. "Wow," he thought, *"dad and Uncle Bruce are going to think I'm a freak. This was supposed to be fun!'* A large cloud passed in front of the sun and shaded the area, and the air felt suddenly chilly to Marshall. He zipped closed his windbreaker.

By the time of the twelfth rifle shot, Marshall had begun to collect himself. His armpits were wet, as was the back of his shirt. The dampness of his shirt beneath his light jacket chilled him. Then he heard the blast of the police whistle. He climbed out of the safety of the gully and examined the target. There was some scattering of small holes in the white area, but there were three holes in the black area of each circular, black orb. Then Marshall answered with his own whistle and climbed down from the target area. Marshall headed back along the faint trail. The Steller's Jay had disappeared, as had the ground squirrel and the chipmunks. He met his dad and Bruce at the stand. The sun was behind a cloud, darkening the woods.

"Whoever was shooting got three in each of the black spots. Hope those were your last and best shots," Marshall added.

"Those were your dad's shots," Bruce said, "I'll take a turn in the pit."

"Uncle Bruce, don't forget the cotton for your ears," Marshall said.

"That noisy back there?"

"Sure is!"

"If the paint is dry enough you can patch those holes in the black area with the tape. Tape over the other holes, too," Newell said. "Otherwise it's a new sheet to start on."

Bruce departed and Newell turned to Marshall. "We put that four power Redfield scope on the Mauser for you. Thought it would remind you of your bombsight. Plus a new trigger guard feature the gunsmith added. It'll hold five cartridges in the magazine, plus one in the chamber, and if you fire one or two, and don't want to fire anymore, you can just slide this little button at the base of the trigger guard and the door falls down and releases the unused cartridges. Beats cranking them out, right?"

"That's a nice feature," Marshall nodded, then said, "This stock is made from a really nice piece of walnut." Suddenly, for some inexplicable reason, Marshall felt the presence of Kristine. He remembered her calling him a Luftgangster, and telling him that Sunder meant sinner in the German language.

"Say Dad, how'd the Sunder family get to America?" Marshall asked.

Surprised by the question, his looked at him quizzically. "What made you think of that," Newell said. "And Son, aren't you hot with that windbreaker on?"

"I just got kind of chilly back in the trees, that's all," Marshall said. He pulled the zipper down a few inches and then continued, "About the Sunder name, I just wondered, you know, talking about the Mauser action being so great."

"Well, your great grandfather was a cobbler, a shoemaker, in a little village called Kitzengen, and back in the '80's if you had a craft you had a good chance of making it to America. Skilled craftsmen were wanted in the States. Up in Minnesota there was a family named Sunder who had known his parents, you know, family friends. They sponsored him, but those jerks at immigration couldn't get it through their thick heads that his name was Sonderzug and that his sponsors were the Sunders, so they wrote Sunder on his papers and he never bothered to try to change it. It was passed along through the years that the guys at immigration didn't know how to write the letter Z. Did it backward a couple of times like an S, then gave up and just wrote his name as Sunder. Obviously a communications problem. After all of the hassle and arguing about how to spell his name, he was so happy to get through immigration he didn't really care what they called him. So goes the story anyway. I was only around old Zug a few times. Quite a character. He loved to sing and dance and played the accordion. Also played the organ at the church. Played Beethoven and Mozart, Bach, Brahms, classical stuff like that."

Newell paused and studied Marshall's face, "This is a strange time to be asking such a question," his dad said, looking at Marshall quizzically.

"Ha! That's really very funny," Marshall said, and laughed, " I like that Zug. Did you know that Sunder translates into sinner?"

"Nope. Didn't know that, and really never gave it a thought, but I've heard of a lot of funny name changes that happened in immigration. Like the guy in town, the author named Fales. One of his sons got involved in genealogy, you know, and learned that the family name was really Sales. The way some of them wrote, the S, it looked like a F, but Fales senior is really upset and insists their name is Fales and now he's trying to verify it, and now he's into genealogy, too." Newell continued, "At one time my folks thought about changing our name to back to Sonderzug, but it was just too complicated, the red tape and all, you know, the social security numbers, marriage licenses, birth certificates, And it is kind of an unwieldy name. Do you care?"

"You know, Dad, I'm going to have to mull that over a bit. Wonder what the English translation happens to be?"

"Never gave it a thought, Son."

The whistle from the target area shrilled loudly. "Your Uncle Bruce is all clear. You want to try out that Mauser?"

"Sure."

"We did a preliminary adjustment of the scope by sighting through the barrel at a door knob and by using those little adjusting wheels on the top and side we lined the cross hairs up. So your first shot ought to be on the paper, at least. And here's some cotton."

Marshall placed a cartridge in the chamber and five more in the holding area and closed the bolt. He rested the rifle on the sandbags and arranged them so that he could kneel down, hold the rifle firmly, partially resting it on his left forearm, and sighted through the scope. Marshall knew that there would be cross hairs, yet he was startled, and found that his mind wanted to place him in the nose of a B-26, and he resented the flush of warmth in his body and especially his neck and face. He hoped that he wasn't blushing.

"Well, Bruce gave us a nice clean target to shoot at. Fire away, lad," his dad said.

Marshall placed the cross hairs in the center of the left target, squeezed the trigger, and felt the recoil, the sharp jab of the rifle against his shoulder.

"See anything through the scope ?"

"No sir."

"Let me take a look with this spotting scope," Newell said. "Here, take a look, Marsh, you're about six inches low and three inches to the right."

"Okay, I see the holes. Now what?"

"According to the manual, all we've got to do is make a few clicks with those little wheels to move the impact area sideways and up."

Newell stepped up beside Marshall and took the rifle from him, removed two quarter-size flat round coverings, and made the adjustments with a small screwdriver. "Give her another try."

Again Marshall leaned across the bench rest, pulled the stock tightly to his shoulder, placed the cross hairs on the center of the black spot and squeezed off a shot, and accepted the sharp jarring against his shoulder.

"Can't make out anything through this scope."

"You've placed that shot in the black, low and to the left. Take a look."

"Well, I hope that's the adjustments you made on the scope and not me weaving the barrel around."

"Give her another go, but don't you allow for the impact position. Just aim dead center."

"Roger, Dad."

The position of the impact was almost identical, so Newell made two very minor adjustments. Again Marshall set the cross hairs as close to dead center as he could, squeezed off a shot and awaited the verdict.

"Hey, Son, take a peek. Great! A shack! Didn't you tell us that was called a bull's eye when you were in cadets?"

"Yes sir, "Marshall said, and he placed the rifle on its side and stepped back from the bench rest, and his mind heard Pop's voice shout over the intercom, *"Shack! The roundhouse is going up. It's on fire. Our flight hit it! Our flight!"*

"Take a few more shots?" Newell asked.

"You go ahead, dad."

"Well, I'm going to try my hand again with the 30-06. Ought to be able to put six in the black on that other target."

"I'll unload the .270," Marshall said, and lifted it from the bench rest.

"Use that new bottom release," Newell said.

"Roger," Marshall said. He held the barrel upwards, pushed on the little slide button and the two cartridges became entangled against the flat springs, jamming together. They wouldn't release.

"Give me a heading," Frank said.

"Three forty. Possible bomb release malfunction. I've got to check the bomb bay."

Marshall placed the Mauser on the bench, worked the cartridges free and clinched them in his fist. He opened his moist palm and stared at them, then replaced them in the cartridge box. Marshall felt ill, felt faint.

"Top two bombs, port side still on the racks, Pop said."

"I'm coming up to take a look," Marshall said. Before he unplugged his head set, John reported from the tail, "Number four still has a smoking engine and is heading for the deck."

"You alright, Marsh?" Newell asked, "You look kind of pale."

"Got chilled back in the woods, now too hot," Marshall said, "and, too many memories, I guess. Hell, dad. I must be getting neurotic about the damn war." He paused, then looked up into his dad's face. Marshall cleared his throat. "You see, dad, I bombed a little bridge. We called it a target of opportunity. Blew it up. Later on, we learned it caused the death of some civilians, and I'm just having a tough time trying to rationalize it, you know, justify it, that sort of thing." And as he said those words he remembered Kris saying something like that to him in the room in Munich. He paused, "But, you know, the book I'm reading is helping though. I'm sorry."

"Hells bells, Son, give us a little credit for understanding that you probably went through ordeals we can't even imagine. Your mom and I and

Bruce want to be supportive, but not interfere. Nothing to be sorry about."

"Thanks, Dad. Why don't you take some shots with this .270? It's really a keen rifle."

"Okay. Hand it over." Newell accepted the rifle, loaded it, found a comfortable position, and fired six shots at the black orb on the right side of the target.

Marshall watched the target through the spotting scope. "Dad, every one of them is in the black. Nice going. Are you going to fire the 30-06 again?"

"No. I'm satisfied. Give the whistle a toot and we'll get Bruce back here for a turn."

Marshall blew the whistle and there was an immediate response from Bruce. In a few minutes he appeared. "Tacked on a new sheet with a couple of new targets." he said. "I brought your sheet to show you," and he held out a rolled up piece of paper.

"Give the .270 a try, Bruce," Newell said. "Marsh and I got it all zeroed in for you."

"Well, I might just have to refine it a bit you know," Bruce said, then laughed, and winked at Newell and Marshall smiled. Newell then headed for the impact area, disappearing through the trees along the narrow path.

"You getting adjusted to civilian life?" Bruce asked. He held the .270 and rubbed the stock with the palm of his right hand. He looked at Marshall, who didn't respond for a few moments.

"Yeah, I guess so," Marshall said, still avoiding Bruce's eyes.

"When you were in high school, before Pearl Harbor, did you ever hear of 'Clean Jeans'? Over in Red Bluff?"

"No, don't think so. Sounds like a laundry."

Bruce laughed. "Now you're folks would kill me, I mean literally, if you went over to Red Bluff with me, later this week, or maybe next week, and they learned that I stopped at 'Clean Jeans.'"

"You're not coming through, Uncle Bruce," Marshall said, and looked at him quizzically.

"Clean Jean lives in the prettiest old Victorian house in Red Bluff. A little bit on the edge of town. Some nice girls live with her, and a bouncer, and there's a big long mahogany bar with good, but inexpensive booze. Can you visualize a great big oil painting in a gold frame of a scantily clad plump lady, over the bar."

"Next you're going to describe this pretty little old antique red lamp behind the lace curtains," Marshall said and laughed and Bruce put his head back and laughed loudly.

"You got it, and Clean Jean has a doctor come to the house every day and gives the girls a physical. Not once a week, but every damn day! And her girls are taught how to examine a customer. Anything questionable with anyone and Jeanette sends them packing. It's a lot safer than some of these girls hanging around the bars in town. You know what I mean?"

"Now you're coming through loud and clear, Uncle Bruce," Marshall said, still laughing.

"Well, I've got to buy some redwood. I want to hand select the planks for a deck I'm building in town. May come as a surprise to you, but this old body of mine needs a little loving about a half dozen times a year to keep my sanity. I'm not suggesting that you partake, but if you want to go along for the ride, just for a little change of pace, I'd love to have you join me. It'll be overnight."

"Uncle Bruce, hell yes, I'll go with you. But maybe I could just peer in and see what's going on. If I walk out, it won't bother you, will it?"

"Hell no! There's a good hotel in town where you can stay. I'm not trying to lead you astray!"

"Come on Unk, I'm a big boy now!" They both laughed.

The shrillness of the whistle startled them. They returned the message and Bruce took the .270 and prepared to shoot it.

"Now remember, not a whisper about this to your folks. They'd kill me!"

"Okay, Uncle Bruce, and don't crawl that stock or that scope will kick you in the eyebrow."

"Well, thanks for the warning."

As Marshall watched through the spotting scope his Uncle Bruce fired the .270 and Bruce agreed that it was well zeroed in as Marshall described the positions of the small holes in the black circles of the target. Bruce stood up and placed the rifle on its side after cranking open the bolt. "Nice checkering job, or checking, as some folks call it," he said, then walked to where he'd placed one of his own guns.

"Going to take a few shots with my Remington pump," Bruce said, as he removed the rifle from a case, loaded it and returned to the bench rest. " I've knocked down a lot of bucks with old iron sights," he said, patting the stock of the rifle, "but I'm sure going to invest in a scope when they're available. Takes about ten years off a man's eyes." Bruce then fired at the other target while Marshall spotted for him.

"You're impact is a little high, Uncle Bruce."

"That's fine. My sights are set so I should be putting those bullets about two inches high. They'll be right on at two hundred yards. Get it?"

"Well, I'd say you're right where you want to be then, " Marshall said, laughing. "Time to blow the whistle."

"Blow away. Get your dad on back here, we'll collect some pine cones for your mom, and then find a nice open spot to throw a few clay birds."

Newell appeared and said, "My, that is noisy back there. The trees and the bank must hold all of the sound in, trap it and magnify it, like an amphitheater. Cool, too."

"Let's fold things up and find a spot to swing the shotguns," Bruce said.

"Don't you want to get in some more practice with the rifles?" Newell looked from one to the other.

"I've had enough," Marshall said. "Up to you and Uncle Bruce," And Marshall could not understand the subtle feeling of resistance building within himself towards a project he thought he'd enjoy. It must be the noise, he felt, because he was with men he admired. He liked it, too, when his Uncle Bruce called him son.

"We can come back a couple of times before we head up to Izee. Let's go break up some of those clay birds," Bruce said.

"I'll go back and get the plywood," Marshall said.

"Leave it there, Son, we'll use it next time out."

The rifles were returned to their cases and the men gathered up their sandbags and tools and the spotting scope and returned to the truck.

They stopped beneath a group of sugar pines and all got out and gathered eighteen of the pine cones, the size of a football, and placed them carefully in a stack in the bed of the truck. "Okay, fellas, pile in, we'll find a nice open field and throw those clay pigeons," Bruce said.

"I tossed in the Remington with the skeet choke I use for quail and doves," Newell said, then added, "Also my old sky scraper, the Model 12 Winchester. It's at the opposite end, a full choke. Good for ducks and geese, but too long a barrel for this stuff."

"Looks like a good open spot," Bruce said, slowing the truck and pulling off of the gravel road, parked and the men climbed down from their seats.

"Marsh, if you want to open that box, there's the bird thrower and a case of clay pigeons. Pass down those shotguns, too, if you don't mind," Bruce said.

Marshall nodded, lowered the tailgate and climbed into the back of the pickup. He handed the carton of clay birds and the shotguns in their cases to his dad and Bruce.

"Nice to have someone young and agile doing the fetching!" Bruce said and laughed loudly. "Okay, I'll throw some," he said, and opened the case and took out two hands full of the round, saucer shaped clay targets. He swung the empty throwing device back and forth, stretching his muscles, while Newell loaded the Remington and handed the shotgun to Marshall.

"Been a long time since we did this," Newell said. "Remember, it's not a rifle-aiming shot. Pull through the bird when you shoot."

"Say throw when you are ready," Bruce advised.

Marshall studied the gun, double-checked the safe and fire positions, then partially raised the shotgun and loudly said, "Throw!"

Instinctively Marshall raised the shotgun, located the flying clay bird and pulled the trigger and saw the bird shatter into dozens of small white pieces. Looks like white flak, he thought, but it isn't, and he was finally growing weary of war reminders. Several more clay birds were flung at various heights and in different directions, and Marshall hit more than half and was satisfied to hand the shotgun to his dad.

"Uncle Bruce," he called out, "I'll take a turn with the thrower."

"It's funny, Dad," Marshall said, "I feel sometimes like I'm living in reverse gear. So many little things now remind me of combat."

"Even shooting at clay pigeons?" Newell said, raising his eyebrows.

"Dad, did you know that the Germans, with their anti-aircraft guns, could estimate our altitude and our course, load and fire their 88's and the projectile traveled a thousand feet a second. So at a true altitude of 13,000' it took thirteen seconds to reach us and explode, sending the flak into us. So if we could change our altitude a bit, and our course a few degrees every twelve seconds, we'd be a little harder to track. That's what throwing these clay birds reminded me of. Only flak is black."

Newell smiled at Marshall and said, "Thanks, Son. Like to share that with Bruce, okay?"

"Why sure. Nothing secret. I'll start throwing for you now," Marshall said, he patted his dad on the shoulder and met Bruce walking towards them.

"Little out of practice, kid!" Bruce said. "We gotta do this often before the bird season opens."

"Guess I need a scope on the shotgun," Marshall said, laughing. He accepted the thrower and walked to the carton of clay pigeons. He threw for both his dad and uncle and finally with a few nods and a little conversation the session was over and they put the shotguns in the cases and headed for the pickup truck.

"Hey, Marshall," Bruce said. "That new surplus store in town had a few boxes of ammo for the .45's. You want to give your dad and me a little lesson?"

"Why sure," Marshall said, grinning, "I didn't even know you brought them!"

"They weren't meant for the mantel, were they?" Newell asked. The three men again laughed.

Pleased that they wanted to fire the .45's, Marshall looked around and spotted a fence post with a steep hill as a background. He scrounged around on the ground until he found a handful of brick-size rocks. He placed one atop the fence post and said, "dad, you've got first try. See how many shots it takes you to split that old rock."

"Mighty small target."

"That weapon is for close up work," Marshall said. "Get about fifteen feet from it and give it a try."

Newell held the gun in his right hand, his arm extended straight out from his shoulder and slowly raised the weapon until the front sight rested in the V of the rear sight, then squeezed off a shot. The recoil caused the gun to lift and they all saw the impact of the bullet as it smacked against the post just beneath the rock.

"Hey, great shooting, dad," Marshall exclaimed. "Keep going until you blast that rock off of the post!"

Newell fired a half dozen more shots, finally hitting the rock. "That's enough for now," He said. "Put another rock up for your Uncle Bruce. He'll probably need a larger rock though." He chuckled and winked at Marshall.

"Step aside, gentlemen. Anyone want to bet four bits I'll hit that little old rock on my first shot?" Bruce said.

"Sure, we'll take you up on that bet, Uncle Bruce!"

Bruce aimed carefully, as had Newell. He pulled the trigger and the recoil lifted the barrel. The rock remained where it rested, and it was not until his eighth shot that Bruce demolished the rock, never once hitting the fence post.

"Alright, show off," he said to Newell, "here's your half a buck." From his trousers pocket he removed the half-dollar piece and tossed it to Newell.

Newell caught the coin, laughed and said, "Hot damn!"

Then Bruce turned to Marshall and said, "You've got to earn that four bits, sonny boy. Let's see what a washed up old bombardier can do with this weapon!"

"Okay, Uncle Bruce." Marshall said, grinning. "Afraid I'm going to embarrass myself though. I can't hit the broad side of a barn with one of these," Marshall took Bruce's weapon, loaded the clip and inserted it. He took a stance similar to that of his dad and uncle, and the impact of his bullets exploded on the fence post eighteen inches below the rock, never hitting it.

Marshall lowered the gun and said, " The Air Corps taught us to aim for the balls, not the head!"

Again the men laughed, and Bruce said, "You didn't learn that BS from your dad!"

"Uncle Bruce," Marshall grinned as he handed the gun back to him, pointing the barrel towards the ground. "If a bombardier survived a crash landing, we were supposed to fire a couple of shots into the Norden. And then try to escape. Hopefully we'd be able to surrender to the Wehrmacht. No telling what the civilians might do. One time they would take care of some wounded guys and others would stick pitchforks into downed fliers. If the SS showed up we'd shoot the bastards, and always keep one shot for ourselves."

"Don't care much for Germans, eh?"

"Make it Nazis. Our C.O., Colonel Schlosser said, 'the only good Germans are the ones who move away from the fatherland!' and he was staying in Germany to try to locate his grandparents somewhere down in Bavaria. Funny, isn't it?"

"Well lad, you're lucky. You've the luck of the Irish on your mom's side and the industriousness of the Germans on your dad's side."

"Dad, Uncle Bruce, only I thing I know for sure is I'm one lucky S.O.B.!"

In the silence that followed, the men walked together toward the truck, each thinking his own private thoughts.

"Well, we can clean the guns tonight. Anyone for coffee? I've got cups for all?" Newell said and obtained the thermos.

"Roger," Marshall said, accepting a cup.

Bruce then took his cup and said, " Wait a minute you guys. I brought my old friend J.D.! We'll just lace that black brew and mellow it out." He reached behind the seat of the pickup truck and brought out a paper bag and then displayed a fifth of Jack Daniel's bourbon. "You like sour mash, Marsh?"

"Uncle Bruce, I don't even know what the heck sour mash bourbon is!" Marshall said, laughing, and he extended his cup towards his dad.

Newell started to pour some coffee and Bruce said, "Not too much, partner, leave a little room for old J.D."

"Sure you want bourbon, Son?" Newell asked, and raised his eyebrows." You're going to ruin two good drinks."

Marshall laughed and once more patted his dad on the shoulder and at the same time extended the cup to Bruce.

"Sour mash me, Uncle Bruce."

Bruce chuckled and poured an ounce or more into the cup. "You mind driving back, Newell?" he said, then continued, " Now, I'm assuming you aren't interested in improving your coffee?"

"You got that right! If I come home smelling like a brewery, especially on Sunday, Martha will keep me in the dog house for a week!"

"We used to get a couple of ounces of whiskey after every mission. Bourbon, I think. We, I mean Frank and Gary and I, and the enlisted men, all of the crews. We would save ours until we'd get enough to get good and high on it," Marshall said. "But, some guys just bolted it down when they got it."

Suddenly three black tail deer bounded out of the woods, crossed the gravel road and leaped a barbed wire fence, and continued to leap highly as they bounded through the chaparral.

"Good four-pointer there, and a doe and a fat little spike hanging around the momma for awhile yet," Bruce said.

Instantly Marshall's mind back-flashed to the crash of a B-26.

"Where's the Spike!" Marshall shouted.

"What do you mean, sir?"

On the runway near the smoldering airplane Marshall saw the body of Spike, the young bombardier, covered with a white tarp. Beside him the chaplain kneeled. Rising from beside the chaplain a medical officer turned and walked towards the ambulance. The chaplain had pulled the tarp over the bombardier's face, then he followed the medical officer. Marshall ran to the body, pulled aside the tarp, and saw the open eyes, saw them lose their color, become white. The medical officer returned and closed the boys' eyes.

"Oh, son of a bitch!" Marshall muttered, and slammed the palm of his left hand down on the hood of the pickup truck, spilling his coffee.

Newell and Bruce were both startled by the loud retort and jumped. Bruce spilled some of his coffee and both looked towards him and stared. "What the heck's the matter, Son?" Newell asked.

Marshall felt ill, and began to tremble. He looked up at them, moisture forming in his eyes, and said, "Please, excuse me. I'm sorry. He turned away from them, then took deep breaths and looked at his father and Uncle Bruce, staring at him. He cleared his throat and began, "This friend of mine, a real young guy, Spike, got killed on a mission, Marshall hesitated, stared back at both men, then said, "I'd rather not talk about it right now. May I have a little more of that J.D., Uncle Bruce?"

"Sure, lad. Can't hurt. Might help," Bruce said, and raised his eyebrows as he looked towards Newell. "Hold that damn cup steady now!" Bruce continued, raising his voice in mock anger. "Don't want to waste any of this old J.D."

"Dad, Uncle Bruce, I'm pretty sure you've heard the expression 'snafu.' Well, that's me, at times, you know, situation normal all fucked up. I'm sorry."

"Guess we ought to think about going home," Newell said. Bruce nodded, and finished his coffee. Newell climbed behind the steering wheel. Marshall balanced his second cup of coffee and again sat between his uncle and father.

"There's an old saying," Bruce said, as he chuckled and elbowed Marshall, "Never drink while you're driving. You might spill some!" Then he guffawed and both Marshall and Newell joined in the laughter.

In silence they drove towards the intersection of the black top road. Suddenly Newell braked the truck. "Well, look there, right there in the middle of the road, sunning itself," Newell exclaimed, "That guy must be nearly three feet long."

Bruce and Marshall leaned forward and saw the rattlesnake stretched out as if had stopped to rest or sun itself as it crossed the gravel road.

"Shall I shoot him?" Bruce said. " We could ask Martha to fry up some nice snake steaks for us. And Marsh, you could skin him, tan the hide and make some hat bands!"

"Why not just honk and see if he'll get out of the way?" Marshall said.

Newell nodded agreement and honked the horn a couple of times, but the rattlesnake didn't budge.

"Well, wait a minute," Bruce said, "I'll toss a couple of little rocks at him and he'll take off. Still think we ought to shoot him. Don't want some kid or dog getting struck." Bruce climbed down from the pickup truck and selected a few small stones and tossed them at the snake.

"There he goes, you guys satisfied?"

"Thanks, Uncle Bruce," Marshall said. "Kids and dogs shouldn't be out here anyway. And my cup is about empty. Little more of your friend, J.D., please."

"Coming up. Want some coffee in with it?" Bruce asked. "I bet there were over a dozen rattles on that guy."

"Thanks, no. The bourbon is better than the coffee," Marshall laughed. "But don't tell mom!"

Newell joined in the laughter, then added, "No, I won't tell your mother, and besides, we never shoot anything we don't eat, and can you imagine asking your mom to fix rattlesnake steaks?"

Bruce leaned forward and looked at Newell, who was keeping his eyes on the road. "Newell, why don't you drop Marsh and me off at my place. I'd like to introduce him to my famous Denver omelet."

"Better yet," Newell said, laughing, "you drop me off at my house. You can come over tomorrow night and unload those pine cones for Martha."

"And that way!" Marshall said, "mom won't be upset when I come in smelling like our old friend J. D.!"

"My Son, it's not your mom that's changed during the past three years."

Marshall chuckled, "Again, you're coming through loud and clear. You sound like Major Crandall," then sipped from the cup. "You've an extra bed at your place, haven't you, Uncle Bruce?"

"It's not the Palace Hotel, but we'll make out. Maybe we'll just drop by the meat market and I'll pick up a couple of T-bones. I've got some dry oak and we'll just have ourselves a little barbecue. Play a little gin after supper, then we'll clean all those guns." Bruce said, "And I'll try out my Denver omelet on you in the morning."

"Hey, that sounds super, Uncle Bruce," Marshall said. "I've got to be at the store by seven, you know."

On the way back to Chico they sat quietly, each pondering the events of the afternoon. Newell pulled into the curved driveway of his home, got out of the pickup and Bruce climbed behind the wheel and they departed, waving at Newell.

X   X   X

Marshall arrived at Sierra Mercantile promptly at seven Monday morning and found the front door unlocked. Both his father and mother were busy putting away merchandise that had arrived Saturday afternoon.

"Howdy, Son," Newell greeted Marshall. "Have a good time at Bruce's?"

"Had a ball. Morning mother," Marshall said.

"Good morning. We've quite a shipment to put away. Loads of wrenches and sockets, screw drivers and hammers, sledges and picks and a variety of shovels. All short-supply items. Torburn and Fox are taking good care of us, I'm happy to say."

"Any bastard files from good old Torburn and Fox, mom?" Marshall asked and looked at his dad and winked. Newell smiled, looked away, and Martha responded, "Without good old Torburn and Fox there would be no Sierra Mercantile!" The sarcasm in her voice annoyed Marshall, but he didn't pursue the subject.

The three of them, father and mother and son worked silently almost side by side. Only one customer entered the store and Newell waited on him, weighing out a few pounds of ten-penny nails. "Got in some nice hammers," Newell told the customer, as he paid for the nails.

"Thanks, Mr. Sunder, I'll pass the word around at the job," the customer said.

"There's sandwiches and milk in the ice box, and some cookies. I'm going home for awhile. Few chores there," Martha said. It was noon. Newell and Marshall washed their hands at a small porcelain sink in the kitchen area, then sat at a table near the cash register and ate their lunch.

"Dad, I think you and I ought to get serious about my future. If you feel you and mom really need me here at the store for awhile, I'll stick around. But I want to get a college education. I can use the G.I. Bill, and when I got discharged they told me I'd probably earned a year's college credit, maybe even more, with all of the Air Corps schools I attended."

"I understand, Son," Newell said. "Quite honestly, the little bit we net out of this business won't permit much of a salary for you, let alone your mom and me." Newell sighed, then spoke again, slowly, "We kind of hoped there would be some growth around here, but nothing big seems to be on the horizon."

"I see," Marshall said. Both of the men sat quietly, washing down their cookies with the last of the milk. "Dad, I get the feeling that mom isn't quite ready to cut the umbilical cord."

"Ha! Ha!" Newell put his head back and guffawed heartily. "Well, shucks Marshall, with you being an only son, I suppose that just comes natural," Newell said, grinning, and chuckled. "She loves you dearly. Just be a little patient with her."

"Roger, Dad," Marshall said and patted his dad on the shoulder. "Guess we better get this stock on the shelves."

"Wait a minute, Son," Newell said and reached out and touched Marshall's forearm, and glancing toward the chair, indicating he'd like him to sit down again.

"What's up, Dad?"

"Before your mother gets back, let me say this. I hope you do go get that college education. Also, I hate to admit it, but I'm slowing down a bit, you know, this heart valve thing. And this place takes as much brawn as it does brains. Your mom's got the brains. No problem there, but the lifting and loading and packing and unpacking is going to get tougher if business does begin to pick up. What used to be a normal day's work is now wearing me out."

"Are you saying I should stay to help mom?"

"No. I'm trying to say the opposite, and not doing a very good job of it. No, but you've got to make a decision very soon. Sort of take a stand. Get your applications off to Cal, or wherever. Just let it be known that this business isn't for you, if that's what you really feel. Level with your mom."

"Geez, I'm surprised, dad. I assumed you wanted me to stay," Marshall said, very quietly, his voice hushed.

"Son, if I was up to full speed, and felt this business could support three people and could grow, I'd urge you stay," Newell said. "All men want to build a business, an estate of sorts, and pass it on to their children. I'm just trying to be realistic, that's all. I don't think your mother has faced up to what I already know."

"Here comes mom," Marshall said, glancing at the front door. "Thanks, dad, we'll kick this around some more, okay?"

"Sure," Newell said, smiling as he stood up and put his hand out for Marshall to give him a lift. "Let's get to work with that stack of shovels."

"Any more cash customers show up while I was gone?" Martha asked.

"It's been very quiet, dear," Newell said.

"I stopped by the *Union* and put in a little ad about new merchandise coming in every day."

A man walked into the store said, "Howdy Newell, Mrs. Sunder, How's it going?" He nodded at Marshall but evidenced no recognition.

"Picking up every day," Newell said. "Got in a big shipment of hand tools, picks and shovels and rakes. Lot's of good stuff. Several kegs of nails and nuts and bolts, all sizes of washers, Ralph."

"Don't expect you have a drum of creosote and a few miles of barbed wire stashed away?"

Marshall laughed, "By golly, we do have a few drums of that creosote out on the dock. How many can I roll into that truck of yours?"

"Say, don't I know you?" Ralph said, and walked closer to Marshall. "Chico High?"

"Yes. Hell, Ralph, we were on the same football team."

"Oh yeah, you're their son," Ralph said. "Quite a few pounds heavier and taller, I'd say?"

"I got back a few months ago. Helped with the harvest wherever I could get on, and been helping the folks get restocked."

"Well, come on down to the Legion meetings. We meet once a week at the Legion Hall. The World War One guys treat us like heroes! Lots of guys there you'll know."

"Thanks, Ralph," Marshall said, and Newell noticed him grinning, which had been rare.

"Well, okay, let's load in that creosote," Ralph said. "Dad's been making posts ever since Pearl, and we're going to try to fence about twenty acres."

"I'll check around for the barbed wire," Martha said. "Guess you'll need four strands per post?"

"Yes mam," Ralph said, " and there's no real big rush. Going to take a lot of digging to get those posts set."

"Believe it not, we got in a few post hole diggers in that last shipment," Newell said.

"Well, throw in a couple with those two drums," Ralph said. He then walked over to Marshall and extended his hand, which Marshall accepted. Ralph pumped vigorously. "You ought to drop by the Elks Lodge too, Sunder. Drinks are two bits, great food and we've a couple of refurbished pool tables. Nice bunch of guys. You come on over."

"Thanks a lot," Marshall said, "Bring your truck around back and we can roll those drums in."

"Right, and put that stuff on dad's bill, Mrs. Sunder. That okay?"

"Certainly. And thank you. Say hi to your mother for me."

Marshall walked to the back of the store and on the open dock sat several drums of creosote. When Ralph arrived with the three-quarter truck, he backed up to the dock, then climbed out, lowered the tail gate, and helped Marshall select a drum and together they balanced it as they rolled it to the truck. They tipped it over, then lowered it into the bed of the truck, again tipping it so that it sat upright. They repeated the chore with the other.

"Here's a couple of post hole diggers," Newell said, carrying them to the truck. "You say hi to your dad, too, and ask him if he'd like to join us for some shooting practice. You, too, of course, Ralph."

"Thanks, and I'll tell dad you're going to check out delivery on that barbed wire."

Newell and Marshall returned to the store and resumed putting away the tools they'd received. "Well, Martha," Newell said, "a few more orders and inquiries like that and we might have a future here!"

"Should be some nice contacts for you at the Legion and the Elks club, too, Marshall."

"Isn't that funny. I really had to scramble to come up with Ralph's name. We didn't see much of each other at school. I wonder how many from my class are in college now?"

"Well, a couple more hours and we can button down this place for the night. Bruce is coming by to have dessert with us," Newell said.

To their delight, two carpenters came in and inquired about hammers. Each selected one from the new inventory. "Nice quality," one of them offered. "Do you have any tool belts, yet?"

"Should be in any day," Martha answered. "Leather goods are a little easier to come by. May I call you when they come in?"

"No mam, thanks, I'll drop by in a day or so." Both carpenters paid cash for their purchases, looked around the store at the inventory, and departed.

"Wow," Newell laughed. "Even a couple of cash sales!"

At six o'clock they closed the front door, checked that everything was locked up in the back, they left on two lights, departed, and locked the front door and with Martha in the middle of the seat of their pickup truck headed for home.

"Be nice to have a sedan," Martha said.

"Well, the new cars are as scarce as hens' teeth. But there are some good used cars out there. I'll look around," Newell said.

"And what would we use for money?" Martha said, then laughed scornfully.

"I'm not accepting any pay, you know. Apply that to a car," Marshall said. "The G.I. Bill awaits and I'm taking advantage of it."

"Is that your way of saying you're not interested in the store?"

"With your education, Martha, you should be the first to understand Marsh's desire to go to college," Newell said. There was a firmness in his voice that ended the conversation. They rode the rest of the way to their home in silence. Marshall was aware of the rigidity of his mother, and she leaned towards Newell, seeming to avoid body contact with him. Newell guided the pickup truck into the curved driveway. As they walked to the front door, Martha said, "I've some left-overs to warm up. Hope that will satisfy you men. I'm sure your uncle fed you well."

"Sure did. We had a good visit."

They took turns washing up and Martha placed slices of cold roast leg of lamb on a platter. She warmed up a dish of mashed potatoes, plus gravy, and string beans, and placed a large pitcher of milk on the table with glasses at each place. Before starting to eat they lowered their heads and Newell quietly said, "Bless this food to our use and us to thy service and make us ever mindful of the needs of others. In Christ's name, Amen."

Martha and Marshall voiced the 'amen' with Newell.

They had barely finished their dinner when they heard the gravel crunching beneath Bruce's tires.

"Who invited Bruce?" Martha asked.

"We did," Newell said, and he nodded towards Marshall. "He's always welcome in our home."

"Well, of course. But what he needs is a wife!"

Bruce entered the house through the back door. "I leaned your guns against the wall, Newell, and we cleaned them up nice and shiny. And look here, Sis, what your men folk collected." He carried in a large gunny-sack stuffed with pinecones, opened the top and displayed one. "Aren't they beauts!"

"That's a nice surprise. Thank you," Martha said, flatly.

Bruce placed the gunnysack on the floor and walked to Newell, grasped his hand, then walked over to Marshall. "That was fun out at the range, eh? You're really getting that rifle zeroed in," Bruce said. He smacked Marshall on the shoulder with the palm of his hand, and laughed loudly.

"You guys getting anxious to go up to Emil's this year?" his dad asked.

"I suppose," Marshall answered, not sure in his own mind that he really wanted to go deer hunting again.

"Heard that Emil's daughter got engaged to some intern where she's going to that nurse's training school. Same hospital," Bruce said.

"Uncle Bruce, I didn't get any mail from her all the time I was overseas."

Bruce shrugged his shoulders and said, "Oh."

"Son," Marshall's mother said, "I mistakenly opened a letter addressed to you. It just had M. Sunder, and in a woman's hand, and I assumed it meant Martha."

"Oh? Where is it?"

"By your dad's chair in the living room."

Marshall said, "Excuse me," and went to the living room and found three letters. He selected the letter with a woman's handwriting. Even without lifting it to look at the return address, he noticed the aroma. He opened it and turned to the bottom of the second page and saw the signature, Eileen.

Marshall sat in his dad's chair and read the letter. "Dear Fly Boy," it started out and Marshall chuckled.

"It's been a couple of months and I thought it about time to let you off the hook. I mean just in case you had any qualms, or worried, you know, that kind of thing, about our little adventure. As the saying goes, the rabbit lived.

I apologize for not being entirely honest with you when I departed rather suddenly. I realize how you feel, shy one, about how ladies are not supposed to talk, however, please try to be a little objective now. You see, my period started during our last night together, and I was startled and relieved and just wanted to go home to be with my mother. I hadn't had a period from the time Billy went over seas until then. For a few months after he left, I thought I was pregnant. I wasn't. So, it was like, well, I really felt alive again when it happened. I was a woman again.

My dad and mom and the lawyers have finally started the paper work for their divorce. I'm not surprised. In fact I'm kind of relieved for dad's sake. We've been playing golf a little. I've taken some lessons. The pro says he's sure I'll be able to break 120 by the end of the year. I guess that's not too bad for a woman, and I've heard Riviera is considered a tough golf course. And yes, mother is in hot pursuit of the rich guy I was telling you about. He doesn't have a chance. I wish I could dislike her, but I can't. School is really interesting. Did you ever hear of Dorothy Draper? Well, I hadn't, and she's another famous designer and architect and redid the famous Greenbrier in White Sulfur Springs. I think it's in West Virginia. Gosh, now I'll have to look that up!

And, dear Fly Boy, we've tabled that book, that collection of men's awful utterings about the fair sex. It got too disgusting even for my ultra liberal sorority sisters. Hope that pleases you.

Marshall, my sweet thing, I told my dad about meeting you at a gathering of aviators and I mentioned your war experiences, and your family business. He volunteered that if you get bored or disenchanted, to come on down. He said he could get you a position as an apprentice stockbroker, after some tests and stuff. Said if you were capable of earning your wings you could handle anything in the brokerage business.

Would love to give you the tour of the SC campus, and show you off to my sisters, too! So hurry south, my darling flyboy. I miss you!

Love and Kisses. Eileen

PS. Yes, Marshall, Billy will have a place in my heart forever, as I know Kristine will in yours."

Marshall reread the letter. He really hadn't expected to hear from her. It had been weeks since he'd written to inquire of her health. What a surprise. He sat back in the chair. Not pregnant. That's a relief. He shook his head and sighed, and thought, I can't believe mom read all of this.

Marshall then picked up another letter. The return address shocked him. It was from Gary McAdam, with a Los Angeles return address.

Marshall ripped open the letter. His eyes rushed through the writing.

"Dear First Lieutenant Sunder! And yep, my 'first' came through too, plus that little old shiny Bronze Star!

So, hi old buddy! Think you'd ever hear from me again? Well, a kraut doctor at Bad Scheidel put me back together again. You'll have to see me to believe it. Anyway, I've lots to tell you. Wanted to visit our old air base at Santa Ana after I got out. While I was there I looked up Pop's wife, Paula. Dated her several times and we fell in love head over heels. We got married. So I'm a daddy for Pop's little boy and Paula has Tim call me daddy. Can you believe it? Will fill in all the details when we arrive. We're planning on being in Chico in a few days, enroute to Seattle. Will stay in a hotel and give you a buzz when we settle in. Okay? My phone number here is Oregon 4023. Absolutely, McAdam."

"Wow," Marshall said aloud.

He looked at the return address of the third letter. It was from Major Crandall at Camp Beale. It can wait, Marshall thought. Probably more recruiting propaganda. He returned to the kitchen.

Newell and Bruce were eating cookies his mother had baked. They all turned to him simultaneously. "Good news?" his dad asked, lowering his glass of milk.

"McAdam married Pop's wife and they are going to be here for a visit in a few days. My God! I didn't think he'd even live through that damn deal! They're bringing their little boy, too. I think. He didn't say. Maybe grandparents or someone will take care of him. Christ, I can't believe it. McAdam and Pop's wife married and coming here! Wow! Good God, dad. Wait until you meet him, and you, mom, and Uncle Bruce. Christ almighty! What we went through together!"

"That's great, Son," his father said. "You know, you've never said much about the war: Your experiences, those sorts of things. We enjoyed what you shared at the rifle range."

"Really?" Marshall said, "I guess no one ever asked."

"Figured you'd tell us when you felt like it," Bruce said.

"We try not to pry, you know," his mother said very softly.

Marshall looked at his mother. Stared into her eyes. She shifted her eyes away from his.

"How much of the letter from Eileen did you read, Mother?"

"I really didn't mean to even open it." She turned her back towards him. "I am sorry."

"How far did you read, Mom?" Marshall prodded.

"Just far enough to know I'm not going to be a grandmother!" She shouted back at him, "Now! Are you satisfied! I didn't read the entire letter! I didn't even mean to read that first paragraph! So, I'm not going to be the grandmother of a bastard child. I'm ashamed that I couldn't put the letter down the second I opened it! So! It's my character that is flawed. Sorry you inherited my defective genes!" Then she started to sob.

"Jesus Christ! I can't believe this is happening. Reading my damn mail! And listen, mother! If she had been pregnant I'd have sure as hell married her and been proud of it." Marshall's face was livid.

"Hey, what the devil is going on with you two!" Marshall's dad spoke. He'd been talking with Bruce, looking at the rifles and discussing the trip to Izee. He heard little of their earlier exchange. "Now, calm down you two! This news about Gary and his wife coming ought to bring some joy to all of us."

"You can all just go to grass!" Martha exclaimed. She removed her glasses and dabbed away the moisture from eyes with her apron. The men realized that her frustration and anger were deep-seated.

Marshall sighed and turned away from her. "I'm sorry, folks. There is just too damn much to explain now."

"And you watch your language in my home, Marshall Sunder! I can't stand your profanity. Every sentence you speak you take the Lord's name in vain!"

"Hey Sis, take it easy. Your little boy is a man, now, remember. Both of you, ease up," Bruce said, quietly, admonishingly. "Come on, calm down."

"And you can mind your own business, too," Martha said, turning towards Bruce and staring at him. Martha found a handkerchief in her apron pocket and blew her nose, then dabbed at her eyes again.

"Enough, enough Martha!" Marshall's dad said, now raising his voice. Then he walked to her and put his arms around her and she removed her glasses and placed her face on his shoulder and sobbed.

Bruce departed in silence. They heard him walk across the porch, heard the retort when the door of his pickup truck slammed shut, the sound of the V-8 engine, and then the noise of the gravel crackling beneath his tires. Marshall and his father went to the living room and Marshall handed the letter from McAdam to him, and placed the letter from Eileen in his hip pocket.

Martha began to gather the dishes and went to the sink with them. Marshall and Newell went to the living room after Newell asked "Can I help you, honey" and Martha replied, emphatically, "No!"

As she turned to the kitchen sink, Marshall and Newell walked towards the living room. Martha heard Newell say, "Maybe we ought to concentrate on that Yosemite jigsaw puzzle for awhile and let things calm down around here."

"Yeah, Dad, and gosh, if you're curious, I'll try to unravel some of this Air Corps crap for you."

A knock was heard on the back door, a few slight taps followed by two short ones and then the door was slowly pushed open and Bruce peeked into the kitchen area.

"Hey, Sis. Truce! No plate throwing now, but little brother's back to hold you and squeeze you up nice and tight, close to me."

Martha turned away from the wet dishes in the sink and stared at him.

"You are not one bit funny."

"Ah, come off it, honey, "Bruce admonished. "Pour me a cup of coffee, please. And don't try to slip any whiskey into it. Any tapioca left?"

"You are impossible, and no. "

"Where are Newell and Marsh?"

"Working on the jigsaw puzzle."

"Okay now, dry your hands, pour two cups of coffee, sit down and please listen to me a minute."

Martha sighed and did as Bruce suggested. He pulled back a chair and nodded for her to sit down.

"Well?" Martha said. Bruce slid in the chair and then sat opposite her.

"Damn it, for a minute or two, let's forget the Kane temper. I want to ask you a couple of questions about Marshall."

"Oh?"

"Your son grew up on you. He's not the same boy you gave a Bible, kissed, and sent off to war three years ago."

"You think I don't know that?"

"Well, you're treating him like a kid."

"I am not!"

"Well, I'm not going to belabor it, but it seems to me you're treating him like a possession, like a piece of property. Do you know what I mean?"

"Frankly Bruce, I don't."

"It's the store. It may be your dream, and Newell's, but it just might not be his."

"Dream? It's now a reality. We managed to keep open during the war and now things are picking up again. It'll be his someday."

"Well, he just may not be interested in a career in the store."

"Newell and I have devoted our lives to that store so that he'll have an inheritance."

"But he wants a college education!"

"He'll get a liberal education running that store."

"Sis, he can go back into the Air Corps and get a free education. He told me he was earning around $300 a month, with room and board, and he's saved a few thousand dollars. What can you and Newell pay him? Not half that, I bet. I sense he wants to go back into the Air Corps."

"You sense?" Martha answered and her voice cracked, her chin quivered, and she turned away from Bruce. "And what does Newell sense? And what about what I feel?"

"Honey, I suspect Newell feels the same, and I don't want to hurt your feelings, dear, but I think what you feel is possessiveness. Come on, sis. Cut the damn umbilical cord!"

"That's mean, Bruce."

"Come on now, you know I wouldn't hurt you for anything. Just let loose of him."

"My God, so now I'm the selfish mother." Martha rested her head in the palms of her hands and with her elbows on the top of the kitchen table and began to sob.

Bruce stood up and walked around the table and placed his large hands on her shoulders and began to massage her tightened muscles. He gently massaged her neck muscles below her hair.

"Bruce?" Martha asked quietly. "Have you been out to the poorhouse to see the Shanks?"

"Nope."

"Have you visited any one at that place?"

"Yeah, I stopped and saw old Sid and his wife a few months ago."

"And what did you think of the place?"

"Smelled bad. That awful urine odor choked me."

"Well, the thought of Newell and I ending up like that, well, it simply terrifies me. I'll commit suicide before I have to end up like that!"

"My God, sis, so that's what this is all about!" Bruce exclaimed. "Damn it to hell, you and Newell aren't going to end up in any poorhouse. I'll see to that. Hells bells, you guys are all I have. I may be five years your junior, but give me some credit. Have a little faith! We'll start thinking about it now. I own a couple of vacant lots. Can borrow on them. When the time comes, I'll build some apartment houses to live in, plus some more to rent. And, this Social Security thing might help. My God, Martha, you're a young, healthy, intelligent woman. And Newell is hanging in there real well, too. Why, you're talking twenty- five years down the road. Marshall won't let that happen, and he'll be a lot better off getting educated than all three of you trying to eke out a living at the store now!"

Martha dried her tears and said, "The future simply frightens me. I can say that to you. I wouldn't allow Newell to know. He's having enough problems with his heart. And we had to take out another mortgage on our home. Oh, I know I shouldn't burden Marshall with all of this. I really thought he'd be anxious to sort of take over, or at least I hoped he would."

"Geez! I'm glad I came back. I honest to God think I'm beginning understand things better now," Bruce said. He sat down again opposite Martha. " Martha, I didn't realize you folks had to take out even one mortgage on this place. And now you're telling me a second one?"

"It takes money to buy all of the tools and supplies we need. Without inventories we might as well close the doors."

Bruce arose and went to the kitchen sink and found the coffeepot was empty.

Martha watched him and said, "I'll make another fresh pot. Newell will want some."

"I really don't need any more, thanks. I've got to get going. Have to get up before daylight. You better get in there and help them with that puzzle."

"Thanks for coming back, Bruce. Really, you've given me some things to think about. Now I've got to get some rest. More inventory arriving tomorrow morning."

"Okay Martha," Bruce said, "and don't you ever mention the poorhouse again. Hear me?"

"How awful to think of needing charity; of accepting charity. Well, what do the fliers say? Roger?"

"That's it. Good night, honey. Come on now, give me a good old Kane hug, and I'll be off. You forget that poorhouse bologna. Okay?"

"All right. And Bruce, you don't believe I'd deliberately open Marshall's mail?"

"Of course not, sis, now let that rest."

She nodded and they embraced briefly. Bruce departed.

Martha returned to the kitchen sink and finished washing and drying the dishes. After putting them away, she pushed open the door into the living room. Marshall and Newell had arisen and were walking away from the card table upon which the puzzle sat. They both headed towards the couch, unaware of Martha.

"Dad, I really don't know how to tell you and mom about three years of service. Where to start? What is important to you folks? I wrote a lot of letters," Marshall said, then hesitated and his dad spoke.

"Well, we haven't the faintest idea about what happened to Gary McAdam. You're expecting all of us to be sympathetic, but you're keeping us in the dark. We're not mind readers. And I just got in on the end of that shouting match with your mother. Are you in trouble with some girl?"

"No, I'm not in trouble. I'm sorry, Dad," Marshall said, "I've felt that some things that happened overseas would be upsetting for you and mom." Marshall sat in a chair facing the couch. "So," he cleared his throat, I will tell you what happened to Gary, and to Pop, and to Frank. Christ, there's so much crap that went on! I'll answer any questions you have, okay?"

"Do you want your mother in on this?"

"Why don't you listen and then decide if you want to tell her in your own way, or have me repeat it. Damn it dad, I just can't believe she'd read my mail!"

"Surprised me too," Newell said, his voice husky. He sighed, " Guess she's human."

Newell leaned back in his chair, raised his arms and ran his fingers through his hair. He looked at Marshall, wondering just how dramatic his revelations might be, that he was so hesitant to share them with Martha. He, too, could not comprehend Martha's act. In his family, no one opened anyone else's mail. Marshall sat facing him.

"Dad, you weren't too subtle when you reminded me that mom hadn't changed," Marshall said, questioning, rather than simply making the statement. "Do you feel I've changed so much?"

"Oh, not really." Newell smiled, "You remember my friend, Jack Herrick. Well, once I was stewing about not being able to please one of our duck hunting acquaintances, I couldn't say the right thing, do anything right, he'd contradict anything and everything I said, no matter how trivial, and as far as he was concerned I even laughed at the wrong time, you know, the harder I tried the worse it got. Finally I avoided getting into the same blind with him. So, one day Jack says, 'Newell, why don't you relax. A nasty adult was a nasty kid and eventually he'll be a nasty old man.' Well, I realized there was a lot of truth in that so I just ignored the son of a gun and I was happier and he didn't even know the difference. So, no, to answer your question, basically you'll always be the same, but," then Newell paused and cleared his throat, "I suppose three years in the service has allowed you to become a little careless with your language. When you left home you were never profane. Now it seems you do curse a lot, and you know how your mom always says that people that swear a lot reveal their ignorance, that they have an inadequate vocabulary."

"I hmm, that's interesting, Dad. I guess you're right. I'll be more aware. And I'm sorry if I've offended you and mom."

"Well, it's only because you asked. Now what say we get on with this bull session, " Newell said and laughed.

For thirty-five minutes Marshall revealed the highlights of the events that still tormented him. As their session continued, Martha appeared with mugs of coffee. Newell thanked her but did not invite her to sit down with them. She hadn't brought a cup for herself, assuming that her husband and son wanted privacy. Marshall found it particularly difficult to describe the death of the young man they called Spike.

Marshall told his dad that Gary was scheduled for surgery the same day he was sent home, but Kristine was never mentioned. As far as he was concerned, their love had been buried with her at Bad Scheidel. He was sorry only that there had been no response when he sent the money for the headstone. Gary never responded. Surely Cal had given him the money. Cal was strange, Marshall thought, but he felt he was honest. But that part of his life involving Kristine was no one's business but his own.

"Well, Dad," Marshall said, "might as well let you know that I met a war widow in San Francisco. Her husband was a P-38 pilot. For a long time she thought he was missing in action. She confronted his squadron commander in Frisco and learned the real truth. Dad, we needed each other at that particular time, I guess. Our paths crossed and we sort of stumbled into each other. Call it an affair if you want. It was short—lived, day or two actually. As far as I'm concerned she's a really a nice gal. She's going to USC. It's her letter that mom read."

"Seems like you've lived a lifetime of tragedies in a few short years," Newell sighed. "Want some more coffee, Son? I don't have any J. D., but I've some good brandy."

Marshall hesitated, then said, his voice now husky, "That would be great, if there's any coffee left."

Newell arose and departed. Marshall heard him speak to Martha. Then he returned with an opened pint bottle of brandy and a pot of hot coffee. While he was gone, Marshall opened and read the letter from Major Crandall.

Newell sat and held the cup in both hands, warming them. He waited for Marshall to speak again.

"Would you listen to this Dad," Marshall said. "Major Crandall wonders if he could spend some weekends working in the store for gratis. He says he's always wanted to own a hardware store since he was a kid, and maybe he could either get the desire out of his system or pursue it further. He owns that Piper Cub now, and could get up here quickly after lunch on Fridays. Work Friday afternoon and Saturdays and if anyone is at the store on Sunday, he could help out, then fly back."

"Amazing offer," Newell said, raising his eyebrows. "I assume you have reason to trust this person."

"I really don't know him all that well. He appears to be an honest man."

"Guess we'll have to kick that around with your mother before you give him an answer."

"Sure, Dad. Maybe I could get him to check me out in that plane while he's here. Always wanted to be a pilot, you know."

"Well, Marshall, this has been an interesting evening to say the least. You know, about the war and all, when you were overseas, about all we had to go on was the newspaper, the Pathe news, Ed Murrow, Gabriel

Heater and of course we read Ernie Pyle. Your letters were always upbeat, you know, on the positive side, so all of these things being condensed into one evening, well, it's, well, I guess I'm just at a loss for words." Newell sighed and again leaned back in his chair and once more raised his arms and ran his fingers through his hair. "Now, unless you have some objections about what you've told me, I'm going to share it with your mother, that is, the gist of what you've told me. Your mother's a wise lady. She'll understand. Okay? And please forgive that little transgression, Son. You know, reading that darn letter. I really think it was the way it was addressed."

"I'll try, Dad, sure. And incidentally, I'm going to take off a couple of days soon, and join Uncle Bruce on a trip up to Red Bluff. He's going to pick up a load of redwood decking and could use some help: next week, or maybe the following one. Okay?"

"Of course," Newell said, "Do you good."

"Night Dad," Marshall said, he arose and patted his dad on the shoulder as he walked past him towards his bedroom, then he paused, looked into his dad's eyes for a second, "I'm having a heck of a time with this death thing, dad. You understand, about Pop, and the kid we called Spike," then he choked up and caught himself before he said Kristine, "And others. You know, they are going to be dead forever."

Tears swelled in Newell's eyes then he spoke, attempting to control the quaver in his voice, "I'm beginning to understand that your wounds aren't from flak or bullets. You know, your mom and I get our answers on things like death and the hereafter at church. We're Christians. At least we try to be. Maybe that author in your book can give you some help?"

Marshall hesitated, then sat down again.

"Strange thing happened back at Bad Scheidel, dad," Marshall started, quietly, wondering if he should tell his dad anything at all about Kristine, then decided not to mention her name. "We had German women, you know, wives and widows and such cleaning our rooms. One of them saw me with my Bible and asked if she could look at it. She studied it a minute. The Germans knew English and French, too, a lot of them. Well educated. Then she said, 'Luftgangster, I can't believe you pray from the same Bible as we pray from. I'll bring mine tomorrow and compare further. All right?'" Marshall continued, "Well, she compared them and they were exactly the same, as you'd expect. Doesn't it seem ironic that the German mothers and wives and children are giving Bibles and new testaments to their loved ones, sending them off to war, and we're all expecting God or Jesus to look after all of us? What's the answer? A German mother gives a Bible to her son and tells him where to read and that God will look after him. Just like my mom."

"Interesting." Newell said, "you know, we heard and read so much about Germans becoming atheists, that I, for one, didn't even think about them having faith in God anymore. Maybe Hitler's ideas didn't get down to what we call 'common folks'. Son, I feel the important thing is that you are sensitive about the irony. And, no, I don't think there's any easy answer. I'll pose the scenario, as you've described it, to Reverend Harms and see what he has to say."

"Dad, I hope you understand that for reasons of my own, I'm not comfortable with Reverend Harms. I hope mom will lay off about me going with you to church."

"I'll handle it," Newell said, then cleared his throat, ran his fingers threw his hair again and said, "Marsh, about that fight you got into over at the *Shuffle Em*. Well, God knows I'm not much of a philosopher, but apparently something happened that made you turn to violence. I know that isn't your nature. But, well, I presume you took a stand, and I'm also guessing that there was a principle involved. You declared your own personal war: A bully? God knows the world has had its fill of bullies! Bully? Isn't that a synonym for Nazi or Fascist? I suspect you recognized evil and did something about it. Son, you know, anger, and violence, retribution and death, well, those are darn complicated subjects."

"Thanks, Dad, for being so patient."

"Hey Marsh, life is a two way street, you know, especially in a family. I'd like to think that you'd make a real effort to understand your mother's viewpoint. No room for chips on the shoulder with either one of you."

"Certainly! Thanks, I love you, Dad." Marshall said, and again gripped his father's shoulder. "Think I'll go have a little visit with Dr. Fosdick right now. Goodnight."

"Night Son."

CHAPTER 27

▼

McAdam's Visit

After the discussion with his father, it soon became obvious to Marshall that his mother had been briefed about the occupation duty occurrences. To him, she now seemed more subdued, revealing empathy, he thought, and was calmer in her communications with him, and while they still maintained a space, they both awkwardly and gingerly avoided a chance for confrontation. He wasn't sure just how much or how little his dad might have covered, but he had reached the point where he didn't much care.

While continuing to put away the incoming merchandise that arrived almost daily now from the wholesale suppliers, and waiting on the customers who were becoming aware that Sierra Mercantile had a bigger variety of goods on their shelves than the other hardware stores in Chico, Marshall had much silent-time to himself, and he mulled over the events of his life since he had been put on inactive duty.

He recalled the bull session he'd had with his Uncle Bruce following their day at the rifle range. While his uncle was barbecuing the T-bones,

Marshall reminded him of the hunting trip where he'd talked about tempering steel, and comparing it to a man's character. "How do you resolve character with going to see Clean Jean?" Marshall had inquired. He remembered that Bruce seemed to squirm a bit, and had then acknowledged that prostitution wasn't a good thing, especially for the girls, but for him it was satisfying a compelling biological urge. He recognized it, the hunger, the drive, when his temper began to get short and he found himself wanting to throw his hammer, that's when he rationalized, or justified in his mind that a trip to Clean Jean's was due. It was therapy, and made him more civilized, he'd concluded.

Then Bruce said, "To my way of thinking, if a man marries a woman just for the bedroom activities, then that's more sinful than paying for it." He told Marshall that if the right woman came along, he'd get hitched again, but in the meantime Clean Jean's girls satisfied him and didn't hurt anyone so far as he could see. As far as he could ascertain, most of the girls seemed to enjoy it as much as he did. If they were just acting, well that didn't bother him. He didn't see as how his not going there would put Clean Jean out of business.

"I hope you aren't too disappointed in your old uncle," Bruce said. He studied his large, callused hands, then added, "Some of my devout Christian friends seem to think that they have been licensed by St. Peter to sit in judgment of their fellow man. So, I guess I wouldn't fare too well."

"Then how about another little sip of JD?" Marshall asked, and they both laughed and Bruce poured the drinks. "And, Uncle Bruce, I hope you don't put me in that category, of playing St. Peter." They raised their drinks, and touched glasses.

"You know, Marsh," Bruce said, after pausing to hold his glass up and stare at the bourbon, "Jeanette is the sort of woman I could marry and love. She makes it clear that she's a businesswoman. One time we shacked up and I was trying to figure how much money I should leave on the dresser, and she sensed it. She came over to me and from behind wrapped her arms around me and really hugged me. Her breasts pushed against my back, and I started to get excited again. I turned and hugged her and kissed her. ' Bruce, honey,' she whispered, 'I'm not a whore. I'm a madam. A businesswoman. We made love because I like you. You don't have enough money to buy me. Nobody does!' she said and laughed. Her voice seemed to sparkle. Oh, it would be impossible, marrying her, but believe me, she's some woman!"

"Will I get to meet her?"

"I reckon," Bruce said. "I'll call before we go over. I take my toolbox. There's always something that needs repairing, and I like to do it for her," Bruce chuckled. "How about one more little snort?"

"Roger," Marshall answered and poured two ounces into their glasses. "I like it when you call me son," Marshall said. "I'm a lucky guy to have both a great dad and you to talk to. Some of the guys in the outfit had pretty shabby home lives." And Marshall thought about the night that Tex came to his room and departed with a new nickname.

"You know what Jeanette says she's going to do?" Bruce asked, then continued without waiting for an answer. "She listens to the advice that some of her educated clientele are happy to offer. I guess they are widowers. A professor down at Cal is telling her what kind of art to buy, you know, those French artists, and gave her a couple of books on fine furniture, antiques and collectibles. And a lawyer from Frisco is advising her on how to invest in blue chip stocks, like IBM and Eastman Kodak and Coca-Cola. And a banker gave her a book on how to keep track of her expenses. Her goal is to eventually move on down to the Frisco and open a fancy antique store."

Marshall had listened carefully. That was admirable, he thought, to have a plan for your life, even if she's in a tawdry business, she obviously wants to better her life. And I am floundering. I've got to set some goals, he concluded.

Furthermore, Marshall did not intend to sit in judgment on anyone, especially his uncle. He recalled Frank reading aloud from one of his books about the Yin Yang of Zen, and shades of gray, about everything not being black and white. If his mother were going to be less judgmental in her everyday association towards him, then he too, would try to avoid subjects that might trigger a renewal of the letter-opening incident. He'd meet her half way. If she'd read the entire letter she must have seen the reference to Eileen's Billy, and to Kristine, but their names never came up. In addition, everyone in the family seemed to have forgotten the word, Model A. Well, Marshall mused, he'd let that sleeping dog lie. And especially Doctor Fosdick seemed to be advising him to forgive and forget.

Then, early one morning right after breakfast, much to Marshall's delight, McAdam telephoned from San Francisco and said they'd be arriving in Chico, would find a hotel and would call again from there. "That's just great. Now hold the line a second," Marshall said, and while they waited, Marshall went to the kitchen and asked his mother if they could stay in his room and he would go to Bruce's place. "Why certainly," she replied without hesitation.

"Okay Gary, now get this. You and Paula are going to bed down with my folks and I'll stay at my uncle's, just a few minutes away. Are you reading me? Good, now, write down how to get to our house. And do you have the little boy, Tim, with you?"

"Tim is staying with Paula's folks. Are you sure this won't be an inconvenience?"

"It's going to be great. Now, have you got something to writer on?

"Wait a second, Marsh, Paula wants to talk to your mom."

"Mother," Marshall called out, "would you come to the phone, please?"

Martha appeared, and it seemed to Marshall she was always drying her hands on her apron." "What is it?" she asked.

"Paula McAdam would like to talk to you."

"Oh?" Martha said She pushed waves of her hair away from her face with the back of her hand, accepted the ear piece in her left hand and lifted the stand with the transmitter, and with her lips almost touching the mouth piece, quietly said, " This is Mrs. Sunder."

"Hello, Mrs. Sunder. First of all, Gary and I are really looking forward to meeting you folks. And are you certain that we won't be in the way?"

"Well, Mr. Sunder and I are looking forward to having you as our guests."

"What can we bring? We've seen fruit stands along the way. Do you like watermelon?

"Now you just bring yourselves. We're all looking forward to this reunion!"

"Thank you so much, and here's Gary."

Martha handed the telephone back to Marshall.

The operator came on the line and said, "Your three minutes are up."

"Thanks, mam, " Gary said, "we'll pay for any extra time. You still there, Marsh?"

"Still connected, ole' buddy. Now write this down carefully so we don't have to send out a search party," Marshall said, and laughed loudly. He then gave detailed instructions on how to reach the Sunder residence. He continued to chuckle as he returned the receiver to the cradle. Marshall went to the kitchen, "Thanks, mom, I really appreciate that."

"All of us, your dad and Bruce and I are looking forward to meeting Gary and Paula. She sounds like a nice girl."

"Well, I guess I'd better straighten out my room a bit," Marshall said, chuckling, "They should get here tomorrow afternoon."

"Marshall, I have to go to the store. Your Uncle Bruce picked up your dad and took him in early. Tomorrow morning, would you mind changing the sheets and pillow cases and get some clean bath towels and hand towels and wash cloths and just put them on the end of your bed." Martha said, "I'll vacuum and dust before I go to the store."

"Consider it done," Marshall said.

"You might want to take a look at the lawn." Martha hinted," Your dad just sharpened the Pennsylvania a couple of days ago."

"Certainly, front and back. I'll edge them, too. Suppose I ought to touch up Uncle Bruce's place a bit. I'll head over to his place, take a look, then I'll see you at the store."

"Son, a couple other things. Would you mind finding those extension leaves for the dining room table and installing them?" She paused then added, "and it would be a big help to me if you could get down the apple pattern platters, bowls and dishes, cups and all. Okay?"

"It's a done deal," Marshall said.

"Bye dear," his mother said, "see you later," She fanned herself with the apron. Her face was flushed.

Martha drove the pick up truck to Sierra Mercantile. Bruce was still there helping Newell put merchandise away.

"Hi honey," Newell said, smiling, as Martha entered the store. "Come on over here a second. Bruce suggested I put my Model 12 back here, along side these shelves, out of the customers' sight. Loaded with buckshot. You know, just in case."

"Let's hope we'll never need it," Martha said. She inspected the placement of the shotgun, nodded, then turned to them and smiled. "Well, Marsh heard from Gary and Paula. They are going to stay at our place, and Marsh said he'd stay with Bruce. They get in tomorrow afternoon, sometime."

"Well, boy howdy!" Newell exclaimed, he slapped his legs, then laughed aloud. "And I'm amazed that the pilot even survived that awful thing."

"What awful thing are you talking about?" Bruce asked.

"Oh," Newell said, "Gosh, Bruce I thought you knew. That poor kid was castrated by some Germans. He was about to be operated on when their C.O. shipped Marsh on home. As I understand it, he was concerned that there was a revenge thing going on because the Germans found out that Marsh's crew bombed the bridge near where they were stationed."

"My God, that is horrible!" Bruce said.

Martha turned and walked across the store and busied herself with an assortment of scissors that just arrived. "We'll have to let some of the ladies know we got in a shipment of Wiss pinking shears," she said.

"Does sis know all about that?" Bruce whispered to Newell.

"She knows."

"Marsh is mowing the lawns," Martha said. "Probably mow your place, too, Bruce, if it needs it."

"Oh, yeah, it needs it. Guess I'll go lend him a hand," Bruce said. "See you folks tomorrow."

"We'll be expecting you for dinner, of course," Martha said.

"Thanks, Sis, and I'll bring a bottle of some expensive dago red!" Bruce laughed and turned, departing from the rear of the store where his truck was parked.

The following day, midmorning, Marshall said he had some errands to run. He took the pickup truck and went to The Tam O'Shanter Liquor store. "I'd like a fifth of Jack Daniel's, Mr. O'Toole, and wonder if you'd recommend a scotch whiskey." Marshall studied the brand names on the shelf behind the proprietor. "My copilot and his wife are due in town this afternoon."

"So why don't you spoil the lad with some fine Irish whiskey? Some Bushmill or I've a nice bottle of Dublin's Dew here," and he pointed to a squat little jug, the dust on the bottles shoulders obvious even from a distance. He winked at Marshall and laughed.

"His name is Gary McAdam."

"No, Marshall, I wouldn't part with Irish liquid gold, however I'll tell you truthfully now, for your friend, you can't go wrong with Johnnie Walker Red Label scotch. A wee bit more costly than some others, but if it's a veteran buddy, then you can loosen the purse strings a bit." Again he laughed, and Marshall said, "Sure, Mr. O'Toole, and what proper thing would you recommend for the ladies, Paula and my mom?"

"Does your mother tend to like sweets?'

"Yes sir."

"Well then, I'd suggest a nice bottle of sherry. I've a fine one on the sweet side from the Napa Valley. You can't go wrong with it, lad. As a matter of fact, if the ladies don't rave about it, you bring it on back and I'll keep it for the Mrs. and I'll refund your cost, too. How about that now?"

"How can I resist such high pressure salesmanship?" Marshall laughed as he reached for his billfold.

"I saw that picture of you in the paper with that general pinning a medal on your chest."

"I think that the Air Corps must have had a surplus of medals after the war, Mr. O'Toole."

"Now I do admire your modesty, now young man," Mr. O'Toole said. He sighed, then continued, "Our Dan survived that Battle of the Bulge, you know. He's not been well since he's come home. His feet were frozen badly and he goes to the VA hospital regularly. And he is deeply depressed, so sad, unhappy, lonely, all of them wrapped into one burden of his own."

"I didn't know that, Mr. O'Toole. I'm real sorry. Will he be able to help in the store?"

"Can't handle too much standing as yet. So, I suppose not for awhile, anyway. We'll know soon enough." Mr. O'Toole sighed deeply, and shook his head. "And he has these awful nightmares. A little German girl died in his arms at Bastogne when her home was shelled and collapsed on top of all of them. Her mother, her little boy, and our Dan, they were all in the same building."

"That's awful," Marshall said. "Mr. O'Toole, when Dan's home, if he wants some ETO vet to shoot the breeze with, have him give me a call at the store, and we'll get together."

"That would be good for him, lad," Mr. O'Toole said. "And now before you leave I want you to accept these two little glasses, courtesy of The Tam O Shanter. I think the sherry will sip well from them." Mr. O'Toole began to wrap them separately in tissue paper.

"Gee, that's not necessary," Marshall said. Mr. O'Toole laughed softly and ignored him.

"So you handle them gently, lad, the stems are fragile. Our gift, from Mrs. O'Toole and me, to your mother."

"Thank you sir. And you have Dan give me a buzz, okay?" Marshall said, then as an after thought added, "If Mrs. O'Toole sews, you might let her know we got in a few Wiss pinking shears."

"I'll be telling the little woman, and thank you."

Marshall paid for the beverages and waved as he departed the store. Smiling, he thought, there are a lot of nice folks in this little burg. He drove to his home, and felt that the front yard looked neat and well trimmed after he'd mowed and edged it. He dragged the hose so that the sprinkler would touch another area of the lawn.

Marshall placed the liquor in a cabinet in the kitchen and unwrapped the two glasses and placed them side-by-side on the breakfast table, then placed the bottle of golden sherry beside them.

Making a bed was a cinch after the cadet days when all beds had to be made with the nurse-type, hospital corners, the sheets and the blankets forming a neat forty five degree angle, as they were tucked in at the foot of the bed. Marshall carefully selected the towels and wash cloths, making certain they had no holes, and all matched, and as his mother had instructed, placed them at the foot of the bed.

He knew his mother wanted to do some more cleaning, so he returned to the store. It was almost noon.

"Did as you asked, Mom. The bedroom is all ready. Dishes are down and the extensions are in."

"Well, I've some shopping to do. I'll prepare a standing rib roast with all the fixin's," Martha said.

"How complicated is it to bake one of your famous pineapple upside down cakes, Mom?"

"I think our guests will be pleased," Martha smiled and they allowed their eyes to make a longer contact than had happened in months.

Marshall's mind turned to the book by Dr. Fosdick and he thought, *maybe I'm like that person in the lighthouse. Instead of looking out at the world, around me, the windows are mirrors and all I see is Marshall, Marshall, Marshall! Well, I hope this visit goes well. Hell! I'll make it go well!*

"I'll stick around the store until about two, Mother, then I'll go home and wait for Gary and Paula," Marshall said. "Dad will be okay here alone for awhile. When they show up I'll show them their room, unless you are home. Then you can. I want to bring them back over to the store while it's still open. Okay?"

"Of course. And I will be home. I have to get that prime rib started, and the rest of the meal."

Again Marshall returned to his home. He turned off the sprinkler and carefully coiled the hose, then swept the porch. He picked up the doormat and took it to the driveway where he shook it vigorously, then returned it to its place at the front door. The word welcome was faded, Marshall observed, and wished he'd thought to have purchased a new one. Something we ought to stock at the store, he mused, then went into the house. He was surprised to see a vase in the middle of the dining room table with multicolored zinnias, the blooms thick and saucer size. The bright reds and yellows and orange colors excited him. Marshall walked to the kitchen and his mother was scrubbing the skins of large Idaho potatoes.

"Flowers are pretty, Mom."

"I cut them over at the Jackson's. June said to help myself. It's about the end of them."

"Everything sure smells good."

"I see you bought some whiskey."

"Yep. Good stuff, too," Marshall said, " And Mr. O'Toole recommended that cream sherry for you and Paula and sent the little glasses with his compliments. Do you like them?"

"Very nice. I'll send him a little thank you note," Martha said. " Well, I hope you men don't drink too much before dinner. Want you all to enjoy it."

"Right. Just some for old times sake, you know."

"Well, your Uncle Bruce does get loud if he has too much."

"Everything will be just fine, mom. You just relax."

"Are all of the waste baskets emptied?"

"Yep."

Immediately Marshall began to chuckle aloud when he heard the gravel crunching on the curved driveway. Without even looking out of the windows he knew it had to be Gary and Paula. Marshall had always felt that Gary's personality was like ragtime music. He was mischievous, he was laughter and adventure, he was fun and Marshall felt Gary had come along in this life too late for the merriment of the Gay Nineties. Gary would have been dancing on tabletops with sexy, young, hip-swaying and body-wriggling girls, in smoky speakeasies with Negro bands playing Dixieland music. It was amazing, how he was handling the cruel thing that happened to him in Bad Scheidel, and Marshall was curious about the operation. No one from the squadron had written to him since his quick departure from Germany. There were a lot of blank spaces that Gary could fill in.

Marshall swung open the front door and the screen door, and the screen door slammed shut loudly behind him. He strode down the stairs, hurrying to the shiny black, four-door '46 Ford sedan parked in front of the house. Dust from the gravel was just beginning to settle when Gary emerged from the driver's side and hurried around to the passenger side, where he met Marshall. They stood, grinning then, staring at each other, then simultaneously extended their right hands and gripped and shook vigorously. Gary released his grip and turned to the car, opened the door and took Paula's hand and she swung her hips and knees in one discreet motion out of the car and stood and reached out for Marshall, who immediately took her in his arms.

"Welcome Paula! Crime-a-nitly, I feel like I've known you all my life." Marshall spoke, almost reverently.

Paula held him close, kissed him on the cheek, and then stood back and studied him for a second. "Why, you are a lot cuter than Gary described." She giggled quietly and Marshall laughed, then looked at Gary.

"Hey, I like that new nose. Heck of lot better than the old one!"

"Hell, I deserved a Purple Heart for that episode. And, hey fella, what's with the dark around your eyes? Overwork?"

"I'm just a peace maker," Marshall grinned. "I'll tell you about it later. Let me give you a hand with your gear. My mom is waiting inside. She's got a nice dinner on the way."

"Didn't know what to bring," Gary said. " Paula selected a two-pound box of *Mrs. See's* candy. Big variety of chocolates, and can you believe this, she bought two loaves of that Frisco bread. You know, the sourdough kind!"

"Terrific!" Marshall said, and he remembered his last remark to Eileen when she said good-bye to him in the lobby of the Fairmont Hotel.

"Nice looking Ford, Gary."

"Company car. How about that?" Gary said, "And are we anxious to see that famous Model A you were always bragging about. Can Paula and I ride in the rumble seat?"

"Sorry, buddy," Marshall said, then sighed, "I'll fill you in later. I'm driving an old pickup truck."

"Well, I'll be darned. As a matter of fact, I'm flabbergasted!"

"Not something I want to get into now," Marshall said.

"I've already forgotten you ever had the car!" Gary said, laughing, and winked at Paula. "Right, honey?"

"Sounds like a family-only subject to me," Paula said.

"Come on in and meet my mother. She's fixing a nice meal in your honor," Marshall said, "Let me help with your suitcase, Paula. I see you're still using the old B-4 bag, Gary."

Marshall carried Paula's small suitcase. At the door he stopped, held open the screen door and pushed the heavy front door open with one foot, nodded for them to enter and followed them into the living room. Marshall noticed that Paula scanned the furnishings quickly. Gary walked towards the kitchen.

Martha emerged from the kitchen, smiling and wiping her hands on her apron, "Welcome to Chico," she said. Without hesitation, McAdam walked straight to her and wrapped his arms around her, hugged her, lifted her off of her feet and sat her back down gently. "I'm sure happy to finally get to meet you, Mom Sunder. Marsh gabbed about you and his father so much I feel like you're my own folks." Taken aback, Martha laughed, then shook his hand, and turned to Paula. They approached each other and Paula extended her hand and quietly said, "How do you do, Mrs. Sunder."

"We've been looking forward to this so much. Newell is at the store."

"I love your home," Paula said. "The oval glass in the front door is beautiful."

"Thank you, dear," Martha said.

"Soon as they get settled, I'd like to take them on over. Do you want to join us, mom?"

"No, Son, I've some things to do in the kitchen."

"May I help with the dinner?" Paula asked.

"No thanks, dear. I'm sure Marsh wants to give both you and Gary the tour," Martha smiled, straightened her apron and returned to the kitchen. "I'll join you at the store in a little while and help Newell lock up."

Marshall helped Gary and Paula with their luggage, showing them the bedroom and bathroom, then retreated to the living room where he waited.

Within a few minutes Gary and Paula reentered the living room. "Comfy bedroom," Paula said.

"I hope so, "Marshall said. "How about a ride in that new Ford?" he added.

They walked to the car. Gary held open the door to the back seat for Paula. "You can be my copilot, Marsh," Gary said. Marshall sat in the front seat and gave directions to Gary and within a few minutes they arrived at Sierra Mercantile.

"It's bigger than you described, Marsh," Gary said.

"That's funny. It seemed smaller to me when I got home. Well, come on in and meet my dad," Marshall said, "and, my Uncle Bruce is here, too. There's his pickup."

The front entrance was almost at street level, but there was a different elevation at the back of the store where trucks could back up and the trucks bed would be level with the dock.

Newell and Bruce were working at the back of the store hoisting kegs of nails, one atop the other.

"Heavy bastards," Bruce said, grunting, , then laughed as he looked up and saw Marshall, Paula and Gary approaching. "Hope she didn't hear me, Newell."

Newell turned then and saw them approaching. He put the palm of his left hand against the small of his back, as if to help him stand erect.

"Welcome to Chico!" Newell exclaimed. "My, we have been looking forward to this day!"

"Dad, Uncle Bruce, meet Gary and Paula," Marshall said, then watched as the men shook hands and his dad and Uncle Bruce both hugged Paula.

"Where's your mother?" Newell asked.

"She was busy in the kitchen and said she'd be along in awhile to help lock up."

"Well, we don't need her to help lock up, however she can show Paula some of the new merchandise that Bruce and I have been putting away. So, why don't you start the big tour with Gary and Paula." Newell said, then laughed and added, "All we need are some customers with a little cash in their pockets."

"Follow me," Marshall said, looking at Gary and Paula, " I'll give you a once-over-lightly tour and if you have any questions, well, heck," Marshall paused, then added, "I'll just ask dad or Uncle Bruce!"

They walked slowly through the store. "Here's the area where everyone needs stuff. I mean our competitors and us. Anything involving steel, or electrical is still hard to come by. You know, the war effort, making all of those tanks and rifles and airplanes and landing ships. Now we wait, like the other hardware stores around the country

"Everyone is retooling, or going back to what they previously made. Mom's trying to set up a kitchen area. You know, cast iron pots, and frying pans, and hopefully she'll be getting in some of those pots and pans with the brass bottoms. I understand that Revere, or whoever made them, were involved in making shells for the navy."

"Always amazes me what a variety of merchandise a hardware store carries," Paula said.

"Anything electrical is awful hard to come by. You know, coffee makers and blenders and things like that. Even curling irons."

"Where's the paint department?" Gary asked.

"We've got to build our inventories. There are so darn many colors to stock. I think lead is still scarce, too."

"Marsh," Gary said, "I sure would like to have a little time with you and your folks to tell you about a new concept in inventorying paint. Rainbow has a new deal that really simplifies inventory. Now, this isn't my territory, but I'd sure like to expose you to this new thinking."

"Certainly, buddy, whenever the time is right."

"Now don't get too aggressive, honey," Paula said, and put her hand on Gary's arm.

Marshall and Gary both laughed and Gary hugged Paula, "Relax sweetheart, you know I just really believe in this product. That's all."

"This is your best friend and his folks," Paula said.

"Come on, doll, if I didn't believe in Rainbow and its products, I wouldn't represent them. You know that!" Gary said, irritation revealed in his voice.

"Okay honey, but this is supposed to be part of our honeymoon trip, too, isn't it?"

"Come on now, you two lovers," Marshall said, laughing, "follow me and I'll show you shovels and wheel barrows and sledge hammers and picks and post hole diggers and heating oil and dynamite and barrels of creosote."

"You must be expecting a building boom?" Gary commented.

"Why the dynamite?" Paula asked, a puzzled expression on her face.

"A lot of the ranchers are beginning to clear some of their land. Blow tree stumps apart. Plant fruit trees. We've one customer that is getting rid of the stumps so he can increase his grazing acreage. Coyotes and foxes like to make their homes in those old stumps and they are death on calves and lambs. Mom's selling him barbed wire fence by the mile," Marshall said, then laughed.

"So you're kidding?" Gary inquired.

"No, I'm serious, really, Gary. But we do have to know how many miles to fence on a big spread, then it's multiplied by four strands to a post."

"There's some figuring to do on painting a warehouse, too," Gary said, then added, "You seem to like what you're doing."

"Well, yes and no. It really is interesting, you know, the tremendous variety of tools, and all of the things for the ranchers, but this is supposed to be the nest egg for my folk's future, not mine. It's their retirement. Their security."

"Not yours too?" Gary said.

"I'm bailing out before long. This operation can't support three people."

"Your folks know that?" Paula asked.

"Dad does. I'm afraid I'm still my mom's little boy. It's as if I hadn't gone away for three years. And my dad's got a heart valve problem. Had rheumatic fever a year ago and it ruined his aortic valve. When he thought I'd stay because of that, he was upset. Wants me to go to college."

"Gee, that's too bad. I think I understand," Gary said. " Chicago isn't for me, but Sean, you remember, my twin, he's settled right into the construction business with dad."

"Well, you've seen a cross section of Sierra Mercantile. Anything you need? The price is right!"

"Nope!" Gary said, then looked towards the front of the store. "Here comes your mother."

Martha walked to where Newell and Bruce were still lifting the kegs of nails. She chatted with them, then turned to Marshall, Paula and Gary.

"So, you got the tour?" she said, smiling, and lifting a hand to push back a wave of hair that fell across her glasses.

"What a tremendous amount of items to try to keep track of," Paula said.

"Well, we have a inventory control system. Everything in the store is recorded on a little three by five card, which we keep in boxes. It's easy to separate them by department. As we sell an item, we reduce the amount from, say ten, to nine and on down until we reach a reorder level that will give us the best price. We'll review the cards regularly. If an item doesn't move, we'll lower the inventory level, and perhaps drop it completely."

"Gary is kind of like Ed, my former husband. The crew called him Pop, you know. They both say they like the industry because a man's word is his bond. Gary has already sold some big jobs just on a handshake."

"That's true in our business, too. However some of the men would rather talk to Newell when it comes time to make payments on a big purchase." Martha smiled, and Paula nodded as if understanding a hidden meaning. "Well, here comes a customer now!"

Both women turned and smiled as the man approached. He was tall, clean shaven, tanned and wore a black and red plaid jacket.

"May I help you?" Martha said.

"No thanks, mam, just shopping. Fellows on the job said you've got a good tool inventory."

"Carpenter tools are over on that wall," Martha said, pointing across the store. "Speak up if you need help."

"Come along, Paula, I'll show you the home section, if you didn't spend much time there." Martha said.

"We didn't even slow down there on the tour," Paula said and laughed.

"Lots of cooking utensils coming in now. Have some nice Boker knives. Don't expect we'll ever see any of those Solingen steel products again. They were excellent."

"My mom has a set of Solingen knives in a little stand on the kitchen sink. Dad takes a delight in keeping them razor sharp for her."

"I'm beginning to get in some china. Not much from England or France yet, and Marshall wrote us about the destruction of the entire city of Dresden. Terrible thing."

"Ed's letters, the V Mail, were censored so severely, I hardly knew what was going on. We read the papers, of course, and the Newsreels were always so grim I hated seeing them."

"Paula, do you like to sew?"

"Would you believe that I make most of Tim's clothes? And I'm taking a sewing class at Frank Wiggins in L.A. My mom takes care of Tim while I'm at school."

"I'd like to give you a little present, from Newell and me," Martha said. "Now, if you already have a good pair of Wiss pinking shears, you tell me, and we'll select something else from the store."

"Oh, Mrs. Sunder! I don't have! Everyone in the class has to use the pair that the school owns! The teacher said that they all disappeared over the years and they haven't been able to buy them. But you must let me pay you for them."

"Oh, hush, these are a gift. I'm delighted you need them! Now let's go over to the counter and I'll put a little wrapping paper around the box."

Paula followed Martha to the counter. Martha opened the box and handed the pinking shears to Paula and she held them, admired them, opened and closed the scissors, listened to the precise meshing of the blades, smiled and handed them back. Martha opened a drawer of the cash register and to Paula's surprise selected a coin, a penny, and taped it to the shears, then looked up at Paula. Martha smiled. "Old custom. Anytime you give a knife or a pair of scissors to a friend, include a coin. Means you won't cut the friendship. Are you superstitious?"

Suddenly Newell shouted. "Hey you! Stop right there!" The man with plaid jacket did not slow as he swiftly walked towards the front door.

Without hesitation Martha jumped to the wall near the cash register. She grabbed the twelve-gauge shotgun and the unmistakable metallic sound, of slick, smooth metal parts rubbing together, pumping a shell into the chamber startled everyone, especially the man whom Newell had confronted.

The man halted in mid-stride. Martha stood with the twelve gauge shotgun pointing above his head, towards the ceiling. Immediately his tanned face paled. He started to raise his arms, and as he did a heavy eighteen-inch adjustable wrench fell from his sleeve, and thudded loudly on the wooden floor.

Marshall and Newell and Bruce walked to the man who now stood with his arms raised above his head.

"Call Sheriff Holcomb, honey," Newell said.

"If it's okay, dear, I'll hang onto this shotgun and Marshall can call."

Wide-eyed, his mouth ajar, Marshall answered with a terse, "Roger !" He telephoned the sheriff and was told a deputy would be right there. "No sir, no need for a siren," Marshall said.

"Might as well lower your arms, fella," Newell said. "I don't recall seeing you around Chico."

Still pale, and shaken, the man lowered his head and said nothing.

Bruce approached and bent over to pick up the adjustable wrench. "Let it lay," Newell said. "Want the officer to see it where it fell. Why don't you relieve Martha, Bruce."

Gary walked to Paula and held her close to him. She was trembling, but she stared at Martha, standing so still, holding the shotgun, her jaw set, and she stared, unblinking at the thief.

Dressed in a house dress with a dark green leaves on a brown pattern, Martha had an earthy look, Paula felt, as she studied Martha with her arms raised high, holding the shotgun, revealing the fullness of her bust, and her rimless eyeglasses resting firmly on her straight, but slightly up-tilted nose. Her trigger finger was outside the trigger guard, not on the trigger. It was beyond Paula's wildest imagination to think that Martha would fire the shotgun.

"Sis, your arms must be getting a little weary. I'll take the gun," Bruce said, gently, and he accepted the weapon, allowing it to rest in the cradle of one arm with the barrel elevated. He looked towards Newell and the thief.

"Paula, dear, I'm so sorry for this ruckus," Martha said. She walked over to Paula and Gary and rested a hand on Paula's arm. "The sheriff will be here soon and then we get can close the store and go home and try to resume our visit," Martha sighed. Her eyeglasses had steamed and she took them off, held them to the light and dried them with a small handkerchief, she slipped them back on and looked back at Paula.

"We work too hard to have our tools stolen right in front of us! The bastard!" Martha whispered, then followed quickly with, "Oh, I'm sorry. Forgive my language, Paula."

They heard the door of the sheriff's car slam shut. A young man in uniform entered the store. "Howdy. I'm Deputy Ted Barta. What's going on here, Mr. Sunder?"

"This bozo tried to leave the store with that adjustable wrench hidden in his sleeve. No telling what else he might have stored in that jacket. I wondered about that jacket when he came in. Too warm for that garb."

"Guess you better take off that jacket, mister," the deputy said.

"I was just heading for the cash register when this jerk lets out a yell and that old lady points that shotgun at me. I was trying to pay for the tool."

"Sure you were," the deputy said, " Now, please take off your jacket."

Reluctantly the man removed it. Beneath his belt near a back pocket were tucked three wooden handle screwdrivers of different lengths. A stapler was in a back pocket. Two paintbrushes were tucked beneath his belt near his left front pocket.

"And the judge is going to believe that you were on the way to the cash register with this other merchandise?"

"Fuck you, you country hick!"

"Well now. We don't use that kind of language around our women folk here in Chico. You just put your hands behind your back, and I'll put these bracelets around your skinny little wrists. When we get to the jail house Sheriff Holcomb will wash out your mouth with soap."

When his hands were behind him, the deputy clasped the handcuffs, jammed them shut and the prisoner yelped. "Ouch! Take it easy, flatfoot."

"Now mister, what I hope is, that you make a run for it as soon as we get to the steps. Please try to escape and you'll be doing Chico a favor!" The deputy pushed the man in the middle of the back with his hand. "Now walk slowly to the door."

"Mr. Sunder, I spoke with Sheriff Holcomb before I came over. Seems there's a regular gang of these guys moving up and down the valley from town to town. Stealing everything they can get their hands on, especially tools and hardware," the officer said.

"They bundle it all up once a week and ship it down to some guy in Fresno. Sheriff said you could come in tonight or in the morning to press charges. Bring any witnesses. I'll have to and take these things with me."

"We'll come in tomorrow morning," Newell said.

"Hey, Sunder, I saw the photo of you in the paper getting that DFC. Nice going."

"Thanks. You in the service, Ted?"

"Flew '17's with the eighth. Got in twenty-five missions without a scratch, then back to Chico, and this."

"Gary here was our pilot in '26's," Marshall said, nodding his head towards Gary and Paula. "The infamous widow maker, eh? Heard that was a bear to land. Well, glad to see you guys are back fat and sassy! Drop by the office some time and we'll shoot the breeze. Now I've got to give this tramp a chance to escape. If you hear some shots, just call the morgue for me. Now, foul mouth, let's head for that car!"

As they left the store, Newell hurried across the store and put his arms around Martha. "You're trembling, dear," he said very softly.

"I'm fine. Kind of nervous now that it's over, I guess."

"Sis, I told you that you should have joined us at the rifle range. You were aiming a little high!"

"Oh, hush, Bruce!" Martha said, then laughed, and the rest of them joined in.

"It's close enough now to lock up," Newell said. "Let's batten this place down, Marsh, and head for home."

"Roger, Dad."

"I'll empty the shotgun," Bruce said, and pumped out the unfired shells. He then replaced the shells and stood the shotgun back in its place behind the door. "So, it did come in handy."

"That sure is a distinctive sound!" Gary said, then asked, " Why don't they just break in at night and steal?"

"Well, someone just might do that. Probably different sentencing for that kind of robbery, you know, burglary, compared to shoplifting," Bruce said. "Really haven't had a lot of burglary problems here in Chico."

"Back door, side door, all bolted and the night lights are on," Marshall said. Together they walked to the front of the store. Newell was last out and locked the front door.

"I'll join you in a little while. Gotta get spruced up a bit," Bruce said.

"Well, hurry it up, Uncle Bruce. We'll wait. I just want you to know your old friend JD is waiting at the house!" Marshall chuckled, then turned to McAdam and said, "And for you, old buddy, a fifth of Johnny Walker Red Label! And hey, Uncle Bruce, bring Tara, will you!"

"Johnny Walker Red? Fantastic! But hey, what about your mom? She just earned a fifth mission Air Medal!" Gary said.

"The ladies are all set!"

Martha joined Newell in their pickup truck. Bruce departed in his and Marshall, Paula and Gary drove away in the black Ford.

"Who's Tara?" Gary asked.

"Uncle Bruce's black Lab. Real well mannered. Hope you like dogs, Paula."

"Woman's best friend!" she said

"I like that!" Marshall said, laughing, then added, "did you have a choice of color on the car?"

"No need for sarcasm!" Gary answered and both he and Paula laughed.

"Didn't Henry Ford say, 'You can have any color you want, as long as it's black.'"

"The P.A. at Rainbow is really furious with the Ford dealer, Hail Motors out in Culver City. Rainbow was on the waiting list all through the war, and our owner was supposed to be a buddy of this man Hail, and told him the ONLY color he didn't want for the company cars was black. So, when they called and said this car came in for us, he was so angry, he almost decided not to accept it. But new cars are scarce, so he re-thought it and Paula is going to pick out a color she likes and we'll paint it with one of our colors. You see, we can use it as a family car, too. A fringe benefit!"

"Sounds like a nice boss," Marshall said.

"Well, Pop was his favorite, so I've got a lot to live up to," Gary said.

"Gary is quickly becoming the fair-haired boy around Rainbow," Paula said and placed her hand on the thigh of his right leg and patted him.

"Jesus, I'm so glad you two got together," Marshall said, admiring her subtle show of affection.

"Have you heard from Kristine?" Gary asked. The car slowed as they reached the curved driveway in front of Marshall's home.

"What did you say?" Marshall said, leaning forward in the seat, staring past Paula at Gary. A sudden chill gripped his body.

"She asked me to give you a watch when I left Bad Scheidel. It's at the house."

"Jesus Christ, Gary!" Marshall shouted, "What are you talking about? The last time I saw Kris she was covered with blood, and under a sheet covering her whole body, it was over her face and head, and the medics said they were taking her to the morgue!" Marshall said, stunned. "Gary, wait. Don't go into my driveway. Turn around. Drive back to that little park we passed and go in there. Please park the car."

"My God! Marsh, holy mackerel! I thought you knew. She was just wounded. But they took her to the morgue because it was a temporary emergency room while they were operating on me!" Gary said.

"For Christ sake, why didn't someone tell me? Did Tex, or Cal, or whatever the hell we finally called him, did he give you the two hundred bucks?"

"Yes, Marsh. Poor Cal. Guess you know he's dead. I'll fill you in on that later. Just when he got his name changed to Hawk: but back to Kris. For God's sake, I gave that money to Kris. I told her you thought she'd been killed and it was supposed to be for a headstone or a memorial. She just shook her head and laughed, as if I was joking. Said she'd use it for books for the base library. I gave her your home address."

"Gary, I just can't believe she's alive. Ever since Cal flew me to Le Havre, I've assumed—have believed—she was dead. Is dead! And just like that you're telling me she's alive! Jesus, this changes everything! I'm shocked! Good lord, I've got to go back to Germany!"

"Well, ole buddy, there's more," Gary said, but before he could continue, Paula pushed her elbow into his side and said, "Gary, honey, you'd better give Marsh a chance to digest this. And I think his folks are probably wondering where we are."

"Oh, Paula, I'm so sorry for upsetting you: my language! You're right. Mom will be waiting. And dad and Uncle Bruce, too. Yes, we'd better head for home," Marshall said, and Paula saw that his face had paled.

"Gary, Paula, please don't mention Kris at home. I never told them about us."

"Okay, fella," Gary said. "Back to your house now?" Gary asked, his voice hushed, "That stuff, about Kris, I mean, that's history. We'll leave it at that."

"For tonight, right. Tomorrow, we've got to talk."

When they arrived back at Marshall's home the pickup truck of his Uncle Bruce's was already in the driveway and his folks' car was parked in the extension of the curved area that led to the garage.

After parking, they entered the house and Paula and Gary went to their bedroom. "Gary, Marshall's face turned from white to red, and back to white," Paula said. "You shocked him terribly!"

"Paula, dear, you've got to believe me. I assumed he knew about Kris. I certainly thought she'd write to him. My God, how is he going to handle the rest? And he didn't even ask about poor Cal."

"Let's sleep on it. Then decide whether you should tell him."

"He'd be insulted if he didn't hear it from us. He'd feel betrayed! I've got to tell him."

"Enough for now. I'm getting freshened up first. Then you can have the bathroom. But we should try to keep him happy this evening."

"Okay, you're right. It'll wait."

Gary, dressed in a red sport shirt and gray slacks and Paula, wearing a light brown, belted shirtmaker dress, entered the living room, and heard the voices in the kitchen and found Marshall, Newell and Bruce volunteering their assistance. Martha was moving around quickly, in the same housedress, but wearing one of the many aprons she owned.

"Mom, I'm going to fix some drinks. Would you like a glass of that sherry now?" Marshall said, then turned to Paula. "I've some sherry, and I've scotch and bourbon and some soda water for mix."

"Yes, Marsh, a little glass of sherry will be fine," Martha said. "My, you young people look so nice," Martha added.

"That sherry sounds good to me," Paula said.

Marshall felt relieved. He sighed. He was concerned that his mother would turn down the sherry and say something critical about the whiskey. Hearing that Kris was alive had set his mind spinning, out of control, as wildly as a runaway merry go-round. "Dad, Uncle Bruce, I've got a bottle of Bruce's buddy, J.D., and some good scotch. I know Gary prefers scotch," he said, and opened the cupboard and placed the bottles on the counter top. "Mr. O'Toole gave these little glasses to mom." He set those aside. "Uncle Bruce, would you pour for the ladies and I'll get glasses and ice for us."

Bruce nodded, smiled, and said, "And isn't Mr. O'Toole a fine Irish lad himself?"

"Not exactly a lad, but as far as the Irish go, he's a good friend and neighbor," Newell said.

"Don't be picking on the Irish, now," Martha said, changing the timbre of her voice, as did Bruce, adding a lilt to it.

All of them laughed now, and Marshall turned to his father and asked, "How much of which would you like, Dad?"

"Couple fingers of JD will be fine, some ice and water with it, please." He held up his hand and showed his index and middle finger closed.

"Make it three fingers for me, Marsh," Bruce laughed. "And a couple of ice cubes and just a wee splash of water."

"Scotch on the rocks for me, Marsh, and I'll follow Bruce's measurement," Gary said, then added, "What's the Irish lingo all about? Somebody here a potato famine victim?" Gary asked.

"My last name is Kane, young man! And the wildness of my little sister Martha here, is due to our wonderful Irish heritage. And too, I'll have you know, in our homeland we were known as those damn Protestants."

"Well, my Scottish ancestors claim possession to the name 'Bruce,'" and then attempting roll his to tongue to produce a brogue, Gary asked, "You must have heard of Robert the Bruce?"

"And surely we have, lad, and Bruce is a name we respect, you see, because there was a certain Bruce McGilveray back some time ago, and he was a Scot who also happened to be the doctor that brought my sweet sister and I into the world. So our gentle parents allowed a wee bit of Scotland into our very own clan."

"It's 'me', that's proper, brother dear, not I," Martha corrected, laughing and the rest of them joined in.

"And laddie, that correction does originate from the educated lassie of the clan." More laughter followed, and Bruce raised his glass and said, " To friendship!"

The men touched glasses and Martha spoke up, "Out of my kitchen, boys. Paula and I have work to do," and then added, "as usual."

The four men nodded and walked out of the kitchen, through the dining room, and stood facing one another, sipping their drinks. "Find a chair, or the couch," Newell said, and Gary and Marshall sat side by side on the couch, as Newell and Bruce sat in chairs. Quietness followed, and they heard the sounds of utensils touching bowls and plates and the quiet, subdued, yet sparkling laughs of the women coming from the kitchen.

"Mom and Paula are sure hitting it off good," Marshall said.

"I'm a lucky guy," Gary said, and raised his glass as if toasting Paula, "Guess you gentlemen know that Paula was married to our engineer, our crew chief, Pop," Gary said, directing his comment to Newell and Bruce.

"Marsh told us, yes, Gary," Newell said. "We're happy for both you and Paula and little Tim, of course."

"I'll raise him as if he's my own flesh and blood," Gary said.

Again the their conversation ebbed and they could hear the laughter of the women. Each sipped his drink, seeming to study the contents. "Good scotch," Gary said.

"Better be, for what I paid for it," Marshall answered and immediately laughed loudly, then stood up and snapped his finger, "Golly, I don't think I showed dad and Uncle Bruce that photo of you in the '26, Gary." He walked to the desk and returned with the eight by ten glossy photo.

"Here's Gary in the captain's seat with his name and *Miss Nausicaa* painted on the nose!"

The men stood and gathered around and studied the photo, and then Newell called out, "Hey ladies, come on out here a minute and see this."

Martha appeared, drying her hands and flipping the apron towards her face and Paula followed. They too, studied the photo.

"I've seen it before," Paula said. She patted Gary's shoulder.

Marshall told them of the sight seeing flight and about Lorelei and Nausicaa and then Martha asked, "My goodness is that the same Nausicaa that helped Odysseus?"

"Who the heck is Odysseus? Bruce asked.

"Oh dear, I assumed all of you probably read Homer's Iliad and The Odyssey." She looked around at all of them and the men stared back blankly, and Paula nodded and smiled, so Martha very quickly gave a short synopsis of the poems.

"See Martha, Newell said, "That's why our son wants to go to college. You don't learn that sort of thing selling barbed wire."

Martha smiled and said, "You are full of it aren't you dear. Come Paula dear, our duties await in the kitchen. Paula smiled at the men, raised her eyebrows and followed Martha back to the kitchen, and they heard Martha's voice, "Would you mind helping me with these baked potatoes. We'll slice them, empty them, mash them and re-stuff them."

Bruce grinned and said, "As for me, it's time for a couple of fingers of ole JD."

"What's with this ole JD stuff?" Gary asked.

"It's Uncle Bruce's pal. Jack Daniel's sour mash whiskey. He introduced me to JD one afternoon when he and dad and I went to our rifle range," Marshall said. "And no, we didn't mix gun powder and booze. JD came after we cased the guns."

"You a hunter, Gary?" Bruce asked.

"Nope. Last guns I fired were fifty-caliber machine guns from our '26' when we strafed a bridge at Bad Scheidel."

Marshall downed his bourbon and suddenly stood up. "Anyone ready for another before supper?"

"I'll pass," Newell said, and Marshall turned to his uncle.

"Don't want your mom down on me," Bruce chuckled, "so, I'll pass."

"I'll join you Marsh," Gary said, and stood and together they returned to the kitchen.

"Oh? More whiskey?" Martha said, raising her eyebrows, when Marshall opened the cupboard. "Supper will be ready in about thirty-five minutes." Marshall ignored her. He poured liberally of the bourbon into his own glass. Gary poured his own scotch. "This is really living high on the hog, folks," Gary said and turned and together they returned to the living room. He winked at Paula.

On the pads that had been placed on the dining room table, Paula had spread a lace tablecloth, and the apple pattern dishware was arranged at the six places. From a large mahogany, felt-lined container, Martha's Roger's International silverware was removed. Paula was aware that Martha was watching her as she set the table, and she chuckled, thinking she should deliberately make a mistake, just to see how Martha would react, but then thought better of the idea. The poor woman had been through enough for one day. Crystal water glasses and wineglasses, and folded linen napkins were all in the correct places.

"Do you want the salad forks beneath the salad plates or next to the dinner forks, Mrs. Sunder?"

"Next to the dinner forks, dear," Martha said. "Would you mind helping me with these baked potatoes. We'll slice them, empty them, mash them and re-stuff them."

Bruce followed Marshall and Gary into the kitchen. "My, what wonderful aromas, Sis. Going to have to have company more often around here." Bruce walked close to Martha and patted her hip. "I'm going to open the red wine and let it breathe."

Martha brushed his hand away and scowled at him, "Out of the kitchen, please. Paula and I have work to do," Martha said. Bruce nodded then uncorked the wine.

Marshall and Gary followed Bruce back to the living room with their drinks. Bruce sat across from Newell and started to say something about the inventory when Gary spoke. Bruce followed Marshall and Gary into the kitchen. "My, what wonderful aromas, Sis. Going to have to have company more often around here," Bruce walked close to Martha and patted her hip. "I'm going to open the red wine and let it breathe."

Martha brushed his hand away and scowled at him, "Out of the kitchen, please. Paula and I have work to do," Martha said. Bruce nodded then uncorked the wine.

Marshall and Gary followed Bruce back to the living room with their drinks. Bruce sat across from Newell and started to say something about the inventory when Gary spoke.

"Wait a second before you sit down, Marsh," Gary said. "While the ladies are busy, I'd like you and your dad and uncle to go to the bedroom with me."

"Why?" Marshall asked.

"Seeing will be believing. I suspect your dad and uncle know about my loss, and I want to share my reconstruction."

Newell and Bruce exchanged glances, then pushed up out of their chairs and followed Gary and Marsh to the bedroom. Gary closed the door and turned the key in the lock. Light filtered in from the one window. Gary walked over to the lamp on the nightstand, and turned it on. Quickly he unbuckled his trousers and allowed them to drop. He then pulled his shorts down, lifted his penis with his right hand and revealed the scrotum that Doctor Friemuth had created.

"See, I've got balls again! Not worth a hell of a lot, I'll admit, but for some strange reason I'm happy to have them here attached to my body. Awful looking still, aren't they, but the redness on the skin, on my thighs, will go away, so the Doc told me," Gary said. He pulled his shorts back up quickly, then said, "And the miracles haven't ceased. We have a sex life! I get shots of testosterone every few weeks and that's what allows me to be a man. Now don't gasp, but yes, not only can I get a hard-on, I have orgasms!"

"Well, how about that!" Bruce said.

"And one more thing before we go back to the living room. I don't like to talk about this in front of the women, you know."

The three men nodded.

"Here's the real miracle. Paula and I are going back to Mayo Clinic next spring and I'll get her pregnant!"

"No more scotch for you, buddy!" Marshall said, laughing nervously.

"Marsh!" Gary said affirmatively. "Remember Sean. My identical twin? According to the medics, he can provide sperm, which would be the same as mine, and they can use it when the time is right for Paula! She's keeping a log of when her periods start and stop, and she's taking her temperature during that time. They feel they'll be able to chart the best time for her to conceive."

"Wow," was all that Marshall could say.

Gary looked at the expressions on the faces of both Newell and Bruce. He laughed and turned away, as he buckled his belt. "It's really true," he said.

"You know," Bruce finally said, "this reminds me of the old story about the farmer that stumbled and fell into a deep, dry well. He dusted himself off and looked up and saw stars and said 'this is too deep for me.'"

Laughter followed. "Well, my show and tell time is over. Better get back to the living room, eh?" Gary said.

"I'll repeat myself, Gary," Newell said. "We're all just happy as the devil for both you and Paula . This has been very enlightening, to say the least! It's a downright miracle."

"Mr. Sunder, believe me, during the past year, my emotions have run the gamut, from suicide to hate, and especially revenge. My hate for the bastard Germans that did this to me, well, it is almost overwhelming. But, now, finally I'm real grateful to that Man upstairs for allowing me to live through it, and especially for my marriage."

"And a friggin kraut doctor put you back together. God, that is ironic!" Marshall said

"Marsh, you know what, the surgeon, a Doctor Friemuth, well, he's now at Mayo Clinic!"

"How'd he manage that?"

"Long story. Tell you tomorrow," Gary said, then pondered how Marshall would handle the other news.

The men had reentered the living room and from the kitchen Martha called out, "Newell, honey, it's time to carve this roast. Better start finding places to sit."

"Well, dad's chair is the one with the arms, at the head of the table, and mom will be at the opposite end."......Marshall was interrupted by Bruce, "And I'm sitting next to Paula and you two guys can take what's left over."

"I'm assuming that you're the uncle that sent those jokes to Marshall, Mr. Kane?" Gary asked.

"Call me Bruce. None of this mister stuff. Right, Newell?" Bruce answered. "Yep, I guess I'm the guilty one."

"Anything current?" Gary asked.

"Well, maybe later. We can slip out on the porch, without the ladies. Okay?

Marshall laughed, "Are you saying you don't know any clean jokes, Uncle Bruce?"

"Anyone that likes the end cut, speak up now," Newell said. Silence followed, and finally Paula said, "I'd love the end cut, Mr. Sunder."

"Include a bone with mine," Bruce said, "for Tara."

"You should have brought her, Uncle Bruce."

"I did. She's in the truck."

"Well, bring the poor girl in," Marshall said.

"What about it, sis?"

"That would be all right, but not at the table."

"Thanks, I'll be right back. You folks sit down. I'll just be a minute."

Gary watched Newell slice thick, one-inch thick slabs of the prime rib. "How do you like yours, Gary? Medium, medium rare, rare?"

"Medium, sir."

"Medium rare for me, dad."

"Medium-well, dear," Martha said.

"Bruce will want it rare," Newell said, "So there you are Martha."

Tara bounded into the living room carrying a tennis ball in her mouth. She dropped it and went to each person, received a pat on the head and on her back, and then Bruce said, "Okay, little lady, into the living room for you. It's sit and stay time." Bruce walked into the living room and indicated with his hand a place for Tara to stay, and she stretched out on her stomach, her back legs spread out behind her, her front legs pointing toward the dining room, her head raised and her eyes staring at them.

"What a beautiful spread," Gary said. Martha had placed each cut of beef on a dinner plate, placed the re-baked, stuffed potatoes with a quarter inch slab of butter on the top, beside the beef and a serving of small boiled white onions, plus fresh green beans. At each place was a tossed green salad upon which Martha had already placed her own special salad dressing.

"Thank you, Gary," Martha said. "Paula has made it easy. Now sit down before things start to cool off. And, I'd appreciate it if you boys would set aside your cocktails until after dinner."

"No problem," Marshall said, and he accepted Gary's drink and sat them together on the counter top.

Marshall held the chair for his mother. When he sat down, Newell spoke, "Let's all hold hands while we give thanks," and they grew silent, reached to each other and touched hands, and lowered their heads, "Dear Lord, we give special thanks this evening for allowing these young men to return to us. Now, as we feel the warmth, the magnetism of your love flowing through our arms, and through our hearts, providing us with your silent, powerful and mysterious strength, we give thanks for this bountiful meal, and for our well being, in the name of Jesus Christ. Amen."

Each person quietly said amen.

"That was very nice, Mr. Sunder," Paula said.

Bruce spoke, "Well, I'm proud to say that Newell and Sis practice what they preach." then paused and added, "Well, now, where's the wine? It's a nice old Cabernet Sauvignon." He arose from the table, located the open bottle and prepared to pour, starting with Martha. He draped a dishtowel over one arm.

"Hey, Uncle Bruce," Marshall said, "would you spell the name of that wine for me?"

"Ha!" Bruce exclaimed, and laughed, " Mr. O'Toole wouldn't let me leave the store until I pronounced it correctly four times! The spelling is right there on the bottle. I suppose that's something you warriors learned in France, eh?"

"No comment," McAdam said, glancing at Marshall and they both chuckled, grinning at Paula.

"Do you want to sample it, Sis?" Bruce asked. He bowed, smiling at his sister.

"Go ahead and pour it, smarty pants. If I turned it down you wouldn't know what to do next," Martha smiled at each of those seated at the table.

"Pass the rolls, please, and the butter," Marshall said, then added, "And no short-stopping, Gary."

"There is homemade strawberry and raspberry jam in that double dish," Martha said.

"Pass it along, please," Marshall said.

"Wow, Sis, where'd you get that horseradish? Careful kids. You can clear your sinuses with that stuff. It's violent."

"You're not supposed to take a tablespoon full," Martha said. "Mr. Scroggins ground it for me this morning."

"Gary, how does this spread compare to some of the Paris food you guys were served?" Bruce asked.

"Why, Mr. Kane, I mean Bruce, the Parisian chefs couldn't touch this meal with a ten-foot pole! Why, this would cost a full carton of Camels! Right, Marsh?"

"Roger, with an exclamation point!"

"Explain the Camel remark, will you, dear?" Paula said.

"Gee, I wasn't trying to be funny or something," Gary said. "You see, cigarettes were more important than money to anyone in Europe. French or Belgians, Dutch or Germans. For instance, we really would get a fine meal anyplace for one pack of cigarettes. And a good tip would be two cigarettes. It was the old barter system. A pack or two of cigarettes might be traded for half a gunny sack of potatoes, or a cigarette for a dozen eggs, you know," Gary said.

"My. Well that was quite a compliment then, wasn't it," Martha said.

"You bet, mam!" Gary said, then added, "Please pass the jam."

"What about chocolate?" Bruce asked.

"Oh, I'd say about the same. Include coffee, too. But I think tobacco was really better for bartering, and they might keep a bit for their own pleasure. Compared to a bite of chocolate a cigarette would last quite awhile."

"A carton of cigarettes cost fifty cents at the P.X.," Marshall volunteered. "Considering what they'd buy, I figured I couldn't afford the habit. So, I don't smoke."

"Bet you'd enjoy one of those fragrant stogies your uncle takes on our hunting trips," Newell said.

"Best thing about them is to keep the mosquitoes away," Marshall said, laughed and pointed his fork at Bruce.

"You going hunting this fall?" Gary asked.

"Well, I'm sure dad and Uncle Bruce will, but it's doubtful for me," Marshall said, and immediately regretted making the statement.

"Why, Emil and Cecil and Mrs. Chubb will sure be disappointed if you don't show up. Bruce said, then continued, "Martha, sweetheart, did you make any extras on those fancy potatoes?"

"Yes, Bruce. Anyone else? I've four more waiting to be eaten. Won't be good tomorrow."

Newell and Marshall quickly accepted and Gary responded with a little urging from Martha.

"Mr. Kane, Bruce that is, well, Marshall, when we were on a mission, he'd just imagine he was on one of those hunting trips he told us about."

"Ha!" Marshall exclaimed, "I wasn't scared on the hunting trips, though."

"Combat pretty scary at times, I imagine," Newell said.

"There was a saying," Gary volunteered, "if a guy said he wasn't afraid of flak, we figured he was stupid, and we didn't want him flying with us."

"Didn't you always fly together as one crew?" Martha asked.

"Well, most of the time. But, you know, someone might get sick, or have an emergency leave, something like that, and you'd fill in on another crew."

As the meal ended, Paula arose and helped Martha clear the table.

"Coffee for everyone?" Martha asked.

The yes answers were followed by a request from Paula. "I'd like tea, Mrs. Sunder."

"Good, dear, and I'll join you," Martha said. "Let me show you the darling little teapot Marshall gave me. I really didn't think I'd ever use it, you know, risk breaking it. But it'll be great for three or four cups." Martha said, " He bought it in Chinatown, in San Francisco, and feels it may be an antique."

"Why, it is just darling!" Paula said, holding the teapot, turning it, admiring it. "Bet there's a book at the library that could identify it, if it is an antique."

"Why didn't I think of that. That'll be a priority, if I can escape from the store for a few hours," Martha said. " And now I've got to whip this cream for the cake."

"I can do that," Paula said.

"Does your mother like to cook?"

"Oh, yes, and so does Gary's mother. His family came out to LA for our wedding. His identical twin, Sean, came too, and if Gary's nose hadn't been broken, you'd never tell them apart."

"Well, maybe I'll be lucky someday and have a sweet girl like you for a daughter-in-law. And I want you to use my Limoges cup and saucer for your tea."

Paula blushed, but did not answer. She used the electric beater to whip the cream.

"Don't get your fingers near those blades, dear," Martha cautioned. "It's funny, Paula. I've heard more about little incidents during the war tonight, with Marshall and Gary talking, than I've heard since Marshall got home."

"Well, that goes for me, too, Mrs. Sunder. Alone with me, Gary never talks about the war," Paula said, then added, "You know Mrs. Sunder, a little of that scotch and JD helps loosen their tongues. Why don't you take those unfinished drinks, the ones setting there, out to them?"

Martha put her head back and laughed. "Sweetheart, if I did that, all three of my men would run for the phone to call the paddy wagon! While I truly discourage drinking, I'll support your idea. But you take the drinks. Might even put some ice in the glasses!" Martha again laughed, then raised her apron and fanned her face. "But what I will do is take that box of *See's* candy out there. That's our favorite and it's getting so expensive."

Paula put ice into the drinks, walked to the porch and delivered the glasses to Marshall and Gary. "Your mom said you might want these," Paula said, chuckling, and handed the glasses to them. She winked at Newell and Bruce.

Both took deep gulps from the glasses then set them on the railing. Newell and Bruce exchanged glances and grinned.

Gary lifted his glass to his lips and said, "Marsh. A toast! Remember this one? Over the lips and through the gums, look out guts, here she comes!"

Gary gulped his drink, wiped his lips and laughed loudly. The men joined in the laughter.

"Let me know if you want those sweetened up a bit, " Bruce said.

"Sure!" Marshall said, "if you don't think mom will be upset."

"Leave that to me laddie," Bruce said. "And for this occasion your dad and I are going to join you. Right, Newell?"

"Guess so," Newell said, grinning. He shrugged his shoulders.

While the ladies prepared to serve the dessert on the porch, Tara joined them and dropped her ball at Marshall's feet, then looked up at him, retreated backwards, appearing ready to pounce, looking at his face, expectantly.

"Okay, Tara, let's get off of this porch." Marshall walked down the steps and stood on the lawn, then faked throwing the ball one way, turned and threw it the other, and Tara spun then lunged across the lawn, catching up to the ball as it bounced and immediately returned to Marshall, dropped the ball at his feet, looked into his face, her tail wagging. Again he faked the direction of his throw, but the dog anticipated the move and bounded after the ball, retrieved it and again dropped it at Marshall's feet. Her long pink tongue hung from her mouth. She waited, anticipated his fake throw, but was surprised when he tossed it up to Gary on the porch.

"Yuck!" Gary said, "It's wet!" Then laughed and stepped down beside Marshall and threw the ball for Tara.

"You'll never wear her out," Bruce said. "Don't know where that dog gets her energy and, I might add, her enthusiasm."

"Okay, you guys, the dessert is on the table," Paula called.

"Excuse me while I wash my hands," Gary said.

"Yeah, me too," Marshall said, then looked at his uncle. "Tara's one hell of dog, Uncle Bruce."

"But you don't care for dog slobber, right?" Bruce said.

The men filed back into the dining room and in front of each chair was a large section of pineapple upside down cake smothered with whipped cream.

"This is my all time favorite dessert! No one, I mean no one, knows how to bake it like mom!" Marshall said.

"Thank you, dear," Martha said as she beamed.

"Man, this is a two-carton dinner!" Gary said, and smiles and laughter followed his remark.

"You can have your coffee now or in the living room later," Martha said.

"Why not both?" Newell said. " And your big brother is fixing us another round."

"Oh?" Martha said, raising her eyebrows.

"Mom, why don't you and Paula join us? That sherry is also nice after dinner, I think."

Before Martha could answer Paula spoke up, "Count me in, Marsh," She said. "How about it, Mrs. Sunder?"

"Well, I guess it would be nice." Still wearing her apron, she lifted it, fanned her face, then took it off and hung it on a hook by the back door.

Martha filled the coffee cups at the sink and served the men. "Tried out the new teapot, Marshall," Martha said, then poured tea into the Limoges cup for Paula and selected another petite china cup for herself.

Marshall thought, I'm going to have to write to Eileen and tell her how well her selection was. He then said, "I was afraid you weren't going to use it. I'm real happy you like it."

Martha smiled at Marshall, then turned to Paula. "Have you ever tasted dried figs, dusted rather heavily with powdered sugar?"

"No, Mrs. Sunder, I haven't."

"They are sweet, but later, when dinner and dessert settles, and after the cocktails, I'll put some on a platter. They're no competition for that *See's* candy though."

"How do you prepare them?"

"It's easy enough. Newell built a platform in the backyard and we spread the ripe figs out on waxed paper then cover them with a sheet of cheese cloth that is elevated so that insects can't get near the fruit. We've a very low humidity here, and they sun-dry fairly fast, and flatten out, then we put the powdered sugar on them and they are like a fruit-cookie. We just don't waste anything, and you can eat just so many figs. I'll show them to you after we've cleaned up the kitchen."

"Guess we'll have to be two fisted drinkers, with both coffee and these toddies," Bruce said.

"You know," Martha said, "Just let me have those coffee mugs back. You haven't touched the coffee. I'm going to pour them back into the per-colator." She gathered the mugs of coffee from the men. "We'll keep the coffee hot for later. Paula and I are going to rinse off and stack these dishes and we'll be right along. Paula, dear, I'll bet you and I can handle both these little glasses, and the tea cups."

Paula nodded, and she and Martha joined the men. "We could hear you guys in the kitchen. What was that laughter all about out on the porch? Can you repeat it?" Paula asked.

"Sure! It's clean." He then repeated the toast, and each of the men raised their glasses and sipped from them, as did Martha and Paula. Everyone smiled and laughed at Gary.

"Lot of funny things happened to us," Marshall said, glancing at Gary. "Remember when we were just putting the crews together down at Lake Charles? We'd met the crewmembers, the engineer, the radioman and the tail gunner, of course, but really didn't know them well. As a matter of fact, Gary and I and Frank were just getting acquainted." Marshall looked again to Gary. "Guess you know, too, that if any crew member was uncomfortable with his assignment, was leery of the pilot's or copilot's skills, he could ask for assignment to a different crew. But there was never a doubt in anyone's minds in our crew about the talents of Frank and Gary. Both competent, skilled, but not quite 'hot pilots'."

Gary stood and bowed at the waist. "I didn't know you cared, buddy!" The group laughed at him.

"You go ahead, Gary. I think you know that story, and Paula will love it," Marshall said.

"Well, Frank and Marsh and I were all dressed up in our greens one evening and heading for the mess hall and we all recognized Pop approaching. We figured we'd stop and chat, but he didn't slow and looked at us kind of sternly, so when he was about five feet from us, all of a sudden, Frank salutes, and simultaneously Marsh and I do, and Pop returns the salutes and goes on past, then yells out, 'Halt!' Well, damned if we didn't! Right on the spot. I think he started to say about face, but hesitated before he could say it, and we turned around and here was Pop bent over at the waist, laughing, holding his sides. He wiped tears away from his cheeks, and said, 'Well, gentlemen, obviously you didn't get exposed to that officer and gentlemen stuff.' His laugh was contagious, so we had to join in. Then he said, 'the enlisted man, guys like me, in this case, he, and I emphasized I,'—— 'I salute first. Officers return the salute! Got it?'

"Well, we nodded, all of us rather embarrassed, then shook hands with him and laughed and knew right then we had a gem for an engineer.

"Well, sirs,' Pop said, 'I'm going to go do some more studying. Lots to know about those big Pratt and Whitneys.' He smiled, clicked his heels and in a very military manner saluted. We all laughed and returned his salute. But, before he leaves, Frank said, 'Wait a minute there, Sergeant Skidmore, this incident had better be a best kept military secret.'

'I gottcha, Lieutenant!' Pop said, laughed, shook his head affirmatively and proceeded on his way, as did we."

"What a guy!" Gary said. He looked around at the faces, smiled and then said, "We tend to recall the events that had sort of a humorous twist. You couldn't perform if you dwelled on the tragic events. Right, Marsh?"

"Roger," Marshall said. "I think we attributed everything to lady luck, whether it was good or bad." Then he continued, "Gary, do you remember that strange mission just a few days before the war ended?" Marshall asked. "Our flight was spread out abreast in the sky, probably a half-block apart, and we were all flying toward the Rhine River. What do you think our bomb load was? What we were carrying into Germany?"

Gary laughed. "All we wanted the krauts to do was give up, turn in the printed sheet to any GI, receive a hot meal, get de-liced and hand over their Mausers or burp guns."

"Our bombs were filled with pamphlets, with instructions on how to surrender," Marshall continued, "And with this peaceful load, all I had to do was find Dusseldorf, across the Rhine River, in the Ruhr Valley, and help end the war with our peaceful mission. We were on a course a little north, of Cologne, and about the time I was nonchalantly pointing out the Cologne Cathedral to the crew, just crossing the Rhine River, six eighty-eight shells exploded around us, front, stern and each wing, dead level with us, but we weren't hit, but we were boxed by the black smoke of the flak. Well, Frank and Gary dove the '26 and we did evasive action the rest of the way to Dusseldorf, found the center of town, dropped the bombs, which were set to explode at a hundred feet or so, and spread the surrender message. Then we got the heck out of there doing evasive action for several miles, until we got well past the Rhine."

Gary and Marshall both laughed, then Gary added, "Of course the krauts didn't know what we were up to. For all they knew we were dropping more real bombs. But those old men manning the 88's sure zeroed in on us!"

"The guys chewed me out good when we got back and I agreed no more guided tours until the war ended!" Marshall said, grinning, looking from face to face.

"Speaking of old men," Gary said, "remember that crew that had to crash land, a wheels up belly landing, a few days before the war ended? Well, they all got out unhurt, which is rare, and luckily some Wehrmacht guys captured them, instead of the SS. They started marching the captives to some little village, but the German men were all seventy or over, tired, underfed, scrawny old guys, obviously weary as heck, and one of the crew members could speak a little German, so he convinced the old soldiers to let the crew members carry the rifles. And they did! They all bedded down that night in a barn filled with hay. The German guard dozed off and our guys quietly slipped off, found a place to swim across the Rhine and in three days were back flying again!"

Chuckles filled the living room. Newell and Bruce shook their heads, and hoped the young fliers would continue. Martha arose and returned with a platter of dried figs and passed the platter around. "The coffee is still hot if you men care for some," she said.

"Sounds good to me," Gary said, then added, "These little devils are good. We'll have to figure out how to prepare them, honey."

"I've already learned."

"Any particular tough mission you want to tell us about?" Bruce asked, then added, "Boy, these *See's* chocolates are really rich!"

Marshall then continued, "Early on we got shot up a bit, and we always knew it would be rough if our C.O., Colonel Schlosser, led the mission. Towards the end the missions were mostly milk runs."

"Remember those guys from that photo unit in town that wanted to go on a mission with us and take pictures?" Gary said.

"Tell them," Marshall said laughing.

"Wasn't legal of course, against regulation, but Frank went along with it. The pilot of the other plane backed out at the last minute when we were about ready to get in the ships. 'Only one of you can go,' I told them. 'Make a decision.'

"So, the fellow named Terry said, 'We'll flip', and with that he took out a French coin about the size of a silver dollar, flipped it into the air, said 'tails' and the coin landed and bounced and stood up vertically, leaning against a stubble of dry grass," Gary said, and both he and Marshall laughed. "Well, there's a lot of superstition involved in flying so we wouldn't have been surprised if both had backed out, but Terry said he wanted to go, and he did. We fixed him up with a flak suit and parachute of course. We'd been out about an hour and he was by the opening with a waist gun, when all of a sudden he breaks silence and says, 'they've zeroed in on us!' but what he saw floating by the opening was what we called 'window', aluminum shreds thrown out by the planes ahead of us to scramble the German radar. Terry thought it was flak."

"Turned out to be a milk run, but it really took a lot of guts for Terry to join us," Marshall said.

"What about that mission where you guys got your medals?" Bruce asked.

Newell said, " That was pretty grim, I guess. You don't need to repeat it, Son."

Marshall cleared his throat, but Gary spoke.

"Yeah," Gary said, "That was a strange mission, really. Marsh got a good hit on the primary, for our flight, but then those bombs hung up in the bomb bay. Marsh found that bridge at Bad Scheidel and busted it up pretty good, but when we finally got back to the base we learned that Spike got it. Everyone was pretty well shook."

Marshall cleared his throat. "The figs are as good as ever, mom," His voice quavered.

"Bet that's something the Air Corps didn't serve you," Martha said. She recalled the incident about the young aviator called Spike. Newell told her how upset Marshall had been.

"Did you say Spike?" Paula asked.

"Yes, honey. I'll tell you about it later," Gary said, recalling, too, that Marshall, of all of them, had taken it quite hard.

"Enough war stories for awhile," Newell said. "Martha, I'm going to get the guitar out. Why don't you and Bruce sing some of those corny Irish songs for us! And of course anyone that knows the words just chime right in." He arose and walked towards a closet in the living room near the front door and returned with a guitar that he handed to Martha.

"Oh, how wonderful," Paula said. "Maybe we can all sing along?"

"I'll hum," Newell said, laughing. " I'd be arrested for issuing fraudulent notes if I sang, but I love to listen!"

"Sis, I'm going to have to float a few drams of JD across my old vocal cords if you want me to join you."

"Any excuse," Martha said, shaking her head, "I know," Martha smiled at Bruce, then accepted the guitar. She balanced it, her left hand resting across the frets, and with her right hand began to pluck the strings. The tone was deep and resonant, and Marshall wished he had asked her to play when he first got home. Her expression seemed more serene. Her lips formed a smile, and she began to hum.

"Let's start with 'My Wild Irish Rose,' Martha said. "Everyone join in now."

They moved quickly through the song and even Newell's voice could be heard. Martha then led them into *Peg O 'My Heart*, and then *Danny Boy*. At the completion of the number they would sit back in satisfaction and applaud their contributions.

"After Newell and I were married and said our marriage vows, Bruce's dear wife, Nedra, sang *'I Love You Truly.'* Martha said."

"Sing it for us, Sis," Bruce said, and nodded at Newell.

Martha smiled at Newell and he winked at her and before she sang an air of quiet reverence settled about all of them.

"Thank you, sis," Bruce said when she had finished.

"I admire people who aren't afraid to be sentimental," Paula said.

"Thank you, Paula," Martha said. "I think we all agree with that, but now here's a lively little ditty. Follow along now!"

Then she strummed the guitar and sang *"Bye, Bye Blackbird,"* and again the words were common to most of them. Newell was content to watch looking from the faces of one to the other, appreciating the gift that seemed to relax and bring Marshall and Martha closer together. Now and then they'd hear him hum or sing a few words.

"Well, I guess that's about the end of my repertoire for one evening," Martha said and started to stand, removing the guitar, when Gary spoke. "Paula's a pretty competent guitarist, too, Mrs. Sunder."

"Really!" Martha said, "Well come dear, please lead us in whatever pleases you."

"Oh, I really don't know any Irish songs," she said, and slowly shook her head.

"We've had enough of Ireland for one evening," Newell said, and encouraged her. "But, please let's continue."

Paula accepted the guitar, and as Martha had done she began very carefully to pluck the strings.

"You know, Paula," Bruce said, "Martha used to teach guitar."

"Well, she certainly has the touch," Paula said.

"Speaking of teachers," Bruce said, laughing, "Did you hear the story about the first day of school?" Again Bruce chuckled, and his audience found his laughter contagious. "Well, some of the little kids were bringing in presents to the teacher, but a few went overboard. She was supposed to guess about a big bouquet, and correctly guessed it was from little Edna's parents that owned the florist shop, and then the next package contained enough apples and oranges and pears for each child, and it obviously came from the fruit market owned by Carlos' father, Mr. Alvarez, and then she picked up a tall box, with the bottom moist. It had a ribbon almost covering the word O'Toole's. She looked at Mike and said, 'Wine from your mommy and daddy?' Mike just smiled. She put her hand to the moisture, then touched her lips and raised her eyebrows and asked, 'Chablis?' And Mike said, 'No, Mam.'" And Bruce laughed loudly and concluded the joke by saying, "Then the little boy answered, 'PUPPY!'"

Everyone joined in the laughter. "I don't think that was with the ones you sent to Marshall," Gary said.

"Heck no!" Bruce said, "Too clean for you studs."

"Well, how about a couple of silly little songs?" Paula asked. "Marsh, you and Gary know these," and then she started to sing, "...*Oh, mares eat oats, and does eat oats and little lambs eat ivy,*" and the young men and Martha chimed in, and Newell and Bruce laughed at them. " *... And a kid will eat ivy, too, wouldn't you?*"

"Now here is really a strange one that needs a translation with it," and she began to strum and started to sing, *The Hut Sut Song,* but before even beginning she started laughing and said, "I'm embarrassed to say I can't put enough of it together in my own mind to make any sense of it. I'm sorry! Gosh!" Paula said, and continued to laughed and looked around at her audience. "Well, I don't think those made the Hit Parade," Paula said. "Some of the WWII songs were kind of melancholy, like '*I'll Walk Alone', 'The Last Time I saw Paris,'* and *'When the Lights Come on Again,'* but I know them, if anyone wants to hear them."

"You just go ahead and sing, sweetheart," Newell said.

"Well, this one is very special because Gary proposed to me when we were dancing at the Palladium. I think it was on our seventh date." Then she began to softly sing the words to *"As Time Goes By."*

"I'd call that 'Seventh Heaven,'" Gary said, "Don't you love the way she sings that," then chuckled and continued, "Would you believe that evening was the first time her mom allowed me to come into the living room after our date! Usually I'd give her a little kiss at the door and then drive off like a high school kid." Again Gary laughed. "As a matter of fact, how come did she let me in that night, Paula?"

"I just plain old told mother you were coming in that night," Paula said, smiling at him.

"Oh," Gary said, then continued. "Well, we sat around on the couch awhile, you know, necking up a storm, when suddenly her dad comes wandering in, wearing slippers and a bathrobe and glasses and his hair all messed up. Boy did he startle us. Her dad cleared his throat and says, 'You interested in guns, Gary? I'd like to show you my collection sometime.' Wow. Was that subtle! And then Paula said, 'Father! Not tonight!'"

"Gary! Hush!" Paula said, feigning a scolding tone.

Paula blushed. She continued to strum the guitar. Her audience listened quietly. "A First World War song that was again popular with soldiers of all countries in our war was *"Lilli of the Lamplight,"* she said. She looked from face to face awaiting encouragement.

"Let's hear it Paula," Bruce said, and clapped his hands, quietly, barely touching them, nodding affirmatively to her.

And she began to strum and sing:
"Underneath the lantern by the barracks gate,
Darling I remember the way you used to wait,
'Twas there that you whispered tenderly,
That you loved me, you'd always be,
My Lilli of the lamplight, my own Lilli Marlene.

"That is very melancholy," Martha said.

"Yes, and there are four verses. I know them, and if you want, I'll just do the last one."

"By all means," Newell said.

Resting in a billet just behind the line,
Even tho' we're parted your lips are close to mine,
You wait where that lantern softly gleams,
Your face seems, to haunt my dreams,
My Lilli of the lamplight, my own Lilli Marlene.

"My golly," Bruce said, "That's a real tearjerker."

"That was a German song," she said, then looked slowly around at each person, "How did the Germans get so messed up with that awful Hitler?" No one answered, and she continued, "You think of their contributions to music, like Mozart, and Beethoven, and on and on. It's so hard to understand," Paula said, then sighed and looked around the room. "You know: I love Brahms, and quite often I sing Tim to sleep with this lullaby." Everyone had grown quiet. She looked around the room and asked, "May I?"

"Yes, dear, please do," Martha said.

Paula picked the notes she desired and sang:

"*Lullaby, and good night. In the sky stars are bright. Close your eyes, start to yawn. Pleasant dreams until the dawn.*" She paused, glanced at her audience, then continued, "*Close your eyes now and rest. Lay your head on my breast. Go to sleep now and rest. May your slumber be blest.*"

"Paula, my dear," Newell said, "that's really very tender."

Marshall felt his chin quiver. Only he knew that in a bed, naked with Kristine, that she sang in German, the Brahms Lullaby. He'd rested his head between her breasts and she had stroked his forehead and the side of his face. Good Lord! And she's alive! With that realization his mind reeled.

But, suddenly, quite abruptly, Gary pushed back his chair and stood up and gazed around the room. His mouth was drawn down at the corners. Perspiration had formed on his forehead and moisture moved down his cheeks near his sideburns. He seemed to be staring at the others. "Excuse me," he said in a hushed tone. "To hell with the damn Germans! I need some fresh air," He walked across the living room and opened the front door, walked out, and quietly pulled the door closed behind him. All of them stared after him, then looked towards Paula.

"Gee, I wonder what triggered that?" Marshall said. "That German song?"

"I'll join him," Paula said, and she removed the strap from her shoulders and handed the guitar to Martha. "You know, you understand, once in awhile Gary gets kind of depressed."

"Do you want me to come, Paula?" Marshall asked.

"Thanks, no, Marshall. Gary needs me now."

Paula followed Gary out on to the front porch of the Sunder home.

"You all right, honey?" Paula asked. She walked to his side and stood close to him, resting her arm across his shoulders.

"Yeah, sure," Gary said. "I'm okay."

"Too much war talk tonight?"

"Christ, honey, you and I have never talked much about the war, or for that matter, my operation. Being with Marsh has kind of brought a lot of thoughts roaring back into my brain," Gary said. He turned and faced her and she moved close to him and she put her arms around him. "If it weren't for you and Tim, I think I'd have gone nuts by now, maybe killed myself with booze, or something. Even being repaired, I'm not handling my hate for Germans very well, am I?"

"Oh I am so sorry, Gary. Those songs triggered this. Sweetheart, you do have us: Tim and me. And I know we'll have a child of our own, with the help of Mayo Clinic," Paula patted his forehead and face with a handkerchief, soaking up the moisture.

"Guess it's like when Marshall said about his Norden bombsight, when it got messed up. 'My gyro tumbled.' Hell, now I've embarrassed you in front of our friends."

"You'll never embarrass me, sweetheart, I love you!"

"Paula, doll, what we do in the bedroom is wonderful." Then Gary sighed deeply. "I suppose I should be grateful I'm even alive. But, I'm just not like a complete man. I hope you understand. Here we are married, and I've never talked to you like this."

"Oh, honey, believe me I do understand!" Paula released her arms, but then stepped close to him, resting the palms of her hands on his chest and gazed up into his face. "Look at me. I love you so much. I just want the kind of love we have to be worth it all, for you." Paula stepped back from him and lightly touched his face and cheeks with her hand. She looked into his eyes.

"I'm ashamed to tell you how I feel about that song." Gary said. "Even the word, German, nauseates me!"

"I'm so sorry. I wasn't thinking. Forgive me, dear."

"Oh, it's not you, Paula. It's me. I'm not handling it. Forget it, honey."

"Do you want to explain to me, your feelings, your thoughts, dear?"

"Well, that Lilli Marlene song just depresses me! Oh, I guess it's a pretty enough song, but any reference to Germans, whether it's that song, or conversation about how great all of those German composers were, well, you see, it's just that the Nazis changed my life, and of course Pop's, too. Now I feel like shouting out a lot of swear words, vulgarisms, and at the same time I'm trying to clean up my act, not cuss, you know, but I really can't understand how those so-called brilliant Germans could have bought Hitler's ideas? If they didn't want to, why did they!"

"Oh, Gary dear, I'm sorry I sang that song, and said that about the composers. I'll learn to be more careful." Paula stammered, "I guess I somehow separate music from all that cruelty."

"Come on, Paula, it's not you. I know I'm too thin-skinned about the bleeping krauts! Being with Marsh sort of brought it all to the surface. And frankly, I think he's nuts to go back on active duty. That little German house Frau, Kristine, isn't worth it! He ought to forget her! She's no more his wife than I'm the man in the moon!"

"Gary, you are proud of that picture of the B-26 with the name *Miss Nausicaa* beneath your name. I know she existed in the book, The Odyssey, and we know she helped Odysseus. So allow me to be the *Nausicaa* in your life. Honey, I know you ARE a strong man, and I do understand your frustrations, and I know we can be happy because we have all of our senses. We can see, we can hear, we can feel, and inhale and enjoy all of the wonderful fragrances of the outdoors, of flowers, and for that matter, that nice cologne you bought me. Just be patient. You'll see how happy I will make you! As with *Nausicaa*, I'll nourish you, help you subdue your anger! And Tim is both of ours now. You are now his role model. We'll share joy together in raising him!"

"Paula, I get nightmares about the night those SS bastards mutilated me," Gary started, but Paula interrupted him. She raised the index finger of her right hand and touched his lips.

"My darling: later. Tonight, when we are in bed, I want you to tell me everything, and I want to you to hold me closely. But we should return now to the others. All right?"

"Paula, I'm such a lucky son of a bitch to have you!" Gary said, then with his own arms he pulled her to him and they hugged. He looked down at her and kissed her.

"Our tears are salty, aren't they," Paula whispered. With her handkerchief she dried his face, then her own.

"Well, you're right. Guess we'd better join the others," Gary sighed. They stood silently, embraced, then returned to the front room and found their seats.

All of them were silent until Bruce said, "Well, all, that fresh air isn't such a bad idea. This has been a beautiful evening, inside and out, but this old Irishman has to go to work tomorrow. You know Gary, if you and your sweetie hadn't shown up, I don't think we'd ever known that Marsh was overseas!" Bruce stood up and looked around the room and grinned at the others. "I'm going to have to say goodnight, and God love you all!"

"I'll go with you, Uncle Bruce." Marshall stood up. "I mean, unless I can stay and help take apart that table and put away the Apple Pattern, or something, mom?"

"That can wait," Martha said. "But, if you want to stay and visit with Gary and Paula you can take your pickup over to Bruce's and then come on back early for breakfast with us."

"No. Think I'll join Uncle Bruce, and hit the sack." Marshall said, "Mom, dad, you folks put on a great dinner and evening for us. I appreciate it. Goodnight. Night Paula. Night buddy."

"He doesn't know it but he'll be sleeping in Tara's bed, if she'll accept him," Bruce turned and whispered. He winked and they laughed quietly. Tara followed as Bruce and Marshall departed.

They heard the thumping of their shoes walking across the porch, then the doors of the pickup closed. The engine purred and the gravel crunched beneath the wheels.

After they departed, Newell, Martha, Paula and Gary returned to the living room Paula picked up the guitar and started to return it to Martha.

"We don't have to stop, do we? " Martha asked. "How about a couple more old American ballads, Paula?"

"Oh, I think Gary and I are going to call it a night. You folks go ahead though."

"I guess you're right. That is enough for one evening," Martha said, sighing. She handed the guitar to Newell, and he returned it to the closet. "Newel and I are early risers. I'll fix his breakfast and get him off to the store. We'll wait for Marshall and then have our breakfast. That sound all right?"

"I'll be up early, too," Gary said. "Maybe in the morning I can give you a quick run down on how to save a bundle on your paint inventories, Mr. Sunder."

"Sure thing," Newell said. "We'd like to hear what you have to say."

"Thanks for a wonderful meal and evening," Paula said, then both she and Gary said goodnight. They went to the guestroom and closed the door behind them. They quickly undressed, took turns in the bathroom and in bed faced each other and embraced. Gary kissed Paula hungrily and caressed her body, tenderly squeezing and exploring.

"Gary! Not here. Not in Marshall's bed, honey! Besides, you are too noisy!" Paula whispered, kissed him and then rested her head on his chest, and again whispered: "now, my sweet, brave warrior, you hold me closely and try to tell me about it."

"Christ, honey, I haven't talked about it to anyone. It was so obvious. I wasn't the first guy that it happened to. Not much to tell the M.P.'s, or Intelligence, but I'm glad to say they caught a couple of SS bastards. I left a few bruises on their goddamn faces!" Gary sighed.

"I was with a German widow who did laundry for us. Oh, I suppose I shouldn't have been there. It was in the evening." Gary sighed deeply, and his voice quavered as he continued. "They held me while they tortured that poor woman. They accused her and cursed her. I didn't sleep with her. I couldn't understand their damn language. It all sounds like they're spitting through false teeth! I fought them, but they held me and made me watch while they tormented the poor woman. She fainted when this guy puts a knife to her throat. Then, right in front of me, they broke her arms. Both of them! Thank God she'd fainted before the guy did it. Then they dragged me outside and threw me down on the ground and ripped my pants and shorts off and forced my legs apart, and pushed that damn tool in my face. They use it on sheep. They gagged me and did it, and I guess I passed out. God, I have such hate in my heart!"

Paula put her lips against his and kissed him. Her tears wetted his cheeks and then his tears blended with hers.

"I never cried about it before," Gary whispered. "Some damn man, eh? You know what. That poor damn German woman came to, and somehow managed to get on her bike and with her broken arms laying in the basket over the handle bars, sort of walked it to the edge of town where our guys found her and took her to our hospital. I guess her neighbors helped her get by after that, until she healed."

"Our tears will wash away your hate. You can't live with that anger inside of you. Transfer it to me, darling. I will handle it. Then we can go on, as we've planned."

In the darkness they could hear the ticking of Marshall's alarm clock on the dresser. Again Gary caressed Paula. "What do you think? If I promise to be real quiet?"

"Oh, Gary," Paula, whispered, then laughed very softly. "Quietly. Promise!"

x   x   x

In the kitchen Newell helped Martha finish up hand-washing and drying her crystal. As she stood on her toes and stretched to place them high in a cupboard, Newell walked close to her and patted her buttocks with his open palm.

"Newell!" she scolded. She brushed his hand away.

They went to their bedroom and began to disrobe. Again Newell approached her, and touched her breasts, then her buttocks. Again she retreated from him, pushing his hands away.

"Thought maybe those glasses of sherry might have relaxed you a bit, dear," Newell whispered.

"And all of that whiskey seems to have aroused you!" Martha said, "Don't get any ideas," Martha turned her back to him, and quickly slipped a cotton gown over her head.

"You arouse me, Martha. I don't need alcohol to want to be close to you."

"Aren't we getting a little old for that sort of thing?" Martha sighed. She went to her side of the bed and turned back the covers, and extinguished the bedside light, leaving just the pink glow of a night light from the adjoining bathroom to illuminate the bedroom. Newell hung his clothes in the closet and pulled a nightgown over his head.

"In my eyes you are a young, beautiful woman," Newell said. Then he continued. "You know, it's an ill wind that doesn't blow some good," he laughed quietly.

"What's that supposed to mean?"

"This new higher blood pressure of mine," he said, chuckling. "I asked the pharmacist if they made a larger size condom, and sure as heck, they do."

"Oh, my God! What pharmacist?"

"Doc Young."

"My God. His wife is in my Circle Group at the church."

"Oh, come off of it. Martha! He's like a MD, or a priest."

"I can't believe you'd do such a thing!" Martha said, raising her voice.

"Hush. Do you want those kids to hear you?"

"I can hardly wait to see the looks I'll get!"

"Well, sweetie, that really won't happen. It's confidential. I know Doc," Newell sighed, then whispered, "So what's it going to be, lovers or fighters?"

Angrily Martha turned over in the bed. She pushed back the sheets and blankets, baring her body from below her breasts and pulled the nightgown almost over her face. She sighed loudly, opened her thighs, turned her face to one side, and waited.

Newell stared at her triangle of darkness, and his passion turned to revulsion. "Well, your enthusiasm has reduced the poor fellow to half mast!" Newell hissed. "Save yourself, Martha. I've heard that if you don't make love for seven years your hymen will grow back. You can be a virgin again, like Mary!"

"Oh, get on with it."

"Hate to tell you, but right now I think a tipped-over saw horse would be more enticing!"

"God, you can be a vulgar man."

"Oh? I just wonder who really is the vulgar one? Some day, if I live long enough, I might just tell Marshall he was a damn accident," Newell said. With one hand, he reached down to the bed and grabbed the sheets and blankets and flung them back down over Martha's legs. He then went to the bathroom, switched on the light, and pulled back the shower curtain, climbed into the tub, turned on the water and adjusted the temperature, pointed the shower head and allowed the warm water to splash against his back and shoulders. He lathered his body with soap, and finally with his right hand relieved the tension that had again risen, and had been rejected. As he stroked, he breathed deeply, gulped in the foggy air, stroked faster, and finally his body shuddered. His legs became taught, then relaxed. He sighed, and again allowed the warm water to pound his neck and back.

After his shower, Newell toweled himself vigorously. He combed his hair, looked into the mirror, then quickly turned away from it, avoiding the reflection of his own eyes. He put on his nightgown, then quietly returned to the bedroom, and from a hook obtained his robe. He found his slippers, and carried them in one hand.

"Are you coming back to bed, Newell?" Martha whispered.

"Ha! Forget it! And you'll sleep better without my heart jarring the bed. I'm going into the living room."

"Oh, Newell, I'm so sorry. Please forgive me. Let me make it up to you."

"Good night, Martha."

Newell was careful to open and close the doors very slowly. The latch clicked. He went to the living room and pulled a footstool up near the overstuffed chair and rested his back against the cushions, his legs raised and supported by the stool, where he dozed off.

x   x   x

Bruce drove towards his home. "Marsh, were all of the members of crews good friends, like you and Gary?"

"Mostly, I'd guess," Marshall said. "Some times a bombardier would have a good friend he'd gone through cadets with, and if they happened to end up in the same outfit they'd hang around together. I got along well with both Frank and Gary. Frank was pretty quiet, more conservative, being married and all. He'd had a couple years of college. Had several books he read, and reread. He was the true-blue guy in our outfit. He was sort of idealistic. He never cheated on Diana. Frank really studied his books more than just read them, if you know what I mean."

"I understand," Bruce replied.

"Geez, Uncle Bruce, one time Gary and I went into Brussels on a three-day pass. Exchanged some American money under the table, in a little Belgian cafe, got eight times the amount in francs. Then we'd deposit the francs in our bank accounts, and it was converted back to dollars. Good way to get ahead if you didn't get too greedy. Some guys bought diamonds. I was afraid they'd pass off some glass junk as a good diamond, so I steered clear of that. Illegal as hell, of course, but everyone was doing it."

"Anyone get caught?"

"Intelligence was after the big shots. Couple of officers somehow got a hold of a boxcar full of butter from Sweden. Could have made them a fortune, but they got caught and I think they ended up in Leavenworth."

"Hmmm," Bruce said.

"We bought gifts for our families, and looked for a little feminine companionship."

"Now you sound like a Kane!"

"In this little bistro, I guess you'd call it, Gary and I were having a couple of beers and it didn't take Gary long to offer to buy drinks for a couple of cute Belgian girls. They accepted and I think their beer was stronger than our three-point-two stuff, so it wasn't long before Gary puts his hand up to his head and circles his head with his index finger and says, ' Me getting zig zig!' Well, the girls both really laughed, and one said, 'No. You mean zig zag!' and they both giggled. Well, another G.I. overheard this exchange, and he moves up close to Gary and me and the guy whispers, 'Zig zig means fuck. Zig Zag means drunk!'

"Well, it was one of the first times I ever saw Gary flabbergasted, but it didn't take him long to suggest another round of beers, which they accepted, and before the night was over we ended up getting both!"

Marshall began to laugh, and Bruce joined in.

"You know, Uncle Bruce, we all considered Gary a cocksman. He didn't just talk about his conquests, he even included me. Frank wouldn't have any part of it, and told both of us to go look at some of those gruesome films the medics would make us watch now and then."

"Films?" Bruce said.

"You know. Or maybe you don't." Marshall said. "The ones that showed the awful diseases some women have, and you'd catch if you fooled around."

Bruce grimaced.

"I sure hope Gary has sowed all of his wild oats," Marshall said, then continued, "Course I guess he really doesn't have any now. Gosh, I'm glad that he and Paula got together. She's really a doll, isn't she, Uncle Bruce."

"Oh, yes, I do agree. She reminds me of Nedra, when she was that age."

"That was sure too bad. About Nedra," Marshall said.

"Yes," Bruce said, very quietly. He paused, then said, "Guess you know the draft board turned me down."

"No, Uncle Bruce, I didn't know that. Why?"

"Guess they wanted younger men," Bruce said, "I even appealed, but got nowhere. But, come on, I'd rather hear about you and Gary!"

Bruce turned into his driveway. "Gosh, I'm happy everyone accepts Tara. When she gets this prime rib bone she'll be a happy puppy!"

"Hell, Uncle Bruce, how could anyone not like Tara? You know, one of our pilots got a hold of a black dog, kind of like a Lab, at our base in Denain. She was a mascot. He named her Flaksy."

"Flaksy?" Bruce asked.

"Flak was black, you know, the powder, when the shell exploded."

"Oh, so, what happened to the dog?"

"He tried like hell to ship her home, but there was no way. Quarantines and stuff. He gave her to one of the local farmers."

When they opened the door, Tara bounded in ahead of Bruce and he told her to "sit and stay." Then he walked to his kitchen, opened the brown bag with the prime rib bone, showed her the bone, and walked to the back porch, turned on an outside light and opened the door, as he handed her the bone. Bruce returned to the kitchen. "Can you stand another little shot of JD?"

"Sure. If you can," Marshall replied. "That was a fun evening. Even mom didn't get on our backs too much about the liquor."

"Too bad I didn't inherit a few of her high morals," Bruce chuckled.

Bruce poured the bourbon into water glasses with ice cubes and water. He raised his glass, "To us, kid," he said. Marshall touched his glass to Bruce's.

"Uncle Bruce, you said you wanted to know more about Gary," Marshall said.

"Oh, just about the mischief you guys got into. No more stuff about combat."

"Well, this is kind of quaint, or funny, or at least different, this little adventure. And you know, Uncle Bruce, I'm sharing things with you that I'm not even telling dad. Not that I don't think he'd get a kick out of it, but, well, I think you understand. And mom, well, I believe she thinks of sex, or anything to do with it, as something that is just plain old dirty."

"Wrong on one count, Marsh. I really don't feel she's a prude. I do think that store is keeping her upset. But anything you tell me stops right here, if that's the way you want it. I kind of like this role of being a confidant."

"Well, one time Gary comes back to the base after a three-day pass. He tells us about this incredibly beautiful redhead, Ginger, that he shacks up with, then adds that her mother, equally beautiful, not only didn't disapprove, but after serving them coffee, climbed naked into bed with Gary and her daughter."

Bruce tipped his head back and laughed loudly.

"So Gary asked me to join him after our next air medal mission, when we'd get a three-day pass." Marshall said, "Frankly I went because I was so sure he was full of BS."

"Was he?" Bruce asked.

"Well, he suggested we take some cigarettes and chocolate and coffee, and I complied. Did you ever hear of an orgy, Uncle Bruce?"

"Go ahead with your story while I fix us another wee nip," Bruce said.

"Uncle Bruce, the whole thing kind of unraveled like a slow motion movie. The four of us had a wonderful dinner at a cozy little Belgian restaurant. The waiter was an old geezer wearing a tux and a bow tie.

"The cigarettes took care of the dinner and the waiter. And it was true. This girl Ginger was a knockout, really stunning. Her mother could have passed for her sister, but with a few little wrinkles around her eyes. I don't know what I expected, but they were well dressed, quiet, whistle clean, and for them, I think sex was the last thing on their minds. I was so damn hard up at the time, that's about all I thought about, and of course Gary was always hard up," Marshall said.

"You see, this little cafe had a small band, and we danced. Gary asked Ginger's mother, so I danced with Ginger and she had the most solid boobs I've ever had pushed into me," Marshall sighed. "We changed partners and her mother was built exactly the same, maybe a little softer around her waist, but she danced cheek to cheek and hummed the words to whatever they were playing. God, was I anxious, but the ladies were relaxed and slow about every thing they did, and there wasn't anything phony about them. Just two women having a good time. Learned later that Ginger's dad had been killed early in the war. With the French Resistance, or something. Both ladies were secretaries.

"Gosh, I don't want to draw this out forever, but I finally ended up in bed with Ginger, and Gary disappeared with her mom. I dozed off after my encounter. When I woke up, she was gone. I dozed off again, and the next thing I know, Ginger is climbing back into bed on one side and her mother is climbing in on the other side, both naked as jaybirds. Uncle

Bruce, I had heard the word ecstasy, but what those two beautiful women did to, and for, me defies description. I'm just asking you to imagine being on your back with one of them on each side, exploring your body with their mouths and hands, and you've only one mouth and two hands to reciprocate. My damn balls ached for a week!"

"Hey, kiddo, you'd better stop or I'll have to take off for Clean Jean's tonight!" Bruce laughed.

"God knows how I survived. We had nice meals with them, went sight-seeing and shacked up for three days! Boy! Did I ever believe Gary!" Marshall sighed, "And you know, Uncle Bruce, there was never a feeling of doing something naughty, irreligious, forbidden, or immoral. It was just downright fun, exhilarating, and normal. We all loved what we were experiencing. No! Gary and I were never in the same bed with both of them at one time. But they did climb in with us."

"Incredible," Bruce said, and again laughed.

"Talk about crazy. You know we had German girls working for us at our base at Bad Scheidel. Well, I got kind of sweet on one of them, a girl named Kristine, and I think it was sort of mutual. She told me she wanted to climb into one of our '26's, to just look around. Well, Gary and Pop and I took her down to the flight line. Told her to wear trousers. Pop borrowed a small flight suit for her. She found out why when we had to hoist her up through the nose wheel opening. She was a curious little thing: kind of proud and feisty. I even helped her down into the nose. Said she wanted to see my office. Pop took her back to the stinger and also helped her climb up into the top turret." Marshall laughed, then said. "That's when I told her that McAdam would marry us. Like a captain of a seagoing ship, he was entitled. Right?"

"Go on," Bruce said, grinning. "If you say so. Must be the Irish in you!"

"Envision this, Gary sits in the pilot's seat, and Pop is in the copilot seat and we kneel side by side between them, and Gary recites some stuff, sounding like a real minister, and then says, 'In my capacity as captain of this ship I now declare you husband and wife. Kiss the bride,' So I did, and so did Pop, our witness, and Gary.

"We all had a great laugh. Kristine told us in her best English, 'You Luftgangsters are all crazy men!'" Again Marshall laughed, "Of course this was before she knew that our crew bombed her fucking town. Can you imagine what mom would say if I told her I married a German maid!"

"Son, I think that German girl pegged you guys right." Bruce laughed loudly. "Kid, you are no more married than your Uncle Bruce!"

"Nope, Uncle Bruce, I really AM married." Then Marshall, too, began to laugh a little louder, but he couldn't stop laughing, and his laughter began to grow even louder, he had a difficult time catching his breath and his laughing seemed like sobs at times, jarred his body and then his laughter became a laughing jag. Tears now flowed across Marshall's cheeks, as he continued to laugh.

Bruce had witnessed the same thing with a friend whose best buddy had been killed. He had begun to reminisce about all of the fun they'd had, and his laughter had finally turned to tears. Bruce now realized that Marshall was actually crying. He put his hands on his shoulders, and massaged them.

"Come on, Son," he said, "Let's go fetch Tara. She's probably cleaned the beef off of that big old bone and buried it by now." He raised Marshall, putting his hands beneath his armpits from behind and helped him stand. Marshall wiped away his laughter-tears and took several deep breaths, then followed Bruce to the back porch. They went outside and Bruce whistled for Tara.

"Christ, Uncle Bruce, I don't know what came over me. Too much of our old buddy JD, I guess." His head swirled. He walked down the back steps, stumbled down the slope to the pond. He held on to the trunk of an alder tree and regurgitated. He kneeled on the gravel and sloshed water onto his face. With his handkerchief he dried his face. He re-washed his hands and tried to dry them on the wet handkerchief. He stuffed it into his back pocket, returned to the tree and steadied himself.

"You going to be okay, Marsh?" Bruce spoke, beyond the porch light, into the blackness.

"Roger," Marshall answered.

x   x   x

Martha and Newell and their guests arose early. Paula helped Martha prepare the breakfast of bacon and eggs, sourdough bread toast, and coffee. Martha had filled glasses with apple juice and placed them it at each setting on the kitchen table.

"Are we waiting for Marshall? Paula asked.

"Probably eating with his uncle. We'd better go ahead without him," Martha said, shrugging her shoulders.

"Mr. Sunder," Gary said, "While we're enjoying our apple juice, let me give you a few facts about inventorying paint. Marshall might be interested, but you and Mrs. Sunder can cover it with him. If you are interested, I can contact the sales rep that covers this area and have him stop by."

"Shoot, Gary," Newell said. He finished drinking his apple juice and looked to see if Martha was listening. He stared at her, as if she was a stranger in their home. She was carefully cracking eggs so the yolks wouldn't break and putting them into a large cast iron frying pan, in which the bacon had already been fried. She lifted her apron, fanned her face, and smiled at Gary and Newell, nodding that she was listening.

"Well, I assume you stock both quarts and gallons of a dozen or more colors, in various amounts according to your sales and inventory cards."

"Correct. Go ahead," Newell said.

"Just for instance, let's say you have fifty of the gallon size and about the same in quarts. How would you like to be able to cut that inventory by at least two thirds, and provide an unlimited choice of colors?"

"We're listening. Keep going."

"Well, Rainbow Paint Company has devised a very exact system that uses combinations of colored powders to mix into a quart-size or a gallon-size of white paint, and a vibrating machine that stirs everything up thoroughly. And with the combination of cards, the color can be duplicated months or even years later. So, instead of inventorying several shades of yellow, and of green, and of blue, or gray, or whatever, you only stock white! And that simply adds up to quite a savings on dollars invested in inventory. Right?"

"Sounds too simple. What's the catch?" Newell said.

"All right boys, here's your bacon and eggs. And the toast is from the loaf Paula and Gary brought from San Francisco," Martha said, as she placed the plates of food on the table.

"Thank you mam," Gary said, then looked to Newell, "The catch?" Gary said. "Well. If you'd call it a catch it would be the exclusivity, I guess. Because Rainbow would provide all of the equipment needed, they've taken a stance that our distributors should be loyal to us. You know, not carry competing brands."

"My, this toast is good," Newell said, then continued, "That sounds reasonable to me. What do you think, Martha?"

"We'd have to consider our overall relations with Torburn and Fox, of course. We really don't inventory a lot of paint. Might not even be a big enough customer to interest your company, Gary."

"Well, if you do decide to talk to a rep, just let me know," Gary said.

"Gary, we appreciate hearing about this. We'll kick it around, Martha and I, and we'll fill Marshall in, too."

"Who, or what is Torburn and Fox?" Gary said, looking towards Newell.

"Biggest wholesale house in Northern Cal. The owner bought Marshall's Model A; collects them."

"Really?" Gary said. He glanced at Paula and raised his eyebrows.

"These eggs really have a nice flavor, Mrs. Sunder," Paula said, and turned and smiled at Gary.

"Thank you. Mrs. Scroggins has Rhode Island Reds and we get them fresh from her."

Gravel crunching announced the arrival of Marshall and Bruce. The men crossed the wooden porch and entered the kitchen after a spirited knock on the front door.

"Just in time for breakfast," Newell said.

"Thank you, no," Bruce responded. " Didn't think you'd be expecting us. We stopped at the diner and had Belgian waffles with a side of ham and eggs. My, it sure does smell good in here."

Gary laughed, "Did you ever hear of a Belgian waffle when we were in Belgium, Marsh?"

"No. But don't knock them. Really good!" Marshall said, "Any coffee left?"

"Coming right up," Martha said, "Gary just gave us a rundown on the Rainbow Paint Company paint-mixing method." She poured coffee into two mugs and handed them to Bruce and Marshall. "Is it hot in here, or is it just me?" Martha added. She again raised her apron and fanned her face. "Suppose we'd still have to carry linseed oil and paint thinner, Gary?"

"Oh sure. That wouldn't change."

"I'm warm, too," Paula said. She smiled and went on, "The stove is hot, plus lots of big-bodied guys in here now."

"The paint subject is very interesting," Newell said. "We'll fill you in later."

"I'm off to work. Tara and I have to submit a bid on a apartment house," Bruce said, grinning at everyone. He then walked to Gary and extended his hand.

Gary arose and said, "My pop always said 'only dogs and ladies shake hands sitting down.'" Both he and Bruce laughed. "I'm going to call you Uncle Bruce if it's okay, and want you to know that you've more than lived up to our expectations."

"Thank you, Marsh," Bruce said, then walked to Paula. "Now honey, I'm not going to shake your hand. I want to give you a nice hug and, well, it's just been great meeting both of you and I hope you'll visit us often. Bring that little tad, Tim, and I'll give him some fishing lessons. What's more, he'll catch fish!" He paused, smiled down at her, then added, "kind of consider us as family, a home away from home up here in the boondocks."

Paula stood up and shared a bear hug with Bruce.

"Thanks for the coffee Newell, sis. See you all soon." He turned to Marshall, "Same goes for you, kiddo."

They heard the sound of his boots as he walked across the porch, and the gravel crunching as he departed. While Paula helped Martha with the kitchen dishes, Newell went to the garage to get the pickup truck.

"We've a lot of unfinished business, Marsh," Gary said. "Paula has a letter from Frank that will interest you, and there's some other stuff that'll wait until we're alone."

"Kitchen is all back in shape," Paula said. "I'm going to finish packing and I'll bring out that letter from Frank for Marsh to read," She departed and returned to the living room where Gary and Marshall sat, still sipping on their coffee.

"Here's the letter, Gary," Paula said, handing it to Gary, who in turn handed it to Marshall and said, "You realize, of course, that Frank thought you and I were still back at Bad Scheidel waiting for our points to come up."

"I'll just read it aloud," Marshall said.

"Dear Paula,

I don't know whether Gary or Marsh told you about my emergency medical leave. The guys said good-bye while I was waiting for a plane home. The shock of learning that Diana had died was almost like an insulation for what was to follow. We'd been overseas eighteen months. She had an abortion and didn't survive hemorrhaging. I was too numb at the funeral to hardly know what went on. Her parents and mine are still devastated. Rightfully, I spent most of the time trying to support them. There's been too much killing going on during the past few years, but if I could identify her lover, I'd kill him in a second. He killed my wife and a baby! But, with the help of a minister, I'm now learning how to forgive Diana. As for now, it stops there. I somehow think the Jews have it right, 'An Eye for an Eye.'

Mostly I'm writing to try to tell you I can now better understand how you must have felt when you learned that Ed was killed. I realize that it is useless to try to deny our grief. It just won't go away, and must be a part of the healing process for survivors such as ourselves.

Paula, you must have your hands full, raising Tim. I assume Ed's folks and yours are helping. In a year or so, I'm going to be out your way for a visit. Please consider me a friend. If there is anything I can do, please call or write.

I've decided the Air Corps isn't for me. I've a couple of high school buddies, also ex-pilots, that are joining me in a trip down the Mississippi from the headwaters to New Orleans. We bought a very seaworthy little vessel and will have our own privacy. One is a photographer, the other a writer, and I'm going to keep a diary and try to find my sanity. My intentions are to go back to Kansas State when we return. I'll check in with my folks every week. I'm sure we'll hear from Gary and Marsh when they finally get home.

Your friend,

Frank Mueller

"Wow," Marshall said, shaking his head. "I haven't even written to him. You know, Gary, I've been feeling so damn sorry for myself since I got back, that, well, I'm just plain ashamed of myself."

"Forget it, buddy. Join the club. I haven't written either." Gary sighed. "Oh shit." He slammed the fist of his right hand in to the open palm of his left. He stood up. "Frank! You poor bastard! How in Christ's name could Diana have done it?" He stared at Marshall, then resumed, "Know what Paula said? She said men aren't ready to believe women have a libido."

Immediately Marshall thought of Eileen, remembering her lack of inhibitions about sex, but then he recalled the stance Frank had taken about marriage vows, and said, his voice barely above a whisper, "I think I understand that, but Diana did take the same vows as Frank."

Gary shrugged, then walked across the room and looked out of the window. He stood there silently, seeming to contemplate his next words, then returned and stared at Marshall, "But, you know, Marsh, good old Frank would probably be the first to understand." He walked around the table three times, tapping his knuckles against the table top, muttering to himself, sighed deeply then walked back into the kitchen.

"Mom Sunder, any more coffee in that pot?" Gary asked. Marshall followed Gary into the kitchen.

Martha said, "I just made a fresh pot. Newell will be taking some to work in a thermos." She went to the stove. "How about you, Son?"

"Yes, please," Marshall answered. His head throbbed. "Let's drink it at the kitchen table, Gary."

"My, you sound subdued."

"Just read a letter that Frank wrote to Paula. I'll fill you and in on it later." Marshall said, "Do you happen to have any aspirin, Mom?"

Martha chuckled, "You and your uncle, eh? Yes, there's a bottle right here in the cupboard." Martha located the bottle, filled a glass with water and handed both to Marshall. "Newell will be back in to say good-bye to Gary and Paula. Then we'll be off to the store."

Paula entered the kitchen. "Mrs. Sunder, I've stripped the bed and the pillows and will put them in the washer if you like. The towels and washcloths are with them."

"Oh, just leave them in the bedroom, Paula," Mrs. Sunder said, "I'll get to them later. And thank you."

Newell entered the kitchen through the back door. "Time for good-byes?" he asked, and walked directly to Paula. "Young lady, I hope you and Gary realize how much we enjoyed having you with us. And as Bruce said, please consider this another home away from home. Give me a hug now." Newell opened his arms and Paula stepped forward and put her arms around him, accepted his hug, and squeezed him tightly. She could feel the strong pulse of his body and wondered if it was because of his defective heart valve. The aroma of his after-shave was refreshing, masculine, and his hair, although thinning, was combed neatly and earlier she had noticed that his hands were strong, always well scrubbed, and his fingernails were closely trimmed and clean.

"I love you both," Paula said, then walked to Martha and they hugged. "In just a couple of days, I feel like I have another set of parents!"

Martha laughed and turned to Gary, "If you can find a duplicate of Paula down south, will you please wrap her up and ship her up here for Marshall?"

"Mom Sunder, that would be quite a challenge!" Gary said. He glanced at Marshall who watched and listened passively. Gary was sure that Martha didn't know that her son would not be staying in Chico.

"Paula spoke for both of us. These have been a couple of great days for us, plus getting to meet Bruce and Tara. We love you all!"

Gary then strode to Newell's side, slapped him on the shoulder, then grasped his hand and shook it vigorously. "Dad Sunder, you take care of yourself, hear. Listen to those medics. Pace yourself. Now do that, will you?"

"Heck Gary, I'm healthy as a pig. Martha spoils me rotten, as you've noticed."

"I filled your thermos, dear," Martha said. Newell walked to the sink and picked it up and turned, grinned, waved, then departed through the back door.

"I'll be right along, Newell. I have to get my purse." She removed her apron and fanned

her face quickly before hanging the apron on the hook by the backdoor. She found her purse, and as she left the kitchen she turned and smiled and lifted her hand and across the upturned palm blew them a kiss.

Marshall was surprised. He'd never seen his mother blow a kiss to anyone and thoughts of Eileen saying good bye at the Fairmont, just a few months ago, flashed across his mind.

They heard the tires on the gravel driveway and all three sat at the kitchen table and sipped their coffee. "You're a lucky guy, Marsh, having parents like those. Remember that session we had back at Bad Scheidel with Cal, alias Tex?"

"Yes, I really am. I realize it more and more," Marshall said. "When you got here a couple of days ago you said there was more to tell me. Want to fill me in on Bad Scheidel? I'm sure you understand that I was really shocked to learn that Kris is alive. What could top that?"

"I advised Gary to just stop there," Paula said. "But Gary felt we should tell you more, especially since you've indicated that you intend to return to Germany."

"First of all, I'm sorry I didn't ask about Cal. What the heck happened to him?"

Gary cleared his throat and glanced at Paula, then shrugged his shoulders. "Well, the other day I told you he had his name legally changed to Hawk, so he was proud and happy about that, but it seems Cal got smitten on some WAC up at Le Havre and every time he'd get some days off he'd fly up, or drive up and see her. Crazy guy insisted he was in love with her, but I think she was stringing him along."

"I think I know who it was. Cute enough."

"Well, he goes up to see her one time and she tells him she is scared of some soldier, a paratrooper, as I understand it. So Cal escorts her to her apartment, probably expecting to get a little lovin' or something of his own. But this guy really does show up, half swacked and he is going to try to beat up on the WAC, so he and Cal go at it, you know, fists, and I guess Cal is getting the upper hand when this maniac guy pulls out one of those Fairbairn daggers, those double-edge deals the British Commandos used, and stabs Cal in the chest. To make a long story short, Cal was put in the hospital. The dagger nicked his heart. Colonel Schlosser and the chaplain, Waldron, fly up to check up on him and then they find out he isn't going survive.

"Guess he must have realized it too, and tells them, 'If I don't make it, sir, please have me cremated and have my ashes scattered at The Alamo.' Last I heard, that's what happened. Can you believe it!"

"My God! Poor Cal. What a hell of a way to go! Gosh, I'm real sorry. So that's the other news you held back, eh?" Marshall said. He sighed, shook his head and stared at Gary.

"Buddy, I don't want to shock you, but there is more."

Marshall looked directly at Gary. "More? Well, come on, Gary, spit it out?" Marshall said, raising his voice, now evidencing his impatience and frustration. "More what?"

"Kristine is pregnant."

"Pregnant!" Marshall pushed away from the table and stood up. He stared at both of them. "Am I the father?" he asked, raising his voice.

"Well, how in the hell would I know!" Gary responded, also raising his own voice. "Hey, old friend, that's something you and Kristine would know!"

"Oh, my God, let me see," Marshall said, and they watched him as he sat back down and could read his lips as he counted to himself. "Do you remember the day and the month when you were attacked, Gary?"

"It was roughly seven months ago."

"Then that was the same week she was shot. God, that was only a couple of weeks after we went to Munich. Then you married us. Remember?"

"Of course! Listen, Marsh! Kristine was just wounded slightly. A little old bullet bounced off a rib and missed anything vital. She bled a lot, and I guess that's what you saw. She was recovering in a room not far from mine, and when she could get around, she'd come visit me."

"Well, what did she say?

"Say? Say about what? She was recovering, and trying to get strong enough to work, and get that library going for the chaplain! You were back in the States! Come on, buddy, what the hell could she say? She happened to say she that she was sorry for me!" Gary looked away from Marshall.

"Honey, you have to go on," Paula said.

"Yeah. It took a couple of months for Kristine to put on weight. You know, to start showing. And then she was busy at the new library and still doing the maid chores. And you can't really be serious about that marriage gag!" Gary said. "And as a matter of fact, Marsh, back then I happened to be having quite a tough friggin time healing, getting my own life back together, plus being worked over by the base psychiatrist. Plus the chaplain. Can you believe suicide actually crossed my mind?"

"Oh, God, Gary, forgive my stupidity," Marshall stammered. "I'm sorry. I should have written to your folks or someone to find out about you. I heard nothing from Schloss or any of the guys in the squadron. Tex, or rather Cal, never got back to me. No wonder. All I knew was that Kris was dead, that I loved her, and that I was responsible for everything that had happened to her."

"I guess all of us involved have been waiting for the dust to settle. Hell, Marsh, I could have written you, but I didn't," Gary said. "And while we're stirring this stew, let me throw in something else that in the long run may have a bearing on your own situation. And I hope you won't take this wrong, or get pissed off at me for telling you."

"My God? What the hell else?" Marshall asked.

Paula left the kitchen table, and went through the dining room to the living room. She found a Good Housekeeping magazine and sat in an overstuffed chair near a window. She wished she had departed earlier.

"Chaplain Waldron was a big help to me. He was also a big help to Kristine, arranging for that library job, and fixing her up with coal. To some of us, it seemed that he was getting sweet on her. It seemed mutual, that is to those of who even noticed, or cared."

Marshall sighed. "Hell Gary, I'm not mad at you. Why would I be mad at you? Jesus! Another surprise. I thought Chaplain Waldron was married?"

"Well, I don't think so," Gary said, "And it's hard to imagine a man of the cloth screwing around if he was, or is, married."

"You're not coming through very loud or clear about the chaplain. I just can't imagine that, but what I'm going to do for sure is call Major Crandall down at Beale. I think he gets brownie points if he signs some of us up for Occupation Duty. He mentioned Heidelberg, and that's not far from Bad Scheidel. If there is one thing I do know, I've got to see Kristine again. I can't tell you how relieved I am to know she's alive. The other stuff will have to sort itself out."

As the voices lowered, Paula decided to return to the kitchen. First she returned to the bedroom and brought back with her the wristwatch that Marshall had purchased in Switzerland for Kristine.

"Getting weary of this barracks language, sweetheart?" Gary asked, then added, "I'm sorry."

"Emotional stuff you guys are dealing with," Paula said, and smiled at both of them. "Here's the watch, Gary. And would it be asking too much to clue me in about you marrying Marshall and Kristine?"

"Oh, honey. That was just a dumb gag. At the time it was funny, I thought. As captain of a ship, a B-26, I married Marshall and Kris. I can't believe he's taken it seriously!"

Paula shook her head from side to side, as if in disbelief.

Gary handed the watch, in its case, to Marshall. He flipped open the case and stared at the watch. The crystal had been re-attached. He then closed the case and slipped it into his side pocket. "Well, I'm going to telephone Beale today and get the paperwork moving." Marshall said.

"Could you write, or get a telephone call through to Bad Scheidel? Maybe your Colonel Schlosser, or even the chaplain, could enlighten you," Paula said.

"Whatever they might say, Paula, and it is a valid idea, I'm definitely going back to Germany," Marshall said.

"What about the store?" Gary asked.

"Major Crandall wants to volunteer his time on weekends to learn the business. That'll take some of the load off of dad. My father knows the store can't support three of us now. If they still own it when I get back I'll be a lot better qualified to take over."

"My mother is going through the same thing as yours, Marsh," Paula said, "so that will make it a little tougher on her."

"What do you mean, Paula?"

"The poor dears are going through their changes. What do you think that fanning is all about?"

"Fanning?" Marshall asked.

"You must have heard about the change of life, about hot flashes!" Paula said, then laughed. "It's really not funny for them. I guess one minute everything is okay, and the next they are burning up. It is actually painful, so my mom says. And they do screwy things, out of character things. Didn't the Air Corps, or even your high school teachers, or the Boy Scouts, warn you about your mothers?"

"Gosh," Marshall whispered, "Maybe that's why my mother opened a letter addressed to me."

"Well, stranger things have happened," Paula said. "Your folks are both really keen, Marsh."

"Honey," Gary said, "we'd better get going. We've got a long drive ahead."

"Everything is packed and ready to load."

"I've a good California map if you need it," Marshall said.

"We're all set. Just point us towards 99, and if you've a favorite gas station, we need to fill up."

"Just head out past that little park a couple of blocks and you'll spot Wally's Garage. It's only a few more blocks to 99. Wally will point the way."

When the car was loaded, Marshall walked to Paula and said, "Everyone in my family wants to hug you, including me." He held her close and she hugged him back. They parted, then she grabbed him and pulled him close to her and said, "How about one from Tara?"

They hugged again; Paula then placed her hand on his neck, pulling his head down, and raised herself on her toes and kissed him. "Good luck in Germany. And be patient with your mom."

Marshall helped Paula into the car, closed the door, and then walked to the other side. "She's too good for you, you lucky bastard!" Marshall said. They gripped hands. "Let's do a little better with our letter writing."

"Right on both counts," Gary said. Then laughed again. " Hell, fella, I've got a secretary for that kind of stuff. But seriously, send us your address when you get settled in. You'd better plot yourself a good course on that mission into Bad Scheidel. You used to know how to guide us through flak alley."

"Roger," Marshall said. "When you get home, how about sending me some photos of the three of you."

"Roger, too. And I guess this is also 'over and out.' It's been fun."

Gary slid behind the steering wheel, as Marshall carefully closed the door. From her side of the car, Paula smiled and waved and Gary drove in the direction of the small park.

They stopped at a gasoline pump at Wally's Garage. Gary rolled down his window when a man approached his car. "Bet you're Wally," Gary said. "Marsh Sunder said you'd look after us and help us get back on 99, towards Medford."

"So the Sunder family are friends of yours?" Wally asked, then said, "Release your hood and I'll check out your vitals."

"Thanks sir, but I think all we need is a full tank of gas."

"Nobody leaves Wally's without a clean bill of car-health!" He smiled broadly at them.

Wally lifted the hood. He checked the oil, the radiator water, and water level in the battery. He made sure the wires to the spark plugs were attached. He let the hood slam down, then double-checked it to make sure if it was secure. He then washed the windshield and back window. Next he uncoiled an air hose from beside a compressor and dragged the hose to each tire. They could hear the compressor cut on and off.

"Manual says 32 pounds on these tires. That's what I put in. Real hot day you might drop back to 30. Make her ride a little easier." He grinned at both of them. "Did I get all of those bugs off of that windshield, miss?"

Paula smiled and nodded.

"Okay, Now we'll fill her up," Wally said. "We've only got one grade, but it's good gas." After he had placed the nozzle in the tank and locked the filling device, he walked back to the side of the car. "Assume you knew Marshall in the service?"

"Yes sir. We were on the same crew. We're up from LA for a visit."

"B-17's?"

"Nope. B-26's"

"Never heard of that airplane You fellas bomb Ploesti?"

"No sir. Out of our range. 26's were mediums."

"Well, we're grateful that you kids got back all in one piece," Wally said, and he heard the meter click off. "Nine gallons, young man. That ought to get you up to the Oregon border. Get good mileage on this new Ford? Old Henry knows how to build a V-8."

"Yes sir, back in one piece," Gary said. "We're still following the engine break-in instructions." Gary handed Wally a ten-dollar bill and waited for his change. *What the hell do you mean, back in one piece! I think I'll drop my fucking trousers and show you my fake balls. One piece, my ass. Am I a man or a woman? I gave my balls for my country! Oh shit! I can't have negative thoughts! I've got to be happy for Paula and Tim!* He leaned forward and rested his forehead on the steering wheel.

Conscious of his sensitivity about anything to do with the castration, Paula asked, "Are you feeling okay, honey?" "We don't want to get too self-absorbed, dear. We can't latch onto every word some one innocently says."

Gary raised his head and looked straight ahead. "Why sure, dear, you're right," Gary said. "That scotch Marsh served was really good! And, I was just thinking about Marshall and Kris."

Wally spoke to Gary, "Well, you drive carefully now. Stay on this street for six blocks, then turn left and it's four more blocks to 99, and you turn right to head north."

"Roger. Thank you, sir," Gary said.

Gary and Paula continued on their journey.

X   X   X

At the store Martha and Newell busied themselves, at opposite ends of the large, open room, putting away merchandise. At ten o'clock Martha walked through the aisles towards Newell. With her she had a thermos of coffee and two cups.

"Newell, I honestly don't know what came over me."

"Well, it's time for twin beds. Let's get on with buying them."

"Newell, I'm trying to apologize."

"Forget it, Martha. We can be friends, husband and wife, but just not lovers."

"Believe me. I love you. I want you close to me. We both said some unkind things to each other last night."

"Come on, Martha. You've made it very clear over the years that pro-creation is one thing, but recreation in bed is somehow sinful or dirty. I'm sure you can quote some line from the Bible to cover it!"

"Newell, I don't believe that at all! Do you honestly think I feel that way?"

"I sure as the devil do!"

"I can't believe you. Don't the previous twenty-five years count for any-thing? I thought I made you happy." Martha sighed, looked up at him and asked, "Will you see a psychiatrist with me?"

"If you want to see a psychiatrist, go to it. Count me out!"

"Won't you just hold me for a second?" Martha asked. She walked up close to Newell. Reluctantly, he placed his arms around her, neither pulling her toward him nor exerting any pressure. She pushed her body against his, feeling the pulsation of his strong heartbeat. He made no effort to hold her, simply stood with his arms taut, almost rigid. Newell looked over her shoulder.

"Excuse me," he said, "here comes a customer." He stepped back.

Martha moved away from him and watched him walk towards the man entering the store. She finished her coffee, then followed Newell holding the cups and the thermos. She set them near the cash register, wiped the moisture from her eyes, dried her glasses, and dabbed at her nose with a white linen handkerchief decorated with tiny, colorful flowers embroidered near the corners. She folded the handkerchief and tucked it into the work-apron pocket. *Oh, dear Lord. I'm the one who needs help.* She replaced her glasses and straightened them and then walked to a space behind the cash register. She stood there, as if awaiting a customer. She stared into space.

CHAPTER 28

▼

ACTIVE DUTY

When Gary and Paula drove out of his driveway, Marshall located his file with his military records. With the orders transferring him to inactive duty, Marshall also found a telephone number. With the assistance of the telephone operator he was connected to the Administration Office at Camp Beale.

"Major Crandall, please."

"Marshall Sunder," he replied to the questioner. And the next voice was that of Major Crandall, revealing the enthusiasm and vigor that Marshall associated with him. "Howdy, Lieutenant Sunder. I bet you are either going to ask me to come to work, or you want to go back on active duty?"

"How about both, Major?"

"You're joshing me, aren't you?"

"No sir. But there are a few 'ifs' involved."

"Well, try me!"

"Procurement Officer School at Heidelberg, flight pay, overseas pay, and a captaincy. And earlier you mentioned one year. I don't want to think beyond one year, sir."

"Wow!" followed by a pause, then, "Marshall, I can say okay on four of the items. The school at Heidelberg will be no problem. Overseas pay is automatic. I'll have to do a little checking about flight pay for bombardier-navigators, and while I admire you for asking for the captaincy, you are going to have to be on active duty for awhile as a first lieutenant. Promotions are coming through fairly quickly, but I can say, providing you sign up for two years, the captaincy is almost a sure thing."

"I'll sign up for one year and see what's going on after that."

"Roger," the major answered, then continued, "As for the paper work to put you back on active duty, I'll get my orderly working on that right now. A phone call should satisfy my question about flight status. Hell, you are automatically a qualified Observer, and that classification should require flight time."

"I need the money."

"Now, as far as my working in the store, I don't recall telling you that I'm married and we have two youngsters. They'll be in their teens soon. That's one reason I'm going to eventually get out, even though I may be wearing a Lt. Colonel's leaf next time you see me. My spouse, Ginny, has had enough of the military life."

"I understand."

"Then, Sunder, you also understand that my desire to learn the hardware business also involves Ginny and the kids. I'd like for her to meet your folks and Uncle Bruce, too. I bought the Piper Cub, so we can be up there in a jiffy. We'll need a small apartment, too, just for the weekends."

"Sir, I'm going to talk to the folks about when to come up, and will get right back by phone very soon."

That evening, after McAdam and Paula departed, following the conversation with Major Crandall, Marshall approached his father and mother.

He asked them to join him in the living room after dinner. Newell and Martha sat on the couch. Martha sat across from them in a stuffed chair.

"I want you both to know that first of all I love you very much." They looked at him curiously, expectantly, and smiled.

"Second, I must tell you that I've telephoned Major Crandall and that I'm going back on active duty. For one year, possibly two."

"You're what?" Martha exclaimed.

"Let him talk, dear, " Newell reached over and held Martha's hand, a move that pleased her.

"I'm going to the University in Heidelberg, where I'll study to be a Procurement Officer. I'll be able to really qualify myself for running a business. I'll probably be getting my flight pay and overseas pay. And now as a first, that'll be a lot more income than I could expect from the store for quite awhile. I have to be a first for awhile before I can expect a captaincy, but Major Crandall says that probably won't take long." Marshall cleared his throat.

"There's another personal matter that I've kept to myself. I am responsible for the predicament of a German girl named Kristine. I'm fond of her. My bombs ended the life of her mother, her little girl, indirectly her grandmother, and another woman, and I learned from Gary that her father wounded her when someone tried to steal their coal. I feel I have to help her get her life back on track. I thought she'd been killed."

"Good Lord," Martha whispered.

"I'm so sorry," Newell said. "But I'm not that surprised that you're going back on active duty."

"You can't be held responsible, Marshall. You were doing your job!" Martha said. Tears again flowed from her eyes, down her cheeks.

"Yeah, for God and country, I know. And I don't mean to sound sarcastic or cynical, but I hope you'll try to understand my viewpoint, and support me."

"You are a man. You've got to do what is right, as you see it. We know that. And of course we support your decision. Right, Martha?"

Martha didn't answer. She turned and put her head on Newell's shoulder, "He's going to be back in danger again!"

"Come on, Mom," Marshall said, "The shooting is over. This will be a flat-out cinch." Then he continued, "Now, I hope you'll both allow me to give the okay to Major Crandall to learn something about the business. He'll bring his wife up to talk with you as soon as you agree. If it doesn't work out, what have you lost? In fact he said he would obtain bonding, for his character, his honesty, in any amount you wish. I trust the man. They have two young children."

"Tell him we'll work out something." Newell said, "Tell him to bring his wife with him, as soon as you want. Understand now Son, if your mother is uneasy about any of this, the deal is off, and I want to be sure that you explain that clearly to him."

"Yes sir."

"Son, of course we'll support you. I'm just so apprehensive about anything to do with the military. Whatever you do, Marshall, you know your dad and I love you," Martha said, very quietly.

"One other thing. I'm taking my truck back to Mr. Bowman. He asked me to sell it back to him if I didn't want it."

"Maybe Mr. Crandall could use it when he's here," Newell said.

"Good thought. But he'll have to buy it from Mr. Bowman."

"All right then. Anytime you want to drop it off, let me know."

Marshall began to feel a sense of urgency. He hadn't asked how much time he'd have before going back on active duty. He felt a desire to share his news with Eileen. He felt that she understood his feelings toward Kristine. He wondered, too, if the news of his discovery might upset Eileen, stimulating thoughts of Billy. He decided to write anyway.

Dear Eileen,

A lot has happened since receiving your letter. I'm glad you are enjoying the challenges of college, and one of the purposes of this note is to let you know I'm going to be back on active duty for one year, as soon as my orders come through. AND, I'm going to college in Heidelberg, Germany. I'll study to become an Air Corps Procurement Officer. Now this news will really startle you. Kristine is alive! Her father only wounded her. Apparently he shot at someone else. He thought he killed her. I learned he's alive, too. I thought he was dead. So, within a few weeks I'll be able to see her. I'll write to you again from Germany.

This I learned from McAdam, who survived successful reconstructive surgery, healed up, returned to the States, married Pop's widow, loves her little boy, Tim, and he believes that Mayo Clinic MD's are going to be able to take sperm from his twin brother, Sean, and implant it into Paula. So, because they are identical twins, the baby will really be his! Can you believe that! For their sakes I hope it works. They were just here for a couple days visit.

Frank wrote to Paula after the funeral for his wife. It was brief. He and a couple of ex-college friends, also pilots, bought a boat. From the headwaters of the Mississippi they'll navigate all the way down the river to New Orleans. They are going to keep a journal, fish, camp out along the way, and take pictures. He said that by the time they reach New Orleans they'll probably be ready to figure out what they want to do with their lives.

My mom and dad are working long hours at the store. Dad understands my decision, my mom is worried about me going back on active duty, and my Uncle Bruce is very supportive. I'm a lot closer to him in some ways, than to my dad. None of my old high school buddies are around. One was killed at Iwo Jima, two others are in college and another stayed in the Marine Corps.

My book reading is pretty well confined to "How to Win Friends and Influence People," by Dale Carnegie. Pop had inscribed in it for me, planning on giving it to me. He'd told me about it, and I found it when we cleaned out his footlocker to send the important stuff home to Paula. It is helping me understand other people. The other book is helping me understand myself (I hope). It's by H.E. Fosdick, and called, "On Being a Real Person." The book by Doctor Fosdick has made me realize just how ignorant I am. I now realize that that are several Marshall's, all in conflict, residing in my body. Doctor Fosdick says it's important to be an integrated person. I'm frustrated. I find

I'm not a very forgiving person. I do want to change. William James says we can change ourselves.

I find it hard to feel anything but hatred towards Germany, on one hand, what with the SS, the Gestapo, and the whole damn Nazi sickness, and yet on an individual basis there is Kristine. I saw Dachau before they sterilized it, and Kristine's grandmother committed suicide when she was forced to tour it. Kristine, too, was violently ill after that experience. I too, was nauseated when our GI guide stopped in this big room and the smelly scum was waist high on the walls. He said, 'see those scratches?' We looked and then he explained that some of the gassed victims were still alive, scratching the wall, for life, while awaiting cremation. Of course, I am guilty of breaking one of the Commandments. I have killed. My involvement in bombing the bridge at Bad Scheidel would have meant very little to me had we completed our tour and been shipped home instead of getting stuck with occupation duty. But that's not the way it happened.

Well, little architect, I didn't mean to ramble on like this. Incidentally, I almost bought a blue blazer and some gray slacks and black shoes. But I'll be back in uniform again for a year, maybe two. I got my first lieutenancy and a Distinguished Flying Cross at Camp Beale when I went on inactive duty. I've been led to believe a captaincy will be in the works. Most important, I'm sure of getting in my four hours flight time a month for the extra pay! And, I've wheels again, but this time I've a little truck, not a Model A, that I want to sell!

PS # 1. I went out the golf ball driving range and hit the hell out of that little white devil. Bought a pair of golf shoes, too. Know what they called me? BANANA-BALL SUNDER! I'm happy to hear you are doing well with your golf lessons. I've taken one lesson and I think I'm hooked! Yes, dearie, I now know that a hook is better than a slice! Seriously, I'm going to take a few days leave and go up to Scotland and get some lessons. I even brought the golf shoes with me!

PS # 2. Back to Dr. Fosdick. In the index he quotes or makes reference to William Sadler seven times, to Gordon Allport eight times, to C. Jung eight times, to William James twelve times, (He was one of the authors Frank was reading.), and Jesus, thirty-three times. I want to go to school because of all of those people. Jesus is the only one I ever heard of, and the index is loaded with the names of others that are famous enough to be quotable.

Well, I hope you will write back before I leave, which will be within a couple of weeks. If I don't hear from you, I'll forward along my air corps address as soon as I know it. Incidentally, if you write to me here, please type my full name on the envelope.

Love and Kisses,

Marsh.

PS # 3. My mom is really thrilled with the little teapot! Thanks for the help!

Marshall folded the letter, put it in an envelope, sealed it and put a three-cent stamp on it. Rather than leave it for the postman to pick up from their own mailbox on the front porch, he took it into the main post office in Chico.

His mother and father had finally approved of the offer of Major Crandall to work without pay in order to learn about the hardware business firsthand. Within a few days he'd be arriving with Mrs. Crandall to look at some of the rooms and small apartments that Martha had located. That decision relieved Marshall of some of his guilt feelings about leaving.

Upon learning that Kristine was alive and pregnant, Marshall felt different about going with his uncle to Red Bluff to pick up the load of redwood. He wrestled with the pseudo-marriage vows made in the cockpit of the B-26. He recalled the expression his Uncle Bruce had used about deciding what's right or wrong. "Needn't complicate things in life Son, when it comes to right or wrong, weigh it like you would the idea of being a little bit pregnant."

Finally he spoke to his uncle, telling him he'd decided to wind down things around home before reporting to Camp Beale. He wouldn't be going to Red Bluff.

"Hey, I understand." Bruce said. "There's plenty of help over there to load the redwood. Sorry though that you won't meet Paula. She's quite a character. You realize, though, damn it, you're going to miss a lot of good fishing and hunting! Dove season's about to open, then there's the pheasants, and the salmon will be shouldering their way up the Sacramento River and the steelhead won't be far behind, and then there's the annual deer hunt up in Oregon!"

"That's not fair, Uncle Bruce!"

"Hey, you'll be back in time for all the good stuff next year. Right?" Bruce walked to Marshall and patted him on the back.

"Right, Uncle Bruce."

Marshall drove into Chico and stopped at Shapiro's, where he was greeted by the owner, who again first looked at Marshall's shoes before smiling at him. "Hi Shap," Marshall said. "Fix me up with a pair of good dark brown shoes that will be comfortable. I'd like them to be shiny, you know, that'll take a good polish, and that'll look good with my uniforms. I'm going back on active duty. I'll be stationed at Heidelberg, in Germany."

"Of your own choice, Marshall?"

"Yes sir. A matter of getting an education and I'll have a good income from my flying status, plus overseas pay. Going to learn Procurement."

"My, my. Let's see. Brown leather, ten and a half, as I recall," Mr. Shapiro, then mumbled, "The military." He shook his head slowly from side to side.

"Yes sir. Of course that was for tennis shoes. I guess the same goes for leather?"

"To be certain, let's take another measurement."

"And, Mr. Shapiro, you mentioned some relatives you hadn't been able to contact. If you'll give me their names and addresses, I'll see what I can find out."

"You are very kind, young man, but we hold little hope." Mr. Shapiro took measurements of both feet and decided that ten and a half was correct. From his inventory he returned with three pairs of brown shoes in different styles.

Marshall selected a pair and paid for them. "If you want to give me a buzz at home or at the store, I'll take the names with me. I'll be around town for a few more days."

"I'm going to phone home as soon as you leave and talk with Sylvia. Yes, Marshall, I'll contact you. Do you realize that over the radio we now hear that over thousands, they report many, many thousands of Jews were executed? It would be a miracle to find someone. Can we be such a threat to anyone?" He looked up at Marshall, his large brown eyes unblinking, questioning.

"Well, I can't believe that is entirely true, Mr. Shapiro. You know the damn papers. But I'll really try to help locate your relatives."

When Marshall drove the pickup truck home he was surprised to see a letter sitting on the dining room table. His name had been typed and the return address didn't include Eileen's name. He knew who it was from.

Dear Fly Boy,

You really know how to shock a girl! Kristine alive! Heidelberg. School. Wow! Gee, sweetheart, keep me posted on this merry-go- round adventure. And all the time I just knew you were going to come down to LA for a visit. But, I really do understand.

Now for the trivial news. The divorce is dragging along, and The Captain, as socialites call him, is staying quietly in the background. Daddy is so calm it's scary! I wish he'd throw something, even a golf club. Have a tantrum or break a vase, or something. He's spending more time with me, and of course long hours at work, plus golf. A few days ago I saw my mother look into a mirror and say aloud, 'I am Cleopatra.' Dear God, if I ever marry again and have children, I swear, their little lives will be different than mine.

At SC there are a lot of vets. They seem so much older than the non-vets of the same age. At the library this young man started talking to me. He's married and they have a little girl. He's taking a Salesmanship Course, a Business Administration requirement, he said. Well, this guy held this book up and said, "This is the kind of thinking I want to be identified with. It's positive! It tells you how to shed all of those damned negative loads placed on you by your parents and society. All the 'can't do' crap I grew up with! By damn, he said,

I'll make something of myself." The book title is "Think and Grow Rich," by Napoleon Hill. I'm going to get a copy and see what it's all about.

And, my idealistic friend, I've resigned from the sorority. I guess my war marriage aged me more than I thought. Forgive my snobbishness, but some of my sisters seem so down right trivial. I live at home now and get to be with my dad more often. He bought me a little Ford Deuce Coupe. It's cute as a bug's ear, and runs great.

You mentioned Dr. Fosdick. Well, I asked my philosophy professor if he knew the name. He very excitedly said, "The man is a genius. Before his time. Brilliant." So, FlyBoy, I'd say you're keeping good company. As time goes on, I too realize how much there is to learn. The same Prof. had to lead us by the hand through "Plato's Republic."

You know, Marsh, I really thought I could pick up a book, read it, and understand what the author was saying. No way! I need help. If you get a chance, get a copy of The Brothers Karamazov, by Dostoevsky, and read the discussion about God and Christianity between Ivan and Alyosha. It's frightening, it's awesome, it's complex, and it has left me befuddled, certainly not enlightened. In my book it's in Part II, Book V, Pro and Contra, Chapter IV, Rebellion. And this author was thinking these kinds of thoughts back in 1880! Our professor says we'll spend more time on the subject matter. I hope so.

Well, sweetheart, I think I'm jealous of Kristine. Aren't I terrible! But, of course I do share your joy that she wasn't killed. God! That is incredible. There just has to be a bright spot in that series of catastrophes you related to me at the Fairmont. I do want to hear from you often. I need some moral support! I honestly don't know if I can handle trigonometry. Geometry makes sense, but I didn't even like high school algebra. Luckily, three dimension drawing I can handle, and some of the boys can't. But, I may be in over my head! I guess that's what school is all about! Good luck.

All my love,
Eileen

X   X   X

When Bruce returned to Chico with his load of redwood, he asked Marshall to help him unload it from the rack atop the truck, and stack it.

"Use these gloves," Bruce told him and gave him a new pair of leather gloves. "Redwood splinters are poisonous."

"You feel better, Uncle Bruce?"

"What do you think, Son?" He chuckled, winked at Marshall, then continued, "Incidentally, I told Jeanette about your assignment in Germany. She wants to talk to you."

"Talk to me?" Marshall looked surprised, then laughed. "What about?"

"A business deal. I told you that she collects antiques and drawings, paintings, all that kind of expensive stuff."

"So?"

"She wants you to buy stuff, have it crated and shipped to her and she'll pay you a commission and start you out with a roll. Europe is loaded with antiques."

"A roll?" Marshall laughed, "Is that the term she used."

"Son, you are incorrigible! A bank roll. An expense account. Whatever you want to call it."

"So what did you tell her?"

"I told her I'd run it by you."

"Guess I could call her."

"No. She covered that. Wants to meet who she's hiring. Talk it over, and if you make a deal, it's a handshake."

"No roll, eh!" Marshall laughed, " Seriously, I don't think that would conflict with my assignment, as long as I did it off duty, or when I'm on a leave."

"Well, I'm going back up in a few days to do some plumbing repairs. God knows they do a lot of washing!" Bruce laughed, "Well, thanks for the help. Take off those gloves now and we'll have a little shot of JD. And I mean a small shot."

"Think you're going have to eighty-six me, Uncle Bruce?"

"No, but I do have a little more experience with JD and his kin than you do." They entered the house, holding open the door for Tara. She dropped a tennis ball at Marshall's feet when they reached the kitchen. Marshall kicked it for her and she scrambled and slipped on the linoleum floor, returned it and dropped it again, and once more Marshall kicked it. Bruce poured two drinks, "I'm diluting yours a wee bit, Lad."

"Roger. I guess I'd better learn how to pace myself. So, when are we going to Red Bluff?"

"We? I'd say that was a quick decision, "Bruce laughed and touched glasses with Marshall. "I guess I really am going to have to buy some more redwood. I sure as hell can't tell your dad I'm doing plumbing repairs at Clean Jean's."

"You think dad knows about the place?"

"Oh, he may have heard rumors, you know, around the lodge or some-place. That's all," Bruce said, lowering his voice. He looked away, avoiding Marshall's eyes.

"Well, keep me posted. The major and his wife are flying up from Beale to look at some little apartments that mom lined up. He asked about you. And, Uncle Bruce, I'm really not anxious about this deal with Clean Jean, but my time is running short, if we're really going to go up there."

"I'll set things up and let you know. And, damn it, this is just between us!"

CHAPTER 29

▼

JEANETTE

It was just after lunch when Bruce and Marshall drove to Sierra Mercantile and dropped off Tara. Newell liked the playful, energetic black Lab, as did Martha, and they were happy to care for her anytime that Bruce went out of town on a business trip. Most of the time the black Lab rode with Bruce inside the cab of the truck, riding with him if it was raining or snowing, but was tethered in the bed of the truck during warm weather. Bruce, with Marshall, drove north out of town towards Red Bluff.

Having signed and returned all of the papers to Major Crandall, Marshall was officially back on active duty. He was allowed two weeks before reporting back to Beale. It felt strange to be back in uniform. Marshall dressed in khakis, and wore his wings and ribbons on his shirt. He draped his necktie beneath his open collar, but didn't tie it. He carried his leather jacket.

"Uncle Bruce," Marshall said, "I'm just amazed at the time and money these ranchers invest in planting and raising all of these nut trees. The walnuts, especially, but pecans and almonds, too. As far as I can see, up ahead and on both sides, there are walnut trees."

"Lots of work, but they thrive here in the valley, and they harvest walnuts by the ton. Must be good money in it."

"Real neat, the way they paint those trunks white."

"Real practical, that's what. That white color discourages bugs and beetles, you know, all kinds of insects, from climbing the trunk."

"No sir, I didn't know that," Marshall said. He cleared his throat, then said, "Uncle Bruce, I've never been to a whorehouse."

Bruce laughed. He rested his arm across the steering wheel and his hand hung from the wrist, over the curve of the wheel.

"I'm not suggesting that you partake of the fruit of the vine. You came along to make, or not make, a business deal with Clean Jean. And I really can use some help loading those redwood planks."

"Roger," Marshall replied. He stared out of the window on the passenger side as they progressed through the tunnel of trees.

"Marsh, let me relate a kind of funny incident: Nedra had been gone over a year. One night I went over to the Refuge Lounge to have some drinks and dinner. Well, frankly I got about three sheets to the wind, and asked a woman sitting alone at the bar to dance. Then I asked her to join me for dinner. I thought some fun might develop, you know. The owner, and bartender, old Tom Logan, who I've known for years, overheard me. Well, I got a table for us, and excused myself to go the rest room. On my way back Tom says, 'hey Bruce, come on over here. Let me tell you a new joke. Just heard it.'

"So, I stopped at the bar and leaned over to hear the joke and he told me an old standby, but he wrote a couple of letters on a tab and pushed the paper to me and pointed at it. "What's that?" I asked, and he said, It's upside down, damn it. Turn it over. Well, staring me in the face were two letters-VD!

"It was instant sobriety for me, Marshall. I bought the lady her dinner and said goodnight. So, the next day I went back to the Refuge, and when

Tom came to work, I thanked him. He says to me 'I've got to look after my clientele, Bruce. As a matter of fact I asked that woman not to come back. I was even bold enough to recommend that she go see Doctor Keith. She was mad as hell, so I probably didn't even need to ask her to stay away.'

"Hell, I'm indebted, Tom, I told him. I'm just looking for some female companionship.

'Well Bruce,' Tom said, 'understand now, and believe this, I'm sure as hell not pimping, but I hear some of the guys talk about a place they call Clean Jean's up in Red Bluff. Apparently from the outside you wouldn't expect it to be a brothel.'

"So, that little encounter scared the hell out of me," Bruce said, "And Marshall, I'm sure there are lots of nice healthy women in Chico, but most of them want to get serious. Be a long time before I get hitched again. You know the rest."

They drove along highway 99, silently, each lost in his own thoughts. When they reached Tehama they crossed the Sacramento River and continued on to Red Bluff, roughly paralleling the course of the river.

"When we get to that big old Kelly-Griggs house we'll be getting close. This is a nice little town. Lots of money, as I understand, from the mining and lumber. Most of the agriculture is south of here."

Bruce turned left on Walnut Street, then right again on Baker Road. There was a scattering of homes similar to his own in Chico, Marshall observed, and then Bruce slowed as they approached a two-story Victorian style house. It sat towards the back of the lot and was surrounded by a wrought iron fence with forged curved spikes atop each post. From the front gate a brick walk led to the porch. On either side of the walk were large areas of freshly mowed grass. In the center of one area adjacent to the walk was a large Japanese maple whose small lavender colored leaves clung to the drooping branches.

On the opposite side of the walk was a clump of three birch trees emanating from one large, bulky common trunk. The bark on the trees was white and the leaves small and pale green. In other circles cut into areas of the lawn were planted bush roses, many of them bearing red and yellow and white blossoms.

"That clump of trees reminds me of Quaking Aspens, Uncle Bruce."

"I think they're birch. Sure are pretty. But Quakers prefer the high country, you know, around eight to ten thousand feet."

The front porch was eight feet deep and forty feet long. It was supported by round columns painted white. On the porch was a lawn swing with green canvas coverings and a group of white wicker chairs situated around a white wicker table.

Supported by two eight inch by eight inch thick posts, a six foot by two feet sign containing the words: Jeanette's Fine Food, in gold lettering, trimmed in black on a white background, and on the second line, at the left end, the word Cocktails, and at the other end, in gold, the word Rooms.

Marshall expected Bruce to park the truck, but he continued on past the house and turned right at the next corner and then pulled into an alley that led to a series of garages set back from the rear of the house. Bruce turned and stopped in front of double doors, climbed out of the truck, and said to Marshall, "This truck is pretty wide for these spaces. Please watch your side."

Bruce carefully guided the truck into the space. Marshall waited, as Bruce stepped out and lowered the gate of the truck and lifted out a large toolbox. He grunted as he lowered it to the ground, "Come on buster, you're going to have to give me a hand with this S.O.B. I've enough pipe fittings in here to build a submarine."

The toolbox had a thick handle long enough for both of them to grasp with one hand from opposite sides. Marshall looked up at a window where curtains had been pulled aside and saw a girl looking at them. "A pretty face from upstairs just smiled at me, Uncle Bruce."

"Well relax, Lieutenant, this place is full of pretty faces. Don't commit yourself too quickly."

They carried the load across the gravel yard and up the steps to the back door. It made a loud clank when they lowered it to the porch. Almost immediately the back door was opened and a woman with a dark complexion, dark brown eyes and black hair pulled back tight and tied in a bun, grinned at them.

"About time you showed up, Bruce." she said, then backed away and laughed heartily. "Where are you going to put that thing?"

"Hi sweetheart!" Bruce said, "Move back a bit, Senorita. My apprentice and I are going to store this on your back porch for awhile. Okay?"

"I guess okay. What choice have I?"

"Little to none, Maria. Damn, you do get prettier and sexier every time I see you! Meet the lieutenant," and he nodded to Marshall.

Marshall removed his overseas cap and tucked it beneath his belt. Maria extended her hand and Marshall held it lightly, until she withdrew. "A soldier boy, eh? With wings. A pilot? My, what a display of ribbons. You must explain them to me. Welcome to Jeanette's." Maria then looked back to Bruce and said, "If I'm beginning to look pretty, you'd better come here more often! And remember, it is Senora, not Senorita!" Then she leaned back and laughed. "Where are your tooth brushes, your jammies and a change of clothes?" Maria asked, but didn't wait for an answer and continued, "Jeanette has been expecting you."

"We'll get our gear later, sweetheart, it's all in the truck. My, something really smells good!" Bruce said. He lifted his chin and sniffed the air.

"Jeanette's favorite. Duckling, ala orange, with all of the trimmings. I'll go tell Jeanette she has company."

Maria disappeared down a hallway and Bruce and Marshall walked after her through the kitchen. "Uncle Bruce," Marshall said, "I didn't think I'd ever see a kitchen as clean as mom's. This whole room is glossy white, even the ceiling and the cupboards. And these big red tiles on the floor, even the grouting is snow white. They look like they've just been scrubbed."

"Now you're beginning to understand why we call her Clean Jean. And by the way, let's forget the 'uncle' part while we're here."

"Roger, Mr. Kane." Marshall answered, laughing.

"It's not that I'm not proud of being your uncle," Bruce stuttered.

"Mr. Kane, you don't have to draw me a picture."

"Okay, let's go the desk and register."

They went through a hallway into a dining room, then into the living room. Four women were in the room. One was sewing, another reading a book, and the other two were playing cards. He heard one of them say "gin, " And the other girl replied, "God you're lucky!" All of the women had casually looked up at them and smiled, but otherwise didn't move. Marshall could feel his cheeks flush as he stared at their snowy white bosoms revealed by low cut blouses. The aroma in the room was faint, subtle and feminine.

There were several armchairs, two couches and a large marble top table. Four tables with seating for two, with white cloths and a candleholder, plus a salt and peppershaker and a sugar bowl, were scattered around the large room. All of the furniture was supported on carved wood legs. A large chandelier hung from the ceiling with three levels, tiers, of bright pieces of shiny crystal A few floor lamps were placed near the chairs. There was a wide fireplace at one end. It was too warm for a fire. Marshall was impressed with the stone work, and the large log that served as a mantle piece. It didn't look like fir or redwood. Above the mantle was a huge painting of a western scene, with horses and riders, mountains and white clouds in a deep blue sky.

Bruce noticed his gaze and offered, "It's mahogany. And Jeanette says that oil painting is an original by Russell."

"Oh really? Where in the heck did she get that huge timber?"

"Story I heard is that some wealthy lumber man friend had it hauled up here from Frisco."

"I expected a mahogany bar and a painting of a beautiful nude behind it."

"Come now, Lieutenant, this is a respectable hotel and restaurant," Bruce said, and poked him in the ribs playfully, "We'd better register, and then I've got to get to work."

Maria was waiting for them at the registration desk, "Okay boys, sign in, and I'm sure you're having dinner with us. Right?"

"Do you have a monthly rate on the rooms?" Bruce asked. He looked at Marshall, winked and grinned broadly.

"Ha, Mr. Kane! Just one week for you and we'd have to call the morgue!"

"Okay. Dinner for both of us, and separate rooms. Awful fresh help around here, Marsh," he said and winked again, "Okay Senorita, guide me to the plumbing problem."

Marshall was aware that Maria was looking over their shoulders, then he heard Jeanette speak.

"Welcome stranger," she said, and both Bruce and Marshall turned around. Bruce opened his arms and she walked up close to him, the top of her head beneath his chin. He hugged her and she hugged back. When he released her he put his face down towards her as if to kiss her, but she turned her cheek and laughed. "Don't get fresh, handsome. Now introduce me to my new business partner."

"Shake hands with Lieutenant Sunder," Bruce said. Jeanette extended her hand and Marshall shook it lightly, felt the warmth in her hand and smiled back at her. Immediately he was struck by her beauty. Her complexion was so fair he wondered if she'd ever been sunburned or wind burned. Her eyes were large and the color deep blue. Her nose, while not small, was well proportioned for the size of her face and chin. Her lips were full, sensuous, and her chin strong, much like his mother's. The color of her wavy hair was a deep red, nearly auburn. She laughed aloud as he stared at her, and then he observed her perfectly spaced teeth, as white as the enamel in the kitchen. It was difficult to keep his eyes looking into hers. Her white blouse was low cut and the cleft suggested ample breasts.

"Hey, Lieutenant," Bruce said, "stop staring. I'm the jealous type, you know."

"Pay him no attention, young man," Jeanette said, and Marshall was pleased to hear the timbre of her voice. *My God, she's prettier than a movie star. Thank gosh she has a soothing voice to match.*

"We've time before dinner to see if we can really put something together on this antique -buying thing," Jeanette said. "My office is upstairs. I've got some refreshments there. We'll go on up, if you like."

"Sure. Anytime," Marshall said. He looked at his uncle.

"Maria is going to lead me to the plumbing problems, Marsh. I'll see you at dinner."

Jeanette led the way back across the living room with Marshall at her side. When they neared the girl who was sewing, Marshall slowed and looked at the material she was working on. "Cross-stitch," the girl said. She glanced up, and smiled at Marshall. She shifted in the chair and leaned forward a bit, then returned to her work.

"The ladies like to relax a little before dinner. Sometimes they have guests for dinner, even all evening. Other men arrive, have dinner, go to bed awhile and disappear. Others don't fool around. They're here for one thing, and want to get to it and go. You know how it is, young man," Jeanette said.

Marshall nodded as if he knew. He laughed and added, "Mam, I wish you wouldn't call me 'young man'."

Jeanette paused, wondering about the young man who didn't want to be called a young man. *Not too subtle, but I like that in a man.* "Here we are then, Lieutenant, and my office is in my boudoir," Jeanette said, and Marshall followed her through the door. At one end of the large room stood a huge canopy bed. The posts appeared to be mahogany with parallel grooves extending from the base through a thicker area, all the way to the canopy top. On another wall was a fireplace. Marshall walked closer to it and looked at the opening. *Probably the extension from the fireplace downstairs. Same chimney. Makes sense.* And over this fireplace was a mirror, easily six feet long and perhaps four feet wide, held in a substantial ornate gold frame. Behind a marble top coffee table was a couch. A small liquor cabinet stood beside the couch. On another smaller table with a marble top was a lamp with a shade made up of dozens of different colored pieces of glass, and Marshall made out the figures of water lilies.

"My gosh," Marshall said, "You've really got beautiful furnishings, Jeanette. Are some of these thing antiques?"

"Lieutenant, I'm investing in good antiques as fast as I can afford them. Every room in my hotel is furnished with antiques. One fine day I'll be a successful antique dealer, hopefully in San Francisco."

"Mr. Kane told me that."

"Oh, come on sweetheart, you can call him Uncle Bruce around me. He's so afraid he's leading you astray," Jeanette said, and laughed, and there was a sultriness in her voice that Marshall hadn't heard before. Then she looked straight into his eyes, and her own eye lids lowered a bit, and Marshall felt a twinge in his groin area.

Marshall chuckled, too, then said, "Well, I really haven't been around much."

"Weren't you in Europe?"

"Yep. Got to see a bit of England, France, Holland and Belgium, and then we had occupation duty in Germany."

"Ha! For a girl that's been to Reno, L.A., Frisco and Portland, I'd say you've been around." Jeanette chuckled and then continued, "Now let's just relax, and we'll talk about our business venture." Jeanette motioned for Marshall to sit down. "I'm going to have a glass of sherry. I've some really smooth brandy, and of course scotch, bourbon, and gin. If you need ice, I'll ring for Maria."

"You sold me on the brandy, Jeanette."

Jeanette poured the drinks into crystal glasses, hers with a long stem, and then sat down beside Marshall, next to his right shoulder. Their shoulders touched. She leaned over in front of him and stared at the two rows of ribbons beneath his wings on his left side. Marshall looked deep into her open blouse, before looking down at his own chest. He rattled off, "DFC, Air Medal, European Theater, Central Europe Campaign, Occupation, Victory Medal, Good Conduct, and this one over here is for our entire Bomb Group, a presidential citation. And we were told that the French Government was coming through with a Croix de Guerre."

"That makes you are a hero!"

"BS." Marshall exclaimed," I'm just one of the lucky ones. That's all."

"Come on, honey. We want to brag on you guys. Modesty is becoming. But, please let me call you a hero."

Marshall was aware of the pressure of her breast against his arm, but then Jeanette sat up, reached for her glass of sherry, raised it, and said, "To our partnership!" Then she touched the glass to Marshall's and he heard the keen tone of the crystal edges meeting.

"Now that I know you haven't been around much, your commissions will be lower. Ha." Jeanette said and laughed loudly. "But if you will share some of those bedroom secrets, that you learned in France, well, then maybe I'll reinstate the rate of commissions."

Marshall felt his face reddening. Jeanette was aware of his discomfort. She said, "Relax, Lieutenant. I'm just teasing. Bring your brandy and I'll give you the tour of my office so you'll get an idea of the kind of things I do collect. And believe me, I'm open to suggestions. I've a couple of books I'm going to loan you. A professor down at Cal is a regular diner here, and he's advising me on what to collect. Good lord, it covers everything from crystal to etchings to rare old rifles and gold inlaid shotguns. Even fly rods. But old can be valuable or it can be junk. I don't want junk."

As Marshall followed her he became more aware of her figure. From tiny feet, and slim ankles, her shapely calves disappeared into her dress. The dress swayed a little as she walked, outlining the shape of her hips, below a tiny waist. Marshall began to feel the swelling in his crotch and hoped it didn't show.

"Now, appreciate this one, partner," Jeanette said, pointing. "See that signature. I paid a damn fortune for that signature, with a guarantee that it is an authentic Renoir." She smiled then added, "I'll get some more of those Frenchmen in my boudoir! You know, there's Degas and Monet, and Gauguin, and that man that slashed off his ear, Van Gogh. They're all covered in one of those books, and the professor says the value will triple, perhaps quadruple, in a few years. But, he also emphasized that there are fakes out there and I must be willing to pay for a professional appraiser."

"You know Jeanette, I may be getting in over my head," Marshall said. "Now if it's nuts and bolts and barbed wire and hammers and nails and wrenches, that's where I'm experienced."

"Don't worry about it, honey, you're going to be where the old stuff is. We'll write. You ask me. We've no deadlines to meet. If I say pass it up, your feelings won't be hurt, will they?"

"Nope."

"Let me show you etchings and watercolors and drawings." She walked to a cabinet that had shallow drawers. She slid open one and took out a pen and ink drawing. "This man creates a lot of crazy things and some of them might be considered vulgar. Ever hear of Aubrey Beardsley?" Jeanette didn't wait for an answer. She held up the drawing and Marshall was astonished to view a bare breasted woman with a flimsy, see-through gown apparently tied at the waist. Her right arm was lowered so that her hand rested where her legs joined, and she wore tiny slippers. A large gown with many tucked tiers of cloth hung from her shoulders and behind her. Her thick black hair was piled high and framed her delicate features. Her left hand rested on the tip of an erect penis that appeared at the edge of the picture, half the size of the girl. Rising from the end of the penis was a stem with leaves that tilted towards the girl's head.

"Shocked, Lieutenant?"

"Yeah," Marshall said, "Frankly I am. You call that art?"

"Well, it had better be art for what I paid for it! I have several of Mr. Beardsley's books-covers and sketches. Many of them are quite humorous. Here's one I had framed," Jeanette said, and he followed along side her. On the wall was a framed black ink drawing of three bare breasted women with another woman at the edge of the picture and from the expression on their faces, she was apparently chastising them, "I think he does justice to a woman's breasts, don't you."

"Oh sure, " Marshall said, lifting his chin and rolling his eyes upward.

"My professor friend refers to them as plates. Not the breasts," Jeanette chuckled, "The entire sketch or drawing."

"Don't you specialize on something?"

"I collect everything: Austrian and Irish crystal, and Chinese vases, and Japanese Cloisonné, quality furniture, and people love these little marble top tables, I'm told. And I think those rich people in San Francisco will come to my store to see the variety of my collection. And speaking of China, let me show you the little collection of ivory carved figures."

Marshall followed Jeanette to a small cabinet on a wall. The cabinet was made of exquisitely inlaid sections of exotic hardwoods, and had a glass door and a mirror in the back. Three shelves held various carved ivory figures, some of cats and dogs and a monkey and one of a Buddha. Then Marshall gasped when he saw one shelf holding eight different figures, male and female, in different positions, performing sexual intercourse.

"You see, my dear, different cultures have different viewpoints about sex. In China, sex is considered desirable and healthy, and respectful. They acknowledge it, and don't apologize to anyone. I resent the American attitude that sex is evil, or somehow sinful. Where did that attitude originate?"

"Well, I don't think all Americans feel that way", and he thought of Eileen. "The French and Belgians, they just seem to consider it good normal fun, recreation so to speak. But I feel they also take marriage very seriously. Especially where there's kids to think of, you know, raising them, being responsible for them, and of course a lot of fights start when some guy thinks his wife is cheating on him, or vice versa. Just like here."

"You're right, sweetie, and I shouldn't really care. After all, I'm in business because of the attitude of a lot of nagging, frigid housewives," Jeanette said, and Marshall thought she suddenly seemed irritated. Then she turned and walked up and stood very closely to Marshall, looking up into his eyes, and again her eyelids lowered a bit. Instinctively he reached out to put his arms around her, but she quickly glided away. *Wow, this is what they mean by sex appeal! She's teasing the hell out of me.*

They heard a light knocking on the door. Jeanette walked across the room and opened it. Maria entered. "Would you like to have your dinner here in your office, Jeanette?" she asked.

Jeanette turned to Marshall, but before she could speak, he said, "I'd like to eat in the dining room with Bruce and all of you."

"Really?" Jeanette said, surprise evident in her voice. " Well, we'll be down in a few minutes, Maria."

"Bruce is still working with those pipes and things in the laundry room. He's made a mess down there, Jeanette! Anyway, I asked him about dinner and he said he'd be through soon. Said he'd eat with me and Mike," Maria said.

"That's fine dear, The lieutenant and I will sit at one of the small tables near the dining room."

Maria nodded and pulled the door closed as she departed.

"Mike is Maria's husband. They have a nice big room of their own downstairs. We seldom have any trouble with our patrons, but once in awhile some young buck will come charging in here drunker than a skunk, wanting to raise hell, and I won't stand for any rowdiness. I go get Mike. So, very diplomatically, Mike will explain the house rules and escort the young man to the back door. Mike is even bigger than Bruce. That generally ends it. He invites him back when he's sobered up."

Jeanette rested her hand on Marshall's arm and guided him across the room to the couch. "See that lamp?" She said, "It's a genuine Tiffany. I paid a top dollar for it. I understand that there are a lot of imitations, and I don't mind buying them to decorate my rooms, but this one is an investment. I treasure it."

"Are they covered in the books?"

"Yes, but they are very fragile, so I don't think we'll look for them. Too many things to buy that are solid, you know unbreakable, that can survive shipping half-way around the world."

They sat on the couch, and Jeanette moved very close to Marshall. "More brandy before dinner?" She poured some sherry into her own glass. She rested her hand on his leg, awaiting his answer.

To Marshall's own surprise, he suddenly blurted out, "Jeanette, you are, well, the most attractive woman I've ever met, but," Marshall stammered, "there's something I want you to know that even Uncle Bruce doesn't know. And please keep it between us."

"My, you sound so upset." Jeanette moved away from his side a little. She removed her hand from the top of his leg and reached for her glass of sherry.

"You see, there's a girl back in Germany that is pregnant, and I'm pretty sure I'm the father. We fell in love, when I met her in the little town that we bombed. It would take a half-hour to tell you all of the details, but the same day I was ordered home, she was shot by someone, and I thought she was dead. I never heard any different from anyone. My copilot came to Chico for a visit a week ago and told me she was only wounded and she is pregnant. That's the main reason I'm back on active duty. Hell, I could go to college on the G.I. Bill right here in California. But, well, the thought of abandoning her, you understand, I just plain can't do that. I've got to go see her. I think I'm the father. I've got to make sure."

"Wow, honey, I'm glad you told me," Jeanette said, and this time she simply patted him on the top of his leg, "Gosh, and I was beginning to think I was too old for you."

"Ha! That's a laugh, Jeanette. If you only knew what your presence does to me! Hells bells, I really do crave you!" Marshall smiled, "But you know Jeanette, Kristine, that's her name, she and I were married in a B-26, by my copilot, who'd been officially checked out as a left-seat pilot, so he was captain of the ship, and our engineer, Pop, was a witness, you understand, it's like a sea captain that can marry people."

Jeanette chuckled, "Somewhere along the line you've lost me, Lieutenant, but if you're telling me you can't sleep with me because you're a married man, well," she sighed, "that IS different, and I sure as hell respect you for it. But you've spoiled my fun! I wanted climb into bed and make love with a real war hero!"

"Come on, Jeanette, a hero I'm not. Survival is pure luck. I just hope you understand my situation. But seriously, is our business deal still on?"

"Of course, silly," Jeanette said, "Now, excuse me for a couple minutes. You just sit there and enjoy that brandy."

Marshall sipped the brandy and stared at the delicate colored, assembled shapes of the Tiffany lamp. *Yee Gods, old McAdam would tell me how stupid I am. I didn't tell him about Eileen. But Christ, I really did think that Kris was dead!*

The room had darkened. Marshall knew the sun must have set, but the light from a floor lamp and the little Tiffany lamp filled the room with a warm, pink glow.

Jeanette returned from the room adjacent to the big canopy bed. She wore what appeared to Marshall to be a sheer pink gown, or a see-through bathrobe. It had a white lace collar. It seemed to float about her, as if weightless. Suddenly he realized he could see the darkness of her nipples, pushing forward through the material, pushed by her firm round breasts, and his eyes darted downward, curious, but by then Jeanette was only two yards from where he sat on the couch.

When she bent over he could see almost all of one of her breasts, but she picked up the wine glass, then turned, pirouetted, and her gown spun up above her knees, revealing to Marshall a glimpse, a hint of her firm buttocks above her slim legs, and when she turned back she lowered one hand and he was denied a view of the dark and silky looking area, concealed by the thin gown. He realized he had seen nothing and had imagined much. Her milk-white figure was like the Petty Girl drawings they'd pinned on the walls of the barracks. It amazed him that a woman, probably near forty, almost twice his age, could posses such a beautiful body. Then

Jeanette, her feet very close together, rising on her toes, again pirouetted swiftly so that the gown elevated itself, lifted waist high and exposed her perfectly formed legs and generous hips. Jeanette again lowered her hand in front of her, as she turned and faced him, the gown swirled to an abrupt stop, settling downward. Jeanette carefully gathered the ties about her waist and lightly knotted them. She smiled at him, lowering her eyelids.

She chuckled, smiled and said, "Just wanted you to see what you missed, Lieutenant! I hope you feel punished?"

"That's not fair. Christ, I am human!" Marshall said, laughing. He lowered his head into his hands, then looked up at her and laughed. "Jeanette, can I change my mind? Yee Gods! You do have a magnificent figure!"

"Ha!" Jeanette laughed heartily, "You made your decision, my sweet young business partner. I don't sleep with happily married men!" She laughed again, and Marshall marveled at the sparkle in her voice, then continued, "But, thank you, my friend, I must have inherited some good genes along the way. I do work out regularly. I've a room in the basement where the girls and I can use our exercise bike, a rowing machine, and a bench with a few light bar bell type weights. You know, women with pretty bodies like to show them off, and I mean in front of men! Lieutenant, try skipping rope, if you want exercise! We girls want to be soft but strong, not muscular, you understand. But, if we want to walk or hike, we have to get out of town. The town fathers tolerate my presence here. They look the other way, but if I ever flaunt it, I'd be closed down in a wink."

Marshall stared at her as she talked, then approached her and whispered, "Jeanette, you know it's pretty damn difficult for me to turn off this desire thing I feel for you. Just let me caress you? Lightly? Touch you, kiss you?" Marshall walked towards her, but she stepped aside. "Let's just take a nice warm shower together and I'll dry you with my tongue."

Jeanette put her head back and laughed loudly, "You are a naughty one aren't you!" She walked up close to him, raised her hand and squeezed his mouth so that his lips puckered, then quickly kissed him and stepped back from his arms, poised to encircle her.

"Oh hell, Jeanette, I'm all talk. Just kidding. I'm trying to be a faithful husband."

"God, that is funny! Hearing that in a whorehouse! Forget it lover boy. However, you are correct, I'm proud of my body, but it's my mind that needs exercise! My professor friend down at Cal once told me, 'beauty fades, dumb is forever.' He's become sort of a mentor, my private tutor. He's trying to educate me beyond antique knowledge. I'm loaded down with the books he brings me, and I'm getting a little less dumb, I think! God, how I do study, especially etiquette, and he's got me reading stuff by the famous Greeks, and a whole selection of books on English literature."

Jeanette backed further away from Marshall, "But, as for us, you can't have it both ways, so let's just be business partners!" Jeanette said. "I guess I'd better change into something uncomfortable. Be back in a minute. And, oh, yes, Lieutenant, if you feel the need of a cold shower, all by yourself, before dinner, there's some nice big towels in the bathroom," Jeanette looked at him and laughed, then puckered her lips and made a kissing sound and returned to her closet. When she returned she wore a black pleated skirt that complimented her hips and legs, and her blouse was white, with frilly folds, and low cut.

Together they walked down the stairs, side by side, and paused, looking into the living room. Marshall was surprised that no one looked their way when they entered. Three men were talking with the young women he'd seen earlier in the day. One couple was dancing to music from the record player. The ladies seemed to be captivated, so attentive, to the conversations of the men. One of the men smoked a cigar, another a cigarette. Marshall liked the aroma, although he'd given up smoking when in Germany. Maria served mixed drinks from a tray. The bar was out of sight. She accepted orders and then returned from the kitchen. The men all signed little slips of paper when the drinks were served. The ladies sipped their drinks from wineglasses. Two of them smoked cigarettes.

"Let's chase down your uncle," Jeanette said.

They walked into the kitchen. Maria was busy with both the dinner meal and fixing cocktails. "Bruce and Mike are in the laundry room," Maria volunteered.

The laundry room was bright, painted a glossy white, as was the kitchen, and it was steamy.

Bruce and Mike turned when they entered. "Hi, sweetheart!" Bruce said, "Hey Marsh, shake hands with Mike, Maria's better half."

Marshall extended his hand, responded to Mike's firm grip, and they exchanged howdy's.

"What did you find?" Jeanette asked.

"Well, you're not in too bad a shape. Cleaned out all of the pipes and I'm going to have to tell you this, you and your ladies are going to have to wash your hair down here in this big sink, unless you want all of the pipes in this place replaced. Jeanette, I've never seen so damn much hair! We can only pour a certain amount of chemicals into this system, can't dissolve everything. You really ought to have a back up septic tank, too, Jeanette."

"Will you take the job?"

"Have to mull that over. You know I've a black Lab, Tara. I can't leave her home."

"Well bring her along. The ladies would love to have a dog to play with."

"Jeanette, that's a hundred miles round trip. I wouldn't want to do that every day. Hell, there's a lot of good plumbers here in Red Bluff."

"Yes, and there are a lot of blabber mouths here in Red Bluff, too."

"Well, let me think it over. I might rent a room in town someplace for a week or so, if you'll take care of Tara. Could be a possibility."

Jeannette shook her head, " Rent a room in town! Rubbish. We'll talk about that. So, Bruce, the lieutenant and I are going to have dinner together. Want to join us?"

"Thanks, no. I've a lot of cleaning up to do. I'll join Mike and Maria, if you don't mind."

Jeanette turned to leave the laundry room and Marshall stayed back. "Mr. Kane, I'd like to use the truck tonight. If you want me to get your gear, I'll bring it in. I'm taking off after dinner, and will meet you anytime in the morning."

"That's the way it is? Sure. If you'll grab my bag of necessities and drop them off with Maria before you leave, I'll see you when you show up. Okay? And here's the combination lock numbers." He jotted them down on a slip of paper.

"Roger," Marshall said, and accepted the note and the truck keys that Bruce tossed to him. Marshall caught up with Jeanette and told her of his plans.

"You know, Lieutenant, we did set aside a room for you."

"No thanks, Jeanette."

"Say no more. After dinner we'll call a nice respectable hotel here in town and fix you up with a room."

When they returned to the front room, two of the ladies, with customers, were having dinners at separate tables. The other couple had disappeared. Marshall and Jeanette sat at a table near the dining room.

"We seldom have dinner in the dining room unless it's Thanksgiving or Christmas. But we have a nice big breakfast together every morning and I want you to know you're invited. About eight."

Maria served duckling with dressing and cranberries plus gravy. Mashed Idaho potatoes, and green beans, a small green salad, and hot rolls were included. "I like the Merlot with duckling. Is that all right with you, Lieutenant?"

"Sure!" Marshall said, then laughed, "When we had a big prime dinner after I got home, Bruce brought over a bottle of Cabernet Sauvignon, and we all teased him, trying to see if he could spell the name, and he finally said, 'hell, it took me ten minutes to learn how to pronounce it.'"

"You're very fond of Bruce."

"Jeanette, it's like having two great dads."

"That's wonderful." *I wish to hell I'd known the only one I had.*

"I'm not positive that I'll have breakfast here, Jeanette, but I want to be really sure I know what you expect of me on this antique buying deal."

"It's really simple, sweetheart. Study the books I'm giving you. If it's fragile, you know packing is very important. I'm sure you'll be able to contact the people that pack and ship things like furniture. Letters of authenticity are very important to me. I hope to attract a clientele that is upper middle class, whatever that is! That's the advice I get from a businessman I trust. I'm starting you out with one thousand dollars, and I expect you to keep an accurate accounting of what you spend, the costs of packing and shipping, insurance, if you can get it, and again, the letters of authenticity. That, I, understand, will be very important when it comes time to selling antiques. I'm going to pay you twenty percent of every transaction, you understand, a commission."

"Hell, the thousand dollars is much as I make in three months!" Marshall said. "The twenty percent is more than fair."

"And this is all on a handshake, and especially because I like your Uncle Bruce, and I'm now a little fond of you, too." Jeanette leaned forward and smiled at him. "And would you like a little more Merlot?"

"You know what I'd like right now, Jeanette? And I understand it isn't an after dinner drink, but, once when I was with another beautiful girl, I was introduced to a dry Martini, on the rocks. How about it? Will you join me?"

"Not on your life, but I'll fix you one. I don't think I've taught Maria how to make them." Maria approached the table and both of them declined the dessert and coffee. "Probably a little coffee later, dear," Jeanette said. When Maria left the table Jeanette arose and went to the bar in the kitchen and returned with a four-inch-deep cocktail glass with three ice cubes, a large green olive and gin. "One of my good customers said to float a little scotch on it, and to use an atomizer to spray dry vermouth above the glass. I hope you like it."

"Terrific," Marshall said, as he sipped from the glass. "A heck of a lot smoother than the ones I had in Frisco."

"The friend who taught me how to make them told me this story one time. He said he took his secretary out to lunch and suggested she have a martini and she declined and told him, 'One might be okay, but two you're under the table, and three you're under the host.'" Jeanette turned her chin upward and laughed loudly. She brushed her wavy hair away from her face and then looked at him, again lowering her eyelids.

Marshall took a gulp of the Martini. It went down smoothly, so he took another sip.

"Jeanette, this is a double, and I bet it's lethal!"

Marshall could not believe that one drink could make him feel giddy. *Maybe I'm allergic to gin.* He did know that he should fetch Bruce's gear from the truck and then find a hotel.

"Maybe someone ought to reserve that room someplace for me, Jeanette?"

"This is difficult for me to comprehend, but I'll do as you ask," Jeanette said. As Maria walked into the room she stopped her. "Maria, would you call the Piute Inn and reserve a room for Lieutenant Sunder. He'll be along within the hour."

"Yes mam," Maria said, then looked at Marshall and shrugged her shoulders.

"Maria thinks I'm nuts, doesn't she?"

"She's a savvy lady. My only real confidant."

Marshall touched his fingers to his lips. *Already numb, you smart ass bastard.* He smiled, and leaned across the table and said, "Jeanette, there's something you ought to know about me," Marshall whispered.

"Oh?" Jeanette said, and leaned across the table to hear him.

"It's against my principles to sleep with my boss!"

"Get out of here! One Bruce is enough in a family! See you tomorrow, Lieutenant!" Jeanette arose and walked back toward the kitchen.

Marshall followed her; he reached down and lightly patted her on the buttocks. "Out with you, devil!" she said, then laughed, "But come back when you are a single man!"

He walked to the back porch. A light above the door illuminated the parking area. Marshall located the garage door and spun the wheel on the combination lock as directed by his uncle, and was amazed when it opened. He retrieved the gear for his uncle, returned to the house, entered and left it on the kitchen sink. Marshall returned to the truck. The evening air was cold, brisk, and he inhaled deeply. *Boy, we really need rain.* He carefully backed out of the space and followed the instructions given to him by Maria and within a few minutes arrived at the Piute Inn. Marshall checked in, was given a key and directions to his room and immediately went to the room, undressed and pulled the covers over his head. *Never again. No more friggin gin. No more martinis. Never again.*

Marshall awakened at six and tried to go back to sleep. But couldn't .He browsed through one of the books given to him, but couldn't concentrate. A hot shower followed by the icy cold spray revived him. Contrary to what he thought he'd do, Marshall drove to Jeanette's and joined them for breakfast.

The ladies and Bruce and Mike all sat at the breakfast table. It seemed to be some sort of tradition that both Jeanette and Maria would prepare the breakfast. They served a platter of scrambled eggs and two different hot plates with bacon and link sausage. Thick biscuits and a bowl of gravy were on the table, as well as jams and jellies, and a bowl of pickled watermelon rinds. Jeanette appeared with a platter stacked high with pancakes. "Butter and hot syrup are on the way," she said, smiling at everyone in the room.

"Well, girls," Bruce said, "How many of you fell in love last night?" Snickers and giggles followed his question.

"One nice guy wanted to save me from all of this," one girl said.

"You tell him you never had it so good?" another girl asked.

"Oh, something like that. But this guy seemed so sincere."

"Did he tip you?"

"No."

"So much for love, eh?"

All of them at the table laughed.

Marshall ate his breakfast and felt his cheeks reddening. "When are we loading that redwood, Mr. Kane?" he asked.

"Right after breakfast, Lieutenant," Bruce said, "And boy, am I glad I brought you along to help me. My back's killing me."

Scattered laughter filled the dining room. "That big tool box is too heavy, Mr. Kane. You should divide all that stuff up. Like two or three boxes that an old man can handle."

"Hey, Maria, cut out that old man stuff or I'll tell Mike about us!"

Again laughter filled the room. Maria shook her head and Bruce grinned at Mike.

"Well dear little friends, unless the lieutenant and I can help with the dishes, we're going to have to go to work," Bruce said, and pushed back from the table. They said their good-byes to the entire crew working for Jeanette.

"You'll get back to me about the plumbing job?" Jeanette asked.

"I'll talk to you as soon as I get the deck assembled."

While they talked, Marshall walked out of the breakfast area towards the reception desk.

When he was out of earshot, Bruce turned to Jeannette and asked, "You guys put together a deal?"

"Yes, honey, and let me tell you something else."

"What?"

"The expression 'wet behind the ears', that's your nephew, but he's a sweet hero!"

Bruce laughed, then walked to the desk and joined Marshall, and Maria presented them with two bills. Bruce grabbed both of them and pulled various bills from his wallet and settled the amount.

"Hey, Mr. Kane," Marshall said, " I can handle my own."

"This trip is on me, apprentice!" Bruce said, and both he and Maria joined in laughter, then Marshall stood aside and Bruce walked across the living room to where a girl with red hair and a gown revealing a plump bosom was seated. He leaned over and whispered in her ear. She smiled and he kissed her cheek. She patted his face. Her hand was pale, her fingers long, and the nails bright red.

Marshall followed Bruce back through the kitchen into the parking area, then drove to a lumberyard where Bruce and Marshall loaded the redwood planks atop the special rig on Bruce's pickup truck. They drove towards Chico, and traveled for a half-hour before either spoke.

"That Jeanette." Marshall said, "She's some woman. Uncle Bruce, she's sexy as hell!"

"Tell me about it, kid. She's also a smart cookie and I think she's going to get what she wants. Give her five years and she'll have the fanciest antique store in Frisco."

"Uncle Bruce, when I get back from Germany, I'll tell you why I didn't stay at Clean Jean's. Hate to admit it, but it looks like wet dreams will be the extent of my sex life for awhile."

"Hell, Son, I respect your decision, whatever it is. You don't owe me any explanations. Wasn't that the way we approached this trip?"

"Yep," Marshall said, his voice hushed, "Uncle Bruce. There's something else I'd like to tell you, in confidence. Do you remember, I mentioned the German maid: how Gary married us in a B-26?"

Bruce looked at him, quizzically, and nodded.

"Well, Gary told me she's pregnant. I love her and I believe I'm the father."

"Oh?" Bruce puckered his lips and whistled.

"Gary thinks I'm nuts: that I couldn't be in love with her: its just sympathy or something."

"Love is a strange thing, Marsh," Bruce said. "It's like understanding why geese mate for life: a mystery. What did you dad say about it?"

"I haven't told my dad."

"You'd better."

"I'm concerned about his heart. Wouldn't want to shock him, you know."

"You'd do more damage by not telling him, at least forewarn him. Your mom, too."

"Hell, I couldn't tell mom."

"Well then, maybe leave that up to your dad. Confiding in your old Uncle Bruce is one thing, Marsh, but this is father and son stuff. You gotta level with him." Bruce cleared his throat, then continued, "Marsh, since you've been back, well, you and me, we've been more like buddies than uncle and nephew." He again cleared his throat.

"Go ahead, Uncle Bruce," Marshall urged.

"This love you have for the girl I can comprehend, but this insisting on your being married, well, it's like your mom now and then says, 'funny ha ha, or funny peculiar' and as a buddy, I feel you ought to forget it. It's peculiar. As your uncle, I'd say, 'come on, Marsh, grow up,'"

Marshall felt the warmth rise in his face. They rode in silence for several miles, neither seeing nor passing another vehicle. Marshall stared at the fruit trees and at open fields and the mountains in the distance. He remembered the words: *when I became a man I put away childish things.* Finally, he spoke.

"I guess you're right, Uncle Bruce. I appreciate your honesty." Marshall laughed quietly, smiled, then looked at his uncle and said, "Thanks, buddy!"

x   x   x

Martha Sunder watched Newell struggle with a bundle of shovels, tied together, but there was no definite center of balance and it was awkward to maneuver. Her first instinct was to go to him and help him, but her second thought was that helping him physically might embarrass him.

From the time of their bedroom debacle, Newell had been aloof. The rift between them worried Martha. She sought the counsel of the family physician, Doctor Keith, and he referred her to Doctor Helen Hummel, a gynecologist who had recently opened her practice in Chico. After two appointments, Martha had a better understanding of her own body chemistry, and the resulting psychological changes that would affect her own attitudes. The togetherness of Newell and Martha was enforced by the demands of Sierra Mercantile.

After two hours of tediously opening the cartons of merchandise from Torburn and Fox, Martha walked to Newell and rested her hand on his arm.

"Let's take a break, dear, I've some coffee in the thermos and some nice fresh chocolate chip cookies."

Without comment, Newell followed her to the counter where they could have their coffee and also have a full view of the entire store, should a customer appear. It was difficult for Newell to resume a life-as-usual routine.

In silence Newell accepted the coffee and munched at a cookie.

"Honey, there's a new movie at the Meralta. A comedy. Laurel and Hardy, and a travelogue, and a cartoon. Why don't we go see them after dinner?"

"Oh?" Newell replied, surprised, because generally he instigated a trip to the picture show. "Well, sure, if that's what you'd like to do."

During dinner, their conversation centered on the growing inventory at the store. It was difficult for both of them to discuss Marshall's decision to go back on active duty. Newell volunteered to help with the dishes after their dinner, and during the ride to the theater, in the darkness of the truck cab, Martha said, "I've had a couple of appointments with a doctor recommended by Doctor Keith. Doctor Helen Hummel. She's a gynecologist that moved up from San Francisco to get away from the hubbub of the city. Doctor Keith recommended her."

"I didn't know that."

"I guess it's pretty obvious I'm going through my change."

"I'm sorry. Is there medication that helps?"

"Not really. I think it's mostly understanding why I have mood changes. I'm sorry to be irritable around you."

"Why heck, Martha. There's nothing to be sorry about. It's like me being sorry about getting rheumatic fever. It's the breaks. With you, it's natures way."

"Newell. We've never been able to talk about, well, you know, sex. I guess that's my fault," Martha said. "Doctor Hummel has given me some insights. If you will be a little patient with me, everything is going to be fine."

"Oh, Martha," Newell stammered, "everything is fine. I love you."

"Thanks, dear," Martha said. "I love you too. I hope you know that." She sat close to him and they were silent the rest of the way to the theater. She pressed closer to him in the cab of the truck, and Newell was pleased to feel the warmth of her leg against his.

x   x   x

Bruce drove the truck into his driveway, leaving room for Marshall to maneuver his own pickup truck when he was ready to depart for home. Marshall removed his belongings from Bruce's truck.

"About the last thing I have to do around town is to sell my truck back to Mr. Bowman, then I'm on way back to the fatherland. Ha! It's going to be interesting. These few months with the folks and you and Tara have been fun. Of course, McAdam's visit, with Paula, that changed a lot of things. But you know, Uncle Bruce, even if I'd stayed in Chico awhile, I couldn't have lived at home."

Bruce looked at Marshall and laughed, "I understand. But believe me, Marsh, it wouldn't have worked out, just in case you thought about moving in with me."

"Oh, hell no. I realize that, and Uncle Bruce, I wouldn't have put you in such a spot."

"I'll look in on your folks, as usual. I really feel that Mr. Crandall is going to turn out to be a blessing. That extra help is going to allow you dad to pace himself better."

Marshall walked close to his uncle and patted his shoulder. "Goodbye. You take care, Uncle Bruce. You know, watch out for those redwood splinters!"

"Sure thing. Tara and I'll be waiting for you. Sorry you'll just miss the dove opener."

Marshall drove home and parked his car in the driveway. The front door was unlocked, and light from a floor lamp by an overstuffed chair revealed the evening paper folded and resting atop a small table. There were no other lights on in the house. Marshall looked at the newspaper, but decided a cookie and a glass of milk would taste good, so went on into the kitchen. Just as he turned on the kitchen light he heard the laughter coming from the master bedroom. Both of his parents were quietly laughing, then there was silence then they could again be heard laughing together.

Marshall was pleased. He hadn't heard them laugh, not when they were together, since he came home with black eyes. He felt badly to have been the cause of their argument. But after a day or two of the routine at Sierra Mercantile—opening boxes and cartons and crates and putting away merchandise—none of them ever brought up the matter. But, his mother did wash the blood out of his shirt. Never said another thing about it. He thanked her, and she had explained that peroxide and cold water was the best way to remove blood. Hearing the laughter was a relief of sorts for Marshall, lessening his guilt feelings about being the cause of their rift.

And finally, tomorrow would be a day of returning his pickup truck and of saying good byes. In the morning, Marshall began to sort out his civilian clothes from his uniforms. He hung his Levi's in his closet, and put his colored shirts in a dresser drawer. His tennis shoes were placed in a corner of the closet. Marshall held his new leather jacket in his hands, then went to the kitchen where his father and mother were drinking coffee as they discussed inventories for the store.

"Dad," Marshall said, "the Air Corps will be providing me with a flight jacket, so I want you to have this one I purchased at the PX in Le Havre. Want to try it on?"

"Well, hot damn!" his dad said, both surprise and delight showed in his face. He pushed away from the table, stood up, and Marshall held the jacket as Newell pushed his arms into the sleeves. He shifted his shoulders a bit, raised and lowered his arms, and said, "Gosh, it feels real good, Son." With the palm of his hand he rubbed the smooth leather sleeve.

"Why it fits you perfectly, Newell," Martha said, smiling at both of them..

"Thank you, Son. I love it. Thank you." He opened his arms wide and Marshall stepped close to him and accepted his hug.

"Great, dad," Marshall said. "I've got to get on with my packing. And, Dad," Marshall whispered, "can we talk privately before you go to the store?"

"Privately? Certainly." Newell nodded, and spoke quietly, "How about out on the porch while your mother cleans up the kitchen?"

They each took a full cup of cup of coffee and walked through the front room onto the porch and rested their cups on the railing.

"Dad, I couldn't seem to find the right time to talk about this, but I want to level with you about something and ask that you'll keep it just between us until I get everything straightened out in Germany."

"Something more than education, right?"

"Dad, when Gary was here he told me the little German girl, our maid, Kristine, was not only alive but is pregnant. I think I'm the father."

Newell sat his cup down so hard some coffee splashed out. "My God, Son, don't you know for sure?"

"Not positive, but the months add up right. Any advice?"

"My goodness. Well Marshall, you've already made your decision to go back on active duty, and of course I thought it was mainly for the education and the good pay you'll receive. As for advice about the girl? Heck, Son, you are a man now, not a kid. We, your mother and I, we taught you right from wrong before you went into the service. Frankly I thought all of that Air Corps officer and gentleman training you got would have sophisticated you a bit, you know; seeing the world, being in all of those European cities, flying combat and winning medals. But a man's basic character doesn't ever change, and it doesn't matter whether she's a German girl, or French or English, or a coed, whatever, if you are responsible, you have to do what you know is right."

"Kinda thought you'd say that, dad," Marshall said, then laughed, and added, "I'm sure happy you like the jacket."

Marshall and Newell returned to the kitchen and sat down their empty coffee cups.

"My, what was that all about?" Martha asked. She backed away from the kitchen sink, dried her hands on a small dishtowel, fanned her face and looked at Newell.

"Marsh wondered if I thought his Uncle Bruce might want a jacket like this and I assured him Bruce would be delighted."

"How sweet," Martha said.

Newell and Martha departed for the store.

Marshall had purchased Greyhound Bus tickets, declining offers to drive him down to Camp Beale. He felt the timing was right for leaving Chico. The following morning he exchanged hugs and kisses with his parents and they dropped him off at the Greyhound Station.

CHAPTER 30

▼

THE REUNION

Marshall entered the officers' club at the air base at Bad Scheidel and paused. There were a number of fliers sitting in comfortable chairs and on couches reading. The bar was open and two fliers were rolling leather dice boxes, playing Ship, Captain and Crew, for drinks. Marshall walked up to the bar and rested his elbows on it and awaited the bartender.

"Help you, sir?"

"Any coffee available?

"Coming up. Cream and sugar?"

"Black, please."

The bartender sat a mug of hot coffee in front of Marshall. "On the house. Big deal, eh?"

"Been stationed here long, Sergeant?" Marshall asked.

"No, sir. About four months now."

"When I drove up I saw all of those apple trees missing that used to be by the barracks, and down the slope. Were they here when you got here?"

"Yes, sir." The sergeant polished the bar top with a white towel. "A new general showed up from the States, new Group Commander, and the first thing he did was have all those trees cut down. Said dead leaves would be unsightly, or something to that affect."

"Unsightly? Apple trees? That's strange. When I was here the German women, the maids, gathered the apples. You know, for food. As a matter of fact some of our guys who grew up on farms pruned them so they'd have a better crop."

"Getting pretty G.I. around here now," The sergeant spoke in a confidential, hushed voice.

Marshall raised his eyebrows, then finished the coffee, set down the mug and said, "Thanks. Know if the library is open?"

"Sure thing," he said and nodded towards the outer room. Marshall walked towards the library and took a deep breath, exhaling it slowly.

Earlier Colonel Schlosser had greeted him warmly. He was now a Bird Colonel. The colonel simply raised his eyebrows when Marshall explained he was back to further his education and said, "Good luck." Chaplain Waldron had been promoted to major, but was not in his office. Marshall felt moisture in the palms of his hands as he made his way across a large room towards the library. Beyond the door, he could see the rows of shelves. They appeared to be well stocked. A sergeant sat at a long table reading a book and writing onto a pad.

He barely recognized Kristine. Instead of the tiny, petite girl he'd last seen, she was now plump, her breasts full, her face almost round, and when he saw her torso he could not believe she could become any larger.

She did not look up from the cart of books until he spoke her name.

"Kristine?" he whispered.

She looked up, recognizing his voice and he thought her face paled.

"You? The luftgangster! What are you doing here?" She walked to the counter and stood opposite him. She did not smile.

"My God, Kris, it will take hours to explain. I thought you were dead! I just found out a few weeks ago that you survived. I'm back on active duty. I'm going to school at Heidelberg."

"So?" Kristine raised her eyebrows and stared at him, blankly.

"What do you mean, 'so'?" Marshall whispered, "I came back because of you! Where can we go to talk?"

Kristine leaned across the counter, resting her elbows on it with her arms resting atop the counter. He felt she was staring into his eyes. Marshall reached out to hold her hands, leaned forward, hoping to kiss her, but she quickly withdrew, pulling her hands away.

"Was ist los?" she said, and frowned at him. "I see you are still wearing silver wings. But no bomb astride them?"

"What is wrong?" Marshall stammered. "You are carrying our baby! My baby!"

"Was? Nein! Absurd! Dummkopf! Luftgangster!" Kristine said, louder than they'd been speaking. She backed away from the counter.

The sergeant at the table looked up from his book and stared at them.

"What the hell is going on? You don't need to speak German," Marshall hissed. "Forget that gibberish. I came back here as your husband, to be to be your husband, and a father to our child!"

"You are crazy. It is my child! I am Frau Schuttenhelm, remember? This is our baby, Paul and me! Verstehen my husband, Paul? This is not your baby. Not your child! And I speak German because I am a German and I am proud to be a German! Verstehen! Auffassen?!"

"Come on, Kristine, for Christ sake. Take it easy! Only a few months ago you said you loved me."

"Ha! Lieutenant Sunder. Lieutenant Sinner! Keep your voice down! You destroy our bridge, you destroy my home and my family, then you go to America and leave me with nothing but my," she paused, then said, "my zerrissenheit. And now you foolishly believe you are the father of my child."

"I can't believe this is happening! Marshall extended his arms and placed his hands down on the counter and shook his head from side to side. "When do you close the library? You're not going to brush me off! You're not leveling with me, Kris! There's something screwy going on here! I've traveled half way around the world because I love you! Verstehen that? You told me your husband died in Russia!"

"Hey, come on, knock it off, will ya! Quiet down, please. This is supposed to be a library," the sergeant said.

Kristine pushed back from the counter. She stared at him, then too shook her head, sighed, then said, "Please do not say that you love me, please, please, just let me be."

"Kristine, listen to me! I've returned from my home, from California, only for one reason. You!" Marshall pleaded.

Kristine stared into his face. Tears filled her eyes. "I cannot believe you have returned, she sighed. "I close the library at five o'clock. I will meet with you, very briefly, in Major Waldron's office."

"Good, good," Marshall said, attempting a smile. Marshall turned and walked towards the bar. *Major Waldron's office. My God, could I be wrong? Her husband is dead. She told me so! Could Waldron be the father?*

Marshall looked at his watch. It was a few minutes past four. He walked to the bar. The bartender smiled at Marshall as he pulled up a stool and sat down. "Another coffee, sir?"

"Nope. Scotch and soda, this time, please," Marshall said.

"We got in a case of single malt, sir? Want to give it a try. Understand it's smoother than a school marm's thigh!" The bartender laughed, then continued, "Give it a try, straight, for a few sips. Okay?" The bartender chuckled.

"That would be fine," Marshall said. *I've heard that expression before. Where? Was it Pop?* Marshall's laugh was hollow.

"Passing through, sir?"

"Oh, I guess you could say that. I was stationed here. Last March. Went home for awhile. Back on active duty again."

The bartender glanced at Marshall's wings. "Observer, eh?"

"I was a bombardier-navigator on a twenty six. Ended up with occupation duty."

"Well, none of those twenty sixes survived those demolition boys. They blew 'em all up, then bull dozed them into stacks and burned whatever would burn. Destroyed them by the hundreds. Couldn't even scrounge an altimeter or a clock out of the wreckage. Criminal, I'd say."

"Yes, hard to believe," Marshall murmured. "What did you call the scotch? It is very smooth."

"Single malt. The Piper's Cache."

"I'll remember that." Marshall paid his tab, left a small tip, and walked through the room, recognizing no one. Across the lounge was the door to the library. He glanced at his wristwatch.

It was a four-thirty. He decided to go to Major Waldron's office, located in the same building, but in another wing, and wait for Kristine.

The door was open. A large cross was on the door with a cast bronze plaque beneath it, spelling out Martin Waldron, and in smaller letters beneath the word, Chaplain. It seemed like yesterday that the Chaplain had been helping them pray before their missions. Marshall recalled the evening of his own despair and drunkenness, and how the chaplain had comforted him. He'd read to him from the Bible. He hadn't criticized him. He'd been sympathetic.

Marshall entered the office. A large desk with a scattering of papers and a stack of correspondence occupied one end, eight feet out from the wall with a similar flat top desk against the wall. A swivel chair was between the desks. Marshall saw the backside of a picture frame. He walked to the side of the desk and peered around the end in order to see what the frame held. A woman with a small child at each side smiled from the frame. *It has to be his wife. He couldn't be the father of Kristine's child!* In his mind Marshall started counting the number of months from February: nine. With his eyes, he continued to explore the contents of the room.

At the opposite end of the room was a blonde-oak altar upon which stood a large bronze cross. There was another oak table, holding a large six pointed star, and on a third table another cross with the figure of Jesus upon it, and there were shiny round trays with lids, that would contain tiny glasses to be used for communion. Several upholstered oak chairs, with arms, were scattered throughout the spacious room. There was a six-foot-tall blonde-oak bookshelf, and most of the books were leather bound. Marshall scanned the shelves to see if there was a copy of Dr. Fosdick's book. He was not surprised when he located four new copies standing side by side.

Marshall selected one of the copies of *On Being A Real Person*, sat down and began to thumb through the pages. He heard the heel clicks in the hallway and arose and waited expectantly. Major Waldron entered the room. Startled to find someone in his office, he hesitated, then loudly said, "Marshall Sunder! For goodness sake! What in the world brings you here?"

"Howdy Chaplain," Marshall said, extended his hand and returned the firm grip of the major. "I decided to go back on active duty, sir. I'm stationed up at Heidelberg. Studying to be a Procurement Officer."

"Why, that is great. Schloss and Doctor Courtright are about the only ones left around here that you'd know. Schloss has located his grandparents and he's trying to help them with a neglected vineyard. Also, I think he's getting his fill of the new general heading up the group, so he may try to transfer out of here. He's trying to get his grandparents back into the winemaking business, before he leaves. Doctor Courtright is sticking around for the Nuremberg Trials."

"I saw Schloss. How come you're still here? I was glad to find you here, sir!"

"Come on Marsh, this 'sir' stuff makes me nervous," the major said, "My first name is Martin." The chaplain hesitated, then continued. "Well, the Corps offered to bring our wives over if we'd sign up for another year of Occupation Duty. A lot of officers turned it down. They were very suspicious of the deal, but as you know, my career is about belief. So, I took a chance and I believed the Air Corps. Gosh, Marshall, Betty arrived here with the kids within a few weeks of my signature, plus they threw in a promotion. Now if I only had flight pay I'd really have it made! I've still got my own jeep, so we get around very well."

"No more prayers before missions, eh?"

"Well, there's always need for prayer. Frankly, I'm working closely with the local Lutheran Pastor, trying to help him with his flock. I think you know that I, too, am Lutheran. The Air Corps is hiring skilled German craftsmen, and for that matter, laborers, to start rebuilding the bridge, restoring it and the few buildings in town that were damaged. There aren't many young German men around: still getting processed out of the POW Camps. Intelligence is trying to weed out the SS and Gestapo people from the Wehrmacht and Luftwaffe vets."

"Martin, I went to the library and tried to have a conversation with Kristine. She's coming to your office when she closes the library. You knew about us, sir. I believe I'm the father of her baby: our baby. That's why I signed up again."

"Marshall, you can't be serious? Surely, you are joshing!"

"You remember McAdam, my copilot? He showed up at my home in California, with his wife, and told me that Kris was alive. I thought she'd been killed. Then he told me she was pregnant."

"Well, he's right on both counts, and Kristine's husband arrived home about the time they operated on McAdam. Wow, do I remember that series of events!"

"Sir, Kris told me that her husband was killed in Russia!"

"I know. I guess that's what she'd heard. And she believed it. But he returned. He was a skinny, decimated kid, but still in uniform. The M.P.'s arrested him the same morning that Kristine was wounded. He had a bladder infection or something. They cured him. So he's alive and back here in Bad Scheidel. As a matter of fact he's working in the motor pool. Intelligence learned from him that he witnessed an SS officer murder a

Wehrmacht officer, and as I understand it, they are trying to trace whom was in command of the SS where he was stationed. Intelligence is after the SS on every accusation, so they show up here now and then and interrogate Paul. But he's a free man."

"Damn it, Chaplain. Kris and I made love, approximately nine months ago and we had our own little wedding ceremony in the cockpit of a '26'. Gary didn't say anything about this guy Paul."

"Gary shipped out before Paul was released from the POW camp, Marshall. And, good Lord! You say you've already talked to Kristine? What in the world did she say?"

"She denied that I could be the father."

"Well, Marshall," the chaplain asked, very carefully, slowly, "just what would she accomplish if she agreed that you are the father? Be realistic, Marsh. And it seems to me you've been gone a lot longer than nine months!"

"Well, she sure looks like she's ready to have a baby right now. I sincerely believe I'm the father. If I am the father, I want her to divorce that guy and marry me! I want to marry her, legally, whenever it's possible. I'd take her, and our baby, back to California when my tour is up."

"Marshall, I never expected to be doing any counseling today, but, I'm going to have to volunteer, maybe be a little blunt, if you will try to calm down and just listen me out."

"I trust you, sir. Go ahead. This is all such a shock to me! Suggesting I'm not the father!'"

"Marshall, I wish all young men could possess your sense of responsibility," the chaplain said, and then dragged a chair across the room and sat by Marshall's side. "Marshall, first of all, do you really believe that Kristine could ever find it in her heart to forgive you and your crew for destroying that bridge?"

"That's your department. You could convince her."

"Come on now! Do you think I would challenge her about who is or isn't the father of the child? She is Frau Schuttenhelm. And in this little village she now has the support, the respect, of her neighbors, and of the townspeople. They know her husband returned. He was there when she was wounded. He was sickly though, but our medics put him back in good shape. No one even considers that the child could be other than his. Her mother, her grandparents, her child, they are all buried in one family plot. She has two jobs, she's still a maid, and she's doing a whale of a job with the library. We're obtaining German language books now and will eventually open it to the local residents. So many of theirs were burned, you know."

"Then you really believe her husband is the father?"

"Certainly. I was there when the M.P.'s arrested him: when she was wounded! Now, what would I accomplish for Kristine, or for that matter for you, if I would, or even desired to believe otherwise? You know her father returned. Other soldiers are returning on a daily basis. Yes, I know that he returned very near the time that McAdam was operated on."

"Hate to ask you this, sir, but what about you and Kris, your relationship, before your wife got here?"

The chaplain shook his head from side to side. "Oh no! So the nasty rumor mills even got as far as California! Incredible! My dear God!" Major Waldron abruptly pushed his chair back away from the table, stood up and his face became livid. The skidding noise made by the chair startled Marshall. The chaplain turned, walked away from the table, then lowered his head, and Marshall could hear him whispering. He sighed deeply and then returned to the table and sat down. "I should be furious with you, Marshall, but, well, please just listen carefully now, dispassionately, and calmly. I assume you understand platonic love?" He paused, staring at Marshall.

"Oh damn, damn! I'm sorry, chaplain. Christ, please accept my apology. Major Waldron, I sincerely apologize!" Marshall said. He sighed, and turned his face away from the chaplain. "I don't know why I said such a stupid thing! The only reason I'm back on active duty is that I'm just trying to do what's right by Kristine. And, honest to God, I do love her, like a husband, not platonically, Martin. It's that I'm just so damn confused!"

Chaplain Waldron stood and paced around the room, then returned to Marshall's side and rested his hand on Marshall's shoulder. "Frankly, it was back after she was taken to Dachau, back when her grandmother hanged herself, that I felt so darn sorry for both of you, and that's how I became involved. You're equally victims of circumstances beyond your control." The chaplain lowered his head, as if to pray, shook his head from side to side, and said, "Dear Jesus, here was this little woman, so young, crushed, yet brave and intelligent. And you, Marsh, you're the one that asked me to go to her, you'll remember. All she had was her pride, and not much of that left after that tour of Dachau. I don't know what you said to her, but she'd thrown out the stuff some GI took to her, and I know she didn't sleep with him, nor did she see anyone else, no other man. I provided coal, some food, and employment and I got the local pastor involved. And some small minds tried to taint even that!"

"Again, I apologize, sir," Marshall whispered. "Do you remember when you read from the Bible about love being the greatest thing? Remember? When I was so damn depressed?" Marshall asked.

"Certainly I remember. And it's true." Chaplain Waldron said. He stood up, walked across the room and returned with a Bible. "Now Marshall, I'm going to read again from First Corinthians, thirteen, but this time I'm going to substitute the word 'responsibility' for love." The chaplain read aloud, and Marshall lowered his chin and listened.

"So?" Marshall said, looking up at the chaplain, "Responsibility in place of love. That's interesting. And I have read it, using the word love. And I've also tried to put away childish things. Are you saying that all I feel is responsibility, or something, about hitting that damn bridge?"

"Marshall," the chaplain said. "believe me, I don't question your feelings for Kristine. As I said, I love her too, but platonically. Perhaps I'm as confused as you, with my own emotions, of empathy, of sympathy, my compassion for all of the beaten up victims of this war. What I do believe is that you, Marshall, cannot cope alone with your own feelings of guilt: the guilt feelings you carry because of your participation in bombing that bridge and all of the subsequent events. Have you ever wondered, ever thought that it's possible that what you really feel for Kristine is pity? But you identify it as love? You feel responsible, and that is admirable, but it isn't necessarily love. Even infatuation, but not love."

"Infatuation, pity, responsibility, guilt? Hell yes, I feel guilty! I feel ugly! I'm the one that broke a Commandment. I killed."

"Hey, now wait a minute. That's a load you don't deserve and one you can't carry."

"Well, seems like that's about all the minister back home cared about. I heard about the Ten Commandments all through Sunday school."

"I'm sure he must have also covered forgiveness."

"Martin, I quit going to Sunday school. All I heard about was eternal damnation and going to hell if we did anything wrong! It upset my mom when I dropped out, but my dad said religion shouldn't be force fed. So, our scout leader and my dad and my Uncle Bruce, they all kind of pointed the way for me to live and think and act. I wanted to be like them. I still do."

"Do you consider yourself a Christian?"

"Yes," Marshall said, then paused. "I guess I never thought about not being a Christian. My mother quotes the Bible quite often. She's a good Christian. Dad's a Christian. We always said grace at mealtime and thanked Jesus, you know, for our blessings. Christmas is always a big celebration. And Easter, of course."

"Did you learn much about Jesus?"

"You know, that's funny. I've learned more about Jesus in Dr. Fosdick's book than anywhere else."

"Do you recall any particular thing he wrote about forgiveness?"

"Not really."

"Well, why don't you check the index when you get back to Heidelberg. But I suspect that Dr. Fosdick will explain some way for you to shed your guilt feelings about bombing the bridge. I feel he'll show you that you've already been forgiven by Jesus. That's what Christianity is all about, Marsh. When you understand that Jesus has forgiven you, then you can get on with your life."

"Are you telling me that those SS guys that wiped out our guys at Malme`dy, that machine-gunned them down while they were unarmed prisoners of war, that they can now turn to Jesus and ask for forgiveness? I don't think I can buy that, sir. To me, that's sort of like white washing over something horrible and ugly, like putting on blinders, putting it out of sight and mind, and then starting over as if nothing happened, Do you see what I mean? I read in the paper and hear over the radio about fifty thousand dying at Hiroshima, and fifty thousand dying at Dresden, and now a million Jews, maybe even more, being gassed and cremated. These numbers are incomprehensible. I can't cope with millions. I'm having a hell of a time coming to grips with my responsibility in the death of Kris's mother and her baby!"

"I understand Marshall, but how are the German soldiers that were ordered to do that terrible thing, different from fliers who were ordered to do what your crew did? If a SS officer held a Luger to the soldiers heads and told them to do it or die, would that make a difference?"

"Come on, Martin, you're the chaplain! If you're telling me that Jesus could forgive them, and that Kristine can't forgive me, but on the other hand that Jesus will forgive me, I'm really one damn confused guy!"

"I feel that anything I can say now will sound like a cliché," Major Waldron said. Then he very slowly spoke, "You know, Marsh, I volunteered. I wasn't drafted. I know and respect other ministers that stayed home because of their personal beliefs. In college I read about a Swiss theologian named Ulrich Zwingli. He was a contemporary of Martin Luther. He was involved with what we call the 'spirit of liberal humanism,' but, to get to the point, he served as a chaplain back when they had mercenary soldiers. I was impressed with his decision and I decided that I belonged with the fighting men, like you. I'm a pacifist, but I couldn't turn my back on the needs of you men involved in combat, whether you volunteered or were drafted and ordered to fight. My wife supported my decision to volunteer."

"So?"

"I feel my experiences with all of you fliers during combat qualifies me to better comprehend the frustrations many of you are having dealing with life and death. You're not alone with your doubts, Marsh. I empathize, and I do feel I'm better qualified than I'd be if I'd stayed in the States with my flock."

"Listen, sir, you are the only man of the cloth I am comfortable with! Is that what you are getting at, you sort of identify with us, because you were with us during combat, that you understand my feelings? Marshall continued, "You know, Martin, Kristine is coming to your office to see me. Would you speak to her about forgiveness? About Kristine forgiving me?"

"So, she's really coming here to see you? I'm a little surprised, but I suppose she feels secure here. Certainly, Marsh, I'll speak with both of you. Together." Major Waldron sighed. "I honestly don't know how Kristine will react. If another crew had bombed that bridge, then we'd have a whole different scenario. But she found out that it was you, and everyone in Bad Scheidel knows. I'm surprised that Schloss didn't ask you to stay away from Bad Scheidel for your own well-being. Isn't that why he ordered you out of here originally?"

"He's not my C.O. now, and I'm not here to cause trouble. I'll be in school. Now I'll wait here with you until Kristine arrives, if that's okay."

"Certainly. Damn, Marshall, you are a persistent one." The chaplain paused, shook his head from side to side, then continued, "Marsh, could you handle a little glass of good brandy? You know that I'm not a drinking man, but a little snifter of brandy now and then is allowable even for Lutheran pastors!"

"Yes, sir. I think I need it. And kind of like breaking bread?"

Major Waldron smiled, nodded, then walked to a cupboard at one end of the room and returned with two short stem wineglasses and a squat bottle of brandy. Nearly filling both glasses, he handed one to Marshall, then sat in a chair beside Marshall. He reached over and touched his glass to that of Marshall's. "Bet this is smoother than the whiskey you guys got after those missions!"

Both of them laughed, then sipped of the brandy.

"Is this what you use for Communion?" Marshall asked, smiled, then stared down into the glass and the chaplain saw the corners of Marshall's mouth droop and he appeared very sad.

"No, I stick to grape juice. But there are some really fine vintners in this region. Schloss and I are chasing them down when we get a little free time." The chaplain looked at the solemn face of Marshall, then added, "You know, Marsh, you fliers abbreviate words and commands, and create a few letters to describe something rather abstruse. For instance, when I look outside and view a bright and shining day, a cloudless sky, no haze or smoke, and I can see for miles in all directions, you use one word for it.

Marshall looked inquisitively at the chaplain and said, "You mean C.A.V.U.?"

"Yes. What's that mean?"

"Ceiling, altitude, visibility unlimited."

"And PX means Post Exchange, and B.O.Q. means Bachelor Officers Quarters, and G2 means Army Intelligence

"Roger."

"Of course I know what snafu means, and I assume that 'roger' transmits over the intercoms more clearly or accurately than saying 'right', and so on with your Air Corps vocabulary?"

"Yes sir."

"Well, when it comes handling the very complex problem of Christian forgiveness," the major paused, "Lets go back to that expression you used, white-wash. Let me assure you that Christian forgiveness doesn't have anything to do with condoning acts of violence." The chaplain looked at Marshall. Their eyes seemed to lock in an unblinking stare. Marshall turned away, lowered his head, and the chaplain continued, "I feel you are asking me to come up with some military like abbreviation to encompass the entire New Testament of the Bible. Understanding Christianity, believing in Christ, isn't easy. Marsh, I've no series of letters like C.A.V.U. to offer, no quick fixes, no panacea. Together, we've read first Corinthians, thirteen, and I've given you a book, and when Kris arrives, I'll share a prayer. But Marshall, what I'd like to suggest is that for a deeper under-standing of the wisdom contained in both the old and new testaments, you should consider joining a Bible study group at the university.

"Oh," Marshall said very quietly, raising his eyes and again looking directly at the chaplain, "Good thought, sir. I'll check that out."

"So, back to our other conversation, we were speaking of the colonel. I'm going to find a little paragraph for you to read that Schloss gave me one time when we were having a bull session about war and religion. He said all West Pointers study military history, campaigns and such, and here he's quoting Napoleon." The chaplain went to his file cabinet and was shuffling through his papers. "Now, Marshall, listen to this, from Napoleon: 'Alexander, Caesar, Charlemagne, and I have founded great empires, but upon what did these creations of our genius depend? Upon force! Jesus founded his empire upon love, and to this very day millions would die for him. I think I understand something of human nature, and I tell you that all these were men and I am a man. None else is like him. Jesus Christ was more than a man.'"

"You're like Doctor Fosdick, with all of the quotations he uses in his book," Marshall said.

"Well, I'm flattered to be compared to him, however I intended to show the respect that Schloss and mighty war generals have for Jesus." The major stared into his brandy glass. "I'm going to give you a list of refer-ences for you to read, that relate to God's forgiveness, for instance, I John 1:9 and Romans 8:1."

"Let me write those down," Marshall said and reached for his fountain pen.

"Don't bother. I'll be writing to you and will include them."

"Kristine should be here soon."

"And, Marshall, when Kristine arrives, I may be a little brief, perhaps seem a bit stern with her."

"Stern?"

"I've my reason. She may resist: be a bit stubborn: her pride, you know." The chaplain smiled and shrugged his shoulders. "Marshall, are you familiar with the name, St. Francis of Assisi?"

"No sir."

"He was closer to being a Protestant in his day, than a Roman Catholic, but he was so Christ-like, so influential, so honest, so dedicated that the Pope latched onto him and made him a Saint. The chaplain smiled, and sipped the brandy. "I'm trying to be facetious, Marsh, but he's also well known for a particular prayer, and I've got copies of it in my desk."

"I'd like to read it. I'd like to copy down that Napoleon saying, too. My folks would find it interesting."

"All right, but as for St. Francis, we'll wait for Kristine," the major said. "Marsh, Schloss advised me many months ago, after you left, that you received a DFC for destroying the bridge in town. It slowed down a contingent of SS troops long enough for the Third Army guys to capture some of the officers responsible for that massacre at Malm`edy."

"That's what the paperwork said," Marshall answered, unsmiling.

"But the good military thing your crew did turned out to be your personal tragedy."

"It's what happened to Kris and her mother and her baby and even her grandmother. That's what is tragic. Hell, I'm okay."

"I understand. And you include your pal, McAdam, as being okay, I suppose," the chaplain said. He studied Marshall's face.

"Sir, believe me, McAdam isn't about to forgive any Germans, the works, Nazis: any of them!"

They heard the light knock at the edge of the open door, and both stood up.

"Major Waldron, Lieutenant Sunder. Hello," Kristine said, hesitatingly. "I told Chico, here, that I would meet him in your office, Major Waldron: just briefly."

Marshall was surprised and heartened to hear her say Chico, wondering though, if it was intended as sarcasm.

"Come in Mrs. Schuttenhelm. Should we be so formal?" The major slid a chair towards her. "We're having a sip of brandy. May I offer you some water, or brandy? Everyone is delighted with the progress with the library."

"Thank you, no sir."

"I never heard anyone call you 'Chico' before, Marsh."

"It's the name of the town in California, where I'm from."

"Tell him, luftgangster, what it means in the Spanish language."

"Mrs. Schuttenhelm," the major said sternly, "in my office there is no room for hostility."

"I apologize. I intended no hostility," Kristine said. She lowered her head. They saw her chin quiver.

"It's okay, Kris," the chaplain said. "And goodness knows we've had enough apologies for one day. However, Kristine, I'd appreciate it if you'd not use the word luftgangster in my presence."

Marshall then spoke softly, "Chico means 'little' in Spanish, Martin. When I was a kid my Uncle Bruce called me Chico Sunder. It's nothing serious. She's teasing."

"I see. Well, good. Now you young people, just remain calm," Major Waldron said. "I love you both. I feel I understand the depths of your frustrations. And Kris, I'm going to assume that you may have learned from your father and from Paul that they may have been involved in acts of violence during the war. I don't want to hear any details, but my point is that if you are able to forgive them, you can also forgive Marshall. So, It's now time for me to ask a favor of both of you."

Marshall and Kristine sat silently. They did not look at one another. Marshall could feel the beating of his heart.

"Do either of you feel that I'm entitled to a favor? Have I earned your trust over the past years?"

"Of course," Marshall said.

"Yes, Major Waldron," Kristine nodded.

"Kristine, you may have read of St. Francis of Assisi. His name ring a bell?"

"I have Catholic friends, nuns, who speak of him."

"Well, I'm going to give each of you a copy of his famous prayer." Major Waldron gave each of them a sheet of paper and held one in his own hand. "And now the favor that I am asking of both of you: do you feel you can handle it? Will you trust me?"

Both of them nodded their heads affirmatively and accepted the sheet of paper with the prayer.

"Now sit in the chairs so that you can hold hands and still have a hand free to hold the prayer."

Eagerly Marshall moved his chair closer to Kristine's. He held the paper in his left hand and extended his right arm allowing it to rest on the table-top. Kristine sat very still, rigid.

"It's up to you Kristine," Major Waldron whispered. "A favor now, for me?"

Kristine sighed. With awkward reluctance she seemed to force her left arm onto the tabletop and allowed her hand to open, palm up.

"Just rest your hand atop hers, Marshall."

Marshall lowered the palm of his right hand very slowly. The warmth of her hand startled him. He made no attempt to squeeze her hand.

"Okay kids, we're half way home." Major Waldron said. "Now, together we are going to read aloud this prayer." The three of them then very quietly read the words: "*Lord, make me an instrument of your peace, Where there is hatred...let me sow love. Where there is injury...pardon, Where there is doubt...faith, Where there is despair...hope, Where there is darkness...light, Where there is sadness...joy, O Divine Master, grant that I may not so much seek to be consoled as to console, To be understood...as to understand, To be loved...as to love, for, It is in giving...that we receive, It is in pardoning, that we are pardoned, It is in dying...that we are born to eternal life."*

Then Marshall very gently squeezed the hand of Kristine and she responded by returning the act.

Major Waldron stared at them and seemed to be holding his breath. Finally he said, "Thanks for the favor, my young friends."

Kristine pulled her hand away and looked up at the chaplain. "That is very beautiful. May I have this copy?"

"Certainly, Kris."

"I can sure buy that philosophy." Marshall said. "May I, too, have this copy?"

"Well, of course. Now I've some business I need to tend to in the lounge. I'll be back in a little while to finish up some business. If you two want to sit and visit for awhile, be my guest. And I am going to pray that you will be friends again."

"Thanks, Martin." Marshall said.

"I, too, thank you Major Waldron. Now I must go home and rest my legs."

"Kris, would you stay for just a second?" Marshall said, "There's something I want to tell you."

Kristine glanced at Major Waldron, hesitated, then said, "All right. Briefly."

The major smiled at them and turned and walked towards the lounge.

"Kris. I realize it's all over. But I will cherish the good times we had and hope you'll try to forgive us. I mean Frank and Pop and Gary and me."

"I am so ashamed that I went to Munich with you." She lowered her head and moved it from side to side. "How could I have done such a thing! Now you must believe that I truly thought my Paul was dead, that I was truly a widow. Ha, Chico, I am the one who seeks forgiveness."

"Come on, Kris. We were all lonely then. I think we just needed each other. And me too, Kris, I wouldn't have asked you to join me in Munich if I thought you were married. You know we both thought you were a widow. God, there must be some answers for us in the prayer we just read?"

"The major is a good man, " Kristine whispered. "If forgiveness is so important to him, then I say it: that I forgive you, Chico. Will you accept that?"

"Thank you Kristine," Marshall said. He felt a sudden release of tension, followed by an involuntary shiver. Marshall sighed, then spoke in a hushed tone, "God, I do love you, you know."

Kristine avoided his eyes. "Our few moments have passed. I must say good night to you, Marshall. My baby is kicking me," Kristine laughed, then said, " I must go home and rest. The time is nearing."

"Kris, wait a second. Let me tell you something that I believe you'll find amusing."

"Oh?"

"Sunder was the name of the family that sponsored my great-grandfather when he moved to the States. He was from Kitzengen. Our immigration guys fouled up his name and called him Sunder. His name was actually Sonderzug. He was called 'Zug' by his family and friends! My last name should be Sonderzug! I know the translation, do you?"

"Ha! It means 'Special'!" Kristine laughed, "You are something special all right, Mr. Luftgangster," Kristine said, looking into his eyes, and laughed again.

"God, it's good to hear you laugh! I've a jeep. Can I drive you home?"

"No, 'Chico.' No, 'Zug.'" Kristine smiled at Marshall, then said, "Whatever your name, zu Ende gehen." Kristine arose. "Now, please understand that I am saying my final good-bye to you."

"Well Kris, I guess good-bye it is," Marshall answered, and sighed.

Kristine folded the sheet of paper given to her by the chaplain, tucked it in a pocket of the loose smock she wore, and walked from the chaplain's office.

Marshall stood and watched her disappear down the corridor. He returned to the office, found the unfinished glass of brandy, and sat, staring at the polished brass cross, and sipped the smooth liquid. It warmed him.

Major Waldron returned to the office. "I saw Kristine on the way out of the club, heading home. I feel you young folks may have solved your own problems. Right?"

"Yes sir. Really," Marshall said. "I do thank you for being so patient. Guess I'm repeating myself, but I mean it, Martin."

"Well, it's time to finish up these brandies, unless you'd like a refill."

"No thanks, Martin, but it is smooth."

"Would you like to join the missus and me for dinner?"

"Gee, that sounds nice. But, how about a rain check?" Marshall said. He laughed. "I'm a student again, and I've a lot of reading to do. I'd better head back to Heidelberg. It's not a long drive."

"Marsh, I'm going to be doing some home work, too. The doubts you expressed, about forgiveness for soldiers, as related to Jesus, are probably even more universal than I thought. For the most part, the men now stationed here weren't involved in combat. They never experienced anything similar to your involvement. They have different needs. But, as with you, other fliers, other vets, back home, must be wondering the same thing." He paused and glanced at the polished brass crucifix on his desk. "Now, this might interest you because Kris is involved. A brilliant German pastor, Dietrich Bonhoeffer, was imprisoned by the Gestapo because of his views, but for some strange reason they allowed him to write philosophical and theological letters, stating his views to his friends. Then, just before the Germans surrendered, the idiots hanged him! The pastor in Bad Scheidel has copies of his letters and has allowed Kris to translate them into English for me. I am eager to read them, to study them. Perhaps I will be able to find additional answers to your questions."

Chaplain Waldron sighed, then looked back to Marshall; "We'll keep in touch! Hey, Lieutenant, do you realize you've thrown down another challenge for me?"

"Ha!" Marshall said, tipping back his head. "I can't ask anything more of you, sir. I know I've lost Kristine, but I honest to God believe that she's forgiven me and I have you to thank."

Marshall stepped close to the pastor and extended his hand. They shook vigorously.

"Well, sir, I'm hitting the road. Mind letting me know when she has her baby?"

"Sure, I'll keep you advised. I'll be writing to you. And, good luck with your studies!"

Marshall walked back out into the lounge. The lights had been turned off in the library. He stared into the darkness, then walked back to the bar and sat at a barstool with armrests. The bartender approached and asked, "Back again the same day, eh? Another sip of the single malt Scotch, sir?"

"I beg you pardon?"

Another scotch, sir?"

"Oh, no, thanks, I think I'll pass. How about a cup of coffee?"

"I've some pretzels, and can order up some slices of a variety of nice cheese, plus crackers, if you like, sir?" The sergeant said.

"If you serve food at the bar, I'd like to have a good old fashioned hamburger with all of the trimmings. I have to hit the road back to Heidelberg, soon."

"Our hamburgers are the best this side of Kansas City, sir. I'll order one for you when you're ready."

"Thanks, I'm ready! Order it now, please."

The bartender walked to a telephone and placed the order. He returned and asked, "You look a bit serious, Lieutenant. Would a dumb blonde joke help?"

"A joke? You bet. Any joke, right now, I'm into!"

"I'm going to read these, there are so many of them. Insulting as hell, of course. But kind of fun."

"Read away."

The bartender took a sheet from behind the bar and began to recite the one-liners:

"How do you make a blonde's eyes light up?"

"I give."

"Shine a flashlight in her ear."

"How do you make a blonde laugh on Friday?"

"Go ahead, you're telling these."

"Tell her a joke on Monday."

"Why don't blondes get coffee breaks?" But the bartender didn't wait for responses from Marshall, and answered each of his questions without hesitation. "Because it takes too long to retrain them."

Marshall laughed along with the bartender as he went through his list of jokes. Finally the sergeant asked, "Have you got a favorite you'll share with me, Lieutenant?" Marshall laughed, and thought of all those jokes that Uncle Bruce had provided, and said, "Well, this old geezer comes into this tavern and walks up to the bar and slaps down a silver dollar, and says, 'barkeep, I'd like a bubble durbin.' And then Marshall completes the joke, laughing as he tells it. The barkeeper, too, laughed, at the punch line and said, "Lieutenant, I'd sure appreciate it if you'd talk that one through slowly so I can write it down."

After telling the joke slowly so the bartender could write it down, Marshall began to think of home and his folks and Uncle Bruce and Tara. He wondered how things were going with Major Crandall working at the store. It had only been a few weeks, but mail from home hadn't caught up with him.

"How are they treating you at that school up at Heidelberg, sir?"

"Fine. Just getting started. Nice quarters. Good food. Competent teachers."

"So, were you in business back home?" the sergeant inquired. He wiped the top of the bar with a towel.

"No thanks. I'm going to have coffee with that hamburger, though," Marshall said. "My folks own a mercantile store. You know, hardware, supplies for farmers and ranchers." *Actually I'm the antique buyer for the madam of a whorehouse.*

"Well, when you get situated I hope you can place a big order for some brooms or picks and shovels or something, with the folks. Keep it in the family, you know!" The bartender laughed and winked at Marshall.

"Interesting thought," Marshall said. "Really!"

"Well, here comes your grub. Hope you enjoy it and I'll have that coffee ready for you in a jiffy."

Two pilots wearing white silk scarves entered the lounge and approached the bar. Colonel Schlosser had mentioned that a P-38 fighter outfit was now attached to the base. It seemed a long time ago that the P-38 had pulled up beside *DIANA*, and the pilot asked if they were okay, back when they bombed the Bad Scheidel Bridge. Marshall chuckled. Schloss wouldn't allow the B-26 pilots to wear white scarves: improper uniform. However, he didn't object to the fliers in his squadron clipping a small section off of the tips of their silver wings. *Wonder what the new general would say.*

Marshall paid his tab and walked to the parking area where his jeep was parked. He stopped at the front bumper, and remembered when a steel pipe had been welded to the front of jeeps to sever the steel piano wire that the Germans stretched across the road to behead any jeep occupants that drove with their windshields down.

As he had been when he arrived again on German soil, Marshall was impressed by the over-all cleanliness and order that had begun to emerge from the staggering piles of debris. He drove towards Heidelberg, and watched the industrious Germans with their little hammers, cleaning and stacking bricks, and separating the timbers and, trimming off any damage, constantly classifying the quality of any material they salvaged and arranging it in neat stacks. No one was idle. Old men and women and youngsters were all busy with shovels or brooms or wheelbarrows.

He wondered whom, if anyone, was directing them. They reminded Marshall of a high school science project where a colony of restless ants could be observed in a huge, dirt-filled glass tank. *I wonder if the U.S. Army is providing the Germans with shovels and wheelbarrows? Maybe I can get the folks on the army's list of suppliers.*

In Heidelberg, Marshall drove to the storage area where jeeps and staff cars were kept for the students and the instructors. He turned over the keys to a young corporal who offered him a picture-perfect military salute. Marshall smiled, returned the salute, and went directly to his room on the second floor of one of the many wings of the University.

To his delight, three letters had been placed on his desk. Quickly he scanned the return addresses and laughed aloud when he read, Eileen O'Ryan. Another was from his mother, and one from Bruce. Marshall sat in the heavy oak chair that had a cushion in the seat and at the back. It was cumbersome and comfortable, and the floor lamp beside it was old, but the light adequate.

Dear Marshall,

Seems strange to be writing to you in Germany. Assume you've started your classes. Of course I'm not going to dilly-dally around! What's happening with you and Kristine? I couldn't believe it when you told me she is alive! Thank God for that. What now, dear Fly Boy? My curiosity is devouring me! Why don't you send a telegram? You can certainly afford it, what with all that overseas pay, and flight pay you say you're getting.

My Daddy is a free man, finally, and I'm going to join him on a trip to England during the Christmas break. I've received permission to miss a couple of weeks, and my Advisor has worked with my Professors, so I can take homework with me. My assignment is to visit Westminster Abbey, then another bridge that is still standing, the Tower Bridge, in London, to study the system of gears, how it all works, and if we can get to the continent, to go to the Eiffel Tower, lots of bridges in Paris I can study, and if we can visit Germany, go to the Cologne Cathedral. That's an awful lot, but daddy is eager. I think he is really anxious to go up to Edinburgh, Scotland, where I can study the castle, but where daddy can visit and play some famous golf courses, like St.Andrews.

Wouldn't it be wonderful if we could meet somewhere? I know you and my dad would hit it off great, maybe get in a round, even if you do hit that awful banana ball! Well, Fly Boy, if you are interested further, let me know and I'll give you the details of our arrival in England, etc. Love and kisses. Eileen.

Marshall reread the letter. *By Gosh. I'll do just that. I'll send her a telegram and advise her that Paul and Kristine Schuttenhelm are expecting their baby any day. Ha! That'll grab her!*

The letter from his mother was brief and he started to read it with some apprehension:

Dear Son, Everything is going along fine at the store now. I was talking to Doctor Keith about the way your dad is coping with his valve problem and he feels that he is getting along fine, certainly not getting any worse. He also suggested that I should seek counseling, from another doctor here in town. Her name is Helen Hummel and she's recently moved up here from San Francisco. I like her very much. I guess an old dog can still learn some new tricks, and yes, Son, I know what females dogs are called!

The Major and his wife are nice, honest people and he is learning the business quickly. Mr. Crandall had been very good with dad. I went to see Mrs. Rodriquez and we had a nice visit. She sends her love. A high school friend of yours, Carla, stopped in. looking for work, but we can't hire anyone, although your uncle said she'd attract a lot of male customers! I offered your address but she said to just say hi. Son, I pray every day that you'll be safe in that hostile environment. We know you'll do well with your studies. Dad will mail a well-wrapped box of chocolate chip cookies in a day or two. Son, I do hope you'll be able to resolve your responsibility problems with the German girl. One more thing Son: Your Uncle Bruce says I can't cut the umbilical cord. That's not true. I do want what is best for you. Your Dad and I taught you to seek high moral standards. Now, I hope this doesn't anger you, but I found that book in your room by D. H. Lawrence. When I was in college, my professor called that book intellectual trash. It was considered lascivious. Please set your standards high. Read the manuscripts of Jefferson and Adams and Lincoln. Bye. Remember, we love you. X X X, Mom.

That's my mother! Marshall shook his head and laughed aloud. Then he opened the letter from his Uncle Bruce.

Howdy partner,

Well, it's still hard for me to believe you left God's country for that beaten up part of the world. Your dad hooked into a 35 pound King over in the Sacramento River the other day and I netted the big son of a bitch for him! I thought about knocking the jig out of its mouth, you know, free it, just to frustrate your dad, but he'd have killed me if that fish had escaped. We smoked it, and canned some. Damn, what a great flavor! Maybe we can ship some to you. I'll check that out. Bird shooting should be great this season, but there seems to be more guys coming up here from L.A. I guess their money is as good as any ones, as long as they mind the rules. Too bad you couldn't have taken a little time off to join us for the dove opener. Had a couple of weeks of good shooting and your mom prepared a batch of them with bacon wrapped around the breasts. A real delicacy. Lots of Ringnecks in the fields! October, as usual, is providing good shooting!

Jeanette feels she shouldn't write to you directly. Why, I don't know. Anyway, in this envelope, there's a note, she says, with instructions about what to buy. I hope she gets that antique store set up in Frisco before the Red Bluff ladies close her down.

Marsh, your dad is hanging in there real good. Over at the store, Mr. Crandall seems to be a real square shooter. Hard worker, and never stops asking questions. Your dad and I are taking him over to the river before the salmon run ends. You know, I get the feeling that Mr. Crandall would like to buy-out your folks. Might not be such a bad idea. Well, time will tell. Tara is still wearing us out with all of that retrieving. I'll give her a good workout when the duck season opens!

Let me know if you need any good jokes. These traveling salesmen never seem to run out. Well, I guess it's about time to go over to Red Bluff for a load of redwood decking!

Keep the faith, your uncle,

Bruce.

Marshall then opened the envelope from Jeanette and enclosed was a check for one thousand dollars. *Dear Lt. Sunder. I realize you probably haven't as yet had time to do any antique searching. One of my U. of C. friends advised that it will be very costly to crate and ship things like furniture, however I am in no rush. But I do want you to have enough funds to select top quality. If it is possible to have an item authenticated, that is desirable, but not mandatory for furniture. I would like you to try to find beautiful inlaid pieces of fine furniture, and I'd also like you to shop for old Bibles. They can be in the German language, or especially Latin. Of course any language is fine, if they are really old and in good shape. Thank you.*

Your friend, Jeanette.

That evening it was difficult for Marshall to concentrate on the subject of Supply and Demand. The theory of Discriminating Pricing interested him. *Sure wouldn't work in Chico. So that's what Gumps does! Price it high and keep the riffraff out of the store to make room for the affluent.* He kept reading paragraphs over and over without assimilating the contents. Finally he closed his books, took a hot shower and climbed into his bed. In the darkness, he stared at the ceiling, became agitated because, in his mind, the counting resumed, from early February into October; nine months. *Shouldn't she have had it by now?* Marshall tossed, then turned onto his side and dozed. When he began to awaken a bluish morning light entered through the rectangular window. He lay there and stared at the bright rectangle and felt a new confidence, sensed that he could now plot his own destiny, after all, he was almost twenty-two. He had his role models, his dad and his Uncle Bruce. Plus, Marshall admired the quiet strength of Chaplain Waldron, appreciated his guidance, and he marveled at the wisdom of Fosdick, men whose mentor was Jesus. *What did they know? There's so much to learn!*

A bird flew upward crossing the window and he wondered if it was a dove or a pigeon. *Probably one of the pigeons that inhabited Heidelberg.* He chuckled when he remembered that his Uncle Bruce referred to pigeons as Polish doves.

Soon he'd have to get busy and see if he could find some of Mr. Shapiro's relatives. *The Star's and Stripes* was now reporting that perhaps more than a million Jews had been killed by the Nazis. *Impossible!*

In the morning, after breakfast and before his first class, Marshall went to the main office, where he was able to compose and send a telegram. He addressed it to Eileen O'Ryan, and wrote: *Mr. Carl and Mrs. Kristine Schuttenhelm are expecting the birth of either a boy or girl. How about that for odds? On my first leave I'm going to Scotland for golf lessons. Enthusiastically awaiting your arrival. Please bring sourdough bread. Love. Marsh.*

Marshall then wrote a short note to Jeanette. *I've received the additional funds and will do as you request. Would you be interested in a really old piece of printing equipment? It's actually a typograph, made in a factory, named Rogers, and I'm told it's very rare, and heavy. Maybe your buddy down at Cal might know something about it. It would require careful packing. Under separate cover I'm mailing a Swiss watch, a little gift from me to you. Hope you like it, and no, it's not an antique. Please let me know what you think about the typograph. Kind regards, your very single friend, Marshall.*

It was nearly time to leave for the classroom. Marshall gathered up his books, his notebook, filled his fountain pen, and pulled the heavy oak door closed behind him and stopped along the elevated walkway at one of the curved arches. Below him a multitude of red tiled roofs of homes, stores and small shops seemed to be a crimson waterfall, splashing down the hillside to the banks of the Neckar River. The red was as intense as a broad blanket of flowing blood. Marshall decided to locate the exact spot where the Neckar joined the Rhine River somewhere down stream.

He thought of the bridge at Bad Scheidel, just a few miles up the Neckar, and then of Kristine, and of Frank and Diana, and of Pop and the troubled Cal, and then his mind returned to the sight-seeing flight along the Rhine River, piloted by Gary, and of the remains of all of the bridges they'd smashed, now crumbled and decaying beneath the surface of the river, wondering too how much human blood flowed down the Neckar to join the Rhine, and then his mind flashed back to the B-26 with the name *Miss Nausicaa* lettered beneath Gary's name, just below the pilots window. His memories wandered now, and flowed along seemingly keeping pace with waters of the German rivers exiting into the North Sea where the bloodied waters would dilute in the salt water, but not be cleansed.

His few months at home seemed like a dream. It all happened too fast. Major Crandall and his folks and Bruce, and he laughed to himself when he recalled his meeting with Jeanette, and he shrugged his shoulders when he wondered what might become of Carla. He thought of his visit to San Francisco and the awe he felt for of the Golden Gate Bridge boldly standing and stretching all the way to Marin County. Then he began to visualize Eileen's face and form, the soft texture and fragrance of her blond hair, her smile and the timbre of her voice.

It was time to go to his classroom.

The End

AFTERWORD

───────────▼───────────

Following my return to civilian life in 1946, I kept in touch with fellow B-26 Marauder friends, and often discussed, and relived events as described in this novel. Over the years, through career changes, and job responsibilities, I communicated with dozens of veterans who experienced combat in the Army, The Navy, The Marine Corps and the Sea Bees.

Remorse was the dominant feeling revealed by all of these men who were aware that they had a personal involvement in taking the life of another human. With the dozens of combat veterans with whom I discussed the war, the theme of regret, of sadness, and of remorse repeated itself. Not a single man "wanted" to kill. The hope for forgiveness was a personal goal sought by all of them in different ways.

ABOUT THE AUTHOR

▼

At San Francisco State University, CA, Jim Folger received a BA in English with a Creative Writing Option. An Associates Degree in Agriculture was earned at California State Polytechnic University. After Pearl Harbor, he enlisted and spent four years in the Air Corps.

As a member of the Outdoor Writers Association of America, and The Outdoor Writers Association of California, he was regularly published in outdoor magazines.

Retirement followed a forty-year business career in sales-management with The L.S. Starrett Co. Presently he is a columnist for *The Wildwood Independent*, and a regular contributor to *The Writers of The Desert Sage*, and *The Shasta Valley Review*.

GLOSSARY

▼

Ack Ack: Also known as flak. An anti-aircraft gun or a group of guns, propels a pineapple shaped object, similar to a large hand grenade, to a pre determined altitude, where in a puff of black smoke, it explodes, sending sharp particles of steel, designed to shred and puncture aluminum, glass, Plexiglas, steel cables, gasoline lines and tanks, and bone and flesh.

Air Corps: Designation of numbered corps, i.e. 8th, 9th, 10th, etc. Shortly after Pearl Harbor, the U.S. Army was recognized. The Air Corps and Air Force Combat Command were merged into the Army Air Forces. On July 26, 1947 The U.S. Air Force was created as a separate entity. During WWII, the common vernacular among fliers was: "I'm in the Ninth Air Corps." (Or 8th, 10th, 12th, etc.)

Air Medal mission: After completion of the fifth combat mission the flier was awarded an Air Medal. After each subsequent combat mission another was awarded in the form of oak leaf cluster, which was attached to the Air Medal ribbon. Depending on the Group or Squadron, a leave, or pass was included.

AWOL: Absent without leave

B.O.C.: Bachelor officers club

B.O.Q.: Bachelor officers' quarters.

Bomb run: After reaching the I.P., the thirty seconds, or so required for the bombardier to make his final adjustments with the Norden bombsight.

Bombs Away: Announcement by the bombardier, over the intercom, that the bombs have left the bomb bay.

CAVU: Ceiling, altitude, visibility unlimited.

Cage the gyro: A sudden lurching of the airplane will cause the gyroscope with the Norden bombsight to tumble, and the bombardier must stabilize it when he uses a knob atop the bombsight, thus he cages the gyro.

Circular error: The bomb impact distance from dead center of a target, averaged at an altitude of 11,000, as rendered by a cadet bombardier.

C.O.: Commanding Officer.

CTD: Civilian pilot training

Eisenhower jacket: Tailored by removing the lower part section, including the pockets, of a standard uniform, resulting in a trim, compact jacket buttoned at the waist.

E.M.C.: Enlisted men's club.

E.M.Q.: Enlisted men's quarters.

ETA: Estimated time of arrival.

ETD: Estimated time of departure.

ETO: European theatre of operations.

Flack: Synonym for ack ack.

Foreign exchange: Rate of exchange: Value of the American dollar to other currencies.

G.I : Government Issue G2: Intelligence.

IP: The point in space from which the bomb run starts.

Leave: A leave of absence from the base. Anything from a three day pass to a two week leave.

Mail call: At a designated time mail is dispersed to a group of service-men as their names are called.

Mess hall: The dining room

MP: Military police.

NCO: Non commissioned officer.

NCOC: Non commissioned officers' club.

OC: Officers' club.

OD: Officer of the day.

Out: In an aircraft, over the intercom, signifies the end of the conversation.

Over: Returning the mic, the intercom use, to the communicator.

PDI: Pilots directional indicator.

Points: Servicemen were awarded points to determine the order in which they would return home. Points were accumulated according time in service, overseas time, combat time, and decorations. Generally more points were required of commissioned officers than of non-commissioned officers and enlisted men.

Pre flight: Cadet training. Schooling at colleges, and physical train-ing, designed to prepare the cadet for a specialty. i.e. pilot, bombardier or navigator.

Pro Kit: Contained a tube of ointment. Venereal disease prevention.

PX : Post exchange (a store).

Rocker: Curved stripes at the lower part of a chevron worn by a non commissioned officer above the rank of sergeant

RON: Remain over night

Roger: A response meaning correct, or right.

Roger, wilco and out: Signing off during a conversation on the intercom meaning, correct, will comply, and signing off, (or end of conversation.)

Roger, wilco, and over: Correct, will comply, and back to you.

Slot: In a six-airplane flight formation, the lead airplane has another airplane behind, and slightly below each wing. Directly below the lead air-plane another airplane is situated in the slot, and off of its wings are another two airplanes, staggered as above.

Six by six : Slang expression designating the size of a three axle truck with front wheel drive, with a canvas canopy, wagon wheel style, capable of carrying a dozen soldiers.

Target of opportunity: When a bomber is unable to drop all or a part of its bombs on the primary target, the bombardier selects a military target of opportunity.

Tour of duty: A combat tour was early on set at twenty five missions, and later raised to fifty. This varied according to the Air Corp, i.e., heavy bombers, fighters, etc.

Tilt: The call of the bombardier when a sudden lurching of the airplane causes the gyro within the Norden bombsight to tumble, or tilt, and it is restored to its upright position when the bombardier cages the gyro.

Throat mic: An elastic band or strap worn around the neck containing two quarter-size vibration sensitive discs that functioned as mics, so the crewman can communicate by depressing a switch, hand held, or situated on pilots stick or wheel.

Wilco: Will comply means the order, or instruction, is understood, and will be obeyed.

88's: A reference to a battery of 80mm anti aircraft guns.

Snafu: Situation normal, all fouled up.

Tour of duty: Originally a tour consisted of twenty-five combat missions. Following D Day, and the new location of B-26 bases on the Continent, the quota was raised to fifty. Many fliers flew sixty-five or more missions.